WALTER SCOTT (1771–1832) wa⸏⸏⸏⸏⸏⸏⸏⸏⸏⸏⸏⸏⸏⸏⸏⸏ ⸏⸏⸏⸏der family. After attending the High ⸏ ⸏⸏⸏⸏ University of Edinburgh he followed his father into the profession of the law, becoming an advocate (barrister) in 1792. In 1799 he was appointed Sheriff-Depute for the county of Selkirk, and in 1806 a Clerk of the Court of Session—appointments which he retained until the end of his life. His first major publication was a collection of ballads entitled *The Minstrelsy of the Scottish Border* (1802–3). He became famous as a poet with *The Lay of the Last Minstrel* (1805), *Marmion* (1808), and *The Lady of the Lake* (1810). In 1814 he published his first novel, *Waverley*, set during the Jacobite rising of 1745. Its success encouraged him to produce more historical novels. With *Ivanhoe* (1820), a romance of medieval England, Scott moved from an early modern Scottish setting to a variety of countries and periods. Scott's work was widely acclaimed in Europe and America. He spent the income from his writings on establishing a house and estate at Abbotsford, near Melrose. He was awarded a baronetcy by the Prince Regent in 1818. Partnership in the printing firm of James Ballantyne and Co. involved him in a financial crash in 1826. His last years were darkened by illness and the need to continue his output of writing to pay off the debts incurred. His *Journal* of those years is the most moving of his works. He died at Abbotsford in 1832; his biography was written by his son-in-law, John Gibson Lockhart.

IAN DUNCAN is Professor of English at the University of California, Berkely and the author of *Modern Romance and Transformations of the Novel: The Gothic, Scott, Dickens* (1992). He has edited Scott's *Ivanhoe* (1996), John Buchan's *The Island of Sheep* (1997), and *Travel Writing 1700–1830* (with Elizabeth A. Bohls) for Oxford World's Classics.

OXFORD WORLD'S CLASSICS

*For over 100 years Oxford World's Classics have brought
readers closer to the world's great literature. Now with over 700
titles—from the 4,000-year-old myths of Mesopotamia to the
twentieth century's greatest novels—the series makes available
lesser-known as well as celebrated writing.*

*The pocket-sized hardbacks of the early years contained
introductions by Virginia Woolf, T. S. Eliot, Graham Greene,
and other literary figures which enriched the experience of reading.
Today the series is recognized for its fine scholarship and
reliability in texts that span world literature, drama and poetry,
religion, philosophy and politics. Each edition includes perceptive
commentary and essential background information to meet the
changing needs of readers.*

OXFORD WORLD'S CLASSICS

SIR WALTER SCOTT

Rob Roy

Edited with an Introduction and Notes by
IAN DUNCAN

OXFORD
UNIVERSITY PRESS

OXFORD
UNIVERSITY PRESS

Great Clarendon Street, Oxford OX2 6DP

Oxford University Press is a department of the University of Oxford.
It furthers the University's objective of excellence in research, scholarship,
and education by publishing worldwide in

Oxford New York

Auckland Bangkok Buenos Aires Cape Town Chennai
Dar es Salaam Delhi Hong Kong Istanbul Karachi Kolkata
Kuala Lumpur Madrid Melbourne Mexico City Mumbai Nairobi
São Paulo Shanghai Taipei Tokyo Toronto

Oxford is a registered trade mark of Oxford University Press
in the UK and in certain other countries

Published in the United States
by Oxford University Press Inc., New York

Editorial matter © Ian Duncan 1998
Chronology © Claire Lamont 1982

The moral rights of the author have been asserted
Database right Oxford University Press (maker)

First published as an Oxford World's Classics paperback 1998
Reissued 2008

British Library Cataloguing in Publication Data

Data available

Library of Congress Cataloging in Publication Data

Scott, Walter, Sir, 1771–1832.
Rob Roy/Sir Walter Scott; edited with an introduction and notes by Ian Duncan.
(Oxford world's classics)
Includes bibliographical references (p.   ).
1. Rob, Roy, 1671–1734—Fiction.   I. Duncan, Ian.   II. Title.
III. Series: Oxford world's classics (Oxford University press)
PR5313.R6   1998   823'.7—dc21   97–37480 CIP

ISBN 978-0-19-954988-7

15

Printed and bound in Great Britain by Clays Ltd, Elcograf S.p.A.

CONTENTS

Acknowledgements   vi

Introduction   vii

Note on the Text   xxix

Select Bibliography   xxxiv

A Chronology of Sir Walter Scott   xxxvii

Map   xl

Advertisement to the First Edition   3

Author's Introduction   5

ROB ROY   65

Scott's Notes   456

Editor's Notes   466

Glossary   498

ACKNOWLEDGEMENTS

I AM grateful to the Trustees of the National Library of Scotland for permission to cite the Interleaved Set of Scott's Waverley Novels. I should also like to thank Dr Iain Gordon Brown and the staff of that library for their assistance, and the staff of the Knight Library at the University of Oregon. Ina Ferris and Janet Sorensen made some helpful suggestions about the introduction; my work on the notes benefited from the expert advice of Dianne Dugaw, Randall McGowen, Fiona Robertson, and Steve Shankman, and—most of all—from the acute and resourceful investigations of Nina Prytula.

INTRODUCTION

Rob Roy (1818) was the third of Scott's romances to feature a Highland setting, after his first novel, *Waverley* (1814), and a narrative poem, *The Lady of the Lake* (1810). These works enjoyed a vast popularity throughout the nineteenth century. Today most people associate them with a cultural rather than strictly literary phenomenon: the reinvention of Scotland for modern tourism. Scott's romances filled the landscape with real readers as well as imaginary characters and events. 'We ought to traverse the district novel in hand,' instructs one Victorian guide to 'Rob Roy's country', 'and fix, if we can, upon the precise spot where Francis Osbaldistone for a moment pressed the flushed cheek of Diana Vernon, or where he started on hearing the deep voice of the MacGregor, saying, "A braw nicht, Maister Osbaldistone."'[1] Besides the Highlands, *Rob Roy* colonized Glasgow, Scotland's second city, for the literary imagination. 'Little did we think that we ourselves were to be immortalized in Rob Roy', wrote a *Blackwood's Magazine* correspondent, signing himself 'Nicol Jarvie, *tertius*'—as though all literary Glaswegians were henceforth to be descendants of characters in Scott's novel.[2] John Galt, a rival novelist from the west of Scotland, acknowledged the foundational status of *Rob Roy* by making Nicol Jarvie a citizen of his Glasgow in *The Entail* (1823), and naming the hero of *Sir Andrew Wylie* (1823) after one of Scott's offstage characters. In the twentieth century Glasgow would eclipse Edinburgh as a centre of cultural production, and no longer have to derive its literary reputation from being a location in *Rob Roy*. But a modern tourist industry has ensured that the Highlands remain Scott's Highlands, the Highlands of *Rob Roy* and *The Lady of the Lake*, well after these works have lost their universal reading public.

Scott himself was a stranger in the Highlands, different only in degree from the tourists who went there to trace the scenery of his fiction. But a 'comparative deficiency in knowledge of Celtic manners' did not disqualify him from attempting *The Lady of the Lake*: 'you are

---

[1] *Ward & Lock's Illustrated Guide to, and Popular History of Loch Lomond, the Trosachs, Loch Katrine, &c.* (London, 1883), 4.

[2] 'Letter to the Author of Rob Roy', *Blackwood's Edinburgh Magazine*, 2 (March 1818), 662–4.

to consider that I have from my youth delighted in all the Highland traditions which I could pick up from the old Jacobites who used to frequent my father's house'.[3] Scott had visited one of the old Jacobites, Alexander Stewart of Invernahyle, on the first of his many jaunts to the Highlands in the autumn of 1787, and been entertained with the tale of a broadsword duel fought between his host and the famous outlaw Rob Roy MacGregor.[4] Another Rob Roy anecdote (collected on a later trip, 1793) suggested the hero's visit to the cave of the robber Donald Bean Lean in *Waverley*. At work on *Rob Roy* itself, in August 1817, Scott went on a short excursion to look over the novel's setting, leading to the guidebook legend that he composed it on the banks of Loch Lomond. As it happens, the descriptions of Glasgow and the Highlands in *Rob Roy* owe less to personal observation than to literary sources, such as Defoe's *Tour of the Whole Island of Great Britain*, Edward Burt's *Letters from a Gentleman in the North of Scotland*, and the Revd Patrick Grahame's *Sketches of Perthshire*. Readers today may find Scott's Highlands all too 'literary', deficient in a sense of felt life or local knowledge, faithfully reproducing their author's cultural distance. That distance, nevertheless, helped make the Highland romances more popular than anything else Scott had written until the appearance of a novel with a still more outlandish setting, *Ivanhoe*.

The combination of distance and fascination has come to define Scott's place in a modern tradition of representations of the Gaelic Highlands. Critics have interpreted that tradition as the literary arm of a historical relationship of 'internal colonialism' between the metropolitan core of the new British state (which included Edinburgh and Glasgow) and its so-called Celtic fringe. After the brutal defeat of the Jacobite insurgency at Culloden in 1746, the Hanoverian government legislated a set of policies to break up the clan system and enforce the assimilation of Scottish Gaelic populations into the modern state. This achievement of national unity upon the suppression of a traditional native culture became the historical premiss for the modern, metropolitan representation of the Highlands, which was founded—in a cloud of scandal—by James Macpherson's 'Ossian' poems in the 1760s. (Not coincidentally, this is the date when Scott's narrator is supposed to be writing the memoir that becomes *Rob Roy*.) The *Poems*

---

[3] *Letters of Sir Walter Scott*, ed. H. J. C. Grierson (1932), i. 324.
[4] For Scott's Highland excursions see J. G. Lockhart, *The Life of Sir Walter Scott, Bart.* (1-vol. edn., 1898), 38–9, 58–9, 181, 196–9, 335–6, 351.

of Ossian defined a new cultural position of *inauthenticity*, somewhere between translation and forgery, which would become the classic position of an 'invented tradition' in modern letters. Antiquarian reconstruction and poetic fantasy combined in the reverie of a vanished ancestral nation, grown glamorously remote and strange.[5]

Scott's contribution to the representation of the Highlands, according to most modern commentators, was to perfect the 'invention of tradition' with the double application of a plausible historicism and a virtuoso rhetoric of fiction. His romances transformed Gaelic history and culture into the trophy of a sentimental Unionist nationalism, exemplified by his stage management of George IV's state visit to Edinburgh in 1822 as a gaudy tartan pageant. Scott's Highlands, in this account, evoke a soothing if melancholy acceptance of the inevitable defeat of those wild elements that resisted Scotland's absorption into the modern state. Recent criticism, alert to the literary complexities of the novels, has analysed the critical strategies with which Scott activates—rather than covers up—his own and his readers' relation of historical difference from the Gaelic world. In *Waverley*, especially, Scott's text insists upon its techniques of inauthenticity, the mediating devices of 'translation and tourism' (in James Buzard's phrase), summed up in the portrait of the polite English hero wearing Highland dress unveiled at the end of the novel. Such devices represent, for the novel's reader, the formation of a distinctively modern kind of national subjectivity, in which the knowledge of our alienation from 'authentic' cultural identities accompanies our privileged repossession of those lost identities as aesthetic effects.[6]

[5] See Michael Hechter, *Internal Colonialism: The Celtic Fringe in British National Development, 1536–1966* (1975); Tom Nairn, *The Break–Up of Britain: Crisis and Neo-Nationalism* (1981); H. Trevor-Roper, 'The Invention of Scotland: The Highland Tradition of Scotland', in E. Hobsbawm and T. Ranger (eds.), *The Invention of Tradition* (1983), 15–42; Peter Womack, *Improvement and Romance: Constructing the Myth of the Highlands* (1989); Murray G. H. Pittock, *The Invention of Scotland: The Stuart Myth and the Scottish Identity, 1638 to the Present* (1991).

[6] On *Waverley* and national representation see, in addition to the sources cited in the previous note, Robert Crawford, *Devolving English Literature* (1992); Ian Duncan, *Modern Romance and Transformations of the Novel: The Gothic, Scott, Dickens* (1992); Saree Makdisi, 'Colonial Space and the Colonization of Time in Scott's *Waverley*', *Studies in Romanticism*, 34 (1995), 155–87; James Buzard, 'Translation and Tourism: Scott's *Waverley* and the Rendering of Culture', *Yale Journal of Criticism*, 8/2 (1995), 31–59; Ina Ferris, 'Translation from the Borders: Encounter and Recalcitrance in *Waverley* and *Clan-Albin*', *Eighteenth-century Fiction*, 9/2 (1997), 203–22; and Katie Trumpener, *Bardic Nationalism: The Romantic Novel and the British Empire* (1997).

These accounts agree that Scott's representation of the Highlands is primarily elegiac in attitude. Whether they are the scenery of nostalgic enchantment or of a more ironical self-fashioning, the Highlands signify an extinct native culture, a lost world confined to the past. Scott himself goes on to question the elegiac, post-historical representation of the Highlands, however, in an article published in the *Quarterly Review* just two years before the appearance of *Rob Roy*. Here Scott traces the modern history of the Highlands to its present-day terminus in the Clearances, the landlords' forced eviction of their tenants to make way for more profitable kinds of farming. History comes to an end as a landscape is emptied of real human lives, and occupied instead by various kinds of literary discourse:

Meanwhile, the highlands may become the faery ground for romance and poetry, or subject of experiment for the professors of speculation, political and economical.—But if the hour of need should come—and it may not, perhaps, be far distant—the pibroch may sound through the deserted region, but the summons will remain unanswered. The children who have left her will re-echo from a distant shore the sounds with which they took leave of their own—Ha til, ha til, ha til, mi tulidh!—'We return—we return—we return—no more!'[7]

Against the competing claims of romance and political economy—both of which will be aired in *Rob Roy*—Scott poses the practical question, scarcely a year after Waterloo, of the future supply of those hardy warriors who have defended the nation against its imperial rivals since Pitt raised Highland regiments in the Seven Years War. The primitive skills of the colonized, whether as soldiers or as colonists in their turn, will be a valuable resource in the progress of empire. In proposing a dynamic part still to be played by the internal colonial fringe in the life of the nation, understood now as an ongoing imperial history, Scott warns that the elegiac attitude may no longer be sufficient—even as he continues to indulge in it. Looking back on the kind of ideological solution represented by *Waverley*, and beginning to turn away from it, the 'Culloden Papers' article indicates the different position *Rob Roy* will occupy in Scott's career. This is useful, since modern discussion of the Highland romances has relied almost exclusively on readings of *Waverley*. *Rob Roy*, in contrast, has proved oddly fugitive or resistant to criticism, partly because of a tendency to interpret Scott's career as

---

[7] 'Culloden Papers', *Quarterly Review*, 28 (1816), 333.

a repetition of the same set of ideological strategies and aesthetic gestures. But in *Rob Roy* Scott attempted something new with the genre
he had established. He made historical romance a medium for viewing,
not the past, but the unrecognizable forms of the present.

Repetition was what Scott most wished to avoid, as he toiled to sustain a one-man novel-writing industry under various anonymous
masks. Scott often described his literary career as a process of restless
territorial expansion: the discovery and colonization of a series of historical topics, or places in time. At the forefront of the fiction boom of
1815–25, he felt driven to open up new frontiers rather than fall back
on ground already settled. Scott worried accordingly that the cultiva-
tion of the Highlands, his most successful enterprise to date, might
have exhausted their romantic capital. 'You are aware the Highlands
are rather a worn-out subject', he confided to James Ballantyne in September 1817.[8] *Rob Roy* marked the return not only to a Highland setting but to the very neighbourhood of *The Lady of the Lake*, and to the
Jacobite historical theme of *Waverley*, this time the 1715 rising rather
than the '45. It also marked the return to public view of Scott's persona
as 'the Author of *Waverley*', who had bowed farewell to his readers at
the end of *The Antiquary* in 1816. Since then Scott had experimented
with a new apparatus of anonymity and a new publisher, William
Blackwood, but Blackwood proved unsatisfactory, and with the new
novel Scott came back (on advantageous terms) to his former publisher Archibald Constable. Ever shrewd, Constable persuaded Scott
that the novel's title should advertise its main attraction, the ingredi-
ent that would set it apart from the run of modern Highland romances.

It was inevitable that someone would write a romance about Rob
Roy in the early nineteenth century. Both *The Lady of the Lake* and
Waverley had featured Highland outlaw chiefs, the warlord Roderick
Dhu and the trickster Donald Bean, without putting either of them at
the centre of the tale in question. Rob Roy MacGregor (1671–1734)
already inhabited the popular imagination as well as the historical
record. Even in his lifetime an industry of ballads and chapbooks had
turned Rob Roy into a type of resistance folk hero, 'the Scottish Robin
Hood', whose fame spread across the different cultural spaces of
the new British nation: *The Highland Rogue*, a pamphlet once attrib-
uted to Defoe, was published in London in 1723. The industrious

---

[8] *Letters*, iv. 504.

cattle-drover, representative of an ancient and persecuted clan, forced outside the law by an aristocratic oppressor, was celebrated as much for his generous spirit as for his skill at fighting and escaping. Polite literature collared the Highland Rogue in 1807 when William Wordsworth published 'Rob Roy's Grave', one of a series of poems inspired by a Scottish tour; Scott would use it ten years later as an epigraph for his novel, and a ballad based on it would become a staple of the dramatic versions of *Rob Roy*.[9] Wordsworth extols Rob Roy as a libertarian noble savage, charged with an ambiguous political nostalgia; the poet must work hard to dispel the shadow of Napoleonic force (we would now call it fascism) from the fantasy of primitive freedom.

Constable's faith in Rob Roy's name as a 'taking title' for Scott's new novel proved well founded. The first edition, published on 31 December 1817, sold out its huge print run of 10,000 copies within two weeks; two more editions were called for by the end of 1818. *Rob Roy* held second place only to *Ivanhoe* as Scott's most popular novel throughout the nineteenth and early twentieth centuries, and it exceeded all his other works (and most novels of the age) in the number of theatrical versions. H. Philip Bolton has counted 1,000 distinct productions of *Rob Roy* since the novel's publication, making up some 20 per cent of all Scott adaptations.[10] The most successful of these, Isaac Pocock's melodrama *Rob Roy MacGregor; or, Auld Lang Syne* (Covent Garden, 12 March 1818), was one of the most popular and influential stage works of the early nineteenth century. Scott himself was delighted with it, especially the performance of Charles Mackay as Nicol Jarvie, when he attended the Edinburgh opening in 1819; it quickly attained the status of national pageant, and was played before George IV on his 1822 visit.

The proliferation of stage versions seems appropriate to the theatricality of Scott's conception of Rob Roy, much of whose part in the novel consists of appearing in different changes of costume, striking poses, and delivering ominous or pithy speeches. Many readers have sensed that he does not entirely belong in the book that bears his name.

[9] See H. Philip Bolton, 'Playing Rob Roy as Robin Hood', in J. H. Alexander and David Hewitt (eds.), *Scott in Carnival: Selected Papers from the Fourth International Scott Conference, Edinburgh, 1991* (1993), 480.

[10] H. Philip Bolton, 'Playing Rob Roy as Robin Hood'. See also the same author's *Scott Dramatized* (1992), and Barbara Bell, 'Sir Walter Scott and the National Drama', in *Scott in Carnival*, 459–77.

Far from occupying the foreground or centre of the narrative he seems to be at once nowhere and everywhere in it, assuming his legendary identity only in the final chapters. Even by the end of the tale Rob's relation to its private and historical plots remains obscure, as does his relation to its ostensible protagonist, Frank Osbaldistone, whose first-person narration supplies the story's climate of emotion and sensation. For much of the book it seems that Scott must have agreed to call it *Rob Roy* mainly in order not to have to call it *Francis Osbaldistone*. In fact Frank—callow, rash, conceited, yet at the same time generous and affectionate—is a rather impressive performance. Some of the best recent criticism of the novel has dwelt on Scott's pioneering rendition of a first-person narrator whose modes of feeling and telling (including his failures of telling) are themselves part of the story.[11] Here is nineteenth-century masculine subjectivity in full, proto-Freudian flood: resentment and yearning towards fathers, desire and fear provoked by strong women, a deadly rage against male siblings, deflected through intricate channels of anxiety and guilt. It seems that the mysterious Scotsman who keeps shifting in and out of the story, Campbell or MacGregor or Rob Roy, must be a figment conjured up by Frank's psychosexual crises—the primitive, violent, yet protective elder brother who is always fading back into the shadows, his dirty work well done. As we shall see, though, Rob Roy also bears an 'objective' identity for the reader, so that ultimately it is his novel rather than Frank's. To adopt a modern distinction: if Frank owns the *récit* (story, narration) of *Rob Roy*, Rob Roy owns the *discours* (its plot, the covert logic of events).

The Rob Roy who appears in the novel is in any case a rather different figure from the subject of the long historical introduction added by Scott in 1829. This gives the reader a thoroughly demystified Mac-Gregor, reduced by historical contingency to bravado, trickery, and an ambiguous pathos. Many of the subsequent adaptations, including the recent film by Michael Caton-Jones, have had to alter or abandon the framework of Scott's novel in order to reclaim a straightforwardly heroic—and sentimentally purified—Rob Roy. (Interestingly, the most successful of them, Pocock's play, keeps quite close to Scott, in

[11] See, in particular, Alexander Welsh, *The Hero of the Waverley Novels* (1963), 118–33; Jane Millgate, *Walter Scott: The Making of the Novelist* (1984), 134–50; Judith Wilt, *Secret Leaves: The Novels of Walter Scott* (1985), 51–70; Diane Elam, *Romancing the Postmodern* (1992), 107–10.

contrast to the first adaptation, George Soane's ridiculous farrago *Rob Roy, The Gregarach*.) Meanwhile, Rob Roy the character embodies a central dislocation in Scott's novel: in order to see him we are forced to look at him askance, as though he appears in the corner of our reading eye.

The popularity of *Rob Roy* has always been at odds with its critical reputation, even more than is usually the case with Scott. Amplifying the theme of a dissociation between *Rob Roy* and Rob Roy, critics have diagnosed a general structural discrepancy in the novel between plot and character. 'The story is in mist throughout,' complained one contemporary reviewer: 'There is everywhere a want of object, of something about which these restless agents may revolve, and which may give meaning and consequence to the preparations which are going on.'[12] At the same time, readers have applauded a succession of vivid characters who step out from the murky, digressive tangle of their narrative origins into something like independent life. Such a criticism identifies *Rob Roy* as the prototype of a distinctively Victorian kind of novel—Dickens's spring to mind—in which an incoherence of plotting appears to be the condition, the literary equivalent of a primal organic ooze, for the spontaneous generation of 'character'—especially comic character, represented here by the self-important, shrewd, and kindly Bailie Jarvie and the devious and sanctimonious Fairservice, although nineteenth-century readers also adored the high-mettled heroine, Diana Vernon.[13] The 'independent life' of these characters is conferred by Scott's turn to a dramatic mode of representation. *Rob Roy* was already poised to take over the stage. Speech, brilliantly stylized, lovingly crafted, rich in inflections of generic register and dialect, takes the place of action for much of the novel, and constitutes its surface interest, its main event. Each character plays his or her role with an energy that fizzes over into melodramatic rant (Helen MacGregor), comic garrulousness (Fairservice, Jarvie), or eye-rolling burlesque (the dying villain, Rashleigh). Scott's 'Shakespearian' rendition of character through speech, and above all comic

---

[12] E. T. Channing, *North American Review*, 7 (July 1818), 149–84; reprinted in John O. Hayden (ed.), *Scott: The Critical Heritage* (1970), 148–64.

[13] John Sutherland traces Die's ancestry in Restoration comedy and her descent through such spirited Victorian heroines as Charlotte Brontë's Shirley Keeldar, Trollope's Glencora Palliser and Meredith's Diana of the Crossways: *The Life of Walter Scott* (1995), 206.

speech (not just Fairservice and Jarvie but, for example, Garschat-tachin, Chs. 28–9), supplies that 'want of object' bemoaned by the critic, and balances the dark intensities of Frank's narrating sensibility.

Much of the official dissatisfaction with *Rob Roy* can be summed up by the complaint that, in one way or another, it isn't *Waverley*.[14] The chronological priority of Scott's first novel, marked in such titles as 'the Author of Waverley' and 'the Waverley novels', has all too easily been interpreted as a paradigmatic priority; as though much of the author's career consisted of attempts to repeat a formula that he him-self barely understood. Such a view has been encouraged, it is true, by Scott's own self-deprecating comments about his art (and he was especially dismissive of *Rob Roy*: 'I did not much write him *con amore* and I think he smells of the cramp . . . I was obliged at last to draw a rough coarse and hasty thread'[15]). Jane Millgate has argued that Scott's novels require their reader to interpret them in relation to one another, as an unfolding pattern of formal and thematic variations. She points out that Scott positively draws attention to his return as the Author of *Waverley* in *Rob Roy*: revisiting not just the earlier novel's setting and topic, but its basic plot of a romantic young Englishman, estranged from his father and profession, who ventures north into Scotland, becomes embroiled with Jacobite rebels and Highland out-laws, and falls in love with a glamorous dark lady.[16] This revisitation signals the opposite of a hapless repetition; it advertises the attempt at something new, a revisionary rethinking of the earlier novel and, in particular, of its cultural achievement as the model of Scottish national historical romance.

The paradigmatic status of *Waverley* has been if anything re-inforced by the twentieth-century rehabilitation of its author's reputa-tion. Georg Lukács, and after him David Daiches, identified Scott's achievement with a serious, innovative historicism; since then, a

[14] Donald Davie condemns *Rob Roy* as a botched repetition of *Waverley: The Heyday of Sir Walter Scott* (1961), 56–64. F. R. Hart, in *Scott's Novels: The Plotting of Historic Sur-vival* (1966), 33–48, and A. O. J. Cockshutt, in *The Achievement of Walter Scott* (1969), 153–70, both concede that Scott is attempting something different in *Rob Roy*, although failing to recapture the earlier novel's thematic coherence.

[15] *Letters* v. 50 (to J. B. S. Morritt, 14 Jan. 1818).

[16] Jane Millgate, *Walter Scott*, 133. Perhaps the most pointed of Scott's internal allusions to *Waverley* in *Rob Roy* involves the reappearance of the Falls of Lediart, the scene of Flora Mac-Ivor's famous 'seduction' of Waverley to the Jacobite cause, as the setting for the picnic at which the MacGregors entertain Frank and Jarvie before they leave the Highlands.

strong tradition of commentary has traced the intellectual programme of the Waverley novels in the sociological historians of the Scottish Enlightenment, such as Adam Smith and Adam Ferguson.[17] This commentary takes its cue from the last chapter of *Waverley*, which frames the historical romance with a meditation on the modernization of Scotland in the period since 1745:

There is no European nation which, within the course of half a century, or little more, has undergone so complete a change as this kingdom of Scotland. The effects of the insurrection of 1745,—the abolition of the heritable jurisdictions of the Lowland nobility and barons,—the total eradication of the Jacobite party, which, averse to intermingle with the English, or adopt their customs, commenced this innovation. The gradual influx of wealth, and extension of commerce, have since united to render the present people of Scotland a class of beings as different from their grandfathers, as the existing English are from those of Queen Elizabeth's time.[18]

Scott rehearses two crucial rhetorical moves here. First, he identifies the political movement of Jacobitism with a vanished Scottish cultural past, which the preceding narrative has located especially in the Gaelic Highlands. Second, Scott aligns the perspective of his narrator and his reader with the temporality of the historical process of modernization, an alignment signalled in the novel's subtitle: ' 'Tis Sixty Years Since'. The title of this last chapter, 'A Postscript, which should have been a Preface', spells out the character of a retrospect that sets the terms through which the preceding narrative is now to be understood.

But in *Rob Roy* Scott undoes both of these rhetorical moves. First, the later novel prises apart the identification of Jacobitism—as a political movement and an ideology—with Highland culture, and in so doing blocks both of these terms from working, together or apart, as representations of 'Scotland'. Second, Scott dissolves the teleological

---

[17] Georg Lukács, *The Historical Novel* (1937); David Daiches, 'Scott's Achievement as a Novelist' (1956). For Scott and Enlightenment historicism, see Duncan Forbes, 'The Rationalism of Sir Walter Scott', *Cambridge Journal*, 7 (1953), 20–35; Peter Garside, 'Scott and the "Philosophical" Historians', *Journal of the History of Ideas*, 36 (1975), 497–512; Graham McMaster, *Scott and Society* (1981); Kathryn Sutherland, 'Fictional Economies: Adam Smith, Sir Walter Scott and the Nineteenth-Century Novel', *English Literary History*, 54/1 (1987), 97–127; Cyrus Vakil, 'Walter Scott and the Historicism of Scottish Enlightenment Philosophical History', *Scott in Carnival*, 404–18; David Kaufmann, *The Business of Common Life: Classical Economics and the Novel from Revolution to Reform* (1995).

[18] Scott, *Waverley* (World's Classics edn., p. 340).

certainty of the narrator–editor who can offer us a postscript so sure of itself that it ought to have been a preface. Notoriously, the first-person narrator of *Rob Roy* fails to give us final access to the meaning of the events he relates. Neither his own life nor the public history with which it intersects arrange themselves into a clear pattern in Frank's telling. Recent criticism has recovered the subtlety of Scott's representation of an unresolved psychology of anxiety, trauma, and repression.[19] The ordeal of a masculinity beset by eloquent Amazons—the lovely Die Vernon, the terrifying Helen MacGregor—culminates not in any clarity of action or self-possession but in a remarkable fit of hysteria, as an archaic feminine energy overwhelms the hero from within (Ch. 33). *Rob Roy* scrambles the lucid alignment of national, psychic, and gender developments upon which the historicism of *Waverley* depended.

At the centre of *Rob Roy* (Ch. 26) the reader encounters an authoritative, 'scientific' analysis of history—the hitherto obscure or illegible referent of this 'historical novel'—according to principles of political economy developed in the Scottish Enlightenment. This analysis is delivered by the Glasgow merchant and magistrate Nicol Jarvie, the character in the novel who personifies an ascendant, modern, cultural order of commerce, legality, and civic virtue. Jarvie's analysis follows (or anticipates) the account of modernity, established by Adam Smith in *The Wealth of Nations*, that identifies it with mercantile capitalism and the institutions of a post-1688 national economy, such as the Stock Exchange, colonial free trade, and a national debt. Explaining both the state of the Highlands and the coming Jacobite rising, this analysis belongs to the genre that will be called (at the end of the eighteenth century) 'the statistical account of Scotland',[20] and it describes 'history' in terms of a dynamic relation between population, productivity, and credit. The overpopulated Highlands have become the equivalent of a third-world debtor economy within the new British state, and a national credit collapse will push the clans into insurrection. Far from signifying a resurgence of ancient cultural loyalties, in this novel the Jacobite and clan risings turn out to be determined by the fluctuations of a modern, imperial economy.

[19] See, in particular, Welsh, *The Hero of the Waverley Novels*, 118–33; Millgate, *Walter Scott*, 134–50.

[20] *The Statistical Account of Scotland* was a 29-vol. series of economic and demographic regional surveys compiled by Sir John Sinclair, 1791–9.

The 'statistical account' would thus appear to occupy a position of authority in Scott's novel, identical with the perspective of modernity from which we are reading, and made possible by the economic and cultural site from which Jarvie, quasi-prophetically, speaks: Glasgow itself, the city where—at the time that Frank is supposed to be writing—Adam Smith holds his professorship, and is indeed composing the lectures that will form *The Wealth of Nations*. We glimpse, through the novel's layering of historical reference, the progress of modernization invoked at the end of *Waverley*. Frank meets Jarvie in Glasgow in 1715, on the eve of its post-Union economic take-off; he is narrating around 1765, when the colonial trade boom is at its height; and Scott himself is writing in 1817, as the city enters the industrial era. Jarvie's account explains not only historical causality in terms of a political economy, but also the conjunction of that political economy and history with the novel's 'private' plot, in which the hero neglects the family business and his wicked cousin makes off with the assets, provoking a nation-wide financial panic and the Jacobite counter-revolutionary attempt. (We also learn that a credit-squeeze lies behind Rob Roy's career in banditry.) Economics seems to be the definitive discourse of the historical novel as well as of history itself.

Rob Roy opens with a ceremonial confrontation between 'commerce' and 'poetry'. The contest, associated with a filial resistance to the disciplines of paternity, replays another topic—the dialogue between 'romance' and 'real history'—familiar from *Waverley*. Frank Osbaldistone defies his father's wish that he succeed him as head of the firm because he would rather be a poet. But the narrative invests commercial enterprise with the peril and glamour of 'romance', and sets up the merchant—in a formulation later developed by John Ruskin in *Unto this Last* (1862)—as the proper hero of modern society. Frank's poetry, by contrast, is a dead letter, imitation in the most lifeless, literal sense. Not only is Frank (like the youthful Scott) translating Ariosto, or replicating the forms of the *ancien régime* in a kind of cultural Jacobitism, but Scott makes one of his efforts echo his own *Marmion*—as if to taunt critics with the spectre of literary repetition. Frank's imagination is incapable of grasping the dynamic energies of modernity. He only dutifully repeats the Smithian maxim: '[Commerce] connects nation with nation, relieves the wants, and contributes to the wealth of all; and is to the general commonwealth of the civilized world what the daily intercourse of ordinary life is to private society, or rather, what air and food are to our bodies' (Ch. 2). It will take another kind of romance than Frank's verses to be adequate to the forces of connection and circulation that mesh together, and so constitute, 'nation', 'world', 'daily life', 'private society', and 'our bodies'. The new romance form of modernity is of course the novel, exemplified by the book we are reading. It is one of the many subtleties of *Rob Roy* that—in contrast to its author—its poet-*manqué* narrator never quite becomes aware of his true vocation as a *novelist*. Frank does not think of his contemporary, Daniel Defoe, who combined a literary career as 'the father of the novel' with the role of economic and political agent, involved, among other enterprises, in the forging of a new nation state through the Union of Scotland and England; but Scott alludes to him more than once, and indeed makes him the source for Jarvie's account of the rising economic energies of Glasgow.[21]

Frank sets out on the Waverley hero's obligatory journey north. His progress is saturated with the topics and tropes of commerce well before it becomes evident how much the plot will turn on the circulation and interception of letters, notes, bills, and other forms of credit and pieces of paper.[22] Diana Vernon, better attuned to metaphor than Frank, rebukes him for spending his stock of polite compliments on her:

they serve fine gentlemen who travel in the country, instead of the toys, beads, and bracelets, which navigators carry to propitiate the inhabitants of newly discovered lands. . . . You remind me . . . of the fairy tale, where the man finds all the money which he had carried to market suddenly changed into pieces of slate. (Ch. 6)

Die's speech understands both the imperial, universal claims of the new system of exchange and the instability it brings as it traverses different cultural epochs. Later, Frank is moved to apologize to the reader for the 'twang of commerce' that pervades his language ('our sympathy, like the funds of a compounding bankrupt, can only be divided' (Ch. 18)). The thematic resonance of the narrator's name, discussed

---

[21] For Scott's role in canonizing Defoe as 'the father of the novel' see Homer O. Brown, *Institutions of the English Novel: From Defoe to Scott* (1997).

[22] For a different view of the 'intercepted letter' in Scott see Nicola Watson, *Revolution and the Form of the Novel: Intercepted Letters, Interrupted Seductions* (1994). Scott's theme reflects contemporary debates about the resumption of cash payments after the long wars with France, and attendant anxieties about deflation and currency depreciation.

by Jane Millgate in her classic essay 'The Limits of Frankness', must be extended then beyond the (important) issue of the hero's psychology to cover his part in the novel's economic scheme—as a character who desires, above all, freedom to circulate and to set his own value, yet who must face at every turn the prospects of depreciation and arrest, as though he himself amounts to no more than what is written on a piece of paper. (A 'frank' is the stamp or wafer that allowed a letter to circulate without payment of a postage fee.) It is no coincidence that the novel's most violent episode culminates in the murder of a revenue officer, accompanied by an icy reiteration of the 'twang of commerce': 'the unit of that life for which he had pleaded so strongly, was for ever withdrawn from the sum of human existence' (Ch. 31).

Frank's journey takes the narrative through a series of different regional sites, each of which represents a specific historical relation to national modernity. The story opens in London, less a thickly described place than a premiss, the centre of the new United Britain and its expanding empire. Then the narrative settles, for an inordinate length (Chs 5–18), at Osbaldistone Hall in Northumberland, before going on to Glasgow (19–26) and at last the Highlands (27–36). Respectively, these are the settings of a rustic feudalism (the crucible of Jacobite intrigue), commercial proto-modernity, and pre-feudal, 'savage', clan society. In short, the novel's settings represent distinct historical stages according to the Scottish Enlightenment model of philosophical or scientific history, which described the production of modernity through an evolutionary sequence of socio-economic formations. We might expect that this arrangement of settings will map the kind of historicist scheme exemplified in *The Wealth of Nations*, with clan society, feudalism, and commerce occupying a teleological progression, in which the obsolescence of one stage—its pastness— guarantees the succession of the next. Frank's sojourn at Osbaldistone Hall (its very length evoking a lethal stagnation) appears to bear this out. The past, residual character of a backwoods feudalism is marked by a conspicuous literary stylization, beginning with the kind of satiric comedy of regional manners perfected by Maria Edgeworth, in *Castle Rackrent*, to signify the obsolescence of the old Irish gentry. Sir Hildebrand's sons are not characters (inhabitants of the new discourse of the novel, psychologically individuated by the complex specificity of a modern economy) but types, generic cases of booby-squire decadence, barely distinguishable by their respective humours. Having made its point, such a representation has nowhere else to go but to record the extinction of the line, which it does in a suitably absurdist key at the end of the novel. As Frank lingers at Osbaldistone Hall, a different literary stylization of feudal obsolescence takes over, this time drawn from the 'Gothic' romance of Horace Walpole, Ann Radcliffe, and Charlotte Smith. Tropes of mystery, fatality, and ghostliness mark the fitful Jacobite theme—in this case, drawn from Walpole's *The Castle of Otranto*:

Diana Vernon stood before me, resting on the arm of a figure so strongly resembling that of the portrait so often mentioned, that I looked hastily at the frame, expecting to see it empty. My first idea was, either that I had gone suddenly distracted, or that the spirits of the dead had arisen and been placed before me. (Ch. 38)

The Gothic register aligns the Jacobites, and especially Die's father, not just with psychological themes of repression and sublimation but with a more drastic condition of spectralization and deathliness.[23] Both styles, the satiric and the Gothic, signify a fated falling into the past.

But the move north into Scotland obscures the teleological certainty—the conviction of pastness—written into the Osbaldistone Hall chapters. Scotland itself is not a unified territorial and cultural entity, a 'nation', since it is split between the very different worlds of Glasgow and the Highlands, nor is it situated as 'provincial' or as 'past' in relation to the metropolitan south. In Glasgow Bailie Jarvie hails the advent of modernity in the form of colonial trade, civic improvement, and a modern politics of legality and credit. Yet here the Gothic shadows associated with Osbaldistone Hall and the Jacobite plot deepen rather than dissipate, to the extent of seeming to belong to the institutional fabric of a far from enlightened city. Frank experiences Glasgow, Jarvie's hospitable parlour aside, as a dangerous sequence of nocturnal, carceral, and labyrinthine spaces: the crypt of the cathedral, the medieval bridge, the town gaol, the 'wilderness' of the College yards. Wild Highlanders infest the burgh, and Rob Roy's outlaw authority reaches into the depths of the prison. These effects exceed the view of Glasgow as a border town, exhibiting a 'transitional' historical character, that marks Frank's arrival there. The Gothic mirk of the cathedral

[23] For a full discussion of Gothic motifs in *Rob Roy* see Fiona Robertson, *Legitimate Histories: Scott, Gothic and the Authority of Fiction* (1994).

crypt evokes a Presbyterian theocratic police state, associated less with the Covenanting past than with a nightmarish intensification of the rule of law that Jarvie himself proclaims.

Glasgow, set just below 'the Highland line', exemplifies the principle of a contrast of cultures and epochs embodied in Rob Roy himself: a figure like 'Robin Hood in the middle ages', as Scott's 1829 introduction puts it, 'blending the wild virtues, the subtle policy, and unrestrained license of an American Indian', yet 'flourishing in Scotland during the Augustan age of Queen Anne and George I', 'within forty miles of . . . a great commercial city, the seat of a learned university.' On more than one occasion Scott would name this contrast of epochs his special topic[24]—except that here the mixture of savage and commercial stages obliterates, instead of clarifying, their status as past and future. Despite their official opposition, savagery and commerce sustain rather than cancel one another, constituting a dark, intricate kind of present. Scott dramatizes this in the 'primitive' bond of kinship that connects Jarvie and Rob Roy, which a number of critics (following Daiches) have seen as the centre of the novel's historical theme.[25] This is so, except that it is not really a historical theme in the sense that it clarifies a relation of chronological progress. The novel does not represent Jarvie's world or values as penetrating or superseding Rob Roy's. The narrative moves towards the mutual reaffirmation of their kinship, and the recognition that both worlds persist alongside, and through, one another—except that Rob Roy is able to move about in the alien society of Glasgow (and England) with far more ease and command than Jarvie could ever hope for in the Highlands. The resolution of this theme arrives in Chapter 34, when Jarvie and Rob settle their accounts. Rob pays his debt to Jarvie, acknowledging the legal and economic claim; but the money comes from an illicit scheme of 'black mail', and Rob burns the receipt, asserting his own code of orality and honour over his cousin's of literacy and credit.[26]

By the end of the Highland adventure it will have become clear to the reader that systems of meaning and value may not necessarily

---

[24] See Scott's 1831 introduction to *The Fortunes of Nigel*.

[25] F. R. Hart, *Scott's Novels*, 33–48; David Brown, *Walter Scott and the Historical Imagination* (1969), 105–8.

[26] Along these lines, Bruce Beiderwell argues that Rob Roy's primitive code of vengeance prevails in the novel against the official, civilized code of legality: *Power and Punishment in Scott's Novels* (1992), 45–61.

prevail outside the cultural site where they are produced. The authority of Jarvie's 'statistical account' belongs to Glasgow; it exerts no
enlightening force over the rest of the narrative. It does not help Jarvie
and Frank, or the reader, to interpret setting or events once the tale
shifts to 'Rob Roy's country'. As Frank and Jarvie cruise down Loch
Lomond, Scott gives them set-piece reactions to the scenery: Jarvie
speaks for economic improvement, Frank for romantic appreciation
(Ch. 36). Jarvie's scheme of improvement seems farcically inappropri-
ate, a crude vision of economic colonization that signifies no more than
the Glasgow Bailie's own provincial foible. This is not simply because
Frank's aesthetic view seems 'truer', reflecting what he conceives to be
the Highlanders' own relation to their setting ('the natural taste which
belongs to mountaineers, and especially to the Scottish Highlanders,
whose feelings I have observed are often allied with the romantic and
poetical' (Ch. 35)). Frank is narrating his adventures in the mid-
1760s, the age not just of Adam Smith but of Macpherson's 'Ossian'
translations, Horace Walpole's Gothic novel, the romance-revival
odes of Gray, the vogue for a sublime aesthetics, and dissertations on
the natural taste of clans and tribes by Hugh Blair and Adam Ferguson. In other words, Frank's aesthetic discourse is no less 'modern'
than Jarvie's utilitarian, economic one; particularly when we consider
that the two discourses—romance and political economy—would
persist alongside each other to constitute the contemporary literary
culture of Scott's readers, in the Waverley Novels and *The Edinburgh
Review*. Indeed, the implication is that a romantic aesthetics is *more*
modern than the raw utilitarianism of the primitive stage of capitalism
for which Jarvie speaks, since the novel, the up-to-date form of
romance, is able to dramatize both perspectives. Scott deploys the
historicist scheme against itself. In contrast to the transcendental
position of a 'postscript which should have been a preface,' the
political–economic analysis of history remains embedded within the
narrative's relative cultural spaces, temporalities and discourses,
framed by them rather than framing them.

The authority of the 'statistical account' withers away once Frank
and Jarvie enter the Highlands, already denominated by Jarvie 'a wild
kind of warld by themsells' (Ch. 26). This may seem paradoxical, since
Scott's representation keeps recurring to the standard Enlightenment
sociological equation of Gaelic clan society with a 'savage' tribalism,
especially that of North American Indians. Rob's kinsman Dougal is

an 'uncouth, wild, and ugly savage' (Ch. 22), the Highlanders are 'the natives' (Ch. 28), Mrs MacAlpine's hut is a 'hospitable wigwam' (Ch. 34), and so on. But Scott gives this savagery a different kind, not degree, of relation to modernity from that of a Jacobite retro-feudalism. Clan culture enjoys a lively autonomy and synchronicity rather than a fated obsolescence; it may look marginal and lawless in the eyes of Glasgow or London, but it is the centre of its own world, and governed by its own laws. If feudalism and Jacobitism together consti-tute the British nation's socio-economic and political past, the High-landers evoke a different order of ancestral relationship to modernity: the order of the primitive. The object of a nascent science, anthro-pology, the primitive signifies an origin still structurally present within modernity, rather than a superseded developmental form. The prim-itive, charged with 'original' virtues—courage, loyalty, pathos, but also violence—belongs to the present as well as to the past; even if it must move in unrecognizable or (in today's jargon of state) 'deniable' forms.

Rob Roy the character, as we might expect, embodies the category of the primitive in the tale that bears his name. The outlaw recurs across the narrative's different sites in a sequence of metamorphic appearances and disappearances, gradually uncloaking his own shape as Frank and the reader approach his 'native heath': the terminus of this revelation being our glimpses (never more than fragmentary) of his wild body. In the Glasgow gaol, Frank observes Rob Roy's preter-naturally broad shoulders and long arms:

I afterwards heard that this length of arm was a circumstance on which he prided himself, that when he wore his native Highland garb, he could tie the garters of his hose without stooping; and that it gave him great advantage in the use of the broadsword, at which he was very dexterous. But certainly this want of symmetry . . . gave something wild, irregular, and, as it were, unearthly, to his appearance, and reminded me involuntarily, of the tales which Mabel used to tell of the old Picts who ravaged Northumberland in ancient times, who, according to her tradition, were a sort of half-goblin half-human beings, distinguished, like this man, for courage, cunning, ferocity, the length of their arms, and the squareness of their shoulders. (Ch. 23)

Over the Highland line, Rob's appearance 'in the dress of his country' allows Frank to notice the 'fell of thick, short, red hair, especially around his knees, which resembled in this respect . . . the limbs of a red-coloured Highland bull' (Ch. 32). He is native yet 'unearthly',

Pictish, 'half-human' and 'half-goblin' but also part animal, simian and bull-like: the tropes for Rob's elemental or aboriginal status are not just mixed but contradictory. Through this figure Scott imagines a heretic or outlaw identity at human and cultural origins, both in the miscegenation of categories (human, animal, demonic) and in the appeal to heterodox discourses: religious-folkloric (goblins as the aboriginal inhabitants of the country) and scientific-anthropological (beasts as human ancestors). Rob Roy has a goblin-like power to shift his shape and appear or disappear at will; such a figure belongs to the traditional imagination of 'folklore', albeit newly recovered (and invested with the aura of tradition) under an anthropologizing rubric. More striking are the glimpses of Rob Roy as a kind of anthropoid ape—broad-shouldered, long-armed, covered in a red pelt—and the allusion to a conspicuously new, and heterodox, scientific discourse of subhuman origins. Edinburgh in the late Enlightenment (until the 1830s) was the British institutional centre for pre-Darwinian theorizing about human origins, and Scott would have been familiar with the polygenetic thesis of Lord Kames, as well as the notorious claims of Lord Monboddo (ridiculed by Dr Johnson) that the orang-utan was a human subspecies and could be taught language. Indeed, this is the kind of ape that Rob Roy resembles. The Romantic vogue for the orang-utan—a figure on the threshold of humanity, language, and culture—extended through Scott's own late romance, *Count Robert of Paris*, as well as Peacock's *Melincourt* (exactly contemporaneous with *Rob Roy*) and Poe's tale 'The Murders in the Rue Morgue'.[27] When, early in the novel, Die Vernon refers disdainfully to 'the Ourang-Outangs, my cousins' (Ch. 9), the metaphor is absorbed in its local satiric context: the primitive is a joke, forecasting the cousins' comic extinction. But in Rob Roy's case the primitive signifies a rugged vitality and cultural integrity ('honour'), quite the opposite of a destiny of extinction—he is quintessentially a survivor, triumphant over the proscription of his clan. Scott makes the point that Rob dies in bed after the end of the adventure, in defiance of Jarvie's prophecy that he will be hanged.

This makes for a striking contrast with *Waverley*, where Scott had identified the failure of the Jacobite rising with the historic end of clan society, ceremonially marked by the execution of the chieftain Fergus

[27] See Clare A. Simmons, 'A Man of Few Words: The Romantic Orang-Outang and Scott's *Count Robert of Paris*', *Scottish Literary Journal*, 17/1 (May 1990), 21–34.

Mac-Ivor. Here, Rob Roy's involvement in the Jacobite plot is oppor-
tunistic, made not out of any love for King James but to advance the
fortunes of his clan: Rob 'is for his ain hand', as Jarvie recognizes—in
an interesting semantic collapse of the communal ethos into an individu-
alist one. Thanks also to the earlier novel, Scott's readers knew about
the end of the clans, but in this text they survive, the secret sharers
of an imaginary present, invigorated rather than depleted by their
station outside the law. Rob Roy's physical energy, his talent for action,
puts him at an opposite pole to the wraith-like figures of the Jacobite
nobility. He enjoys a preternatural ability to turn up in any scene, or
scenario, without being confined to it; breaking in and out of the story
at its crisis points, he inhabits a recursive rather than linear, interrup-
tive rather than continuous, narrative time. This signifies resilience
and potency, rather than the typical vulnerability of the savage, incar-
cerated in his 'other time' by the edicts of Western anthropology.[28]
Adept in all cultural sites and roles, the master of appearances and languages, Rob Roy is expert, above all, in the 'modern' arts of commerce
and negotiation, which may extend to robbery and homicide—for who
better than a freebooter should thrive in the new capitalist economy?
In short, the primitive Highlander is also the archetype of economic
man, since the new age requires an ideological recovery of 'natural
man' at the same time that actual 'savages' are being figured into the
expanding horizon of an imperial economy. (Mungo Park, the African
explorer, had been Scott's friend and neighbour in the Borders.) That
is just, of course, what theorists of capitalism-as-modernity then and
now have wanted to insist; whether they formulate the original principle of human nature as a propensity to exchange or barter (Smith's
Wealth of Nations) or as an insatiable desire (Ferguson's *History of
Civil Society*).

If Scott's novel endows Highland savagery with a specific historical
context, it is surely—but only partly—that of colonial empire. More
than any other Scott novel (except, perhaps, *The Heart of Mid-Lothian*)
Rob Roy represents the Highlands as a colonial frontier. The tale's single episode of military violence follows the historical-romance convention, described by Lukács, of dramatizing a clash between different
epochs, but it is significant (again, in contrast to *Waverley*) that the

---

[28] See the classic analysis by Johannes Fabian, *Time and the Other: How Anthropology
Makes its Object* (New York, 1983).

ambush of Thornton's troop by Helen MacGregor does not belong to the history of the Jacobite rising. This overthrow of disciplined red-coats by a rabble of wild 'natives' (most of them women and youths, led not by Rob Roy but his frightening Amazon wife), complete with 'bar-baric' atrocity, belongs to the theatre of colonial resistance rather than of national history. For Scott's readers, the military role of Highland regiments in the modern British army would have compounded the episode's allusive force; most recently, in Wellington's Peninsular cam-paign, such troops had supported mountaineer guerrilla fighters against the Napoleonic empire. Scott revives a traditional rhetoric of Highland 'savagery' to insist not on the obsolescence but on the con-temporaneity of these figures—'the indispensable atavistic natives', as Womack calls them, 'in the Victorian triumph of peace and progress.'[29] Here, though, complicating the formula, Scott also insists on the Mac-Gregors' ferocious resistance to the military and legal apparatus of the British state. These Highlanders may not be drafted; Rob Roy's sup-port of Frank, like his kinship with Jarvie, remains illicit, covert, un-accountable. Through the figure of the up-to-date primitive we glimpse instead the shadow of a 'world-system'—sublime, dynamic, 'outlaw'— that exceeds the official, enlightened boundaries, historical and ideo-logical as well as territorial, of civil society and the nation state.[30] The British condition of modernity does not after all consist of an internally unified, civilized nation, the product of an evolutionary graduation of discrete historical stages. It consists of a global network of uneven, heterogeneous times and spaces bound together by commerce and military force, the dynamism of which flows among, precisely, the economic and cultural differences of the local parts. This sublime imperial dynamism, rather than their elegiac absorption by the mod-ern state, informs the aesthetic glamour of the Highlanders in *Rob Roy*.

The traditional complaint about the incoherence of *Rob Roy* rehearses terms Scott has already set in play in his marvellously shifty romance. The exemplary criticism of Nassau Senior (Professor of Political Economy at Oxford) is already enclosed by, rather than stand-ing outside, Scott's text:

The author himself, as he goes on, finds himself so thoroughly involved in the meshes of his plot, that seeing no legitimate extrication, he clears

[29] Womack, *Improvement and Romance*, 60.

[30] See Immanuel Wallerstein, *The Modern World-System III: The Second Era of Great Expansion of the Capitalist World-Economy, 1730–1840s* (1989).

himself at last by the most absolute, we had almost said the most tyrannical, exercise of the empire which authors must be acknowledged to have over their personages and events, which we recollect, even in the annals of that despotic class of sovereigns. C'est un vrai coup d'état—and one which we should have expected rather from an Asiatic writer, than from a novelist 'in this free country.'[31]

It is the critic, protesting against an Asiatic despotism on the part of the author, who remains thoroughly involved in these meshes, in his reluctant acknowledgement that the novel performs an 'exotic' induction into the barbaric psychic and political relations of empire. To be compelled by *Rob Roy*—as tens of thousands of readers were compelled—is to find oneself outside the fiction of modernity as a 'free country', and spellbound by those narrative effects of obscurity, disjunctiveness, illogic, and bewilderment deplored by critics. It seems we still need to revise our assumptions about the cultural work of fiction, and abandon an easy language of 'nostalgia' and 'escapism', when we talk about Scott.

---

[31] *Quarterly Review*, 26 (October 1821); repr. in Hayden (ed.), *Scott: The Critical Heritage*, 215.

NOTE ON THE TEXT

In April 1817 Scott informed his agent, John Ballantyne, that he had
'a good subject for a work of fiction in petto' to mark his return to the
firm of Archibald Constable; on 3 May he signed an agreement to
receive £600 for an edition of 6,000 copies, increased to 10,000 as he set
to work on the new novel over the summer (*Letters* i. 514–15). Scott
completed the first volume by the end of August; composition was
retarded, however, by attacks of the 'stomach cramps' (gallstones) that
had made his life a misery since the early spring. *Rob Roy* eventually
appeared on 31 December 1817, bearing the publication date 1818. It
went through two subsequent 'editions' (i.e. printings) in the three-
volume format before the end of the year, and was reissued in two large
octavo volumes in the series *Novels and Tales of the Author of Waverley*
in 1820. From 1828 until shortly before his death in 1832 Scott edited
all his novels for republication in a collected edition, writing new
introductions and additional notes for them and correcting and revis-
ing the texts. This, the so-called 'Magnum Opus' edition (published
by Constable's erstwhile partner, Robert Cadell), established the texts
of the Waverley novels as they have been read since Scott's death. Like
most other Scott titles in World's Classics, the present edition of *Rob
Roy* is based on the 1829 Magnum Opus text.

Scott used the second edition, 1822, of *Novels and Tales of the
Author of Waverley* as his base text for the first 12 volumes of the Magnum Opus edition. His working copy, the so-called 'Interleaved Set' of
the Waverley Novels containing corrections and insertions in his
hand, was acquired by the National Library of Scotland in 1986, after
more than 50 years' absence from the public domain. *Rob Roy*, cata-
logued as MSS 23005–23006, occupies part of Volume 5 and all of Volume 6 of the Interleaved Set. Two nineteenth-century editions of the
Waverley Novels, the Centenary (1871) and the Dryburgh (1892–94),
were corrected against the Interleaved Set. The present edition is the
first modern *Rob Roy* to take account of Scott's preparatory materials.

Anyone seriously interested in *Rob Roy* will want to consult John
and Winifred MacQueen's forthcoming volume in the new Edinburgh
Edition of the Waverley Novels, based on the early editions collated
with Scott's manuscripts and proofs. (There are many variants

between 1818 and 1822.) The Magnum Opus edition represents a different historical state of the text, with a different kind of cultural presence and influence. Scott's revisions of *Rob Roy*, undertaken in the autumn of 1828, fall into two categories: alterations of the 1822 text of the novel, and the addition of new editorial matter. 'It will differ from the others in having a long Introduction History of Rob and but few notes', Scott informed Cadell (*Letters* xi. 34). Scott's exuberant antiquarianism, Jane Millgate has argued, led him to insert more notes than he had at first intended, notably the long account of the Revd Robert Kirk and the fairies (Chapter XXVIII). The introduction with its several appendices, filling almost half the first volume, is the most distinctive—some may find it obtrusive—of the 1829 innovations. The reader now approaches the shadowy Rob of the tale through the demystifying detail of an Enlightenment historical essay, drawn from primary sources both oral and literary, and still one of the most authoritative accounts of its subject. Many readers, of course, have always skipped Scott's introductory material—which does not justify the bad habit of some modern editions of dumping it at the back of the book or omitting it altogether.

Textual revision in 1829 is profuse but light, addressing stylistic detail rather than main event. Scott took the opportunity to bring his prose into sharper focus, inserting words and phrases to balance syntax and clarify grammatical antecedents, eliminating verbal repetition by variation, and shaping emphasis, most of the time to happy effect. The printed text, in addition, brings spelling, punctuation, and syntax into conformity with house style and English conventions. Some of the results, such as an increased density of punctuation and the identification (often supererogatory) of speakers in dialogue, can seem fussy to modern taste. Many of the changes, however, restore readings from the first edition of 1818, and in general the Magnum Opus text of this particular novel represents a clarification of the first edition rather than any new tilt or emphasis. Only a few of Scott's revisions are substantive. Frank and Andrew Fairservice now arrive in Glasgow on a Saturday evening rather than a Thursday morning (Chapter XIX); rather than leave his English readers puzzled by references to the Presbyterian fast-Thursday which preceded a communion Sunday, or explain it in a new note, Scott found it simpler to make his characters arrive on the eve of the Sabbath. Scott also adjusts his orientation of Glasgow geography, so that the Clyde now flows through the city from east to west instead of north–south (Chapter XXI). At a moment of crisis in Chapter XXII Rob Roy's speech is elevated from Lowland dialect to a grander, more theatrical manner. In Chapter XXX Frank, London-bred, had compared the ignominiously dangling Jarvie to a sign in front of a shop on 'Ludgate-hill'; in 1829 the association is with 'the Trongate of his native city'. In Chapter XXXI Scott corrects the birth order of Rob Roy's sons, which he had the wrong way around in earlier editions.

In the present edition of *Rob Roy* I have adopted a conservative stance, retaining the 1829 text except where, in my judgement, typographic errors have crept in (the omission of the comma after 'Mr Rashleigh' in Chapter X, 1829, redirects Frank's speech to the wrong interlocutor) or where the copyist or compositor has misread Scott's holograph ('Haig' for 'Ilay', 'medical' for 'mutual'), or neglected the Interleaved Set revision for no apparent good reason. For example, Scott took care to correct the Scots 'hinderlans' and Gaelic 'brochan' (early editions) to 'hinderlins' and 'brechan', in Chapter XXIII. Failure to transmit the correction meant that, such was Scott's authority, the corrupt usage became canonical in nineteenth-century Scottish literature: the *Scottish National Dictionary* tracks the progress of 'hinderlans' from *Rob Roy* through Hogg's *The Three Perils of Man*, Stevenson's *Underwoods*, and Buchan's *The Thirty-Nine Steps*. Of the many discrepancies between Scott's holograph introduction and the printed text, almost all can be accounted for by the imposition of house conventions and general tidying-up on the part of publisher or printers, which the author would have expected; I have accordingly corrected very little there, except for some obvious errors and omissions. A paragraph left out of the published text is printed in the explanatory notes.

Scott's Notes are marked in the text by superior figures; my Explanatory Notes are marked by asterisks. A useful account of the Magnum Opus edition can be found in Jane Millgate, *Scott's Last Edition: A Study in Publishing History* (1987), which contains an extensive discussion of the notes and introduction to *Rob Roy* (pp. 82–8). See also Iain Gordon Brown (ed.), *Scott's Interleaved Waverley Novels: An Introduction and Commentary* (1987), especially J. H. Alexander, 'Descriptive Guide to the Interleaved Set' (pp. 11–26), and Iain Gordon Brown, 'An Illustrated Commentary on the Interleaved Set', which reproduces several folios showing Scott's revisions and additions to *Rob Roy* (Plates 21–3).

Emendation List

The 1829 edition text is printed in the left-hand column and the emendation in the right. 'IS' marks the restoration of a revision in Scott's hand from the Interleaved Set that was altered or unincorporated in the 1829 edition, and '1822' marks the restoration of a reading from the 1822 edition, unemended in the Interleaved Set but altered in the 1829 edition.

p. 8 l. 31 *Raid*	*Raad* (Gaelic *radh*, road)
p. 22 l. 5 'Since then,' said Robin, 'right is plain	Since then the rule of right is plain (IS)
p. 39 l. 9 1738	1733 (IS)
p. 40 ll. 29–30 Até stirring up to blood and strife	Até 'stirring up to blood and strife' (IS)
p. 42 l. 3 France	France. (IS)
p. 59 l. 22 noa	no (IS)
p. 59 l. 25 affec	affect (IS)
p. 59 l. 27 ROB ROY	Ro: Roy (IS)
p. 59 l. 29 Haig	Ilay (IS)
p. 61 l. 7 Poets	poets (IS)
p. 76 ll. 18–19 stoch-fish	stock-fish (1822)
p. 81 l. 22 pobration	probation (1822)
p. 90 l. 6 Content sir	Content, sir (1822)
p. 115 l. 1 Although,	Although (1822)
p. 128 l. 16 the zeal of his assistant	his alert assistant (IS)
p. 142 l. 6 seem-|be	seemed (1822)
p. 154 ll. 29–30 accomplishments, that	accomplishments that (1822)
p. 158 l. 23 Mr Rashleigh has	Mr Rashleigh, has (1822)
p. 162 l. 18 enough of all	enough of all these (1822)
p. 221 ll. 5–6 amicable passion?	amiable passion. (1822)

p. 227 l. 13 spear   speer (1822)

p. 244 l. 13 listening   hearkening (IS)

p. 262 l. 24 deeply engaged   engaged deep (IS)

p. 270 l. 30 hinderlans   hinderlins (IS)

p. 272 l. 25 brochan   brechan (IS)

p. 303 l. 25 the Rob   sae Rob (1822)

p. 335 l. 1 seem'd   seemed (1822)

p. 351 l. 2 up and town   up and down (1822)

p. 361 l. 6 hung on their left   hung on the left shoulder (IS)
         shoulder

p. 463 l. 32 medical   mutual (IS)

SELECT BIBLIOGRAPHY

Biographical, Bibliographical, and Other Reference Works

Anderson, W. E. K. (ed.), *The Journal of Sir Walter Scott*, 1972.

Bolton, H. Philip, *Scott Dramatized*, 1992.

Brown, Iain Gordon (ed.), *Scott's Interleaved Waverley Novels: An Introduction and Commentary*, 1987.

[Cochrane, J. G.], *Catalogue of the Library at Abbotsford*, 1938.

Corson, James C., *A Bibliography of Sir Walter Scott, 1797–1940*, 1943.

—— *Notes and Index to Sir Herbert Grierson's Edition of the Letters of Sir Walter Scott*, 1979.

Johnson, Edgar, *Sir Walter Scott: The Great Unknown*, 2 vols., 1970.

Lockhart, John Gibson, *Memoirs of the Life of Sir Walter Scott, Bart*, 10 vols., 1839.

Millgate, Jane, *Scott's Last Edition: A Study in Publishing History*, 1987.

Rubenstein, Jill, *Sir Walter Scott: A Reference Guide*, 1978.

Ruddick, William, 'Sir Walter Scott's Northumberland', in J. H. Alexander and David Hewitt (eds.), *Scott and his Influence: The Papers of the Aberdeen Scott Conference, 1982*, 1983, 20–30.

Scott, Walter, *The Letters of Sir Walter Scott*, ed. H. J. C. Grierson, 12 vols., 1932–7.

Sutherland, John, *The Life of Walter Scott: A Critical Biography*, 1995.

Criticism

Beiderwell, Bruce, *Power and Punishment in Scott's Novels*, 1992.

Bolton, H. Philip, 'Playing Rob Roy as Robin Hood', in J. H. Alexander and David Hewitt (eds.), *Scott in Carnival: Selected Papers from the Fourth International Scott Conference, Edinburgh, 1991*, 1993, 478–90.

Brown, David, *Walter Scott and the Historical Imagination*, 1979.

Cadbury, William, 'The Two Structures of Rob Roy', *Modern Language Quarterly*, 29 (1968), 42–60.

Cockshut, A. O. J., *The Achievement of Walter Scott*, 1969.

Cottom, Daniel, *The Civilised Imagination: A Study of Ann Radcliffe, Jane Austen, and Sir Walter Scott*, 1985.

Daiches, David, 'Scott's Achievement as a Novelist', in D. D. Devlin (ed.), *Modern Judgements: Walter Scott*, 1969, 33–62.

Duncan, Ian, *Modern Romance and Transformations of the Novel: The Gothic, Scott, Dickens*, 1992.

Elam, Diane, *Romancing the Postmodern*, 1992.

Ferris, Ina, *The Achievement of Literary Authority: Gender, History, and the Waverley Novels*, 1991.

Fielding, Penny, *Writing and Orality: Nationality, Culture and Nineteenth-Century Scottish Fiction*, 1996.

Forbes, Duncan, 'The Rationalism of Sir Walter Scott', *Cambridge Journal*, 7 (1953), 20–35.

Garside, P. D., 'Scott and the "Philosophical" Historians', *Journal of the History of Ideas*, 36 (1975), 497–512.

Gordon, Robert C., *Under Which King? A Study of the Scottish Waverley Novels*, 1969.

Hart, Francis R., *Scott's Novels: The Plotting of Historic Survival*, 1966.

Hartveit, Lars, 'Interaction between Genre and Social Content in Sir Walter Scott, *Rob Roy*', in Sven Backman and Goran Kjellmar (eds.), *Papers on Language and Literature Presented to Alvar Ellegard and Erik Frykman*, 1985, 165–83.

——'The Hero in the Melting Pot: A Reading of Sir Walter Scott's *Rob Roy*', in Karsten Engelberg (ed.), *The Romantic Heritage: A Collection of Critical Essays*, 1983, 53–80.

Hayden, John O. (ed.), *Scott: The Critical Heritage*, 1970.

Hewitt, David, '*Rob Roy* and First Person Narratives', in J. H. Alexander and David Hewitt (eds.), *Scott and his Influence: The Papers of the Aberdeen Scott Conference, 1982*, 1983, 372–81.

Hillhouse, James T., *The Waverley Novels and their Critics*, 1936.

Howard, William, 'The Symbolic Structure of Scott's *Rob Roy*', *Studies in Scottish Literature*, 14 (1979), 72–89.

Kaufmann, David, *The Business of Common Life: Classical Economics and the Novel from Revolution to Reform*, 1995.

Kelly, Gary, *English Fiction of the Romantic Period, 1789–1830*, 1989.

Kerr, James, *Fiction Against History: Scott as Storyteller*, 1989.

Kropf, David, *Authorship as Alchemy: Subversive Writing in Pushkin, Scott, Hoffmann*, 1994.

Lascelles, Mary, *The Story-Teller Retrieves the Past*, 1980.

Lukács, Georg, *The Historical Novel*, 1937, trans. Hannah Mitchell and Stanley Mitchell, 1962.

McClure, J. Derrick, 'Linguistic Characterisation in *Rob Roy*', in J. H. Alexander and David Hewitt (eds.), *Scott and his Influence: The Papers of the Aberdeen Scott Conference, 1982*, 1983, 129–39.

McMaster, Graham, *Scott and Society*, 1981.

Millgate, Jane, *Walter Scott: The Making of the Novelist*, 1984.

Punter, David, 'To Cheat the Time, a Powerful Spell: Scott, History and the Double', in J. H. Alexander and David Hewitt (eds.), *Scott in*

Carnival: Selected Papers from the Fourth International Scott Conference, Edinburgh, 1991, 1993, 1–18.

Robertson, Fiona, *Legitimate Histories: Scott, Gothic, and the Authority of Fiction*, 1994.

Shaw, Harry E., *The Forms of Historical Fiction: Sir Walter Scott and his Successors*, 1983.

Sutherland, Kathleen, 'Fictional Economies: Adam Smith, Sir Walter Scott and the Nineteenth-Century Novel', *English Literary History*, 54/1 (1987), 97–127.

Trumpener, Katie, *Bardic Nationalism: The Romantic Novel and the British Empire*, 1997.

Tulloch, Graham, *The Language of Walter Scott: A Study of his Scottish and Period Language*, 1980.

Watson, Nicola, *Revolution and the Form of the British Novel, 1790–1825: Intercepted Letters, Interrupted Seductions*, 1994.

Welsh, Alexander, *The Hero of the Waverley Novels; With New Essays on Scott*, 1992 (1st publ. 1963).

Wilt, Judith, *Secret Leaves: The Novels of Walter Scott*, 1985.

Related Historical and Cultural Studies

Chapman, Malcolm, *The Gaelic Vision in Scottish Culture*, 1978.

Crawford, Robert, *Devolving English Literature*, 1992.

Fry, Michael, *The Dundas Despotism*, 1992.

Hechter, Michael, *Internal Colonialism: The Celtic Fringe in British National Development, 1536–1966*, 1975.

Hobsbawm, E. J., and Terence Ranger (eds.), *The Invention of Tradition*, 1983.

Lenman, Bruce, *The Jacobite Risings in Britain, 1689–1746*, 1980.

Murray, W. H., *Rob Roy MacGregor: His Life and Times*, 1982.

Nairn, Tom, *The Break-up of Britain: Crisis and Neo-Nationalism*, 1977.

Pittock, Murray G. H., *The Invention of Scotland: The Stuart Myth and the Scottish Identity, 1638 to the Present*, 1991.

Scott, Walter, 'Culloden Papers', *Quarterly Review*, 28 (1816), 283–333.

Smout, T. C., *A History of the Scottish People, 1560–1830*, 1972.

Szechi, Daniel, *Jacobitism and Tory Politics, 1710–14*, 1984.

Womack, Peter, *Improvement and Romance: Constructing the Myth of the Highlands*, 1989.

A CHRONOLOGY OF
SIR WALTER SCOTT

1771   Born in Edinburgh, son of Walter Scott, W. S., and Anne Rutherford.

1772–3   Suffers from poliomyelitis which leaves him lame.

1779–83   Attends the High School, Edinburgh.

1783–6   Attends classes at Edinburgh University; 1786, is apprenticed to his father.

1792   Is admitted to Faculty of Advocates.

1796   *The Chase, and William and Helen*, translated from Bürger, is issued anonymously.

1797   Marries Charlotte Charpentier.

1799   *Goetz of Berlichingen*, translated from Goethe; *Tales of Terror*; appointed Sheriff-Depute of Selkirkshire.

1801   Contributes to M. G. Lewis's *Tales of Wonder*.

1802–3   *The Minstrelsy of the Scottish Border*.

1804   Moves to Ashestiel.

1805   *The Lay of the Last Minstrel*; enters into partnership with James Ballantyne & Co., printers; starts *Waverley*.

1806   Is appointed a Principal Clerk of Session.

1808   *Marmion*; edition of *The Works of John Dryden*; completes Joseph Strutt's *Queen-Hoo Hall*.

1810   *The Lady of the Lake*; resumes *Waverley*, but puts it aside again.

1812   Moves to Abbotsford.

1813   *Rokeby*; declines offer of Poet Laureateship.

1814   *Waverley*; edition of *The Works of Jonathan Swift*.

1815   *The Lord of the Isles*; *Guy Mannering*.

1816   *The Antiquary*; *The Black Dwarf* and *Old Mortality* (*Tales of My Landlord*, 1st series).

1817   *Rob Roy*.

1818   *The Heart of Mid-Lothian* (*Tales of My Landlord*, 2nd series); accepts Baronetcy (gazetted 1820).

1819   *The Bride of Lammermoor* and *A Legend of Montrose* (*Tales of My Landlord*, 3rd series); *Ivanhoe*.

1820   *The Monastery*; *The Abbot*; daughter, Sophia, marries J. G. Lockhart.

1821   *Kenilworth*.

1822   *The Pirate*; *The Fortunes of Nigel*; *Peveril of the Peak*.

1823   *Quentin Durward*.

1824   *St Ronan's Well*; *Redgauntlet*.

1825   *The Betrothed* and *The Talisman* (*Tales of the Crusaders*); begins *Journal*.

1826   Financial collapse, caused by the bankruptcy of Archibald Constable & Co., and James Ballantyne & Co.; *Woodstock*.

1827   Acknowledges authorship of Waverley novels; *Life of Napoleon*.

1827–8 *Chronicles of the Canongate* (two series).

1828–31 *Tales of a Grandfather* (four series).

1829   *Anne of Geierstein*; Magnum series of Waverley Novels starts to appear.

1830   *Letters on Demonology and Witchcraft*.

1831   Travels to the Mediterranean in search of health.

1832   *Count Robert of Paris* and *Castle Dangerous* (*Tales of My Landlord*, 4th series).

        Dies at Abbotsford, 21 September.

Rob Roy's Country

ROB ROY

For why? Because the good old rule
   Sufficeth them; the simple plan,
That they should take who have the power,
   And they should keep who can.

     Rob Roy's Grave.—WORDSWORTH*

ADVERTISEMENT

TO THE FIRST EDITION

WHEN the Editor of the following volumes published, about two years since, the work called 'The Antiquary,' he announced that he was, for the last time, intruding upon the public in his present capacity.* He might shelter himself under the plea that every anonymous writer is, like the celebrated Junius,* only a phantom, and that therefore, although an apparition of a more benign, as well as much meaner description, he cannot be bound to plead to a charge of inconsistency. A better apology may be found in the imitating the confession of honest Benedict, that, when he said he would die a bachelor, he did not think he should live to be married.* The best of all would be, if, as has eminently happened in the case of some distinguished contemporaries,* the merit of the work should, in the reader's estimation, form an excuse for the author's breach of promise. Without presuming to hope that this may prove the case, it is only further necessary to mention, that my resolution, like that of Benedict, fell a sacrifice, to temptation at least, if not to stratagem.

It is now about six months since the Author, through the medium of his respectable Publishers, received a parcel of Papers, containing the Outlines of this narrative, with a permission, or rather with a request, couched in highly flattering terms, that they might be given to the Public, with such alterations as should be found suitable.[1] These were of course so numerous, that, besides the suppression of names, and of incidents approaching too much to reality, the work may in a great measure be said to be new written. Several anachronisms have probably crept in during the course of these changes; and the mottoes for the Chapters have been selected without any reference to the supposed date of the incidents. For these, of course, the Editor is responsible. Some others occurred in the original materials, but they are of little consequence. In point of minute accuracy, it may be stated, that the bridge over the Forth, or rather the Avondhu, (or Black River,) near the hamlet of Aberfoil, had not an existence thirty years ago. It does not, however, become the Editor to be the first to point out these errors; and he takes this public opportunity to thank the unknown and nameless correspondent, to whom the reader will owe the principal share of any amusement which he may derive from the following pages.

1st December, 1817

INTRODUCTION

WHEN the author projected this further encroachment on the patience of an indulgent public, he was at some loss for a title; a good name being very nearly of as much consequence in literature as in life. The title of ROB ROY was suggested by the late Mr Constable,* whose sagacity and experience foresaw the germ of popularity which it included.

No introduction can be more appropriate to the work than some account of the singular character whose name is given to the title-page, and who, through good report and bad report, has maintained a wonderful degree of importance in popular recollection. This cannot be ascribed to the distinction of his birth, which, though that of a gentleman, had in it nothing of high destination, and gave him little right to command in his clan. Neither, though he lived a busy, restless, and enterprising life, were his feats equal to those of other freebooters who have been less distinguished. He owed his fame in a great measure to his residing on the very verge of the Highlands, and playing such pranks in the beginning of the 18th century, as are usually ascribed to Robin Hood in the middle ages,—and that within forty miles of Glasgow, a great commercial city, the seat of a learned university. Thus a character like his, blending the wild virtues, the subtle policy, and unrestrained license of an American Indian,* was flourishing in Scotland during the Augustan age of Queen Anne and George I. Addison, it is probable, or Pope, would have been considerably surprised if they had known that there existed in the same island with them a personage of Rob Roy's peculiar habits and profession. It is this strong contrast betwixt the civilized and cultivated mode of life on the one side of the Highland line,* and the wild and lawless adventures which were habitually undertaken and achieved by one who dwelt on the opposite side of that ideal boundary, which creates the interest attached to his name. Hence it is that even yet,

'Far and near, through vale and hill,
    Are faces that attest the same,
And kindle like a fire new stirr'd,
    At sound of Rob Roy's name.'*

There were several advantages which Rob Roy enjoyed, for sustaining to advantage the character which he assumed.

The most prominent of these was his descent from, and connexion with, the clan MacGregor, so famous for their misfortunes, and the indomitable spirit with which they maintained themselves as a clan, linked and banded together in spite of the most severe laws, executed with unheard-of rigour against those who bore this forbidden surname. Their history was that of several others of the original Highland clans, who were suppressed by more powerful neighbours, and either extirpated, or forced to secure themselves by renouncing their own family appellation, and assuming that of the conquerors. The peculiarity in the story of the MacGregors, is their retaining, with such tenacity, their separate existence and union as a clan under circumstances of the utmost urgency. The history of the tribe is briefly as follows: But we must premise that the tale depends in some degree on tradition; therefore, excepting when written documents are quoted, it must be considered as in some degree dubious.

The sept of MacGregor claimed a descent from Gregor, or Gregorius, third son, it is said, of Alpin King of Scots, who flourished about 787. Hence their original patronymic is MacAlpine, and they are usually termed the Clan Alpine. An individual tribe of them retains the same name. They are accounted one of the most ancient clans in the Highlands, and it is certain they were a people of original Celtic descent, and occupied at one period very extensive possessions in Perthshire and Argyleshire, which they imprudently continued to hold by the *coir a glaive*,* that is, the right of the sword. Their neighbours, the Earls of Argyle and Breadalbane, in the meanwhile, managed to have the lands occupied by the MacGregors engrossed in those charters which they easily obtained from the Crown; and thus constituted a legal right in their own favour, without much regard to its justice. As opportunity occurred of annoying or extirpating their neighbours, they gradually extended their own domains, by usurping, under the pretext of such royal grants, those of their more uncivilized neighbours. A Sir Duncan Campbell of Lochow, known in the Highlands by the name of *Donacha Dhu nan Churraichd*, that is, Black Duncan with the Cowl, it being his pleasure to wear such a head-gear, is said to have been peculiarly successful in those acts of spoliation upon the clan MacGregor.

The devoted sept, ever finding themselves iniquitously driven from their possessions, defended themselves by force, and occasionally gained advantages, which they used cruelly enough. This conduct, though natural, considering the country and time, was studiously represented at the capital as arising from an untamable and innate ferocity, which nothing, it was said, could remedy, save cutting off the tribe of MacGregor root and branch.

In an act of Privy Council at Stirling, 22d September, 1563, in the reign of Queen Mary, commission is granted to the most powerful nobles, and chiefs of the clans, to pursue the clan Gregor with fire and sword. A similar warrant in 1563, not only grants the like powers to Sir John Campbell of Glenorchy, the descendant of Duncan with the Cowl, but discharges the lieges to receive or assist any of the clan Gregor, or afford them, under any colour whatever, meat, drink, or clothes.

An atrocity which the clan Gregor committed in 1589, by the murder of John Drummond of Drummond-ernoch, a forester of the royal forest of Glenartney, is elsewhere given, with all its horrid circumstances.* The clan swore upon the severed head of the murdered man, that they would make common cause in avowing the deed. This led to an act of the Privy Council, directing another crusade against the 'wicked clan Gregor, so long continuing in blood, slaughter, theft, and robbery,' in which letters of fire and sword are denounced against them for the space of three years. The reader will find this particular fact illustrated in the Introduction to the Legend of Montrose in the present edition of these Novels.

Other occasions frequently occurred, in which the MacGregors testified contempt for the laws, from which they had often experienced severity, but never protection. Though they were gradually deprived of their possessions, and of all ordinary means of procuring subsistence, they could not, nevertheless, be supposed likely to starve for famine, while they had the means of taking from strangers what they considered as rightfully their own. Hence they became versed in predatory forays, and accustomed to bloodshed. Their passions were eager, and, with a little management on the part of some of their most powerful neighbours, they could easily be *hounded out*, to use an expressive Scottish phrase,* to commit violence, of which the wily instigators took the advantage, and left the ignorant MacGregors an undivided portion of blame and punishment. This policy of pushing on the fierce clans of the Highlands and Borders to break the peace of the country, is accounted by the historian one of the most dangerous practices of his own period, in which the MacGregors were considered as ready agents.

Notwithstanding these severe denunciations, which were acted upon in the same spirit in which they were conceived, some of the clan still possessed property, and the chief of the name in 1592 is designed Allaster MacGregor of Glenstrae. He is said to have been a brave and active man; but, from the tenor of his confession at his death, appears to have been engaged in many and desperate feuds, one of which finally proved fatal to himself and many of his followers. This was the celebrated conflict at Glenfruin, near the south-western extremity of Loch Lomond, in the vicinity of which the MacGregors continued to exercise much authority by the *coir a glaive*, or right of the strongest, which we have already mentioned.

There had been a long and bloody feud betwixt the MacGregors and the Laird of Luss, head of the family of Colquhoun, a powerful race on the lower part of Loch Lomond. The MacGregors' tradition affirms that the quarrel began on a very trifling subject. Two of the MacGregors being benighted, asked shelter in a house belonging to a dependent of the Colquhouns, and were refused. They then retreated to an out-house, took a wedder from the fold, killed it, and supped off the carcass, for which (it is said) they offered payment to the proprietor. The Laird of Luss seized on the offenders, and, by the summary process which feudal barons had at their command, had them both condemned and executed. The MacGregors verify this account of the feud by appealing to a proverb current amongst them, execrating the hour (*Mult dhu an Carbail ghil*) that the black wedder with the white tail was ever lambed. To avenge this quarrel, the Laird of MacGregor assembled his clan, to the number of three or four hundred men, and marched towards Luss from the banks of Loch Long, by a pass called *Raad na Gael*, or the Highlandman's Pass.

Sir Humphrey Colquhoun* received early notice of this incursion, and collected a strong force, more than twice the number of that of the invaders. He had with him the gentlemen of the name of Buchanan, with the Grahams, and other gentry of the Lennox, and a party of the citizens of Dunbarton, under command of Tobias Smollett, a magistrate, or bailie, of that town, and ancestor of the celebrated author.

The parties met in the valley of Glenfruin, which signifies the Glen of Sorrow, a name that seemed to anticipate the event of the day, which, fatal to the conquered party, was at least equally so to the victors, the 'babe unborn'* of clan Alpine having reason to repent it. The Mac-Gregors, somewhat discouraged by the appearance of a force much superior to their own, were cheered on to the attack by a Seer, or second-sighted person, who professed that he saw the shrouds of the dead wrapt around their principal opponents. The clan charged with great fury on the front of the enemy, while John MacGregor, with a strong party, made an unexpected attack on the flank. A great part of the Colquhouns' force consisted in cavalry, which could not act in the boggy ground. They were said to have disputed the field manfully, but were at length completely routed, and a merciless slaughter was exercised on the fugitives, of whom betwixt two and three hundred fell on the field, and in the pursuit. If the MacGregors lost, as is averred, only two men slain in the action, they had slight provocation for an indiscriminate massacre. It is said that their fury extended itself to a party of students for clerical orders, who had imprudently come to see the battle. Some doubt is thrown on this fact, from the indictment against the chief of the clan Gregor being silent on the subject, as is the historian Johnston, and a Professor Ross,* who wrote an account of the battle twenty-nine years after it was fought. It is, however, constantly averred by the tradition of the country, and a stone where the deed was done is called *Leck-a-Mhinisteir*, the Minister or Clerk's Flag-stone. The MacGregors impute this cruel action to the ferocity of a single man of their tribe, renowned for size and strength, called Dugald, *Ciar Mhor*, or the great Mouse-coloured Man. He was MacGregor's foster-brother, and the chief committed the youths to his charge, with directions to keep them safely till the affray was over. Whether fearful of their escape, or incensed by some sarcasms which they threw on his tribe, or whether out of mere thirst of blood, this savage, while the other MacGregors were engaged in the pursuit, poniarded his helpless and defenceless prisoners. When the chieftain, on his return, demanded where the youths were, the *Ciar* (pronounced Kiar) *Mhor* drew out his bloody dirk, saying in Gaelic, 'Ask that, and God save me!' The latter words allude to the exclamation which his victims used when he was murdering them. It would seem, therefore, that this horrible part of the story is founded on fact, though the number of the youths so slain is probably exaggerated in the Lowland accounts. The common people say that the blood of the Ciar Mhor's victims can never be washed off the stone. When MacGregor learnt their fate, he expressed the utmost horror at the deed, and upbraided his foster-brother with having done that which would occasion the destruction of him and his clan. This homicide was the ancestor of Rob Roy, and the tribe from which he was descended. He lies buried at the church of Fortingal, where his sepulchre, covered with a large stone,[2] is still shown, and where his great strength and courage are the theme of many traditions.[3]

MacGregor's brother was one of the very few of the tribe who was slain. He was buried near the field of battle, and the place is marked by a rude stone, called the Grey Stone of MacGregor.

Sir Humphrey Colquhoun, being well mounted, escaped for the time to the castle of Banochar, or Benechra. It proved no sure defence, however, for he was shortly after murdered in a vault of the castle, the family annals say by the MacGregors, though other accounts charge the deed upon the MacFarlanes.

This battle of Glenfruin, and the severity which the victors exercised in the pursuit, was reported to King James VI. in a manner the most unfavourable to the clan Gregor, whose general character, being that of lawless though brave men, could not much avail them in such a case. That James might fully understand the extent of the slaughter, the widows of the slain to the number of eleven score, in deep mourning, riding upon white palfreys, and each bearing her husband's bloody shirt on a spear, appeared at Stirling, in presence of a monarch peculiarly accessible to such sights of fear and sorrow, to demand vengeance for the death of their husbands, upon those by whom they had been made desolate.*

The remedy resorted to was at least as severe as the cruelties which it was designed to punish. By an act of the Privy Council, dated 3d April, 1603, the name of MacGregor was expressly abolished, and those who had hitherto borne it were commanded to change it for other surnames, the pain of death being denounced against those who should call themselves Gregor or MacGregor, the names of their fathers. Under the same penalty, all who had been at the conflict of Glenfruin, or accessory to other marauding parties charged in the act, were prohibited from carrying weapons, except a pointless knife to eat their victuals. By a subsequent act of Council, 24th June, 1613, death was denounced against any persons of the tribe formerly called Mac-Gregor, who should presume to assemble in greater numbers than four. Again, by an act of Parliament, 1617, chap. 26, these laws were continued, and extended to the rising generation, in respect that great numbers of the children of those against whom the acts of Privy Council had been directed, were stated to be then approaching to maturity, who, if permitted to resume the name of their parents, would render the clan as strong as it was before.

The execution of those severe acts was chiefly intrusted in the west to the Earl of Argyle, and the powerful clan of Campbell, and to the Earl of Athole and his followers, in the more eastern Highlands of Perthshire. The MacGregors failed not to resist with the most determined courage; and many a valley in the West and North Highlands retains memory of the severe conflicts, in which the proscribed clan sometimes obtained transient advantages, and always sold their lives dearly. At length the pride of Allaster MacGregor, the chief of the clan, was so much lowered by the sufferings of his people, that he resolved to surrender himself to the Earl of Argyle, with his principal followers, on condition that they should be sent out of Scotland. If the unfortunate chief's own account be true, he had more reasons than one for expecting some favour from the Earl, who had in secret advised and encouraged him to many of the desperate actions for which he was now called to so severe a reckoning. But Argyle, as old Birrell expresses himself, kept a Highlandman's promise with them,* fulfilling it to the ear, and breaking it to the sense. MacGregor was sent under a strong guard to the frontier of England, and being thus, in the literal sense, sent out of Scotland, Argyle was judged to have kept faith with him, though the same party which took him there brought him back to Edinburgh in custody.

MacGregor of Glenstrae was tried before the Court of Justiciary, 20th January, 1604, and found guilty. He appears to have been instantly conveyed from the bar to the gallows; for Birrell, of the same date, reports that he was hanged at the Cross, and, for distinction's sake, was suspended higher by his own height than two of his kindred and friends. On the 18th of February following, more men of the Mac-Gregors were executed, after a long imprisonment, and several others in the beginning of March.

The Earl of Argyle's service, in conducing to the surrender of the insolent and wicked race and name of MacGregor, notorious common malefactors, and in the in-bringing of MacGregor, with a great many of the leading men of the clan, worthily executed to death for their offences, is thankfully acknowledged by act of Parliament, 1607, chap. 16, and rewarded with a grant of twenty chalders of victual out of the lands of Kintire.

The MacGregors, notwithstanding the letters of fire and sword, and orders for military execution repeatedly directed against them by the Scottish legislature, who apparently lost all the calmness of conscious dignity and security, and could not even name the outlawed clan without vituperation, showed no inclination to be blotted out of the roll of clanship. They submitted to the law, indeed, so far as to take the names of the neighbouring families amongst whom they happened to live, nominally becoming, as the case might render it most convenient, Drummonds, Campbells, Grahams, Buchanans, Stewarts, and the like; but to all intents and purposes of combination and mutual attachment, they remained the clan Gregor, united together for right or wrong, and menacing with the general vengeance of their race, whomsoever committed aggressions against any individual of their number.

They continued to take and give offence with as little hesitation as before the legislative dispersion which had been attempted, as appears from the preamble to statute 1633, chapter 30, setting forth, that the clan Gregor, which had been suppressed and reduced to quietness by the great care of the late King James of eternal memory, had nevertheless broken out again, in the counties of Perth, Stirling, Clackmannan, Monteith, Lennox, Angus, and Mearns; for which reason the statute re-establishes the disabilities attached to the clan, and grants a new commission for enforcing the laws against that wicked and rebellious race.

Notwithstanding the extreme severities of King James I. and Charles I. against this unfortunate people, who were rendered furious by proscription, and then punished for yielding to the passions which had been wilfully irritated, the MacGregors to a man attached themselves during the civil war to the cause of the latter monarch. Their bards have ascribed this to the native respect of the MacGregors for the crown of Scotland, which their ancestors once wore, and have appealed to their armorial bearings, which display a pine-tree, crossed saltire wise* with a naked sword, the point of which supports a royal crown. But, without denying that such motives may have had their weight, we are disposed to think, that a war which opened the low country to the raids of the clan Gregor would have more charms for them than any inducement to espouse the cause of the Covenanters, which would have brought them into contact with Highlanders as fierce as themselves, and having as little to lose. Patrick MacGregor, their leader, was the son of a distinguished chief, named Duncan Abbarach, to whom Montrose wrote letters as to his trusty and special friend, expressing his reliance on his devoted loyalty, with an assurance, that when once his Majesty's affairs were placed upon a permanent footing, the grievances of the clan MacGregor should be redressed.

At a subsequent period of these melancholy times, we find the clan Gregor claiming the immunities of other tribes, when summoned by the Scottish Parliament to resist the invasion of the Commonwealth's army, in 1651. On the last day of March in that year, a supplication to the King and Parliament, from Calum MacCondachie Vich Euen, and Euen MacCondachie Euen, in their own name, and that of the whole name of MacGregor, set forth, that while, in obedience to the orders of Parliament, enjoining all clans to come out in the present service under their chieftains, for the defence of religion, king, and kingdoms, the petitioners were drawing their men to guard the passes at the head of the river Forth, they were interfered with by the Earl of Athole and the Laird of Buchanan, who had required the attendance of many of the clan Gregor upon their arrays. This interference was, doubtless, owing to the change of name, which seems to have given rise to the claim of the Earl of Athole and the Laird of Buchanan to muster the MacGregors under their banners, as Murrays or Buchanans. It does not appear that the petition of the MacGregors, to be permitted to come out in a body as other clans, received any answer. But upon the Restoration, King Charles, in the first Scottish Parliament of his reign, (statute 164, chap. 195,) annulled the various acts against the clan Gregor, and restored them to the full use of their family name, and the other privileges of liege subjects, setting forth, as a reason for this lenity, that those who were formerly designed MacGregors, had, during the late troubles, conducted themselves with such loyalty and affection to his Majesty, as might justly wipe off all memory of former miscarriages, and take away all marks of reproach for the same.

It is singular enough, that it seems to have aggravated the feelings of the non-conforming Presbyterians, when the penalties which were most unjustly imposed upon themselves were relaxed towards the poor MacGregors; so little are the best men, any more than the worst, able to judge with impartiality of the same measures, as applied to themselves, or to others. Upon the Restoration, an influence inimical to this unfortunate clan, said to be the same with that which afterwards dictated the massacre of Glencoe,* occasioned the re-enaction of the penal statutes against the MacGregors. There are no reasons given why these highly penal acts should have been renewed; nor is it alleged that the clan had been guilty of late irregularities. Indeed, there is some reason to think that the clause was formed of set purpose, in a shape which should elude observation; for, though containing conclusions fatal to the rights of so many Scottish subjects, it is neither mentioned in the title nor the rubric of the Act of Parliament in which it occurs, and is thrown briefly in at the close of the statute 1693, chap. 61, entitled, an Act for the Justiciary in the Highlands.

It does not, however, appear that after the Revolution the acts against the clan were severely enforced; and in the latter half of the eighteenth century, they were not enforced at all. Commissioners of supply* were named in Parliament by the proscribed title of Mac-Gregor, and decrees of courts of justice were pronounced, and legal deeds entered into, under the same appellative. The MacGregors, however, while the laws continued in the statute book, still suffered under the deprivation of the name which was their birth-right, and some attempts were made for the purpose of adopting another, MacAlpine or Grant being proposed as the title of the whole clan in future. No agreement, however, could be entered into; and the evil was submitted to as a matter of necessity, until full redress was obtained from the British Parliament, by an act abolishing for ever the penal statutes which had been so long imposed upon this ancient race. This statute, well merited by the services of many a gentleman of the clan in behalf of their King and country, was passed,* and the clan proceeded to act upon it with the same spirit of ancient times, which had made them suffer severely under a deprivation that would have been deemed of little consequence by a great part of their fellow subjects.

They entered into a deed recognising John Murray of Lanrick, Esq. (afterwards Sir John MacGregor, Baronet), representative of the family of Glencarnock, as lawfully descended from the ancient stock and blood of the Lairds and Lords of MacGregor, and therefore acknowledged him as their chief on all lawful occasions and causes whatsoever. This deed was subscribed by eight hundred and twenty-six persons of the name of MacGregor, capable of bearing arms. A great many of the clan during the last war formed themselves into what was called the Clan Alpine regiment, raised in 1799, under the command of their Chief, and his brother Colonel MacGregor.

Having briefly noticed the history of this clan, which presents a rare and interesting example of the indelible character of the patriarchal system, the author must now offer some notices of the individual who gives name to these volumes.

In giving an account of a Highlander, his pedigree is first to be considered. That of Rob Roy was deduced from Ciar Mohr, the great mouse-coloured man, who is accused by tradition of having slain the young students at the battle of Glenfruin.

Without puzzling ourselves and our readers with the intricacies of Highland genealogy, it is enough to say, that after the death of Allaster MacGregor of Glenstrae, the clan, discouraged by the unremitting persecution of their enemies, seem not to have had the means of placing themselves under the command of a single CHIEF. According to their places of residence and immediate descent, the several families were led and directed by *Chieftains*, which, in the Highland acceptation, signifies the head of a particular branch of a tribe, in opposition to *Chief*, who is the leader and commander of the whole name.

The family and descendants of Dugald Ciar Mohr lived chiefly in the mountains between Loch Lomond and Loch Katrine, and occupied a good deal of property there, whether by sufferance, by the right of the sword, which it was never safe to dispute with them, or by legal titles of various kinds, it would be useless to enquire and unnecessary to detail. Enough, there they certainly were; a people whom their most powerful neighbours were desirous to conciliate, their friendship in peace being very necessary to the quiet of the vicinage, and their assistance in war equally prompt and effectual.

Rob Roy MacGregor Campbell, which last name he bore in consequence of the Acts of Parliament abolishing his own, was the younger son of Donald MacGregor of Glengyle, said to have been a Lieutenant-Colonel, (probably in the service of James II.) by his wife, a daughter of Campbell of Glenfalloch.* Rob's own designation was of Inversnaid; but he appears to have acquired a right of some kind or other to the property or possession of Craig Royston, a domain of rock and forest, lying on the east side of Loch Lomond, where that beautiful lake stretches into the dusky mountains of Glenfalloch.

The time of his birth is uncertain. But he is said to have been active in the scenes of war and plunder which succeeded the Revolution; and tradition affirms him to have been the leader in a predatory incursion into the parish of Kippen, in the Lennox, which took place in the year

1691. It was of almost a bloodless character, only one person losing his life; but from the extent of the depredation, it was long distinguished by the name of the Her'-ship, or devastation, of Kippen.[4] The time of his death is also uncertain, but as he is said to have survived the year 1733, and died an aged man, it is probable he may have been twenty-five about the time of the Her'-ship of Kippen, which would assign his birth to the middle of the 17th century.*

In the more quiet times which succeeded the Revolution, Rob Roy, or Red Robert,* seems to have exerted his active talents, which were of no mean order, as a drover or trader in cattle to a great extent. It may well be supposed that in those days no Lowland, much less English drovers, ventured to enter the Highlands. The cattle, which were the staple commodity of the mountains, were escorted down to fairs, on the borders of the Lowlands, by a party of Highlanders, with their arms rattling around them; and who dealt, however, in all honour and good faith with their Southern customers. A fray, indeed, would some-times arise, when the Lowlandmen, chiefly Borderers, who had to supply the English market, used to dip their bonnets in the next brook, and wrapping them round their hands, oppose their cudgels to the naked broadswords, which had not always the superiority. I have heard from aged persons, who had been engaged in such affrays, that the Highlanders used remarkably fair play, never using the point of the sword, far less their pistols or daggers; so that

> With many a stiff thwack and many a bang,
> Hard crabtree and cold iron rang.*

A slash or two, or a broken head, was easily accommodated, and as the trade was of benefit to both parties, trifling skirmishes were not allowed to interrupt its harmony. Indeed it was of vital interest to the Highlanders, whose income, so far as derived from their estates, depended entirely on the sale of black cattle; and a sagacious and ex-perienced dealer benefited not only himself, but his friends and neigh-bours, by his speculations. Those of Rob Roy were for several years so successful, as to inspire general confidence, and raise him in the esti-mation of the country in which he resided.

His importance was increased by the death of his father, in conse-quence of which he succeeded to the management of his nephew Gregor MacGregor of Glengyle's property, and, as his tutor, to such influence with the clan and following as was due to the representative of Dougal Ciar. Such influence was the more uncontrolled, that this family of the MacGregors seem to have refused adherence to Mac-Gregor of Glencarnock, the ancestor of the present Sir Ewan Mac-Gregor, and asserted a kind of independence.

It was at this time that Rob Roy acquired an interest by purchase, wadset, or otherwise, to the property of Craig Royston already mentioned.* He was in particular favour, during this prosperous period of his life, with his nearest and most powerful neighbour, James first Duke of Montrose,* from whom he received many marks of regard. His Grace consented to give his nephew and himself a right of property on the estates of Glengyle and Inversnaid, which they had till then only held as kindly tenants. The Duke, also, with a view to the interest of the country and his own estate, supported our adventurer by loans of money to a considerable amount, to enable him to carry on his speculations in the cattle trade.

Unfortunately, that species of commerce was and is liable to sudden fluctuations; and Rob Roy was—by a sudden depression of markets, and, as a friendly tradition adds, by the bad faith of a partner named MacDonald, whom he had imprudently received into his confidence, and intrusted with a considerable sum of money—rendered totally insolvent.* He absconded, of course,—not empty-handed, if it be true, as stated in an advertisement for his apprehension, that he had in his possession sums to the amount of L.1000 sterling, obtained from several noblemen and gentlemen under pretence of purchasing cows for them in the Highlands. This advertisement appeared in June 1712, and was several times repeated. It fixes the period when Rob Roy exchanged his commercial adventures for speculations of a very different complexion.[5]

He appears at this period first to have removed, from his ordinary dwelling at Inversnaid, ten or twelve Scots miles (which is double the number of English) farther into the Highlands, and commenced the lawless sort of life which he afterwards followed. The Duke of Montrose, who conceived himself deceived and cheated by Mac-Gregor's conduct, employed legal means to recover the money lent to him. Rob Roy's landed property was attached by the regular form of legal procedure, and his stock and furniture made the subject of arrest and sale.

It is said that this diligence of the law, as it is called in Scotland, which the English more bluntly term distress, was used in this case with uncommon severity, and that the legal satellites, not usually the gentlest persons in the world, had insulted MacGregor's wife, in a manner which would have aroused a milder man than he to thoughts of unbounded vengeance. She was a woman of fierce and haughty temper, and is not unlikely to have disturbed the officers in the execution of their duty, and thus to have incurred ill treatment, though, for the sake of humanity, it is to be hoped that the story sometimes told is a popular exaggeration.* It is certain that she felt extreme anguish at being expelled from the banks of Loch Lomond, and gave vent to her feelings in a fine piece of pipe-music, still well known to amateurs by the name of 'Rob Roy's Lament.'

The fugitive is thought to have found his first place of refuge in Glen Dochart, under the Earl of Breadalbane's protection; for though that family had been active agents in the destruction of the MacGregors in former times, they had of late years sheltered a great many of the name in their old possessions. The Duke of Argyle* was also one of Rob Roy's protectors, so far as to afford him, according to the Highland phrase, wood and water—the shelter, namely, that is afforded by the forests and lakes of an inaccessible country.

The great men of the Highlands in that time, besides being anxiously ambitious to keep up what was called their Following, or military retainers, were also desirous to have at their disposal men of resolute character, to whom the world and the world's law were no friends, and who might at times ravage the lands or destroy the tenants of a feudal enemy, without bringing responsibility on their patrons. The strife between the names of Campbell and Graham, during the civil wars of the seventeenth century, had been stamped with mutual loss and inveterate enmity. The death of the great Marquis of Montrose on the one side, the defeat at Inverlochy, and cruel plundering of Lorn, on the other, were reciprocal injuries not likely to be forgotten.* Rob Roy was, therefore, sure of refuge in the country of the Campbells, both as having assumed their name, as connected by his mother with the family of Glenfalloch, and as an enemy to the rival house of Montrose. The extent of Argyle's possessions, and the power of retreating thither in any emergency, gave great encouragement to the bold schemes of revenge which he had adopted.

This was nothing short of the maintenance of a predatory war against the Duke of Montrose, whom he considered as the author of his exclusion from civil society, and of the outlawry to which he had been sentenced by letters of horning and caption,* (legal writs so called,) as well as the seizure of his goods, and adjudication of his landed property. Against his Grace, therefore, his tenants, friends, allies, and relatives, he disposed himself to employ every means of annoyance in his power; and though this was a circle sufficiently extensive for active depredation, Rob, who professed himself a Jacobite,* took the liberty of extending his sphere of operations against all whom he chose to consider as friendly to the revolutionary government, or to that most obnoxious of measures—the Union of the Kingdoms. Under one or other of these pretexts, all his neighbours of the Lowlands who had any thing to lose, or were unwilling to compound for security, by paying him an annual sum for protection or forbearance, were exposed to his ravages.

The country in which this private warfare, or system of depredation, was to be carried on, was, until opened up by roads, in the highest degree favourable for his purpose. It was broken up into narrow valleys, the habitable part of which bore no proportion to the huge wildernesses of forest, rocks, and precipices by which they were encircled, and which was, moreover, full of inextricable passes, morasses, and natural strengths, unknown to any but the inhabitants themselves, where a few men acquainted with the ground were capable, with ordinary address, of baffling the pursuit of numbers.

The opinions and habits of the nearest neighbours to the Highland line were also highly favourable to Rob Roy's purpose. A large proportion of them were of his own clan of MacGregor, who claimed the property of Balquhidder, and other Highland districts, as having been part of the ancient possessions of their tribe; though the harsh laws, under the severity of which they had suffered so deeply, had assigned the ownership to other families. The civil wars of the seventeenth century had accustomed these men to the use of arms, and they were peculiarly brave and fierce from remembrance of their sufferings. The vicinity of a comparatively rich Lowland district gave also great temptations to incursion. Many belonging to other clans, habituated to contempt of industry, and to the use of arms, drew towards an unprotected frontier which promised facility of plunder; and the state of the country, now so peaceable and quiet, verified at that time the opinion which Dr Johnson heard with doubt and suspicion, that the most disorderly and lawless districts of the Highlands were those which lay nearest to the Lowland line.* There was, therefore, no difficulty in Rob Roy, descended of a tribe which was widely dispersed in the country we have described, collecting any number of followers whom he might be able to keep in action, and to maintain by his proposed operations.

He himself appears to have been singularly adapted for the profession which he proposed to exercise. His stature was not of the tallest, but his person was uncommonly strong and compact. The greatest peculiarities of his frame were the breadth of his shoulders, and the great and almost disproportioned length of his arms; so remarkable, indeed, that it was said he could, without stooping, tie the garters of his Highland hose, which are placed two inches below the knee. His countenance was open, manly, stern at periods of danger, but frank and cheerful in his hours of festivity. His hair was dark red, thick, and frizzled, and curled short around the face. His fashion of dress showed, of course, the knees and upper part of the leg, which was described to me as resembling that of a Highland bull, hirsute, with red hair, and evincing muscular strength similar to that animal. To these personal qualifications must be added a masterly use of the Highland sword, in which his length of arm gave him great advantage, and a perfect and intimate knowledge of all the recesses of the wild country in which he harboured, and the character of the various individuals, whether friendly or hostile, with whom he might come in contact.

His mental qualities seem to have been no less adapted to the circumstances in which he was placed. Though the descendant of the blood-thirsty Ciar Mohr, he inherited none of his ancestor's ferocity. On the contrary, Rob Roy avoided every appearance of cruelty, and it is not averred that he was ever the means of unnecessary bloodshed, or the actor in any deed which could lead the way to it. His schemes of plunder were contrived and executed with equal boldness and sagacity, and were almost universally successful, from the skill with which they were laid, and the secrecy and rapidity with which they were executed. Like Robin Hood of England, he was a kind and gentle robber, and, while he took from the rich, was liberal in relieving the poor. This might in part be policy; but the universal tradition of the country speaks it to have arisen from a better motive. All whom I have conversed with, and I have in my youth seen some who knew Rob Roy personally, gave him the character of a benevolent and humane man 'in his way.'

His ideas of morality were those of an Arab chief, being such as naturally arose out of his wild education. Supposing Rob Roy to have argued on the tendency of the life which he pursued, whether from choice or from necessity, he would doubtless have assumed to himself the character of a brave man, who, deprived of his natural rights by the partiality of laws, endeavoured to assert them by the strong hand of natural power; and he is most felicitously described as reasoning thus, in the high-toned poetry of my gifted friend Wordsworth:*

> Say, then, that he was wise as brave,
>   As wise in thought as bold in deed;
> For in the principles of things
>   *He* sought his moral creed.
>
> Said generous Rob, 'What need of Books?
>   Burn all the statutes and their shelves!
> They stir us up against our kind,
>   And worse, against ourselves.
>
> 'We have a passion, make a law,
>   Too false to guide us or control;
> And for the law itself we fight
>   In bitterness of soul.
>
> 'And puzzled, blinded, then we lose
>   Distinctions that are plain and few;
> These find I graven on my heart,
>   That tells me what to do.
>
> 'The creatures see of flood and field,
>   And those that travel on the wind;
> With them no strife can last; they live
>   In peace, and peace of mind.
>
> 'For why? Because the good old rule
>   Sufficeth them; the simple plan,
> That they should take who have the power,
>   And they should keep who can.
>
> 'A lesson which is quickly learn'd,
>   A signal through which all can see;
> Thus, nothing here provokes the strong
>   To wanton cruelty.
>
> 'And freakishness of mind is check'd,
>   He tamed who foolishly aspires,
> While to the measure of his might
>   Each fashions his desires.

'All kinds and creatures stand and fall
   By strength of prowess or of wit;
'Tis God's appointment who must sway,
   And who is to submit.

'Since then the rule of right is plain
   And longest life is but a day,
To have my ends, maintain my rights,
   I'll take the shortest way.'

And thus among these rocks he lived,
   Through summer's heat and winter's snow:
The eagle, he was lord above,
   And Rob was lord below.

We are not, however, to suppose the character of this distinguished outlaw to be that of an actual hero, acting uniformly and consistently on such moral principles as the illustrious bard who, standing by his grave, has vindicated his fame. On the contrary, as is common with barbarous chiefs, Rob Roy appears to have mixed his professions of principle with a large alloy of craft and dissimulation, of which his conduct during the civil war is sufficient proof. It is also said, and truly, that although his courtesy was one of his strongest characteristics, yet sometimes he assumed an arrogance of manner which was not easily endured by the high-spirited men to whom it was addressed, and drew the daring outlaw into frequent disputes, from which he did not always come off with credit. From this it has been inferred, that Rob Roy was more of a bully than a hero, or at least that he had, according to the common phrase, his fighting days. Some aged men who knew him well, have described him also as better at a *taich-tulzie*, or scuffle within doors, than in mortal combat. The tenor of his life may be quoted to repel this charge; while, at the same time, it must be allowed, that the situation in which he was placed rendered him prudently averse to maintaining quarrels, where nothing was to be had save blows, and where success would have raised up against him new and powerful enemies, in a country where revenge was still considered as a duty rather than a crime. The power of commanding his passions, on such occasions, far from being inconsistent with the part which MacGregor had to perform, was essentially necessary, at the period when he lived, to prevent his career from being cut short.

I may here mention one or two occasions on which Rob Roy appears to have given way in the manner alluded to. My late venerable friend, John Ramsay of Ochtertyre,* alike eminent as a classical scholar and as an authentic register of the ancient history and manners of Scotland, informed me, that on occasion of a public meeting at a bonfire in the town of Doune, Rob Roy gave some offence to James Edmondstone of Newton, the same gentleman who was unfortunately concerned in the slaughter of Lord Rollo, (See Maclaurin's Criminal Trials, No. IX.,) when Edmondstone compelled MacGregor to quit the town on pain of being thrown by him into the bonfire. 'I broke one of your ribs on a former occasion,' said he, 'and now, Rob, if you provoke me farther, I will break your neck.' But it must be remembered that Edmondstone was a man of consequence in the Jacobite party, as he carried the royal standard of James VII. at the battle of Sherrif-muir, and also, that he was near the door of his own mansion-house, and probably sur-rounded by his friends and adherents. Rob Roy, however, suffered in reputation for retiring under such a threat.

Another well-vouched case is that of Cunningham of Boquhan.

Henry Cunningham, Esq. of Boquhan, was a gentleman of Stir-lingshire, who, like many *exquisites* of our own time, united a natural high spirit and daring character with an affectation of delicacy of address and manners amounting to foppery.[6] He chanced to be in company with Rob Roy, who, either in contempt of Boquhan's supposed effeminacy, or because he thought him a safe person to fix a quarrel on, (a point which Rob's enemies alleged he was wont to con-sider,) insulted him so grossly that a challenge passed between them. The goodwife of the clachan had hidden Cunningham's sword, and, while he rummaged the house in quest of his own or some other, Rob Roy went to the Shieling Hill, the appointed place of combat, and paraded there with great majesty, waiting for his antagonist. In the meantime, Cunningham had rummaged out an old sword, and, enter-ing the ground of contest in all haste, rushed on the outlaw with such unexpected fury that he fairly drove him off the field, nor did he show himself in the village again for some time. Mr MacGregor Stirling has a softened account of this anecdote in his new edition of Nimmo's Stirlingshire*; still he records Rob Roy's discomfiture.

Occasionally Rob Roy suffered disasters, and incurred great per-sonal danger. On one remarkable occasion he was saved by the cool-ness of his lieutenant, Macanaleister, or Fletcher, the *Little John* of his band*—a fine active fellow, of course, and celebrated as a marksman.

It happened that MacGregor and his party had been surprised and dispersed by a superior force of horse and foot, and the word was given to 'split and squander.' Each shifted for himself, but a bold dragoon attached himself to pursuit of Rob, and overtaking him, struck at him with his broadsword. A plate of iron in his bonnet saved the MacGregor from being cut down to the teeth; but the blow was heavy enough to bear him to the ground, crying as he fell, 'O, Macanaleister, is there naething in her?' (*i.e.* in the gun.) The trooper, at the same time exclaiming, 'D—n ye, your mother never wrought your night-cap!' had his arm raised for a second blow, when Macanaleister fired, and the ball pierced the dragoon's heart.

Such as he was, Rob Roy's progress in his occupation is thus described by a gentleman of sense and talent, who resided within the circle of his predatory wars, had probably felt their effects, and speaks of them, as might be expected, with little of the forbearance with which, from their peculiar and romantic character, they are now regarded.

'This man (Rob Roy MacGregor) was a person of sagacity, and neither wanted stratagem nor address; and, having abandoned himself to all licentiousness, set himself at the head of all the loose, vagrant, and desperate people of that clan, in the west end of Perth and Stirlingshires, and infested those whole countries with thefts, robberies, and depredations. Very few who lived within his reach (that is, within the distance of a nocturnal expedition) could promise to themselves security, either for their persons or effects, without subjecting themselves to pay him a heavy and shameful tax of *black-mail*. He at last proceeded to such a degree of audaciousness, that he committed robberies, raised contributions, and resented quarrels, at the head of a very considerable body of armed men, in open day, and in the face of the government.'[7]

The extent and success of these depredations cannot be surprising, when we consider that the scene of them was laid in a country where the general law was neither enforced nor respected.

Having recorded that the general habit of cattle-stealing had blinded even those of the better classes to the infamy of the practice, and that as men's property consisted entirely in herds, it was rendered in the highest degree precarious, Mr Grahame adds,—

'On these accounts there is no culture of ground, no improvement of pastures, and, from the same reasons, no manufactures, no trade; in short, no industry. The people are extremely prolific, and therefore so numerous, that there is not business in that country, according to its present order and economy, for the one-half of them. Every place is full of idle people, accustomed to arms, and lazy in every thing but rapines and depredations. As *buddel* or *aquavitæ* houses are to be found every where through the country, so in these they saunter away their time, and frequently consume there the returns of their illegal purchases. Here the laws have never been executed, nor the authority of the magistrate ever established. Here the officer of the law neither dare nor can execute his duty, and several places are about thirty miles from lawful persons. In short, here is no order, no authority, no government.'

The period of the Rebellion, 1715, approached soon after Rob Roy had attained celebrity. His jacobite partialities were now placed in opposition of his sense of the obligations which he owed to the indirect protection of the Duke of Argyle. But the desire of 'drowning his sounding steps amid the din of general war,'* induced him to join the forces of the Earl of Mar, although his patron, the Duke of Argyle, was at the head of the army opposed to the Highland insurgents.

The MacGregors, a large sept of them at least, that of Ciar Mohr, on this occasion, were not commanded by Rob Roy, but by his nephew already mentioned, Gregor MacGregor, otherwise called James Grahame of Glengyle, and still better remembered by the Gaelic epithet of *Ghlune Dhu, i.e.* Black Knee, from a black spot on one of his knees, which his Highland garb rendered visible. There can be no question, however, that being then very young, Glengyle must have acted on most occasions by the advice and direction of so experienced a leader as his uncle.

The MacGregors assembled in numbers at that period, and began even to threaten the Lowlands towards the lower extremity of Loch Lomond. They suddenly seized all the boats which were upon the lake, and, probably with a view to some enterprise of their own, drew them overland to Inversnaid, in order to intercept the progress of a large body of west-country whigs who were in arms for the government, and moving in that direction.

The whigs made an excursion for the recovery of the boats. Their forces consisted of volunteers from Paisley, Kilpatrick, and elsewhere, who, with the assistance of a body of seamen, were towed up the river Leven in long-boats belonging to the ships of war then lying in the Clyde. At Luss they were joined by the forces of Sir Humphry

Colquhoun, and James Grant, his son-in-law, with their followers, attired in the Highland dress of the period, which is picturesquely described.[8] The whole party crossed to Craig-Royston, but the Mac-Gregors did not offer combat. If we are to believe the account of the expedition given by the historian Rae, they leaped on shore at Craig-Royston with the utmost intrepidity, no enemy appearing to oppose them, and, by the noise of their drums, which they beat incessantly, and the discharge of their artillery and small arms, terrified the Mac-Gregors, whom they appear never to have seen, out of their fastnesses, and caused them to fly in a panic to the general camp of the Highlanders at Strath Fillan.[9] The low-country men succeeded in getting possession of the boats, at a great expenditure of noise and courage, and little risk of danger.*

After this temporary removal from his old haunts, Rob Roy was sent by the Earl of Mar to Aberdeen, to raise, it is believed, a part of the clan Gregor, which is settled in that country. These men were of his own family (the race of the Ciar Mohr). They were the descendants of about three hundred MacGregors whom the Earl of Murray, about the year 1624, transported from his estates in Monteith to oppose against his enemies the MacIntoshes, a race as hardy and restless as they were themselves.

But while in the city of Aberdeen, Rob Roy met a relation of a very different class and character from those whom he was sent to summon to arms. This was Dr James Gregory, (by descent a MacGregor,) the patriarch of a dynasty of professors distinguished for literary and scientific talent, and the grandfather of the late eminent physician and accomplished scholar, Professor Gregory of Edinburgh. This gentleman was at the time Professor of Medicine in King's College, Aberdeen, and son of Dr James Gregory, distinguished in science as the inventor of the reflecting telescope.* With such a family it may seem our friend Rob could have had little communion. But civil war is a species of misery which introduces men to strange bedfellows. Dr Gregory thought it a point of prudence to claim kindred, at so critical a period, with a man so formidable and influential. He invited Rob Roy to his house, and treated him with so much kindness, that he produced in his generous bosom a degree of gratitude which seemed likely to occasion very inconvenient effects.

The Professor had a son about eight or nine years old,—a lively, stout boy of his age,—with whose appearance our Highland Robin

Hood was much taken. On the day before his departure from the house of his learned relative, Rob Roy, who had pondered deeply how he might requite his cousin's kindness, took Dr Gregory aside, and addressed him to this purport:—'My dear kinsman, I have been thinking what I could do to show my sense of your hospitality. Now, here you have a fine spirited boy of a son, whom you are ruining by cramming him with your useless book-learning, and I am determined, by way of manifesting my great good-will to you and yours, to take him with me, and make a man of him.' The learned Professor was utterly overwhelmed when his warlike kinsman announced his kind purpose, in language which implied no doubt of its being a proposal which would be, and ought to be, accepted with the utmost gratitude. The task of apology or explanation was of a most delicate description; and there might have been considerable danger in suffering Rob Roy to perceive that the promotion with which he threatened the son was, in the father's eyes, the ready road to the gallows. Indeed, every excuse which he could at first think of—such as regret for putting his friend to trouble with a youth who had been educated in the Lowlands, and so on—only strengthened the chieftain's inclination to patronise his young kinsman, as he supposed they arose entirely from the modesty of the father. He would for a long time take no apology, and even spoke of carrying off the youth by a certain degree of kindly violence, whether his father consented or not. At length the perplexed Professor pleaded that his son was very young, and in an infirm state of health, and not yet able to endure the hardships of a mountain life; but that in another year or two he hoped his health would be firmly established, and he would be in a fitting condition to attend on his brave kinsman, and follow out the splendid destinies to which he opened the way. This agreement being made, the cousins parted,—Rob Roy pledging his honour to carry his young relation to the hills with him on his next return to Aberdeenshire, and Dr Gregory, doubtless, praying in his secret soul that he might never see Rob's Highland face again.

James Gregory, who thus escaped being his kinsman's recruit, and in all probability his henchman, was afterwards Professor of Medicine in the College, and, like most of his family, distinguished by his scientific acquirements. He was rather of an irritable and pertinacious disposition; and his friends were wont to remark, when he showed any symptom of these foibles, 'Ah! this comes of not having been educated by Rob Roy.'*

The connexion between Rob Roy and his classical kinsman did not end with the period of Rob's transient power. At a period considerably subsequent to the year 1715, he was walking in the Castle Street of Aberdeen, arm in arm with his host, Dr James Gregory, when the drums in the barracks suddenly beat to arms, and soldiers were seen issuing from the barracks. 'If these lads are turning out,' said Rob, taking leave of his cousin with great composure, 'it is time for me to look after my safety.' So saying, he dived down a close, and, as John Bunyan says, 'went upon his way and was seen no more.'[10]*

We have already stated that Rob Roy's conduct during the insurrection of 1715 was very equivocal. His person and followers were in the Highland army, but his heart seems to have been with the Duke of Argyle's. Yet the insurgents were constrained to trust to him as their only guide, when they marched from Perth towards Dumblane, with the view of crossing the Forth at what are called the Fords of Frew, and when they themselves said he could not be relied upon.

This movement to the westward, on the part of the insurgents, brought on the battle of Sherriff-muir,* indecisive indeed in its immediate results, but of which the Duke of Argyle reaped the whole advantage. In this action, it will be recollected that the right wing of the Highlanders broke and cut to pieces Argyle's left wing, while the clans on the left of Mar's army, though consisting of Stewarts, Mackenzies, and Camerons, were completely routed. During this medley of flight and pursuit, Rob Roy retained his station on a hill in the centre of the Highland position; and though it is said his attack might have decided the day, he could not be prevailed upon to charge. This was the more unfortunate for the insurgents, as the leading of a party of the Macphersons had been committed to MacGregor. This, it is said, was owing to the age and infirmity of the chief of that name, who, unable to lead his clan in person, objected to his heir apparent, Macpherson of Nord, discharging his duty on that occasion; so that the tribe, or a part of them, were brigaded with their allies the MacGregors. While the favourable moment for action was gliding away unemployed, Mar's positive orders reached Rob Roy that he should presently attack. To which he coolly replied, 'No, no! if they cannot do it without me, they cannot do it with me.' One of the Macphersons, named Alexander, one of Rob's original profession, *videlicet* a drover, but a man of great strength and spirit, was so incensed at the inactivity of his temporary leader, that he threw off his plaid, drew his sword, and called out to his clansmen, 'Let us endure this no longer! if he will not lead you, I will.' Rob Roy replied, with great coolness, 'Were the question about driving Highland stots or kyloes, Sandie, I would yield to your superior skill; but as it respects the leading of men, I must be allowed to be the better judge.'—'Did the matter respect driving Glen-Eigas stots,' answered the Macpherson, 'the question with Rob would not be, which was to be last, but which was to be foremost.' Incensed at this sarcasm, MacGregor drew his sword, and they would have fought upon the spot if their friends on both sides had not interfered. But the moment of attack was completely lost. Rob did not, however, neglect his own private interest on the occasion. In the confusion of an undecided field of battle, he enriched his followers by plundering the baggage and the dead on both sides.*

The fine old satirical ballad on the battle of Sherriff-muir* does not forget to stigmatize our hero's conduct on this memorable occasion.

> Rob Roy he stood watch
> On a hill for to catch
>   The booty, for aught that I saw, man;
> For he ne'er advanced
> From the place where he stanced,
>   Till nae mair was to do there at a', man.

Notwithstanding the sort of neutrality which Rob Roy had continued to observe during the progress of the Rebellion, he did not escape some of its penalties. He was included in the act of attainder, and the house in Breadalbane, which was his place of retreat, was burned by General Lord Cadogan, when, after the conclusion of the insurrection, he marched through the Highlands to disarm and punish the offending clans.* But upon going to Inverary with about forty or fifty of his followers, Rob obtained favour, by an apparent surrender of their arms of Col. Patrick Campbell of Finnah,* who furnished them and their leader with protections under his hand. Being thus in a great measure secured from the resentment of government, Rob Roy established his residence at Craig-Royston, near Loch Lomond, in the midst of his own kinsmen, and lost no time in resuming his private quarrel with the Duke of Montrose. For this purpose, he soon got on foot as many men, and well armed too, as he had yet commanded. He never stirred without a body-guard of ten or twelve picked followers, and without much effort could increase them to fifty or sixty.

The Duke was not wanting in efforts to destroy this troublesome adversary. His Grace applied to General Carpenter, commanding the forces in Scotland, and by his orders three parties of soldiers were directed from the three different points of Glasgow, Stirling, and Finlarig near Killin. Mr Graham of Killearn, the Duke of Montrose's relation and factor, Sheriff-depute also of Dumbartonshire, accompanied the troops, that they might act under the civil authority, and have the assistance of a trusty guide well acquainted with the hills. It was the object of these several columns to arrive about the same time in the neighbourhood of Rob Roy's residence, and surprise him and his followers. But heavy rains, the difficulties of the country, and the good intelligence which the Outlaw was always supplied with, disappointed their well-concerted combination. The troops, finding the birds were flown, avenged themselves by destroying the nest. They burned Rob Roy's house, though not with impunity, for the MacGregors, concealed among the thickets and cliffs, fired on them, and killed a grenadier.

Rob Roy avenged himself for the loss which he sustained on this occasion by an act of singular audacity. About the middle of November, 1716, John Graham of Killearn, already mentioned as factor of the Montrose family, went to a place called Chapel Errock, where the tenants of the Duke were summoned to appear with their termly rents. They appeared accordingly, and the factor had received ready money to the amount of about L.300, when Rob Roy entered the room at the head of an armed party. The steward endeavoured to protect the Duke's property by throwing the books of accounts and money into a garret, trusting they might escape notice. But the experienced freebooter was not to be baffled where such a prize was at stake. He recovered the books and cash, placed himself calmly in the receipt of custom, examined the accounts, pocketed the money, and gave receipts on the Duke's part, saying he would hold reckoning with the Duke of Montrose out of the damages which he had sustained by his Grace's means, in which he included the losses he had suffered, as well by the burning of his house by General Cadogan, as by the later expedition against Craig-Royston. He then requested Mr Graham to attend him; nor does it appear that he treated him with any personal violence or even rudeness, although he informed him he regarded him as a hostage, and menaced rough usage in case he should be pursued, or in danger of being overtaken. Few more audacious feats have been performed. After some rapid changes of place, (the fatigue attending which was the only annoyance that Mr Graham seems to have complained of,) he carried his prisoner to an island on Loch Katrine, and caused him to write to the Duke, to state that his ransom was fixed at 3400 merks, being the balance which MacGregor pretended remained due to him, after deducting all that he owed to the Duke of Montrose.

However, after detaining Mr Graham five or six days in custody on the island, which is still called Rob Roy's Prison, and could be no comfortable dwelling for November nights, the Outlaw seems to have despaired of attaining further advantage from his bold attempt, and suffered his prisoner to depart uninjured, with the account-books, and bills granted by the tenants, taking especial care to retain the cash.[11]

Other pranks are told of Rob, which argue the same boldness and sagacity as the seizure of Killearn. The Duke of Montrose, weary of his insolence, procured a quantity of arms, and distributed them among his tenantry, in order that they might defend themselves against future violences. But they fell into different hands from those they were intended for. The MacGregors made separate attacks on the houses of the tenants, and disarmed them all one after another, not, as was supposed, without the consent of many of the persons so disarmed.

As a great part of the Duke's rents were payable in kind, there were girnels (granaries) established for storing up the corn at Moulin, and elsewhere on the Buchanan estate. To these storehouses Rob Roy used to repair with a sufficient force, and of course when he was least expected, and insist upon the delivery of quantities of grain, sometimes for his own use, and sometimes for the assistance of the country people, always giving regular receipts in his own name, and pretending to reckon with the Duke for what sums he received.

In the meanwhile a garrison was established by government, the ruins of which may be still seen about half way betwixt Loch Lomond and Loch Katrine, upon Rob Roy's original property of Inversnaid. Even this military establishment could not bridle the restless MacGregor. He contrived to surprise the little fort, disarm the soldiers, and destroy the fortification.* It was afterwards re-established and again taken by the MacGregors under Rob Roy's nephew, Ghlune Dhu, previous to the insurrection of 1745–6. Finally, the fort of Inversnaid was a third time repaired after the extinction of civil

discord; and when we find the celebrated General Wolfe* commanding in it, the imagination is strongly affected by the variety of time and
events which the circumstance brings simultaneously to recollection.
It is now totally dismantled.[12]

It was not, strictly speaking, as a professed depredator that Rob Roy
now conducted his operations, but as a sort of contractor for the police;
in Scottish phrase, a lifter of black-mail. The nature of this contract
has been described in the Novel of Waverley, and in the notes on that
work.* Mr Graham of Gartmore's description of the character may be
here transcribed.

'The confusion and disorders of the country were so great, and the
government so absolutely neglected it, that the sober people there
were obliged to purchase some security to their effects by shameful
and ignominious contracts of *black-mail*. A person who had the greatest correspondence with the thieves was agreed with to preserve the
lands contracted for from thefts, for certain sums to be paid yearly.
Upon this fund he employed one half of the thieves to recover stolen
cattle, and the other half of them to steal, in order to make this agreement and black-mail contract necessary. The estates of those gentlemen who refused to contract, or give countenance to that pernicious
practice, are plundered by the thieving part of the watch, in order to
force them to purchase their protection. Their leader calls himself the
Captain of the *Watch*, and his banditti go by that name. And as this
gives them a kind of authority to traverse the country, so it makes them
capable of doing any mischief. These corps through the Highlands
make altogether a very considerable body of men, inured from their
infancy to the greatest fatigues, and very capable to act in a military
way when occasion offers.

'People who are ignorant and enthusiastic, who are in absolute
dependence upon their chief or landlord, who are directed in their
consciences by Roman Catholic priests, or non-juring clergymen, and
who are not masters of any property, may easily be formed into any
mould. They fear no dangers, as they have nothing to lose, and so can
with ease be induced to attempt any thing. Nothing can make their
condition worse; confusions and troubles do commonly indulge them
in such licentiousness, that by these they better it.'[13]

As the practice of contracting for black-mail was an obvious encouragement to rapine, and a great obstacle to the course of justice, it was,
by the statute 1567, chap. 21, declared a capital crime, both on the part

of him who levied and him who paid this sort of tax. But the necessity of the case prevented the execution of this severe law, I believe, in any one instance; and men went on submitting to a certain unlawful imposition rather than run the risk of utter ruin,—just as it is now found difficult or impossible to prevent those who have lost a very large sum of money by robbery, from compounding with the felons for restoration of a part of their booty.

At what rate Rob Roy levied black-mail, I never heard stated; but there is a formal contract by which his nephew, in 1741, agreed with various landholders of estates in the counties of Perth, Stirling, and Dumbarton, to recover cattle stolen from them, or to pay the value within six months of the loss being intimated, if such intimation were made to him with sufficient dispatch, in consideration of a payment of L.5 on each L.100 of valued rent, which was not a very heavy insurance. Petty thefts were not included in the contract; but the theft of one horse, or one head of black cattle, or of sheep exceeding the number of six, fell under the agreement.

Rob Roy's profits upon such contracts brought him in a considerable revenue in money or cattle, of which he made a popular use; for he was publicly liberal, as well as privately beneficent. The minister of the parish of Balquhidder, whose name was Robison, was at one time threatening to pursue the parish for an augmentation of his stipend. Rob Roy took an opportunity to assure him that he would do well to abstain from this new exaction,—a hint which the minister did not fail to understand. But to make him some indemnification, MacGregor presented him every year with a cow and a fat sheep; and no scruples as to the mode in which the donor came by them, are said to have affected the reverend gentleman's conscience.

The following account of the proceedings of Rob Roy, on an application to him from one of his contractors, had in it something very interesting to me, as told by an old countryman in the Lennox who was present on the expedition. But as there is no point or marked incident in the story, and as it must necessarily be without the half-frightened, half-bewildered look with which the narrator accompanied his recollections, it may possibly lose its effect when transferred to paper.

My informant stated himself to have been a lad of fifteen, living with his father on the estate of a gentleman in the Lennox, whose name I have forgotten, in the capacity of herd. On a fine morning in the end of October, the period when such calamities were almost always to be apprehended, they found the Highland thieves had been down upon them, and swept away ten or twelve head of cattle. Rob Roy was sent for, and came with a party of seven or eight armed men. He heard with great gravity all that could be told him of the circumstances of the *creagh*, and expressed his confidence that the *herd-widdiefows*[14] could not have carried their booty far, and that he should be able to recover them. He desired that two Lowlanders should be sent on the party, as it was not to be expected that any of his gentlemen would take the trouble of driving the cattle when he should recover possession of them. My informant and his father were dispatched on the expedition. They had no good-will to the journey; nevertheless, provided with a little food, and with a dog to help them to manage the cattle, they set off with MacGregor. They travelled a long day's journey in the direction of the mountain Benvoirlich, and slept for the night in a ruinous hut or bothy. The next morning they resumed their journey among the hills, Rob Roy directing their course by signs and marks on the heath, which my informant did not understand.

About noon, Rob commanded the armed party to halt, and to lie couched in the heather where it was thickest. 'Do you and your son,' he said to the oldest Lowlander, 'go boldly over the hill. You will see beneath you, in a glen on the otherside, your master's cattle feeding, it may be, with others; gather your own together, taking care to disturb no one else, and drive them to this place. If any one speak to, or threaten you, tell them that I am here, at the head of twenty men.'— 'But what if they abuse us, or kill us?' said the Lowland peasant, by no means delighted at finding the embassy imposed on him and his son. 'If they do you any wrong,' said Rob, 'I will never forgive them as long as I live.' The Lowlander was by no means content with this security, but did not think it safe to dispute Rob's injunctions.

He and his son climbed the hill, therefore, found a deep valley, where there grazed, as Rob had predicted, a large herd of cattle. They cautiously selected those which their master had lost, and took measures to drive them over the hill. As soon as they began to remove them, they were surprised by hearing cries and screams; and looking around in fear and trembling, they saw a woman, seeming to have started out of the earth, who *flyted* at them, that is, scolded them, in Gaelic. When they contrived, however, in the best Gaelic they could muster, to deliver the message Rob Roy told them, she became silent, and disappeared without offering them any further annoyance. The chief heard their story on their return, and spoke with great complacency of the art which he possessed of putting such things to rights without any unpleasant bustle. The party were now on their road home, and the danger, though not the fatigue, of the expedition was at an end.

They drove on the cattle with little repose until it was nearly dark, when Rob proposed to halt for the night upon a wide moor, across which a cold north-east wind, with frost on its wing, was whistling to the tune of the Pipers of Strath-Dearn.[15] The Highlanders, sheltered by their plaids, lay down in the heath comfortably enough, but the Lowlanders had no protection whatever. Rob Roy observing this, directed one of his followers to afford the old man a portion of his plaid; 'for the callant (boy), he may,' said the freebooter, 'keep himself warm by walking about and watching the cattle.' My informant heard this sentence with no small distress; and as the frost wind grew more and more cutting, it seemed to freeze the very blood in his young veins. He had been exposed to weather all his life, he said, but never could forget the cold of that night; in so much that, in the bitterness of his heart, he cursed the bright moon for giving no heat with so much light. At length the sense of cold and weariness became so intolerable, that he resolved to desert his watch to seek some repose and shelter. With that purpose, he couched himself down behind one of the most bulky of the Highlanders, who acted as lieutenant to the party. Not satisfied with having secured the shelter of the man's large person, he coveted a share of his plaid, and by imperceptible degrees drew a corner of it round him. He was now comparatively in paradise, and slept sound till daybreak, when he awoke, and was terribly afraid on observing that his nocturnal operations had altogether uncovered the dhuiniewassell's neck and shoulders, which, lacking the plaid which should have protected them, were covered with *cranreuch* (*i.e.* hoar frost). The lad rose in great dread of a beating, at least, when it should be found how luxuriously he had been accommodated at the expense of a principal person of the party. Good Mr Lieutenant, however, got up and shook himself, rubbing off the hoar frost with his plaid, and muttering something of a *cauld neight*. They then drove on the cattle, which were restored to their owner without farther adventure. The above can hardly be termed a tale, but yet it contains materials both for the poet and artist.

It was perhaps about the same time that, by a rapid march into the Balquhidder hills at the head of a body of his own tenantry, the Duke of Montrose actually surprised Rob Roy, and made him prisoner. He was mounted behind one of the Duke's followers, named James Stewart, and made fast to him by a horse-girth. The person who had him thus in charge was grandfather of the intelligent man of the same name, now deceased, who lately kept the inn in the vicinity of Loch Katrine, and acted as a guide to visitors through that beautiful scenery. From him I learned the story many years before he was either a publican, or a guide, except to moorfowl shooters.—It was evening, (to resume the story,) and the Duke was pressing on to lodge his prisoner, so long sought after in vain, in some place of security, when, in crossing the Teith or Forth, I forget which, MacGregor took an opportunity to conjure Stewart, by all the ties of old acquaintance and good-neighbourhood, to give him some chance of an escape from an assured doom. Stewart was moved with compassion, perhaps with fear. He slipped the girth-buckle, and Rob, dropping down from behind the horse's croupe, dived, swam, and escaped, pretty much as described in the Novel. When James Stewart came on shore, the Duke hastily demanded where his prisoner was; and as no distinct answer was returned, instantly suspected Stewart's connivance at the escape of the outlaw; and, drawing a steel pistol from his belt, struck him down with a blow on the head, from the effects of which, his descendant said, he never completely recovered.

In the success of his repeated escapes from the pursuit of his powerful enemy, Rob Roy at length became wanton and facetious. He wrote a mock challenge to the Duke, which he circulated among his friends to amuse them over a bottle. The reader will find this document in the Appendix.[16] It is written in a good hand, and not particularly deficient in grammar or spelling. Our Southern readers must be given to understand that it was a piece of humour,—a *quiz*, in short,—on the part of the outlaw, who was too sagacious to propose such a rencontre in reality. This letter was written in the year 1719.

In the following year Rob Roy composed another epistle, very little to his own reputation, as he therein confesses having played booty during the civil war of 1715. It is addressed to General Wade, at that time engaged in disarming the Highland clans, and making military roads through the country. The letter is a singular composition.* It sets out the writer's real and unfeigned desire to have offered his service to King George, but for his liability to be thrown into jail for a civil debt, at the instance of the Duke of Montrose. Being thus debarred from taking the right side, he acknowledged he embraced the wrong one, upon Falstaff's principle, that since the King wanted men and the rebels soldiers, it were worse shame to be idle in such a stirring world, than to embrace the worst side, were it as black as rebellion could make it.* The impossibility of his being neutral in such a debate, Rob seems to lay down as an undeniable proposition. At the same time, while he acknowledges having been forced into an unnatural rebellion against King George, he pleads that he not only avoided acting offensively against his Majesty's forces on all occasions, but, on the contrary, sent to them what intelligence he could collect from time to time; for the truth of which he refers to his Grace the Duke of Argyle. What influence this plea had on General Wade we have no means of knowing.

Rob Roy appears to have continued to live very much as usual. His fame, in the mean while, passed beyond the narrow limits of the country in which he resided. A pretended history of him appeared in London during his lifetime, under the title of the Highland Rogue.* It is a catch-penny publication, bearing in front the effigy of a species of ogre, with a beard of a foot in length; and his actions are as much exaggerated as his personal appearance. Some few of the best known adventures of the hero are told, though with little accuracy; but the greater part of the pamphlet is entirely fictitious. It is great pity so excellent a theme for a narrative of the kind had not fallen into the hands of De Foe, who was engaged at the time on subjects somewhat similar, though inferior in dignity and interest.

As Rob Roy advanced in years he became more peaceable in his habits, and his nephew Ghlune Dhu, with most of his tribe, renounced those peculiar quarrels with the Duke of Montrose, by which his uncle had been distinguished. The policy of that great family had latterly been rather to attach this wild tribe by kindness than to follow the mode of violence which had been hitherto ineffectually resorted to. Leases at a low rent were granted to many of the MacGregors, who had heretofore held possessions in the Duke's Highland property merely by occupancy; and Glengyle, (or Black-knee,) who continued to act as collector of black-mail, managed his police, as a commander of the Highland watch arrayed at the charge of government. He is said to have strictly abstained from the open and lawless depredations which his kinsman had practised.

It was probably after this state of temporary quiet had been obtained, that Rob Roy began to think of the concerns of his future state. He had been bred, and long professed himself, a Protestant; but in his later years he embraced the Roman Catholic faith,—perhaps on Mrs Cole's principle,* that it was a comfortable religion for one of his calling. He is said to have alleged as the cause of his conversion, a desire to gratify the noble family of Perth, who were then strict Catholics. Having, as he observed, assumed the name of the Duke of Argyle, his first protector, he could pay no compliment worth the Earl of Perth's acceptance, save complying with his mode of religion.* Rob did not pretend, when pressed closely on the subject, to justify all the tenets of Catholicism, and acknowledged that extreme unction always appeared to him a great waste of *ulzie*, or oil.[17]

In the last years of Rob Roy's life his clan was involved in a dispute with one more powerful than themselves. Stewart of Appin, a chief of the tribe so named, was proprietor of a hill-farm in the Braes of Balquhidder, called Invernenty. The MacGregors of Rob Roy's tribe claimed a right to it by ancient occupancy, and declared they would oppose to the uttermost the settlement of any person upon the farm not being of their own name. The Stewarts came down with two hundred men, well armed, to do themselves justice by main force. The MacGregors took the field, but were unable to muster an equal strength. Rob Roy, finding himself the weaker party, asked a parley, in which he represented that both clans were friends to the *King*, and that he was unwilling they should be weakened by mutual conflict, and thus made a merit of surrendering to Appin the disputed territory of Invernenty. Appin, accordingly, settled as tenants there, at an easy quit-rent,* the MacLarens, a family dependent on the Stewarts, and from whose character for strength and bravery, it was expected that they would make their right good if annoyed by the MacGregors. When all this had been amicably adjusted, in presence of the two clans drawn up in arms near the Kirk of Balquhidder, Rob Roy, apparently fearing his tribe might be thought to have conceded too much upon the occasion, stepped forward and said, that where so many gallant men were met in arms, it would be shameful to part without a trial of skill, and therefore he took the freedom to invite any gentleman of the Stewarts present to exchange a few blows with him for the honour of their respective clans. The brother-in-law of Appin, and second chieftain of the clan, Alaster Stewart of Invernahyle,* accepted the challenge, and they encountered with broadsword and target before their respective kinsmen.[18] The combat lasted till Rob received a slight wound in the arm, which was the usual termination of such a combat when fought for honour only, and not with a mortal purpose. Rob Roy dropped his point, and congratulated his adversary on having been the first man who ever drew blood from him. The victor generously acknowledged, that without the advantage of youth, and the agility accompanying it, he probably could not have come off with advantage.

This was probably one of Rob Roy's last exploits in arms. The time of his death is not known with certainty, but he is generally said to have survived 1733, and to have died an aged man. When he found himself approaching his final change, he expressed some contrition for particular parts of his life. His wife laughed at these scruples of conscience, and exhorted him to die like a man, as he had lived. In reply, he rebuked her for her violent passions, and the counsels she had given him. 'You have put strife,' he said, 'betwixt me and the best men of the country, and now you would place enmity between me and my God.'

There is a tradition, no way inconsistent with the former, if the character of Rob Roy be justly considered, that while on his death-bed, he learned that a person, with whom he was at enmity, proposed to visit him. 'Raise me from my bed,' said the invalid; 'throw my plaid around me, and bring me my claymore, dirk, and pistols—it shall never be said that a foeman saw Rob Roy MacGregor defenceless and unarmed.' His foeman, conjectured to be one of the MacLarens before and after mentioned, entered and paid his compliments, enquiring after the health of his formidable neighbour. Rob Roy maintained a cold, haughty civility during their short conference, and so soon as he had left the house, 'Now,' he said, 'all is over—let the piper play *Ha til mi tulidh*, (we return no more,)' and he is said to have expired before the dirge was finished.*

This singular man died in bed in his own house, in the parish of Balquhidder. He was buried in the churchyard of the same parish, where his tombstone is only distinguished by a rude attempt at the figure of a broadsword.

The character of Rob Roy is, of course, a mixed one. His sagacity, boldness, and prudence, qualities so highly necessary to success in war, became in some degree vices from the manner in which they were employed. The circumstances of his education, however, must be admitted as some extenuation of his habitual transgressions against the law; and for his political tergiversations, he might in that distracted period plead the example of men far more powerful, and less excusable in becoming the sport of circumstances, than the poor and desperate outlaw. On the other hand, he was in the constant exercise of virtues, the more meritorious as they seem inconsistent with his general character. Pursuing the occupation of a predatory chieftain,—in modern phrase, a captain of banditti,—Rob Roy was moderate in his revenge, and humane in his successes. No charge of cruelty or bloodshed, unless in battle, is brought against his memory. In like manner, the formidable outlaw was the friend of the poor, and, to the utmost of his ability, the support of the widow and the orphan—kept his word when pledged—and died lamented in his own wild country, where there were hearts grateful for his beneficence, though their minds were not sufficiently instructed to appreciate his errors.

The author perhaps ought to stop here; but the fate of a part of Rob Roy's family was so extraordinary, as to call for a continuation of this somewhat prolix account, as affording an interesting chapter, not on Highland manners alone, but on every stage of society in which the people of a primitive and half-civilized tribe are brought into close contact with a nation, in which civilization and polity has attained a complete superiority.

Rob had five sons,—Coll, Ronald, James, Duncan, and Robert. Nothing occurs worth notice concerning three of them; but James, who was a very handsome man, seems to have had a good deal of his father's spirit, and the mantle of Dougal Ciar Mohr had apparently descended on the shoulders of Robin Oig, that is, young Robin. Shortly after Rob Roy's death, the ill-will which the MacGregors entertained against the MacLarens again broke out, at the instigation, it was said, of Rob's widow, who seems thus far to have deserved the character given to her by her husband, as an Até 'stirring up to blood and strife.'* Robin Oig, under her instigation, swore that as soon as he could get back a certain gun which had belonged to his father, and had been lately at Doune to be repaired, he would shoot MacLaren, for having presumed to settle on his mother's land.[19] He was as good as his word, and shot MacLaren when between the stilts of his plough, wounding him mortally.

The aid of a Highland leech was procured, who probed the wound with a probe made out of a castock, *i.e.* the stalk of a cole-wort or cabbage. This learned gentleman declared he would not venture to prescribe, not knowing with what shot the patient had been wounded.

MacLaren died, and about the same time his cattle were houghed and his live stock destroyed in a barbarous manner.

Robin Oig, after this feat—which one of his biographers represents as the unhappy discharge of a gun—retired to his mother's house, to boast that he had drawn the first blood in the quarrel aforesaid. On the approach of troops, and a body of the Stewarts, who were bound to take up the cause of their tenant, Robin Oig absconded, and escaped all search.

The doctor already mentioned, by name Callam MacInleister, with James and Ronald, brothers to the actual perpetrator of the murder, were brought to trial. But as they contrived to represent the action as a rash deed committed by the 'daft callant Rob,' to which they were not accessary, the jury found their accession to the crime was Not Proven.* The alleged acts of spoil and violence on the MacLarens' cattle were also found to be unsupported by evidence. As it was proved, however, that the two brothers, Ronald and James, were held and reputed thieves, they were appointed to find caution to the extent of L.200, for their good behaviour for seven years.[20]

The spirit of clanship was at that time so strong—to which must be added the wish to secure the adherence of stout, able-bodied, and, as the Scotch phrase then went, *pretty* men—that the representative of the noble family of Perth condescended to act openly as patron of the MacGregors, and appeared as such upon their trial. So at least the author was informed by the late Robert MacIntosh, Esq. advocate. The circumstance may, however, have occurred later than 1736—the year in which this first trial took place.

Robin Oig served for a time in the 42d regiment, and was present at the battle of Fontenoy, where he was made prisoner and wounded. He was exchanged, returned to Scotland, and obtained his discharge. He afterwards appeared openly in the MacGregor's country; and, not-withstanding his outlawry, married a daughter of Graham of Drunkie, a gentleman of some property. His wife died a few years afterwards.

The insurrection of 1745 soon afterwards called the MacGregors to arms. Robert MacGregor of Glencarnoch, generally regarded as the chief of the whole name, and grandfather of Sir John, whom the clan received in that character, raised a MacGregor regiment, with which he joined the standard of the Chevalier. The race of Ciar Mohr, how-ever, affecting independence, and commanded by Glengyle and his cousin James Roy MacGregor, did not join this kindred corps, but united themselves to the levies of the titular Duke of Perth, until William MacGregor Drummond of Bolhaldin, whom they regarded as head of their branch of Clan-Alpine, should come over from France. To cement the union after the Highland fashion, James laid down the name of Campbell and assumed that of Drummond, in compliment to Lord Perth. He was also called James Roy, after his father, and James Mohr, or Big James, from his height. His corps, the relics of his father Rob's band, behaved with great activity; with only twelve men he succeeded in surprising and burning, for the second time, the fort at Inversnaid, constructed for the express purpose of bridling the country of the MacGregors.

What rank or command James MacGregor had, is uncertain. He calls himself Major; and Chevalier Johnstone* calls him Captain. He must have held rank under Ghlune Dhu, his kinsman, but his active and audacious character placed him above the rest of his brethren. Many of his followers were unarmed; he supplied the want of guns and swords with scythe-blades set straight upon their handles.

At the battle of Prestonpans, James Roy distinguished himself. 'His company,' says Chevalier Johnstone, 'did great execution with their scythes.' They cut the legs of the horses in two; the riders through the middle of their bodies. MacGregor was brave and intrepid, but, at the same time, somewhat whimsical and singular. When advancing to the charge with his company, he received five wounds, two of them from balls that pierced his body through and through. Stretched on the ground, with his head resting on his hand, he called out loudly to the Highlanders of his company, 'My lads, I am not dead. By G——, I shall see if any of you does not do his duty.' The victory, as is well known, was instantly obtained.

In some curious letters of James Roy,[21] it appears that his thigh bone was broken on this occasion, and that he, nevertheless, rejoined the army with six companies, and was present at the battle of Culloden. After that defeat the clan MacGregor kept together in a body, and did not disperse till they had returned into their own country. They brought James Roy with them in a litter; and, without being particularly molested, he was permitted to reside in the MacGregor's country along with his brothers.

James MacGregor Drummond was attainted for high treason with persons of more importance. But it appears he had entered into some communication with government, as, in the letters quoted, he mentions having obtained a pass from the Lord Justice Clerk in 1747, which was a sufficient protection to him from the military. The circumstance is obscurely stated in one of the letters already quoted, but may perhaps, joined to subsequent incidents, authorise the suspicion that James, like his father, could look at both sides of the cards. As the confusion of the country subsided, the MacGregors, like foxes which had baffled the hounds, drew back to their old haunts, and lived unmolested. But an atrocious outrage, in which the sons of Rob Roy were concerned, brought at length on the family the full vengeance of the law.

James Roy was a married man, and had fourteen children. But his brother, Robin Oig, was now a widower; and it was resolved, if possible, that he should make his fortune by carrying off and marrying, by force if necessary, some woman of fortune from the Lowlands.

The imagination of the half-civilized Highlanders was less shocked at the idea of this particular species of violence, than might be expected from their general kindness to the weaker sex when they make part of their own families. But all their views were tinged with the idea that they lived in a state of war; and in such a state, from the time of the siege of Troy to 'the moment when Previsa fell,'[22]* the female captives are, to uncivilized victors, the most valuable part of the booty.

'The wealthy are slaughter'd, the lovely are spared.'

We need not refer to the rape of the Sabines, or to a similar instance in the Book of Judges,* for evidence that such deeds of violence have been committed upon a large scale. Indeed, this sort of enterprise was so common along the Highland line as to give rise to a variety of songs and ballads.[23] The annals of Ireland, as well as those of Scotland, prove the crime to have been common in the more lawless parts of both countries; and any woman who happened to please a man of spirit who came of a good house, and possessed a few chosen friends, and a retreat in the mountains, was not permitted the alternative of saying him nay. What is more, it would seem that the women themselves, most interested in the immunities of their sex, were, among the lower classes, accustomed to regard such marriages as that which is presently to be detailed as 'pretty Fanny's way,'* or rather, the way of Donald with pretty Fanny. It is not a great many years since a respectable woman,* above the lower rank of life, expressed herself very warmly to the author on his taking the freedom to censure the behaviour of the Mac-Gregors on the occasion in question. She said 'that there was no use in giving a bride too much choice upon such occasions; that the marriages were the happiest lang syne which had been done off hand.' Finally, she averred that her 'own mother had never seen her father till the night he brought her up from the Lennox, with ten head of black cattle, and there had not been a happier couple in the country.'

James Drummond and his brethren having similar opinions with the author's old acquaintance, and debating how they might raise the fallen fortunes of their clan, formed a resolution to settle their brother's fortune by striking up an advantageous marriage betwixt Robin Oig and one Jean Key, or Wright, a young woman scarce twenty years old, and who had been left about two months a widow by the death of her husband. Her property was estimated at only from 16,000 to 18,000 merks, but it seems to have been sufficient temptation to these men to join in the commission of a great crime.

This poor young victim lived with her mother in her own house at Edinbilly, in the parish of Balfron and shire of Stirling. At this place, in the night of 3d December 1750, the sons of Rob Roy, and particularly James Mohr and Robin Oig, rushed into the house where the object of their attack was resident, presented guns, swords, and pistols to the males of the family, and terrified the women by threatening to break open the doors if Jean Key was not surrendered, as, said James Roy, 'his brother was a young fellow determined to make his fortune.' Having, at length, dragged the object of their lawless purpose from her place of concealment, they tore her from her mother's arms, mounted her on a horse before one of the gang, and carried her off in spite of her screams and cries, which were long heard after the terrified spectators of the outrage could no longer see the party retreat through the darkness. In her attempts to escape, the poor young woman threw herself from the horse on which they had placed her, and in so doing wrenched her side. They then laid her double over the pummel of the saddle, and transported her through the mosses and moors till the pain of the injury she had suffered in her side, augmented by the uneasiness of her posture, made her consent to sit upright. In the execution of this crime they stopped at more houses than one, but none of the inhabitants dared interrupt their proceedings. Amongst others who saw them was that classical and accomplished scholar the late Professor William Richardson of Glasgow,* who used to describe as a terrible dream their violent and noisy entrance into the house where he was then residing. The Highlanders filled the little kitchen, brandishing their arms, demanding what they pleased, and receiving whatever they demanded. James Mohr, he said, was a tall, stern, and soldier-like man. Robin Oig looked more gentle; dark, but yet ruddy in complexion—a good-looking young savage. Their victim was so dishevelled in her dress, and forlorn in her appearance and demeanour, that he could hardly tell whether she was alive or dead.

The gang carried the unfortunate woman to Rowerdennan, where they had a priest unscrupulous enough to read the marriage service, while James Mohr forcibly held the bride up before him; and the priest declared the couple man and wife, even while she protested against the infamy of his conduct. Under the same threats of violence, which had been all along used to enforce their scheme, the poor victim was compelled to reside with the pretended husband who was thus forced upon her. They even dared to carry her to the public church of Balquhidder, where the officiating clergyman (the same who had been Rob Roy's pensioner) only asked them if they were married persons. Robert MacGregor answered in the affirmative; the terrified female was silent.

The country was now too effectually subjected to the law for this vile outrage to be followed by the advantages proposed by the actors. Military parties were sent out in every direction to seize the Mac-Gregors, who were for two or three weeks compelled to shift from one place to another in the mountains, bearing the unfortunate Jean Key along with them. In the mean while, the Supreme Civil Court issued a warrant sequestrating the property of Jean Key, or Wright, which removed out of the reach of the actors in the violence the prize which they expected. They had, however, adopted a belief of the poor woman's spirit being so far broken that she would prefer submitting to her condition, and adhering to Robin Oig as her husband, rather than incur the disgrace of appearing in such a cause in an open court. It was, indeed, a delicate experiment, but their kinsman Glengyle, chief of their immediate family, was of a temper averse to lawless proceedings;[24] and the captive's friends having had recourse to his advice, they feared that he would withdraw his protection if they refused to place the prisoner at liberty.

The brethren resolved therefore to liberate the unhappy woman, but previously had recourse to every measure which should oblige her, either from fear or otherwise, to own her marriage with Robin Oig. The cailliachs (old Highland hags) administered drugs, which were designed to have the effect of philtres, but were probably deleterious. James Mohr at one time threatened, that if she did not acquiesce in the match, she would find that there were enough of men in the Highlands to bring the heads of two of her uncles who were pursuing the civil law-suit. At another time he fell down on his knees, and confessed he had been accessory to wronging her, but begged she would not ruin his innocent wife and large family. She was made to swear she would not prosecute the brethren for the offence they had committed; and she was obliged, by threats, to subscribe papers which were tendered to her, intimating that she was carried off in consequence of her own previous request.

James Mohr Drummond, accordingly, brought his pretended sister-in-law to Edinburgh, where, for some little time, she was carried about from one house to another, watched by those with whom she was lodged, and never permitted to go out alone, or even to approach the window. The Court of Session, considering the peculiarity of the case, and regarding Jean Key as being still under some forcible restraint, took her person under their own special charge, and appointed her to reside in the family of Mr Wightman of Mauldsley, a gentleman of respectability, who was married to one of her near relatives. Two sentinels kept guard on the house day and night,—a precaution not deemed superfluous when the MacGregors were in question. She was allowed to go out whenever she chose, and to see whomsoever she had a mind, as well as the men of law employed in the civil suit on either side. When she first came to Mr Wightman's house, she seemed broken down with affright and suffering, so changed in features that her mother hardly knew her, and so shaken in mind that she scarce could recognise her parent. It was long before she could be assured that she was in perfect safety. But when she at length received confidence in her situation, she made a judicial declaration, or affidavit, telling the full history of her wrongs, imputing to fear her former silence on the subject, and expressing her resolution not to prosecute those who had injured her, in respect of the oath which she had been compelled to take. From the possible breach of such an oath, though a compulsory one, she was relieved by the forms of Scottish jurisprudence, in that respect more equitable than those of England, prosecutions for crimes being always conducted at the expense and charge of the King, without inconvenience or cost to the private party who has sustained the wrong. But the unhappy sufferer did not live to be either accuser or witness against those who had so deeply injured her.*

James Mohr Drummond had left Edinburgh so soon as his half-dead prey had been taken from his clutches. Mrs Key, or Wright, was released from her species of confinement there, and removed to Glasgow, under the escort of Mr Wightman. As they passed the Hill of Shotts, her escort chanced to say, 'This is a very wild spot; what if the MacGregors should come upon us?'—'God forbid!' was her immediate answer, 'the very sight of them would kill me.' She continued to reside at Glasgow, without venturing to return to her own house at Edinbilly. Her pretended husband made some attempts to obtain an interview with her, which she steadily rejected. She died on the 4th October, 1751. The information for the crown hints that her decease might be the consequence of the usage she received. But there is a general report that she died of the small-pox.

In the meantime, James Mohr, or Drummond, fell into the hands of justice. He was considered as the instigator of the whole affair. Nay, the deceased had informed her friends that, on the night of her being carried off, Robin Oig, moved by her cries and tears, had partly consented to let her return, when James came up, with a pistol in his hand, and, asking whether he was such a coward as to relinquish an enterprise in which he had risked every thing to procure him a fortune, in a manner compelled his brother to persevere. James's trial took place on 13th July, 1752, and was conducted with the utmost fairness and impartiality. Several witnesses, all of the MacGregor family, swore that the marriage was performed with every appearance of acquiescence on the woman's part; and three or four witnesses, one of them sheriff-substitute of the county, swore she might have made her escape if she wished, and the magistrate stated that he offered her assistance if she felt desirous to do so. But when asked why he, in his official capacity, did not arrest the MacGregors, he could only answer, that he had not force sufficient to make the attempt.

The judicial declarations of Jean Key, or Wright, stated the violent manner in which she had been carried off, and they were confirmed by many of her friends, from her private communications with them, which the event of her death rendered good evidence. Indeed, the fact of her abduction (to use a Scottish law term) was completely proved by impartial witnesses. The unhappy woman admitted that she had pretended acquiescence in her fate on several occasions, because she dared not trust such as offered to assist her to escape, not even the sheriff-substitute.

The jury brought in a special verdict,* finding that Jean Key, or Wright, had been forcibly carried off from her house, as charged in the indictment, and that the accused had failed to show that she was herself privy and consenting to this act of outrage. But they found the forcible marriage, and subsequent violence, was not proved; and also found, in alleviation of the panel's guilt in the premises, that Jean Key did afterwards acquiesce in her condition. Eleven of the jury, using the names of other four who were absent, subscribed a letter to the Court, stating it was their purpose and desire, by such special verdict, to take the panel's case out of the class of capital crimes.

Learned informations (written arguments) on the import of the verdict, which must be allowed a very mild one in the circumstances, were laid before the High Court of Justiciary. This point is very learnedly debated in these pleadings by Mr Grant, Solicitor for the Crown, and the celebrated Mr Lockhart, on the part of the prisoner; but James Mohr did not wait the event of the Court's decision.

He had been committed to the Castle of Edinburgh on some reports that an escape would be attempted. Yet he contrived to achieve his liberty even from that fortress. His daughter had the address to enter the prison, disguised as a cobbler, bringing home work as she pretended. In this cobbler's dress her father quickly arrayed himself. The wife and daughter of the prisoner were heard by the sentinels scolding the supposed cobbler for having done his work ill, and the man came out with his hat slouched over his eyes, and grumbling, as if at the manner in which they had treated him. In this way the prisoner passed all the guards without suspicion, and made his escape to France. He was afterwards outlawed by the Court of Justiciary, which proceeded to the trial of Duncan MacGregor, or Drummond, his brother, 15th January, 1753. The accused had unquestionably been with the party which carried off Jean Key; but no evidence being brought which applied to him individually and directly, the jury found him not guilty, and nothing more is known of his fate.

That of James MacGregor, who, from talent and activity, if not by seniority, may be considered as head of the family, has been long misrepresented, as it has been generally averred in Law Reports, as well as elsewhere, that his outlawry was reversed, and that he returned and died in Scotland. But the curious letters published in Blackwood's Magazine for December, 1817, show this to be an error. The first of these documents is a petition to Charles Edward. It is dated 20th September, 1753, and pleads his service to the cause of the Stewarts, ascribing his exile to the persecution of the Hanoverian Government, without any allusion to the affair of Jean Key, or the Court of Justiciary. It is stated to be forwarded by MacGregor Drummond of Bohaldie, whom, as before mentioned, James Mohr acknowledged as his chief.

The effect which this petition produced does not appear. Some temporary relief was perhaps obtained. But, soon after, this daring adventurer was engaged in a very dark intrigue against an exile of his own country, and placed pretty nearly in his own circumstances. A remarkable Highland story must be here briefly alluded to.* Mr Campbell, of Glenure, who had been named factor for Government on the forfeited estates of Stewart of Ardshiel, was shot dead by an assassin as he passed through the wood of Lettermore, after crossing the ferry of Ballichulish. A gentleman, named James Stewart, a natural brother of Ardshiel the forfeited person, was tried as being accessory to the murder, and condemned and executed upon very doubtful evidence; the heaviest part of which only amounted to the accused person having assisted a nephew of his own, called Allan Breck Stewart, with money to escape after the deed was done. Not satisfied with this vengeance, which was obtained in a manner little to the honour of the dispensation of justice at the time, the friends of the deceased Glenure were eagerly desirous to obtain possession of the person of Allan Breck Stewart, supposed to be the actual homicide. James Mohr Drummond was secretly applied to to trepan Stewart to the sea-coast, and bring him over to Britain to almost certain death. Drummond MacGregor had kindred connexions with the slain Glenure; and, besides, the MacGregors and Campbells had been friends of late, while the former clan and the Stewarts had, as we have seen, been recently at feud; lastly, Robert Oig was now in custody at Edinburgh, and James was desirous to do some service by which his brother might be saved. The joint force of these motives may, in James's estimation of right and wrong, have been some vindication for engaging in such an enterprise, although, as must be necessarily supposed, it could only be executed by treachery of a gross description. MacGregor stipulated for a license to return to England, promising to bring Allan

Breck thither along with him. But the intended victim was put upon his guard by two countrymen, who suspected James's intentions towards him. He escaped from his kidnapper, after, as MacGregor alleged, robbing his portmanteau of some clothes and four snuffboxes. Such a charge, it may be observed, could scarce have been made unless the parties had been living on a footing of intimacy, and had access to each other's baggage.

Although James Drummond had thus missed his blow in the matter of Allan Breck Stewart, he used his license to make a journey to London, and had an interview, as he avers, with Lord Holdernesse. His Lordship, and the Under-Secretary, put many puzzling questions to him; and, as he says, offered him a situation, which would bring him bread, in the Government's service. This office was advantageous as to emolument; but in the opinion of James Drummond, his acceptance of it would have been a disgrace to his birth, and have rendered him a scourge to his country. If such a tempting offer and sturdy rejection had any foundation in fact, it probably relates to some plan of espionage on the Jacobites, which the Government might hope to carry on by means of a man who, in the matter of Allan Breck Stewart, had shown no great nicety of feeling. Drummond MacGregor was so far accommodating as to intimate his willingness to act in any station in which other gentlemen of honour served, but not otherwise; an answer which, compared with some passages of his past life, may remind the reader of Ancient Pistol standing upon his reputation.*

Having thus proved intractable, as he tells the story, to the proposals of Lord Holdernesse, James Drummond was ordered instantly to quit England.

On his return to France his condition seems to have been utterly disastrous. He was seized with fever and gravel, ill consequently in body, and weakened and dispirited in mind. Allan Breck Stewart threatened to put him to death in revenge of the designs he had harboured against him.[25] The Stewart clan were in the highest degree unfriendly to him; and his late expedition to London had been attended with many suspicious circumstances, amongst which it was not the slightest that he had kept his purpose secret from his chief Bohaldie. His intercourse with Lord Holdernesse was suspicious. The Jacobites were probably, like Don Bernard de Castel Blazo, in Gil Blas, little disposed to like those who kept company with Alguazils.* MacDonnell, of Lochgarry, a man of unquestioned honour, lodged an information against James Drummond before the High Bailie of Dunkirk, accusing him of being a spy, so that he found himself obliged to leave that town and come to Paris, with only the sum of thirteen livres for his immediate subsistence, and with absolute beggary staring him in the face.

We do not offer the convicted common thief, the accomplice in MacLaren's assassination, or the manager of the outrage against Jean Key, as an object of sympathy; but it is melancholy to look on the dying struggles even of a wolf or tiger, creatures of a species directly hostile to our own; and, in like manner, the utter distress of this man, whose faults may have sprung from a wild system of education, working on a haughty temper, will not be perused without some pity. In his last letter to Bohaldie, dated Paris, 25th September, 1754, he describes his state of destitution as absolute, and expresses himself willing to exercise his talents in breaking or breeding horses, or as a hunter or fowler, if he could only procure employment in such an inferior capacity till something better should occur. An Englishman may smile, but a Scotsman will sigh at the postscript, in which the poor starving exile asks the loan of his patron's bagpipes that he might play over some of the melancholy tunes of his own land. But the effect of music arises, in a great degree, from association, and sounds which might jar the nerves of a Londoner or Parisian, bring back to the Highlander his lofty mountain, wild lake, and the deeds of his fathers of the glen. To prove MacGregor's claim to our reader's compassion, we here insert the last part of the letter alluded to.

'By all appearance I am born to suffer crosses, and it seems they're not at an end; for such is my wretched case at present, that I do not know earthly where to go or what to do, as I have no subsistence to keep body and soul together. All that I have carried here is about 13 livres, and have taken a room at my old quarters in Hotel St Pierre, Rue de Cordier. I send you the bearer, begging of you to let me know if you are to be in town soon, that I may have the pleasure of seeing you, for I have none to make application to but you alone; and all I want is, if it was possible you could contrive where I could be employed without going to entire beggary. This probably is a difficult point, yet, unless it's attended with some difficulty, you might think nothing of it, as your long head can bring about matters of much more difficulty and consequence than this. If you'd disclose this matter to your friend Mr Buttler, it's possible he might have some employ wherein I could be of use, as I pretend to know as much of breiding and riding of horses as any in France, besides that I am a good hunter, either on horseback or by footing. You may judge my reduction, as I propose the meanest things to lend a turn till better cast up. I am sorry that I am obliged to give you so much trouble, but I hope you are very well assured that I am grateful for what you have done for me, and I leave you to judge of my present wretched case. I am, and shall for ever continue,

> 'Dear Chief, your own to command,
> 'JAS. MACGREGOR.

'P.S.—If you'd send your pipes by the bearer, and all the other little trinkims belonging to it, I would put them in order, and play some melancholy tunes, which I may now with safety, and in real truth. Forgive my not going directly to you, for if I could have borne the seeing of yourself, I could not choose to be seen by my friends in my wretchedness, nor by any of my acquaintance.'

While MacGregor wrote in this disconsolate manner, Death, the sad but sure remedy for mortal evils, and decider of all doubts and uncertainties, was hovering near him. A memorandum on the back of the letter says the writer died about a week after, in October, 1754.

It now remains to mention the fate of Robin Oig, for the other sons of Rob Roy seem to have been no way distinguished. Robin was apprehended by a party of military from the fort of Inversnaid, at the foot of Gartmore, and was conveyed to Edinburgh 26th May, 1753. After a delay, which may have been protracted by the negotiations of James for delivering up Allan Breck Stewart, upon promise of his brother's life, Robin Oig, on the 24th December, 1753, was brought to the bar of the High Court of Justiciary, and indicted by the name of Robert Mac-Gregor, *alias* Campbell, *alias* Drummond, *alias* Robert Oig; and the evidence led against him resembled exactly that which was brought by the Crown on the former trial. Robert's case was in some degree more favourable than his brother's; for, though the principal in the forcible marriage, he had yet to plead that he had shown symptoms of relenting while they were carrying Jean Key off, which were silenced by the remonstrances and threats of his harder natured brother James. Four years had also elapsed since the poor woman died, which is always a strong circumstance in favour of the accused; for there is a sort of perspective in guilt, and crimes of an old date seem less odious than those of recent occurrence. But notwithstanding these considerations, the jury, in Robert's case, did not express any solicitude to save his life, as they had done that of James. They found him guilty of being art and part in the forcible abduction of Jean Key from her own dwelling.[26]

Robin Oig was condemned to death, and executed on 14th February, 1754. At the place of execution he behaved with great decency; and professing himself a Catholic, imputed all his misfortunes to his swerving from the true church two or three years before. He confessed the violent methods he had used to gain Mrs Key, or Wright, and hoped his fate would stop further proceedings against his brother James.[27]

The newspapers observe that his body, after hanging the usual time, was delivered to his friends to be carried to the Highlands. To this the recollection of a venerable friend, recently taken from us in the fulness of years, then a schoolboy at Linlithgow, enables the author to add, that a much larger body of MacGregors than had cared to advance to Edinburgh, received the corpse at that place with the coronach, and other wild emblems of Highland mourning, and so escorted it to Balquhidder. Thus, we may conclude this long account of Rob Roy and his family, with the classic phrase,

'ITE. CONCLAMATUM EST.'*

I have only to add, that I have selected the above from many anecdotes of Rob Roy, which were, and may still be, current among the mountains where he flourished; but I am far from warranting their exact authenticity. Clannish partialities were very apt to guide the tongue and pen as well as the pistol and claymore, and the features of an anecdote are wonderfully softened or exaggerated, as the story is told by a MacGregor or a Campbell.

APPENDIX

No. I

ROB ROY

(From the Edinburgh Evening Courant, June 18 to June 21,
A.D. 1712. No. 1058)

'THAT Robert Campbell, commonly known by the name of Rob Roy MacGregor, being lately intrusted by several noblemen and gentlemen with considerable sums for buying cows for them in the Highlands, has treacherously gone off with the money, to the value of L.1000 sterling, which he carries along with him. All Magistrates and Officers of his Majesty's forces are intreated to seize upon the said Rob Roy, and the money which he carries with him, until the persons concerned in the money be heard against him; and that notice be given, when he is apprehended, to the keepers of the Exchange Coffee-house at Edinburgh, and the keeper of the Coffee-house at Glasgow, where the parties concerned will be advertised, and the seizers shall be very reasonably rewarded for their pains.'

———————

It is unfortunate that this Hue and Cry, which is afterwards repeated in the same paper, contains no description of Rob Roy's person, which, of course, we must suppose to have been pretty generally known. As it is directed against Rob Roy personally, it would seem to exclude the idea of the cattle being carried off by his partner, MacDonald, who would certainly have been mentioned in the advertisement, if the creditors concerned had supposed him to be in possession of the money.

No. II

LETTERS

FROM AND TO

THE DUKE OF MONTROSE,

RESPECTING

ROB ROY'S ARREST OF MR GRAHAME OF KILLEARN

THE DUKE OF MONTROSE TO————[28]

'*Glasgow, the 21st November*, 1716

'MY LORD,—I was surprised last night with the account of a very remarkable instance of the insolence of that very notorious rogue Rob Roy, whom your lordship has often heard named. The honour of his Majesty's government being concerned in it, I thought it my duty to acquaint your lordship of the particulars by an express.

'Mr Grahame of Killearn (whom I have had occasion to mention frequently to you, for the good service he did last winter during the rebellion) having the charge of my Highland estate, went to Monteath, which is a part of it, on Monday last, to bring in my rents, it being usual for him to be there for two or three nights together at this time of the year, in a country house, for the conveniency of meeting the tenants, upon that account. The same night, about 9 of the clock, Rob Roy, with a party of those ruffians whom he has still kept about him since the late rebellion, surrounded the house where Mr Grahame was with some of my tenants doing his business, ordered his men to present their guns in att the windows of the room where he was sitting, while he himself at the same time with others entered at the door, with cocked pistols, and made Mr Grahame prisoner, carreing him away to the hills with the money he had got, his books and papers, and my tenants' bonds for their fines, amounting to above a thousand pounds sterling, whereof the one-half had been paid last year, and the other was to have been paid now; and att the same time had the insolence to cause him to write a letter to me (the copy of which is enclosed) offering me terms of a treaty.

'That your Lordship may have the better view of this matter, it will be necessary that I should inform you, that this fellow has now, of a long time, put himself at the head of the Clan M'Gregor, a race of people who, in all ages, have distinguished themselves beyond others, by robberies, depredations, and murders, and have been the constant harbourers and entertainers of vagabonds and loose people. From the time of the Revolution he has taken every opportunity to appear against the government, acting rather as a robber than doing any real service to those whom he pretended to appear for, and has really done more mischief to the countrie than all the other Highlanders have done.

'Some three or four years before the last rebellion broke out, being overburdened with debts, he quitted his ordinary residence, and removed some twelve or sixteen miles farther into the Highlands, putting himself under the protection of the Earl of Bredalbin. When my Lord Cadogan was in the Highlands, he ordered his house att this place to be burnt, which your Lordship sees he now places to my account.

'This obliges him to return to the same countrie he went from, being a most rugged inaccessible place, where he took up his residence anew amongst his own friends and relations; but well judging that it was possible to surprise him, he, with about forty-five of his followers, went to Inverary, and made a sham surrender of their arms to Coll. Campbell of Finab, Commander of one of the Independant Companies, and returned home with his men, each of them having the Coll.'s protection. This happened in the beginning of summer last; yet not long after he appeared with his men twice in arms, in opposition to the King's troops; and one of those times attackt them, rescued a prisoner from them, and all this while sent abroad his party through the countrie, plundering the countrie people, and amongst the rest some of my tenants.

'Being informed of these disorders after I came to Scotland, I applied to Lieut. Genll. Carpenter, who ordered three parties from Glasgow, Stirling, and Finlarig, to march in the night by different routes, in order to surprise him and his men in their houses, which would have had its effect certainly, if the great rains that happened to fall that verie night had not retarded the march of the troops, so as some of the parties came too late to the stations that they were ordered for. All that could be done upon the occasion was to burn a countrie house, where Rob Roy then resided, after some of his clan had, from the rocks, fired upon the king's troops, by which a grenadier was killed.

'Mr Grahame, of Killearn, being my deputy-sheriff in that countrie, went along with the party that marched from Stirling; and, doubtless, will now meet with the worse treatment from that barbarous people on that account. Besides, that he is my relation, and that they know how active he has been in the service of the government—all which, your Lordship may believe, puts me under very great concern for the gentleman, while, at the same time, I can forsee no manner of way how to relieve him, other than to leave him to chance and his own management.

'I had my thoughts before of proposing to government the building of some barracks, as the only expedient for suppressing these rebels, and securing the peace of the countrie; and in that view I spoke to Genll. Carpenter, who has now a scheme of it in his hands; and I am persuaded that will be the true method for restraining them effectually; but, in the meantime, it will be necessary to lodge some of the troops in those places, upon which I intend to write to the Generall.

'I am sensible I have troubled your Lordship with a very long letter, which I should be ashamed of, were I myself singly concerned; but where the honour of the King's Government is touched, I need make no apologie, and I shall only beg leave to add, that I am, with great respect, and truth,

> 'My Lord,
> 'yr. Lords^s. most humble and
> 'obedient servant,
> 'MONTROSE.'

COPY OF GRAHAME OF KILLEARN'S LETTER
ENCLOSED IN THE PRECEDING

'*Chappellarroch, Nov.* 19*th*, 1716

'MAY IT PLEASE YOUR GRACE,—I am obliged to give your Grace the trouble of this, by Robert Roy's commands, being so unfortunate at present as to be his prisoner. I refer the way and manner I was apprehended, to the bearer, and shall only, in short, acquaint your Grace with the demands, which are, that your Grace shall discharge him of all soumes he owes your Grace, and give him the soume of 3400 merks for his loss and damages sustained by him, both at Craigrostown and at his house, Auchinchisallen; and that your Grace shall give your word not to trouble or prosecute him afterwards; till which time he carries me, all the money I received this day, my books and bonds for entress, not yet paid, along with him, with assurances of hard usage, if any party are sent after him. The soume I received this day, conform to the nearest computation I can make before several of the gentlemen, is 3227L. 2sh. 8d. Scots, of which I gave them notes. I shall wait your Grace's return, and ever am,

> 'Your Grace's most obedient, faithful,
> 'humble servant,
> *Sic subscribitur*, 'JOHN GRAHAME.'

THE DUKE OF MONTROSE TO———
28th Nov. 1716.—KILLEARN'S RELEASE

> '*Glasgow*, 28*th Nov.* 1716

'SIR,—Having acquainted you by my last, of the 21st instant, of what had happened to my friend Mr Grahame of Killearn, I'm very glad now to tell you, that last night I was very agreeably surprised with Mr Grahame's coming here himself, and giving me the first account I had had of him from the time of his being carried away. It seems Rob Roy, when he came to consider a little better of it, found that he could not mend his matters by retaining Killearn his prisoner, which could only expose him still the more to the justice of the government; and therefore thought fit to dismiss him on Sunday evening last, having kept him from the Monday night before, under a very uneasy kind of restraint, being obliged to change continually from place to place. He gave him back the books, papers, and bonds, but kept the money.

> 'I am, with great truth, Sir,
> 'your most humble servant,
> 'MONTROSE'

No. III

CHALLENGE BY ROB ROY

ROB ROY *to ain hie and mighty Prince*, JAMES DUKE OF MONTROSE

'IN charity to your Grace's couradge and conduct, please know, the only way to retrive both is to treat Rob Roy like himself, in appointing your place and choice of arms, that at once you may extirpate your inveterate enemy, or put a period to your punny (puny?) life in falling gloriously by his hands. That impertinent criticks or flatterers may not brand me for challenging a man that's repute of a poor dastardly soul, let such know that I admit of the two great supporters of his character and the captain of his bands to joyne with him in the combate. Then sure your Grace wont have the impudence to clamour att court for multitudes to hunt me like a fox, under pretence that I am not to be found above ground. This saves your Grace and the troops any further trouble of searching; that is, if your ambition of glory press you to embrace this unequald venture offerd of Rob's head. But if your Grace's piety, prudence, and cowardice, forbids hazarding this gentlemanly expedient, then let your design of peace restore what you have robed from me by the tyranny of your present cituation, otherwise your overthrow as a man is determined; and advertise your friends never more to look for the frequent civility payed them, of sending them home without their arms only. Even their former cravings wont purchase that favour; so your Grace by this has peace in your offer, if the sound of war be frightful, and chuse you whilk, your good friend or mortal enemy.'

[This singular rhodomontade is enclosed in a letter to a friend of Rob Roy, probably a retainer of the Duke of Argyle in Isla, which is in these words:—]

'Sir,—Receive the enclosed paper, q^n you are taking your botle; it will divert yourself and comrades. I got no news since I saw you, only q^t we had before about the Spanyards is like to continue. If I get any account about them I'll be sure to let you hear of it, and till then I will not write any more till I have more account. I am, Sir, your affect C^n [cousin,] and most humble servant,

'*Argyle*, 1719.   'RO: ROY.'

Addressed, To Mr Patrick Anderson,⎱
            at Ilay—These.   ⎰

The seal, a stag—no bad emblem ⎱
            of a wild catteran.   ⎰

It appears from the envelope that Rob Roy still continued to act as intelligencer to the Duke of Argyle and his agents. The war he alludes to is probably some vague report of invasion from Spain.* Such rumours were likely enough to be afloat, in consequence of the disembarkation of the troops who were taken at Glensheal in the preceding year, 1718.

No. IV

'SIR,—The great humanity with which you have constantly acted in the discharge of the trust reposed in you, and your ever having made use of the great powers with which you were vested, as the means of doing good and charitable offices to such as ye found proper objects of compassion, will, I hope, excuse my importunity in endeavouring to approve myself not absolutely unworthy of that mercy and favour which your Excellency has so generously procured from his Majesty for others in my unfortunate circumstances. I am very sensible nothing can be alledged sufficient to excuse so great a crime as I have been guilty of, that of Rebellion. But I humbly beg leave to lay before your Excellency some particulars in the circumstance of my guilt, which, I hope, will extenuate it in some measure. It was my misfortune, at the time the Rebellion broke out, to be liable to legal diligence and caption, at the Duke of Montrose's instance, for debt alledged due to him. To avoid being flung into prison, as I must certainly have been, had I followed my real inclinations in joining the King's troops at Stirling, I was forced to take party with the adherents of the Pretender; for the country being all in arms, it was neither safe nor indeed possible for me to stand neuter. I should not, however, plead my being forced into that unnatural Rebellion against his Majesty, King George, if I could not at the same time assure your Excellency, that I not only avoided acting offensively against his Majesty's forces upon all occasions, but on the contrary, sent his Grace the Duke of Argyle all the intelligence I could from time to time, of the strength and situation of the Rebels; which I hope his Grace will do me the justice to acknowledge. As to the debt to the Duke of Montrose, I have discharged it to the utmost farthing. I beg your Excellency would be persuaded that, had it been in my power, as it was in my inclination, I should always have acted for the service of his Majesty King George, and that one reason of my begging the favour of your intercession with his Majesty for the pardon of my life,

is the earnest desire I have to employ it in his service, whose goodness, justice, and humanity, are so conspicuous to all mankind.

> 'I am, with all duty and respect,
> 'Your Excellency's most, &c.
> 'ROBERT CAMPBELL.'

No. V

There are many productions of the Scottish Ballad poets upon the
lion-like mode of wooing practised by the ancient Highlanders when
they had a fancy for the person (or property) of a Lowland damsel.
One example is found in Mr Robert Jamieson's Popular Scottish
Songs:*—

> Bonny Babby Livingstone
>   Gaed out to see the kye,
> And she has met with Glenlyon,
>   Who has stolen her away.
>
> He took frae her her sattin coat,
>   But an her silken gown,
> Syne roud her in his tartan plaid,
>   And happd her round and roun'.

In another ballad we are told how

> Four-and-twenty Hieland men
>   Came doun by Fiddoch side,
> And they have sworn a deadly aith,
>   Jean Muir suld be a bride:
>
> And they have sworn a deadly aith,
>   Ilke man upon his durke,
> That she should wed with Duncan Ger,
>   Or they'd make bloody worke.

This last we have from tradition, but there are many others in the
collections of Scottish Ballads to the same purpose.

The achievement of Robert Oig, or young Rob Roy, as the Lowlanders called him, was celebrated in a ballad, of which there are
twenty different and various editions. The tune is lively and wild, and
we select the following words from memory:

Rob Roy is frae the Hielands come,
　　Down to the Lowland border;
And he has stolen that lady away,
　　To haud his house in order.

He set her on a milk-white steed,
　　Of none he stood in awe;
Untill they reached the Hieland hills,
　　Aboon the Balmaha'![30]

Saying, Be content, be content,
　　Be content with me, lady;
Where will ye find in Lennox land,
　　Sae braw a man as me, lady?

Rob Roy, he was my father called,
　　MacGregor was his name, lady;
A' the country, far and near,
　　Have heard MacGregor's fame, lady.

He was a hedge about his friends,
　　A heckle to his foes, lady;
If any man did him gainsay,
　　He felt his deadly blows, lady.

I am as bold, I am as bold,
　　I am as bold and more, lady;
Any man that doubts my word,
　　May try my gude claymore, lady.

Then be content, be content,
　　Be content with me, lady;
For now you are my wedded wife,
　　Until the day ye die, lady.

No. VI

GHLUNE DHU

THE following notices concerning this Chief fell under the Author's eye while the sheets were in the act of going through the press. They occur in manuscript memoirs, written by a person intimately acquainted with the incidents of 1745.

This Chief had the important task intrusted to him of defending the castle of Doune, in which the Chevalier placed a garrison to protect his communication with the Highlands, and to repel any sallies which might be made from Stirling Castle. Ghlune Dhu distinguished himself by his good conduct in this charge.

Ghlune Dhu is thus described:—'Glengyle is, in person, a tall handsome man, and has more of the mien of the ancient heroes than our modern fine gentlemen are possessed of. He is honest and disinterested to a proverb—extremely modest—brave and intrepid—and born one of the best partisans in Europe. In short, the whole people of that country declared that never did men live under so mild a government as Glengyle's, not a man having so much as lost a chicken while he continued there.'

It would appear from this curious passage that Glengyle—not Stewart of Balloch, as averred in a note on Waverley*—commanded the garrison of Doune. Balloch might, no doubt, succeed MacGregor in the situation.

ROB ROY

CHAPTER I

How have I sinn'd, that this affliction
Should light so heavy on me? I have no more sons,
And this no more mine own.—My grand curse
Hang o'er his head that thus transform'd thee!—Travel?
I'll send my horse to travel next.

MONSIEUR THOMAS*

YOU have requested me, my dear friend, to bestow some of that leisure, with which Providence has blessed the decline of my life, in registering the hazards and difficulties which attended its commencement. The recollection of those adventures, as you are pleased to term them, has indeed left upon my mind a chequered and varied feeling of pleasure and of pain, mingled, I trust, with no slight gratitude and veneration to the Disposer of human events, who guided my early course through much risk and labour, that the ease with which he has blessed my prolonged life, might seem softer from remembrance and contrast. Neither is it possible for me to doubt, what you have often affirmed, that the incidents which befell me among a people singularly primitive in their government and manners, have something interesting and attractive for those who love to hear an old man's stories of a past age.

Still, however, you must remember, that the tale told by one friend, and listened to by another, loses half its charms when committed to paper; and that the narratives to which you have attended with interest, as heard from the voice of him to whom they occurred, will appear less deserving of attention when perused in the seclusion of your study. But your greener age and robust constitution promise longer life than will, in all human probability, be the lot of your friend. Throw, then, these sheets into some secret drawer of your escritoir till we are separated from each other's society by an event which may happen at any moment, and which must happen within the course of a few—a very few years. When we are parted in this world, to meet, I hope, in a better, you will, I am well aware, cherish more than it

deserves the memory of your departed friend, and will find in those
details which I am now to commit to paper, matter for melancholy, but
not unpleasing reflection. Others bequeath to the confidents of their
bosom portraits of their external features—I put into your hands a
faithful transcript of my thoughts and feelings, of my virtues and of my
failings, with the assured hope, that the follies and headstrong
impetuosity of my youth will meet the same kind construction and forgiveness which have so often attended the faults of my matured age.

One advantage, among the many, of addressing my Memoirs (if I
may give these sheets a name so imposing) to a dear and intimate
friend, is, that I may spare some of the details, in this case unnecessary,
with which I must needs have detained a stranger from what I have to
say of greater interest. Why should I bestow all my tediousness upon
you,* because I have you in my power, and have ink, paper, and time
before me? At the same time, I dare not promise that I may not abuse
the opportunity so temptingly offered me, to treat of myself and my
own concerns, even though I speak of circumstances as well known to
you as to myself. The seductive love of narrative, when we ourselves
are the heroes of the events which we tell, often disregards the attention due to the time and patience of the audience, and the best and wisest have yielded to its fascination. I need only remind you of the
singular instance evinced by the form of that rare and original edition
of Sully's Memoirs,* which you (with the fond vanity of a book-
collector) insist upon preferring to that which is reduced to the useful
and ordinary form of Memoirs, but which I think curious, solely as
illustrating how far so great a man as the author was accessible to the
foible of self-importance. If I recollect rightly, that venerable peer and
great statesman had appointed no fewer than four gentlemen of his
household to draw up the events of his life, under the title of Memorials
of the Sage and Royal Affairs of State, Domestic, Political, and Military,
transacted by Henry IV., and so forth. These grave recorders, having
made their compilation, reduced the Memoirs containing all the
remarkable events of their master's life into a narrative, addressed to
himself in *propria persona*. And thus, instead of telling his own story, in
the third person, like Julius Cæsar, or in the first person, like most who,
in the hall, or the study, undertake to be the heroes of their own tale,
Sully enjoyed the refined, though whimsical pleasure, of having the
events of his life told over to him by his secretaries, being himself the
auditor, as he was also the hero, and probably the author, of the whole

book. It must have been a great sight to have seen the ex-minister, as bolt upright as a starched ruff and laced cassock could make him, seated in state beneath his canopy, and listening to the recitation of his compilers, while, standing bare in his presence, they informed him gravely, 'Thus said the duke—so did the duke infer—such were your grace's sentiments upon this important point—such were your secret counsels to the king on that other emergency,'—circumstances, all of which must have been much better known to their hearer than to themselves, and most of which could only be derived from his own special communication.

My situation is not quite so ludicrous as that of the great Sully, and yet there would be something whimsical in Frank Osbaldistone giving Will Tresham a formal account of his birth, education, and connexions in the world. I will, therefore, wrestle with the tempting spirit of P. P., Clerk of our Parish,* as I best may, and endeavour to tell you nothing that is familiar to you already. Some things, however, I must recall to your memory, because, though formerly well known to you, they may have been forgotten through lapse of time, and they afford the ground-work of my destiny.

You must remember my father well; for as your own was a member of the mercantile house, you knew him from infancy. Yet you hardly saw him in his best days, before age and infirmity had quenched his ardent spirit of enterprise and speculation. He would have been a poorer man indeed, but perhaps as happy, had he devoted to the extension of science those active energies, and acute powers of observation, for which commercial pursuits found occupation. Yet, in the fluctuations of mercantile speculation, there is something captivating to the adventurer, even independent of the hope of gain. He who embarks on that fickle sea, requires to possess the skill of the pilot and the fortitude of the navigator, and after all may be wrecked and lost, unless the gales of fortune breathe in his favour. This mixture of necessary attention and inevitable hazard,—the frequent and awful uncertainty whether prudence shall overcome fortune, or fortune baffle the schemes of prudence, affords full occupation for the powers, as well as for the feelings of the mind, and trade has all the fascination of gambling without its moral guilt.

Early in the 18th century, when I (Heaven help me) was a youth of some twenty years old, I was summoned suddenly from Bourdeaux to attend my father on business of importance. I shall never forget our first interview. You recollect the brief, abrupt, and somewhat stern mode in which he was wont to communicate his pleasure to those around him. Methinks I see him even now in my mind's eye;*—the firm and upright figure,—the step, quick and determined,—the eye, which shot so keen and so penetrating a glance,—the features, on which care had already planted wrinkles,—and hear his language, in which he never wasted word in vain, expressed in a voice which had sometimes an occasional harshness, far from the intention of the speaker.

When I dismounted from my post-horse, I hastened to my father's apartment. He was traversing it with an air of composed and steady deliberation, which even my arrival, although an only son unseen for four years, was unable to discompose. I threw myself into his arms. He was a kind, though not a fond father, and the tear twinkled in his dark eye, but it was only for a moment.

'Dubourg writes to me that he is satisfied with you, Frank.'

'I am happy, sir'——

'But I have less reason to be so,' he added, sitting down at his bureau.

'I am sorry, sir'——

'Sorry and happy, Frank, are words that, on most occasions, signify little or nothing—Here is your last letter.'

He took it out from a number of others tied up in a parcel of red tape, and curiously labelled and filed. There lay my poor epistle, written on the subject the nearest to my heart at the time, and couched in words which I had thought would work compassion, if not conviction,—there, I say, it lay, squeezed up among the letters on miscellaneous business in which my father's daily affairs had engaged him. I cannot help smiling internally when I recollect the mixture of hurt vanity, and wounded feeling, with which I regarded my remonstrance, to the penning of which there had gone, I promise you, some trouble, as I beheld it extracted from amongst letters of advice, of credit, and all the commonplace lumber, as I then thought them, of a merchant's correspondence. Surely, thought I, a letter of such importance (I dared not say, even to myself, so well written) deserved a separate place, as well as more anxious consideration, than those on the ordinary business of the counting-house.

But my father did not observe my dissatisfaction, and would not have minded it if he had. He proceeded, with the letter in his hand. 'This, Frank, is yours of the 21st ultimo, in which you advise me, (reading from my letter,) that in the most important business of forming a plan, and adopting a profession for life, you trust my paternal goodness will hold you entitled to at least a negative voice; that you have insuperable—ay, insuperable is the word—I wish, by the way, you would write a more distinct current hand—draw a score through the tops of your t's, and open the loops of your l's—insuperable objections to the arrangements which I have proposed to you. There is much more to the same effect, occupying four good pages of paper, which a little attention to perspicuity and distinctness of expression might have comprised within as many lines. For, after all, Frank, it amounts but to this, that you will not do as I would have you.'

'That I cannot, sir, in the present instance; not that I will not.'

'Words avail very little with me, young man,' said my father, whose inflexibility always possessed the air of the most perfect calmness and self-possession. '*Can not* may be a more civil phrase than *will not*, but the expressions are synonymous where there is no moral impossibility. But I am not a friend to doing business hastily; we will talk this matter over after dinner.—Owen!'

Owen appeared, not with the silver locks which you were used to venerate, for he was then little more than fifty; but he had the same, or an exactly similar uniform suit of light brown clothes,—the same pearl-grey silk stockings,—the same stock, with its silver buckle,—the same plaited cambric ruffles, drawn down over his knuckles in the parlour, but in the counting-house carefully folded back under the sleeves, that they might remain unstained by the ink which he daily consumed;—in a word, the same grave, formal, yet benevolent cast of features, which continued to his death to distinguish the head clerk of the great house of Osbaldistone and Tresham.

'Owen,' said my father, as the kind old man shook me affectionately by the hand, 'you must dine with us to-day, and hear the news Frank has brought us from our friends in Bourdeaux.'

Owen made one of his stiff bows of respectful gratitude; for, in those days, when the distance between superiors and inferiors was enforced in a manner to which the present times are strangers, such an invitation was a favour of some little consequence.

I shall long remember that dinner-party. Deeply affected by feelings of anxiety, not unmingled with displeasure, I was unable to take that active share in the conversation which my father seemed to expect from me; and I too frequently gave unsatisfactory answers to the

questions with which he assailed me. Owen, hovering betwixt his
respect for his patron, and his love for the youth he had dandled on his
knee in childhood, like the timorous, yet anxious ally of an invaded
nation, endeavoured at every blunder I made to explain my no-
meaning, and to cover my retreat; manœuvres which added to my
father's pettish displeasure, and brought a share of it upon my kind
advocate, instead of protecting me. I had not, while residing in the
house of Dubourg, absolutely conducted myself like

> A clerk condemn'd his father's soul to cross,
> Who penn'd a stanza when he should engross;—*

but, to say truth, I had frequented the counting-house no more than I
had thought absolutely necessary to secure the good report of the
Frenchman, long a correspondent of our firm, to whom my father had
trusted for initiating me into the mysteries of commerce. In fact, my
principal attention had been dedicated to literature and manly exercises. My father did not altogether discourage such acquirements,
whether mental or personal. He had too much good sense not to perceive, that they sate gracefully upon every man, and he was sensible
that they relieved and dignified the character to which he wished me to
aspire. But his chief ambition was, that I should succeed not merely to
his fortune, but to the views and plans by which he imagined he could
extend and perpetuate the wealthy inheritance which he designed for
me.

Love of his profession was the motive which he chose should be
most ostensible, when he urged me to tread the same path; but he had
others with which I only became acquainted at a later period. Impetuous in his schemes, as well as skilful and daring, each new adventure,
when successful, became at once the incentive, and furnished the
means, for farther speculation. It seemed to be necessary to him, as to
an ambitious conqueror, to push on from achievement to achievement,
without stopping to secure, far less to enjoy, the acquisitions which he
made. Accustomed to see his whole fortune trembling in the scales of
chance, and dexterous at adopting expedients for casting the balance in
his favour, his health and spirits and activity seemed ever to increase
with the animating hazards on which he staked his wealth; and he
resembled a sailor, accustomed to brave the billows and the foe, whose
confidence rises on the eve of tempest or of battle. He was not, however, insensible to the changes which increasing age or supervening

malady might make in his own constitution; and was anxious in good time to secure in me an assistant, who might take the helm when his hand grew weary, and keep the vessel's way according to his counsel and instruction. Paternal affection, as well as the furtherance of his own plans, determined him to the same conclusion. Your father, though his fortune was vested in the house, was only a sleeping partner, as the commercial phrase goes; and Owen, whose probity and skill in the details of arithmetic rendered his services invaluable as a head clerk, was not possessed either of information or talents sufficient to conduct the mysteries of the principal management. If my father were suddenly summoned from life, what would become of the world of schemes which he had formed, unless his son were moulded into a commercial Hercules, fit to sustain the weight when relinquished by the falling Atlas?* and what would become of that son himself, if, a stranger to business of this description, he found himself at once involved in the labyrinth of mercantile concerns, without the clew of knowledge necessary for his extraction? For all these reasons, avowed and secret, my father was determined I should embrace his profession; and when he was determined, the resolution of no man was more immovable. I, however, was also a party to be consulted, and, with something of his own pertinacity, I had formed a determination precisely contrary.

It may, I hope, be some palliative for the resistance which, on this occasion, I offered to my father's wishes, that I did not fully understand upon what they were founded, or how deeply his happiness was involved in them. Imagining myself certain of a large succession in future, and ample maintenance in the meanwhile, it never occurred to me that it might be necessary, in order to secure these blessings, to submit to labour and limitations unpleasant to my taste and temper. I only saw in my father's proposal for my engaging in business, a desire that I should add to those heaps of wealth which he had himself acquired; and imagining myself the best judge of the path to my own happiness, I did not conceive that I should increase that happiness by augmenting a fortune which I believed was already sufficient, and more than sufficient, for every use, comfort, and elegant enjoyment.

Accordingly, I am compelled to repeat, that my time at Bourdeaux had not been spent as my father had proposed to himself. What he considered as the chief end of my residence in that city, I had postponed for every other, and would (had I dared) have neglected it altogether. Dubourg, a favoured and benefited correspondent of our mercantile house, was too much of a shrewd politician to make such reports to the head of the firm concerning his only child, as would excite the displeasure of both; and he might also, as you will presently hear, have views of selfish advantage in suffering me to neglect the purposes for which I was placed under his charge. My conduct was regulated by the bounds of decency and good order, and thus far he had no evil report to make, supposing him so disposed; but, perhaps, the crafty Frenchman would have been equally complaisant, had I been in the habit of indulging worse feelings than those of indolence and aversion to mercantile business. As it was, while I gave a decent portion of my time to the commercial studies he recommended, he was by no means envious of the hours which I dedicated to other and more classical attainments, nor did he ever find fault with me for dwelling upon Corneille and Boileau,* in preference to Postlethwayte, (supposing his folio to have then existed, and Monsieur Dubourg able to have pronounced his name,) or Savary,* or any other writer on commercial economy. He had picked up somewhere a convenient expression, with which he rounded off every letter to his correspondent,—'I was all,' he said, 'that a father could wish.'

My father never quarrelled with a phrase, however frequently repeated, provided it seemed to him distinct and expressive; and Addison himself* could not have found expressions so satisfactory to him as, 'Yours received, and duly honoured the bills enclosed, as per margin.'

Knowing, therefore, very well what he desired me to be, Mr Osbaldistone made no doubt, from the frequent repetition of Dubourg's favourite phrase, that I was the very thing he wished to see me; when, in an evil hour, he received my letter, containing my eloquent and detailed apology for declining a place in the firm, and a desk and stool in the corner of the dark counting-house in Crane Alley, surmounting in height those of Owen, and the other clerks, and only inferior to the tripod of my father himself. All was wrong from that moment. Dubourg's reports became as suspicious as if his bills had been noted for dishonour. I was summoned home in all haste, and received in the manner I have already communicated to you.

CHAPTER II

I begin shrewdly to suspect the young man of a terrible taint—
Poetry; with which idle disease if he be infected, there's no hope
of him in a state course. *Actum est* of him for a commonwealth's
man, if he go to't in rhyme once.

BEN JONSON'S *Bartholomew Fair**

MY father had, generally speaking, his temper under complete self-
command, and his anger rarely indicated itself by words, except in a
sort of dry testy manner, to those who had displeased him. He never
used threats, or expressions of loud resentment. All was arranged with
him on system, and it was his practice to do 'the needful' on every
occasion, without wasting words about it. It was, therefore, with a bitter smile that he listened to my imperfect answers concerning the state
of commerce in France, and unmercifully permitted me to involve
myself deeper and deeper in the mysteries of agio, tariffs, tare and
tret;* nor can I charge my memory with his having looked positively
angry, until he found me unable to explain the exact effect which the
depreciation of the louis d'or* had produced on the negotiation of
bills of exchange. 'The most remarkable national occurrence in my
time,' said my father, (who nevertheless had seen the Revolution,)
'and he knows no more of it than a post on the quay!'

'Mr Francis,' suggested Owen, in his timid and conciliatory manner, 'cannot have forgotten, that by an *arret* of the King of France,
dated 1st May, 1700, it was provided that the *porteur*,* within ten days
after due, must make demand'——

'Mr Francis,' said my father, interrupting him, 'will, I dare say, recollect for the moment anything you are so kind as hint to him.—But,
body o' me! how Dubourg could permit him!—Hark ye, Owen, what
sort of a youth is Clement Dubourg, his nephew there, in the office,
the black-haired lad?'

'One of the cleverest clerks, sir, in the house; a prodigious young
man for his time,' answered Owen; for the gaiety and civility of the
young Frenchman had won his heart.

'Ay, ay, I suppose *he* knows something of the nature of exchange.
Dubourg was determined I should have one youngster at least about
my hand who understood business; but I see his drift, and he shall find

that I do so when he looks at the balance-sheet. Owen, let Clement's salary be paid up to next quarter-day, and let him ship himself back to Bourdeaux in his father's ship, which is clearing out yonder.'

'Dismiss Clement Dubourg, sir?' said Owen, with a faltering voice.

'Yes, sir, dismiss him instantly; it is enough to have a stupid Englishman in the counting-house to make blunders, without keeping a sharp Frenchman there to profit by them.'

I had lived long enough in the territories of the *Grand Monarque** to contract a hearty aversion to arbitrary exertion of authority, even if it had not been instilled into me with my earliest breeding; and I could not refrain from interposing, to prevent an innocent and meritorious young man from paying the penalty of having acquired that proficiency which my father had desired for me.

'I beg pardon, sir,' when Mr Osbaldistone had done speaking, 'but I think it but just, that if I have been negligent of my studies, I should pay the forfeit myself. I have no reason to charge Monsieur Dubourg with having neglected to give me opportunities of improvement, however little I may have profited by them; and, with respect to Monsieur Clement Dubourg'——

'With respect to him, and to you, I shall take the measures which I see needful,' replied my father; 'but it is fair in you, Frank, to take your own blame on your own shoulders—very fair, that cannot be denied.—I cannot acquit old Dubourg,' he said, looking to Owen, 'for having merely afforded Frank the means of useful knowledge, without either seeing that he took advantage of them, or reporting to me if he did not. You see, Owen, he has natural notions of equity becoming a British merchant.'

'Mr Francis,' said the head clerk, with his usual formal inclination of the head, and a slight elevation of his right hand, which he had acquired by a habit of sticking his pen behind his ear before he spoke— 'Mr Francis seems to understand the fundamental principle of all moral accounting, the great ethic rule of three. Let A do to B, as he would have B do to him; the product will give the rule of conduct required.'

My father smiled at this reduction of the golden rule* to arithmetical form, but instantly proceeded.

'All this signifies nothing, Frank; you have been throwing away your time like a boy, and in future you must learn to live like a man. I shall put you under Owen's care for a few months, to recover the lost ground.'

I was about to reply, but Owen looked at me with such a supplicatory and warning gesture, that I was involuntarily silent.

'We will then,' continued my father, 'resume the subject of mine of the 1st ultimo, to which you sent me an answer which was unadvised and unsatisfactory. So now, fill your glass, and push the bottle to Owen.'

Want of courage—of audacity, if you will—was never my failing. I answered firmly, 'I was sorry that my letter was unsatisfactory, unadvised it was not; for I had given the proposal his goodness had made me my instant and anxious attention, and it was with no small pain that I found myself obliged to decline it.'

My father bent his keen eye for a moment on me, and instantly withdrew it. As he made no answer, I thought myself obliged to proceed, though with some hesitation, and he only interrupted me by monosyllables.

'It is impossible, sir, for me to have higher respect for any character than I have for the commercial, even were it not yours.'

'Indeed!'

'It connects nation with nation, relieves the wants, and contributes to the wealth of all; and is to the general commonwealth of the civilized world what the daily intercourse of ordinary life is to private society, or rather, what air and food are to our bodies.'

'Well, sir?'

'And yet, sir, I find myself compelled to persist in declining to adopt a character which I am so ill qualified to support.'

'I will take care that you acquire the qualifications necessary. You are no longer the guest and pupil of Dubourg.'

'But, my dear sir, it is no defect of teaching which I plead, but my own inability to profit by instruction.'

'Nonsense; have you kept your journal in the terms I desired?'

'Yes, sir.'

'Be pleased to bring it here.'

The volume thus required was a sort of commonplace book, kept by my father's recommendation, in which I had been directed to enter notes of the miscellaneous information which I had acquired in the course of my studies. Foreseeing that he would demand inspection of this record, I had been attentive to transcribe such particulars of information as he would most likely be pleased with, but too often the pen had discharged the task without much correspondence with the head.

And it had also happened, that, the book being the receptacle nearest to my hand, I had occasionally jotted down memoranda which had little regard to traffic. I now put it into my father's hand, devoutly hoping he might light on nothing that would increase his displeasure against me. Owen's face, which had looked something blank when the question was put, cleared up at my ready answer, and wore a smile of hope, when I brought from my apartment, and placed before my father, a commercial-looking volume, rather broader than it was long, having brazen clasps and a binding of rough calf. This looked businesslike, and was encouraging to my benevolent well-wisher. But he actually smiled with pleasure as he heard my father run over some part of the contents, muttering his critical remarks as he went on.

'*Brandies—Barils and barricants, also tonneaux.**—*At Nantz 29—Velles to the barique at Cognac and Rochelle 27—At Bourdeaux 32—*Very right, Frank—*Duties on tonnage and custom-house, see Saxby's Tables**—That's not well; you should have transcribed the passage; it fixes the thing in the memory—*Reports outward and inward—Corn debentures—Over-sea Cockets—Linens—Isingham—Gentish—Stockfish—Titling—Cropling—Lub-fish.* You should have noted that they are all, nevertheless, to be entered as titlings.—How many inches long is a titling?'

Owen, seeing me at fault, hazarded a whisper, of which I fortunately caught the import.

'Eighteen inches, sir'——

'And a lub-fish is twenty-four—very right. It is important to remember this, on account of the Portugueze trade.—But what have we here?—*Bourdeaux founded in the year—Castle of the Trompette—Palace of Gallienus**—Well, well, that's very right too.—This is a kind of waste-book, Owen, in which all the transactions of the day, emptions, orders, payments, receipts, acceptances, draughts, commissions, and advices, are entered miscellaneously.'

'That they may be regularly transferred to the day-book and ledger,' answered Owen; 'I am glad Mr Francis is so methodical.'

I perceived myself getting so fast into favour, that I began to fear the consequence would be my father's more obstinate perseverance in his resolution that I must become a merchant; and, as I was determined on the contrary, I began to wish I had not, to use my friend Mr Owen's phrase, been so methodical. But I had no reason for apprehension on that score; for a blotted piece of paper dropped out of the book, and, being taken up by my father, he interrupted a hint from Owen, on the propriety of securing loose memoranda with a little paste, by exclaiming, 'To the memory of Edward the Black Prince—What's all this?—verses!—By Heaven, Frank, you are a greater blockhead than I supposed you!'

My father, you must recollect, as a man of business, looked upon the labour of poets with contempt; and as a religious man, and of the dissenting persuasion, he considered all such pursuits as equally trivial and profane. Before you condemn him, you must recall to remembrance how too many of the poets in the end of the seventeenth century had led their lives and employed their talents.* The sect also to which my father belonged, felt, or perhaps affected, a puritanical aversion to the lighter exertions of literature. So that many causes contributed to augment the unpleasant surprise occasioned by the ill-timed discovery of this unfortunate copy of verses. As for poor Owen, could the bob-wig which he then wore have uncurled itself, and stood on end with horror, I am convinced the morning's labour of the friseur would have been undone, merely by the excess of his astonishment at this enormity. An inroad on the strong-box, or an erasure in the ledger, or a mis-summation in a fitted account, could hardly have surprised him more disagreeably. My father read the lines sometimes with an affectation of not being able to understand the sense,—sometimes in a mouthing tone of mock heroic,—always with an emphasis of the most bitter irony, most irritating to the nerves of an author.

> ' "O for the voice of that wild horn,
> On Fontarabian echoes borne,*
> The dying hero's call,
> That told imperial Charlemagne,
> How Paynim sons of swarthy Spain
> Had wrought his champion's fall."

'*Fontarabian echoes!*' continued my father, interrupting himself; 'the Fontarabian Fair would have been more to the purpose.—*Paynim?*—What's Paynim?—Could you not say Pagan as well, and write English, at least, if you must needs write nonsense?—

> ' "Sad over earth and ocean sounding,
> And England's distant cliffs astounding,
> Such are the notes should say

> How Britain's hope, and France's fear,
> Victor of Cressy and Poitier,
> In Bourdeaux dying lay."

'Poitiers, by the way, is always spelt with an *s*, and I know no reason why orthography should give place to rhyme.——

> ' "Raise my faint head, my squires," he said,
> "And let the casement be display'd,
> That I may see once more
> The splendour of the setting sun
> Gleam on thy mirror'd wave, Garonne,
> And Blaye's empurpled shore."

'*Garonne* and *sun* is a bad rhyme. Why, Frank, you do not even understand the beggarly trade you have chosen.——

> ' "Like me, he sinks to Glory's sleep,
> His fall the dews of evening steep,
> As if in sorrow shed.
> So soft shall fall the trickling tear,
> When England's maids and matrons hear
> Of their Black Edward dead.

> ' "And though my sun of glory set,
> Nor France, nor England shall forget
> The terror of my name;
> And oft shall Britain's heroes rise,
> New planets in these southern skies,
> Through clouds of blood and flame."

'A cloud of flame is something new—Good-morrow, my masters all, and a merry Christmas to you!—Why, the bellman writes better lines.'* He then tossed the paper from him with an air of superlative contempt, and concluded,—'Upon my credit, Frank, you are a greater blockhead than I took you for.'

What could I say, my dear Tresham?—There I stood, swelling with indignant mortification, while my father regarded me with a calm but stern look of scorn and pity; and poor Owen, with uplifted hands and eyes, looked as striking a picture of horror as if he had just read his patron's name in the Gazette.* At length I took courage to speak, endeavouring that my tone of voice should betray my feelings as little as possible.

'I am quite aware, sir, how ill qualified I am to play the conspicuous part in society you have destined for me; and, luckily, I am not ambitious of the wealth I might acquire. Mr Owen would be a much more effective assistant.' I said this in some malice, for I considered Owen as having deserted my cause a little too soon.

'Owen?' said my father—'The boy is mad, actually insane. And, pray, sir, if I may presume to enquire, having coolly turned me over to Mr Owen, (although I may expect more attention from any one than from my son,) what may your own sage projects be?'

'I should wish, sir,' I replied, summoning up my courage, 'to travel for two or three years, should that consist with your pleasure; otherwise, although late, I would willingly spend the same time at Oxford or Cambridge.'

'In the name of common sense! was the like ever heard?—to put yourself to school among pedants and Jacobites,* when you might be pushing your fortune in the world! Why not go to Westminster or Eton at once, man, and take to Lilly's Grammar and Accidence,* and to the birch, too, if you like it?'

'Then, sir, if you think my plan of improvement too late, I would willingly return to the Continent.'

'You have already spent too much time there to little purpose, Mr Francis.'

'Then I would choose the army, sir, in preference to any other active line of life.'

'Choose the d—l,' answered my father, hastily, and then checking himself—'I profess you make me as great a fool as you are yourself.— Is he not enough to drive one mad, Owen?'—Poor Owen shook his head, and looked down. 'Hark ye, Frank,' continued my father, 'I will cut all this matter very short—I was at your age when my father turned me out of doors, and settled my legal inheritance on my younger brother. I left Osbaldistone Hall on the back of a broken-down hunter, with ten guineas in my purse. I have never crossed the threshold again, and I never will. I know not, and I care not, if my fox-hunting brother is alive, or has broken his neck; but he has children, Frank, and one of them shall be my son if you cross me farther in this matter.'

'You will do your pleasure,' I answered, rather, I fear, with more sullen indifference than respect, 'with what is your own.'

'Yes, Frank, what I have *is* my own, if labour in getting, and care in augmenting, can make a right of property; and no drone shall feed on my honeycomb. Think on it well; what I have said is not without reflection, and what I resolve upon I will execute.'

'Honoured sir—dear sir,' exclaimed Owen, tears rushing into his eyes, 'you are not wont to be in such a hurry in transacting business of importance. Let Mr Francis run up the balance before you shut the account; he loves you, I am sure; and when he puts down his filial obedience to the *per contra*, I am sure his objections will disappear.'

'Do you think I will ask him twice,' said my father sternly, 'to be my friend, my assistant, and my confident?—to be a partner of my cares and of my fortune?—Owen, I thought you had known me better.'

He looked at me as if he meant to add something more, but turned instantly away, and left the room abruptly. I was, I own, affected by this view of the case, which had not occurred to me; and my father would probably have had little reason to complain of me, had he commenced the discussion with this argument.

But it was too late. I had much of his own obduracy of resolution, and Heaven had decreed that my sin should be my punishment, though not to the extent which my transgression merited. Owen, when we were left alone, continued to look at me with eyes, which tears from time to time moistened, as if to discover, before attempting the task of intercessor, upon what point my obstinacy was most assailable. At length he began, with broken and disconcerted accents,—' O L—d, Mr Francis!—Good Heavens, sir!—My stars, Mr Osbaldistone!— that I should ever have seen this day—and you so young a gentleman, sir—For the love of Heaven! look at both sides of the account—Think what you are going to lose—a noble fortune, sir—one of the finest houses in the City, even under the old firm of Tresham and Trent, and now Osbaldistone and Tresham—You might roll in gold, Mr Francis—And, my dear young Mr Frank, if there was any particular thing in the business of the house which you disliked, I would' (sinking his voice to a whisper) 'put it in order for you termly, or weekly, or daily, if you will—Do, my dear Mr Francis, think of the honour due to your father, that your days may be long in the land.'

'I am much obliged to you, Mr Owen,' said I,—'very much obliged indeed; but my father is best judge how to bestow his money. He talks of one of my cousins—let him dispose of his wealth as he pleases, I will never sell my liberty for gold.'

'Gold, sir?—I wish you saw the balance-sheet of profits at last term—It was in five figures—five figures to each partner's sum total,

Mr Frank—And all this is to go to a Papist, and a north-country booby, and a disaffected person besides—It will break my heart, Mr Francis, that have been toiling more like a dog than a man, and all for love of the firm.—Think how it will sound, Osbaldistone, Tresham, and Osbaldistone—or, perhaps, who knows,' (again lowering his voice,) 'Osbaldistone, Osbaldistone, and Tresham, for our Mr Osbaldistone can buy them all out.'

'But, Mr Owen, my cousin's name being also Osbaldistone, the name of the company will sound every bit as well in your ears.'

'O, fie upon you, Mr Francis, when you know how well I love you— Your cousin, indeed!—a Papist, no doubt, like his father, and a disaffected person to the Protestant succession—that's another item, doubtless.'

'There are many very good men Catholics, Mr Owen,' rejoined I.

As Owen was about to answer with unusual animation, my father re-entered the apartment.

'You were right,' he said, 'Owen, and I was wrong; we will take more time to think over this matter.—Young man, you will prepare to give me an answer on this important subject this day month.'

I bowed in silence, sufficiently glad of a reprieve, and trusting it might indicate some relaxation in my father's determination.

The time of probation passed slowly, unmarked by any accident whatever. I went and came, and disposed of my time as I pleased, without question or criticism on the part of my father. Indeed, I rarely saw him, save at meal-times, when he studiously avoided a discussion which you may well suppose I was in no hurry to press onward. Our conversation was of the news of the day, or on such general topics as strangers discourse upon to each other; nor could any one have guessed, from its tenor, that there remained undecided betwixt us a dispute of such importance. It haunted me, however, more than once, like the nightmare. Was it possible he would keep his word, and disinherit his only son in favour of a nephew, whose very existence he was not perhaps quite certain of? My grandfather's conduct, in similar circumstances, boded me no good, had I considered the matter rightly. But I had formed an erroneous idea of my father's character, from the importance which I recollected I maintained with him and his whole family before I went to France. I was not aware, that there are men who indulge their children at an early age, because to do so interests and amuses them, and who can yet be sufficiently severe when the same children cross their expectations at a more advanced period. On the contrary, I persuaded myself, that all I had to apprehend, was some temporary alienation of affection;—perhaps a rustication of a few weeks, which I thought would rather please me than otherwise, since it would give me an opportunity of setting about my unfinished version of Orlando Furioso,* a poem which I longed to render into English verse. I suffered this belief to get such absolute possession of my mind, that I had resumed my blotted papers, and was busy in meditation on the oft-recurring rhymes of the Spenserian stanza, when I heard a low and cautious tap at the door of my apartment. 'Come in,' I said, and Mr Owen entered. So regular were the motions and habits of this worthy man, that in all probability this was the first time he had ever been in the second story of his patron's house, however conversant with the first; and I am still at a loss to know in what manner he discovered my apartment.

'Mr Francis,' he said, interrupting my expressions of surprise and pleasure at seeing him, 'I do not know if I am doing well in what I am about to say—it is not right to speak of what passes in the comptinghouse out of doors—one should not tell, as they say, to the post in the warehouse, how many lines there are in the ledger. But young Twineall has been absent from the house for a fortnight and more, until two days since.'

'Very well, my dear sir, and how does that concern us?'

'Stay, Mr Francis—your father gave him a private commission; and I am sure he did not go down to Falmouth about the pilchard affair; and the Exeter business with Blackwell and company has been settled; and the mining people in Cornwall, Trevanion and Treguilliam, have paid all they are likely to pay; and any other matter of business must have been put through my books:—in short, it's my faithful belief that Twineall has been down in the north.'

'Do you really suppose so?' said I, somewhat startled.

'He has spoken about nothing, sir, since he returned, but his new boots, and his Rippon spurs, and a cock-fight at York—it's as true as the multiplication-table. Do, Heaven bless you, my dear child, make up your mind to please your father, and to be a man and a merchant at once.'

I felt at that instant a strong inclination to submit, and to make Owen happy by requesting him to tell my father, that I resigned myself to his disposal. But pride—pride, the source of so much that is good

and so much that is evil in our course of life, prevented me. My acquiescence stuck in my throat;* and while I was coughing to get it up, my
father's voice summoned Owen. He hastily left the room, and the
opportunity was lost.

My father was methodical in every thing. At the very same time of
the day, in the same apartment, and with the same tone and manner
which he had employed an exact month before, he recapitulated the
proposal he had made for taking me into partnership, and assigning
me a department in the counting-house, and requested to have my
final decision. I thought at the time there was something unkind in
this; and I still think that my father's conduct was injudicious. A more
conciliatory treatment would, in all probability, have gained his purpose. As it was, I stood fast, and, as respectfully as I could, declined the
proposal he made to me. Perhaps,—for who can judge of their own
heart?—I felt it unmanly to yield on the first summons, and expected
farther solicitation, as at least a pretext for changing my mind. If so, I
was disappointed; for my father turned coolly to Owen, and only said,
'You see it is as I told you.—Well, Frank,' (addressing me,) 'You are
nearly of age, and as well qualified to judge of what will constitute your
own happiness as you ever are like to be; therefore, I say no more. But
as I am not bound to give in to your plans, any more than you are compelled to submit to mine, may I ask to know if you have formed any
which depend on my assistance?'

I answered, not a little abashed, 'That being bred to no profession,
and having no funds of my own, it was obviously impossible for me to
subsist without some allowance from my father; that my wishes were
very moderate; and that I hoped my aversion for the profession to
which he had designed me, would not occasion his altogether with-
drawing his paternal support and protection.'

'That is to say, you wish to lean on my arm, and yet to walk your own
way? That can hardly be, Frank;—however, I suppose you mean to
obey my directions, so far as they do not cross your own humour?'

I was about to speak—'Silence, if you please,' he continued. 'Supposing this to be the case, you will instantly set out for the North of
England, to pay your uncle a visit, and see the state of his family. I have
chosen from among his sons (he has six, I believe) one who, I understand, is most worthy to fill the place I intended for you in the
counting-house. But some farther arrangements may be necessary,
and for these your presence may be requisite. You shall have farther

instructions at Osbaldistone Hall, where you will please to remain
until you hear from me. Every thing will be ready for your departure
to-morrow morning.'

With these words my father left the apartment.

'What does all this mean, Mr Owen?' said I to my sympathetic
friend, whose countenance wore a cast of the deepest dejection.

'You have ruined yourself, Mr Frank, that's all; when your father
talks in that quiet determined manner, there will be no more change in
him than in a fitted account.'

And so it proved; for the next morning, at five o'clock, I found
myself on the road to York, mounted on a reasonably good horse, and
with fifty guineas in my pocket; travelling, as it would seem, for the
purpose of assisting in the adoption of a successor to myself in my
father's house and favour, and, for aught I knew, eventually in his fortune also.

CHAPTER III

The slack sail shifts from side to side,
The boat, untrimm'd, admits the tide,
Borne down, adrift, at random tost,
The oar breaks short, the rudder's lost.

GAY's *Fables**

I HAVE tagged with rhyme and blank verse the subdivisions of this important narrative, in order to seduce your continued attention by powers of composition of stronger attraction than my own. The preceding lines refer to an unfortunate navigator, who daringly unloosed from its moorings a boat, which he was unable to manage, and thrust it off into the full tide of a navigable river. No school-boy, who, betwixt frolic and defiance, has executed a similar rash attempt, could feel himself, when adrift in a strong current, in a situation more awkward than mine, when I found myself driving, without a compass, on the ocean of human life. There had been such unexpected ease in the manner in which my father slipt a knot, usually esteemed the strongest which binds society together, and suffered me to depart as a sort of outcast from his family, that it strangely lessened the confidence in my own personal accomplishments, which had hitherto sustained me. Prince Prettyman,* now a prince, and now a fisher's son, had not a more awkward sense of his degradation. We are so apt, in our engrossing egotism, to consider all those accessories which are drawn around us by prosperity, as pertaining and belonging to our own persons, that the discovery of our unimportance, when left to our own proper resources, becomes inexpressibly mortifying. As the hum of London died away on my ear, the distant peal of her steeples more than once sounded to my ears the admonitory 'Turn again,' erst heard by her future Lord Mayor;* and when I looked back from Highgate on her dusky magnificence, I felt as if I were leaving behind me comfort, opulence, the charms of society, and all the pleasures of cultivated life.

But the die was cast. It was, indeed, by no means probable that a late and ungracious compliance with my father's wishes would have reinstated me in the situation which I had lost. On the contrary, firm and strong of purpose as he himself was, he might rather have been disgusted than conciliated by my tardy and compulsory acquiescence in his desire that I should engage in commerce. My constitutional obstinacy came also to my aid, and pride whispered how poor a figure I should make, when an airing of four miles from London had blown away resolutions formed during a month's serious deliberation. Hope, too, that never forsakes the young and hardy, lent her lustre to my future prospects. My father could not be serious in the sentence of foris-familiation,* which he had so unhesitatingly pronounced. It must be but a trial of my disposition, which, endured with patience and steadiness on my part, would raise me in his estimation, and lead to an amicable accommodation of the point in dispute between us. I even settled in my own mind how far I would concede to him, and on what articles of our supposed treaty I would make a firm stand; and the result was, according to my computation, that I was to be reinstated in my full rights of filiation, paying the easy penalty of some ostensible compliances to atone for my past rebellion.

In the meanwhile, I was lord of my person, and experienced that feeling of independence which the youthful bosom receives with a thrilling mixture of pleasure and apprehension. My purse, though by no means amply replenished, was in a situation to supply all the wants and wishes of a traveller. I had been accustomed, while at Bourdeaux, to act as my own valet; my horse was fresh, young, and active, and the buoyancy of my spirits soon surmounted the melancholy reflections with which my journey commenced.

I should have been glad to have journeyed upon a line of road better calculated to afford reasonable objects of curiosity, or a more interesting country, to the traveller. But the north road* was then, and perhaps still is, singularly deficient in these respects; nor do I believe you can travel so far through Britain in any other direction without meeting more of what is worthy to engage the attention. My mental ruminations, notwithstanding my assumed confidence, were not always of an unchequered nature. The Muse too,—the very coquette who had led me into this wilderness,—like others of her sex, deserted me in my utmost need; and I should have been reduced to rather an uncomfortable state of dulness, had it not been for the occasional conversation of strangers who chanced to pass the same way. But the characters whom I met with were of a uniform and uninteresting description. Country parsons, jogging homewards after a visitation; farmers, or graziers, returning from a distant market; clerks of traders, travelling to collect what was due to their masters in provincial towns; with now and then an officer going down into the country upon the recruiting service, were, at this period, the persons by whom the turnpikes and tapsters were kept in exercise. Our speech, therefore, was of tithes and creeds, of beeves and grain, of commodities wet and dry, and the solvency of the retail dealers, occasionally varied by the description of a siege, or battle, in Flanders,* which, perhaps, the narrator only gave me at second hand. Robbers, a fertile and alarming theme, filled up every vacancy; and the names of the Golden Farmer, the Flying Highwayman, Jack Needham, and other Beggar's Opera heroes,* were familiar in our mouths as household words.* At such tales, like children closing their circle round the fire when the ghost story draws to its climax, the riders drew near to each other, looked before and behind them, examined the priming of their pistols, and vowed to stand by each other in case of danger; an engagement which, like other offensive and defensive alliances, sometimes glided out of remembrance when there was an appearance of actual peril.

Of all the fellows whom I ever saw haunted by terrors of this nature, one poor man, with whom I travelled a day and a half, afforded me most amusement. He had upon his pillion a very small, but apparently a very weighty portmanteau, about the safety of which he seemed particularly solicitous; never trusting it out of his own immediate care, and uniformly repressing the officious zeal of the waiters and ostlers, who offered their services to carry it into the house. With the same precaution he laboured to conceal, not only the purpose of his journey, and his ultimate place of destination, but even the direction of each day's route. Nothing embarrassed him more than to be asked by any one, whether he was travelling upwards or downwards, or at what stage he intended to bait. His place of rest for the night he scrutinized with the most anxious care, alike avoiding solitude, and what he considered as bad neighbourhood; and at Grantham, I believe, he sate up all night to avoid sleeping in the next room to a thick-set squinting fellow, in a black wig, and a tarnished gold-laced waistcoat. With all these cares on his mind, my fellow traveller, to judge by his thewes and sinews, was a man who might have set danger at defiance with as much impunity as most men. He was strong, and well-built; and, judging from his gold-laced hat and cockade, seemed to have served in the army, or, at least, to belong to the military profession in one capacity or other. His conversation also, though always sufficiently vulgar, was that of a man of sense, when the terrible bugbears which haunted his imagination for a moment ceased to occupy his attention. But every accidental association recalled them. An open heath, a close plantation, were alike subjects of apprehension; and the whistle of a shepherd lad was instantly converted into the signal of a depredator. Even the sight of a gibbet, if it assured him that one robber was safely disposed of by justice, never failed to remind him how many remained still unhanged.

I should have wearied of this fellow's company, had I not been still more tired of my own thoughts. Some of the marvellous stories, however, which he related, had in themselves a cast of interest, and another whimsical point of his peculiarities afforded me the occasional opportunity of amusing myself at his expense. Among his tales, several of the unfortunate travellers who fell among thieves, incurred that calamity from associating themselves on the road with a well-dressed and entertaining stranger, in whose company they trusted to find protection as well as amusement; who cheered their journey with tale and song, protected them against the evils of overcharges and false reckonings, until at length, under pretext of showing a near path over a desolate common, he seduced his unsuspicious victims from the public road into some dismal glen, where, suddenly blowing his whistle, he assembled his comrades from their lurking-place, and displayed himself in his true colours, the captain, namely, of the band of robbers to whom his unwary fellow-travellers had forfeited their purses, and perhaps their lives. Towards the conclusion of such a tale, and when my companion had wrought himself into a fever of apprehension by the progress of his own narrative, I observed that he usually eyed me with a glance of doubt and suspicion, as if the possibility occurred to him, that he might, at that very moment, be in company with a character as dangerous as that which his tale described. And ever and anon, when such suggestions pressed themselves on the mind of this ingenious self-tormentor, he drew off from me to the opposite side of the high road, looked before, behind, and around him, examined his arms, and seemed to prepare himself for flight or defence, as circumstances might require.

The suspicion implied on such occasions seemed to me only momentary, and too ludicrous to be offensive. There was, in fact, no particular reflection on my dress or address, although I was thus mistaken for a robber. A man in those days might have all the external appearance of a gentleman, and yet turn out to be a highwayman. For the division of labour* in every department not having then taken place so fully as since that period, the profession of the polite and accomplished adventurer, who nicked you out of your money at White's, or bowled you out of it at Marybone,* was often united with that of the professed ruffian, who, on Bagshot Heath, or Finchley Common, commanded his brother beau to stand and deliver. There was also a touch of coarseness and hardness about the manners of the times, which has since, in a great degree, been softened and shaded away. It seems to me, on recollection, as if desperate men had less reluctance then, than now, to embrace the most desperate means of retrieving their fortune. The times were indeed past, when Anthony-a-Wood* mourned over the execution of two men, goodly in person, and of undisputed courage and honour, who were hanged without mercy at Oxford, merely because their distress had driven them to raise contributions on the highway. We were still farther removed from the days of 'the mad Prince and Poins.'* And yet, from the number of unenclosed and extensive heaths in the vicinity of the metropolis, and from the less populous state of remote districts, both were frequented by that species of mounted highwaymen, that may possibly become one day unknown, who carried on their trade with something like courtesy; and, like Gibbet in the Beaux Stratagem,* piqued themselves on being the best behaved men on the road, and on conducting themselves with all appropriate civility in the exercise of their vocation. A young man, therefore, in my circumstances, was not entitled to be highly indignant at the mistake which confounded him with this worshipful class of depredators.

Neither was I offended. On the contrary, I found amusement in alternately exciting, and lulling to sleep, the suspicions of my timorous companion, and in purposely so acting as still farther to puzzle a brain which nature and apprehension had combined to render none of the clearest. When my free conversation had lulled him into complete security, it required only a passing enquiry concerning the direction of his journey, or the nature of the business which occasioned it, to put his suspicions once more in arms. For example, a conversation on the comparative strength and activity of our horses took such a turn as follows:—

'O sir,' said my companion, 'for the gallop, I grant you; but allow me to say, your horse (although he is a very handsome gelding—that must

be owned) has too little bone to be a good roadster. The trot, sir,'
(striking his Bucephalus* with his spurs,) 'the trot is the true pace for
a hackney; and, were we near a town, I should like to try that daisy-
cutter of yours upon a piece of level road (barring canter) for a quart of
claret at the next inn.'

'Content, sir,' replied I; 'and here is a stretch of ground very
favourable.'

'Hem, ahem,' answered my friend with hesitation; 'I make it a rule
of travelling never to blow my horse between stages; one never knows
what occasion he may have to put him to his mettle: and besides, sir,
when I said I would match you, I meant with even weight; you ride four
stone lighter than I.'

'Very well; but I am content to carry weight. Pray what may that
portmanteau of yours weigh?'

'My p—p—portmanteau?' replied he hesitating—'O very little—a
feather—just a few shirts and stockings.'

'I should think it heavier, from its appearance. I'll hold you the quart
of claret it makes the odds betwixt our weight.'

'You're mistaken, sir, I assure you—quite mistaken,' replied my
friend, edging off to the side of the road, as was his wont on these
alarming occasions.

'Well, I'm willing to venture the wine; or, I will bet you ten pieces to
five, that I carry your portmanteau on my croupe, and out-trot you into
the bargain.'

This proposal raised my friend's alarm to the uttermost. His nose
changed from the natural copper hue which it had acquired from
many a comfortable cup of claret, or sack, into a palish brassy tint,
and his teeth chattered with apprehension at the unveiled audacity of
my proposal, which seemed to place the bare-faced plunderer before
him in full atrocity. As he faltered for an answer, I relieved him in
some degree by a question concerning a steeple, which now became
visible, and an observation that we were now so near the village as to
run no risk from interruption on the road. At this his countenance
cleared up: but I easily perceived that it was long ere he forgot a
proposal which seemed to him so fraught with suspicion as that
which I had now hazarded. I trouble you with this detail of the man's
disposition, and the manner in which I practised upon it, because,
however trivial in themselves, these particulars were attended by an
important influence on future incidents which will occur in this

narrative. At the time, this person's conduct only inspired me with contempt, and confirmed me in an opinion, which I already entertained, that of all the propensities which teach mankind to torment themselves, that of causeless fear is the most irritating, busy, painful, and pitiable.

CHAPTER IV

The Scots are poor, cries surly English pride.
True is the charge; nor by themselves denied.
Are they not, then, in strictest reason clear,
Who wisely come to mend their fortunes here?

CHURCHILL*

THERE was, in the days of which I write, an old-fashioned custom on the English road, which I suspect is now obsolete, or practised only by the vulgar. Journeys of length being made on horseback, and, of course, by brief stages, it was usual always to make a halt on the Sunday in some town where the traveller might attend divine service, and his horse have the benefit of the day of rest, the institution of which is as humane to our brute labourers as profitable to ourselves. A counterpart to this decent practice, and a remnant of old English hospitality, was, that the landlord of a principal inn laid aside his character of publican on the seventh day, and invited the guests who chanced to be within his walls to take a part of his family beef and pudding. This invitation was usually complied with by all whose distinguished rank did not induce them to think compliance a derogation; and the proposal of a bottle of wine after dinner, to drink the landlord's health, was the only recompense ever offered or accepted.

I was born a citizen of the world, and my inclination led me into all scenes where my knowledge of mankind could be enlarged; I had, besides, no pretensions to sequester myself on the score of superior dignity, and therefore seldom failed to accept of the Sunday's hospitality of mine host, whether of the Garter, Lion, or Bear. The honest publican, dilated into additional consequence by a sense of his own importance, while presiding among the guests on whom it was his ordinary duty to attend, was in himself an entertaining spectacle; and around his genial orbit, other planets of inferior consequence performed their revolutions. The wits and humorists, the distinguished worthies of the town or village, the apothecary, the attorney, even the curate himself, did not disdain to partake of this hebdomadal festivity. The guests, assembled from different quarters, and following different professions, formed, in language, manners, and sentiments, a curious contrast to each other, not indifferent to those who desired to possess a knowledge of mankind in its varieties.

It was on such a day, and such an occasion, that my timorous acquaintance and I were about to grace the board of the ruddy-faced host of the Black Bear, in the town of Darlington, and bishoprick of Durham, when our landlord informed us, with a sort of apologetic tone, that there was a Scotch gentleman to dine with us.

'A gentleman?—what sort of a gentleman?' said my companion, somewhat hastily, his mind, I suppose, running on gentlemen of the pad, as they were then termed.

'Why, a Scotch sort of a gentleman, as I said before,' returned mine host; 'they are all gentle, ye mun know, though they ha' narra shirt to back; but this is a decentish hallion—a canny North Briton* as e'er cross'd Berwick bridge—I trow he's a dealer in cattle.'

'Let us have his company, by all means,' answered my companion; and then, turning to me, he gave vent to the tenor of his own reflections. 'I respect the Scotch, sir; I love and honour the nation for their sense of morality. Men talk of their filth and their poverty: but commend me to sterling honesty, though clad in rags, as the poet saith.* I have been credibly assured, sir, by men on whom I can depend, that there was never known such a thing in Scotland as a highway robbery.'

'That's because they have nothing to lose,' said mine host, with the chuckle of a self-applauding wit.

'No, no, landlord,' answered a strong deep voice behind him, 'it's e'en because your English gaugers and supervisors,[31] that you have sent down benorth the Tweed, have taen up the trade of thievery over the heads of the native professors.'

'Well said, Mr Campbell!' answered the landlord; 'I did nat think thoud'st been sae near us, mon. But thou kens I'm an outspoken Yorkshire tyke—And how go markets in the south?'

'Even in the ordinar,' replied Mr Campbell; 'wise folks buy and sell, and fools are bought and sold.'

'But wise men and fools both eat their dinner,' answered our jolly entertainer; 'and here a comes—as prime a buttock of beef as e'er hungry mon stuck fork in.'

So saying, he eagerly whetted his knife, assumed his seat of empire at the head of the board, and loaded the plates of his sundry guests with his good cheer.

This was the first time I had heard the Scottish accent, or, indeed, that I had familiarly met with an individual of the ancient nation by whom it was spoken. Yet, from an early period, they had occupied and interested my imagination. My father, as is well known to you, was of an ancient family in Northumberland, from whose seat I was while eating the aforesaid dinner, not very many miles distant. The quarrel betwixt him and his relatives was such, that he scarcely ever mentioned the race from which he sprung, and held as the most contemptible species of vanity, the weakness which is commonly termed family pride. His ambition was only to be distinguished as William Osbaldistone, the first, at least one of the first, merchants on Change;* and to have proved him the lineal representative of William the Conqueror, would have far less flattered his vanity than the hum and bustle which his approach was wont to produce among the bulls, bears, and brokers of Stock-alley. He wished, no doubt, that I should remain in such ignorance of my relatives and descent as might insure a correspondence between my feelings and his own on this subject. But his designs, as will happen occasionally to the wisest, were, in some degree at least, counteracted by a being whom his pride would never have supposed of importance adequate to influence them in any way. His nurse, an old Northumbrian woman, attached to him from his infancy, was the only person connected with his native province for whom he retained any regard; and when fortune dawned upon him, one of the first uses which he made of her favours, was to give Mabel Rickets a place of residence within his household. After the death of my mother, the care of nursing me during my childish illnesses, and of rendering all those tender attentions which infancy exacts from female affection, devolved on old Mabel. Interdicted by her master from speaking to him on the subject of the heaths, glades, and dales of her beloved Northumberland, she poured herself forth to my infant ear in descriptions of the scenes of her youth, and long narratives of the events which tradition declared to have passed amongst them. To these I inclined my ear much more seriously* than to graver, but less animated instructors. Even yet, methinks I see old Mabel, her head slightly agitated by the palsy of age, and shaded by a close cap, as white as the driven snow,—her face wrinkled, but still retaining the healthy tinge which it had acquired in rural labour,—I think I see her look around on the brick walls and narrow street which presented themselves from our windows, as she concluded with a sigh the favourite old ditty, which I then preferred, and—why should I not tell the truth?—which I still prefer to all the opera airs ever minted by the capricious brain of an Italian Mus. D.—

> Oh, the oak, the ash, and the bonny ivy tree,
> They flourish best at home in the North Country!*

Now, in the legends of Mabel, the Scottish nation was ever freshly remembered, with all the embittered declamation of which the narrator was capable. The inhabitants of the opposite frontier served in her narratives to fill up the parts which ogres and giants with seven-leagued boots occupy in the ordinary nursery tales. And how could it be otherwise? Was it not the Black Douglas* who slew with his own hand the heir of the Osbaldistone family the day after he took possession of his estate, surprising him and his vassals while solemnizing a feast suited to the occasion? Was it not Wat the Devil* who drove all the year-old hogs off the braes of Lanthorn-side, in the very recent days of my grandfather's father? And had we not many a trophy, but, according to old Mabel's version of history, far more honourably gained, to mark our revenge of these wrongs? Did not Sir Henry Osbaldistone, fifth baron of the name, carry off the fair maid of Fairnington, as Achilles did his Chryseis and Briseis of old,* and detain her in his fortress against all the power of her friends, supported by the most mighty Scottish chiefs of warlike fame? And had not our swords shone foremost at most of those fields in which England was victorious over her rival? All our family renown was acquired,—all our family misfortunes were occasioned,—by the northern wars.

Warmed by such tales, I looked upon the Scottish people during my childhood, as a race hostile by nature to the more southern inhabitants of this realm; and this view of the matter was not much corrected by the language which my father sometimes held with respect to them. He had engaged in some large speculations concerning oak-woods, the property of Highland proprietors, and alleged, that he found them much more ready to make bargains, and extort earnest of the purchase-money, than punctual in complying on their side with the terms of the engagements. The Scotch mercantile men, whom he was under the necessity of employing as a sort of middle-men on these occasions, were also suspected by my father of having secured, by one means or other, more than their own share of the profit which ought to have accrued. In short, if Mabel complained of the Scottish arms in ancient times, Mr Osbaldistone inveighed no less against the arts of these modern Sinons;* and between them, though without any fixed purpose of doing so, they impressed my youthful mind with a sincere aversion to the northern inhabitants of Britain, as a people blood-thirsty in time of war, treacherous during truce, interested, selfish, avaricious, and tricky in the business of peaceful life, and having few good qualities, unless there should be accounted such, a ferocity which resembled courage in martial affairs, and a sort of wily craft, which supplied the place of wisdom in the ordinary commerce of mankind. In justification, or apology, for those who entertained such prejudices, I must remark, that the Scotch of that period were guilty of similar injustice to the English, whom they branded universally as a race of purse-proud arrogant epicures. Such seeds of national dislike remained between the two countries, the natural consequences of their existence as separate and rival states. We have seen recently the breath of a demagogue blow these sparks into a temporary flame, which I sincerely hope is now extinguished in its own ashes.[32]

It was, then, with an impression of dislike, that I contemplated the first Scotchman I chanced to meet in society. There was much about him that coincided with my previous conceptions. He had the hard features and athletic form, said to be peculiar to his country, together with the national intonation and slow pedantic mode of expression, arising from a desire to avoid peculiarities of idiom or dialect. I could also observe the caution and shrewdness of his country in many of the observations which he made, and the answers which he returned. But I was not prepared for the air of easy self-possession and superiority, with which he seemed to predominate over the company into which he was thrown, as it were by accident. His dress was as coarse as it could be, being still decent; and, at a time when great expense was lavished upon the wardrobe, even of the lowest who pretended to the character of gentlemen, this indicated mediocrity of circumstances, if not poverty. His conversation intimated, that he was engaged in the cattle-trade, no very dignified professional pursuit. And yet, under these dis-advantages, he seemed, as a matter of course, to treat the rest of the company with the cool and condescending politeness, which implies a real, or imagined, superiority over those towards whom it is used. When he gave his opinion on any point, it was with that easy tone of confidence used by those superior to their society in rank or informa-tion, as if what he said could not be doubted, and was not to be ques-tioned. Mine host and his Sunday guests, after an effort or two to support their consequence by noise and bold averment, sunk grad-ually under the authority of Mr Campbell, who thus fairly possessed himself of the lead in the conversation. I was tempted from curiosity, to dispute the ground with him myself, confiding in my knowledge of the world, extended as it was by my residence abroad, and in the stores with which a tolerable education had possessed my mind. In the latter respect, he offered no competition, and it was easy to see that his natural powers had never been cultivated by education. But I found him much better acquainted than I was myself with the present state of France, the character of the Duke of Orleans, who had just succeeded to the regency of that kingdom,* and that of the statesmen by whom he was surrounded; and his shrewd, caustic, and somewhat satirical remarks, were those of a man who had been a close observer of the affairs of that country.

On the subject of politics, Campbell observed a silence and moderation which might arise from caution. The divisions of Whig and Tory then shook England to her very centre, and a powerful party, engaged in the Jacobite interest, menaced the dynasty of Hanover, which had been just established on the throne.* Every alehouse resounded with the brawls of contending politicians, and as mine host's politics were of that liberal description which quarrelled with no good customer, his hebdomadal visitants were often divided in their opinion as irreconcilably as if he had feasted the Common Council.* The curate and the apothecary, with a little man, who made no boast of his vocation, but who, from the flourish and snap of his fingers, I believe to have been the barber,* strongly espoused the cause of high church and the Stewart line. The exciseman, as in duty bound, and the attorney, who looked to some petty office under the crown, together with my fellow-traveller, who seemed to enter keenly into the contest, stanchly supported the cause of King George and the Protestant succession. Dire was the screaming—deep the oaths! Each party appealed to Mr Campbell, anxious, it seemed, to elicit his approbation.

'You are a Scotchman, sir; a gentleman of your country must stand up for hereditary right,' cried one party.

'You are a Presbyterian,' assumed the other class of disputants; 'you cannot be a friend to arbitrary power.'

'Gentlemen,' said our Scotch oracle, after having gained, with some difficulty, a moment's pause, 'I havena much dubitation that King George weel deserves the predilection of his friends; and if he can haud the grip he has gotten, why, doubtless, he may make the gauger, here, a commissioner of the revenue, and confer on our friend,

Mr Quitam, the preferment of solicitor-general; and he may also grant some good deed or reward to this honest gentleman who is sitting upon his portmanteau, which he prefers to a chair: And, questionless, King James is also a grateful person, and when he gets his hand in play, he may, if he be so minded, make this reverend gentleman archprelate of Canterbury, and Dr Mixit, chief physician to his household, and commit his royal beard to the care of my friend Latherum. But as I doubt mickle whether any of the competing sovereigns would give Rob Campbell a tass of aquavitæ, if he lacked it, I give my vote and interest to Jonathan Brown, our landlord, to be the King and Prince of Skinkers,* conditionally that he fetches us another bottle as good as the last.'

This sally was received with general applause, in which the landlord cordially joined; and when he had given orders for fulfilling the condition on which his preferment was to depend, he failed not to acquaint them, 'that, for as peaceable a gentleman as Mr Campbell was, he was, moreover, as bold as a lion—seven highwaymen had he defeated with his single arm, that beset him as he came from Whitson-Tryste.'*

'Thou art deceived, friend Jonathan,' said Campbell, interrupting him; 'they were but barely two, and two cowardly loons as man could wish to meet withal.'

'And did you, sir, really,' said my fellow-traveller, edging his chair (I should have said his portmanteau) nearer to Mr Campbell, 'really and actually beat two highwaymen yourself alone?'

'In troth did I, sir,' replied Campbell; 'and I think it nae great thing to make a sang about.'

'Upon my word, sir,' replied my acquaintance, 'I should be happy to have the pleasure of your company on my journey—I go northward, sir.'

This piece of gratuitous information concerning the route he proposed to himself, the first I had heard my companion bestow upon any one, failed to excite the corresponding confidence of the Scotchman.

'We can scarce travel together,' he replied, dryly. 'You, sir, doubtless, are well mounted, and I, for the present, travel on foot, or on a Highland shelty, that does not help me much faster forward.'

So saying, he called for a reckoning for the wine, and throwing down the price of the additional bottle which he had himself introduced, rose as if to take leave of us. My companion made up to him, and taking him by the button, drew him aside into one of the windows. I could not help overhearing him pressing something;—I supposed his company upon the journey, which Mr Campbell seemed to decline.

'I will pay your charges, sir,' said the traveller, in a tone, as if he thought the argument should bear down all opposition.

'It is quite impossible,' said Campbell, somewhat contemptuously; 'I have business at Rothbury.'

'But I am in no great hurry; I can ride out of the way, and never miss a day or so for good company.'

'Upon my faith, sir,' said Campbell, 'I cannot render you the service you seem to desiderate. I am,' he added, drawing himself up haughtily, 'travelling on my own private affairs, and if ye will act by my advisement, sir, ye will neither unite yourself with an absolute stranger on the road, nor communicate your line of journey to those who are asking ye no questions about it.' He then extricated his button, not very ceremoniously, from the hold which detained him, and, coming up to me as the company were dispersing, observed, 'Your friend, sir, is too communicative, considering the nature of his trust.'

'That gentleman,' I replied, looking towards the traveller, 'is no friend of mine, but an acquaintance whom I picked up on the road. I know neither his name nor business, and you seem to be deeper in his confidence than I am.'

'I only meant,' he replied hastily, 'that he seems a thought rash in conferring the honour of his company on those who desire it not.'

'The gentleman,' replied I, 'knows his own affairs best, and I should be sorry to constitute myself a judge of them in any respect.'

Mr Campbell made no farther observation, but merely wished me a good journey, and the party dispersed for the evening.

Next day I parted company with my timid companion, as I left the great northern road to turn more westerly in the direction of Osbaldistone Manor, my uncle's seat.* I cannot tell whether he felt relieved or embarrassed by my departure, considering the dubious light in which he seemed to regard me. For my own part, his tremors ceased to amuse me, and, to say the truth, I was heartily glad to get rid of him.

CHAPTER V

How melts my beating heart, as I behold
Each lovely nymph, our island's boast and pride,
Push on the generous steed, that sweeps along
O'er rough, o'er smooth, nor heeds the steepy hill,
Nor falters in the extended vale below!

*The Chase**

I APPROACHED my native north, for such I esteemed it, with that enthusiasm which romantic and wild scenery inspires in the lovers of nature. No longer interrupted by the babble of my companion, I could now remark the difference which the country exhibited from that through which I had hitherto travelled. The streams now more properly deserved the name, for, instead of slumbering stagnant among reeds and willows, they brawled along beneath the shade of natural copsewood; were now hurried down declivities, and now purled more leisurely, but still in active motion, through little lonely valleys, which, opening on the road from time to time, seemed to invite the traveller to explore their recesses. The Cheviots rose before me in frowning majesty; not, indeed, with the sublime variety of rock and cliff which characterises mountains of the primary class, but huge, round-headed, and clothed with a dark robe of russet, gaining, by their extent and desolate appearance, an influence upon the imagination, as a desert district possessing a character of its own.

The abode of my fathers, which I was now approaching, was situated in a glen, or narrow valley, which ran up among those hills. Extensive estates, which once belonged to the family of Osbaldistone, had been long dissipated by the misfortunes or misconduct of my ancestors; but enough was still attached to the old mansion, to give my uncle the title of a man of large property. This he employed (as I was given to understand by some enquiries which I made on the road) in maintaining the prodigal hospitality of a northern squire of the period, which he deemed essential to his family dignity.

From the summit of an eminence, I had already had a distant view of Osbaldistone Hall, a large and antiquated edifice, peeping out from a Druidical grove of huge oaks; and I was directing my course towards it, as straightly and as speedily as the windings of a very indifferent road would permit, when my horse, tired as he was, pricked up his ears at the enlivening notes of a pack of hounds in full cry, cheered by the occasional bursts of a French horn, which in those days was a constant accompaniment to the chase. I made no doubt that the pack was my uncle's, and drew up my horse with the purpose of suffering the hunters to pass without notice, aware that a hunting-field was not the proper scene to introduce myself to a keen sportsman, and determined, when they had passed on, to proceed to the mansion-house at my own pace, and there to await the return of the proprietor from his sport. I paused, therefore, on a rising ground, and, not unmoved by the sense of interest which that species of silvan sport is so much calculated to inspire, (although my mind was not at the moment very accessible to impressions of this nature,) I expected with some eagerness the appearance of the huntsmen.

The fox, hard run, and nearly spent, first made his appearance from the copse which clothed the right-hand side of the valley. His drooping brush, his soiled appearance, and jaded trot, proclaimed his fate impending; and the carrion crow, which hovered over him, already considered poor Reynard as soon to be his prey. He crossed the stream which divides the little valley, and was dragging himself up a ravine on the other side of its wild banks, when the headmost hounds, followed by the rest of the pack in full cry, burst from the coppice, followed by the huntsman, and three or four riders. The dogs pursued the trace of Reynard with unerring instinct; and the hunters followed with reckless haste, regardless of the broken and difficult nature of the ground. They were tall, stout young men, well mounted, and dressed in green and red, the uniform of a sporting association, formed under the auspices of old Sir Hildebrand Osbaldistone. My cousins! thought I, as they swept past me. The next reflection was, what is my reception likely to be among these worthy successors of Nimrod? and how improbable is it, that I, knowing little or nothing of rural sports, shall find myself at ease, or happy, in my uncle's family. A vision that passed me interrupted these reflections.

It was a young lady, the loveliness of whose very striking features was enhanced by the animation of the chase and the glow of the exercise, mounted on a beautiful horse, jet black, unless where he was flecked by spots of the snow-white foam which embossed his bridle. She wore, what was then somewhat unusual, a coat, vest, and hat, resembling those of a man, which fashion has since called a riding-habit. The mode had been introduced while I was in France, and was perfectly new to me.* Her long black hair streamed on the breeze, having in the hurry of the chase escaped from the ribbon which bound it. Some very broken ground, through which she guided her horse with the most admirable address and presence of mind, retarded her course, and brought her closer to me than any of the other riders had passed. I had, therefore, a full view of her uncommonly fine face and person, to which an inexpressible charm was added by the wild gaiety of the scene, and the romance of her singular dress and unexpected appearance. As she passed me, her horse made, in his impetuosity, an irregular movement, just while, coming once more upon open ground, she was again putting him to his speed. It served as an apology for me to ride close up to her, as if to her assistance. There was, however, no cause for alarm; it was not a stumble, nor a false step; and, if it had, the fair Amazon had too much self-possession to have been deranged by it. She thanked my good intentions, however, by a smile, and I felt encouraged to put my horse to the same pace, and to keep in her immediate neighbourhood. The clamour of 'Whoop, dead, dead!' and the corresponding flourish of the French horn, soon announced to us that there was no more occasion for haste, since the chase was at a close. One of the young men whom we had seen approached us, waving the brush of the fox in triumph, as if to upbraid my fair companion.

'I see,' she replied,—'I see; but make no noise about it; if Phœbe,'* she said, patting the neck of the beautiful animal on which she rode, 'had not got among the cliffs, you would have had little cause for boasting.'

They met as she spoke, and I observed them both look at me and converse a moment in an under tone, the young lady apparently pressing the sportsman to do something which he declined shyly, and with a sort of sheepish sullenness. She instantly turned her horse's head towards me, saying,—'Well, well, Thornie, if you won't, I must, that's all.—Sir,' she continued, addressing me, 'I have been endeavouring to persuade this cultivated young gentleman to make enquiry of you, whether, in the course of your travels in these parts, you have heard any thing of a friend of ours, one Mr Francis Osbaldistone, who has been for some days expected at Osbaldistone Hall?'

I was too happy to acknowledge myself to be the party enquired after, and to express my thanks for the obliging enquiries of the young lady.

'In that case, sir,' she rejoined, 'as my kinsman's politeness seems to be still slumbering, you will permit me (though I suppose it is highly improper) to stand mistress of ceremonies, and to present to you young Squire Thorncliff Osbaldistone, your cousin, and Die Vernon, who has also the honour to be your accomplished cousin's poor kinswoman.'

There was a mixture of boldness, satire, and simplicity in the manner in which Miss Vernon pronounced these words. My knowledge of life was sufficient to enable me to take up a corresponding tone as I expressed my gratitude to her for her condescension, and my extreme pleasure at having met with them. To say the truth, the compliment was so expressed, that the lady might easily appropriate the greater share of it, for Thorncliff seemed an arrant country bumpkin, awkward, shy, and somewhat sulky withal. He shook hands with me, however, and then intimated his intention of leaving me that he might help the huntsman and his brothers to couple up the hounds, a purpose which he rather communicated by way of information to Miss Vernon than as apology to me.

'There he goes,' said the young lady, following him with eyes in which disdain was admirably painted,—'the prince of grooms and cock-fighters, and blackguard horse-coursers. But there is not one of them to mend another.—Have you read Markham?'* said Miss Vernon.

'Read whom, ma'am?—I do not even remember the author's name.'

'O lud! on what a strand are you wrecked!' replied the young lady. 'A poor forlorn and ignorant stranger, unacquainted with the very Alcoran* of the savage tribe whom you are come to reside among— Never to have heard of Markham, the most celebrated author on farriery! then I fear you are equally a stranger to the more modern names of Gibson and Bartlett?'*

'I am, indeed, Miss Vernon.'

'And do you not blush to own it?' said Miss Vernon. 'Why, we must forswear your alliance. Then, I suppose, you can neither give a ball, nor a mash, nor a horn?'*

'I confess I trust all these matters to an ostler, or to my groom.'

'Incredible carelessness!—And you cannot shoe a horse, or cut his mane and tail; or worm a dog, or crop his ears, or cut his dew-claws;* or reclaim a hawk, or give him his casting-stones, or direct his diet when he is sealed;* or'——

'To sum up my insignificance in one word,' replied I, 'I am profoundly ignorant in all these rural accomplishments.'

'Then, in the name of Heaven, Mr Francis Osbaldistone, what *can* you do?'

'Very little to the purpose, Miss Vernon; something, however, I can pretend to—When my groom has dressed my horse, I can ride him, and when my hawk is in the field I can fly him.'

'Can you do this?' said the young lady, putting her horse to a canter.

There was a sort of rude overgrown fence crossed the path before us, with a gate, composed of pieces of wood rough from the forest; I was about to move forward to open it, when Miss Vernon cleared the obstruction at a flying leap. I was bound, in point of honour, to follow, and was in a moment again at her side.

'There are hopes of you yet,' she said. 'I was afraid you had been a very degenerate Osbaldistone. But what on earth brings you to Cub-Castle?—for so the neighbours have christened this hunting-hall of ours. You might have staid away, I suppose, if you would?'

I felt I was by this time on a very intimate footing with my beautiful apparition, and therefore replied in a confidential under tone,—'Indeed, my dear Miss Vernon, I might have considered it as a sacrifice to be a temporary resident in Osbaldistone Hall, the inmates being such as you describe them; but I am convinced there is one exception that will make amends for all deficiencies.'

'O, you mean Rashleigh?' said Miss Vernon.

'Indeed I do not; I was thinking—forgive me—of some person much nearer me.'

'I suppose it would be proper not to understand your civility?—But that is not my way—I don't make a curtsey for it, because I am sitting on horseback. But, seriously, I deserve your exception, for I am the only conversible being about the Hall, except the old priest and Rashleigh.'

'And who is Rashleigh, for Heaven's sake?'

'Rashleigh is one who would fain have every one like him for his own sake.—He is Sir Hildebrand's youngest son—about your own age, but not so—not well looking, in short. But nature has given him a mouthful of common sense, and the priest has added a bushelful of learning—he is what we call a very clever man in this country, where clever men are scarce. Bred to the church, but in no hurry to take orders.'

'To the Catholic Church?'

'The Catholic Church! what Church else?' said the young lady. 'But I forgot, they told me you are a heretic. Is that true, Mr Osbaldistone?'

'I must not deny the charge.'

'And yet you have been abroad, and in Catholic countries?'

'For nearly four years.'

'You have seen convents?'

'Often; but I have not seen much in them which recommended the Catholic religion.'

'Are not the inhabitants happy?'

'Some are unquestionably so, whom either a profound sense of devotion, or an experience of the persecutions and misfortunes of the world, or a natural apathy of temper, has led into retirement. Those who have adopted a life of seclusion from sudden and overstrained enthusiasm, or in hasty resentment of some disappointment or mortification, are very miserable. The quickness of sensation soon returns, and, like the wilder animals in a menagerie, they are restless under confinement, while others muse or fatten in cells of no larger dimensions than theirs.'

'And what,' continued Miss Vernon, 'becomes of those victims who are condemned to a convent by the will of others? what do they resemble? especially, what do they resemble, if they are born to enjoy life, and feel its blessings?'

'They are like imprisoned singing-birds,' replied I, 'condemned to wear out their lives in confinement, which they try to beguile by the exercise of accomplishments, which would have adorned society, had they been left at large.'

'I shall be,' returned Miss Vernon—'that is,' said she, correcting herself,—'I should be rather like the wild hawk, who, barred the free exercise of his soar through heaven, will dash himself to pieces against the bars of his cage. But to return to Rashleigh,' said she, in a more lively tone, 'you will think him the pleasantest man you ever saw in your life, Mr Osbaldistone, that is, for a week at least. If he could find out a blind mistress, never man would be so secure of conquest; but the eye breaks the spell that enchants the ear. But here we are in the court of the old hall, which looks as wild and old-fashioned as any of its inmates. There is no great toilette kept at Osbaldistone Hall, you must know; but I must take off these things, they are so unpleasantly warm, and the hat hurts my forehead too,' continued the lively girl, taking it off, and shaking down a profusion of sable ringlets, which, half laughing, half blushing, she separated with her white slender fingers, in order to clear them away from her beautiful face and piercing hazel eyes. If there was any coquetry in the action, it was well disguised by the careless indifference of her manner. I could not help saying, 'that, judging of the family from what I saw, I should suppose the toilette a very unnecessary care.'

'That's very politely said; though, perhaps, I ought not to understand in what sense it was meant,' replied Miss Vernon; 'but you will see a better apology for a little negligence, when you meet the Orsons* you are to live amongst, whose forms no toilette could improve. But, as I said before, the old dinner-bell will clang, or rather clank, in a few minutes—it cracked of its own accord on the day of the landing of King Willie,* and my uncle, respecting its prophetic talent, would never permit it to be mended. So do you hold my palfrey, like a duteous knight, until I send some more humble squire to relieve you of the charge.'

She threw me the rein as if we had been acquainted from our childhood, jumped from her saddle, tripped across the court-yard, and entered at a side-door, leaving me in admiration of her beauty, and astonished with the overfrankness of her manners, which seemed the more extraordinary, at a time when the dictates of politeness, flowing from the court of the Grand Monarque Louis XIV., prescribed to the fair sex an unusual severity of decorum.* I was left awkwardly enough stationed in the centre of the court of the old hall, mounted on one horse, and holding another in my hand.

The building afforded little to interest a stranger, had I been disposed to consider it attentively; the sides of the quadrangle were of various architecture, and with their stone-shafted latticed windows, projecting turrets, and massive architraves, resembled the inside of a convent, or of one of the older and less splendid colleges of Oxford. I called for a domestic, but was for some time totally unattended to; which was the more provoking, as I could perceive I was the object of curiosity to several servants, both male and female, from different parts of the building, who popped out their heads and withdrew them, like rabbits in a warren, before I could make a direct appeal to the attention of any individual. The return of the huntsmen and hounds relieved me from my embarrassment, and with some difficulty I got one clown to relieve me of the charge of the horses, and another stupid boor to guide me to the presence of Sir Hildebrand. This service he performed with much such grace and good-will, as a peasant who is compelled to act as guide to a hostile patrol; and in the same manner I was obliged to guard against his deserting me in the labyrinth of low vaulted passages which conducted to 'Stun Hall,' as he called it, where I was to be introduced to the gracious presence of my uncle.

We did, however, at length reach a long vaulted room, floored with stone, where a range of oaken tables, of a weight and size too massive ever to be moved aside, were already covered for dinner. This venerable apartment, which had witnessed the feasts of several generations of the Osbaldistone family, bore also evidence of their success in field-sports. Huge antlers of deer, which might have been trophies of the hunting of Chevy Chace,* were ranged around the walls, interspersed with the stuffed skins of badgers, otters, martins, and other animals of the chase. Amidst some remnants of old armour, which had, perhaps, served against the Scotch, hung the more valued weapons of silvan war, cross-bows, guns of various device and construction, nets, fishing-rods, otter-spears, hunting-poles, with many other singular devices and engines for taking or killing game. A few old pictures, dimmed with smoke, and stained with March beer, hung on the walls, representing knights and ladies, honoured, doubtless, and renowned in their day; those frowning fearfully from huge bushes of wig and of beard; and these looking delightfully with all their might at the roses which they brandished in their hands.

I had just time to give a glance at these matters, when about twelve blue-coated servants burst into the hall with much tumult and talk, each rather employed in directing his comrades than in discharging his own duty. Some brought blocks and billets to the fire, which roared, blazed, and ascended, half in smoke, half in flame, up a huge tunnel, with an opening wide enough to accommodate a stone-seat within its ample vault, and which was fronted, by way of chimney-piece, with a huge piece of heavy architecture, where the monsters of heraldry, embodied by the art of some Northumbrian chisel, grinned and ramped in red free-stone, now japanned by the smoke of centuries. Others of these old-fashioned serving-men bore huge smoking dishes, loaded with substantial fare; others brought in cups, flagons, bottles, yea barrels of liquor. All tramped, kicked, plunged, shouldered, and jostled, doing as little service with as much tumult as could well be imagined. At length, while the dinner was, after various

efforts, in the act of being arranged upon the board, 'the clamour much
of men and dogs,'* the cracking of whips, calculated for the intimidation of the latter, voices loud and high, steps which, impressed by the
heavy-heeled boots of the period, clattered like those in the statue of
the *Festin de pierre*,[33] announced the arrival of those for whose benefit
the preparations were made. The hubbub among the servants rather
increased than diminished as this crisis approached,—some called to
make haste,—others to take time,—some exhorted to stand out of the
way, and make room for Sir Hildebrand and the young squires,—some
to close round the table, and be *in* the way,—some bawled to open,
some to shut a pair of folding-doors, which divided the hall from a sort
of gallery, as I afterwards learned, or withdrawing-room, fitted up with
black wainscot. Opened the doors were at length, and in rushed curs
and men,—eight dogs, the domestic chaplain, the village doctor, my
six cousins, and my uncle.

CHAPTER VI

The rude hall rocks—they come, they come,—
The din of voices shakes the dome;—
In stalk the various forms, and, drest
In varying morion, varying vest,
All march with haughty step—all proudly shake the crest.

PENROSE*

IF Sir Hildebrand Osbaldistone was in no hurry to greet his nephew, of whose arrival he must have been informed for some time, he had important avocations to allege in excuse. 'Had seen thee sooner, lad,' he exclaimed, after a rough shake of the hand, and a hearty welcome to Osbaldistone Hall, 'but had to see the hounds kennelled first. Thou art welcome to the Hall, lad—here is thy cousin Percie, thy cousin Thornie, and thy cousin John—your cousin Dick, your cousin Wilfred, and—stay, where's Rashleigh—ay, here's Rashleigh—take thy long body aside, Thornie, and let's see thy brother a bit—your cousin Rashleigh.—So, thy father has thought on the old Hall, and old Sir Hildebrand at last—better late than never—Thou art welcome, lad, and there's enough.—Where's my little Die?—ay, here she comes—this is my niece Die, my wife's brother's daughter—the prettiest girl in our dales, be the other who she may—and so now let's to the sirloin.'—

To gain some idea of the person who held this language, you must suppose, my dear Tresham, a man aged about sixty, in a hunting suit which had once been richly laced, but whose splendour had been tarnished by many a November and December storm. Sir Hildebrand, notwithstanding the abruptness of his present manner, had, at one period of his life, known courts and camps; had held a commission in the army which encamped on Hounslow Heath previous to the Revolution,* and, recommended perhaps by his religion, had been knighted about the same period by the unfortunate and ill-advised James II. But the Knight's dreams of further preferment, if he ever entertained any, had died away at the crisis which drove his patron from the throne, and since that period he had spent a sequestered life upon his native domains. Notwithstanding his rusticity, however, Sir Hildebrand retained much of the exterior of a gentleman, and appeared among his sons as the remains of a Corinthian pillar, defaced and overgrown with moss and lichen, might have looked, if contrasted with the rough, unhewn masses of upright stones in Stonhenge, or any other druidical temple. The sons were, indeed, heavy unadorned blocks as the eye would desire to look upon. Tall, stout, and comely, all and each of the five eldest seemed to want alike the Promethean fire of intellect, and the exterior grace and manner, which, in the polished world, sometimes supply mental deficiency. Their most valuable moral quality seemed to be the good-humour and content which was expressed in their heavy features, and their only pretence to accomplishment was their dexterity in field sports, for which alone they lived. The strong Gyas, and the strong Cloanthus,* are not less distinguished by the poet, than the strong Percival, the strong Thorncliff, the strong John, Richard, and Wilfred Osbaldistones, were by outward appearance.

But, as if to indemnify herself for a uniformity so uncommon in her productions, Dame Nature had rendered Rashleigh Osbaldistone a striking contrast in person and manner, and, as I afterwards learned, in temper and talents, not only to his brothers, but to most men whom I had hitherto met with. When Percie, Thornie, and Co. had respectively nodded, grinned, and presented their shoulder, rather than their hand, as their father named them to their new kinsman, Rashleigh stepped forward, and welcomed me to Osbaldistone Hall, with the air and manner of a man of the world. His appearance was not in itself prepossessing. He was of low stature, whereas all his brethren seemed to be descendants of Anak;* and, while they were handsomely formed, Rashleigh, though strong in person, was bull-necked and cross-made, and, from some early injury in his youth, had an imperfection in his gait, so much resembling an absolute halt, that many alleged that it formed the obstacle to his taking orders; the church of Rome, as is well known, admitting none to the clerical profession who labours under any personal deformity. Others, however, ascribed this unsightly defect to a mere awkward habit, and contended, that it did not amount to a personal disqualification from holy orders.

The features of Rashleigh were such, as, having looked upon, we in vain wish to banish from our memory, to which they recur as objects of painful curiosity, although we dwell upon them with a feeling of dislike, and even of disgust. It was not the actual plainness of his face, taken separately from the meaning, which made this strong impression.

His features were, indeed, irregular, but they were by no means vulgar; and his keen dark eyes, and shaggy eyebrows, redeemed his face from the charge of commonplace ugliness. But there was in these eyes an expression of art and design, and, on provocation, a ferocity tempered by caution, which nature had made obvious to the most ordinary physiognomist, perhaps with the same intention that she has given the rattle to the poisonous snake. As if to compensate him for these disadvantages of exterior, Rashleigh Osbaldistone was possessed of a voice the most soft, mellow, and rich in its tones that I ever heard, and was at no loss for language of every sort suited to so fine an organ. His first sentence of welcome was hardly ended, ere I internally agreed with Miss Vernon, that my new kinsman would make an instant conquest of a mistress whose ears alone were to judge his cause. He was about to place himself beside me at dinner, but Miss Vernon, who, as the only female in the family, arranged all such matters according to her own pleasure, contrived that I should sit betwixt Thorncliff and herself; and it can scarce be doubted that I favoured this more advantageous arrangement.

'I want to speak with you,' she said, 'and I have placed honest Thornie betwixt Rashleigh and you on purpose. He will be like—

> Feather-bed 'twixt castle wall
> And heavy brunt of cannon ball;*

while I, your earliest acquaintance in this intellectual family, ask of you how you like us all?'

'A very comprehensive question, Miss Vernon, considering how short while I have been at Osbaldistone Hall.'

'O, the philosophy of our family lies on the surface—there are minute shades distinguishing the individuals, which require the eye of an intelligent observer; but the species, as naturalists I believe call it, may be distinguished and characterised at once.'

'My five elder cousins, then, are, I presume, of pretty nearly the same character.'

'Yes, they form a happy compound of sot, gamekeeper, bully, horse-jockey, and fool; but as they say there cannot be found two leaves on the same tree exactly alike, so these happy ingredients, being mingled in somewhat various proportions in each individual, make an agreeable variety for those who like to study character.'

'Give me a sketch, if you please, Miss Vernon.'

'You shall have them all in a family-piece, at full length—the favour is too easily granted to be refused. Percie, the son and heir, has more of the sot than of the gamekeeper, bully, horse-jockey, or fool—My precious Thornie is more of the bully than the sot, gamekeeper, jockey, or fool—John, who sleeps whole weeks amongst the hills, has most of the gamekeeper—The jockey is powerful with Dickon, who rides two hundred miles by day and night to be bought and sold at a horse-race—And the fool predominates so much over Wilfred's other qualities, that he may be termed a fool positive.'*

'A goodly collection, Miss Vernon, and the individual varieties belong to a most interesting species. But is there no room on the canvass for Sir Hildebrand?'

'I love my uncle,' was her reply: 'I owe him some kindness, (such it was meant for at least,) and I will leave you to draw his picture yourself, when you know him better.'

Come, thought I to myself, I am glad there is some forbearance. After all, who would have looked for such bitter satire from a creature so young and so exquisitely beautiful?

'You are thinking of me,' she said, bending her dark eyes on me, as if she meant to pierce through my very soul.

'I certainly was,' I replied with some embarrassment at the determined suddenness of the question, and then endeavouring to give a complimentary turn to my frank avowal. 'How is it possible I should think of anything else, seated as I have the happiness to be?'

She smiled with such an expression of concentrated haughtiness as she alone could have thrown into her countenance. 'I must inform you at once, Mr Osbaldistone, that compliments are entirely lost upon me; do not, therefore, throw away your pretty sayings—they serve fine gentlemen who travel in the country, instead of the toys, beads, and bracelets, which navigators carry to propitiate the savage inhabitants of newly discovered lands. Do not exhaust your stock in trade—you will find natives in Northumberland to whom your fine things will recommend you—on me they would be utterly thrown away, for I happen to know their real value.'

I was silenced and confounded.

'You remind me at this moment,' said the young lady, resuming her lively and indifferent manner, 'of the fairy tale, where the man finds all the money which he had carried to market suddenly changed into pieces of slate.* I have cried down and ruined your whole stock of complimentary discourse by one unlucky observation. But, come, never mind it—You are belied, Mr Osbaldistone, unless you have much better conversation than these *fadeurs*, which every gentleman with a toupet thinks himself obliged to recite to an unfortunate girl, merely because she is dressed in silk and gauze, while he wears superfine cloth with embroidery. Your natural paces, as any of my five cousins might say, are far preferable to your complimentary amble. Endeavour to forget my unlucky sex; call me Tom Vernon, if you have a mind, but speak to me as you would to a friend and companion; you have no idea how much I shall like you.'

'That would be a bribe indeed,' returned I.

'Again!' replied Miss Vernon, holding up her finger; 'I told you I would not bear the shadow of a compliment. And now, when you have pledged my uncle, who threatens you with what he calls a brimmer, I will tell you what you think of me.'

The bumper being pledged by me, as a dutiful nephew, and some other general intercourse of the table having taken place, the continued and business-like clang of knives and forks, and the devotion of cousin Thorncliff on my right hand, and cousin Dickon, who sate on Miss Vernon's left, to the huge quantities of meat with which they heaped their plates, made them serve as two occasional partitions, separating us from the rest of the company, and leaving us to our *tête-à-tête*. 'And now,' said I, 'give me leave to ask you frankly, Miss Vernon, what you suppose I am thinking of you?—I could tell you what I really *do* think, but you have interdicted praise.'

'I do not want your assistance. I am conjurer enough to tell your thoughts without it. You need not open the casement of your bosom; I see through it. You think me a strange bold girl, half coquette, half romp; desirous of attracting attention by the freedom of her manners and loudness of her conversation, because she is ignorant of what the Spectator* calls the softer graces of the sex; and perhaps you think I have some particular plan of storming you into admiration. I should be sorry to shock your self-opinion, but you were never more mistaken. All the confidence I have reposed in you, I would have given as readily to your father, if I thought he could have understood me. I am in this happy family as much secluded from intelligent listeners as Sancho in the Sierra Morena,* and when opportunity offers, I must speak or die. I assure you I would not have told you a word of all this curious intelligence, had I cared a pin who knew it or knew it not.'

'It is very cruel in you, Miss Vernon, to take away all particular marks of favour from your communications, but I must receive them on your own terms.—You have not included Mr Rashleigh Osbaldistone in your domestic sketches.'

She shrunk, I thought, at this remark, and hastily answered, in a much lower tone, 'Not a word of Rashleigh! His ears are so acute when his selfishness is interested, that the sounds would reach him even through the mass of Thorncliff's person, stuffed as it is with beef, venison-pasty, and pudding.'

'Yes,' I replied; 'but peeping past the living screen which divides us, before I put the question, I perceived that Mr Rashleigh's chair was empty—he has left the table.'

'I would not have you be too sure of that,' Miss Vernon replied. 'Take my advice, and when you speak of Rashleigh, get up to the top of Otterscope-hill, where you can see for twenty miles round you in every direction—stand on the very peak, and speak in whispers; and, after all, don't be too sure that the bird of the air will not carry the matter.* Rashleigh has been my tutor for four years; we are mutually tired of each other, and we shall heartily rejoice at our approaching separation.'

'Mr Rashleigh leaves Osbaldistone-Hall, then?'

'Yes, in a few days;—did you not know that?—Your father must keep his resolutions much more secret than Sir Hildebrand. Why, when my uncle was informed that you were to be his guest for some time, and that your father desired to have one of his hopeful sons to fill up the lucrative situation in his counting-house, which was vacant by your obstinacy, Mr Francis, the good knight held a *cour plénière** of all his family, including the butler, housekeeper, and gamekeeper. This reverend assembly of the peers and household officers of Osbaldistone Hall was not convoked, as you may suppose, to elect your substitute, because, as Rashleigh alone possessed more arithmetic than was necessary to calculate the odds on a fighting-cock, none but he could be supposed qualified for the situation. But some solemn sanction was necessary for transforming Rashleigh's destination from starving as a Catholic priest, to thriving as a wealthy banker; and it was not without some reluctance that the acquiescence of the assembly was obtained to such an act of degradation.'

'I can conceive the scruples—but how were they got over?'

'By the general wish, I believe, to get Rashleigh out of the house,' replied Miss Vernon. 'Although youngest of the family, he has some-how or other got the entire management of all the others; and every one is sensible of the subjection, though they cannot shake it off. If any one opposes him, he is sure to rue having done so before the year goes about; and if you do him a very important service, you may rue it still more.'

'At that rate,' answered I, smiling, 'I should look about me; for I have been the cause, however unintentionally, of his change of situation.'

'Yes! and whether he regards it as an advantage or disadvantage, he will owe you a grudge for it—But here come cheese, radishes, and a bumper to church and king, the hint for chaplains and ladies to disappear; and I, the sole representative of womanhood at Osbaldistone Hall, retreat, as in duty bound.'

She vanished as she spoke, leaving me in astonishment at the mingled character of shrewdness, audacity, and frankness, which her conversation displayed. I despair conveying to you the least idea of her manner, although I have, as nearly as I can remember, imitated her language. In fact, there was a mixture of untaught simplicity, as well as native shrewdness and haughty boldness in her manner, and all were modified and recommended by the play of the most beautiful features I had ever beheld. It is not to be thought that, however strange and uncommon I might think her liberal and unreserved communications, a young man of two-and-twenty was likely to be severely critical on a beautiful girl of eighteen, for not observing a proper distance towards him. On the contrary, I was equally diverted and flattered by Miss Vernon's confidence; and that notwithstanding her declaration of its being conferred on me solely because I was the first auditor who occurred, of intelligence enough to comprehend it. With the presumption of my age, certainly not diminished by my residence in France, I imagined, that well-formed features, and a handsome person, both which I conceived myself to possess, were not unsuitable qualifications for the confident of a young beauty. My vanity thus enlisted in Miss Vernon's behalf, I was far from judging her with severity, merely for a frankness which, I supposed, was in some degree justified by my own personal merit; and the feelings of partiality, which her beauty, and the singularity of her situation, were of themselves calculated to excite, were enhanced by my opinion of her penetration and judgment in her choice of a friend.

After Miss Vernon quitted the apartment, the bottle circulated, or rather flew around the table in unceasing revolution. My foreign education had given me a distaste to intemperance, then and yet too common a vice among my countrymen. The conversation which seasoned such orgies was as little to my taste, and, if any thing could render it more disgusting, it was the relationship of the company. I therefore seized a lucky opportunity, and made my escape through a side-door, leading I knew not whither, rather than endure any longer the sight of father and sons practising the same degrading intemperance, and holding the same coarse and disgusting conversation. I was pursued, of course, as I had expected, to be reclaimed by force, as a deserter from the shrine of Bacchus. When I heard the whoop and hollo, and the tramp of the heavy boots of my pursuers on the winding stair which I was descending, I plainly foresaw I should be overtaken unless I could get into the open air. I therefore threw open a casement in the staircase, which looked into an old-fashioned garden; and, as the height did not exceed six feet, I jumped out without hesitation, and soon heard, far behind, the 'hey whoop! stole away! stole away!' of my baffled pursuers. I ran down one alley, walked fast up another; and then, conceiving myself out of all danger of pursuit, I slackened my pace into a quiet stroll, enjoying the cool air which the heat of the wine I had been obliged to swallow, as well as that of my rapid retreat, rendered doubly grateful.

As I sauntered on, I found the gardener hard at his evening employment, and saluted him, as I paused to look at his work. 'Good even, my friend.'

'Gude e'en—gude e'en t'ye,' answered the man, without looking up, and in a tone which at once indicated his northern extraction.

'Fine weather for your work, my friend.'

'It's no that muckle to be compleened o',' answered the man, with that limited degree of praise which gardeners and farmers usually bestow on the very best weather. Then raising his head, as if to see who spoke to him, he touched his Scotch bonnet with an air of respect, as he observed, 'Eh, gude safe us!—it's a sight for sair een, to see a gold-laced jeistiecor in the Ha' garden sae late at e'en.'

'A gold-laced what, my good friend?'

'Ou, a jeistiecor[34]—that's a jacket like your ain, there. They hae other things to do wi' them up yonder—unbuttoning them to make room for the beef and the bag-puddings, and the claret-wine, nae doubt—that's the ordinary for evening lecture on this side the Border.'

'There's no such plenty of good cheer in your country, my good friend,' I replied, 'as to tempt you to sit so late at it.'

'Hout, sir, ye ken little about Scotland; it's no for want of gude vivers—the best of fish, flesh, and fowl hae we, by sybos, ingans, turneeps, and other garden fruit. But we hae mense and discretion, and are moderate of our mouths; but here, frae the kitchen to the ha', it's fill and fetch mair, frae the tae end of the four-and twenty till the tother. Even their fast days—they ca' it fasting when they hae the best o' sea-fish frae Hartlepool and Sunderland by land carriage, forbye trouts, grilses, salmon, and a' the lave o't, and so they make their very fasting a kind of luxury and abomination; and then the awfu' masses and matins of the puir deceived souls—but I shouldna speak about them, for your honour will be a Roman, I'se warrant, like the lave.'

'Not I, my friend; I was bred an English presbyterian, or dissenter.'

'The right hand of fellowship to your honour then,' quoth the gardener, with as much alacrity as his hard features were capable of expressing, and, as if to show that his good-will did not rest on words, he plucked forth a huge horn snuff-box, or mull, as he called it, and proffered me a pinch with a most fraternal grin.

Having accepted his courtesy, I asked him if he had been long a domestic at Osbaldistone Hall?

'I have been fighting with wild beasts at Ephesus,'* said he, looking towards the building, 'for the best part of these four-and-twenty years, as sure as my name's Andrew Fairservice.'

'But, my excellent friend Andrew Fairservice, if your religion and your temperance are so much offended by Roman rituals and southern hospitality, it seems to me that you must have been putting yourself to an unnecessary penance all this while, and that you might have found a service where they eat less, and are more orthodox in their worship. I dare say it cannot be want of skill which prevented your being placed more to your satisfaction.'

'It disna become me to speak to the point of my qualifications,' said Andrew, looking round him with great complacency; 'but nae doubt I should understand my trade of horticulture, seeing I was bred in the parish of Dreepdaily, where they raise lang-kale under glass, and force the early nettles for their spring kale.—And, to speak truth, I hae been flitting every term these four-and-twenty years; but when the time comes, there's aye something to saw that I would like to see sawn,—or something to maw that I would like to see mawn,—or something to ripe that I would like to see ripen,—and sae I e'en daiker on wi' the family frae year's end to year's end. And I wad say for certain, that I am gaun to quit at Cannlemas, only I was just as positive on it twenty years syne, and I find mysell still turning up the mouls here, for a' that. For-bye that, to tell your honour the even-down truth, there's nae better place ever offered to Andrew. But if your honour wad wush me to ony place where I wad hear pure doctrine, and hae a free cow's grass, and a cot, and a yard, and mair than ten punds of annual fee, and where there's nae leddy about the town to count the apples, I'se hold mysell muckle indebted t'ye.'

'Bravo, Andrew; I perceive you'll lose no preferment for want of asking patronage.'

'I canna see what for I should,' replied Andrew; 'it's no a generation to wait till ane's worth's discovered, I trow.'

'But you are no friend, I observe, to the ladies.'

'Na, by my troth, I keep up the first gardener's quarrel to them.*
They're fasheous bargains—aye crying for apricocks, pears, plums, and apples, summer and winter, without distinction o' seasons; but we hae nae slices o'the spare rib here, be praised for't! except auld Martha, and she's weel eneugh pleased wi' the freedom o' the berry-bushes to her sister's weans, when they come to drink tea in a holiday in the housekeeper's room, and wi' a wheen codlings now and then for her ain private supper.'

'You forget your young mistress.'

'What mistress do I forget?—whae's that?'

'Your young mistress, Miss Vernon.'

'What! the lassie Vernon?—She's nae mistress o' mine, man. I wish she was her ain mistress; and I wish she mayna be some other body's mistress or it's lang—She's a wild slip that.'

'Indeed!' said I, more interested than I cared to own to myself, or to show to the fellow—'why, Andrew, you know all the secrets of this family.'

'If I ken them, I can keep them,' said Andrew; 'they winna work in my wame like barm in a barrel, I'se warrant ye. Miss Die is—but it's neither beef nor brose o' mine.'

And he began to dig with a great semblance of assiduity.

'What is Miss Vernon, Andrew? I am a friend of the family, and should like to know.'

'Other than a gude ane, I'm fearing,' said Andrew, closing one eye hard, and shaking his head with a grave and mysterious look—'something glee'd—your honour understands me?'

'I cannot say I do,' said I, 'Andrew; but I should like to hear you explain yourself;' and therewithal I slipped a crown-piece into Andrew's horn-hard hand. The touch of the silver made him grin a ghastly smile, as he nodded slowly, and thrust it into his breeches pocket; and then, like a man who well understood that there was value to be returned, stood up, and rested his arms on his spade, with his features composed into the most important gravity, as for some serious communication.

'Ye maun ken, then, young gentleman, since it imports you to know, that Miss Vernon is'—

Here breaking off, he sucked in both his cheeks, till his lantern jaws and long chin assumed the appearance of a pair of nut-crackers; winked hard once more, frowned, shook his head, and seemed to think his physiognomy had completed the information which his tongue had not fully told.

'Good God!' said I, 'so young, so beautiful, so early lost!'

'Troth, ye may say sae—she's in a manner lost, body and saul; forby being a Papist, I'se uphaud her for'—and his northern caution prevailed, and he was again silent.

'For what, sir?' said I, sternly. 'I insist on knowing the plain meaning of all this.'

'Ou, just for the bitterest Jacobite in the haill shire.'

'Pshaw! a Jacobite?—is that all?'

Andrew looked at me with some astonishment, at hearing his information treated so lightly; and then muttering, 'Aweel, it's the warst thing I ken aboot the lassie, howsoe'er,' he resumed his spade, like the King of the Vandals, in Marmontel's late novel.*

CHAPTER VII

Bardolph. The sheriff, with a monstrous watch, is at the door.

*Henry IV. First Part**

I FOUND out with some difficulty the apartment which was destined for my accommodation; and, having secured myself the necessary good-will and attention from my uncle's domestics, by using the means they were most capable of comprehending, I secluded myself there for the remainder of the evening, conjecturing, from the fair way in which I had left my new relatives, as well as from the distant noise which continued to echo from the stone-hall, (as their banqueting-room was called,) that they were not likely to be fitting company for a sober man.

What could my father mean by sending me to be an inmate in this strange family? was my first and most natural reflection. My uncle, it was plain, received me as one who was to make some stay with him, and his rude hospitality rendered him as indifferent as King Hal to the number of those who fed at his cost.* But it was plain my presence or absence would be of as little importance in his eyes as that of one of his blue-coated serving-men. My cousins were mere cubs, in whose company I might, if I liked it, unlearn whatever decent manners, or elegant accomplishments, I had acquired, but where I could attain no information beyond what regarded worming dogs, rowelling horses,* and following foxes. I could only imagine one reason, which was probably the true one. My father considered the life which was led at Osbaldistone Hall as the natural and inevitable pursuits of all country gentlemen, and he was desirous, by giving me an opportunity of seeing that with which he knew I should be disgusted, to reconcile me, if possible, to take an active share in his own business. In the meantime, he would take Rashleigh Osbaldistone into the counting-house. But he had an hundred modes of providing for him, and that advantageously, whenever he chose to get rid of him. So that, although I did feel a certain qualm of conscience at having been the means of introducing Rashleigh, being such as he was described by Miss Vernon, into my father's business—perhaps into his confidence—I subdued it by the reflection, that my father was complete master of his own affairs—a man not to be imposed upon, or influenced by any one, and that all I knew to the young gentleman's prejudice was through the medium of a singular and giddy girl, whose communications were made with an injudicious frankness, which might warrant me in supposing her conclusions had been hastily or inaccurately formed. Then my mind naturally turned to Miss Vernon herself; her extreme beauty; her very peculiar situation, relying solely upon her reflections, and her own spirit, for guidance and protection; and her whole character offering that variety and spirit which piques our curiosity, and engages our attention in spite of ourselves. I had sense enough to consider the neighbourhood of this singular young lady, and the chance of our being thrown into very close and frequent intercourse, as adding to the dangers, while it relieved the dulness, of Osbaldistone Hall; but I could not, with the fullest exertion of my prudence, prevail upon myself to regret excessively this new and particular hazard to which I was to be exposed. This scruple I also settled as young men settle most difficulties of the kind—I would be very cautious, always on my guard, consider Miss Vernon rather as a companion than an intimate; and all would do well enough. With these reflections I fell asleep, Miss Vernon, of course, forming the last subject of my contemplation.

Whether I dreamed of her or not, I cannot satisfy you, for I was tired, and slept soundly. But she was the first person I thought of in the morning, when waked at dawn by the cheerful notes of the hunting-horn. To start up, and direct my horse to be saddled, was my first movement; and in a few minutes I was in the court-yard, where men, dogs, and horses, were in full preparation. My uncle, who, perhaps, was not entitled to expect a very alert sportsman in his nephew, bred as he had been in foreign parts, seemed rather surprised to see me, and I thought his morning salutation wanted something of the hearty and hospitable tone which distinguished his first welcome. 'Art there, lad?—ay, youth's aye rathe—but look to thysell—mind the old song, lad—

> "He that gallops his horse on Blackstone edge
> May chance to catch a fall." ' *

I believe there are few young men, and those very sturdy moralists, who would not rather be taxed with some moral peccadillo than with want of knowledge in horsemanship. As I was by no means deficient either in skill or courage, I resented my uncle's insinuation accordingly, and assured him he would find me up with the hounds.

'I doubtna, lad,' was his reply; 'thou'rt a rank rider, I'se warrant thee—but take heed. Thy father sent thee here to me to be bitted, and I doubt I must ride thee on the curb, or we'll hae some one to ride thee on the halter, if I takena the better heed.'

As this speech was totally unintelligible to me; as, besides, it did not seem to be delivered for my use, or benefit, but was spoken as it were aside, and as if expressing aloud something which was passing through the mind of my much-honoured uncle, I concluded it must either refer to my desertion of the bottle on the preceding evening, or that my uncle's morning hours being a little discomposed by the revels of the night before, his temper had suffered in proportion. I only made the passing reflection, that if he played the ungracious landlord, I would remain the shorter while his guest, and then hastened to salute Miss Vernon, who advanced cordially to meet me. Some show of greeting also passed between my cousins and me; but as I saw them maliciously bent upon criticising my dress and accoutrements, from the cap to the stirrup-irons, and sneering at whatever had a new or foreign appearance, I exempted myself from the task of paying them much attention; and assuming, in requital of their grins and whispers, an air of the utmost indifference and contempt, I attached myself to Miss Vernon as the only person in the party whom I could regard as a suitable companion. By her side, therefore, we sallied forth to the destined cover, which was a dingle or copse on the side of an extensive common. As we rode thither, I observed to Diana, that I did not see my cousin Rashleigh in the field; to which she replied,—'O no—he's a mighty hunter, but it's after the fashion of Nimrod,* and his game is man.'

The dogs now brushed into the cover, with the appropriate encouragement from the hunters—all was business, bustle, and activity. My cousins were soon too much interested in the business of the morning to take any further notice of me, unless that I overheard Dickon the horse-jockey whisper to Wilfred the fool—'Look thou, an our French cousin be nat off a' first burst.'

To which Wilfred answered, 'Like enow, for he has a queer outlandish binding on's castor.'

Thorncliff, however, who, in his rude way, seemed not absolutely insensible to the beauty of his kinswoman, appeared determined to keep us company more closely than his brothers, perhaps to watch what passed betwixt Miss Vernon and me—perhaps to enjoy my expected mishaps in the chase. In the last particular he was disappointed. After beating in vain for the greater part of the morning, a fox was at length found, who led us a chase of two hours, in the course of which, notwithstanding the ill-omened French binding upon my hat, I sustained my character as a horseman to the admiration of my uncle and Miss Vernon, and the secret disappointment of those who expected me to disgrace it. Reynard, however, proved too wily for his pursuers, and the hounds were at fault. I could at this time observe in Miss Vernon's manner an impatience of the close attendance which we received from Thorncliff Osbaldistone; and, as that active-spirited young lady never hesitated at taking the readiest means to gratify any wish of the moment, she said to him, in a tone of reproach—'I wonder, Thornie, what keeps you dangling at my horse's crupper all this morning, when you know the earths above Woolverton-mill are not stopt.'

'I know no such an thing then, Miss Die, for the miller swore himself as black as night, that he stopt them at twelve o'clock, midnight that was.'

'O fie upon you, Thornie, would you trust to a miller's word?*— and these earths, too, where we lost the fox three times this season, and you on your grey mare that can gallop there and back in ten minutes!'

'Well, Miss Die, I'se go to Woolverton then, and if the earths are not stopt, I'se raddle Dick the miller's bones for him.'

'Do, my dear Thornie; horsewhip the rascal to purpose—via*—fly away, and about it;'—Thorncliff went off at the gallop—'or get horse-whip yourself, which will serve my purpose just as well.—I must teach them all discipline and obedience to the word of command. I am raising a regiment, you must know. Thornie shall be my sergeant-major, Dickon my riding-master, and Wilfred, with his deep dub-a-dub tones, that speak but three syllables at a time, my kettle-drummer.'

'And Rashleigh?'

'Rashleigh shall be my scout-master.'*

'And will you find no employment for me, most lovely colonel?'

'You shall have the choice of being paymaster, or plunder-master, to the corps. But see how the dogs puzzle about there. Come, Mr Frank, the scent's cold; they won't recover it there this while; follow me, I have a view to show you.'

And, in fact, she cantered up to the top of a gentle hill, commanding an extensive prospect. Casting her eyes around, to see that no one was near us, she drew up her horse beneath a few birch-trees, which screened us from the rest of the hunting-field,—'Do you see yon peaked, brown, heathy hill, having something like a whitish speck upon the side?'

'Terminating that long ridge of broken moorish uplands?—I see it distinctly.'

'That whitish speck is a rock called Hawkesmore-crag, and Hawkesmore-crag is in Scotland.'

'Indeed? I did not think we had been so near Scotland.'

'It is so, I assure you, and your horse will carry you there in two hours.'

'I shall hardly give him the trouble; why, the distance must be eighteen miles as the crow flies.'

'You may have my mare, if you think her less blown—I say, that in two hours you may be in Scotland.'

'And I say, that I have so little desire to be there, that if my horse's head were over the Border, I would not give his tail the trouble of following. What should I do in Scotland?'

'Provide for your safety, if I must speak plainly. Do you understand me now, Mr Frank?'

'Not a whit; you are more and more oracular.'

'Then, on my word, you either mistrust me most unjustly, and are a better dissembler than Rashleigh Osbaldistone himself, or you know nothing of what is imputed to you; and then no wonder you stare at me in that grave manner, which I can scarce see without laughing.'

'Upon my word of honour, Miss Vernon,' said I, with an impatient feeling of her childish disposition to mirth, 'I have not the most distant conception of what you mean. I am happy to afford you any subject of amusement, but I am quite ignorant in what it consists.'

'Nay, there's no sound jest after all,' said the young lady, composing herself, 'only one looks so very ridiculous when he is fairly perplexed; but the matter is serious enough. Do you know one Moray, or Morris, or some such name?'

'Not that I can at present recollect.'

'Think a moment—Did you not lately travel with somebody of such a name?'

'The only man with whom I travelled for any length of time was a fellow whose soul seemed to lie in his portmanteau.'

'Then it was like the soul of the licentiate Pedro Garcias,* which lay among the ducats in his leathern purse. That man has been robbed, and he has lodged an information against you, as connected with the violence done to him.'

'You jest, Miss Vernon!'

'I do not, I assure you—the thing is an absolute fact.'

'And do you,' said I, with strong indignation, which I did not attempt to suppress, 'do you suppose me capable of meriting such a charge?'

'You would call me out for it, I suppose, had I the advantage of being a man—You may do so as it is, if you like it—I can shoot flying, as well as leap a five-barred gate.'*

'And are colonel of a regiment of horse besides,' replied I, reflecting how idle it was to be angry with her—'But do explain the present jest to me!'

'There's no jest whatever,' said Diana; 'you are accused of robbing this man, and my uncle believes it as well as I did.'

'Upon my honour, I am greatly obliged to my friends for their good opinion!'

'Now do not, if you can help it, snort, and stare, and snuff the wind, and look so exceedingly like a startled horse—There's no such offence as you suppose—you are not charged with any petty larceny, or vulgar felony—by no means. This fellow was carrying money from government, both specie and bills, to pay the troops in the north; and it is said he has been also robbed of some dispatches of great consequence.'

'And so it is high treason, then, and not simple robbery, of which I am accused?'

'Certainly; which, you know, has been in all ages accounted the crime of a gentleman. You will find plenty in this country, and one not far from your elbow, who think it a merit to distress the Hanoverian government by every means possible.'

'Neither my politics nor my morals, Miss Vernon, are of a description so accommodating.'

'I really begin to believe that you are a presbyterian and Hanoverian in good earnest. But what do you propose to do?'

'Instantly to refute this atrocious calumny.—Before whom,' I asked, 'was this extraordinary accusation laid?'

'Before old Squire Inglewood, who had sufficient unwillingness to receive it. He sent tidings to my uncle, I suppose, that he might smuggle you away into Scotland, out of reach of the warrant. But my uncle is sensible that his religion and old predilections render him obnoxious to government, and that, were he caught playing booty,* he would be disarmed, and probably dismounted, (which would be the worse evil of the two,) as a Jacobite, Papist, and suspected person.'[35]

'I can conceive that, sooner than lose his hunters, he would give up his nephew.'

'His nephew, nieces, sons—daughters, if he had them, and whole generation,' said Diana; 'therefore trust not to him, even for a single moment, but make the best of your way before they can serve the warrant.'

'That I shall certainly do; but it shall be to the house of this Squire Inglewood—Which way does it lie?'

'About five miles off, in the low ground, behind yonder plantations—you may see the tower of the clock-house.'

'I will be there in a few minutes,' said I, putting my horse in motion.

'And I will go with you, and show you the way,' said Diana, putting her palfrey also to the trot.

'Do not think of it, Miss Vernon,' I replied. 'It is not—permit me the freedom of a friend—it is not proper, scarcely even delicate, in you to go with me on such an errand as I am now upon.'

'I understand your meaning,' said Miss Vernon, a slight blush crossing her haughty brow;—'it is plainly spoken,'—and after a moment's pause she added, 'and I believe kindly meant.'

'It is indeed, Miss Vernon; can you think me insensible of the interest you show me, or ungrateful for it?' said I, with even more earnestness than I could have wished to express. 'Yours is meant for true kindness, shown best at the hour of need. But I must not, for your own sake—for the chance of misconstruction—suffer you to pursue the dictates of your generosity; this is so public an occasion—it is almost like venturing into an open court of justice.'

'And if it were not almost, but altogether entering into an open court of justice, do you think I would not go there if I thought it right, and wished to protect a friend? You have no one to stand by you—you are a stranger; and here, in the outskirts of the kingdom, country justices do odd things. My uncle has no desire to embroil himself in your affair;— Rashleigh is absent, and were he here, there is no knowing which side he might take; the rest are all more stupid and brutal one than another. I will go with you, and I do not fear being able to serve you. I am no fine lady, to be terrified to death with law books, hard words, or big wigs.'

'But, my dear Miss Vernon'——

'But, my dear Mr Francis, be patient and quiet, and let me take my own way; for when I take the bit between my teeth, there is no bridle will stop me.'

Flattered with the interest so lovely a creature seemed to take in my fate, yet vexed at the ridiculous appearance I should make, by carrying a girl of eighteen along with me as an advocate, and seriously concerned for the misconstruction to which her motives might be exposed, I endeavoured to combat her resolution to accompany me to Squire Inglewood's. The self-willed girl told me roundly, that my dissuasions were absolutely in vain; that she was a true Vernon, whom no consideration, not even that of being able to do but little to assist him, should induce to abandon a friend in distress; and that all I could say on the subject might be very well for pretty, well-educated, well-behaved misses from a town boarding-school, but did not apply to her, who was accustomed to mind nobody's opinion but her own.

While she spoke thus, we were advancing hastily towards Inglewood-Place, while, as if to divert me from the task of farther remonstrance, she drew a ludicrous picture of the magistrate and his clerk. Inglewood was, according to her description, a white-washed Jacobite, that is, one who, having been long a non-juror,* like most of the other gentlemen of the country, had lately qualified himself to act as a justice, by taking the oaths to government. 'He had done so,' she said, 'in compliance with the urgent request of most of his brother squires, who saw, with regret, that the palladium* of silvan sport, the game-laws, were likely to fall into disuse for want of a magistrate who would enforce them; the nearest acting justice being the Mayor of Newcastle, and he, as being rather inclined to the consumption of the game when properly dressed, than to its preservation when alive, was more partial, of course, to the cause of the poacher than of the sportsman. Resolving, therefore, that it was expedient some one of their number should sacrifice the scruples of Jacobitical loyalty to the good of the community, the Northumbrian country gentlemen imposed the duty on Inglewood, who, being very inert in most of his feelings and sentiments, might, they thought, comply with any political creed without much repugnance. Having thus procured the body of justice, they proceeded,' continued Miss Vernon, 'to attach to it a clerk, by way of soul, to direct and animate its movements. Accordingly, they got a sharp Newcastle attorney, called Jobson, who, to vary my metaphor, finds it a good thing enough to retail justice at the sign of Squire Inglewood, and, as his own emoluments depend on the quantity of business which he transacts, he hooks in his principal for a great deal more employment in the justice line than the honest squire had ever bargained for; so that no apple-wife within the circuit of ten miles can settle her account with a coster-monger without an audience of the reluctant Justice and his alert clerk, Mr Joseph Jobson. But the most ridiculous scenes occur when affairs come before him, like our business of to-day, having any colouring of politics. Mr Joseph Jobson (for which, no doubt, he has his own very sufficient reasons) is a prodigious zealot for the Protestant religion, and a great friend to the present establishment in church and state. Now, his principal, retaining a sort of instinctive attachment to the opinions which he professed openly, until he relaxed his political creed, with the patriotic view of enforcing the law against unauthorized destroyers of black-game, grouse, partridges, and hares, is peculiarly embarrassed when his alert assistant involves him in judicial proceedings connected with his earlier faith; and, instead of seconding his zeal, he seldom fails to oppose to it a double dose of indolence and lack of exertion. And this inactivity does not by any means arise from actual stupidity. On the contrary, for one whose principal delight is in eating and drinking, he is an alert, joyous, and lively old soul, which makes his assumed dulness the more diverting. So you may see Jobson on such occasions, like a bit of a broken-down blood-tit condemned to drag an overloaded cart, puffing, strutting, and spluttering, to get the Justice put in motion, while, though the wheels groan, creak, and revolve slowly, the great and preponderating weight of the vehicle fairly frustrates the efforts of the willing quadruped, and prevents its being brought into a state of actual progression. Nay more, the unfortunate pony, I understand, has been heard to complain, that this same car of justice, which he finds it so hard to put in motion on some occasions, can on others run fast enough down hill of its own accord, dragging his reluctant self backwards along with it, when any thing can be done of service to Squire Inglewood's quondam friends. And then Mr Jobson talks big about reporting his principal to the Secretary of State for the Home Department, if it were not for his particular regard and friendship for Mr Inglewood and his family.'

As Miss Vernon concluded this whimsical description, we found ourselves in front of Inglewood Place, a handsome, though old-fashioned building, which showed the consequence of the family.

CHAPTER VIII

'Sir,' quoth the Lawyer, 'not to flatter ye,
You have as good and fair a battery
As heart could wish, and need not shame
The proudest man alive to claim.'

BUTLER*

OUR horses were taken by a servant in Sir Hildebrand's livery, whom we found in the court-yard, and we entered the house. In the entrance-hall I was somewhat surprised, and my fair companion still more so, when we met Rashleigh Osbaldistone, who could not help showing equal wonder at our rencontre.

'Rashleigh,' said Miss Vernon, without giving him time to ask any question, 'you have heard of Mr Francis Osbaldistone's affair, and you have been talking to the Justice about it?'

'Certainly,' said Rashleigh, composedly, 'it has been my business here. I have been endeavouring,' he said, with a bow to me, 'to render my cousin what service I can. But I am sorry to meet him here.'

'As a friend and relation, Mr Osbaldistone, you ought to have been sorry to have met me anywhere else, at a time when the charge of my reputation required me to be on this spot as soon as possible.'

'True; but, judging from what my father said, I should have supposed a short retreat into Scotland—just till matters should be smoothed over in a quiet way'——

I answered with warmth, 'That I had no prudential measures to observe, and desired to have nothing smoothed over; on the contrary, I was come to enquire into a rascally calumny, which I was determined to probe to the bottom.'

'Mr Francis Osbaldistone is an innocent man, Rashleigh,' said Miss Vernon, 'and he demands an investigation of the charge against him, and I intend to support him in it.'

'You do, my pretty cousin?—I should think, now, Mr Francis Osbaldistone was likely to be as effectually, and rather more delicately, supported by my presence than by yours.'

'O certainly; but two heads are better than one, you know.'

'Especially such a head as yours, my pretty Die,' advancing, and

taking her hand with a familiar fondness, which made me think him
fifty times uglier than nature had made him. She led him, however, a
few steps aside; they conversed in an under voice, and she appeared to
insist upon some request, which he was unwilling or unable to comply
with. I never saw so strong a contrast betwixt the expression of two
faces. Miss Vernon's from being earnest became angry. Her eyes and
cheeks became more animated, her colour mounted, she clenched her
little hand, and, stamping on the ground with her tiny foot, seemed to
listen with a mixture of contempt and indignation to the apologies,
which, from his look of civil deference, his composed and respectful
smile, his body rather drawing back than advanced, and other signs of
look and person, I concluded him to be pouring out at her feet. At
length she flung away from him, with 'I *will* have it so.'

'It is not in my power—there is no possibility of it.—Would you
think it, Mr Osbaldistone?' said he, addressing me——

'You are not mad?' said she, interrupting him.

'Would you think it?' said he, without attending to her hint—'Miss
Vernon insists, not only that I know your innocence, (of which, indeed,
it is impossible for any one to be more convinced,) but that I must also
be acquainted with the real perpetrators of the outrage on this fellow—if, indeed, such an outrage has been committed. Is this reasonable, Mr Osbaldistone?'

'I will not allow any appeal to Mr Osbaldistone, Rashleigh,' said
the young lady; 'he does not know, as I do, the incredible extent and
accuracy of your information on all points.'

'As I am a gentleman, you do me more honour than I deserve.'

'Justice, Rashleigh—only justice—and it is only justice which I
expect at your hands.'

'You are a tyrant, Diana,' he answered, with a sort of sigh—'a capricious tyrant, and rule your friends with a rod of iron. Still, however, it
shall be as you desire. But you ought not to be here—you know you
ought not—you must return with me.'

Then turning from Diana, who seemed to stand undecided, he
came up to me in the most friendly manner, and said, 'Do not doubt my
interest in what regards you, Mr Osbaldistone. If I leave you just at this
moment, it is only to act for your advantage. But you must use your
influence with your cousin to return; her presence cannot serve you,
and must prejudice herself.'

'I assure you, sir,' I replied, 'you cannot be more convinced of this than I; I have urged Miss Vernon's return as anxiously as she would permit me to do.'

'I have thought on it,' said Miss Vernon, after a pause, 'and I will not go till I see you safe out of the hands of the Philistines. Cousin Rashleigh, I dare say, means well; but he and I know each other well.— Rashleigh, I will NOT go;—I know,' she added, in a more soothing tone, 'my being here will give you more motive for speed and exertion.'

'Stay, then, rash, obstinate girl,' said Rashleigh; 'you know but too well to whom you trust;' and hastening out of the hall, we heard his horse's feet a minute afterwards in rapid motion.

'Thank Heaven, he is gone!' said Diana. 'And now, let us seek out the Justice.'

'Had we not better call a servant?'

'O, by no means; I know the way to his den—we must burst on him suddenly—follow me.'

I did follow her accordingly, as she tripped up a few gloomy steps, traversed a twilight passage, and entered a sort of anteroom, hung round with old maps, architectural elevations, and genealogical trees. A pair of folding-doors opened from this into Mr Inglewood's sitting apartment, from which was heard the fag-end of an old ditty, chanted by a voice which had been in its day fit for a jolly bottle-song.

> 'O, in Skipton-in-Craven,*
> Is never a haven,
>   But many a day foul weather;
> And he that would say
> A pretty girl nay,
>   I wish for his cravat a tether.'—

'Hey day!' said Miss Vernon, 'the genial Justice must have dined already—I did not think it had been so late.'

It was even so. Mr Inglewood's appetite having been sharpened by his official investigations, he had ante-dated his meridian repast, having dined at twelve instead of one o'clock, then the general dining hour in England. The various occurrences of the morning occasioned our arriving some time after this hour, to the Justice the most important of the four-and-twenty, and he had not neglected the interval.

'Stay you here,' said Diana; 'I know the house, and I will call a servant; your sudden appearance might startle the old gentleman even to choking;' and she escaped from me, leaving me uncertain whether I ought to advance or retreat. It was impossible for me not to hear some part of what passed within the dinner apartment, and particularly several apologies for declining to sing, expressed in a dejected croaking voice, the tones of which, I conceived, were not entirely new to me.

'Not sing, sir? by our Lady! but you must—What! you have cracked my silver-mounted cocoa-nut of sack, and tell me that you cannot sing!—Sir, sack will make a cat sing, and speak too; so up with a merry stave, or trundle yourself out of my doors—Do you think you are to take up all my valuable time with your d—d declarations, and then tell me you cannot sing?'

'Your worship is perfectly in rule,' said another voice, which, from its pert conceited accent, might be that of the clerk, 'and the party must be conformable; he hath *canet** written on his face in court hand.'

'Up with it, then,' said the Justice, 'or, by St Christopher, you shall crack the cocoa-nut full of salt-and-water, according to the statute for such effect made and provided.'

Thus exhorted and threatened, my quondam fellow-traveller, for I could no longer doubt that he was the recusant in question, uplifted, with a voice similar to that of a criminal singing his last psalm on the scaffold, a most doleful stave to the following effect:

> 'Good people all, I pray give ear,*
> A woful story you shall hear,
> 'Tis of a robber as stout as ever
> Bade a true man stand and deliver.
>   With his foodle doo fa loodle loo

> 'This knave, most worthy of a cord,
> Being arm'd with pistol and with sword,
> 'Twixt Kensington and Brentford then
> Did boldly stop six honest men.
>   With his foodle doo, &c.

> 'These honest men did at Brentford dine,
> Having drank each man his pint of wine,
> When this bold thief, with many curses,
> Did say, You dogs, your lives or purses.
>   With his foodle doo,' &c.

I question if the honest men, whose misfortune is commemorated in this pathetic ditty, were more startled at the appearance of the bold thief, than the songster was at mine; for, tired of waiting for some one to announce me, and finding my situation as a listener rather awkward, I presented myself to the company just as my friend Mr Morris, for such, it seems, was his name, was uplifting the fifth stave of his doleful ballad. The high tone, with which the tune started, died away in a quaver of consternation, on finding himself so near one whose character he supposed to be little less suspicious than that of the hero of his madrigal, and he remained silent, with a mouth gaping as if I had brought the Gorgon's head* in my hand.

The Justice, whose eyes had closed under the influence of the somniferous lullaby of the song, started up in his chair as it suddenly ceased, and stared with wonder at the unexpected addition which the company had received, while his organs of sight were in abeyance. The clerk, as I conjectured him to be from his appearance, was also commoved; for, sitting opposite to Mr Morris, that honest gentleman's terror communicated itself to him, though he wotted not why.

I broke the silence of surprise occasioned by my abrupt entrance.—— 'My name, Mr Inglewood, is Francis Osbaldistone; I understand that some scoundrel has brought a complaint before you, charging me with being concerned in a loss which he says he has sustained.'

'Sir,' said the Justice, somewhat peevishly, 'these are matters I never enter upon after dinner—there is a time for every thing, and a justice of peace must eat as well as other folks.'

The goodly person of Mr Inglewood, by the way, seemed by no means to have suffered by any fasts, whether in the service of the law or of religion.

'I beg pardon for an ill-timed visit, sir; but as my reputation is concerned, and as the dinner appears to be concluded'——

'It is not concluded, sir,' replied the magistrate; 'man requires digestion as well as food, and I protest I cannot have benefit from my victuals, unless I am allowed two hours of quiet leisure, intermixed with harmless mirth, and a moderate circulation of the bottle.'

'If your honour will forgive me,' said Mr Jobson, who had produced and arranged his writing implements in the brief space that our conversation afforded; 'as this is a case of felony, and the gentleman seems something impatient, the charge is *contra pacem domini regis*'*——

'D——n *dominie regis*!' said the impatient Justice—'I hope it's no treason to say so;—but it's enough to make one mad to be worried in this way—have I a moment of my life quiet, for warrants, orders, directions, acts, bails, bonds, and recognisances?—I pronounce to you, Mr Jobson, that I shall send you and the justice-ship to the devil one of these days.'

'Your honour will consider the dignity of the office—one of the quorum and custos rotulorum,* an office of which Sir Edward Coke wisely saith, The whole Christian world hath not the like of it, so it be duly executed.'*

'Well,' said the Justice, partly reconciled by this eulogium on the dignity of his situation, and gulping down the rest of his dissatisfaction in a huge bumper of claret, 'let us to this gear then, and get rid of it as fast as we can.—Here you, sir—you, Morris—you, knight of the sorrowful countenance*—is this Mr Francis Osbaldistone the gentleman whom you charge with being art and part of* felony?'

'I, sir?' replied Morris, whose scattered wits had hardly yet reassembled themselves—'I charge nothing—I say nothing against the gentleman.'

'Then we dismiss your complaint, sir, that's all, and a good riddance—Push about the bottle—Mr Osbaldistone, help yourself.'

Jobson, however, was determined that Morris should not back out of the scrape so easily. 'What do you mean, Mr Morris?—Here is your own declaration—the ink scarce dried—and you would retract it in this scandalous manner!'

'How do I know,' whispered the other, in a tremulous tone, 'how many rogues are in the house to back him?—I have read of such things in Johnson's Lives of the Highwaymen.* I protest the door opens'——

And it did open, and Diana Vernon entered—'You keep fine order here, Justice—not a servant to be seen or heard of.'

'Ah!' said the Justice, starting up with an alacrity, which showed that he was not so engrossed by his devotions to Themis, or Comus,* as to forget what was due to beauty—'Ah, ha! Die Vernon, the heath-bell of Cheviot, and the blossom of the Border, come to see how the old bachelor keeps house?—Art welcome, girl, as flowers in May.'

'A fine, open, hospitable house you do keep, Justice, that must be allowed—not a soul to answer a visitor.'

'Ah! the knaves, they reckoned themselves secure of me for a couple of hours—But why did you not come earlier?—Your cousin Rashleigh dined here, and ran away like a poltroon after the first bottle was out—But you have not dined—we'll have something nice and ladylike—sweet and pretty, like yourself, tossed up in a trice.'

'I may eat a crust in the anteroom before I set out,' answered Miss Vernon—'I have had a long ride this morning; but I can't stay long, Justice—I came with my cousin, Frank Osbaldistone, there, and I must show him the way back again to the Hall, or he'll lose himself in the wolds.'

'Whew! sits the wind in that quarter?'* enquired the Justice.

> 'She show'd him the way, and she show'd him the way,
>   She show'd him the way to woo.'*

What! no luck for old fellows, then, my sweet bud of the wilderness?'

'None whatever, Squire Inglewood; but if you will be a good kind Justice, and dispatch young Frank's business, and let us canter home again, I'll bring my uncle to dine with you next week, and we'll expect merry doings.'

'And you shall find them, my pearl of the Tyne—Zookers, lass, I never envy these young fellows their rides and scampers, unless when you come across me. But I must not keep you just now, I suppose?—I am quite satisfied with Mr Francis Osbaldistone's explanation—here has been some mistake, which can be cleared at greater leisure.'

'Pardon me, sir,' said I, 'but I have not heard the nature of the accusation yet.'

'Yes, sir,' said the clerk, who, at the appearance of Miss Vernon, had given up the matter in despair, but who picked up courage to press farther investigation, on finding himself supported from a quarter whence assuredly he expected no backing—'Yes, sir, and Dalton* saith, That he who is apprehended as a felon shall not be discharged upon any man's discretion, but shall be held either to bail or commitment, paying to the clerk of the peace the usual fees for recognisance or commitment.'

The Justice, thus goaded on, gave me at length a few words of explanation.

It seems the tricks which I had played to this man, Morris, had made a strong impression on his imagination; for I found they had been arrayed against me in his evidence, with all the exaggerations which a timorous and heated imagination could suggest. It appeared also, that, on the day he parted from me, he had been stopped on a solitary spot, and eased of his beloved travelling-companion, the portmanteau, by two men, well mounted and armed, having their faces covered with vizards.

One of them, he conceived, had much of my shape and air, and in a whispering conversation which took place betwixt the freebooters, he heard the other apply to him the name of Osbaldistone. The declaration farther set forth, that upon enquiring into the principles of the family so named, he, the said declarant, was informed, that they were of the worst description, the family, in all its members, having been Papists and Jacobites, as he was given to understand by the dissenting clergyman at whose house he stopped after his rencontre, since the days of William the Conqueror.

Upon all, and each of these weighty reasons, he charged me with being accessory to the felony committed upon his person; he, the said declarant, then travelling in the special employment of government, and having charge of certain important papers, and also a large sum in specie, to be paid over, according to his instructions, to certain persons of official trust and importance in Scotland.

Having heard this extraordinary accusation, I replied to it, that the circumstances on which it was founded were such as could warrant no justice, or magistrate, in any attempt on my personal liberty. I admitted that I had practised a little upon the terrors of Mr Morris, while we travelled together, but in such trifling particulars as could have excited apprehension in no one who was one whit less timorous and jealous than himself. But I added, that I had never seen him since we parted, and if that which he feared had really come upon him, I was in nowise accessory to an action so unworthy of my character and station in life. That one of the robbers was called Osbaldistone, or that such a name was mentioned in the course of the conversation betwixt them, was a trifling circumstance, to which no weight was due. And concerning the disaffection alleged against me, I was willing to prove, to the satisfaction of the Justice, the clerk, and even the witness himself, that I was of the same persuasion as his friend the dissenting clergyman; had been educated as a good subject in the principles of the Revolution, and as such now demanded the personal protection of the laws which had been assured by that great event.

The Justice fidgeted, took snuff, and seemed considerably embarrassed, while Mr Attorney Jobson, with all the volubility of his profession, ran over the statute of the 34 Edward III.,* by which justices of the peace are allowed to arrest all those whom they find by indictment or suspicion, and to put them into prison. The rogue even turned my own admissions against me, alleging, 'that since I had confessedly, upon my own showing, assumed the bearing or deportment of a robber or malefactor, I had voluntarily subjected myself to the suspicions of which I complained, and brought myself within the compass of the act, having wilfully clothed my conduct with all the colour and livery of guilt.'

I combated both his arguments and his jargon with much indignation and scorn, and observed, 'that I should, if necessary, produce the bail of my relations, which I conceived could not be refused, without subjecting the magistrate in a misdemeanour.'

'Pardon me, my good sir,—pardon me,' said the insatiable clerk, 'this is a case in which neither bail nor mainprize can be received, the felon who is liable to be committed on heavy grounds of suspicion, not being replevisable under the statute of the 3d of King Edward,* there being in that act an express exception of such as be charged of commandment, or force, and aid of felony done;' and he hinted, that his worship would do well to remember that such were no way replevisable by common writ, nor without writ.

At this period of the conversation a servant entered, and delivered a letter to Mr Jobson. He had no sooner run it hastily over, than he exclaimed, with the air of one who wished to appear much vexed at the interruption, and felt the consequence attached to a man of multifarious avocations—'Good God!—why, at this rate, I shall have neither time to attend to the public concerns nor my own—no rest—no quiet—I wish to Heaven another gentleman in our line would settle here!'

'God forbid!' said the Justice, in a tone of *sotto-voce* deprecation; 'some of us have enough of one of the tribe.'

'This is a matter of life and death, if your worship pleases.'

'In God's name! no more justice business, I hope,' said the alarmed magistrate.

'No—no,' replied Mr Jobson, very consequentially; 'old Gaffer Rutledge of Grime's-hill, is sub-pœna'd for the next world; he has sent an express for Dr Kill-down to put in bail—another for me to arrange his worldly affairs.'

'Away with you, then,' said Mr Inglewood hastily; 'his may not be a replevisable case under the statute, you know, or Mr Justice Death may not like the doctor for a *main pernor*, or bailsman.'*

'And yet,' said Jobson, lingering as he moved towards the door, 'if my presence here be necessary—I could make out the warrant for committal in a moment, and the constable is below—And you have heard,' he said, lowering his voice, 'Mr Rashleigh's opinion'—the rest was lost in a whisper.

The Justice replied aloud, 'I tell thee no, man, no—we'll do nought till thou return, man; 'tis but a four-mile ride—Come, push the bottle, Mr Morris—Don't be cast down, Mr Osbaldistone—And you, my rose of the wilderness—one cup of claret to refresh the bloom of your cheeks.'

Diana started, as if from a reverie, in which she appeared to have been plunged while we held this discussion. 'No, Justice, I should be afraid of transferring the bloom to a part of my face where it would show to little advantage. But I will pledge you in a cooler beverage;' and, filling a glass with water, she drank it hastily, while her hurried manner belied her assumed gaiety.

I had not much leisure to make remarks upon her demeanour, however, being full of vexation at the interference of fresh obstacles to an instant examination of the disgraceful and impertinent charge which was brought against me. But there was no moving the Justice to take the matter up in absence of his clerk, an incident which gave him apparently as much pleasure as a holiday to a schoolboy. He persisted in his endeavours to inspire jollity into a company, the individuals of which, whether considered with reference to each other, or to their respective situations, were by no means inclined to mirth. 'Come, Master Morris, you're not the first man that's been robbed, I trow—grieving ne'er brought back loss, man.—And you, Mr Frank Osbaldistone, are not the first bully-boy that has said stand to a true man. There was Jack Winterfield, in my young days, kept the best company in the land—at horse-races and cock-fights who but he—hand and glove was I with Jack.—Push the bottle, Mr Morris, it's dry talking—Many quart bumpers have I cracked, and thrown many a merry main with poor Jack—good family—ready wit—quick eye—as honest a fellow, barring the deed he died for—we'll drink to his memory, gentlemen—Poor Jack Winterfield—And since we talk of him, and of those sort of things, and since that d—d clerk of mine has taken his gibberish elsewhere, and since we're snug among ourselves, Mr Osbaldistone, if you will have my best advice, I would take up this matter*—the law's hard—very severe—hanged poor Jack Winterfield at York, despite family connexions and great interest—all for easing a fat west-country grazier of the price of a few beasts—Now, here is honest

Mr Morris has been frightened, and so forth—D—n it, man, let the poor fellow have back his portmanteau, and end the frolic at once.'

Morris's eyes brightened up at this suggestion, and he began to hesitate forth an assurance that he thirsted for no man's blood, when I cut the proposed accommodation short, by resenting the Justice's suggestion as an insult, that went directly to suppose me guilty of the very crime which I had come to his house with the express intention of disavowing. We were in this awkward predicament, when a servant, opening the door, announced, 'A strange gentleman to wait upon his honour;' and the party whom he thus described entered the room without farther ceremony.

CHAPTER IX

One of the thieves come back again! I'll stand close.
He dares not wrong me now, so near the house,
And call in vain 'tis, till I see him offer it.

*The Widow**

'A STRANGER!' echoed the Justice,—'not upon business, I trust, for I'll be'——

His protestation was cut short by the answer of the man himself. 'My business is of a nature somewhat onerous and particular,' said my acquaintance Mr Campbell,—for it was he, the very Scotchman whom I had seen at Northallerton,—'and I must solicit your honour to give instant and heedful consideration to it—I believe, Mr Morris,' he added, fixing his eye on that person with a look of peculiar firmness and almost ferocity—'I believe ye ken brawly what I am—I believe ye cannot have forgotten what passed at our last meeting on the road?' Morris's jaw dropped—his countenance became the colour of tallow—his teeth chattered, and he gave visible signs of the utmost consternation. 'Take heart of grace, man,' said Campbell, 'and dinna sit clattering your jaws there like a pair of castanets! I think there can be nae difficulty in your telling Mr Justice, that ye have seen me of yore, and ken me to be a cavalier of fortune, and a man of honour.—Ye ken fu'weel ye will be some time resident in my vicinity, when I may have the power, as I will possess the inclination, to do you as good a turn.'

'Sir—sir—I believe you to be a man of honour, and, as you say, a man of fortune.—Yes, Mr Inglewood,' he added, clearing his voice, 'I really believe this gentleman to be so.'

'And what are this gentleman's commands with me?' said the Justice, somewhat peevishly. 'One man introduces another, like the rhymes in the "house that Jack built," and I get company without either peace or conversation!'

'Both shall be yours, sir,' answered Campbell, 'in a brief period of time. I come to release your mind from a piece of troublesome duty, not to make increment to it.'

'Body o' me! then you are welcome as ever Scot was to England, and that's not saying much—but get on, man, let's hear what you have got to say at once.'

'I presume this gentleman,' continued the North Briton, 'told you there was a person of the name of Campbell with him, when he had the mischance to lose his valise?'

'He has not mentioned such a name, from beginning to end of the matter,' said the Justice.

'Ah! I conceive—I conceive,' replied Mr Campbell; 'Mr Morris was kindly afeared of committing a stranger into collision wi' the judicial forms of the country; but as I understand my evidence is necessary to the compurgation of ane honest gentleman here, Mr Francis Osbaldistone, wha has been most unjustly suspected, I will dispense with the precaution—Ye will, therefore, (he added, addressing Morris with the same determined look and accent,) please tell Mr Justice Inglewood, whether we did not travel several miles together on the road, in consequence of your own anxious request and suggestion, reiterated ance and again, baith on the evening that we were at Northallerton, and there declined by me, but afterwards accepted, when I overtook ye on the road near Cloberry Allers, and was prevailed on by you to resign my ain intentions of proceeding to Rothbury; and, for my misfortune, to accompany you on your proposed route.'

'It's a melancholy truth,' answered Morris, holding down his head, as he gave this general assent to the long and leading question which Campbell put to him, and seeming to acquiesce in the statement it contained with rueful docility.

'And I presume you can also asseverate to his worship, that no man is better qualified than I am to bear testimony in this case, seeing that I was by you, and near you, constantly during the whole occurrence?'

'No man better qualified, certainly,' said Morris, with a deep and embarrassed sigh.

'And why the devil did you not assist him then,' said the Justice, 'since, by Mr Morris's account, there were but two robbers; so you were two to two, and you are both stout likely men?'

'Sir, if it please your worship,' said Campbell, 'I have been all my life a man of peace and quietness, no ways given to broils or batteries. Mr Morris, who belongs, as I understand, or hath belonged, to his Majesty's army, might have used his pleasure in resistance, he travelling, as I also understand, with a great charge of treasure; but for me, who had but my own small peculiar to defend, and who am, moreover, a man of a pacific occupation, I was unwilling to commit myself to hazard in the matter.'

I looked at Campbell as he uttered these words, and never recollect to have seen a more singular contrast than that between the strong daring sternness expressed in his harsh features, and the air of composed meekness and simplicity which his language assumed. There was even a slight ironical smile lurking about the corners of his mouth, which seemed, involuntarily as it were, to intimate his disdain of the quiet and peaceful character which he thought proper to assume, and which led me to entertain strange suspicions that his concern in the violence done to Morris had been something very different from that of a fellow-sufferer, or even of a mere spectator.

Perhaps some such suspicions crossed the Justice's mind at the moment, for he exclaimed, as if by way of ejaculation, 'Body o' me! but this is a strange story.'

The North Briton seemed to guess at what was passing in his mind; for he went on, with a change of manner and tone, dismissing from his countenance some part of the hypocritical affectation of humility which had made him obnoxious to suspicion, and saying, with a more frank and unconstrained air, 'To say the truth, I am just ane o' those canny folks wha care not to fight, but when they hae gotten something to fight for, which did not chance to be my predicament when I fell in wi' these loons. But, that your worship may know that I am a person of good fame and character, please to cast your eye over that billet.'

Mr Inglewood took the paper from his hands, and read half aloud, 'These are to certify, that the bearer, Robert Campbell of——of some place which I cannot pronounce,' interjected the Justice,—'is a person of good lineage, and peaceable demeanour, travelling towards England on his own proper affairs, &c. &c. &c. Given under our hand, at our Castle of Inver—Invera—rara—ARGYLE.'

'A slight testimonial, sir, which I thought fit to impetrate from that worthy nobleman, (here he raised his hand to his head, as if to touch his hat,) MacCallum More.'

'MacCallum who, sir?' said the Justice.

'Whom the Southern call the Duke of Argyle.'*

'I know the Duke of Argyle very well to be a nobleman of great worth and distinction, and a true lover of his country. I was one of those that stood by him in 1714, when he unhorsed the Duke of Marlborough out of his command. I wish we had more noblemen like him. He was an honest Tory in those days, and hand and glove with Ormond. And he has acceded to the present government, as I have done myself, for the peace and quiet of his country; for I cannot presume that great man to have been actuated, as violent folks pretend, with the fear of losing his places and regiment. His testimonial, as you call it, Mr Campbell, is perfectly satisfactory; and now, what have you got to say to this matter of the robbery?'

'Briefly this, if it please your worship; that Mr Morris might as weel charge it against the babe yet to be born, or against myself even, as against this young gentleman, Mr Osbaldistone; for I am not only free to depone that the person for whom he took him was a shorter man, and a thicker man, but also, for I chanced to obtain a glisk of his visage, as his fause-face slipped aside, that he was a man of other features and complexion than those of this young gentleman, Mr Osbaldistone. And I believe,' he added, turning round with a natural, yet somewhat sterner air, to Mr Morris, 'that the gentleman will allow I had better opportunity to take cognizance wha were present on that occasion than he, being, I believe, much the cooler o' the twa.'

'I agree to it, sir—I agree to it perfectly,' said Morris, shrinking back, as Campbell moved his chair towards him to fortify his appeal— 'And I incline, sir,' he added, addressing Mr Inglewood, 'to retract my information as to Mr Osbaldistone; and I request, sir, you will permit him, sir, to go about his business, and me to go about mine also; your worship may have business to settle with Mr Campbell, and I am rather in haste to be gone.'

'Then, there go the declarations,' said the Justice, throwing them into the fire—'And now you are at perfect liberty, Mr Osbaldistone— And you, Mr Morris, are set quite at your ease.'

'Ay,' said Campbell, eyeing Morris as he assented with a rueful grin to the Justice's observations, 'much like the ease of a toad under a pair of harrows—But fear nothing, Mr Morris; you and I maun leave the house thegither. I will see you safe—I hope you will not doubt my honour, when I say sae—to the next highway, and then we part company; and if we do not meet as friends in Scotland, it will be your ain fault.'

With such a lingering look of terror as the condemned criminal throws, when he is informed that the cart awaits him, Morris arose; but when on his legs, appeared to hesitate. 'I tell thee, man, fear nothing,' reiterated Campbell; 'I will keep my word with you—Why, thou sheep's heart, how do ye ken but we may can pick up some speerings of your valise, if ye will be amenable to gude counsel?—Our horses are ready. Bid the Justice fareweel, man, and show your southern breeding.'

Morris, thus exhorted and encouraged, took his leave, under the escort of Mr Campbell; but, apparently, new scruples and terrors had struck him before they left the house, for I heard Campbell reiterating assurances of safety and protection as they left the anteroom—'By the soul of my body, man, thou'rt as safe as in thy father's kail-yard—Zounds! that a chield wi' sic a black beard, should hae nae mair heart than a hen-partridge!—Come on wi' ye, like a frank fallow, anes and for aye.'

The voices died away, and the subsequent trampling of their horses announced to us that they had left the mansion of Justice Inglewood.

The joy which that worthy magistrate received at this easy conclusion of a matter which threatened him with some trouble in his judicial capacity, was somewhat damped by reflection on what his clerk's views of the transaction might be at his return. 'Now, I shall have Jobson on my shoulders about these d——d papers—I doubt I should not have destroyed them, after all—But, hang it, it is only paying his fees, and that will make all smooth—And now, Miss Die Vernon, though I have liberated all the others, I intend to sign a writ for committing you to the custody of Mother Blakes, my old housekeeper, for the evening, and we will send for my neighbour Mrs Musgrave, and the Miss Dawkins, and your cousins, and have old Cobs the fiddler, and be as merry as the maids; and Frank Osbaldistone and I will have a carouse that will make us fit company for you in half an hour.'

'Thanks, most worshipful,' returned Miss Vernon; 'but, as matters stand, we must return instantly to Osbaldistone Hall, where they do not know what has become of us, and relieve my uncle of his anxiety on my cousin's account, which is just the same as if one of his own sons were concerned.'

'I believe it truly,' said the Justice; 'for when his eldest son, Archie, came to a bad end, in that unlucky affair of Sir John Fenwick's,* old Hildebrand used to hollow out his name as readily as any of the remaining six, and then complain that he could not recollect which of his sons had been hanged. So, pray hasten home, and relieve his paternal solicitude, since go you must.—But, hark thee hither, heath-blossom,' he said, pulling her towards him by the hand, and in a good-humoured tone of admonition, 'another time let the law take its course, without putting your pretty finger into her old musty pie, all full of fragments of law gibberish—French and dog-Latin—And, Die, my beauty, let young fellows show each other the way through the moors, in case you should lose your own road, while you are pointing out theirs, my pretty Will o' the Wisp.'

With this admonition, he saluted and dismissed Miss Vernon, and took an equally kind farewell of me.

'Thou seems to be a good tight lad, Mr Frank, and I remember thy father too—he was my play-fellow at school. Hark thee, lad, ride early at night, and don't swagger with chance passengers on the king's highway. What, man! all the king's liege subjects are not bound to understand joking, and it's ill cracking jests on matters of felony. And here's poor Die Vernon too—in a manner alone and deserted on the face of this wide earth, and left to ride, and run, and scamper at her own silly pleasure. Thou must be careful of Die, or, egad, I will turn a young fellow again on purpose, and fight thee myself, although I must own it would be a great deal of trouble. And now, get ye both gone, and leave me to my pipe of tobacco, and my meditations; for what says the song—

> 'The Indian leaf doth briefly burn;
> So doth man's strength to weakness turn;—
> The fire of youth extinguish'd quite,
> Comes age, like embers, dry and white.
>   Think of this as you take tobacco.'*

I was much pleased with the gleams of sense and feeling which escaped from the Justice through the vapours of sloth and self-indulgence, assured him of my respect to his admonitions, and took a friendly farewell of the honest magistrate and his hospitable mansion.

We found a repast prepared for us in the ante-room, which we partook of slightly, and rejoined the same servant of Sir Hildebrand who had taken our horses at our entrance, and who had been directed, as he informed Miss Vernon, by Mr Rashleigh, to wait and attend upon us home. We rode a little way in silence, for, to say truth, my mind was too much bewildered with the events of the morning to permit me to be the first to break it. At length Miss Vernon exclaimed, as if giving vent to her own reflections, 'Well, Rashleigh is a man to be feared and wondered at, and all but loved; he does whatever he pleases, and makes all others his puppets—has a player ready to perform every part which he imagines, and an invention and readiness which supply expedients for every emergency.'

'You think, then,' said I, answering rather to her meaning, than to the express words she made use of, 'that this Mr Campbell, whose appearance was so opportune, and who trussed up and carried off my accuser as a falcon trusses a partridge,* was an agent of Mr Rashleigh Osbaldistone's?'

'I do guess as much,' replied Diana, 'and shrewdly suspect, moreover, that he would hardly have appeared so very much in the nick of time, if I had not happened to meet Rashleigh in the hall at the Justice's.'

'In that case, my thanks are chiefly due to you, my fair preserver.'

'To be sure they are,' returned Diana; 'and pray, suppose them paid, and accepted with a gracious smile, for I do not care to be troubled with hearing them in good earnest, and am much more likely to yawn than to behave becoming. In short, Mr Frank, I wished to serve you, and I have fortunately been able to do so, and have only one favour to ask in return, and that is, that you will say no more about it.—But who comes here to meet us, "bloody with spurring, fiery-red with haste?"* It is the subordinate man of law, I think; no less than Mr Joseph Jobson.'

And Mr Joseph Jobson it proved to be, in great haste, and, as it speedily appeared, in most extreme bad humour. He came up to us, and stopped his horse, as we were about to pass with a slight salutation.

'So, sir—so, Miss Vernon—ay—I see well enough how it is—bail put in during my absence, I suppose—I should like to know who drew the recognizance, that's all. If his worship uses this form of procedure often, I advise him to get another clerk, that's all, for I shall certainly demit.'

'Or suppose he get his present clerk stitched to his sleeve, Mr Jobson,' said Diana, 'would not that do as well? And pray how does Farmer Rutledge, Mr Jobson? I hope you found him able to sign, seal, and deliver?'

This question seemed greatly to increase the wrath of the man of law. He looked at Miss Vernon with such an air of spite and resentment, as laid me under a strong temptation to knock him off his horse with the but of my whip, which I only suppressed in consideration of his insignificance.

'Farmer Rutledge, ma'am?' said the clerk, so soon as his indignation permitted him to articulate, 'Farmer Rutledge is in as handsome enjoyment of his health as you are—it's all a bam, ma'am—all a bamboozle and a bite* that affair of his illness; and if you did not know as much before, you know it now, ma'am.'

'La you there now!' replied Miss Vernon, with an affectation of extreme and simple wonder, 'sure you don't say so, Mr Jobson?'

'But I *do* say so, ma'am,' rejoined the incensed scribe; 'and moreover I say, that the old miserly clod-breaker called me pettifogger—pettifogger, ma'am—and said I came to hunt for a job, ma'am—which I have no more right to have said to me than any other gentleman of my profession, ma'am—especially as I am clerk to the peace, having and holding said office under *Trigesimo Septimo Henricj Octavi*, and *Primo Gulielmi*,*—the first of King William, ma'am, of glorious and immortal memory—our immortal deliverer from papists and pretenders, and wooden shoes and warming pans,* Miss Vernon.'

'Sad things, these wooden shoes and warming pans,' retorted the young lady, who seemed to take pleasure in augmenting his wrath;—'and it is a comfort you don't seem to want a warming pan at present, Mr Jobson. I am afraid Gaffer Rutledge has not confined his incivility to language—Are you sure he did not give you a beating?'

'Beating, ma'am!—no'—(very shortly) 'no man alive shall beat me, I promise you, ma'am.'

'That is according as you happen to merit, sir,' said I; 'for your mode of speaking to this young lady is so unbecoming, that, if you do not change your tone, I shall think it worth while to chastise you myself.'

'Chastise, sir? and—me, sir?—Do you know whom you speak to, sir?'

'Yes, sir,' I replied; 'you say yourself you are clerk of peace to the county; and Gaffer Rutledge says you are a pettifogger; and in neither capacity are you entitled to be impertinent to a young lady of fashion.'

Miss Vernon laid her hand on my arm, and exclaimed, 'Come, Mr Osbaldistone, I will have no assaults and battery on Mr Jobson; I am not in sufficient charity with him to permit a single touch of your whip—why, he would live on it for a term at least. Besides, you have already hurt his feelings sufficiently—you have called him impertinent.'

'I don't value his language, Miss,' said the clerk, somewhat crestfallen; 'besides, impertinent is not an actionable word; but pettifogger is slander in the highest degree, and that I will make Gaffer Rutledge know to his cost, and all who maliciously repeat the same to the breach of the public peace, and the taking away of my private good name.'

'Never mind that, Mr Jobson,' said Miss Vernon; 'you know, where there is nothing, your own law allows that the king himself must lose his rights; and, for the taking away of your good name, I pity the poor fellow who gets it, and wish you joy of losing it with all my heart.'*

'Very well, ma'am—good evening, ma'am—I have no more to say— only there are laws against papists, which it would be well for the land were they better executed. There's third and fourth Edward VI., of antiphoners, missals, grailes, processionals, manuals, legends, pies, portuasses,* and those that have such trinkets in their possession, Miss Vernon—and there's summoning of papists to take the oaths—and there are popish recusant convicts under the first of his present Majesty—ay, and there are penalties for hearing mass. See twenty-third of Queen Elizabeth, and third James First, chapter twenty-fifth.—And there are estates to be registered, and deeds and wills to be enrolled, and double taxes to be made, according to the acts in that case made and provided'——

'See the new edition of the Statutes at Large, published under the careful revision of Joseph Jobson, Gent., Clerk of the Peace,' said Miss Vernon.

'Also, and above all,' continued Jobson,—'for I speak to your warning—you, Diana Vernon, spinstress, not being a *femme couverte*;* and being a convict popish recusant, are bound to repair to your own dwelling, and that by the nearest way, under penalty of being held felon to the king—and diligently to seek for passage at common ferries, and to tarry there but one ebb and flood; and unless you can have it in such places, to walk every day into the water up to the knees, assaying to pass over.'

'A sort of Protestant penance for my Catholic errors, I suppose,' said Miss Vernon, laughing. 'Well, I thank you for the information, Mr Jobson, and will hie me home as fast as I can, and be a better house-keeper in time coming. Good night, my dear Mr Jobson, thou mirror of clerical courtesy.'

'Good night, ma'am, and remember the law is not to be trifled with.'

And we rode on our separate ways.

'There he goes for a troublesome mischief-making tool,' said Miss Vernon, as she gave a glance after him; 'it is hard that persons of birth and rank and estate should be subjected to the official impertinence of such a paltry pick-thank as that, merely for believing as the whole world believed not much above a hundred years ago—for certainly our Catholic faith has the advantage of antiquity at least.'

'I was much tempted to have broken the rascal's head,' I replied.

'You would have acted very like a hasty young man,' said Miss Vernon; 'and yet, had my own hand been an ounce heavier than it is, I think I should have laid its weight upon him.—Well, it does not signify complaining, but there are three things for which I am much to be pitied, if any one thought it worth while to waste any compassion upon me.'

'And what are these three things, Miss Vernon, may I ask?'

'Will you promise me your deepest sympathy, if I tell you?'

'Certainly;—can you doubt it?' I replied, closing my horse nearer to hers as I spoke, with an expression of interest which I did not attempt to disguise.

'Well, it is very seducing to be pitied, after all; so here are my three grievances—In the first place, I am a girl, and not a young fellow, and would be shut up in a mad-house, if I did half the things that I have a mind to; and that, if I had your happy prerogative of acting as you list, would make all the world mad with imitating and applauding me.'

'I can't quite afford you the sympathy you expect upon this score,' I replied; 'the misfortune is so general, that it belongs to one half of the species; and the other half'——

'Are so much better cared for, that they are jealous of their prerogatives,' interrupted Miss Vernon; 'I forgot you were a party interested. Nay,' said she, as I was going to speak, 'that soft smile is intended to be the preface of a very pretty compliment respecting the peculiar advantages which Die Vernon's friends and kinsmen enjoy, by her being born one of their Helots;* but spare me the utterance, my good friend, and let us try whether we shall agree better on the second count of my indictment against fortune, as that quill-driving puppy would call it. I belong to an oppressed sect and antiquated religion, and, instead of getting credit for my devotion, as is due to all good girls beside, my kind friend, Justice Inglewood, may send me to the house of correction, merely for worshipping God in the way of my ancestors, and say, as old Pembroke did to the Abbess of Wilton,[36] when he usurped her convent and establishment, "Go spin, you jade,—Go spin."'

'This is not a cureless evil,' said I gravely. 'Consult some of our learned divines, or consult your own excellent understanding,

Miss Vernon; and surely the particulars in which our religious creed differs from that in which you have been educated'——

'Hush!' said Diana, placing her fore-finger on her mouth,—'Hush! no more of that. Forsake the faith of my gallant fathers!—I would as soon, were I a man, forsake their banner, when the tide of battle pressed hardest against it, and turn, like a hireling recreant, to join the victorious enemy.'

'I honour your spirit, Miss Vernon; and as to the inconveniences to which it exposes you, I can only say, that wounds sustained for the sake of conscience carry their own balsam with the blow.'

'Ay; but they are fretful and irritating, for all that. But I see, hard of heart as you are, my chance of beating hemp, or drawing out flax* into marvellous coarse thread, affects you as little as my condemnation to coif and pinners, instead of beaver and cockade; so I will spare myself the fruitless pains of telling my third cause of vexation.'

'Nay, my dear Miss Vernon, do not withdraw your confidence, and I will promise you, that the threefold sympathy due to your very unusual causes of distress shall be all duly and truly paid to account of the third, providing you assure me, that it is one which you neither share with all womankind, nor even with every Catholic in England, who, God bless you, are still a sect more numerous than we Protestants, in our zeal for church and state, would desire them to be.'

'It is, indeed,' said Diana, with a manner greatly altered, and more serious than I had yet seen her assume, 'a misfortune that well merits compassion. I am by nature, as you may easily observe, of a frank and unreserved disposition*—a plain true-hearted girl, who would willingly act openly and honestly by the whole world, and yet fate has involved me in such a series of nets, and toils, and entanglements, that I dare hardly speak a word for fear of consequences—not to myself, but to others.'

'That is indeed a misfortune, Miss Vernon, which I do most sincerely compassionate, but which I should hardly have anticipated.'

'O, Mr Osbaldistone, if you but knew—if any one knew, what difficulty I sometimes find in hiding an aching heart with a smooth brow, you would indeed pity me. I do wrong, perhaps, in speaking to you even thus far on my own situation; but you are a young man of sense and penetration—you cannot but long to ask me a hundred questions on the events of this day—on the share which Rashleigh has in your deliverance from this petty scrape—upon many other points which cannot but excite your attention—and I cannot bring myself to answer with the necessary falsehood and finesse—I should do it awkwardly, and lose your good opinion, if I have any share of it, as well as my own. It is best to say at once, Ask me no questions, I have it not in my power to reply to them.'

Miss Vernon spoke these words with a tone of feeling which could not but make a corresponding impression upon me. I assured her she had neither to fear my urging her with impertinent questions, nor my misconstruing her declining to answer those which might in themselves be reasonable, or at least natural.

'I was too much obliged,' I said, 'by the interest she had taken in my affairs, to misuse the opportunity her goodness had afforded me of prying into hers—I only trusted and entreated, that if my services could at any time be useful, she would command them, without doubt or hesitation.'

'Thank you—thank you,' she replied; 'your voice does not ring the cuckoo chime of compliment, but speaks like that of one who knows to what he pledges himself. If—but it is impossible—but yet, *if* an opportunity should occur, I will ask you if you remember this promise; and I assure you, I shall not be angry if I find you have forgotten it, for it is enough that you are sincere in your intentions just now—much may occur to alter them ere I call upon you, should that moment ever come, to assist Die Vernon, as if you were Die Vernon's brother.'

'And if I were Die Vernon's brother,' said I, 'there could not be less chance that I should refuse my assistance—And now I am afraid I must not ask whether Rashleigh was willingly accessory to my deliverance?'

'Not of me; but you may ask it of himself, and, depend upon it, he will say *yes*; for rather than any good action should walk through the world like an unappropriated adjective in an ill-arranged sentence, he is always willing to stand noun substantive to it himself.'

'And I must not ask whether this Campbell be himself the party who eased Mr Morris of his portmanteau, or whether the letter, which our friend the attorney received, was not a finesse to withdraw him from the scene of action, lest he should have marred the happy event of my deliverance? And I must not ask'——

'You must ask nothing of me,' said Miss Vernon; 'so it is quite in vain to go on putting cases. You are to think just as well of me, as if

I had answered all these queries, and twenty others besides, as glibly as Rashleigh could have done; and observe, whenever I touch my chin just so, it is a sign that I cannot speak upon the topic which happens to occupy your attention. I must settle signals of correspondence with you, because you are to be my confident and my counsellor, only you are to know nothing whatever of my affairs.'

'Nothing can be more reasonable,' I replied, laughing; 'and the extent of your confidence will, you may rely upon it, only be equalled by the sagacity of my counsels.'

This sort of conversation brought us, in the highest good-humour with each other, to Osbaldistone Hall, where we found the family far advanced in the revels of the evening.

'Get some dinner for Mr Osbaldistone and me in the library,' said Miss Vernon to a servant.—'I must have some compassion upon you,' she added, turning to me, 'and provide against your starving in this mansion of brutal abundance; otherwise I am not sure that I should show you my private haunts. This same library is my den—the only corner of the Hall-house where I am safe from the Ourang-Outangs,* my cousins. They never venture there, I suppose, for fear the folios should fall down and crack their skulls; for they will never affect their heads in any other way—So follow me.'

And I followed through hall and bower, vaulted passage and winding stair, until we reached the room where she had ordered our refreshments.

CHAPTER X

In the wide pile, by others heeded not,
Hers was one sacred solitary spot,
Whose gloomy aisles and bending shelves contain
For moral hunger food, and cures for moral pain.

*Anonymous**

THE library at Osbaldistone Hall was a gloomy room, whose antique oaken shelves bent beneath the weight of the ponderous folios so dear to the seventeenth century, from which, under favour be it spoken, we have distilled matter for our quartos and octavos, and which, once more subjected to the alembic, may, should our sons be yet more frivolous than ourselves, be still farther reduced into duodecimos and pamphlets.* The collection was chiefly of the classics, as well foreign as ancient history, and, above all, divinity. It was in wretched order. The priests, who, in succession, had acted as chaplains at the Hall, were, for many years, the only persons who entered its precincts, until Rashleigh's thirst for reading had led him to disturb the venerable spiders, who had muffled the fronts of the presses with their tapestry. His destination for the church rendered his conduct less absurd in his father's eyes, than if any of his other descendants had betrayed so strange a propensity, and Sir Hildebrand acquiesced in the library receiving some repairs, so as to fit it for a sitting room. Still an air of dilapidation, as obvious as it was uncomfortable, pervaded the large apartment, and announced the neglect from which the knowledge which its walls contained had not been able to exempt it. The tattered tapestry, the worm-eaten shelves, the huge and clumsy, yet tottering, tables, desks, and chairs, the rusty grate, seldom gladdened by either sea-coal or fagots, intimated the contempt of the lords of Osbaldistone Hall for learning, and for the volumes which record its treasures.

'You think this place somewhat disconsolate, I suppose?' said Diana, as I glanced my eye round the forlorn apartment; 'but to me it seems like a little paradise, for I call it my own, and fear no intrusion. Rashleigh was joint proprietor with me, while we were friends.'

'And are you no longer so?' was my natural question.

Her fore-finger immediately touched her dimpled chin, with an arch look of prohibition.

'We are still *allies*,' she continued, 'bound, like other confederate powers, by circumstances of mutual interest; but I am afraid, as will happen in other cases, the treaty of alliance has survived the amicable dispositions in which it had its origin. At any rate, we live less together; and when he comes through that door there, I vanish through this door here; and so, having made the discovery that we two were one too many for this apartment, as large as it seems, Rashleigh, whose occasions frequently call him elsewhere, has generously made a cession of his rights in my favour; so that I now endeavour to prosecute alone the studies in which he used formerly to be my guide.'

'And what are those studies, if I may presume to ask?'

'Indeed you may, without the least fear of seeing my fore-finger raised to my chin. Science and history are my principal favourites; but I also study poetry and the classics.'

'And the classics? Do you read them in the original?'

'Unquestionably; Rashleigh, who is no contemptible scholar, taught me Greek and Latin, as well as most of the languages of modern Europe. I assure you, there has been some pains taken in my education, although I can neither sew a tucker, nor work cross-stitch, nor make a pudding, nor, as the vicar's fat wife, with as much truth as elegance, good-will, and politeness, was pleased to say in my behalf, do any other useful thing in the varsal world.'*

'And was this selection of studies Rashleigh's choice, or your own, Miss Vernon?' I asked.

'Um!' said she, as if hesitating to answer my question,—'it's not worth while lifting my finger about, after all—why, partly his, and partly mine. As I learned out of doors to ride a horse, and bridle and saddle him in case of necessity, and to clear a five-barred gate, and fire a gun without winking, and all other of those masculine accomplishments that my brute cousins run mad after, I wanted, like my rational cousin, to read Greek and Latin within doors, and make my complete approach to the tree of knowledge, which you men-scholars would engross to yourselves, in revenge, I suppose, for our common mother's share in the great original transgression.'

'And Rashleigh readily indulged your propensity to learning?'

'Why, he wished to have me for his scholar, and he could but teach me that which he knew himself—he was not likely to instruct me in the mysteries of washing lace-ruffles, or hemming cambric-handkerchiefs, I suppose.'

'I admit the temptation of getting such a scholar, and have no doubt that it made a weighty consideration on the tutor's part.'

'O, if you begin to investigate Rashleigh's motives, my finger touches my chin once more. I can only be frank where my own are enquired into. But to resume—he has resigned the library in my favour, and never enters without leave had and obtained; and so I have taken the liberty to make it the place of deposit for some of my own goods and chattels, as you may see by looking round you.'

'I beg pardon, Miss Vernon, but I really see nothing around these walls which I can distinguish as likely to claim you as mistress.'

'That is, I suppose, because you neither see a shepherd or shepherdess wrought in worsted, and handsomely framed in black ebony,—or a stuffed parrot,—or a breeding-cage, full of canary-birds,—or a housewife-case, broidered with tarnished silver,—or a toilette-table, with a nest of japanned boxes, with as many angles as Christmas mincedpies,—or a broken-backed spinet,—or a lute with three strings,—or rock-work,—or shell-work,—or needle-work, or work of any kind,—or a lap-dog, with a litter of blind puppies—None of these treasures do I possess,' she continued, after a pause, in order to recover the breath she had lost in enumerating them—'But there stands the sword of my ancestor Sir Richard Vernon, slain at Shrewsbury, and sorely slandered by a sad fellow called Will Shakspeare,* whose Lancastrian partialities, and a certain knack at embodying them, has turned history upside down, or rather inside out;—and by that redoubted weapon hangs the mail of the still older Vernon, squire to the Black Prince, whose fate is the reverse of his descendant's, since he is more indebted to the bard, who took the trouble to celebrate him, for good-will, than for talents,—

> "Amiddes the route you might descern one
> Brave knight, with pipes on shield, ycleped Vernon;
> Like a borne fiend along the plain he thundered,
> Prest to be carving throtes, while others plundered."*

Then there is a model of a new martingale which I invented myself—a great improvement on the Duke of Newcastle's;* and there are the hood and bells of my falcon Cheviot, who spitted himself on a heron's bill at Horsely-moss—poor Cheviot, there is not a bird on the perches below, but are kites and riflers compared to him; and there is my own light fowling-piece, with an improved fire-lock; with twenty other treasures, each more valuable than another—And there, that speaks for itself.'

She pointed to the carved oak-frame of a full-length portrait by Vandyke, on which were inscribed, in Gothic letters, the words *Vernon semper viret*.* I looked at her for explanation—'Do you not know,' said she, with some surprise, 'our motto—the Vernon motto, where,

> "Like the solemn vice, Iniquity,
> We moralize two meanings in one word?"*

And do you not know our cognizance, the pipes?' pointing to the armorial bearings sculptured on the oaken scutcheon, around which the legend was displayed.

'Pipes!—they look more like penny-whistles—But, pray, do not be angry with my ignorance,' I continued, observing the colour mount to her cheeks, 'I can mean no affront to your armorial bearings, for I do not even know my own.'

'You an Osbaldistone, and confess so much!' she exclaimed. 'Why, Percie, Thornie, John, Dickon—Wilfred himself, might be your instructor—Even ignorance itself is a plummet over you.'

'With shame I confess it, my dear Miss Vernon, the mysteries couched under the grim hieroglyphics of heraldry are to me as unintelligible as those of the pyramids of Egypt.'*

'What! is it possible?—Why, even my uncle reads Gwillym* sometimes of a winter night—Not know the figures of heraldry?—of what could your father be thinking?'

'Of the figures of arithmetic,' I answered; 'the most insignificant unit of which he holds more highly than all the blazonry of chivalry. But, though I am ignorant to this inexpressible degree, I have knowledge and taste enough to admire that splendid picture, in which I think I can discover a family likeness to you. What ease and dignity in the attitude—what richness of colouring—what breadth and depth of shade!'

'Is it really a fine painting?' she asked.

'I have seen many works of the renowned artist,' I replied, 'but never beheld one more to my liking.'

'Well, I know as little of pictures as you do of heraldry,' replied Miss Vernon; 'yet I have the advantage of you, because I have always admired the painting without understanding its value.'

'While I have neglected pipes and tabors, and all the whimsical combinations of chivalry, still I am informed that they floated in the fields of ancient fame. But you will allow their exterior appearance is not so peculiarly interesting to the uninformed spectator as that of a fine painting.—Who is the person here represented?'

'My grandfather—he shared the misfortunes of Charles I.;* and, I am sorry to add, the excesses of his son. Our patrimonial estate was greatly impaired by his prodigality, and was altogether lost by his successor, my unfortunate father. But peace be with them who have got it—it was lost in the cause of loyalty.'

'Your father, I presume, suffered in the political dissensions of the period?'

'He did indeed; he lost his all. And hence is his child a dependent orphan; eating the bread of others; subjected to their caprices, and compelled to study their inclinations: Yet prouder of having had such a father, than if, playing a more prudent, but less upright part, he had left me possessor of all the rich and fair baronies which his family once possessed.'

As she thus spoke, the entrance of the servants with dinner cut off all conversation but that of a general nature.

When our hasty meal was concluded, and the wine placed on the table, the domestic informed us, 'that Mr Rashleigh had desired to be told when our dinner was removed.'

'Tell him,' said Miss Vernon, 'we shall be happy to see him if he will step this way—place another wine-glass and chair, and leave the room.—You must retire with him when he goes away,' she continued, addressing herself to me; 'even *my* liberality cannot spare a gentleman above eight hours out of the twenty-four; and I think we have been together for at least that length of time.'

'The old scythe-man has moved so rapidly,' I answered, 'that I could not count his strides.'

'Hush!' said Miss Vernon, 'here comes Rashleigh;' and she drew off her chair, to which I had approached mine rather closely, so as to place a greater distance between us.

A modest tap at the door,—a gentle manner of opening when invited to enter,—a studied softness and humility of step and deportment, announced that the education of Rashleigh Osbaldistone at the College of St Omers* accorded well with the ideas I entertained of the manners of an accomplished Jesuit. I need not add, that, as a sound Protestant, these ideas were not the most favourable. 'Why should you use the ceremony of knocking,' said Miss Vernon, 'when you knew that I was not alone?'

This was spoken with a burst of impatience, as if she had felt that Rashleigh's air of caution and reserve covered some insinuation of impertinent suspicion. 'You have taught me the form of knocking at this door so perfectly, my fair cousin,' answered Rashleigh, without change of voice or manner, 'that habit has become a second nature.'

'I prize sincerity more than courtesy, sir, and you know I do,' was Miss Vernon's reply.

'Courtesy is a gallant gay, a courtier by name and by profession,' replied Rashleigh, 'and therefore most fit for a lady's bower.'

'But Sincerity is the true knight,' retorted Miss Vernon, 'and therefore much more welcome, cousin. But, to end a debate not over amusing to your stranger kinsman, sit down, Rashleigh, and give Mr Francis Osbaldistone your countenance to his glass of wine. I have done the honours of the dinner, for the credit of Osbaldistone Hall.'

Rashleigh sate down, and filled his glass, glancing his eye from Diana to me, with an embarrassment which his utmost efforts could not entirely disguise. I thought he appeared to be uncertain concerning the extent of confidence she might have reposed in me, and hastened to lead the conversation into a channel which should sweep away his suspicion that Diana might have betrayed any secrets which rested between them. 'Miss Vernon,' I said, 'Mr Rashleigh, has recommended me to return my thanks to you for my speedy disengagement from the ridiculous accusation of Morris; and, unjustly fearing my gratitude might not be warm enough to remind me of this duty, she has put my curiosity on its side, by referring me to you for an account, or rather explanation, of the events of the day.'

'Indeed?' answered Rashleigh; 'I should have thought,' (looking keenly at Miss Vernon,) 'that the lady herself might have stood interpreter;' and his eye, reverting from her face, sought mine, as if to search, from the expression of my features, whether Diana's communication had been as narrowly limited as my words had intimated. Miss Vernon retorted his inquisitorial glance with one of decided scorn; while I, uncertain whether to deprecate or resent his obvious suspicion, replied, 'If it is your pleasure, Mr Rashleigh, as it has been Miss Vernon's, to leave me in ignorance, I must necessarily submit; but, pray, do not withhold your information from me, on the ground of imagining that I have already obtained any on the subject. For I tell you as a man of honour, I am as ignorant as that picture of any thing relating to the events I have witnessed to-day, excepting that I understand from Miss Vernon, that you have been kindly active in my favour.'

'Miss Vernon has overrated my humble efforts,' said Rashleigh, 'though I claim full credit for my zeal. The truth is, that as I galloped back to get some one of our family to join me in becoming your bail, which was the most obvious, or, indeed, I may say, the only way of serving you which occurred to my stupidity, I met the man Cawmil— Colville—Campbell, or whatsoever they call him. I had understood from Morris that he was present when the robbery took place, and had the good fortune to prevail on him, (with some difficulty, I confess,) to tender his evidence in your exculpation, which I presume was the means of your being released from an unpleasant situation.'

'Indeed?—I am much your debtor for procuring such a seasonable evidence in my behalf. But I cannot see why, (having been, as he said, a fellow-sufferer with Morris,) it should have required much trouble to persuade him to step forth and bear evidence, whether to convict the actual robber, or free an innocent person.'

'You do not know the genius of that man's country, sir,' answered Rashleigh; 'discretion, prudence, and foresight, are their leading qualities; these are only modified by a narrow-spirited, but yet ardent patriotism, which forms as it were the outmost of the concentric bulwarks with which a Scotchman fortifies himself against all the attacks of a generous philanthropical principle. Surmount this mound, you find an inner and still dearer barrier—the love of his province, his village, or, most probably, his clan; storm this second obstacle, you have a third—his attachment to his own family—his father, mother, sons, daughters, uncles, aunts, and cousins, to the ninth generation. It is within these limits that a Scotchman's social affection expands itself, never reaching those which are outermost, till all means of discharging itself in the interior circles have been exhausted. It is within these circles that his heart throbs, each pulsation being fainter and fainter, till, beyond the widest boundary, it is almost unfelt. And what is worst of all, could you surmount all these concentric outworks, you have an inner citadel, deeper, higher, and more efficient than them all—a Scotchman's love for himself.'

'All this is extremely eloquent and metaphorical, Rashleigh,' said Miss Vernon, who listened with unrepressed impatience; 'there are only two objections to it: first, it is *not* true; secondly, if true, it is nothing to the purpose.'

'It *is* true, my fairest Diana,' returned Rashleigh; 'and moreover, it is most instantly to the purpose. It is true, because you cannot deny that I know the country and people intimately, and the character is drawn from deep and accurate consideration; and it is to the purpose, because it answers Mr Francis Osbaldistone's question, and shows why this same wary Scotchman, considering our kinsman to be neither his countryman, nor a Campbell, nor his cousin in any of the inextricable combinations by which they extend their pedigree; and, above all, seeing no prospect of personal advantage, but, on the contrary, much hazard of loss of time and delay of business'——

'With other inconveniences, perhaps, of a nature yet more formidable,' interrupted Miss Vernon.

'Of which, doubtless, there might be many,' said Rashleigh, continuing in the same tone—'In short, my theory shows why this man, hoping for no advantage, and afraid of some inconvenience, might require a degree of persuasion ere he could be prevailed on to give his testimony in favour of Mr Osbaldistone.'

'It seems surprising to me,' I observed, 'that during the glance I cast over the declaration, or whatever it is termed, of Mr Morris, he should never have mentioned that Campbell was in his company when he met the marauders.'

'I understood from Campbell, that he had taken his solemn promise not to mention that circumstance,' replied Rashleigh; 'his reason for exacting such an engagement you may guess from what I have hinted—he wished to get back to his own country, undelayed and unembarrassed by any of the judicial enquiries which he would have been under the necessity of attending, had the fact of his being present at the robbery taken air while he was on this side of the Border. But let him once be as distant as the Forth, Morris will, I warrant you, come forth with all he knows about him, and, it may be, a good deal more. Besides, Campbell is a very extensive dealer in cattle, and has often occasion to send great droves into Northumberland; and, when driving such a trade, he would be a great fool to embroil himself with our Northumbrian thieves, than whom no men who live are more vindictive.'

'I dare be sworn of that,' said Miss Vernon, with a tone which implied something more than a simple acquiescence in the proposition.

'Still,' said I, resuming the subject, 'allowing the force of the reasons which Campbell might have for desiring that Morris should be silent with regard to his promise when the robbery was committed, I cannot yet see how he could attain such an influence over the man, as to make him suppress his evidence in that particular, at the manifest risk of subjecting his story to discredit.'

Rashleigh agreed with me, that it was very extraordinary, and seemed to regret that he had not questioned the Scotchman more closely on that subject, which he allowed looked extremely mysterious. 'But,' he asked, immediately after this acquiescence, 'are you very sure the circumstance of Morris's being accompanied by Campbell, is really not alluded to in his examination?'

'I read the paper over hastily,' said I; 'but it is my strong impression, that no such circumstance is mentioned; at least it must have been touched on very slightly, since it failed to catch my attention.'

'True, true,' answered Rashleigh, forming his own inference while he adopted my words; 'I incline to think with you, that the circumstance must in reality have been mentioned, but so slightly, that it failed to attract your attention. And then, as to Campbell's interest with Morris, I incline to suppose that it must have been gained by playing upon his fears. This chicken-hearted fellow, Morris, is bound, I understand, for Scotland, destined for some little employment under government; and, possessing the courage of the wrathful dove, or most magnanimous mouse,* he may have been afraid to encounter the ill-will of such a kill-cow as Campbell, whose very appearance would be enough to fright him out of his little wits. You observed that Mr Campbell has at times a keen and animated manner—something of a martial cast in his tone and bearing.'

'I own,' I replied, 'that his expression struck me as being occasionally fierce and sinister, and little adapted to his peaceable professions. Has he served in the army?'

'Yes—no—not, strictly speaking, *served;* but he has been, I believe, like most of his countrymen, trained to arms. Indeed, among the hills, they carry them from boyhood to the grave. So, if you know any thing of your fellow-traveller, you will easily judge, that, going to such a country, he will take care to avoid a quarrel, if he can help it, with any of the natives.—But, come, I see you decline your wine—and I too am a degenerate Osbaldistone, so far as respects the circulation of the bottle. If you will go to my room, I will hold you a hand at piquet.'

We rose to take leave of Miss Vernon, who had from time to time suppressed, apparently with difficulty, a strong temptation to break in upon Rashleigh's details. As we were about to leave the room, the smothered fire broke forth.

'Mr Osbaldistone,' she said, 'your own observation will enable you to verify the justice, or injustice, of Rashleigh's suggestions concerning such individuals as Mr Campbell and Mr Morris. But, in slandering Scotland, he has borne false witness against a whole country; and I request you will allow no weight to his evidence.'

'Perhaps,' I answered, 'I may find it somewhat difficult to obey your injunction, Miss Vernon; for I must own I was bred up with no very favourable idea of our northern neighbours.'

'Distrust that part of your education, sir,' she replied, 'and let the daughter of a Scotchwoman pray you to respect the land which gave her parent birth, until your own observation has proved them to be unworthy of your good opinion. Preserve your hatred and contempt for dissimulation, baseness, and falsehood, wheresoever they are to be met with. You will find enough of all these without leaving England.— Adieu, gentlemen,—I wish you good evening.'

And she signed to the door, with the manner of a princess dismissing her train.

We retired to Rashleigh's apartment, where a servant brought us coffee and cards. I had formed my resolution to press Rashleigh no farther on the events of the day. A mystery, and, as I thought, not of a favourable complexion, appeared to hang over his conduct; but to ascertain if my suspicions were just, it was necessary to throw him off his guard. We cut for the deal, and were soon earnestly engaged in our play. I thought I perceived in this trifling for amusement (for the stake which Rashleigh proposed was a mere trifle) something of a fierce and ambitious temper. He seemed perfectly to understand the beautiful game at which he played, but preferred, as it were on principle, the risking bold and precarious strokes to the ordinary rules of play; and neglecting the minor and better-balanced chances of the game, he hazarded every thing for the chance of piqueing, repiqueing, or capotting his adversary.* So soon as the intervention of a game or two at piquet, like the music between the acts of a drama, had completely interrupted our previous course of conversation, Rashleigh appeared to tire of the game, and the cards were superseded by discourse, in which he assumed the lead.

More learned than soundly wise—better acquainted with men's minds than with the moral principles that ought to regulate them, he had still powers of conversation which I have rarely seen equalled, never excelled. Of this his manner implied some consciousness; at least, it appeared to me that he had studied hard to improve his natural advantages of a melodious voice, fluent and happy expression, apt language, and fervid imagination. He was never loud, never overbearing, never so much occupied with his own thoughts, as to outrun either the patience or the comprehension of those he conversed with. His ideas succeeded each other with the gentle but unintermitting flow of a plentiful and bounteous spring; while I have heard those of others, who aimed at distinction in conversation, rush along like the turbid gush from the sluice of a mill-pond, as hurried, and as easily exhausted. It was late at night ere I could part from a companion so fascinating; and, when I gained my own apartment, it cost me no small effort to recall to my mind the character of Rashleigh, such as I had pictured him previous to this tête-à-tête.

So effectual, my dear Tresham, does the sense of being pleased and amused blunt our faculties of perception and discrimination of character, that I can only compare it to the taste of certain fruits, at once luscious and poignant, which renders our palate totally unfit for relishing or distinguishing the viands which are subsequently subjected to its criticism.

CHAPTER XI

What gars ye gaunt, my merrymen a'?
    What gars ye look sae dreary?
What gars ye hing your head sae sair
    In the castle of Balwearie?

Old Scotch Ballad*

THE next morning chanced to be Sunday, a day peculiarly hard to be got rid of at Osbaldistone Hall; for after the formal religious service of the morning had been performed, at which all the family regularly attended, it was hard to say upon which individual, Rashleigh and Miss Vernon excepted, the fiend of ennui descended with the most abundant outpouring of his spirit. To speak of my yesterday's embarrassment amused Sir Hildebrand for several minutes, and he congratulated me on my deliverance from Morpeth or Hexham jail, as he would have done if I had fallen in attempting to clear a five-barred gate, and got up without hurting myself.

'Hast had a lucky turn, lad; but do na be over venturous again. What, man! the king's road is free to all men, be they Whigs, be they Tories.'

'On my word, sir, I am innocent of interrupting it; and it is the most provoking thing on earth, that every person will take it for granted that I am accessory to a crime which I despise and detest, and which would, moreover, deservedly forfeit my life to the laws of my country.'

'Well, well, lad; even so be it; I ask no questions—no man bound to tell on himsell—that's fair play, or the devil's in't.'

Rashleigh here came to my assistance; but I could not help thinking that his arguments were calculated rather as hints to his father to put on a show of acquiescence in my declaration of innocence, than fully to establish it.

'In your own house, my dear sir—and your own nephew—you will not surely persist in hurting his feelings, by seeming to discredit what he is so strongly interested in affirming. No doubt, you are fully deserving of all his confidence, and I am sure, were there any thing you could do to assist him in this strange affair, he would have recourse to your goodness. But my cousin Frank has been dismissed as an innocent man, and no one is entitled to suppose him otherwise. For my part,

I have not the least doubt of his innocence; and our family honour, I conceive, requires that we should maintain it with tongue and sword against the whole country.'

'Rashleigh,' said his father, looking fixedly at him, 'thou art a sly loon—thou hast ever been too cunning for me, and too cunning for most folks. Have a care thou proven a too cunning for thysell—two faces under one hood is no true heraldry.—And since we talk of heraldry, I'll go and read Gwillym.'

This resolution he intimated with a yawn, resistless as that of the Goddess in the Dunciad,* which was responsively echoed by his giant sons, as they dispersed in quest of the pastimes to which their minds severally inclined them—Percie to discuss a pot of March beer with the steward in the buttery,—Thorncliff to cut a pair of cudgels, and fix them in their wicker hilts,—John to dress May-flies,—Dickon to play at pitch and toss by himself, his right hand against his left,—and Wilfred to bite his thumbs, and hum himself into a slumber which should last till dinner time, if possible. Miss Vernon had retired to the library.

Rashleigh and I were left alone in the old hall, from which the servants, with their usual bustle and awkwardness, had at length contrived to hurry the remains of our substantial breakfast. I took the opportunity to upbraid him with the manner in which he had spoken of my affair to his father, which I frankly stated was highly offensive to me, as it seemed rather to exhort Sir Hildebrand to conceal his suspicions, than to root them out.

'Why, what can I do, my dear friend?' replied Rashleigh; 'my father's disposition is so tenacious of suspicions of all kinds, when once they take root, which, to do him justice, does not easily happen, that I have always found it the best way to silence him upon such subjects, instead of arguing with him. Thus I get the better of the weeds which I cannot eradicate, by cutting them over as often as they appear, until at length they die away of themselves. There is neither wisdom nor profit in disputing with such a mind as Sir Hildebrand's, which hardens itself against conviction, and believes in its own inspirations as firmly as we good Catholics do in those of the Holy Father of Rome.'

'It is very hard though, that I should live in the house of a man, and he a near relation too, who will persist in believing me guilty of a highway robbery.'

'My father's foolish opinion, if one may give that epithet to any opinion of a father's, does not affect your real innocence; and as to the disgrace of the fact, depend on it, that, considered in all its bearings, political as well as moral, Sir Hildebrand regards it as a meritorious action—a weakening of the enemy—a spoiling of the Amalekites*— and you will stand the higher in his regard for your supposed accession to it.'

'I desire no man's regard, Mr Rashleigh, on such terms as must sink me in my own; and I think these injurious suspicions will afford a very good reason for quitting Osbaldistone Hall, which I shall do whenever I can communicate on the subject with my father.'

The dark countenance of Rashleigh, though little accustomed to betray its master's feelings, exhibited a suppressed smile, which he instantly chastened by a sigh.

'You are a happy man, Frank—you go and come, as the wind bloweth where it listeth.* With your address, taste, and talents, you will soon find circles where they will be more valued, than amid the dull inmates of this mansion; while I——' he paused.

'And what is there in your lot that can make you or any one envy mine,—an outcast, as I may almost term myself, from my father's house and favour?'

'Ay, but,' answered Rashleigh, 'consider the gratified sense of inde-pendence which you must have attained by a very temporary sacrifice, for such I am sure yours will prove to be—consider the power of act-ing as a free agent, of cultivating your own talents in the way to which your taste determines you, and in which you are well qualified to dis-tinguish yourself—Fame and freedom are cheaply purchased by a few weeks' residence in the North, even though your place of exile be Osbaldistone Hall.—A second Ovid in Thrace, you have not his reasons for writing Tristia.'*

'I do not know,' said I, blushing as became a young scribbler, 'how you should be so well acquainted with my truant studies.'

'There was an emissary of your father's here some time since, a young coxcomb, one Twineall, who informed me concerning your secret sacrifices to the muses, and added, that some of your verses had been greatly admired by the best judges.'

Tresham, I believe you are guiltless of having ever essayed to build the lofty rhyme;* but you must have known in your day many an apprentice and fellow-craft, if not some of the master-masons, in the temple of Apollo. Vanity is their universal foible, from him who decor-ated the shades of Twickenham,* to the veriest scribbler whom he has lashed in his Dunciad. I had my own share of this common failing, and without considering how little likely this young fellow Twineall was, by taste and habits, either to be acquainted with one or two little pieces of poetry, which I had at times insinuated into Button's coffee-house,* or to report the opinion of the critics who frequented that resort of wit and literature, I almost instantly gorged the bait; which Rashleigh perceiving, improved his opportunity by a diffident, yet apparently very anxious request, to be permitted to see some of my manuscript productions.

'You shall give me an evening in my own apartment,' he continued; 'for I must soon lose the charms of literary society for the drudgery of commerce, and the coarse every-day avocations of the world. I repeat it, that my compliance with my father's wishes for the advantage of my family, is indeed a sacrifice, especially considering the calm and peaceful profession to which my education destined me.'

I was vain, but not a fool, and this hypocrisy was too strong for me to swallow—'You would not persuade me,' I replied, 'that you really regret to exchange the situation of an obscure Catholic priest, with all its privations, for wealth and society, and the pleasures of the world?'

Rashleigh saw that he had coloured his affectation of moderation too highly, and, after a second's pause, during which, I suppose, he calculated the degree of candour which it was necessary to use with me, (that being a quality of which he was never needlessly profuse,) he answered with a smile,—'At my age, to be condemned, as you say, to wealth and the world, does not, indeed, sound so alarming as perhaps it ought to do. But, with pardon be it spoken, you have mistaken my destination—a Catholic priest, if you will, but not an obscure one—No, sir, Rashleigh Osbaldistone will be more obscure, should he rise to be the richest citizen in London, than he might have been as a member of a church, whose ministers, as some one says, 'set their sandall'd feet on princes.'*—My family interest at a certain exiled court is high, and the weight which that court ought to possess, and does possess, at Rome, is yet higher—my talents not altogether inferior to the education I have received. In sober judgment, I might have looked forward to high eminence in the church—in the dream of fancy, to the very highest—Why might not,' (he added, laughing, for it was part of his manner to keep much of his discourse apparently betwixt jest and earnest,)—'why might not Cardinal Osbaldistone have swayed the fortunes of empires, well-born and well-connected, as well as the low-born Mazarin, or Alberoni,* the son of an Italian gardener?'

'Nay, I can give you no reason to the contrary; but in your place I should not much regret losing the chance of such precarious and invidious elevation.'

'Neither would I,' he replied, 'were I sure that my present establishment was more certain; but that must depend upon circumstances, which I can only learn by experience—the disposition of your father, for example.'

'Confess the truth without finesse, Rashleigh; you would willingly know something of him from me?'

'Since, like Die Vernon, you make a point of following the banner of the good knight Sincerity, I reply—certainly.'

'Well, then, you will find in my father a man who has followed the paths of thriving more for the exercise they afforded to his talents, than for the love of the gold with which they are strewed. His active mind would have been happy in any situation which gave it scope for exertion, though that exertion had been its sole reward. But his wealth has accumulated, because, moderate and frugal in his habits, no new sources of expense have occurred to dispose of his increasing income. He is a man who hates dissimulation in others; never practises it himself; and is peculiarly alert in discovering motives through the colouring of language. Himself silent by habit, he is readily disgusted by great talkers; the rather, that the circumstances by which he is most interested afford no great scope for conversation. He is severely strict in the duties of religion; but you have no reason to fear his interference with yours, for he regards toleration as a sacred principle of political economy. But if you have any Jacobitical partialities, as is naturally to be supposed, you will do well to suppress them in his presence, as well as the least tendency to the highflying or Tory principles;* for he holds both in utter detestation. For the rest, his word is his own bond, and must be the law of all who act under him. He will fail in his duty to no one, and will permit no one to fail towards him; to cultivate his favour, you must execute his commands, instead of echoing his sentiments. His greatest failings arise out of prejudices connected with his own profession, or rather his exclusive devotion to it, which makes him see little worthy of praise or attention, unless it be in some measure connected with commerce.'

'O rare-painted portrait!' exclaimed Rashleigh, when I was silent—

'Vandyke was a dauber to you, Frank. I see thy sire before me in all his strength and weakness; loving and honouring the King as a sort of lord mayor of the empire, or chief of the board of trade;—venerating the Commons, for the acts regulating the export trade;—and respecting the Peers, because the Lord Chancellor sits on a woolsack.'

'Mine was a likeness, Rashleigh; yours is a caricature. But in return for the *carte du pays* which I have unfolded to you, give me some lights on the geography of the unknown lands'——

'On which you are wrecked,' said Rashleigh. 'It is not worth while; it is no Isle of Calypso,* umbrageous with shade and intricate with silvan labyrinth—but a bare ragged Northumbrian moor, with as little to interest curiosity as to delight the eye—you may descry it in all its nakedness in half an hour's survey, as well as if I were to lay it down before you by line and compass.'

'O, but something there is, worthy a more attentive survey—What say you to Miss Vernon? Does not she form an interesting object in the landscape, were all round as rude as Iceland's coast?'

I could plainly perceive that Rashleigh disliked the topic now presented to him; but my frank communication had given me the advantageous title to make enquiries in my turn. Rashleigh felt this, and found himself obliged to follow my lead, however difficult he might find it to play his cards successfully. 'I have known less of Miss Vernon,' he said, 'for some time, than I was wont to do formerly. In early age I was her tutor; but as she advanced towards womanhood, my various avocations,—the gravity of the profession to which I was destined,—the peculiar nature of her engagements,—our mutual situation, in short, rendered a close and constant intimacy dangerous and improper. I believe Miss Vernon might consider my reserve as unkindness, but it was my duty; I felt as much as she seemed to do, when compelled to give way to prudence. But where was the safety in cultivating an intimacy with a beautiful and susceptible girl, whose heart, you are aware, must be given either to the cloister or to a betrothed husband?'

'The cloister or a betrothed husband?' I echoed—'Is that the alternative destined for Miss Vernon?'

'It is indeed,' said Rashleigh, with a sigh. 'I need not, I suppose, caution you against the danger of cultivating too closely the friendship of Miss Vernon; you are a man of the world, and know how far you can indulge yourself in her society, with safety to yourself and justice to her. But I warn you, that, considering her ardent temper, you must let your experience keep guard over her as well as yourself, for the specimen of yesterday may serve to show her extreme thoughtlessness and neglect of decorum.'

There was something, I was sensible, of truth, as well as good sense, in all this; it seemed to be given as a friendly warning, and I had no right to take it amiss; yet I felt I could with pleasure have run Rashleigh Osbaldistone through the body all the time he was speaking.

The deuce take his insolence! was my internal meditation. Would he wish me to infer, that Miss Vernon had fallen in love with that hatchet-face of his, and become degraded so low as to require his shyness to cure her of an imprudent passion? I will have his meaning from him, was my resolution, if I should drag it out with cart-ropes.

For this purpose, I placed my temper under as accurate a guard as I could, and observed, 'That, for a lady of her good sense and acquired accomplishments, it was to be regretted that Miss Vernon's manners were rather blunt and rustic.'

'Frank and unreserved, at least, to the extreme,' replied Rashleigh; 'yet, trust me, she has an excellent heart. To tell you the truth, should she continue her extreme aversion to the cloister, and to her destined husband, and should my own labours in the mine of Plutus* promise to secure me a decent independence, I shall think of renewing our acquaintance, and sharing it with Miss Vernon.'

With all his fine voice, and well-turned periods, thought I, this same Rashleigh Osbaldistone is the ugliest and most conceited coxcomb I ever met with.

'But,' continued Rashleigh, as if thinking aloud, 'I should not like to supplant Thorncliff.'

'Supplant Thorncliff!—Is your brother Thorncliff,' I enquired, with great surprise, 'the destined husband of Diana Vernon?'

'Why, ay; her father's commands, and a certain family-contract, destine her to marry one of Sir Hildebrand's sons. A dispensation has been obtained from Rome to Diana Vernon to marry *Blank* Osbaldistone, Esq., son of Sir Hildebrand Osbaldistone, of Osbaldistone Hall, Bart., and so forth; and it only remains to pitch upon the happy man, whose name shall fill the gap in the manuscript. Now, as Percie is seldom sober, my father pitched on Thorncliff, as the second prop of the family, and therefore most proper to carry on the line of the Osbaldistones.'

'The young lady,' said I, forcing myself to assume an air of pleasantry, which, I believe, became me extremely ill, 'would perhaps have been inclined to look a little lower on the family-tree, for the branch to which she was desirous of clinging.'

'I cannot say,' he replied. 'There is room for little choice in our family; Dick is a gambler, John a boor, and Wilfred an ass. I believe my father really made the best selection for poor Die, after all.'

'The present company,' said I, 'being always expected.'

'O, my destination to the church placed me out of the question; otherwise I will not affect to say, that, qualified by my education both to instruct and guide Miss Vernon, I might not have been a more creditable choice than any of my elders.'

'And so thought the young lady, doubtless?'

'You are not to suppose so,' answered Rashleigh, with an affectation of denial, which was contrived to convey the strongest affirmation the case admitted of—'Friendship—only friendship—formed the tie betwixt us, and the tender affection of an opening mind to its only instructor—Love came not near us—I told you I was wise in time.'

I felt little inclination to pursue this conversation any farther, and, shaking myself clear of Rashleigh, withdrew to my own apartment, which I recollect I traversed with much vehemence of agitation, repeating aloud the expressions which had most offended me. 'Susceptible—ardent—tender affection—Love!—Diana Vernon, the most beautiful creature I ever beheld, in love with him, the bandy-legged, bull-necked, limping scoundrel!—Richard the Third in all but his hump-back!—And yet the opportunities he must have had during his cursed course of lectures; and the fellow's flowing and easy strain of sentiment; and her extreme seclusion from every one who spoke and acted with common sense; ay, and her obvious pique at him, mixed with admiration of his talents, which looked as like the result of neglected attachment as any thing else—Well, and what is it to me that I should storm and rage at it? Is Diana Vernon the first pretty girl that has loved or married an ugly fellow? And if she were free of every Osbaldistone of them, what concern is it of mine?—A Catholic—a Jacobite—a termagant into the boot—for me to look that way were utter madness.'

By throwing such reflections on the flame of my displeasure, I subdued it into a sort of smouldering heart-burning, and appeared at the dinner-table in as sulky a humour as could well be imagined.

CHAPTER XII

Drunk?—and speak parrot?—and squabble?—swagger?—
Swear?—and discourse fustian with one's own shadow?

OTHELLO*

I HAVE already told you, my dear Tresham, what probably was no news to you, that my principal fault was an unconquerable pitch of pride, which exposed me to frequent mortification. I had not even whispered to myself, that I loved Diana Vernon; yet no sooner did I hear Rashleigh talk of her as a prize which he might stoop to carry off, or neglect, at his pleasure, than every step which the poor girl had taken, in the innocence and openness of her heart, to form a sort of friendship with me, seemed in my eyes the most insulting coquetry. 'Soh! she would secure me as a *pis aller*, I suppose, in case Mr Rashleigh Osbaldistone should not take compassion upon her! but I will satisfy her that I am not a person to be trepanned in that manner—I will make her sensible that I see through her arts, and that I scorn them.'

I did not reflect for a moment, that all this indignation, which I had no right whatever to entertain, proved that I was anything but indifferent to Miss Vernon's charms; and I sate down to table in high ill-humour with her and all the daughters of Eve.

Miss Vernon heard me, with surprise, return ungracious answers to one or two playful strokes of satire which she threw out with her usual freedom of speech; but, having no suspicion that offence was meant, she only replied to my rude repartees with jests somewhat similar, but polished by her good temper, though pointed by her wit. At length she perceived I was really out of humour, and answered one of my rude speeches thus:

'They say, Mr Frank, that one may gather sense from fools—I heard cousin Wilfred refuse to play any longer at cudgels the other day with cousin Thornie, because cousin Thornie got angry, and struck harder than the rules of amicable combat, it seems, permitted. "Were I to break your head in good earnest," quoth honest Wilfred, "I care not how angry you are, for I should do it so much the more easily;—but it's hard I should get raps over the costard, and only pay you back in make-believes"—Do you understand the moral of this, Frank?'

'I have never felt myself under the necessity, madam, of studying how to extract the slender portion of sense with which this family season their conversation.'

'Necessity! and madam!—You surprise me, Mr Osbaldistone.'

'I am unfortunate in doing so.'

'Am I to suppose that this capricious tone is serious; or is it only assumed, to make your good-humour more valuable?'

'You have a right to the attention of so many gentlemen in this family, Miss Vernon, that it cannot be worth your while to enquire into the cause of my stupidity and bad spirits.'

'What!' she said, 'am I to understand, then, that you have deserted my faction, and gone over to the enemy?'

Then, looking across the table, and observing that Rashleigh, who was seated opposite, was watching us with a singular expression of interest on his harsh features, she continued,

> 'Horrible thought!—Ay, now I see 'tis true,
> For the grim-visaged Rashleigh smiles on me,
> And points at thee for his!——*

Well, thank Heaven, and the unprotected state which has taught me endurance, I do not take offence easily; and that I may not be forced to quarrel, whether I like it or no, I have the honour, earlier than usual, to wish you a happy digestion of your dinner and your bad humour.'

And she left the table accordingly.

Upon Miss Vernon's departure, I found myself very little satisfied with my own conduct. I had hurled back offered kindness, of which circumstances had but lately pointed out the honest sincerity, and I had but just stopped short of insulting the beautiful, and, as she had said with some emphasis, the unprotected being by whom it was proffered. My conduct seemed brutal in my own eyes. To combat or drown these painful reflections, I applied myself more frequently than usual to the wine which circulated on the table.

The agitated state of my feelings combined with my habits of temperance to give rapid effect to the beverage. Habitual topers, I believe, acquire the power of soaking themselves with a quantity of liquor that does little more than muddy those intellects, which, in their sober state, are none of the clearest; but men who are strangers to the vice of drunkenness as a habit, are more powerfully acted upon by intoxicating liquors. My spirits, once aroused, became extravagant; I talked a great deal, argued upon what I knew nothing of, told stories of which I forgot the point, then laughed immoderately at my own forgetfulness; I accepted several bets without having the least judgment; I challenged the giant John to wrestle with me, although he had kept the ring at Hexham for a year, and I never tried so much as a single fall.

My uncle had the goodness to interpose and prevent this consummation of drunken folly, which, I suppose, would have otherwise ended in my neck being broken.

It has even been reported by maligners, that I sung a song while under this vinous influence; but, as I remember nothing of it, and never attempted to turn a tune in all my life before or since, I would willingly hope there is no actual foundation for the calumny. I was absurd enough without this exaggeration. Without positively losing my senses, I speedily lost all command of my temper, and my impetuous passions whirled me onward at their pleasure. I had sate down sulky and discontented, and disposed to be silent—the wine rendered me loquacious, disputatious, and quarrelsome. I contradicted whatever was asserted, and attacked, without any respect to my uncle's table, both his politics and his religion. The affected moderation of Rashleigh, which he well knew how to qualify with irritating ingredients, was even more provoking to me than the noisy and bullying language of his obstreperous brothers. My uncle, to do him justice, endeavoured to bring us to order; but his authority was lost amidst the tumult of wine and passion. At length, frantic at some real, or supposed injurious insinuation, I actually struck Rashleigh with my fist. No Stoic philosopher, superior to his own passion and that of others, could have received an insult with a higher degree of scorn. What he himself did not think it apparently worth while to resent, Thorncliff resented for him. Swords were drawn, and we exchanged one or two passes, when the other brothers separated us by main force; and I shall never forget the diabolical sneer which writhed Rashleigh's wayward features, as I was forced from the apartment by the main strength of two of these youthful Titans. They secured me in my apartment by locking the door, and I heard them, to my inexpressible rage, laugh heartily as they descended the stairs. I essayed in my fury to break out; but the window-grates, and the strength of a door clenched with iron, resisted my efforts. At length I threw myself on my bed, and fell asleep amidst vows of dire revenge to be taken in the ensuing day.

But with the morning cool repentance came.* I felt, in the keenest manner, the violence and absurdity of my conduct, and was obliged to confess that wine and passion had lowered my intellects even below those of Wilfred Osbaldistone, whom I held in so much contempt. My uncomfortable reflections were by no means soothed by meditating the necessity of an apology for my improper behaviour, and recollecting that Miss Vernon must be a witness of my submission. The impropriety and unkindness of my conduct to her personally, added not a little to these galling considerations, and for this I could not even plead the miserable excuse of intoxication.

Under all these aggravating feelings of shame and degradation, I descended to the breakfast-hall, like a criminal to receive sentence. It chanced that a hard frost had rendered it impossible to take out the hounds, so that I had the additional mortification to meet the family, excepting only Rashleigh and Miss Vernon, in full divan,* surrounding the cold venison-pasty and chine of beef. They were in high glee as I entered, and I could easily imagine that the jests were furnished at my expense. In fact, what I was disposed to consider with serious pain, was regarded as an excellent good joke by my uncle, and the greater part of my cousins. Sir Hildebrand, while he rallied me on the exploits of the preceding evening, swore he thought a young fellow had better be thrice drunk in one day, than sneak sober to bed like a presbyterian, and leave a batch of honest fellows, and a double quart of claret. And to back this consolatory speech, he poured out a large bumper of brandy, exhorting me to swallow 'a hair of the dog that had bit me.'

'Never mind these lads laughing, nevoy,' he continued; 'they would have been all as great milksops as yourself, had I not nursed them, as one may say, on the toast and tankard.'*

Ill-nature was not the fault of my cousins in general; they saw I was vexed and hurt at the recollections of the preceding evening, and endeavoured, with clumsy kindness, to remove the painful impression they had made on me. Thorncliff alone looked sullen and unreconciled. This young man had never liked me from the beginning; and in the marks of attention occasionally shown me by his brothers, awkward as they were, he alone had never joined. If it was true, of which, however, I began to have my doubts, that he was considered by the family, or regarded himself, as the destined husband of Miss Vernon, a sentiment of jealousy might have sprung up in his mind from the marked predilection which it was that young lady's pleasure to show for one, whom Thorncliff might, perhaps, think likely to become a dangerous rival.

Rashleigh at last entered, his visage as dark as mourning weed, brooding, I could not but doubt, over the unjustifiable and disgraceful insult I had offered to him. I had already settled in my own mind how I was to behave on the occasion, and had schooled myself to believe, that true honour consisted not in defending, but in apologizing for, an injury so much disproportioned to any provocation I might have to allege.

I therefore hastened to meet Rashleigh, and to express myself in the highest degree sorry for the violence with which I had acted on the preceding evening.

'No circumstances,' I said, 'could have wrung from me a single word of apology, save my own consciousness of the impropriety of my behaviour. I hoped my cousin would accept of my regrets so sincerely offered, and consider how much of my misconduct was owing to the excessive hospitality of Osbaldistone Hall.'

'He shall be friends with thee, lad,' cried the honest knight, in the full effusion of his heart; 'or d—n me, if I call him son more!—Why, Rashie, dost stand there like a log? *Sorry for it* is all a gentleman can say, if he happens to do any thing awry, especially over his claret.—I served in Hounslow, and should know something, I think, of affairs of honour. Let me hear no more of this, and we'll go in a body and rummage out the badger in Birkenwood-bank.'

Rashleigh's face resembled, as I have already noticed, no other countenance that I ever saw. But this singularity lay not only in the features, but in the mode of changing their expression. Other countenances, in altering from grief to joy, or from anger to satisfaction, pass through some brief interval, ere the expression of the predominant passion supersedes entirely that of its predecessor. There is a sort of twilight, like that between the clearing up of the darkness and the rising of the sun, while the swollen muscles subside, the dark eye clears, the forehead relaxes and expands itself, and the whole countenance loses its sterner shades, and becomes serene and placid. Rashleigh's face exhibited none of these gradations, but changed almost instantaneously from the expression of one passion to that of the contrary. I can compare it to nothing but the sudden shifting of a scene in the theatre, where, at the whistle of the prompter, a cavern disappears, and a grove arises.

My attention was strongly arrested by this peculiarity on the present occasion. At Rashleigh's first entrance, 'black he stood as night!'* With the same inflexible countenance he heard my excuse and his father's exhortation; and it was not until Sir Hildebrand had done speaking, that the cloud cleared away at once, and he expressed, in the kindest and most civil terms, his perfect satisfaction with the very handsome apology I had offered.

'Indeed,' he said, 'I have so poor a brain myself, when I impose on it the least burden beyond my usual three glasses, that I have only, like honest Cassio, a very vague recollection of the confusion of last night—remember a mass of things, but nothing distinctly—a quarrel, but nothing wherefore*—So, my dear cousin,' he continued, shaking me kindly by the hand, 'conceive how much I am relieved, by finding that I have to receive an apology, instead of having to make one—I will not have a word said upon the subject more; I should be very foolish to institute any scrutiny into an account, when the balance, which I expected to be against me, has been so unexpectedly and agreeably struck in my favour. You see, Mr Osbaldistone, I am practising the language of Lombard Street,* and qualifying myself for my new calling.'

As I was about to answer, and raised my eyes for the purpose, they encountered those of Miss Vernon, who, having entered the room unobserved during the conversation, had given it her close attention. Abashed and confounded, I fixed my eyes on the ground, and made my escape to the breakfast-table, where I herded among my busy cousins.

My uncle, that the events of the preceding day might not pass out of our memory without a practical moral lesson, took occasion to give Rashleigh and me his serious advice to correct our milksop habits, as he termed them, and gradually to inure our brains to bear a gentlemanlike quantity of liquor, without brawls or breaking of heads. He recommended that we should begin piddling with a regular quart of claret per day, which, with the aid of March beer and brandy, made a handsome competence for a beginner in the art of toping. And for our encouragement, he assured us that he had known many a man who had lived to our years without having drunk a pint of wine at a sitting, who yet, by falling into honest company, and following hearty example, had afterwards been numbered among the best good fellows of the time, and could carry off their six bottles under their belt quietly and comfortably, without brawling or babbling, and be neither sick nor sorry the next morning.

Sage as this advice was, and comfortable as was the prospect it held out to me, I profited but little by the exhortation; partly, perhaps, because, as often as I raised my eyes from the table, I observed Miss Vernon's looks fixed on me, in which I thought I could read grave compassion blended with regret and displeasure. I began to consider how I should seek a scene of explanation and apology with her also, when she gave me to understand she was determined to save me the trouble of soliciting an interview. 'Cousin Francis,' she said, addressing me by the same title she used to give to the other Osbaldistones, although I had, properly speaking, no title to be called her kinsman, 'I have encountered this morning a difficult passage in the Divína Commédia of Dante;* will you have the goodness to step to the library and give me your assistance? and when you have unearthed for me the meaning of the obscure Florentine, we will join the rest at Birkenwood-bank, and see their luck at unearthing the badger.'

I signified, of course, my readiness to wait upon her. Rashleigh made an offer to accompany us. 'I am something better skilled,' he said, 'at tracking the sense of Dante through the metaphors and elisions of his wild and gloomy poem, than at hunting the poor inoffensive hermit yonder out of his cave.'

'Pardon me, Rashleigh,' said Miss Vernon; 'but as you are to occupy Mr Francis's place in the counting-house, you must surrender to him the charge of your pupil's education at Osbaldistone Hall. We shall call you in, however, if there is any occasion; so pray do not look so grave upon it. Besides, it is a shame to you not to understand field-sports— What will you do should our uncle in Crane-Alley ask you the signs by which you track a badger?'

'Ay, true, Die,—true,' said Sir Hildebrand, with a sigh. 'I misdoubt Rashleigh will be found short at the leap when he is put to the trial. An he would ha' learned useful knowledge like his brothers, he was bred up where it grew, I wuss; but French antics, and book-learning, with the new turnips, and the rats, and the Hanoverians,* ha' changed the world that I ha' known in Old England—But come along with us, Rashie, and carry my hunting-staff, man; thy cousin lacks none of thy company as now, and I wonna ha' Die crossed—It's ne'er be said there was but one woman in Osbaldistone Hall, and she died for lack of her will.'

Rashleigh followed his father, as he commanded, not, however, ere he had whispered to Diana, 'I suppose I must in discretion bring the courtier, Ceremony, in my company, and knock when I approach the door of the library?'

'No, no, Rashleigh,' said Miss Vernon; 'dismiss from your company the false archimage* Dissimulation, and it will better ensure your free access to our classical consultations.'

So saying, she led the way to the library, and I followed—like a criminal, I was going to say, to execution; but, as I bethink me, I have used the simile once, if not twice before. Without any simile at all, then, I followed, with a sense of awkward and conscious embarrassment, which I would have given a great deal to shake off. I thought it a degrading and unworthy feeling to attend one on such an occasion, having breathed the air of the Continent long enough to have imbibed the notion that lightness, gallantry, and something approaching to well-bred self-assurance, should distinguish the gentleman whom a fair lady selects for her companion in a *tête-à-tête*.

My English feelings, however, were too many for my French education, and I made, I believe, a very pitiful figure, when Miss Vernon, seating herself majestically in a huge elbow-chair in the library, like a judge about to hear a cause of importance, signed to me to take a chair opposite to her, (which I did, much like the poor fellow who is going to be tried,) and entered upon conversation in a tone of bitter irony.

CHAPTER XIII

Dire was his thought, who first in poison steep'd
The weapon form'd for slaughter—direr his,
And worthier of damnation, who instill'd
The mortal venom in the social cup,
To fill the veins with death instead of life.

*Anonymous**

'UPON my word, Mr Francis Osbaldistone,' said Miss Vernon, with the air of one who thought herself fully entitled to assume the privilege of ironical reproach, which she was pleased to exert, 'your character improves upon us, sir—I could not have thought that it was in you. Yesterday might be considered as your assay-piece, to prove yourself entitled to be free of the corporation of Osbaldistone Hall. But it was a masterpiece.'

'I am quite sensible of my ill-breeding, Miss Vernon, and I can only say for myself, that I had received some communications by which my spirits were unusually agitated. I am conscious I was impertinent and absurd.'

'You do yourself great injustice,' said the merciless monitor—'you have contrived, by what I saw and have since heard, to exhibit in the course of one evening a happy display of all the various masterly qualifications which distinguish your several cousins;—the gentle and generous temper of the benevolent Rashleigh,—the temperance of Percie,—the cool courage of Thorncliff,—John's skill in dog-breaking,—Dickon's aptitude to betting,—all exhibited by the single individual Mr Francis, and that with a selection of time, place, and circumstance, worthy the taste and sagacity of the sapient Wilfred.'

'Have a little mercy, Miss Vernon,' said I; for I confess I thought the schooling as severe as the case merited, especially considering from what quarter it came, 'and forgive me if I suggest, as an excuse for follies I am not usually guilty of, the custom of this house and country. I am far from approving of it; but we have Shakspeare's authority* for saying, that good wine is a good familiar creature, and that any man living may be overtaken at some time.'

'Ay, Mr Francis, but he places the panegyric and the apology in the mouth of the greatest villain his pencil has drawn. I will not, however, abuse the advantage your quotation has given me, by overwhelming you with the refutation with which the victim Cassio replies to the tempter Iago. I only wish you to know, that there is one person at least sorry to see a youth of talents and expectations sink into the slough, in which the inhabitants of this house are nightly wallowing.'

'I have but wet my shoe, I assure you, Miss Vernon, and am too sensible of the filth of the puddle to step farther in.'

'If such be your resolution,' she replied, 'it is a wise one. But I was so much vexed at what I heard, that your concerns have pressed before my own.—You behaved to me yesterday, during dinner, as if something had been told you which lessened or lowered me in your opinion—I beg leave to ask you what it was?'

I was stupified—the direct bluntness of the demand was much in the style one gentleman uses to another, when requesting explanation of any part of his conduct in a good-humoured yet determined manner, and was totally devoid of the circumlocutions, shadings, softenings, and periphrasis, which usually accompany explanations betwixt persons of different sexes in the higher orders of society.

I remained completely embarrassed; for it pressed on my recollection, that Rashleigh's communications, supposing them to be correct, ought to have rendered Miss Vernon rather an object of my compassion, than of my pettish resentment; and had they furnished the best apology possible for my own conduct, still I must have had the utmost difficulty in detailing what inferred such necessary and natural offence to Miss Vernon's feelings. She observed my hesitation, and proceeded in a tone somewhat more peremptory, but still temperate and civil.

'I hope Mr Osbaldistone does not dispute my title to request this explanation. I have no relative who can protect me; it is, therefore, just that I be permitted to protect myself.'

I endeavoured with hesitation to throw the blame of my rude behaviour upon indisposition—upon disagreeable letters from London. She suffered me to exhaust my apologies, and fairly to run myself aground, listening all the while with a smile of absolute incredulity.

'And now, Mr Francis, having gone through your prologue of excuses, with the same bad grace with which all prologues are delivered, please to draw the curtain, and show me that which I desire to see. In a word, let me know what Rashleigh says of me; for he is the grand engineer and first mover of all the machinery of Osbaldistone Hall.'

'But, supposing there was any thing to tell, Miss Vernon, what does he deserve that betrays the secrets of one ally to another?—Rashleigh, you yourself told me, remained your ally, though no longer your friend.'

'I have neither patience for evasion, nor inclination for jesting, on the present subject. Rashleigh cannot—ought not—dare not, hold any language respecting me, Diana Vernon, but what I may demand to hear repeated. That there are subjects of secrecy and confidence between us, is most certain; but to such, his communications to you could have no relation; and with such, I, as an individual, have no concern.'

I had by this time recovered my presence of mind, and hastily determined to avoid making any disclosure of what Rashleigh had told me in a sort of confidence. There was something unworthy in retailing private conversation; it could, I thought, do no good, and must necessarily give Miss Vernon great pain. I therefore replied, gravely, 'that nothing but frivolous talk had passed between Mr Rashleigh Osbaldistone and me on the state of the family at the Hall; and I protested, that nothing had been said which left a serious impression to her disadvantage. As a gentleman, I said, I could not be more explicit in reporting private conversation.'

She started up with the animation of a Camilla* about to advance into battle. 'This shall not serve your turn, sir,—I must have another answer from you.' Her features kindled—her brow became flushed—her eye glanced wild-fire as she proceeded. 'I demand such an explanation, as a woman basely slandered has a right to demand from every man who calls himself a gentleman—as a creature, motherless, friendless, alone in the world, left to her own guidance and protection, has a right to require from every being having a happier lot, in the name of that God who sent *them* into the world to enjoy, and *her* to suffer. You shall not deny me—or,' she added, looking solemnly upwards, 'you will rue your denial, if there is justice for wrong either on earth or in heaven.'

I was utterly astonished at her vehemence, but felt, thus conjured, that it became my duty to lay aside scrupulous delicacy, and gave her briefly, but distinctly, the heads of the information which Rashleigh had conveyed to me.

She sate down and resumed her composure, as soon as I entered upon the subject, and when I stopped to seek for the most delicate turn of expression, she repeatedly interrupted me, with 'Go on—pray, go on; the first word which occurs to you is the plainest, and must be the best. Do not think of my feelings, but speak as you would to an unconcerned third party.'

Thus urged and encouraged, I stammered through all the account which Rashleigh had given of her early contract to marry an Osbaldistone, and of the uncertainty and difficulty of her choice; and there I would willingly have paused. But her penetration discovered that there was still something behind, and even guessed to what it related.

'Well, it was ill-natured of Rashleigh to tell this tale on me. I am like the poor girl in the fairy tale, who was betrothed in her cradle to the Black Bear of Norway,* but complained chiefly of being called Bruin's bride by her companions at school. But besides all this, Rashleigh said something of himself with relation to me—Did he not?'

'He certainly hinted, that were it not for the idea of supplanting his brother, he would now, in consequence of his change of profession, be desirous that the word Rashleigh should fill up the blank in the dispensation, instead of the word Thorncliff.'

'Ay? indeed?' she replied; 'was he so very condescending?—Too much honour for his humble handmaid, Diana Vernon—And she, I suppose, was to be enraptured with joy could such a substitute be effected?'

'To confess the truth, he intimated as much, and even farther insinuated'——

'What?—Let me hear it all!' she exclaimed hastily.

'That he had broken off your mutual intimacy, lest it should have given rise to an affection by which his destination to the church would not permit him to profit.'

'I am obliged to him for his consideration,' replied Miss Vernon, every feature of her fine countenance taxed to express the most supreme degree of scorn and contempt. She paused a moment, and then said, with her usual composure, 'There is but little I have heard from you which I did not expect to hear, and which I ought not to have expected; because, bating one circumstance, it is all very true. But as there are some poisons so active, that a few drops, it is said, will infect a whole fountain, so there is one falsehood in Rashleigh's communication, powerful enough to corrupt the whole well in which Truth herself is said to have dwelt. It is the leading and foul falsehood, that, knowing Rashleigh as I have reason too well to know him, any circumstance on earth could make me think of sharing my lot with him. No,' she continued, with a sort of inward shuddering that seemed to express involuntary horror, 'any lot rather than that—the sot, the gambler, the bully, the jockey, the insensate fool, were a thousand times preferable to Rashleigh;—the convent—the jail—the grave, shall be welcome before them all.'

There was a sad and melancholy cadence in her voice, corresponding with the strange and interesting romance of her situation. So young, so beautiful, so untaught, so much abandoned to herself, and deprived of all the support which her sex derives from the countenance and protection of female friends, and even of that degree of defence which arises from the forms with which the sex are approached in civilized life,—it is scarce metaphorical to say, that my heart bled for her. Yet there was an expression of dignity in her contempt of ceremony—of upright feeling in her disdain of falsehood—of firm resolution in the manner in which she contemplated the dangers by which she was surrounded, which blended my pity with the warmest admiration. She seemed a princess deserted by her subjects, and deprived of her power, yet still scorning those formal regulations of society which are created for persons of an inferior rank; and, amid her difficulties, relying boldly and confidently on the justice of Heaven, and the unshaken constancy of her own mind.

I offered to express the mingled feelings of sympathy and admiration with which her unfortunate situation and her high spirit combined to impress me, but she imposed silence on me at once.

'I told you in jest,' she said, 'that I disliked compliments—I now tell you in earnest, that I do not ask sympathy, and that I despise consolation. What I have borne, I have borne—What I am to bear, I will sustain as I may; no word of commiseration can make a burden feel one feather's weight lighter to the slave who must carry it. There is only one human being who could have assisted me, and that is he who has rather chosen to add to my embarrassment—Rashleigh Osbaldistone.—Yes! the time once was that I might have learned to love that man—But, great God! the purpose for which he insinuated himself into the confidence of one already so forlorn—the undeviating and continued assiduity with which he pursued that purpose from year to year, without one single momentary pause of remorse or compassion—the purpose for which he would have converted into poison the food he administered to my mind—Gracious Providence! what should

I have been in this world and the next, in body and soul, had I fallen under the arts of this accomplished villain!'

I was so much struck with the scene of perfidious treachery which these words disclosed, that I rose from my chair, hardly knowing what I did, laid my hand on the hilt of my sword, and was about to leave the apartment in search of him on whom I might discharge my just indignation. Almost breathless, and with eyes and looks in which scorn and indignation had given way to the most lively alarm, Miss Vernon threw herself between me and the door of the apartment.

'Stay,' she said,—'stay; however just your resentment, you do not know half the secrets of this fearful prison-house.' She then glanced her eyes anxiously round the room, and sunk her voice almost to a whisper—'He bears a charmed life; you cannot assail him without endangering other lives, and wider destruction. Had it been otherwise, in some hour of justice he had hardly been safe, even from this weak hand. I told you,' she said, motioning me back to my seat, 'that I needed no comforter—I now tell you, I need no avenger.'

I resumed my seat mechanically, musing on what she said, and recollecting also, what had escaped me in my first glow of resentment, that I had no title whatever to constitute myself Miss Vernon's champion. She paused to let her own emotions and mine subside, and then addressed me with more composure.

'I have already said, that there is a mystery connected with Rashleigh, of a dangerous and fatal nature. Villain as he is, and as he knows he stands convicted in my eyes, I cannot—dare not, openly break with or defy him. You also, Mr Osbaldistone, must bear with him with patience, foil his artifices by opposing to them prudence, not violence; and, above all, you must avoid such scenes as that of last night, which cannot but give him perilous advantages over you. This caution I designed to give you, and it was the object with which I desired this interview; but I have extended my confidence farther than I proposed.'

I assured her it was not misplaced.

'I do not believe that it is,' she replied. 'You have that in your face and manners which authorizes trust. Let us continue to be friends. You need not fear,' she said, laughing, while she blushed a little, yet speaking with a free and unembarrassed voice, 'that friendship with us should prove only a specious name, as the poet says,* for another feeling. I belong, in habits of thinking and acting, rather to your sex, with which I have always been brought up, than to my own. Besides, the fatal veil was wrapt round me in my cradle; for you may easily believe I have never thought of the detestable condition under which I may remove it. The time,' she added, 'for expressing my final determination is not arrived, and I would fain have the freedom of wild heath and open air with the other commoners of nature, as long as I can be permitted to enjoy them. And now that the passage in Dante is made so clear, pray go and see what is become of the badger-baiters—My head aches so much that I cannot join the party.'

I left the library, but not to join the hunters. I felt that a solitary walk was necessary to compose my spirits, before I again trusted myself in Rashleigh's company, whose depth of calculating villainy had been so strikingly exposed to me. In Dubourg's family, (as he was of the reformed persuasion,) I had heard many a tale of Romish priests, who gratified, at the expense of friendship, hospitality, and the most sacred ties of social life, those passions, the blameless indulgence of which is denied by the rules of their order. But the deliberate system of undertaking the education of a deserted orphan of noble birth, and so intimately allied to his own family, with the perfidious purpose of ultimately seducing her, detailed as it was by the intended victim with all the glow of virtuous resentment, seemed more atrocious to me than the worst of the tales I had heard at Bourdeaux, and I felt it would be extremely difficult for me to meet Rashleigh, and yet to suppress the abhorrence with which he impressed me. Yet this was absolutely necessary, not only on account of the mysterious charge which Diana had given me, but because I had, in reality, no ostensible ground for quarrelling with him.

I therefore resolved, as far as possible, to meet Rashleigh's dissimulation with equal caution on my part during our residence in the same family; and when he should depart for London, I resolved to give Owen at least such a hint of his character as might keep him on his guard over my father's interests. Avarice or ambition, I thought, might have as great, or greater charms, for a mind constituted like Rashleigh's, than unlawful pleasure; the energy of his character, and his power of assuming all seeming good qualities, were likely to procure him a high degree of confidence, and it was not to be hoped, that either good faith or gratitude would prevent him from abusing it. The task was somewhat difficult, especially in my circumstances, since the caution which I threw out might be imputed to jealousy of my rival, or rather my successor, in my father's favour. Yet I thought it absolutely necessary to frame such a letter, leaving it to Owen, who, in his own line, was wary, prudent, and circumspect, to make the necessary use of his knowledge of Rashleigh's true character. Such a letter, therefore, I indited, and dispatched to the post-house by the first opportunity.

At my meeting with Rashleigh, he, as well as I, appeared to have taken up distant ground, and to be disposed to avoid all pretext for collision. He was probably conscious that Miss Vernon's communications had been unfavourable to him, though he could not know that they extended to discovering his meditated villainy towards her. Our intercourse, therefore, was reserved on both sides, and turned on subjects of little interest. Indeed, his stay at Osbaldistone Hall did not exceed a few days after this period, during which I only remarked two circumstances respecting him. The first was, the rapid and almost intuitive manner in which his powerful and active mind seized upon and arranged the elementary principles necessary in his new profession, which he now studied hard, and occasionally made parade of his progress, as if to show me how light it was for him to lift the burden which I had flung down from very weariness and inability to carry it. The other remarkable circumstance was, that, notwithstanding the injuries with which Miss Vernon charged Rashleigh, they had several private interviews together of considerable length, although their bearing towards each other in public did not seem more cordial than usual.

When the day of Rashleigh's departure arrived, his father bade him farewell with indifference; his brothers, with the ill-concealed glee of schoolboys, who see their taskmaster depart for a season, and feel a joy which they dare not express; and I myself with cold politeness. When he approached Miss Vernon, and would have saluted her, she drew back with a look of haughty disdain; but said, as she extended her hand to him, 'Farewell, Rashleigh; God reward you for the good you have done, and forgive you for the evil you have meditated.'

'Amen, my fair cousin,' he replied, with an air of sanctity, which belonged, I thought, to the seminary of Saint Omers; 'happy is he whose good intentions have borne fruit in deeds, and whose evil thoughts have perished in the blossom.'

These were his parting words. 'Accomplished hypocrite!' said Miss Vernon to me, as the door closed behind him—'how nearly can what we most despise and hate approach in outward manner to that which we most venerate!'

I had written to my father by Rashleigh, and also a few lines to Owen, besides the confidential letter which I have already mentioned, and which I thought it more proper and prudent to dispatch by another conveyance. In these epistles, it would have been natural for me to have pointed out to my father and my friend, that I was at present in a situation where I could improve myself in no respect, unless in the mysteries of hunting and hawking; and where I was not unlikely to forget, in the company of rude grooms and horse-boys, any useful knowledge or elegant accomplishments which I had hitherto acquired. It would also have been natural that I should have expressed the disgust and tædium which I was likely to feel among beings, whose whole souls were centred in field-sports or more degrading pastimes—that I should have complained of the habitual intemperance of the family in which I was a guest, and the difficulty and almost resentment with which my uncle Sir Hildebrand received any apology for deserting the bottle. This last, indeed, was a topic on which my father, himself a man of severe temperance, was likely to be easily alarmed, and to have touched upon this spring would to a certainty have opened the doors of my prison-house, and would either have been the means of abridging my exile, or at least would have procured me a change of residence during my rustication.

I say, my dear Tresham, that, considering how very unpleasant a prolonged residence at Osbaldistone Hall must have been to a young man of my age, and with my habits, it might have seemed very natural that I should have pointed out all these disadvantages to my father, in order to obtain his consent for leaving my uncle's mansion. Nothing, however, is more certain, than that I did not say a single word to this purpose in my letters to my father and Owen. If Osbaldistone Hall had been Athens in all its pristine glory of learning, and inhabited by sages, heroes, and poets, I could not have expressed less inclination to leave it.

If thou hast any of the salt of youth left in thee, Tresham, thou wilt be at no loss to account for my silence on a topic seemingly so obvious. Miss Vernon's extreme beauty, of which she herself seemed so little conscious,—her romantic and mysterious situation,—the evils to which she was exposed,—the courage with which she seemed to face them,—her manners, more frank than belonged to her sex, yet, as it seemed to me, exceeding in frankness only from the dauntless consciousness of her innocence,—above all, the obvious and flattering distinction which she made in my favour over all other persons, were at once calculated to interest my best feelings, to excite my curiosity, awaken my imagination, and gratify my vanity. I dared not, indeed, confess to myself the depth of the interest with which Miss Vernon inspired me, or the large share which she occupied in my thoughts. We read together, walked together, rode together, and sate together. The studies which she had broken off upon her quarrel with Rashleigh, she now resumed under the auspices of a tutor, whose views were more sincere, though his capacity was far more limited.

In truth, I was by no means qualified to assist her in the prosecution of several profound studies which she had commenced with Rashleigh, and which appeared to me more fitted for a churchman than for a beautiful female. Neither can I conceive with what view he should have engaged Diana in the gloomy maze of casuistry which schoolmen called philosophy, or in the equally abstruse, though more certain sciences of mathematics and astronomy; unless it were to break down and confound in her mind the difference and distinction between the sexes, and to habituate her to trains of subtile reasoning, by which he might at his own time invest that which is wrong with the colour of that which is right. It was in the same spirit, though in the latter case the evil purpose was more obvious, that the lessons of Rashleigh had encouraged Miss Vernon in setting at nought and despising the forms and ceremonial limits which are drawn round females in modern society. It is true, she was sequestered from all female company, and could not learn the usual rules of decorum, either from example or precept; yet such was her innate modesty, and accurate sense of what was right and wrong, that she would not of herself have adopted the bold uncompromising manner which struck me with so much surprise on our first acquaintance, had she not been led to conceive, that a contempt of ceremony indicated at once superiority of understanding, and the confidence of conscious innocence. Her wily instructor had, no doubt, his own views in levelling those outworks which reserve and caution erect around virtue. But for these, and for his other crimes, he has long since answered at a higher tribunal.

Besides the progress which Miss Vernon, whose powerful mind readily adopted every means of information offered to it, had made in more abstract science, I found her no contemptible linguist, and well acquainted both with ancient and modern literature. Were it not that strong talents will often go farthest when they seem to have least assistance, it would be most incredible to tell the rapidity of Miss Vernon's progress in knowledge; and it was still more extraordinary, when her stock of mental acquisitions from books was compared with her total ignorance of actual life. It seemed as if she saw and knew every thing, except what passed in the world around her; and I believe it was this very ignorance and simplicity of thinking upon ordinary subjects, so strikingly contrasted with her fund of general knowledge and information, which rendered her conversation so irresistibly fascinating, and riveted the attention to whatever she said or did; since it was absolutely impossible to anticipate whether her next word or action was to display the most acute perception, or the most profound simplicity. The degree of danger which necessarily attended a youth of my age and keen feelings from remaining in close and constant intimacy with an object so amiable, and so peculiarly interesting, all who remember their own sentiments at my age may easily estimate.

CHAPTER XIV*

Yon lamp its line of quivering light
Shoots from my lady's bower;
But why should Beauty's lamp be bright
At midnight's lonely hour?

*Old Ballad**

THE mode of life at Osbaldistone Hall was too uniform to admit of description. Diana Vernon and I enjoyed much of our time in our mutual studies; the rest of the family killed theirs in such sports and pastimes as suited the seasons, in which we also took a share. My uncle was a man of habits, and by habit became so much accustomed to my presence and mode of life, that, upon the whole, he was rather fond of me than otherwise. I might probably have risen yet higher in his good graces, had I employed the same arts for that purpose which were used by Rashleigh, who, availing himself of his father's disinclination to business, had gradually insinuated himself into the management of his property. But although I readily gave my uncle the advantage of my pen and my arithmetic so often as he desired to correspond with a neighbour, or settle with a tenant, and was, in so far, a more useful inmate in his family than any of his sons, yet I was not willing to oblige Sir Hilderbrand, by relieving him entirely from the management of his own affairs; so that, while the good knight admitted that nevoy Frank was a steady, handy lad, he seldom failed to remark in the same breath, that he did not think he should ha' missed Rashleigh so much as he was like to do.

As it is particularly unpleasant to reside in a family where we are at variance with any part of it, I made some efforts to overcome the ill-will which my cousins entertained against me. I exchanged my laced hat for a jockey-cap, and made some progress in their opinion; I broke a young colt in a manner which carried me further into their good graces. A bet or two opportunely lost to Dickon, and an extra health pledged with Percie, placed me on an easy and familiar footing with all the young squires, except Thorncliff.

I have already noticed the dislike entertained against me by this young fellow, who, as he had rather more sense, had also a much worse temper, than any of his brethren. Sullen, dogged, and quarrelsome, he regarded my residence at Osbaldistone Hall as an intrusion, and viewed, with envious and jealous eyes, my intimacy with Diana Vernon, whom the effect proposed to be given to a certain family-compact assigned to him as an intended spouse. That he loved her could scarcely be said, at least without much misapplication of the word; but he regarded her as something appropriated to himself, and resented internally the interference which he knew not how to prevent or interrupt. I attempted a tone of conciliation towards Thorncliff on several occasions; but he rejected my advances with a manner about as gracious as that of a growling mastiff, when the animal shuns and resents a stranger's attempts to caress him. I therefore abandoned him to his ill-humour, and gave myself no further trouble about the matter.

Such was the footing upon which I stood with the family at Osbaldistone Hall; but I ought to mention another of its inmates with whom I occasionally held some discourse. This was Andrew Fairservice, the gardener, who (since he had discovered that I was a Protestant) rarely suffered me to pass him without proffering his Scotch mull for a social pinch. There were several advantages attending this courtesy. In the first place, it was made at no expense, for I never took snuff; and, secondly, it afforded an excellent apology to Andrew (who was not particularly fond of hard labour) for laying aside his spade for several minutes. But, above all, these brief interviews gave Andrew an opportunity of venting the news he had collected, or the satirical remarks which his shrewd northern humour suggested.

'I am saying, sir,' he said to me one evening, with a face obviously charged with intelligence, 'I hae been doun at the Trinlay-knowe.'

'Well, Andrew, and I suppose you heard some news at the alehouse?'

'Na, sir; I never gang to the yillhouse—that is, unless ony neighbour was to gie me a pint, or the like o' that; but to gang there on ane's ain coat tail, is a waste o' precious time and hard-won siller.—But I was doun at the Trinlay-knowe, as I was saying, about a wee bit business o' my ain wi' Mattie Simpson, that wants a forpit or twa o' peers, that will never be missed in the Ha'-house—and when we were at the thrangest o' our bargain, wha suld come in but Pate Macready the travelling merchant?'

'Pedlar, I suppose you mean?'

'E'en as your honour likes to ca' him; but it's a creditable calling and a gainfu', and has been lang in use wi' our folk. Pate's a far-awa cousin o' mine, and we were blythe to meet wi' ane anither.'

'And you went and had a jug of ale together, I suppose, Andrew?—
For Heaven's sake, cut short your story.'

'Bide a wee—bide a wee; you southrons are aye in sic a hurry, and
this is something concerns yoursell, an ye wad tak patience to hear't—
Yill?—deil a drap o' yill did Pate offer me; but Mattie gae us baith a
drap skimmed milk, and ane o' her thick ait jannocks, that was as wat
and raw as a divot.—O, for the bonnie girdle cakes o' the North!—and
sae we sat doun and took out our clavers.'

'I wish you would take them out just now. Pray, tell me the news, if
you have got any worth telling, for I can't stop here all night.'

'Than, if ye maun hae't, the folk in Lunnun are a' clean wud about
this bit job in the north here.'

'Clean wood! what's that?'

'Ou, just real daft—neither to haud nor to bind—a' hirdy-girdy—
clean through ither—the deil's over Jock Wabster.'*

'But what does all this mean? or what business have I with the devil
or Jack Webster?'

'Umph!' said Andrew, looking extremely knowing, 'it's just
because—just that the dirdum's a' about yon man's pokmanty.'

'Whose portmanteau? or what do you mean?'

'Ou, just the man Morris's, that he said he lost yonder; but if it's no
your honour's affair, as little is it mine; and I maunna lose this gracious
evening.'

And, as if suddenly seized with a violent fit of industry, Andrew
began to labour most diligently.

My attention, as the crafty knave had foreseen, was now arrested,
and unwilling, at the same time, to acknowledge any particular interest in that affair, by asking direct questions, I stood waiting till the
spirit of voluntary communication should again prompt him to
resume his story. Andrew dug on manfully, and spoke at intervals, but
nothing to the purpose of Mr Macready's news; and I stood and listened, cursing him in my heart, and desirous, at the same time, to see
how long his humour of contradiction would prevail over his desire of
speaking upon the subject, which was obviously uppermost in his
mind.

'Am trenching up the sparry-grass, and am gaun to saw sum Misegun beans;* they winna want them to their swine's flesh, I'se warrant—muckle gude may it do them. And sicklike dung as the grieve
has gien me; it should be wheat-strae, or aiten at the warst o't, and it's

pease-dirt, as fizzenless as chuckie-stanes. But the huntsman guides a'
as he likes about the stable-yard, and he's selled the best o' the litter,
I'se warrant. But, howsoever, we maunna lose a turn o' this Saturday at
e'en, for the wather's sair broken, and if there's a fair day in seven,
Sunday's sure to come and lick it up—Howsomever, I'm no denying
that it may settle, if it be Heaven's will, till Monday morning, and
what's the use o' my breaking my back at this rate—I think, I'll e'en
awa' hame, for yon's the curfew, as they ca' their jowing-in bell.'

Accordingly, applying both his hands to his spade, he pitched it
upright in the trench which he had been digging, and, looking at me
with the air of superiority of one who knows himself possessed of
important information, which he may communicate or refuse at his
pleasure, pulled down the sleeves of his shirt, and walked slowly
towards his coat, which lay carefully folded up upon a neighbouring
garden-seat.

I must pay the penalty of having interrupted the tiresome rascal,
thought I to myself, and even gratify Mr Fairservice by taking his communication on his own terms. Then raising my voice, I addressed
him,—'And after all, Andrew, what are these London news you had
from your kinsman, the travelling merchant?'

'The pedlar, your honour means?' retorted Andrew—'but ca' him
what ye wull, they're a great convenience in a country-side that's scant
o' borough-towns, like this Northumberland—That's no the case,
now, in Scotland—There's the kingdom o' Fife, frae Culross to the
East Nuik,* it's just like a great combined city—Sae mony royal bor-
oughs yoked on end to end, like ropes of ingans, with their hie-streets,
and their booths, nae doubt, and their kræmes, and houses of stane and
lime and forestairs—Kirkcaldy, the sell o't, is langer than ony town in
England.'

'I dare say it is all very splendid and very fine—but you were talking
of the London news a little while ago, Andrew.'

'Ay,' replied Andrew; 'but I dinna think your honour cared to hear
about them—howsoever,' (he continued, grinning a ghastly smile,)
'Pate Macready does say, that they are sair mistrysted yonder in their
Parliament-House about this rubbery o' Mr Morris, or whatever they
ca' the chiel.'

'In the House of Parliament, Andrew! How came they to mention it
there?'

'Ou, that's just what I said to Pate; if it like your honour, I'll tell you the very words; it's no worth making a lie for the matter—"Pate," said I, "what ado had the lords and lairds and gentles at Lunnun wi' the carle and his walise?—When we had a Scotch Parliament, Pate," says I, (and deil rax their thrapples that reft us o't!) "they sate dousely down and made laws for a haill country and kinrick, and never fashed their beards about things that were competent to the judge ordinar o' the bounds; but I think," said I, "that if ae kail-wife pou'd aff her neighbour's mutch, they wad hae the twasome o' them into the Parliament-House o' Lunnun. It's just," said I, "amaist as silly as our auld daft laird here and his gomerils o' sons, wi' his huntsmen and his hounds, and his hunting cattle and horns, riding haill days after a bit beast that winna weigh sax punds when they hae catched it." '

'You argued most admirably, Andrew,' said I, willing to encourage him to get into the marrow of his intelligence; 'and what said Pate?'

'Ou,' he said, 'what better cou'd be expected of a wheen pock-pudding English folk?—But as to the robbery, it's like that when they're a' at the thrang o' their Whig and Tory wark, and ca'ing ane anither, like unhanged blackguards—up gets ae lang-tongued chield, and he says, that a' the north of England were rank Jacobites, (and, quietly, he wasna far wrang maybe,) and that they had levied amaist open war, and a king's messenger had been stoppit and rubbit on the highway, and that the best bluid o' Northumberland had been at the doing o't—and mickle gowd ta'en aff him, and mony valuable papers; and that there was nae redress to be gotten by remeed of law, for the first justice o' the peace that the rubbit man gaed to, he had fund the twa loons that did the deed birling and drinking wi' him, wha but they; and the justice took the word o' the tane for the compearance o' the tither; and that they e'en gae him leg-bail, and the honest man that had lost his siller was fain to leave the country for fear that waur had come of it.'

'Can this be really true?' said I.

'Pate swears it's as true as that his ellwand is a yard lang—(and so it is, just bating an inch, that it may meet the English measure)*—And when the chield had said his warst, there was a terrible cry for names, and out comes he wi' this man Morris's name, and your uncle's, and Squire Inglewood's, and other folk's beside,' (looking sly at me)— 'And then another dragon o' a chield got up on the other side, and said, wad they accuse the best gentlemen in the land on the oath of a broken coward,—for it's like that Morris had been drummed out o' the army for rinning awa in Flanders; and he said, it was like the story had been made up between the minister and him or ever he had left Lunnun; and that, if there was to be a search-warrant granted, he thought the siller wad be fund some gate near to St James's Palace. Aweel, they trailed up Morris to their bar, as they ca't, to see what he could say to the job; but the folk that were again him, gae him sic an awfu' throughgaun about his rinnin' awa, and about a' the ill he had ever dune or said for a' the forepart o' his life, that Patie says, he looked mair like ane dead than living; and they cou'dna get a word o' sense out o' him, for downright fright at their gowling and routing.——He maun be a saft sap, wi' a head nae better than a fozy frosted turnip——it wad hae ta'en a hantle o' them to scaur Andrew Fairservice out o' his tale.'

'And how did it all end, Andrew? did your friend happen to learn?'

'Ou, ay; for as his walk's in this country, Pate put aff his journey for the space of a week or thereby, because it wad be acceptable to his customers to bring down the news. It just a' gaed aff like moonshine in water. The fallow that began it drew in his horns and said, that though he believed the man had been rubbit, yet he acknowledged he might hae been mista'en about the particulars. And then the other chield got up, and said, he cared na whether Morris was rubbit or no, provided it wasna to become a stain on ony gentleman's honour and reputation, especially in the north of England; for, said he before them, I come frae the north mysell, and I carena a boddle wha kens it. And this is what they ca' explaining——the tane gies up a bit, and the tither gies up a bit, and a' friends again. Aweel, after the Commons' Parliament had tuggit, and rived, and ruggit at Morris and his rubbery till they were tired o't, the Lord's Parliament they behoved to hae their spell o't. In puir auld Scotland's Parliament they a' sate thegither, cheek by choul, and than they didna need to hae the same blethers twice ower again. But till't their lordships went wi' as muckle teeth and gude-will, as if the matter had been a' speck and span new. Forbye, there was something said about ane Campbell, that suld hae been concerned in the rubbery, mair or less, and that he suld hae had a warrant frae the Duke of Argyle, as a testimonial o' his character. And this put MacCallum More's beard in a bleize, as gude reason there was; and he gat up wi' an unco bang, and garr'd them a' look about them, and wad ram it even doun their throats, there was never ane o' the Campbells but was as wight, wise, warlike, and worthy trust, as auld Sir John the Græme.* Now, if your honour's sure ye arena a drap's bluid a-kin to a Campbell, as I am nane mysell, sae far as I can count my kin, or hae had it counted to me, I'll gie ye my mind on that matter.'

'You may be assured I have no connexion whatever with any gentleman of the name.'

'Ou, than we may speak it quietly amang oursells. There's baith gude and bad o' the Campbells, like other names. But this MacCallum More has an unco sway and say baith, amang the grit folk at Lunnun even now; for he canna preceesely be said to belang to ony o' the twa sides o' them, sae deil ane o' them likes to quarrel wi' him; sae they e'en voted Morris's tale a fause calumnious libel, as they ca't, and if he hadna gien them leg-bail, he was likely to hae ta'en the air on the pillory for leasing-making.'

So speaking, honest Andrew collected his dibbles, spades, and hoes, and threw them into a wheel-barrow,—leisurely, however, and allowing me full time to put any farther questions which might occur to me before he trundled them off to the tool-house, there to repose during the ensuing day. I thought it best to speak out at once, lest this meddling fellow should suppose there were more weighty reasons for my silence than actually existed.

'I should like to see this countryman of yours, Andrew; and to hear his news from himself directly. You have probably heard that I had some trouble from the impertinent folly of this man Morris,' (Andrew grinned a most significant grin,) 'and I should wish to see your cousin the merchant, to ask him the particulars of what he heard in London, if it could be done without much trouble.'

'Naething mair easy,' Andrew observed; 'he had but to hint to his cousin that I wanted a pair or twa o' hose, and he wad be wi' me as fast as he could lay leg to the grund.'

'O yes, assure him I shall be a customer; and as the night is, as you say, settled and fair, I shall walk in the garden until he comes; the moon will soon rise over the fells. You may bring him to the little back-gate; and I shall have pleasure, in the meanwhile, in looking on the bushes and evergreens by the bright frosty moon-light.'

'Vara right—vara right—that's what I hae aften said; a kail-blaid, or a colliflour, glances sae glegly by moonlight, it's like a leddy in her diamonds.'

So saying, off went Andrew Fairservice with great glee. He had to walk about two miles, a labour he undertook with the greatest pleasure, in order to secure to his kinsman the sale of some articles of his trade, though it is probable he would not have given him sixpence to treat him to a quart of ale. The good-will of an Englishman would have displayed itself in a manner exactly the reverse of Andrew's, thought I, as I paced along the smooth cut velvet walks, which, embowered with high hedges of yew and of holly, intersected the ancient garden of Osbaldistone Hall.

As I turned to retrace my steps, it was natural that I should lift up my eyes to the windows of the old library; which, small in size, but several in number, stretched along the second story of that side of the house which now faced me. Light glanced from their casements. I was not surprised at this, for I knew Miss Vernon often sate there of an evening, though from motives of delicacy I put a strong restraint upon myself, and never sought to join her at a time when I knew, all the rest of the family being engaged for the evening, our interviews must necessarily have been strictly *tête-à-tête*. In the mornings we usually read together in the same room; but then it often happened that one or other of our cousins entered to seek some parchment duodecimo that could be converted into a fishing-book, despite its gildings and illumination, or to tell us of some 'sport toward,'* or from mere want of knowing where else to dispose of themselves. In short, in the mornings the library was a sort of public room, where man and woman might meet as on neutral ground. In the evening it was very different; and, bred in a country where much attention is paid, or was at least then paid, to *bienséance*, I was desirous to think for Miss Vernon concerning those points of propriety where her experience did not afford her the means of thinking for herself. I made her therefore comprehend, as delicately as I could, that when we had evening lessons, the presence of a third party was proper.

Miss Vernon first laughed, then blushed, and was disposed to be displeased; and then, suddenly checking herself, said, 'I believe you are very right; and when I feel inclined to be a very busy scholar, I will bribe old Martha with a cup of tea to sit by me and be my screen.'

Martha, the old housekeeper, partook of the taste of the family at the Hall. A toast and tankard would have pleased her better than all the tea in China. However, as the use of this beverage was then confined to the higher ranks, Martha felt some vanity in being asked to partake of it; and by dint of a great deal of sugar, many words scarce less sweet, and abundance of toast and butter, she was sometimes prevailed upon to give us her countenance. On other occasions, the servants almost unanimously shunned the library after nightfall, because it was their foolish pleasure to believe that it lay on the haunted side of the house. The more timorous had seen sights and heard sounds there when all the rest of the house was quiet; and even the young squires were far from having any wish to enter these formidable precincts after nightfall without necessity.

That the library had at one time been a favourite resource of Rashleigh—that a private door out of one side of it communicated with the sequestered and remote apartment which he chose for himself, rather increased than disarmed the terrors which the household had for the dreaded library of Osbaldistone Hall. His extensive information as to what passed in the world,—his profound knowledge of science of every kind,—a few physical experiments which he occasionally showed off, were, in a house of so much ignorance and bigotry, esteemed good reasons for supposing him endowed with powers over the spiritual world. He understood Greek, Latin, and Hebrew; and, therefore, according to the apprehension, and in the phrase, of his brother Wilfred, needed not to care 'for ghaist or barghaist, devil or dobbie.'* Yea, the servants persisted that they had heard him hold conversations in the library, when every varsal soul in the family were gone to bed; and that he spent the night in watching for bogles, and the morning in sleeping in his bed, when he should have been heading the hounds like a true Osbaldistone.

All these absurd rumours I had heard in broken hints and imperfect sentences, from which I was left to draw the inference; and, as easily may be supposed, I laughed them to scorn. But the extreme solitude to which this chamber of evil fame was committed every night after curfew time, was an additional reason why I should not intrude on Miss Vernon when she chose to sit there in the evening.

To resume what I was saying, I was not surprised to see a glimmering of light from the library windows; but I was a little struck when I distinctly perceived the shadows of two persons pass along and intercept the light from the first of the windows, throwing the casement for a moment into shade. It must be old Martha, thought I, whom Diana has engaged to be her companion for the evening, or I must have been mistaken, and taken Diana's shadow for a second person. No, by Heaven! it appears on the second window,—two figures distinctly traced; and now it is lost again—it is seen on the third—on the fourth—the darkened forms of two persons distinctly seen in each window as they pass along the room, betwixt the windows and the lights. Whom can Diana have got for a companion?—The passage of the shadows between the lights and the casements was twice repeated, as if to satisfy me that my observation served me truly; after which the lights were extinguished, and the shades, of course, were seen no more.

Trifling as this circumstance was, it occupied my mind for a considerable time. I did not allow myself to suppose, that my friendship for Miss Vernon had any directly selfish view; yet it is incredible the displeasure I felt at the idea of her admitting any one to private interviews, at a time, and in a place, where, for her own sake, I had been at some trouble to show her, that it was improper for me to meet with her.

'Silly, romping, incorrigible girl!' said I to myself, 'on whom all good advice and delicacy are thrown away! I have been cheated by the simplicity of her manner, which I suppose she can assume just as she could a straw bonnet, were it the fashion, for the mere sake of celebrity. I suppose, notwithstanding the excellence of her understanding, the society of half a dozen of clowns to play at whisk and swabbers* would give her more pleasure than if Ariosto himself were to awake from the dead.'

This reflection came the more powerfully across my mind, because, having mustered up courage to show to Diana my version of the first books of Ariosto, I had requested her to invite Martha to a teaparty in the library that evening, to which arrangement Miss Vernon had refused her consent, alleging some apology which I thought frivolous at the time. I had not long speculated on this disagreeable subject, when the back garden-door opened, and the figures of Andrew and his countryman, bending under his pack, crossed the moonlight alley, and called my attention elsewhere.

I found Mr Macready, as I expected, a tough, sagacious, long-headed Scotchman, and a collector of news both from choice and profession. He was able to give me a distinct account of what had passed in the House of Commons and House of Lords on the affair of Morris, which, it appears, had been made by both parties a touchstone to ascertain the temper of the Parliament. It appeared also, that, as I had learned from Andrew by second hand, the ministry had proved too weak to support a story, involving the character of men of rank and importance, and resting upon the credit of a person of such indifferent fame as Morris, who was, moreover, confused and contradictory in his mode of telling the story. Macready was even able to supply me with a copy of a printed journal, or News-Letter,* seldom extending beyond the capital, in which the substance of the debate was mentioned; and with a copy of the Duke of Argyle's speech, printed upon a broadside, of which he had purchased several from the hawkers, because, he said, it would be a saleable article on the north of the Tweed. The first was a meagre statement, full of blanks and asterisks, and which added little or nothing to the information I had from the Scotchman; and the Duke's speech, though spirited and eloquent, contained chiefly a panegyric on his country, his family, and his clan, with a few compliments, equally sincere, perhaps, though less glowing, which he took so favourable an opportunity of paying to himself. I could not learn whether my own reputation had been directly implicated, although I perceived that the honour of my uncle's family had been impeached, and that this person Campbell, stated by Morris to have been the most active robber of the two by whom he was assailed, was said by him to have appeared in the behalf of a Mr Osbaldistone, and by the connivance of the Justice, procured his liberation. In this particular, Morris's story jumped with my own suspicions, which had attached to Campbell from the moment I saw him appear at Justice Inglewood's. Vexed upon the whole, as well as perplexed with this extraordinary story, I dismissed the two Scotchmen, after making some purchases from Macready, and a small compliment to Fairservice, and retired to my own apartment to consider what I ought to do in defence of my character thus publicly attacked.

CHAPTER XV

Whence, and what art thou?
MILTON*

AFTER exhausting a sleepless night in meditating on the intelligence I had received, I was at first inclined to think that I ought, as speedily as possible, to return to London, and by my open appearance repel the calumny which had been spread against me. But I hesitated to take this course on recollection of my father's disposition, singularly absolute in his decisions as to all that concerned his family. He was most able, certainly, from experience, to direct what I ought to do, and from his acquaintance with the most distinguished Whigs then in power, had influence enough to obtain a hearing for my cause. So, upon the whole, I judged it most safe to state my whole story in the shape of a narrative, addressed to my father; and as the ordinary opportunities of intercourse between the Hall and the post-town recurred rarely, I determined to ride to the town, which was about ten miles' distance, and deposit my letter in the post-office, with my own hands.

Indeed I began to think it strange, that though several weeks had elapsed since my departure from home, I had received no letter, either from my father or Owen, although Rashleigh had written to Sir Hildebrand of his safe arrival in London, and of the kind reception he had met with from his uncle. Admitting that I might have been to blame, I did not deserve, in my own opinion at least, to be so totally forgotten by my father; and I thought my present excursion might have the effect of bringing a letter from him to hand more early than it would otherwise have reached me. But before concluding my letter concerning the affair of Morris, I failed not to express my earnest hope and wish that my father would honour me with a few lines, were it but to express his advice and commands in an affair of some difficulty, and where my knowledge of life could not be supposed adequate to my own guidance. I found it impossible to prevail on myself to urge my actual return to London as a place of residence, and I disguised my unwillingness to do so under apparent submission to my father's will, which, as I imposed it on myself as a sufficient reason for not urging my final departure from Osbaldistone Hall, would, I doubted not, be received as such by my parent. But I begged permission to come to London, for a short time at least, to meet and refute the infamous calumnies which had been circulated concerning me in so public a manner. Having made up my packet, in which my earnest desire to vindicate my character was strangely blended with reluctance to quit my present place of residence, I rode over to the post-town, and deposited my letter in the office. By doing so, I obtained possession, somewhat earlier than I should otherwise have done, of the following letter from my friend Mr Owen.

'DEAR MR FRANCIS,

'Yours received per favour of Mr R. Osbaldistone, and note the contents. Shall do Mr R. O. such civilities as are in my power, and have taken him to see the Bank and Custom-house. He seems a sober, steady young gentleman, and takes to business; so will be of service to the firm. Could have wished another person had turned his mind that way; but God's will be done. As cash may be scarce in those parts, have to trust you will excuse my enclosing a goldsmith's bill at six days' sight, on Messrs Hooper and Girder of Newcastle, for L.100, which I doubt not will be duly honoured.—I remain, as in duty bound, dear Mr Frank, your very respectful and obedient servant,

'JOSEPH OWEN.

'*Postscriptum.*—Hope you will advise the above coming safe to hand. Am sorry we have so few of yours. Your father says he is as usual, but looks poorly.'

From this epistle, written in old Owen's formal style, I was rather surprised to observe that he made no acknowledgment of that private letter which I had written to him, with a view to possess him of Rashleigh's real character, although, from the course of post, it seemed certain that he ought to have received it. Yet I had sent it by the usual conveyance from the Hall, and had no reason to suspect that it could miscarry upon the road. As it comprised matters of great importance, both to my father and to myself, I sat down in the post-office, and again wrote to Owen, recapitulating the heads of my former letter, and requesting to know, in course of post, if it had reached him in safety. I also acknowledged the receipt of the bill, and promised to make use of the contents, if I should have any occasion for money. I thought, indeed, it was odd that my father should leave the care of supplying my necessities to his clerk; but I concluded it was a matter arranged between them. At any rate, Owen was a bachelor, rich in his way, and passionately attached to me, so that I had no hesitation in being obliged to him for a small sum, which I resolved to consider as a loan, to be returned with my earliest ability, in case it was not previously repaid by my father; and I expressed myself to this purpose to Mr Owen. A shop-keeper in a little town, to whom the post-master directed me, readily gave me in gold the amount of my bill on Messrs Hooper and Girder, so that I returned to Osbaldistone Hall a good deal richer than I had set forth. This recruit to my finances was not a matter of indifference to me, as I was necessarily involved in some expenses at Osbaldistone Hall; and I had seen, with some uneasy impatience, that the sum which my travelling expenses had left unexhausted at my arrival there, was imperceptibly diminishing. This source of anxiety was for the present removed. On my arrival at the Hall, I found that Sir Hildebrand and all his offspring had gone down to the little hamlet, called Trinlay-Knowes, 'to see,' as Andrew Fairservice expressed it, 'a wheen midden cocks pike ilk ithers harns out.'

'It is indeed a brutal amusement, Andrew; I suppose you have none such in Scotland?'

'Na, na,' answered Andrew boldly; then shaded away his negative with, 'unless it be on Fastern's-e'en, or the like o' that—But, indeed, it's no muckle matter what the folk do to the midden pootry, for they haud siccan a skarting and scraping in the yard, that there's nae getting a bean or pea keepit for them.—But I am wondering what it is that leaves that turret-door open; now that Mr Rashleigh's away, it canna be him, I trow.'

The turret-door, to which he alluded, opened to the garden at the bottom of a winding-stair, leading down from Mr Rashleigh's apartments. This, as I have already mentioned, was situated in a sequestered part of the house, communicating with the library by a private entrance, and by another intricate and dark vaulted passage with the rest of the house. A long narrow turf-walk led, between two high holly hedges, from the turret-door to a little postern in the wall of the garden. By means of these communications, Rashleigh, whose movements were very independent of those of the rest of his family, could leave the Hall or return to it at pleasure, without his absence or presence attracting any observation. But during his absence the stair and the turret-door were entirely disused, and this made Andrew's observation somewhat remarkable.

'Have you often observed that door open?' was my question.

'No just that often neither; but I hae noticed it ance or twice. I'm thinking it maun hae been the priest, Father Vaughan, as they ca' him. Ye'll no catch ane o' the servants ganging up that stair, puir frightened heathens that they are, for fear of bogles and brownies, and lang-nebbit things frae the neist warld. But Father Vaughan thinks himsell a privileged person—set him up and lay him down!—I'se be caution the warst stibbler that ever stickit a sermon out ower the Tweed yonder, wad lay a ghaist twice as fast as him, wi' his holy water and his idolatrous trinkets. I dinna believe he speaks gude Latin neither; at least he disna take me up when I tell him the learned names o' the plants.'*

Of Father Vaughan, who divided his time and his ghostly care between Osbaldistone Hall, and about half-a-dozen mansions of Catholic gentlemen in the neighbourhood, I have as yet said nothing, for I had seen but little. He was aged about sixty, of a good family, as I was given to understand, in the north; of a striking and imposing presence, grave in his exterior, and much respected among the Catholics of Northumberland, as a worthy and upright man. Yet Father Vaughan did not altogether lack those peculiarities which distinguish his order. There hung about him an air of mystery, which, in Protestant eyes, savoured of priestcraft. The natives (such they might be well termed) of Osbaldistone Hall looked up to him with much more fear, or at least more awe, than affection. His condemnation of their revels was evident, from their being discontinued in some measure when the priest was a resident at the Hall. Even Sir Hildebrand himself put some restraint upon his conduct at such times, which, perhaps, rendered Father Vaughan's presence rather irksome than otherwise. He had the well-bred, insinuating, and almost flattering address, peculiar to the clergy of his persuasion, especially in England, where the lay Catholic, hemmed in by penal laws, and by the restrictions of his sect and recommendation of his pastor, often exhibits a reserved, and almost a timid manner, in the society of Protestants; while the priest, privileged by his order to mingle with persons of all creeds, is open, alert, and liberal in his intercourse with them, desirous of popularity, and usually skilful in the mode of obtaining it.

Father Vaughan was a particular acquaintance of Rashleigh's, otherwise, in all probability, he would scarce have been able to maintain his footing at Osbaldistone Hall. This gave me no desire to cultivate his intimacy, nor did he seem to make any advances towards mine; so our occasional intercourse was confined to the exchange of mere civility. I considered it as extremely probable that Mr Vaughan might occupy Rashleigh's apartment during his occasional residence at the Hall; and his profession rendered it likely that he should occasionally be a tenant of the library. Nothing was more probable than that it might have been his candle which had excited my attention on a preceding evening. This led me involuntarily to recollect that the intercourse between Miss Vernon and the priest was marked with something like the same mystery which characterized her communications with Rashleigh. I had never heard her mention Vaughan's name, or even allude to him, excepting on the occasion of our first meeting, when she mentioned the old priest and Rashleigh as the only conversible beings, besides herself, in Osbaldistone Hall. Yet although silent with respect to Father Vaughan, his arrival at the Hall never failed to impress Miss Vernon with an anxious and fluttering tremor, which lasted until they had exchanged one or two significant glances.

Whatever the mystery might be which overclouded the destinies of this beautiful and interesting female, it was clear that Father Vaughan was implicated in it; unless, indeed, I could suppose that he was the agent employed to procure her settlement in the cloister, in the event of her rejecting a union with either of my cousins,—an office which would sufficiently account for her obvious emotion at his appearance. As to the rest, they did not seem to converse much together, or even to seek each other's society. Their league, if any subsisted between them, was of a tacit and understood nature, operating on their actions without any necessity of speech. I recollected, however, on reflection, that I had once or twice discovered signs pass betwixt them, which I had at the time supposed to bear reference to some hint concerning Miss Vernon's religious observances, knowing how artfully the Catholic clergy maintain, at all times and seasons, their influence over the mind of their followers. But now I was disposed to assign to these communications a deeper and more mysterious import. Did he hold private meetings with Miss Vernon in the library? was a question which occupied my thoughts; and if so, for what purpose? And why should she have admitted an intimate of the deceitful Rashleigh to such close confidence?

These questions and difficulties pressed on my mind with an interest which was greatly increased by the impossibility of resolving them. I had already begun to suspect that my friendship for Diana Vernon was not altogether so disinterested as in wisdom it ought to have been. I had already felt myself becoming jealous of the contemptible lout Thorncliff, and taking more notice, than in prudence or dignity of feeling I ought to have done, of his silly attempts to provoke me. And now I was scrutinizing the conduct of Miss Vernon with the most close and eager observation, which I in vain endeavoured to palm on myself as the offspring of idle curiosity. All these, like Benedick's brushing his hat of a morning, were signs that the sweet youth was in love;* and while my judgment still denied that I had been guilty of forming an attachment so imprudent, she resembled those ignorant guides, who, when they have led the traveller and themselves into irretrievable error, persist in obstinately affirming it to be impossible that they can have missed the way.

CHAPTER XVI

'It happened one day about noon, going to my boat, I was exceedingly surprised with the print of a man's naked foot on the shore,
which was very plain to be seen on the sand.'

*Robinson Crusoe**

WITH the blended feelings of interest and jealousy which were
engendered by Miss Vernon's singular situation, my observations of
her looks and actions became acutely sharpened, and that to a degree,
which, notwithstanding my efforts to conceal it, could not escape her
penetration. The sense that she was observed, or, more properly
speaking, that she was watched by my looks, seemed to give Diana a
mixture of embarrassment, pain, and pettishness. At times it seemed
that she sought an opportunity of resenting a conduct which she could
not but feel as offensive, considering the frankness with which she had
mentioned the difficulties that surrounded her. At other times she
seemed prepared to expostulate upon the subject. But either her
courage failed, or some other sentiment impeded her seeking an eclaircissement. Her displeasure evaporated in repartee, and her expostulations died on her lips. We stood in a singular relation to each other,
spending, and by mutual choice, much of our time in close society with
each other, yet disguising our mutual sentiments, and jealous of, or
offended by, each other's actions. There was betwixt us intimacy without confidence; on one side love without hope or purpose, and curiosity without any rational or justifiable motive; and on the other
embarrassment and doubt, occasionally mingled with displeasure. Yet
I believe that this agitation of the passions, such is the nature of the
human bosom, as it continued by a thousand irritating and interesting,
though petty circumstances, to render Miss Vernon and me the constant objects of each other's thoughts, tended, upon the whole, to
increase the attachment with which we were naturally disposed to
regard each other. But although my vanity early discovered that my
presence at Osbaldistone Hall had given Diana some additional reason
for disliking the cloister, I could by no means confide in an affection
which seemed completely subordinate to the mysteries of her singular
situation. Miss Vernon was of a character far too formed and determined, to permit her love for me to overpower either her sense of duty

or of prudence, and she gave me a proof of this in a conversation which we had together about this period.

We were sitting together in the library. Miss Vernon, in turning over a copy of the Orlando Furioso, which belonged to me, shook a piece of written paper from between the leaves. I hastened to lift it, but she prevented me.

'It is verse,' she said, on glancing at the paper; and then unfolding it, but as if to wait my answer before proceeding—'May I take the liberty?—nay, nay, if you blush and stammer, I must do violence to your modesty, and suppose that permission is granted.'

'It is not worthy your perusal—a scrap of a translation—My dear Miss Vernon, it would be too severe a trial, that you, who understand the original so well, should sit in judgment.'

'Mine honest friend,' replied Diana, 'do not, if you will be guided by my advice, bait your hook with too much humility; for, ten to one, it will not catch a single compliment. You know I belong to the unpopular family of Tell-truths, and would not flatter Apollo for his lyre.'

She proceeded to read the first stanza, which was nearly to the following purpose:—

'Ladies, and knights, and arms, and love's fair flame,
   Deeds of emprize and courtesy, I sing;*
What time the Moors from sultry Africk came,
   Led on by Agramant, their youthful king—
He whom revenge and hasty ire did bring
   O'er the broad wave, in France to waste and war;
Such ills from old Trojano's death did spring,
   Which to avenge he came from realms afar,
And menaced Christian Charles, the Roman Emperor.

'Of dauntless Roland, too, my strain shall sound,
   In import never known in prose or rhyme,
How He, the chief, of judgment deem'd profound,
   For luckless love was crazed upon a time—'

'There is a great deal of it,' said she, glancing along the paper, and interrupting the sweetest sounds which mortal ears can drink in,—those of a youthful poet's verses, namely, read by the lips which are dearest to them.

'Much more than ought to engage your attention, Miss Vernon,' I replied, something mortified; and I took the verses from her unreluctant hand—'and yet,' I continued, 'shut up as I am in this retired situation, I have felt sometimes I could not amuse myself better than by carrying on, merely for my own amusement you will of course understand, the version of this fascinating author, which I began some months since, when I was on the banks of the Garonne.'

'The question would only be,' said Diana, gravely, 'whether you could not spend your time to better purpose?'

'You mean in original composition,' said I, greatly flattered; 'but, to say truth, my genius rather lies in finding words and rhymes than ideas; and, therefore, I am happy to use those which Ariosto has prepared to my hand. However, Miss Vernon, with the encouragement you give——'

'Pardon me, Frank; it is encouragement not of my giving, but of your taking. I meant neither original composition nor translation, since I think you might employ your time to far better purpose than in either. You are mortified,' she continued, 'and I am sorry to be the cause.'

'Not mortified,—certainly not mortified,' said I, (with the best grace I could muster, and it was but indifferently assumed;) 'I am too much obliged by the interest you take in me.'

'Nay, but,' resumed the relentless Diana, 'there is both mortification and a little grain of anger in that constrained tone of voice; do not be angry if I probe your feelings to the bottom—perhaps what I am about to say will affect them still more.'

I felt the childishness of my own conduct, and the superior manliness of Miss Vernon's, and assured her, that she need not fear my wincing under criticism which I knew to be kindly meant.

'That was honestly meant and said,' she replied; 'I knew full well that the fiend of poetical irritability flew away with the little preluding cough which ushered in the declaration. And now I must be serious.— Have you heard from your father lately?'

'Not a word,' I replied; 'he has not honoured me with a single line during the several months of my residence here.'

'That is strange;—you are a singular race, you bold Osbaldistones. Then you are not aware that he has gone to Holland, to arrange some pressing affairs which required his own immediate presence?'

'I never heard a word of it until this moment.'

'And farther, it must be news to you, and I presume scarcely the most agreeable, that he has left Rashleigh in the almost uncontrolled management of his affairs until his return?'

I started, and could not suppress my surprise and apprehension.

'You have reason for alarm,' said Miss Vernon, very gravely; 'and were I you, I would endeavour to meet and obviate the dangers which arise from so undesirable an arrangement.'

'And how is it possible for me to do so?'

'Every thing is possible for him who possesses courage and activity,' she said, with a look resembling one of those heroines of the age of chivalry, whose encouragement was wont to give champions double valour at the hour of need; 'and to the timid and hesitating every thing is impossible, because it seems so.'

'And what would you advise, Miss Vernon?' I replied, wishing, yet dreading, to hear her answer.

She paused a moment, then answered firmly,—'That you instantly leave Osbaldistone Hall, and return to London. You have perhaps already,' she continued, in a softer tone, 'been here too long; that fault was not yours. Every succeeding moment you waste here will be a crime. Yes, a crime: for I tell you plainly, that if Rashleigh long manages your father's affairs, you may consider his ruin as consummated.'

'How is this possible?'

'Ask no questions,' she said; 'but, believe me, Rashleigh's views extend far beyond the possession or increase of commercial wealth: He will only make the command of Mr Osbaldistone's revenues and property the means of putting in motion his own ambitious and extensive schemes. While your father was in Britain this was impossible; during his absence, Rashleigh will possess many opportunities, and he will not neglect to use them.'

'But how can I, in disgrace with my father, and divested of all control over his affairs, prevent this danger by my mere presence in London?'

'That presence alone will do much. Your claim to interfere is a part of your birthright, and is inalienable. You will have the countenance, doubtless, of your father's head-clerk, and confidential friends and partners. Above all, Rashleigh's schemes are of a nature that'—(she stopped abruptly, as if fearful of saying too much)—'are, in short,' she resumed, 'of the nature of all selfish and unconscientious plans, which are speedily abandoned as soon as those who frame them perceive their arts are discovered and watched. Therefore, in the language of your favourite poet—

"To horse! to horse! urge doubts to those that fear." '*

A feeling, irresistible in its impulse, induced me to reply,—'Ah! Diana, can *you* give me advice to leave Osbaldistone Hall?—then indeed I have already been a resident here too long!'

Miss Vernon coloured, but proceeded with great firmness; 'Indeed, I do give you this advice—not only to quit Osbaldistone Hall, but never to return to it more. You have only one friend to regret here,' she continued, forcing a smile, 'and she has been long accustomed to sacrifice her friendships and her comforts to the welfare of others. In the world you will meet a hundred whose friendship will be as disinterested—more useful—less encumbered by untoward circumstances—less influenced by evil tongues and evil times.'

'Never!' I exclaimed, 'never! the world can afford me nothing to repay what I must leave behind me.' Here I took her hand, and pressed it to my lips.

'This is folly!' she exclaimed—'This is madness!' and she struggled to withdraw her hand from my grasp, but not so stubbornly as actually to succeed, until I had held it for nearly a minute. 'Hear me, sir!' she said, 'and curb this unmanly burst of passion. I am, by a solemn contract, the bride of Heaven, unless I could prefer being wedded to villainy in the person of Rashleigh Osbaldistone, or brutality in that of his brother. I am, therefore, the bride of Heaven, betrothed to the convent from the cradle. To me, therefore, these raptures are misapplied—they only serve to prove a farther necessity for your departure, and that without delay.' At these words she broke suddenly off, and said, but in a suppressed tone of voice, 'Leave me instantly—we will meet here again, but it must be for the last time.'

My eyes followed the direction of hers as she spoke, and I thought I saw the tapestry shake, which covered the door of the secret passage from Rashleigh's room to the library. I conceived we were observed, and turned an enquiring glance on Miss Vernon.

'It is nothing,' said she, faintly; 'a rat behind the arras.'

'Dead for a ducat,'* would have been my reply, had I dared to give way to the feelings which rose indignant at the idea of being subjected to an eve's-dropper on such an occasion. Prudence, and the necessity of suppressing my passion, and obeying Diana's reiterated command of 'Leave me! leave me!' came in time to prevent any rash action. I left the apartment in a wild whirl and giddiness of mind, which I in vain attempted to compose when I returned to my own.

A chaos of thoughts intruded themselves on me at once, passing hastily through my brain, intercepting and overshadowing each other, and resembling those fogs which in mountainous countries are wont to descend in obscure volumes, and disfigure or obliterate the usual marks by which the traveller steers his course through the wilds. The dark and undefined idea of danger arising to my father from the machinations of such a man as Rashleigh Osbaldistone,—the half-declaration of love which I had offered to Miss Vernon's acceptance,—the acknowledged difficulties of her situation, bound by a previous contract to sacrifice herself to a cloister, or to an ill-assorted marriage,—all pressed themselves at once upon my recollection, while my judgment was unable deliberately to consider any of them in their just light and bearings. But chiefly, and above all the rest, I was perplexed by the manner in which Miss Vernon had received my tender of affection, and by her manner, which, fluctuating betwixt sympathy and firmness, seemed to intimate that I possessed an interest in her bosom, but not of force sufficient to counterbalance the obstacles to her avowing a mutual affection. The glance of fear, rather than surprise, with which she had watched the motion of the tapestry over the concealed door, implied an apprehension of danger which I could not but suppose well-grounded; for Diana Vernon was little subject to the nervous emotions of her sex, and totally unapt to fear without actual and rational cause. Of what nature could those mysteries be with which she was surrounded as with an enchanter's spell, and which seemed continually to exert an active influence over her thoughts and actions, though their agents were never visible? On this subject of doubt my mind finally rested, as if glad to shake itself free from investigating the propriety or prudence of my own conduct, by transferring the enquiry to what concerned Miss Vernon. I will be resolved, I concluded, ere I leave Osbaldistone Hall, concerning the light in which I must in future regard this fascinating being, over whose life frankness and mystery seem to have divided their reign, the former inspiring her words and sentiments, the latter spreading in misty influence over all her actions.

Joined to the obvious interests which arose from curiosity and anxious passion, there mingled in my feelings a strong, though unavowed and undefined, infusion of jealousy. This sentiment, which springs up with love as naturally as the tares with the wheat, was excited by the degree of influence which Diana appeared to concede to those unseen beings by whom her actions were limited. The more I reflected upon her character, the more I was internally though unwillingly convinced, that she was formed to set at defiance all control, excepting that which arose from affection; and I felt a strong, bitter, and gnawing suspicion, that such was the foundation of that influence by which she was overawed.

These tormenting doubts strengthened my desire to penetrate into the secret of Miss Vernon's conduct, and in the prosecution of this sage adventure I formed a resolution, of which, if you are not weary of these details, you will find the result in the next Chapter.

CHAPTER XVII

I hear a voice you cannot hear,
   Which says, I must not stay;
I see a hand you cannot see,
   Which beckons me away.

                                        TICKELL*

I HAVE already told you, Tresham, if you deign to bear it in remembrance, that my evening visits to the library had seldom been made except by appointment, and under the sanction of old Dame Martha's presence. This, however, was entirely a tacit conventional arrangement of my own instituting. Of late, as the embarrassments of our relative situation had increased, Miss Vernon and I had never met in the evening at all. She had therefore no reason to suppose that I was likely to seek a renewal of these interviews, and especially without some previous notice or appointment betwixt us, that Martha might, as usual, be placed upon duty; but, on the other hand, this cautionary provision was a matter of understanding, not of express enactment. The library was open to me, as to the other members of the family, at all hours of the day and night, and I could not be accused of intrusion, however suddenly and unexpectedly I might make my appearance in it. My belief was strong, that in this apartment Miss Vernon occasionally received Vaughan, or some other person, by whose opinion she was accustomed to regulate her conduct, and that at the times when she could do so with least chance of interruption. The lights which gleamed in the library at unusual hours,—the passing shadows which I had myself remarked,—the footsteps which might be traced in the morning dew from the turret-door to the postern-gate in the garden,—sounds and sights which some of the servants, and Andrew Fairservice in particular, had observed and accounted for in their own way,—all tended to show that the place was visited by some one different from the ordinary inmates of the hall. Connected as this visitant must probably be with the fates of Diana Vernon, I did not hesitate to form a plan of discovering who or what he was,—how far his influence was likely to produce good or evil consequences to her on whom he acted,—above all, though I endeavoured to persuade myself that this was a mere subordinate consideration, I desired to know by what means this person had acquired or maintained his influence over Diana, and whether he ruled over her by fear or by affection. The proof that this jealous curiosity was uppermost in my mind, arose from my imagination always ascribing Miss Vernon's conduct to the influence of some one individual agent, although, for aught I knew about the matter, her advisers might be as numerous as Legion. I remarked this over and over to myself, but I found that my mind still settled back in my original conviction, that one single individual, of the masculine sex, and in all probability young and handsome, was at the bottom of Miss Vernon's conduct; and it was with a burning desire of discovering, or rather of detecting, such a rival, that I stationed myself in the garden to watch the moment when the lights should appear in the library windows.

So eager, however, was my impatience, that I commenced my watch for a phenomenon, which could not appear until darkness, a full hour before the daylight disappeared, on a July evening. It was Sabbath, and all the walks were still and solitary. I walked up and down for some time, enjoying the refreshing coolness of a summer evening, and meditating on the probable consequences of my enterprise. The fresh and balmy air of the garden, impregnated with fragrance, produced its usual sedative effects on my over-heated and feverish blood; as these took place, the turmoil of my mind began proportionally to abate, and I was led to question the right I had to interfere with Miss Vernon's secrets, or with those of my uncle's family. What was it to me whom my uncle might choose to conceal in his house, where I was myself a guest only by tolerance? And what title had I to pry into the affairs of Miss Vernon, fraught, as she had avowed them to be, with mystery, into which she desired no scrutiny?

Passion and self-will were ready with their answers to these questions. In detecting this secret, I was in all probability about to do service to Sir Hildebrand, who was probably ignorant of the intrigues carried on in his family; and a still more important service to Miss Vernon, whose frank simplicity of character exposed her to so many risks in maintaining a private correspondence, perhaps with a person of doubtful or dangerous character. If I seemed to intrude myself on her confidence, it was with the generous and disinterested (yes, I even ventured to call it the *disinterested*) intention of guiding, defending, and protecting her against craft,—against malice,—above all, against the secret counsellor whom she had chosen for her confident. Such were the arguments which my will boldly preferred to my conscience, as coin which ought to be current; and which conscience, like a grumbling shopkeeper, was contented to accept, rather than come to an open breach with a customer, though more than doubting that the tender was spurious.

While I paced the green alleys, debating these things *pro* and *con*, I suddenly lighted upon Andrew Fairservice, perched up like a statue by a range of bee-hives, in an attitude of devout contemplation; one eye, however, watching the motions of the little irritable citizens, who were settling in their straw-thatched mansion for the evening, and the other fixed on a book of devotion, which much attrition had deprived of its corners, and worn into an oval shape; a circumstance, which, with the close print and dingy colour of the volume in question, gave it an air of most respectable antiquity.

'I was e'en taking a spell o' worthy Mess John Quackleben's* Flower of a Sweet Savour sawn on the Middenstead of this World,' said Andrew, closing his book at my appearance, and putting his horn spectacles, by way of mark, at the place where he had been reading.

'And the bees, I observe, were dividing your attention, Andrew, with the learned author?'

'They are a contumacious generation,' replied the gardener; 'they hae sax days in the week to hive on, and yet it's a common observe that they will aye swarm on the Sabbath-day, and keep folk at hame frae hearing the word—But there's nae preaching at Graneagain Chapel the e'en—that's aye ae mercy.'

'You might have gone to the parish church as I did, Andrew, and heard an excellent discourse.'

'Clauts o' cauld parritch—clauts o' cauld parritch,' replied Andrew, with a most supercilious sneer,—'gude aneuch for dogs, begging your honour's pardon—Ay! I might nae doubt hae heard the curate linking awa at it in his white sark yonder, and the musicians playing on whistles, mair like a penny wedding than a sermon—and to the boot of that, I might hae gane to even-song, and heard Daddie Docharty mumbling his mass—muckle the better I wad hae been o' that!'

'Docharty!' said I, (this was the name of an old priest, an Irishman, I think, who sometimes officiated at Osbaldistone Hall,) 'I thought Father Vaughan had been at the Hall. He was here yesterday.'

'Ay,' replied Andrew; 'but he left it yestreen, to gang to Greystock, or some o' thae west-country haulds. There's an unco stir amang them a' e'enow. They are as busy as my bees are—God sain them! that I suld even the puir things to the like o' papists. Ye see this is the second swarm, and whiles they will swarm off in the afternoon. The first swarm set off sune in the morning. But I am thinking they are settled in their skeps for the night. Sae I wuss your honour good-night, and grace, and muckle o't.'

So saying, Andrew retreated; but often cast a parting glance upon the *skeps*, as he called the bee-hives.

I had indirectly gained from him an important piece of information, that Father Vaughan, namely, was not supposed to be at the Hall. If, therefore, there appeared light in the windows of the library this evening, it either could not be his, or he was observing a very secret and suspicious line of conduct. I waited with impatience the time of sunset and of twilight. It had hardly arrived, ere a gleam from the windows of the library was seen, dimly distinguishable amidst the still enduring light of the evening. I marked its first glimpse, however, as speedily as the benighted sailor descries the first distant twinkle of the light-house which marks his course. The feelings of doubt and propriety, which had hitherto contended with my curiosity and jealousy, vanished when an opportunity of gratifying the former was presented to me. I re-entered the house, and, avoiding the more frequented apartments with the consciousness of one who wishes to keep his purpose secret, I reached the door of the library,—hesitated for a moment as my hand was upon the latch,—heard a suppressed step within,—opened the door,—and found Miss Vernon alone.

Diana appeared surprised,—whether at my sudden entrance, or from some other cause, I could not guess; but there was in her appearance a degree of flutter, which I had never before remarked, and which I knew could only be produced by unusual emotion. Yet she was calm in a moment; and such is the force of conscience, that I, who studied to surprise her, seemed myself the surprised, and was certainly the embarrassed person.

'Has any thing happened?' said Miss Vernon. 'Has any one arrived at the Hall?'

'No one that I know of,' I answered, in some confusion; 'I only sought the Orlando.'

'It lies there,' said Miss Vernon, pointing to the table.

In removing one or two books to get at that which I pretended to seek, I was, in truth, meditating to make a handsome retreat from an investigation to which I felt my assurance inadequate, when I perceived a man's glove lying upon the table. My eyes encountered those of Miss Vernon, who blushed deeply.

'It is one of my relics,' she said, with hesitation, replying not to my words, but to my looks; 'it is one of the gloves of my grandfather, the original of the superb Vandyke which you admire.'

As if she thought something more than her bare assertion was necessary to prove her statement true, she opened a drawer of the large oaken table, and, taking out another glove, threw it towards me. When a temper naturally ingenuous stoops to equivocate or to dissemble, the anxious pain with which the unwonted task is laboured, often induces the hearer to doubt the authenticity of the tale. I cast a hasty glance on both gloves, and then replied gravely—'The gloves resemble each other, doubtless, in form and embroidery; but they cannot form a pair, since they both belong to the right hand.'

She bit her lip with anger, and again coloured deeply.

'You do right to expose me,' she replied, with bitterness; 'some friends would have only judged from what I said, that I chose to give no particular explanation of a circumstance which calls for none—at least to a stranger. You have judged better, and have made me feel, not only the meanness of duplicity, but my own inadequacy to sustain the task of a dissembler. I now tell you distinctly, that that glove is not the fellow, as you have acutely discerned, to the one which I just now produced. It belongs to a friend yet dearer to me than the original of Vandyke's picture—a friend by whose counsels I have been, and will be, guided—whom I honour—whom I'—She paused.

I was irritated at her manner, and filled up the blank in my own way. 'Whom she *loves*, Miss Vernon would say.'

'And if I do say so,' she replied, haughtily, 'by whom shall my affection be called to account?'

'Not by me, Miss Vernon, assuredly. I entreat you to hold me acquitted of such presumption. *But*,' I continued, with some emphasis, for I was now piqued in return, 'I hope Miss Vernon will pardon a friend, from whom she seems disposed to withdraw the title, for observing'——

'Observe nothing, sir,' she interrupted, with some vehemence, 'except that I will neither be doubted nor questioned. There does not exist one by whom I will be either interrogated or judged; and if you sought this unusual time of presenting yourself, in order to spy upon my privacy, the friendship or interest with which you pretend to regard me, is a poor excuse for your uncivil curiosity.'

'I relieve you of my presence,' said I, with pride equal to her own; for my temper has ever been a stranger to stooping, even in cases where my feelings were most deeply interested—'I relieve you of my presence. I awake from a pleasant, but a most delusive dream; and—but we understand each other.'

I had reached the door of the apartment, when Miss Vernon, whose movements were sometimes so rapid as to seem almost instinctive, overtook me, and, catching hold of my arm, stopped me with that air of authority which she could so whimsically assume, and which, from the naiveté and simplicity of her manner, had an effect so peculiarly interesting.

'Stop, Mr Frank,' she said; 'you are not to leave me in that way neither; I am not so amply provided with friends, that I can afford to throw away even the ungrateful and the selfish. Mark what I say, Mr Francis Osbaldistone. You shall know nothing of this mysterious glove,' and she held it up as she spoke—'nothing—no, not a single iota more than you know already; and yet I will not permit it to be a gauntlet of strife and defiance betwixt us. My time here,' she said, sinking into a tone somewhat softer, 'must necessarily be very short; yours must be still shorter: We are soon to part, never to meet again; do not let us quarrel, or make any mysterious miseries the pretext for farther embittering the few hours we shall ever pass together on this side of eternity.'

I do not know, Tresham, by what witchery this fascinating creature obtained such complete management over a temper, which I cannot at all times manage myself. I had determined, on entering the library, to seek a complete explanation with Miss Vernon. I had found that she refused it with indignant defiance, and avowed to my face the preference of a rival; for what other construction could I put on her declared preference of her mysterious confident? And yet, while I was on the point of leaving the apartment, and breaking with her for ever, it cost her but a change of look and tone, from that of real and haughty resentment to that of kind and playful despotism, again shaded off into melancholy and serious feeling, to lead me back to my seat, her willing subject, on her own hard terms.

'What does this avail?' said I, as I sate down. 'What can this avail, Miss Vernon? Why should I witness embarrassments which I cannot relieve, and mysteries which I offend you even by attempting to penetrate? Inexperienced as you are in the world, you must still be aware, that a beautiful young woman can have but one male friend. Even in a male friend I will be jealous of a confidence shared with a third party unknown and concealed; but with *you*, Miss Vernon'——

'You are, of course, jealous, in all the tenses and moods of that amiable passion. But, my good friend, you have all this time spoke nothing but the paltry gossip which simpletons repeat from play-books and romances, till they give mere cant a real and powerful influence over their minds. Boys and girls prate themselves into love; and when their love is like to fall asleep, they prate and teaze themselves into jealousy. But you and I, Frank, are rational beings, and neither silly nor idle enough to talk ourselves into any other relation, than that of plain honest disinterested friendship. Any other union is as far out of our reach as if I were man, or you woman.——To speak truth,' she added, after a moment's hesitation, 'even though I am so complaisant to the decorum of my sex as to blush a little at my own plain dealing, we cannot marry, if we would; and we ought not, if we could.'

And certainly, Tresham, she did blush most angelically as she made this cruel declaration. I was about to attack both her positions, entirely forgetting those very suspicions which had been confirmed in the course of the evening, but she proceeded with a cold firmness which approached to severity.

'What I say is sober and indisputable truth, on which I will neither hear question nor explanation. We are therefore friends, Mr Osbaldistone—are we not?' She held out her hand, and taking mine, added,—'And nothing to each other now, or henceforward, except as friends.'

She let go my hand. I sunk it and my head at once, fairly *overcrowed*, as Spenser would have termed it,* by the mingled kindness and firmness of her manner. She hastened to change the subject.

'Here is a letter,' she said, 'directed for you, Mr Osbaldistone, very duly and distinctly; but which, notwithstanding the caution of the person who wrote and addressed it, might perhaps never have reached your hands, had it not fallen into the possession of a certain Pacolet,* or enchanted dwarf of mine, whom, like all distressed damsels of romance, I retain in my secret service.'

I opened the letter and glanced over the contents—the unfolded sheet of paper dropped from my hands, with the involuntary exclamation of 'Gracious Heaven! my folly and disobedience have ruined my father!'

Miss Vernon rose with looks of real and affectionate alarm—'You grow pale—you are ill—shall I bring you a glass of water? Be a man, Mr Osbaldistone, and a firm one. Is your father—is he no more?'

'He lives,' said I, 'thank God! but to what distress and difficulty'——

'If that be all, despair not. May I read this letter?' she said, taking it up.

I assented, hardly knowing what I said. She read it with great attention.

'Who is this Mr Tresham, who signs the letter?'

'My father's partner,' (your own good father, Will,) 'but he is little in the habit of acting personally in the business of the house.'

'He writes here,' said Miss Vernon, 'of various letters sent to you previously.'

'I have received none of them,' I replied.

'And it appears,' she continued, 'that Rashleigh, who has taken the full management of affairs during your father's absence in Holland, has some time since left London for Scotland, with effects and remittances to take up large bills granted by your father to persons in that country, and that he has not since been heard of.'

'It is but too true.'

'And here has been,' she added, looking at the letter, 'a head-clerk, or some such person,—Owenson—Owen—dispatched to Glasgow, to find out Rashleigh, if possible, and you are entreated to repair to the same place, and assist him in his researches.'

'It is even so, and I must depart instantly.'

'Stay but one moment,' said Miss Vernon. 'It seems to me that the worst which can come of this matter will be the loss of a certain sum of money; and can that bring tears into your eyes? For shame, Mr Osbaldistone!'

'You do me injustice, Miss Vernon,' I answered. 'I grieve not for the loss, but for the effect which I know it will produce on the spirits and health of my father, to whom mercantile credit is as honour; and who, if declared insolvent, would sink into the grave, oppressed by a sense of grief, remorse, and despair, like that of a soldier convicted of cowardice, or a man of honour who had lost his rank and character in society. All this I might have prevented by a trifling sacrifice of the foolish pride and indolence which recoiled from sharing the labours of his honourable and useful profession. Good Heaven! how shall I redeem the consequences of my error!'

'By instantly repairing to Glasgow, as you are conjured to do by the friend who writes this letter.'

'But if Rashleigh,' said I, 'has really formed this base and unconscientious scheme of plundering his benefactor, what prospect is there that I can find means of frustrating a plan so deeply laid?'

'The prospect,' she replied, 'indeed, may be uncertain; but, on the other hand, there is no possibility of your doing any service to your father by remaining here.—Remember, had you been on the post destined for you, this disaster could not have happened; hasten to that which is now pointed out, and it may possibly be retrieved.—Yet stay—do not leave this room until I return.'

She left me in confusion and amazement; amid which, however, I could find a lucid interval to admire the firmness, composure, and presence of mind, which Miss Vernon seemed to possess on every crisis, however sudden.

In a few minutes she returned with a sheet of paper in her hand, folded and sealed like a letter, but without address. 'I trust you,' she said, 'with this proof of my friendship, because I have the most perfect confidence in your honour. If I understand the nature of your distress rightly, the funds in Rashleigh's possession must be recovered by a certain day—the 12th of September, I think, is named—in order that they may be applied to pay the bills in question; and, consequently, that, if adequate funds be provided before that period, your father's credit is safe from the apprehended calamity.'

'Certainly—I so understand Mr Tresham'—I looked at your father's letter again, and added, 'There cannot be a doubt of it.'

'Well,' said Diana, 'in that case my little Pacolet may be of use to you.—You have heard of a spell contained in a letter. Take this packet; do not open it until other and ordinary means have failed; if you succeed by your own exertions, I trust to your honour for destroying it without opening or suffering it to be opened. But if not, you may break the seal within ten days of the fated day, and you will find directions which may possibly be of service to you.—Adieu, Frank; we never meet more—but sometimes think on your friend Die Vernon.'

She extended her hand, but I clasped her to my bosom. She sighed as she extricated herself from the embrace which she permitted, escaped to the door which led to her own apartment, and I saw her no more.

CHAPTER XVIII

And hurry, hurry, off they rode,
    As fast as fast might be;
Hurra, hurra, the dead can ride,
    Dost fear to ride with me?

BURGHER*

THERE is one advantage in an accumulation of evils, differing in cause and character, that the distraction which they afford by their contradictory operation prevents the patient from being overwhelmed under either. I was deeply grieved at my separation from Miss Vernon, yet not so much so as I should have been, had not my father's apprehended distresses forced themselves on my attention; and I was distressed by the news of Mr Tresham, yet less so than if they had fully occupied my mind. I was neither a false lover nor an unfeeling son; but man can give but a certain portion of distressful emotions to the causes which demand them, and if two operate at once, our sympathy, like the funds of a compounding bankrupt, can only be divided between them. Such were my reflections when I gained my apartment—it seems, from the illustration, they already began to have a twang of commerce in them.

I set myself seriously to consider your father's letter. It was not very distinct, and referred for several particulars to Owen, whom I was entreated to meet with as soon as possible at a Scotch town, called Glasgow; being informed, moreover, that my old friend was to be heard of at Messrs Macvittie, Macfin, and Company, merchants in the Gallowgate of the said town. It likewise alluded to several letters, which, as it appeared to me, must have miscarried or have been intercepted, and complained of my obdurate silence in terms which would have been highly unjust, had my letters reached their purposed destination. I was amazed as I read. That the spirit of Rashleigh walked around me, and conjured up these doubts and difficulties by which I was surrounded, I could not doubt for one instant; yet it was frightful to conceive the extent of combined villainy and power which he must have employed in the perpetration of his designs. Let me do myself justice in one respect; the evil of parting from Miss Vernon, however distressing it might in other respects and at another time have appeared to me, sunk into a subordinate consideration when I thought of the dangers impending over my father. I did not myself set a high estimation on wealth, and had the affectation of most young men of lively imagination, who suppose that they can better dispense with the possession of money, than resign their time and faculties to the labour necessary to acquire it. But in my father's case, I knew that bankruptcy would be considered as an utter and irretrievable disgrace, to which life would afford no comfort, and death the speediest and sole relief.

My mind, therefore, was bent on averting this catastrophe, with an intensity which the interest could not have produced had it referred to my own fortunes; and the result of my deliberation was a firm resolution to depart from Osbaldistone Hall the next day, and wend my way without loss of time to meet Owen at Glasgow. I did not hold it expedient to intimate my departure to my uncle, otherwise than by leaving a letter of thanks for his hospitality, assuring him that sudden and important business prevented my offering them in person. I knew the blunt old knight would readily excuse ceremony, and I had such a belief in the extent and decided character of Rashleigh's machinations, that I had some apprehension of his having provided means to intercept a journey which was undertaken with a view to disconcert them, if my departure were publicly announced at Osbaldistone Hall.

I therefore determined to set off on my journey with daylight in the ensuing morning, and to gain the neighbouring kingdom of Scotland before any idea of my departure was entertained at the Hall; but one impediment of consequence was likely to prevent that speed which was the soul of my expedition. I did not know the shortest, nor indeed any road to Glasgow; and as, in the circumstances in which I stood, dispatch was of the greatest consequence, I determined to consult Andrew Fairservice on the subject, as the nearest and most authentic authority within my reach. Late as it was, I set off with the intention of ascertaining this important point, and after a few minutes' walk reached the dwelling of the gardener.

Andrew's dwelling was situated at no great distance from the exterior wall of the garden, a snug comfortable Northumbrian cottage, built of stones roughly dressed with the hammer, and having the windows and doors decorated with huge heavy architraves, or lintels, as they are called, of hewn stone, and its roof covered with broad grey flags, instead of slates, thatch, or tiles. A jargonelle pear-tree at one end of the cottage, a rivulet, and flower-plot of a rood in extent, in front, and a kitchen-garden behind; a paddock for a cow, and a small field, cultivated with several crops of grain, rather for the benefit of the cottager than for sale, announced the warm and cordial comforts which Old England, even at her most northern extremity, extends to her meanest inhabitants.

As I approached the mansion of the sapient Andrew, I heard a noise, which, being of a nature peculiarly solemn, nasal, and prolonged, led me to think that Andrew, according to the decent and meritorious custom of his countrymen, had assembled some of his neighbours to join in family exercise, as he called evening devotion. Andrew had indeed neither wife, child, nor female inmate in his family. 'The first of his trade,' he said, 'had had eneugh o' thae cattle.' But, notwithstanding, he sometimes contrived to form an audience for himself out of the neighbouring Papists and Church-of-England-men, brands, as he expressed it, snatched out of the burning, on whom he used to exercise his spiritual gifts, in defiance alike of Father Vaughan, Father Docharty, Rashleigh, and all the world of Catholics around him, who deemed his interference on such occasions an act of heretical interloping. I conceived it likely, therefore, that the well-disposed neighbours might have assembled to hold some chapel of ease of this nature. The noise, however, when I listened to it more accurately, seemed to proceed entirely from the lungs of the said Andrew; and when I interrupted it by entering the house, I found Fairservice alone, combating, as he best could, with long words and hard names, and reading aloud, for the purpose of his own edification, a volume of controversial divinity. 'I was just taking a spell,' said he, laying aside the huge folio volume as I entered, 'of the worthy Doctor Lightfoot.'*

'Lightfoot!' I replied, looking at the ponderous volume with some surprise; 'surely your author was unhappily named.'

'Lightfoot was his name, sir; a divine he was, and another kind of a divine than they hae now-a-days. Always, I crave your pardon for keeping ye standing at the door, but having been mistrysted (gude preserve us!) with ae bogle the night already, I was dubious o' opening the yett till I had gaen through the e'ening worship; and I had just finished the fifth chapter of Nehemiah—if that winna gar them keep their distance, I wotna what will.'

'Trysted with a bogle!' said I; 'what do you mean by that, Andrew?'

'I said mistrysted,' replied Andrew; 'that is as muckle as to say, fley'd wi' a ghaist—gude preserve us, I say again!'

'Flay'd by a ghost, Andrew! how am I to understand that?'

'I did not say flay'd,' replied Andrew, 'but *fley'd*, that is, I got a fleg, and was ready to jump out o' my skin, though naebody offered to whirl it aff my body as a man wad bark a tree.'

'I beg a truce to your terrors in the present case, Andrew, and I wish to know whether you can direct me the nearest way to a town in your country of Scotland, called Glasgow?'

'A town ca'd Glasgow!' echoed Andrew Fairservice. 'Glasgow's a ceety, man.—And is't the way to Glasgow ye were speering if I kend?—What suld ail me to ken it?—it's no that dooms far frae my ain parish of Dreepdaily, that lies a bittock farther to the west. But what may your honour be gaun to Glasgow for?'

'Particular business,' replied I.

'That's as muckle as to say, speer nae questions, and I'll tell ye nae lees—To Glasgow?'—he made a short pause—'I am thinking ye wad be the better o' some ane to show you the road.'

'Certainly, if I could meet with any person going that way.'

'And your honour, doubtless, wad consider the time and trouble?'

'Unquestionably—my business is pressing, and if you can find any guide to accompany me, I'll pay him handsomely.'

'This is no a day to speak o' carnal matters,' said Andrew, casting his eyes upwards; 'but if it werena Sabbath at e'en, I wad speer what ye wad be content to gie to ane that wad bear ye pleasant company on the road, and tell ye the names of the gentlemen's and noblemen's seats and castles, and count their kin to ye?'

'I tell you, all I want to know is the road I must travel; I will pay the fellow to his satisfaction—I will give him any thing in reason.'

'Ony thing,' replied Andrew, 'is naething; and this lad that I am speaking o' kens a' the short cuts and queer bye-paths through the hills, and'——

'I have no time to talk about it, Andrew ; do you make the bargain for me your own way.'

'Aha! that's speaking to the purpose,' answered Andrew.—'I am thinking, since sae be that sae it is, I'll be the lad that will guide you mysell.'

'You, Andrew? how will you get away from your employment?'

'I tell'd your honour a while syne, that it was lang that I hae been thinking o' flitting, maybe as lang as frae the first year I came to Osbaldistone Hall; and now I am o' the mind to gang in gude earnest—better soon as syne—better a finger aff as aye wagging.'*

'You leave your service then?—but will you not lose your wages?'

'Nae doubt there will be a certain loss ; but then I hae siller o' the laird's in my hands that I took for the apples in the auld orchyard—and a sair bargain the folk had that bought them—a wheen green trash— and yet Sir Hildebrand's as keen to hae the siller (that is, the steward is as pressing about it) as if they had been a' gowden pippins—and then there's the siller for the seeds—I'm thinking the wage will be in a manner decently made up.—But doubtless your honour will consider my risk of loss when we won to Glasgow—and ye'll be for setting out forthwith?'

'By day-break in the morning,' I answered.

'That's something o' the suddenest—whare am I to find a naig?— Stay—I ken just the beast that will answer me.'

'At five in the morning, then, Andrew, you will meet me at the head of the avenue.'

'Deil a fear o' me (that I suld say sae) missing my tryste,' replied Andrew very briskly; 'and, if I might advise, we wad be aff twa hours earlier. I ken the way, dark or light, as weel as blind Ralph Ronaldson, that's travelled ower every moor in the country-side, and disna ken the colour of a heather-cowe when a's dune.'

I highly approved of Andrew's amendment on my original proposal, and we agreed to meet at the place appointed at three in the morning. At once, however, a reflection came across the mind of my intended travelling companion.

'The bogle! the bogle! what if it should come out upon us?—I downa forgather wi' thae things twice in the four-and-twenty hours.'

'Pooh! pooh!' I exclaimed, breaking away from him, 'fear nothing from the next world—the earth contains living fiends, who can act for themselves without assistance, were the whole host that fell with Lucifer to return to aid and abet them.'

With these words, the import of which was suggested by my own situation, I left Andrew's habitation, and returned to the Hall.

I made the few preparations which were necessary for my proposed journey, examined and loaded my pistols, and then threw myself on my bed, to obtain, if possible, a brief sleep before the fatigue of a long and anxious journey. Nature, exhausted by the tumultuous agitations of the day, was kinder to me than I expected, and I sunk into a deep and profound slumber, from which, however, I started as the old clock struck two from a turret adjoining to my bedchamber. I instantly arose, struck a light, wrote the letter I proposed to leave for my uncle, and leaving behind me such articles of dress as were cumbrous in carriage, I deposited the rest of my wardrobe in my valise, glided down stairs, and gained the stable without impediment. Without being quite such a groom as any of my cousins, I had learned at Osbaldistone Hall to dress and saddle my own horse, and in a few minutes I was mounted and ready for my sally.

As I paced up the old avenue, on which the waning moon threw its light with a pale and whitish tinge, I looked back with a deep and boding sigh towards the walls which contained Diana Vernon, under the despondent impression that we had probably parted to meet no more. It was impossible, among the long and irregular lines of Gothic casements, which now looked ghastly white in the moonlight, to distinguish that of the apartment which she inhabited. She is lost to me already, thought I, as my eye wandered over the dim and indistinguishable intricacies of architecture offered by the moonlight view of Osbaldistone Hall—She is lost to me already, ere I have left the place which she inhabits! What hope is there of my maintaining any correspondence with her when leagues shall lie between?

While I paused in a reverie of no very pleasing nature, the 'iron tongue of time told three upon the drowsy ear of night,'* and reminded me of the necessity of keeping my appointment with a person of a less interesting description and appearance—Andrew Fairservice.

At the gate of the avenue I found a horseman stationed in the shadow of the wall, but it was not until I had coughed twice, and then called 'Andrew,' that the horticulturist replied, 'I'se warrant it's Andrew.'

'Lead the way, then,' said I, 'and be silent if you can till we are past the hamlet in the valley.'

Andrew led the way accordingly, and at a much brisker pace than I would have recommended; and so well did he obey my injunctions of keeping silence, that he would return no answer to my repeated enquiries into the cause of such unnecessary haste. Extricating ourselves by short cuts, known to Andrew, from the numerous stony lanes and by-paths which intersected each other in the vicinity of the Hall, we reached the open heath; and riding swiftly across it, took our course among the barren hills which divide England from Scotland on what are called the Middle Marches.* The way, or rather the broken track which we occupied, was a happy interchange of bog and shingles; nevertheless, Andrew relented nothing of his speed, but trotted manfully forward at the rate of eight or ten miles an hour. I was surprised and provoked at the fellow's obstinate persistence, for we made abrupt ascents and descents over ground of a very break-neck character, and traversed the edge of precipices, where a slip of the horse's feet would have consigned the rider to certain death. The moon, at best, afforded a dubious and imperfect light; but in some places we were so much under the shade of the mountain as to be in total darkness, and then I could only trace Andrew by the clatter of his horse's feet, and the fire which they struck from the flints. At first, this rapid motion, and the attention which, for the sake of personal safety, I was compelled to give to the conduct of my horse, was of service, by forcibly diverting my thoughts from the various painful reflections which must otherwise have pressed on my mind. But at length, after hallooing repeatedly to Andrew to ride slower, I became seriously incensed at his impudent perseverance in refusing either to obey or to reply to me. My anger was, however, quite impotent. I attempted once or twice to get up along-side of my self-willed guide, with the purpose of knocking him off his horse with the but-end of my whip; but Andrew was better mounted than I, and either the spirit of the animal which he bestrode, or more probably some presentiment of my kind intentions towards him, induced him to quicken his pace whenever I attempted to make up to him. On the other hand, I was compelled to exert my spurs to keep him in sight, for without his guidance I was too well aware that I should never find my way through the howling wilderness which we now traversed at such an unwonted pace. I was so angry at length, that I threatened to have recourse to my pistols, and send a bullet after the Hotspur* Andrew, which should stop his fiery-footed career, if he did not abate it of his own accord. Apparently this threat made some impression on the tympanum of his ear, however deaf to all my milder entreaties; for he relaxed his pace upon hearing it, and suffering me to close up to him, observed, 'There wasna muckle sense in riding at sic a daft-like gate.'

'And what did you mean by doing so at all, you self-willed scoundrel?' replied I; for I was in a towering passion, to which, by the way, nothing contributes more than the having recently undergone a spice of personal fear, which, like a few drops of water flung on a glowing fire, is sure to inflame the ardour which it is insufficient to quench.

'What's your honour's wull?' replied Andrew, with impenetrable gravity.

'My will, you rascal?—I have been roaring to you this hour to ride slower, and you have never so much as answered me—Are you drunk or mad to behave so?'

'An it like your honour, I am something dull o' hearing; and I'll no deny but I might have maybe taen a stirrup-cup at parting frae the auld bigging whare I hae dwalt sae lang; and having nae-body to pledge, nae doubt I was obliged to do mysell reason, or else leave the end o' the brandy stoup to thae papists,—and that wad be a waste, as your honour kens.'

This might be all very true, and my circumstances required that I should be on good terms with my guide; I therefore satisfied myself with requiring of him to take his directions from me in future concerning the rate of travelling.

Andrew, emboldened by the mildness of my tone, elevated his own into the pedantic, conceited octave, which was familiar to him on most occasions.

'Your honour winna persuade me, and naebody shall persuade me, that it's either halesome or prudent to tak the night air on thae moors without a cordial o' clow-gilliflower water, or a tass of brandy or aqua-vitæ, or sic-like creature-comfort. I hae taen the bent ower the Otter-scape-rigg a hundred times, day and night, and never could find the way unless I had taen my morning;* mair by token that I had whiles twa bits o' ankers o' brandy on ilk side o' me.'—

'In other words, Andrew,' said I, 'you were a smuggler—how does a man of your strict principles reconcile yourself to cheat the revenue?'

'It's a mere spoiling o' the Egyptians,' replied Andrew; 'puir auld Scotland suffers eneugh by thae blackguard loons o' excisemen and gaugers, that hae come down on her like locusts since the sad and sorrowfu' Union; it's the part of a kind son to bring her a soup o' something that will keep up her auld heart, and that will they nill they, the ill-fa'ard thieves.'

Upon more particular enquiry, I found Andrew had frequently travelled these mountain-paths as a smuggler, both before and after his establishment at Osbaldistone Hall; a circumstance which was so far of importance to me, as it proved his capacity as a guide, notwithstanding the escapade of which he had been guilty at his outset. Even now, though travelling at a more moderate pace, the stirrup-cup, or whatever else had such an effect in stimulating Andrew's motions, seemed not totally to have lost its influence. He often cast a nervous and startled look behind him; and whenever the road seemed at all practicable, showed symptoms of a desire to accelerate his pace, as if he feared some pursuit from the rear. These appearances of alarm gradually diminished as we reached the top of a high bleak ridge, which ran nearly east and west for about a mile, with a very steep descent on either side. The pale beams of the morning were now enlightening the horizon, when Andrew cast a look behind him, and not seeing the appearance of a living being on the moors which he had travelled, his hard features gradually unbent, as he first whistled, then sung, with much glee and little melody, the end of one of his native songs:

> 'Jenny, lass! I think I hae her
> Ower the moor amang the heather;
> All their clan shall never get her.'*

He patted at the same time the neck of the horse which had carried him so gallantly; and my attention being directed by that action to the animal, I instantly recognised a favourite mare of Thorncliff Osbaldistone. 'How is this, sir?' said I sternly; 'that is Mr Thorncliff's mare!'

'I'll no say but she may aiblins hae been his honour's Squire Thorncliff's in her day—but she's mine now.'

'You have stolen her, you rascal.'

'Na, na, sir, nae man can wyte me wi' theft—The thing stands this gate, ye see—Squire Thorncliff borrowed ten punds o' me to gang to York Races—deil a boddle wad he pay me back again, and spake o' raddling my banes, as he ca'd it, when I asked him but for my ain back again—now I think it will riddle him or he gets his horse ower the Border again—unless he pays me plack and bawbee, he sall never see a hair o' her tail. I ken a canny chield at Loughmaben, a bit writer lad, that will put me in the way to sort him—Steal the mear! na, na, far be the sin o' theft frae Andrew Fairservice—I have just arrested her *jurisdictiones fandandy causey*.* Thae are bonny writer words—amaist like the language o' huz gardeners and other learned men—it's a pity they're sae dear—thae three words were a' that Andrew got for a lang law-plea, and four ankers o' as gude brandy as was e'er coupit ower craig—Hech, sirs! but law's a dear thing.'

'You are likely to find it much dearer than you suppose, Andrew, if you proceed in this mode of paying yourself, without legal authority.'

'Hout tout, we're in Scotland now (be praised for't,) and I can find baith friends and lawyers, and judges too, as weel as ony Osbaldistone o' them a'. My mither's mither's third cousin was cousin to the Provost o' Dumfries, and he winna see a drap o' her blude wranged. Hout awa, the laws are indifferently administered here to a' men alike; it's no like on yon side, when a chield may be whuppit awa' wi' ane o' Clerk Jobson's warrants, afore he kens where he is. But they will hae little eneugh law amang them by and by, and that is ae grand reason that I hae gi'en them gude day.'

I was highly provoked at the achievement of Andrew, and considered it as a hard fate, which a second time threw me into collision with a person of such irregular practices. I determined, however, to buy the mare of him, when we should reach the end of our journey, and send her back to my cousin at Osbaldistone Hall; and with this purpose of reparation I resolved to make my uncle acquainted from the next post-town. It was needless, I thought, to quarrel with Andrew in the meantime, who had, after all, acted not very unnaturally for a person in his circumstances. I therefore smothered my resentment, and asked him what he meant by his last expressions, that there would be little law in Northumberland by and by?

'Law!' said Andrew, 'hout, ay—there will be club-law* eneugh. The priests and the Irish officers, and thae papist cattle that hae been sodgering abroad, because they durstna bide at hame, are a' fleeing thick in Northumberland e'enow—and thae corbies dinna gather without they smell carrion. As sure as ye live, his honour Sir Hildebrand is gaun to stick his horn in the bog—there's naething but gun and pistol, sword and dagger, amang them—and they'll be laying on, I'se warrant; for they're fearless fules the young Osbaldistone squires, aye craving your honour's pardon.'

This speech recalled to my memory some suspicions that I myself had entertained, that the jacobites were on the eve of some desperate enterprise. But, conscious it did not become me to be a spy on my uncle's words and actions, I had rather avoided than availed myself of any opportunity which occurred of remarking upon the signs of the times. Andrew Fairservice felt no such restraint, and doubtless spoke very truly in stating his conviction, that some desperate plots were in agitation, as a reason which determined his resolution to leave the Hall.

'The servants,' he stated, 'with the tenantry and others, had been all regularly enrolled and mustered, and they wanted me to take arms also. But I'll ride in nae siccan troop—they little kend Andrew that asked him. I'll fight when I like mysell, but it sall neither be for the hure o' Babylon,* nor ony hure in England.'

CHAPTER XIX

Where longs to fall yon rifted spire,
 As weary of the insulting air,—
The poet's thoughts, the warrior's fire,
 The lover's sighs, are sleeping there.

LANGHORNE*

AT the first Scotch town which we reached, my guide sought out his friend and counsellor, to consult upon the proper and legal means of converting into his own lawful property the 'bonny creature,' which was at present his own only by one of those slight-of-hand arrangements, which still sometimes took place in that once lawless district. I was somewhat diverted with the dejection of his looks on his return. He had, it seems, been rather too communicative to his confidential friend, the attorney; and learned with great dismay, in return for his unsuspecting frankness, that Mr Touthope had, during his absence, been appointed clerk to the peace of the county, and was bound to communicate to justice all such achievements as that of his friend, Mr Andrew Fairservice. There was a necessity, this alert member of the police stated, for arresting the horse, and placing him in Bailie Trumbull's stable, therein to remain at livery, at the rate of twelve shillings (Scotch)* per diem, until the question of property was duly tried and debated. He even talked as if, in strict and rigorous execution of his duty, he ought to detain honest Andrew himself; but on my guide's most piteously entreating his forbearance, he not only desisted from this proposal, but made a present to Andrew of a broken-winded and spavined pony, in order to enable him to pursue his journey. It is true, he qualified this act of generosity by exacting from poor Andrew an absolute cession of his right and interest in the gallant palfrey of Thorncliff Osbaldistone; a transference which Mr Touthope represented as of very little consequence, since his unfortunate friend, as he facetiously observed, was likely to get nothing of the mare excepting the halter.

Andrew seemed woful and disconcerted, as I screwed out of him these particulars; for his northern pride was cruelly pinched by being compelled to admit that attorneys were attorneys on both sides of the Tweed; and that Mr Clerk Touthope was not a farthing more sterling coin than Mr Clerk Jobson.

'It wadna hae vexed him half sae muckle to hae been cheated out o' what might amaist be said to be won with the peril o' his craig, had it happened amang the Inglishers; but it was an unco thing to see hawks pike out hawks' een, or ae kindly Scot cheat anither. But nae doubt things were strangely changed in his country sin' the sad and sorrowfu' Union;' an event to which Andrew referred every symptom of depravity or degeneracy which he remarked among his countrymen, more especially the inflammation of reckonings, the diminished size of pint-stoups, and other grievances, which he pointed out to me during our journey.

For my own part, I held myself, as things had turned out, acquitted of all charge of the mare, and wrote to my uncle the circumstances under which she was carried into Scotland, concluding with informing him that she was in the hands of justice, and her worthy representatives, Bailie Trumbull and Mr Clerk Touthope, to whom I referred him for farther particulars. Whether the property returned to the Northumbrian fox-hunter, or continued to bear the person of the Scottish attorney, it is unnecessary for me at present to say.

We now pursued our journey to the north-westward, at a rate much slower than that at which we had achieved our nocturnal retreat from England. One chain of barren and uninteresting hills succeeded another, until the more fertile vale of Clyde opened upon us; and with such dispatch as we might we gained the town, or, as my guide pertinaciously termed it, the city, of Glasgow. Of late years, I understand, it has fully deserved the name, which, by a sort of political second-sight, my guide assigned to it. An extensive and increasing trade with the West Indies and American colonies, has, if I am rightly informed, laid the foundation of wealth and prosperity, which, if carefully strengthened and built upon, may one day support an immense fabric of commercial prosperity; but, in the earlier time of which I speak, the dawn of this splendour had not arisen. The union had, indeed, opened to Scotland the trade of the English colonies; but, betwixt want of capital, and the national jealousy of the English, the merchants of Scotland were as yet excluded, in a great measure, from the exercise of the privileges which that memorable treaty conferred on them. Glasgow lay on the wrong side of the island for participating in the east country or continental trade, by which the trifling commerce as yet possessed by Scotland chiefly supported itself. Yet, though she then gave small promise of the commercial eminence to which, I am informed, she seems now likely one day to attain, Glasgow, as the principal central town of the western district of Scotland, was a place of considerable rank and importance.* The broad and brimming Clyde, which flows so near its walls, gave the means of an inland navigation of some importance. Not only the fertile plains in its immediate neighbour-hood, but the districts of Ayr and Dumfries, regarded Glasgow as their capital, to which they transmitted their produce, and received in return such necessaries and luxuries as their consumption required.

The dusky mountains of the Western Highlands often sent forth wilder tribes to frequent the marts of St Mungo's favourite city.* Hordes of wild, shaggy, dwarfish cattle and ponies, conducted by Highlanders, as wild, as shaggy, and sometimes as dwarfish, as the animals they had in charge, often traversed the streets of Glasgow. Strangers gazed with surprise on the antique and fantastic dress, and listened to the unknown and dissonant sounds of their language, while the mountaineers, armed even while engaged in this peaceful occupa-tion with musket and pistol, sword, dagger, and target, stared with astonishment on the articles of luxury of which they knew not the use, and with an avidity which seemed somewhat alarming on the articles which they knew and valued. It is always with unwillingness that the Highlander quits his deserts, and at this early period it was like tear-ing a pine from its rock, to plant him elsewhere. Yet even then the mountain glens were over-peopled, although thinned occasionally by famine or by the sword, and many of their inhabitants strayed down to Glasgow—there formed settlements—there sought and found employment, although different, indeed, from that of their native hills. This supply of a hardy and useful population was of conse-quence to the prosperity of the place, furnished the means of carrying on the few manufactures which the town already boasted, and laid the foundation of its future prosperity.

The exterior of the city corresponded with these promising cir-cumstances.* The principal street was broad and important, decor-ated with public buildings, of an architecture rather striking than correct in point of taste, and running between rows of tall houses, built of stone, the fronts of which were occasionally richly ornamented with mason-work; a circumstance which gave the street an imposing air of dignity and grandeur, of which most English towns are in some measure deprived, by the slight, unsubstantial, and perishable quality and appearance of the bricks with which they are constructed.

In the western metropolis of Scotland, my guide and I arrived on a Saturday evening,* too late to entertain thoughts of business of any kind. We alighted at the door of a jolly hostler-wife, as Andrew called her, the Ostelere of old father Chaucer,* by whom we were civilly received.

On the following morning the bells pealed from every steeple, announcing the sanctity of the day. Notwithstanding, however, what I had heard of the severity with which the Sabbath is observed in Scotland, my first impulse, not unnaturally, was to seek out Owen; but on enquiry I found that my attempt would be in vain, 'until kirk-time was ower.' Not only did my landlady and guide jointly assure me that 'there wadna be a living soul either in the counting-house or dwelling-house of Messrs MacVittie, Macfin, and Company,' to which Owen's letter referred me, but, moreover, 'far less would I find any of the partners there. They were serious men, and wad be where a' gude Christians ought to be at sic a time, and that was in the Barony Laigh Kirk.'*

Andrew Fairservice, whose disgust at the law of his country had fortunately not extended itself to the other learned professions of his native land, now sung forth the praises of the preacher who was to perform the duty, to which my hostess replied with many loud amens. The result was, that I determined to go to this popular place of worship, as much with the purpose of learning, if possible, whether Owen had arrived in Glasgow, as with any great expectation of edification. My hopes were exalted by the assurance, that, if Mr Ephraim MacVittie (worthy man) were in the land of life, he would surely honour the Barony Kirk that day with his presence; and if he chanced to have a stranger within his gates, doubtless he would bring him to the duty along with him. This probability determined my motions, and, under the escort of my faithful Andrew, I set forth for the Barony Kirk.

On this occasion, however, I had little need of his guidance; for the crowd, which forced its way up a steep and rough-paved street, to hear the most popular preacher in the west of Scotland, would of itself have swept me along with it. On attaining the summit of the hill, we turned to the left, and a large pair of folding doors admitted us, amongst others, into the open and extensive burying-place which surrounds the Minster, or Cathedral Church of Glasgow. The pile is of a gloomy and massive, rather than of an elegant, style of Gothic architecture; but its peculiar character is so strongly preserved, and so well suited with the accompaniments that surround it, that the impression of the first view was awful and solemn in the extreme. I was indeed so much struck, that I resisted for a few minutes all Andrew's efforts to drag me into the interior of the building, so deeply was I engaged in surveying its outward character.

Situated in a populous and considerable town, this ancient and massive pile has the appearance of the most sequestered solitude. High walls divide it from the buildings of the city on one side; on the other, it is bounded by a ravine, at the bottom of which, and invisible to the eye, murmurs a wandering rivulet, adding, by its gentle noise, to the imposing solemnity of the scene. On the opposite side of the ravine rises a steep bank, covered with fir-trees closely planted, whose dusky shade extends itself over the cemetery with an appropriate and gloomy effect. The churchyard itself had a peculiar character; for though in reality extensive, it is small in proportion to the number of respectable inhabitants who are interred within it, and whose graves are almost all covered with tombstones. There is therefore no room for the long rank grass, which, in most cases, partially clothes the surface of those retreats, where the wicked cease from troubling, and the weary are at rest. The broad flat monumental stones are placed so close to each other, that the precincts appear to be flagged with them, and, though roofed only by the heavens, resemble the floor of one of our old English churches, where the pavement is covered with sepulchral inscriptions. The contents of these sad records of mortality, the vain sorrows which they preserve, the stern lesson which they teach of the nothingness of humanity, the extent of ground which they so closely cover, and their uniform and melancholy tenor, reminded me of the roll of the prophet, which was 'written within and without, and there was written therein lamentations and mourning and woe.'*

The Cathedral itself corresponds in impressive majesty with these accompaniments. We feel that its appearance is heavy, yet that the effect produced would be destroyed were it lighter or more ornamental. It is the only metropolitan church in Scotland, excepting, as I am informed, the cathedral of Kirkwall, in the Orkneys, which remained uninjured at the Reformation; and Andrew Fairservice, who saw with great pride the effect which it produced upon my mind, thus accounted for its preservation. 'Ah! it's a brave kirk—nane o' yere whigmaleeries and curliewurlies and open-steek hems about it—a' solid, weel-jointed mason-wark, that will stand as lang as the warld, keep hands and gunpowder aff it. It had amaist a douncome lang syne at the Reformation, when they pu'd doun the kirks of St Andrews and Perth, and there-awa', to cleanse them o' Papery, and idolatry, and image worship, and surplices, and sic like rags o' the muckle hure that sitteth on seven hills, as if ane wasna braid eneugh for her auld hinder end. Sae the commons o' Renfrew, and o' the Barony, and the Gorbals, and a' about, they behoved to come into Glasgow ae fair morning, to try their hand on purging the High Kirk o' Popish nick-nackets. But the townsmen o' Glasgow, they were feared their auld edifice might slip the girths in gaun through siccan rough physic, sae they rang the common bell, and assembled the train-bands wi' took o' drum—by good luck, the worthy James Rabat was Dean o' Guild that year—(and a gude mason he was himsell, made him the keener to keep up the auld bigging,) and the trades assembled, and offered downright battle to the commons, rather than their kirk should coup the crans, as others had done elsewhere.* It wasna for luve o' Paperie—na, na!—nane could ever say that o' the trades o' Glasgow—Sae they sune came to an agreement to take a' the idolatrous statues of sants (sorrow be on them) out o' their neuks—And sae the bits o' stane idols were broken in pieces by Scripture warrant, and flung into the Molendinar burn, and the auld kirk stood as crouse as a cat when the flaes are kaimed aff her, and a' body was alike pleased. And I hae heard wise folk say, that if the same had been done in ilka kirk in Scotland, the Reform wad just hae been as pure as it is e'en now, and we wad hae mair Christian-like kirks; for I hae been sae lang in England, that naething will drived out o' my head, that the dog-kennel at Osbaldistone Hall is better than mony a house o' God in Scotland.'

Thus saying, Andrew led the way into the place of worship.

CHAPTER XX

——It strikes an awe
And terror on my aching sight; the tombs
And monumental caves of death look cold,
And shoot a chillness to the trembling heart.

*Mourning Bride**

NOTWITHSTANDING the impatience of my conductor, I could not forbear to pause and gaze for some minutes on the exterior of the building, rendered more impressively dignified by the solitude which ensued when its hitherto open gates were closed, after having, as it were, devoured the multitudes which had lately crowded the church-yard, but now, enclosed within the building, were engaged, as the choral swell of voices from within announced to us, in the solemn exercises of devotion. The sound of so many voices, united by the dis-tance into one harmony, and freed from those harsh discordances which jar the ear when heard more near, combining with the mur-muring brook, and the wind which sung among the old firs, affected me with a sense of sublimity. All nature, as invoked by the Psalmist whose verses they chanted, seemed united in offering that solemn praise in which trembling is mixed with joy as she addresses her Maker. I had heard the service of high mass in France, celebrated with all the eclat which the choicest music, the richest dresses, the most imposing ceremonies, could confer on it; yet it fell short in effect of the simplicity of the Presbyterian worship. The devotion, in which every one took a share, seemed so superior to that which was recited by musicians, as a lesson which they had learned by rote, that it gave the Scottish worship all the advantage of reality over acting.

As I lingered to catch more of the solemn sound, Andrew, whose impatience became ungovernable, pulled me by the sleeve—'Come awa', sir—Come awa', we maunna be late o' gaun in to disturb the worship; if we bide here, the searchers will be on us, and carry us to the guard-house for being idlers in kirk-time.'*

Thus admonished, I followed my guide, but not, as I had supposed, into the body of the cathedral. 'This gate—this gate, sir!' he exclaimed, dragging me off as I made towards the main entrance of the building,—'There's but cauldrife law-wark gaun on yonder—carnal morality, as dow'd and as fusionless as rue leaves at Yule—Here's the real savour of doctrine.'

So saying, we entered a small low-arched door, secured by a wicket, which a grave-looking person seemed on the point of closing, and descended several steps as if into the funeral vaults beneath the church. It was even so; for in these subterranean precincts, why chosen for such a purpose I knew not, was established a very singular place of worship.

Conceive, Tresham, an extensive range of lowbrowed, dark, and twilight vaults, such as are used for sepulchres in other countries, and had long been dedicated to the same purpose in this, a portion of which was seated with pews, and used as a church. The part of the vaults thus occupied, though capable of containing a congregation of many hundreds, bore a small proportion to the darker and more extensive caverns which yawned around what may be termed the inhabited space. In those waste regions of oblivion, dusky banners and tattered escutcheons indicated the graves of those who were once, doubtless, 'princes in Israel.'* Inscriptions, which could only be read by the painful antiquary, in language as obsolete as the act of devotional charity which they implored, invited the passengers to pray for the souls of those whose bodies rested beneath. Surrounded by these receptacles of the last remains of mortality, I found a numerous congregation engaged in the act of prayer. The Scotch perform this duty in a standing, instead of a kneeling posture, more, perhaps, to take as broad a distinction as possible from the ritual of Rome than for any better reason, since I have observed that in their family worship, as doubtless in their private devotions, they adopt, in their immediate address to the Deity, that posture which other Christians use as the humblest and most reverential. Standing, therefore, the men being uncovered, a crowd of several hundreds of both sexes, and all ages, listened with great reverence and attention to the extempore, at least the unwritten, prayer of an aged clergyman,[37] who was very popular in the city. Educated in the same religious persuasion, I seriously bent my mind to join in the devotion of the day, and it was not till the congregation resumed their seats that my attention was diverted to the consideration of the appearance of all around me.

At the conclusion of the prayer, most of the men put on their hats or bonnets, and all who had the happiness to have seats sate down. Andrew and I were not of this number, having been too late of entering the church to secure such accommodation. We stood among a number of other persons in the same situation, forming a sort of ring around the seated part of the congregation. Behind and around us were the vaults I have already described; before us the devout audience, dimly shown by the light which streamed on their faces through one or two low Gothic windows, such as give air and light to charnel-houses. By this were seen the usual variety of countenances, which are generally turned towards a Scotch pastor on such occasions, almost all composed to attention, unless where a father or mother here and there recalls the wandering eyes of a lively child, or disturbs the slumbers of a dull one. The high-boned and harsh countenance of the nation, with the expression of intelligence and shrewdness which it frequently exhibits, is seen to more advantage in the act of devotion, or in the ranks of war, than on lighter and more cheerful occasions of assemblage. The discourse of the preacher was well qualified to call forth the various feelings and faculties of his audience.

Age and infirmities had impaired the powers of a voice originally strong and sonorous. He read his text with a pronunciation somewhat inarticulate; but when he closed the Bible, and commenced his sermon, his tones gradually strengthened, as he entered with vehemence into the arguments which he maintained. They related chiefly to the abstract points of the Christian faith, subjects grave, deep, and fathomless by mere human reason, but for which, with equal ingenuity and propriety, he sought a key in liberal quotations from the inspired writings. My mind was unprepared to coincide in all his reasoning, nor was I sure that in some instances I rightly comprehended his positions. But nothing could be more impressive than the eager enthusiastic manner of the good old man, and nothing more ingenious than his mode of reasoning. The Scotch, it is well known, are more remarkable for the exercise of their intellectual powers, than for the keenness of their feelings; they are, therefore, more moved by logic than by rhetoric, and more attracted by acute and argumentative reasoning on doctrinal points, than influenced by the enthusiastic appeals to the heart and to the passions, by which popular preachers in other countries win the favour of their hearers.

Among the attentive group which I now saw, might be distinguished various expressions similar to those of the audience in the famous cartoon of Paul preaching at Athens.* Here sat a zealous and intelligent Calvinist, with brows bent just as much as to indicate profound attention; lips slightly compressed; eyes fixed on the minister, with an expression of decent pride, as if sharing the triumph of his argument; the forefinger of the right hand touching successively those of the left, as the preacher, from argument to argument, ascended towards his conclusion. Another, with fiercer and sterner look, intimated at once his contempt of all who doubted the creed of his pastor, and his joy at the appropriate punishment denounced against them. A third, perhaps belonging to a different congregation, and present only by accident or curiosity, had the appearance of internally impeaching some link of the reasoning; and you might plainly read, in the slight motion of his head, his doubts as to the soundness of the preacher's argument. The greater part listened with a calm satisfied countenance, expressive of a conscious merit in being present, and in hearkening to such an ingenious discourse, although, perhaps, unable entirely to comprehend it. The women in general belonged to this last division of the audience; the old, however, seeming more grimly intent upon the abstract doctrines laid before them; while the younger females permitted their eyes occasionally to make a modest circuit around the congregation; and some of them, Tresham, (if my vanity did not greatly deceive me,) contrived to distinguish your friend and servant, as a handsome young stranger, and an Englishman. As to the rest of the congregation, the stupid gaped, yawned, or slept, till awakened by the application of their more zealous neighbours' heels to their shins; and the idle indicated their inattention by the wandering of their eyes, but dared give no more decided token of weariness. Amid the Lowland costume of coat and cloak, I could here and there discern a Highland plaid, the wearer of which, resting on his basket-hilt, sent his eyes among the audience with the unrestrained curiosity of savage wonder; and who, in all probability, was inattentive to the sermon, for a very pardonable reason—because he did not understand the language in which it was delivered. The martial and wild look, however, of these stragglers, added a kind of character which the congregation could not have exhibited without them. They were more numerous, Andrew afterwards observed, owing to some cattle-fair in the neighbourhood.

Such was the group of countenances, rising tier on tier, discovered to my critical inspection by such sunbeams as forced their way through the narrow Gothic lattices of the Laigh Kirk of Glasgow; and, having illuminated the attentive congregation, lost themselves in the vacuity of the vaults behind, giving to the nearer part of their labyrinth a sort of imperfect twilight, and leaving their recesses in an utter darkness, which gave them the appearance of being interminable.

I have already said that I stood with others in the exterior circle, with my face to the preacher, and my back to those vaults which I have so often mentioned. My position rendered me particularly obnoxious to any interruption which arose from any slight noise occurring amongst these retiring arches, where the least sound was multiplied by a thousand echoes. The occasional sound of rain-drops, which, admitted through some cranny in the ruined roof, fell successively, and plashed upon the pavement beneath, caused me to turn my head more than once to the place from whence it seemed to proceed; and when my eyes took that direction, I found it difficult to withdraw them; such is the pleasure our imagination receives from the attempt to penetrate as far as possible into an intricate labyrinth, imperfectly lighted, and exhibiting objects which irritate our curiosity, only because they acquire a mysterious interest from being undefined and dubious. My eyes became habituated to the gloomy atmosphere to which I directed them, and insensibly my mind became more interested in their discoveries than in the metaphysical subtleties which the preacher was enforcing.

My father had often checked me for this wandering mood of mind, arising perhaps from an excitability of imagination to which he was a stranger; and the finding myself at present solicited by these temptations to inattention, recalled the time when I used to walk, led by his hand, to Mr Shower's chapel, and the earnest injunctions which he then laid on me to redeem the time, because the days were evil. At present, the picture which my thoughts suggested, far from fixing my attention, destroyed the portion I had yet left, by conjuring up to my recollection the peril in which his affairs now stood. I endeavoured, in the lowest whisper I could frame, to request Andrew to obtain information, whether any of the gentlemen of the firm of MacVittie & Co. were at present in the congregation. But Andrew, wrapped in profound attention to the sermon, only replied to my suggestion by hard punches with his elbow, as signals to me to remain silent. I next strained my eyes, with equally bad success, to see if, among the sea of up-turned faces which bent their eyes on the pulpit as a common centre, I could discover the sober and business-like physiognomy of Owen. But not among the broad beavers of the Glasgow citizens, or the yet broader brimmed Lowland bonnets of the peasants of Lanarkshire, could I see any thing resembling the decent periwig, starched ruffles, or the uniform suit of light brown garments, appertaining to the head clerk of the establishment of Osbaldistone and Tresham. My anxiety now returned on me with such violence, as to overpower not only the novelty of the scene around me, by which it had hitherto been diverted, but moreover my sense of decorum. I pulled Andrew hard by the sleeve, and intimated my wish to leave the church, and pursue my investigation as I could. Andrew, obdurate in the Laigh Kirk of Glasgow as on the mountains of Cheviot, for some time deigned me no answer; and it was only when he found I could not otherwise be kept quiet that he condescended to inform me, that, being once in the church, we could not leave it till service was over, because the doors were locked so soon as the prayers began. Having thus spoken in a brief and peevish whisper, Andrew again assumed the air of intelligent and critical importance, and attention to the preacher's discourse.

While I endeavoured to make a virtue of necessity, and recall my attention to the sermon, I was again disturbed by a singular interruption. A voice from behind whispered distinctly in my ear, 'You are in danger in this city.'—I turned round as if mechanically.

One or two starched and ordinary-looking mechanics stood beside and behind me, stragglers, who, like ourselves, had been too late in obtaining entrance. But a glance at their faces satisfied me, though I could hardly say why, that none of these was the person who had spoken to me. Their countenances seemed all composed to attention to the sermon, and not one of them returned any glance of intelligence to the inquisitive and startled look with which I surveyed them. A massive round pillar, which was close behind us, might have concealed the speaker the instant he uttered his mysterious caution; but wherefore it was given in such a place, or to what species of danger it directed my attention, or by whom the warning was uttered, were points on which my imagination lost itself in conjecture. It would, however, I concluded, be repeated, and I resolved to keep my countenance turned towards the clergyman, that the whisperer might be tempted to renew his communication under the idea that the first had passed unobserved.

My plan succeeded. I had not resumed the appearance of attention to the preacher for five minutes, when the same voice whispered, 'Listen—but do not look back.' I kept my face in the same direction. 'You are in danger in this place,' the voice proceeded; 'so am I—Meet me to-night on the Brigg, at twelve preceesely—keep at home till the gloaming, and avoid observation.'

Here the voice ceased, and I instantly turned my head. But the speaker had, with still greater promptitude, glided behind the pillar, and escaped my observation. I was determined to catch a sight of him, if possible, and, extricating myself from the outer circle of hearers, I also stepped behind the column. All there was empty; and I could only see a figure wrapped in a mantle, whether a Lowland cloak, or Highland plaid, I could not distinguish, which traversed, like a phantom, the dreary vacuity of vaults which I have described.

I made a mechanical attempt to pursue the mysterious form, which glided away, and vanished in the vaulted cemetery, like the spectre of one of the numerous dead who rested within its precincts. I had little chance of arresting the course of one obviously determined not to be spoken with; but that little chance was lost by my stumbling and falling before I had made three steps from the column. The obscurity which occasioned my misfortune covered my disgrace; which I accounted rather lucky, for the preacher, with that stern authority which the Scottish ministers assume for the purpose of keeping order in their congregations, interrupted his discourse, to desire the 'proper officer' to take into custody the causer of this disturbance in the place of worship. As the noise, however, was not repeated, the beadle, or whatever else he was called, did not think it necessary to be rigorous in searching out the offender; so that I was enabled, without attracting farther observation, to place myself by Andrew's side in my original position. The service proceeded, and closed without the occurrence of any thing else worthy of notice.

As the congregation departed and dispersed, my friend Andrew exclaimed, 'See, yonder is worthy Mr MacVittie and Mrs MacVittie, and Miss Alison MacVittie, and Mr Thamas MacFin, that they say is to marry Miss Alison, if a' bowls row right—she'll hae a hantle siller, if she's no that bonny.'

My eyes took the direction he pointed out. Mr MacVittie was a tall, thin, elderly man, with hard features, thick grey eyebrows, light eyes, and, as I imagined, a sinister expression of countenance, from which my heart recoiled. I remembered the warning I had received in the church, and hesitated to address this person, though I could not allege to myself any rational ground of dislike or suspicion.

I was yet in suspense, when Andrew, who mistook my hesitation for bashfulness, proceeded to exhort me to lay it aside. 'Speak till him—speak till him, Mr Francis—he's no provost yet, though they say he'll be my lord neist year. Speak till him, then—he'll gie ye a decent answer for as rich as he is, unless ye were wanting siller frae him—they say he's dour to draw his purse.'

It immediately occurred to me, that if this merchant were really of the churlish and avaricious disposition which Andrew intimated, there might be some caution necessary in making myself known, as I could not tell how accounts might stand between my father and him. This consideration came in aid of the mysterious hint which I had received, and the dislike which I had conceived at the man's countenance. Instead of addressing myself directly to him, as I had designed to have done, I contented myself with desiring Andrew to enquire at Mr MacVittie's house the address of Mr Owen, an English gentleman; and I charged him not to mention the person from whom he received the commission, but to bring me the result to the small inn where we lodged. This Andrew promised to do. He said something of the duty of my attending the evening service; but added, with a causticity natural to him, that 'in troth, if folk couldna keep their legs still, but wad needs be couping the creels ower through-stanes, as if they wad raise the very dead folk wi' the clatter, a kirk wi' a chimley in't* was fittest for them.'

CHAPTER XXI

On the Rialto, every night at twelve,
I take my evening's walk of meditation:
There we two will meet.

*Venice Preserved**

FULL of sinister augury, for which, however, I could assign no satisfactory cause, I shut myself up in my apartment at the inn, and having dismissed Andrew, after resisting his importunity to accompany
him to St Enoch's Kirk,[38] where, he said, 'a soul-searching divine was
to haud forth,' I set myself seriously to consider what were best to be
done. I never was, what is properly called, superstitious; but I suppose
all men, in situations of peculiar doubt and difficulty, when they have
exercised their reason to little purpose, are apt, in a sort of despair, to
abandon the reins to their imagination, and be guided either altogether by chance, or by those whimsical impressions which take
possession of the mind, and to which we give way as if to involuntary
impulses. There was something so singularly repulsive in the hard
features of the Scotch trader, that I could not resolve to put myself
into his hands without transgressing every caution which could be
derived from the rules of physiognomy; while, at the same time, the
warning voice, the form which flitted away like a vanishing shadow
through those vaults, which might be termed 'the valley of the shadow
of death,'* had something captivating for the imagination of a young
man, who, you will farther please to remember, was also a young poet.

If danger was around me, as the mysterious communication intimated, how could I learn its nature, or the means of averting it, but by
meeting my unknown counsellor, to whom I could see no reason for
imputing any other than kind intentions. Rashleigh and his machinations occurred more than once to my remembrance; but so rapid had
my journey been, that I could not suppose him apprized of my arrival
in Glasgow, much less prepared to play off any stratagem against my
person. In my temper also I was bold and confident, strong and active
in person, and in some measure accustomed to the use of arms, in
which the French youth of all kinds were then initiated. I did not fear
any single opponent; assassination was neither the vice of the age nor
of the country; the place selected for our meeting was too public to

admit any suspicion of meditated violence. In a word, I resolved to meet my mysterious counsellor on the bridge, as he had requested, and to be afterwards guided by circumstances. Let me not conceal from you, Tresham, what at the time I endeavoured to conceal from myself—the subdued, yet secretly-cherished hope, that Diana Vernon might—by what chance I knew not—through what means I could not guess—have some connexion with this strange and dubious intimation, conveyed at a time and place, and in a manner so surprising. She alone—whispered this insidious thought—she alone knew of my journey; from her own account, she possessed friends and influence in Scotland; she had furnished me with a talisman, whose power I was to invoke when all other aid failed me: who, then, but Diana Vernon, possessed either means, knowledge, or inclination for averting the dangers, by which, as it seemed, my steps were surrounded? This flattering view of my very doubtful case pressed itself upon me again and again. It insinuated itself into my thoughts, though very bashfully, before the hour of dinner; it displayed its attractions more boldly during the course of my frugal meal, and became so courageously intrusive during the succeeding half hour, (aided perhaps by the flavour of a few glasses of most excellent claret,) that, with a sort of desperate attempt to escape from a delusive seduction, to which I felt the danger of yielding, I pushed my glass from me, threw aside my dinner, seized my hat, and rushed into the open air with the feeling of one who would fly from his own thoughts. Yet perhaps I yielded to the very feelings from which I seemed to fly, since my steps insensibly led me to the bridge over the Clyde, the place assigned for the rendezvous by my mysterious monitor.

Although I had not partaken of my repast until the hours of evening church-service were over,—in which, by the way, I complied with the religious scruples of my landlady, who hesitated to dress a hot dinner between sermons, and also with the admonition of my unknown friend, to keep my apartment till twilight,—several hours had still to pass away betwixt the time of my appointment and that at which I reached the assigned place of meeting. The interval, as you will readily credit, was wearisome enough; and I can hardly explain to you how it passed away. Various groups of persons, all of whom, young and old, seemed impressed with a reverential feeling of the sanctity of the day, passed along the large open meadow which lies on the northern bank of the Clyde,* and serves at once as a bleaching-field and pleasure-walk for the inhabitants, or paced with slow steps the long bridge which communicates with the southern district of the county. All that I remember of them was the general, yet not unpleasing, intimation of a devotional character impressed on each little party, formally assumed perhaps by some, but sincerely characterising the greater number, which hushed the petulant gaiety of the young into a tone of more quiet, yet more interesting, interchange of sentiments, and suppressed the vehement argument and protracted disputes of those of more advanced age. Notwithstanding the numbers who passed me, no general sound of the human voice was heard; few turned again to take some minutes' voluntary exercise, to which the leisure of the evening, and the beauty of the surrounding scenery, seemed to invite them: all hurried to their homes and resting-places. To one accustomed to the mode of spending Sunday evenings abroad, even among the French Calvinists, there seemed something Judaical, yet at the same time striking and affecting, in this mode of keeping the Sabbath holy. Insensibly, I felt my mode of sauntering by the side of the river, and crossing successively the various persons who were passing homeward, and without tarrying or delay, must expose me to observation at least, if not to censure, and I slunk out of the frequented path, and found a trivial occupation for my mind in marshalling my revolving walk in such a manner as should least render me obnoxious to observation. The different alleys lined out through this extensive meadow, and which are planted with trees, like the Park of St James's in London, gave me facilities for carrying into effect these childish manœuvres.

As I walked down one of these avenues, I heard, to my surprise, the sharp and conceited voice of Andrew Fairservice, raised by a sense of self-consequence to a pitch somewhat higher than others seemed to think consistent with the solemnity of the day. To slip behind the row of trees under which I walked was perhaps no very dignified proceeding; but it was the easiest mode of escaping his observation, and perhaps his impertinent assiduity, and still more intrusive curiosity. As he passed, I heard him communicate to a grave-looking man, in a black coat, a slouched hat, and Geneva cloak, the following sketch of a character, which my self-love, while revolting against it as a caricature, could not, nevertheless, refuse to recognise as a likeness.

'Ay, ay, Mr Hammorgaw, it's e'en as I tell ye. He's no a'thegether sae void o' sense neither; he has a gloaming sight o' what's reasonable— that is anes and awa'—a glisk and nae mair—but he's crack-brained and cockle-headed about his nipperty-tipperty poetry nonsense—He'll glowr at an auld-warld barkit aik-snag as if it were a queez-maddam in full bearing; and a naked craig, wi' a burn jawing ower't, is unto him as a garden garnisht with flowering knots and choice pot-herbs; then, he wad rather claver wi' a daft quean they ca' Diana Vernon (weel I wot they might ca' her Diana of the Ephesians,* for she's little better than a heathen—better? she's waur—a Roman—a mere Roman)—he'll claver wi' her, or ony other idle slut, rather than hear what might do him gude a' the days of his life, frae you or me, Mr Hammorgaw, or ony ither sober and sponsible person. Reason, sir, is what he canna endure—he's a' for your vanities and volubilities; and he ance tell'd me, (puir blinded creature,) that the Psalms of David were excellent poetry!* as if the holy Psalmist thought o' rattling rhymes in a blether, like his ain silly clinkum-clankum things that he ca's verse. Gude help him! twa lines o' Davie Lindsay* wad ding a' he ever clerkit.'

While listening to this perverted account of my temper and studies, you will not be surprised if I meditated for Mr Fairservice the unpleasant surprise of a broken pate on the first decent opportunity. His friend only intimated his attention by 'Ay, ay!' and 'Is't e'en sae?' and such like expressions of interest, at the proper breaks in Mr Fairservice's harangue, until at length, in answer to some observation of greater length, the import of which I only collected from my trusty guide's reply, honest Andrew answered, 'Tell him a bit o' my mind, quoth ye?—Wha wad be fule then but Andrew?—He's a red-wud deevil, man!—He's like Giles Heathertap's auld boar; ye need but shake a clout at him to make him turn and gore. Bide wi' him, say ye?—Troth, I kenna what for I bide wi' him mysell—But the lad's no a bad lad after a'; and he needs some carefu' body to look after him. He hasna the right grip o' his hand—the gowd slips through't like water, man; and it's no that ill a thing to be near him when his purse is in his hand, and it's seldom out o't. And then he's come o' guid kith and kin—My heart warms to the puir thoughtless callant, Mr Hammorgaw—and then the penny fee'——

In the latter part of this instructive communication, Mr Fairservice lowered his voice to a tone better beseeming the conversation in a place of public resort on a Sabbath evening, and his companion and he were soon beyond my hearing. My feelings of hasty resentment soon subsided under the conviction, that, as Andrew himself might have said, 'A hearkener always hears a bad tale of himself,' and that whoever should happen to overhear their character discussed in their own servants'-hall, must prepare to undergo the scalpel of some such anatomist as Mr Fairservice. The incident was so far useful, as, including the feelings to which it gave rise, it sped away a part of the time which hung so heavily on my hand.

Evening had now closed, and the growing darkness gave to the broad, still, and deep expanse of the brimful river, first a hue sombre and uniform, then a dismal and turbid appearance, partially lighted by a waning and pallid moon. The massive and ancient bridge which stretches across the Clyde, was now but dimly visible, and resembled that which Mirza, in his unequalled vision, has described as traversing the valley of Bagdad.* The low-browed arches, seen as imperfectly as the dusky current which they bestrode, seemed rather caverns which swallowed up the gloomy waters of the river, than apertures contrived for their passage. With the advancing night the stillness of the scene increased. There was yet a twinkling light occasionally seen to glide along by the stream, which conducted home one or two of the small parties, who, after the abstinence and religious duties of the day, had partaken of a social supper, the only meal at which the rigid presbyterians made some advance to sociality on the Sabbath. Occasionally, also, the hoofs of a horse were heard, whose rider, after spending the Sunday in Glasgow, was directing his steps towards his residence in the country. These sounds and sights became gradually of more rare occurrence. At length they altogether ceased, and I was left to enjoy my solitary walk on the shores of the Clyde in solemn silence, broken only by the tolling of the successive hours from the steeples of the churches.

But as the night advanced, my impatience at the uncertainty of the situation in which I was placed increased every moment, and became nearly ungovernable. I began to question whether I had been imposed upon by the trick of a fool, the raving of a madman, or the studied machination of a villain, and paced the little quay or pier adjoining the entrance to the bridge in a state of incredible anxiety and vexation. At length the hour of twelve o'clock swung its summons over the city from the belfry of the metropolitan church of St Mungo, and was answered and vouched by all the others like dutiful diocesans. The echoes had scarcely ceased to repeat the last sound, when a human form—the first I had seen for two hours—appeared passing along the bridge from the southern shore of the river. I advanced to meet him with a feeling as if my fate depended on the result of the interview, so much had my anxiety been wound up by protracted expectation. All that I could remark of the passenger as we advanced towards each other was, that his frame was rather beneath than above the middle size, but apparently strong, thick-set, and muscular; his dress a horseman's wrapping coat. I slackened my pace, and almost paused as I advanced, in expectation that he would address me. But to my inexpressible disappointment, he passed without speaking, and I had no pretence for being the first to address one, who, notwithstanding his appearance at the very hour of appointment, might nevertheless be an absolute stranger. I stopped when he had passed me, and looked after him, uncertain whether I ought not to follow him. The stranger walked on till near the northern end of the bridge, then paused, looked back, and, turning round, again advanced towards me. I resolved that this time he should not have the apology for silence proper to apparitions, who, it is vulgarly supposed, cannot speak until they are spoken to. 'You walk late, sir,' said I, as we met a second time.

'I bide tryste,' was the reply, 'and so I think do you, Mr Osbaldistone.'

'You are then the person who requested to meet me here at this unusual hour?'

'I am,' he replied. 'Follow me, and you shall know my reasons.'

'Before following you, I must know your name and purpose,' I answered.

'I am a man,' was the reply; 'and my purpose is friendly to you.'

'A man!' I repeated. 'That is a very brief description.'

'It will serve for one who has no other to give,' said the stranger. 'He that is without name, without friends, without coin, without country, is still at least a man; and he that has all these is no more.'

'Yet this is still too general an account of yourself, to say the least of it, to establish your credit with a stranger.'

'It is all I mean to give, howsoe'er; you may choose to follow me, or to remain without the information I desire to afford you.'

'Can you not give me that information here?' I demanded.

'You must receive it from your eyes, not from my tongue—you must follow me, or remain in ignorance of the information which I have to give you.'

There was something short, determined, and even stern in the man's manner, not certainly well calculated to conciliate undoubting confidence.

'What is it you fear?' he said impatiently. 'To whom, think ye, your life is of such consequence, that they should seek to bereave ye of it?'

'I fear nothing,' I replied firmly, though somewhat hastily. 'Walk on—I attend you.'

We proceeded, contrary to my expectation, to re-enter the town, and glided like mute spectres, side by side, up its empty and silent streets. The high and gloomy stone fronts, with the variegated ornaments and pediments of the windows, looked yet taller and more sable by the imperfect moonshine. Our walk was for some minutes in perfect silence. At length my conductor spoke.

'Are you afraid?'

'I retort your own words,' I replied; 'wherefore should I fear?'

'Because you are with a stranger—perhaps an enemy, in a place where you have no friends and many enemies.'

'I neither fear you nor them; I am young, active, and armed.'

'I am not armed,' replied my conductor; 'but no matter, a willing hand never lacked weapon. You say you fear nothing; but if you knew who was by your side, perhaps you might underlie a tremor.'

'And why should I?' replied I. 'I again repeat, I fear nought that you can do.'

'Nought that I can do?—Be it so. But do you not fear the consequences of being found with one, whose very name whispered in this lonely street would make the stones themselves rise up to apprehend him—on whose head half the men in Glasgow would build their fortune as on a found treasure, had they the luck to grip him by the collar—the sound of whose apprehension were as welcome at the Cross of Edinburgh as ever the news of a field stricken and won in Flanders?'

'And who then are you, whose name should create so deep a feeling of terror?' I replied.

'No enemy of yours, since I am conveying you to a place, where, were I myself recognised and identified, iron to the heels, and hemp to the craig, would be my brief dooming.'

I paused and stood still on the pavement, drawing back so as to have the most perfect view of my companion which the light afforded, and which was sufficient to guard me against any sudden motion of assault.

'You have said,' I answered, 'either too much or too little—too much to induce me to confide in you as a mere stranger, since you avow yourself a person amenable to the laws of the country in which we are—and too little, unless you could show that you are unjustly subjected to their rigour.'

As I ceased to speak, he made a step towards me. I drew back instinctively, and laid my hand on the hilt of my sword.

'What,' said he, 'on an unarmed man, and your friend?'

'I am yet ignorant if you are either the one or the other,' I replied; 'and, to say the truth, your language and manner might well entitle me to doubt both.'

'It is manfully spoken,' replied my conductor; 'and I respect him whose hand can keep his head.—I will be frank and free with you—I am conveying you to prison.'

'To prison!' I exclaimed; 'by what warrant, or for what offence?—You shall have my life sooner than my liberty—I defy you, and I will not follow you a step farther.'

'I do not,' he said, 'carry you there as a prisoner. I am,' he added, drawing himself haughtily up, 'neither a messenger nor sheriff's officer; I carry you to see a prisoner from whose lips you will learn the risk in which you presently stand. *Your* liberty is little risked by the visit; mine is in some peril; but that I readily encounter on your account, for I care not for risk, and I love a free young blood, that kens no protector but the cross o' the sword.'

While he spoke thus, we had reached the principal street, and were pausing before a large building of hewn stone, garnished, as I thought I could perceive, with gratings of iron before the windows.

'Muckle,' said the stranger, whose language became more broadly national as he assumed a tone of colloquial freedom—'Muckle wad the provost and bailies o' Glasgow gie to hae him sitting with iron garters to his hose within their tolbooth, that now stands wi' his legs as free as the red-deer's on the outside on't. And little wad it avail them; for an if they had me there wi' a stane's weight o' iron at every ancle, I would show them a toom room and a lost lodger before to-morrow—But come on, what stint ye for?'

As he spoke thus, he tapped at a low wicket, and was answered by a sharp voice, as of one awakened from a dream or reverie,—'Fa's tat?—Wha's that, I wad say?—and fat a deil want ye at this hour at e'en?—Clean again rules—clean again rules, as they ca' them.'

The protracted tone in which the last words were uttered, betokened that the speaker was again composing himself to slumber. But my guide spoke in a loud whisper, 'Dougal, man! hae ye forgotten Ha nun Gregarach?'*

'Deil a bit, deil a bit,' was the ready and lively response, and I heard the internal guardian of the prison-gate bustle up with great alacrity. A few words were exchanged between my conductor and the turnkey, in a language to which I was an absolute stranger. The bolts revolved, but with a caution which marked the apprehension that the noise might be overheard, and we stood within the vestibule of the prison of Glasgow, a small, but strong guard-room, from which a narrow stair-case led upwards, and one or two low entrances conducted to apartments on the same level with the outward gate, all secured with the jealous strength of wickets, bolts, and bars. The walls, otherwise naked, were not unsuitably garnished with iron fetters, and other uncouth implements, which might be designed for purposes still more inhuman, interspersed with partisans, guns, pistols of antique manufacture, and other weapons of defence and offence.

At finding myself so unexpectedly, fortuitously, and, as it were, by stealth, introduced within one of the legal fortresses of Scotland, I could not help recollecting my adventure in Northumberland, and fretting at the strange incidents which again, without any demerits of my own, threatened to place me in a dangerous and disagreeable collision with the laws of a country, which I visited only in the capacity of a stranger.

CHAPTER XXII

'Look round thee, young Astolpho: Here's the place
Which men (for being poor) are sent to starve in;—
Rude remedy, I trow, for sore disease.
Within these walls, stifled by damp and stench,
Doth Hope's fair torch expire; and at the snuff,
Ere yet 'tis quite extinct, rude, wild, and wayward,
The desperate revelries of wild despair,
Kindling their hell-born cressets, light to deeds
That the poor captive would have died ere practised,
Till bondage sunk his soul to his condition.'

*The Prison, Scene III. Act I**

AT my first entrance I turned an eager glance towards my conductor;
but the lamp in the vestibule was too low in flame to give my curiosity
any satisfaction by affording a distinct perusal of his features. As the
turnkey held the light in his hand, the beams fell more full on his own
scarce less interesting figure. He was a wild shock-headed looking
animal, whose profusion of red hair covered and obscured his features,
which were otherwise only characterised by the extravagant joy that
affected him at the sight of my guide. In my experience I have met
nothing so absolutely resembling my idea of a very uncouth, wild, and
ugly savage, adoring the idol of his tribe. He grinned, he shivered, he
laughed, he was near crying, if he did not actually cry. He had a 'Where
shall I go?—What can I do for you?' expression of face; the complete,
surrendered, and anxious subservience and devotion of which it is
difficult to describe, otherwise than by the awkward combination
which I have attempted. The fellow's voice seemed choking in his
ecstasy, and only could express itself in such interjections as 'Oigh,
oigh,—Ay, ay—it's lang since she's seen ye!' and other exclamations
equally brief, expressed in the same unknown tongue in which he had
communicated with my conductor while we were on the outside of the
jail door. My guide received all this excess of joyful gratulation much
like a prince too early accustomed to the homage of those around him
to be much moved by it, yet willing to requite it by the usual forms of
royal courtesy. He extended his hand graciously towards the turnkey,
with a civil enquiry of 'How's a' wi' you, Dougal?'

'Oigh, oigh!' exclaimed Dougal, softening the sharp exclamations

of his surprise as he looked around with an eye of watchful alarm—
'Oigh, to see you here—to see you here—Oigh, what will come o' ye
gin the bailies suld come to get witting—ta filthy, gutty hallions, tat
they are?'

My guide placed his finger on his lip, and said, 'Fear nothing,
Dougal; your hands shall never draw a bolt on me.'

'Tat sall they no,' said Dougal; 'she suld—she wad—that is, she
wishes them hacked aff by the elbows first—But when are ye gaun
yonder again? and ye'll no forget to let her ken—she's your puir
cousin, God kens, only seven times removed.'

'I will let you ken, Dougal, as soon as my plans are settled.'

'And, by her sooth, when you do, an it were twal o' the Sunday at
e'en, she'll fling her keys at the provost's head or she gie them anither
turn, and that or ever Monday morning begins—see if she winna.'

My mysterious stranger cut his acquaintance's ecstasies short by
again addressing him, in what I afterwards understood to be the Irish,
Earse, or Gaelic,* explaining, probably, the services which he required
at his hand. The answer, 'Wi' a' her heart—wi' a' her soul,' with a
good deal of indistinct muttering in a similar tone, intimated the
turnkey's acquiescence in what he proposed. The fellow trimmed his
dying lamp, and made a sign to me to follow him.

'Do you not go with us?' said I, looking to my conductor.

'It is unnecessary,' he replied; 'my company may be inconvenient
for you, and I had better remain to secure our retreat.'

'I do not suppose you mean to betray me to danger,' said I.

'To none but what I partake in doubly,' answered the stranger, with
a voice of assurance which it was impossible to mistrust.

I followed the turnkey, who, leaving the inner wicket unlocked
behind him, led me up a *turnpike*, (so the Scotch call a winding stair,)
then along a narrow gallery,—then opening one of several doors which
led into the passage, he ushered me into a small apartment, and casting
his eye on the pallet bed which occupied one corner, said with an under
voice, as he placed the lamp on a little deal table, 'She's sleeping.'*

'She!—who?—can it be Diana Vernon in this abode of misery?'

I turned my eye to the bed, and it was with a mixture of disappointment oddly mingled with pleasure, that I saw my first suspicion had
deceived me. I saw a head neither young nor beautiful, garnished with
a grey beard of two days' growth, and accommodated with a red night-
cap. The first glance put me at ease on the score of Diana Vernon; the

second, as the slumberer awoke from a heavy sleep, yawned, and rubbed his eyes, presented me with features very different indeed—even those of my poor friend Owen. I drew back out of view an instant, that he might have time to recover himself; fortunately recollecting that I was but an intruder on these cells of sorrow, and that any alarm might be attended with unhappy consequences.

Meantime, the unfortunate formalist, raising himself from the pallet-bed with the assistance of one hand, and scratching his cap with the other, exclaimed, in a voice in which as much peevishness as he was capable of feeling, contended with drowsiness, 'I'll tell you what, Mr Dugwell, or whatever your name may be, the sum total of the matter is, that if my natural rest is to be broken in this manner, I must complain to the lord mayor.'

'Shentlemans to speak wi' her,' replied Dougal, resuming the true dogged sullen tone of a turnkey, in exchange for the shrill clang of Highland congratulation with which he had welcomed my mysterious guide; and, turning on his heel, he left the apartment.

It was some time before I could prevail upon the unfortunate sleeper awakening to recognise me; and when he did so, the distress of the worthy creature was extreme, at supposing, which he naturally did, that I had been sent thither as a partner of his captivity.

'O, Mr Frank, what have you brought yourself and the house to?—I think nothing of myself, that am a mere cipher, so to speak; but you, that was your father's sum total—his omnium*—you that might have been the first man in the first house in the first city, to be shut up in a nasty Scotch jail, where one cannot even get the dirt brushed off their clothes!'

He rubbed, with an air of peevish irritation, the once stainless brown coat, which had now shared some of the impurities of the floor of his prison-house,—his habits of extreme punctilious neatness acting mechanically to increase his distress.

'O Heaven be gracious to us!' he continued. 'What news this will be on 'Change! There has not the like come there since the battle of Almanza,* where the total of the British loss was summed up to five thousand men killed and wounded, besides a floating balance of missing—but what will that be to the news that Osbaldistone and Tresham have stopped!'

I broke in on his lamentations to acquaint him, that I was no prisoner, though scarce able to account for my being in that place at such an hour. I could only silence his enquiries by persisting in those which his own situation suggested; and at length obtained from him such information as he was able to give me. It was none of the most distinct; for, however clear-headed in his own routine of commercial business, Owen, you are well aware, was not very acute in comprehending what lay beyond that sphere.

The sum of his information was, that of two correspondents of my father's firm at Glasgow, where, owing to engagements in Scotland formerly alluded to, he transacted a great deal of business, both my father and Owen had found the house of MacVittie MacFin and Company, the most obliging and accommodating. They had deferred to the great English house on every possible occasion; and in their bargains and transactions acted, without repining, the part of the jackall, who only claims what the lion is pleased to leave him. However small the share of profit allotted to them, it was always, as they expressed it, 'enough for the like of them;' however large the portion of trouble, 'they were sensible they could not do too much to deserve the continued patronage and good opinion of their honoured friends in Crane Alley.'

The dictates of my father were to MacVittie and MacFin the laws of the Medes and Persians, not to be altered, innovated, or even discussed; and the punctilios exacted by Owen in their business transactions, for he was a great lover of form, more especially when he could dictate it *ex cathedra*, seemed scarce less sanctimonious in their eyes. This tone of deep and respectful observance went all currently down with Owen; but my father looked a little closer into men's bosoms, and whether suspicious of this excess of deference, or, as a lover of brevity and simplicity in business, tired with these gentlemen's long-winded professions of regard, he had uniformly resisted their desire to become his sole agents in Scotland. On the contrary, he transacted many affairs through a correspondent of a character perfectly different,—a man whose good opinion of himself amounted to self-conceit, and who, disliking the English in general as much as my father did the Scotch, would hold no communication but on a footing of absolute equality; jealous, moreover; captious occasionally; as tenacious of his own opinions in point of form as Owen could be of his; and totally indifferent, though the authority of all Lombard-Street had stood against his own private opinion.

As these peculiarities of temper rendered it difficult to transact business with Mr Nicol Jarvie,—as they occasioned at times disputes and coldness between the English house and their correspondent, which were only got over by a sense of mutual interest,—as, moreover, Owen's personal vanity sometimes suffered a little in the discussions to which they gave rise, you cannot be surprised, Tresham, that our old friend threw at all times the weight of his influence in favour of the civil, discreet, accommodating concern of MacVittie and MacFin, and spoke of Jarvie as a petulant, conceited Scotch pedlar, with whom there was no dealing.

It was also not surprising, that in these circumstances, which I only learned in detail some time afterwards, Owen, in the difficulties to which the house was reduced by the absence of my father, and the disappearance of Rashleigh, should, on his arrival in Scotland, which took place two days before mine, have recourse to the friendship of those correspondents, who had always professed themselves obliged, gratified, and devoted to the service of his principal. He was received at Messrs MacVittie and MacFin's counting-house in the Gallowgate, with something like the devotion a Catholic would pay to his tutelar saint. But, alas! this sunshine was soon overclouded, when, encouraged by the fair hopes which it inspired, he opened the difficulties of the house to his friendly correspondents, and requested their counsel and assistance. MacVittie was almost stunned by the communication; and MacFin, ere it was completed, was already at the ledger of their firm, and engaged deep in the very bowels of the multitudinous accounts between their house and that of Osbaldistone and Tresham, for the purpose of discovering on which side the balance lay. Alas! the scale depressed considerably against the English firm; and the faces of MacVittie and MacFin, hitherto only blank and doubtful, became now ominous, grim, and lowering. They met Mr Owen's request of countenance and assistance, with a counter-demand of instant security against imminent hazard of eventual loss; and at length, speaking more plainly, required that a deposit of assets, destined for other purposes, should be placed in their hands for that purpose. Owen repelled this demand with great indignation, as dishonourable to his constituents, unjust to the other creditors of Osbaldistone and Tresham, and very ungrateful on the part of those by whom it was made.

The Scotch partners gained, in the course of this controversy, what is very convenient to persons who are in the wrong, an opportunity and pretext for putting themselves in a violent passion, and for taking, under the pretext of the provocation they had received, measures to which some sense of decency, if not of conscience, might otherwise have deterred them from resorting.

Owen had a small share, as I believe is usual, in the house to which he acted as head clerk, and was therefore personally liable for all its obligations. This was known to Messrs MacVittie and MacFin; and, with a view of making him feel their power, or rather in order to force him, at this emergency, into those measures in their favour, to which he had expressed himself so repugnant, they had recourse to a summary process of arrest and imprisonment, which it seems the law of Scotland (therein surely liable to much abuse) allows to a creditor, who finds his conscience at liberty to make oath that the debtor meditates departing from the realm.* Under such a warrant had poor Owen been confined to durance on the day preceding that when I was so strangely guided to his prison-house.

Thus possessed of the alarming outline of facts, the question remained, what was to be done? and it was not of easy determination. I plainly perceived the perils with which we were surrounded, but it was more difficult to suggest any remedy. The warning which I had already received seemed to intimate, that my own personal liberty might be endangered by an open appearance in Owen's behalf. Owen entertained the same apprehension, and, in the exaggeration of his terror, assured me that a Scotchman, rather than run the risk of losing a farthing by an Englishman, would find law for arresting his wife, children, man-servant, maid-servant, and stranger within his household. The laws concerning debt, in most countries, are so unmercifully severe, that I could not altogether disbelieve his statement; and my arrest, in the present circumstances, would have been a *coup-de-grace* to my father's affairs. In this dilemma, I asked Owen if he had not thought of having recourse to my father's other correspondent in Glasgow, Mr Nicol Jarvie?

'He had sent him a letter,' he replied, 'that morning; but if the smooth-tongued and civil house in the Gallowgate had used him thus, what was to be expected from the cross-grained crab-stock in the Salt-Market? You might as well ask a broker to give up his per centage, as expect a favour from him without the *per contra*. He had not even,' Owen said, 'answered his letter, though it was put into his hand that morning as he went to church.' And here the despairing man-of-figures threw himself down on his pallet, exclaiming,—'My poor dear master!—My poor dear master! O, Mr Frank, Mr Frank, this is all your obstinacy!—But God forgive me for saying so to you in your distress! It's God's disposing, and man must submit.'

My philosophy, Tresham, could not prevent my sharing in the honest creature's distress, and we mingled our tears, the more bitter on my part, as the perverse opposition to my father's will, with which the kind-hearted Owen forbore to upbraid me, rose up to my conscience as the cause of all this affliction.

In the midst of our mingled sorrow, we were disturbed and surprised by a loud knocking at the outward door of the prison. I ran to the top of the staircase to listen, but could only hear the voice of the turnkey, alternately in a high tone, answering to some person without, and in a whisper, addressed to the person who had guided me hither: 'She's coming—she's coming,' aloud; then in a low key, 'O hon-a-ri! O hon-a-ri!* what'll she do now?—Gang up ta stair, and hide yoursell ahint ta Sassenach shentleman's ped.—She's coming as fast as she can—Ahellanay! it's my lord provosts, and ta pailies, and ta guard— and ta captain's coming toon stairs too—Got pless her! gang up or he meets her.—She's coming—she's coming—ta lock's sair roosted.'

While Dougal unwillingly, and with as much delay as possible, undid the various fastenings to give admittance to those without, whose impatience became clamorous, my guide ascended the winding stair, and sprang into Owen's apartment, into which I followed him. He cast his eyes hastily round as if looking for a place of concealment, then said to me, 'Lend me your pistols—yet it's no matter, I can do without them—Whatever you see, take no heed, and do not mix your hand in another man's feud—This gear's mine, and I must manage it as I dow; but I have been as hard bested, and worse, than I am even now.'

As the stranger spoke these words, he stripped from his person the cumbrous upper coat in which he was wrapt, confronted the door of the apartment, on which he fixed a keen and determined glance, drawing his person a little back to concentrate his force, like a fine horse brought up to the leaping-bar. I had not a moment's doubt that he meant to extricate himself from his embarrassment, whatever might be the cause of it, by springing full upon those who should appear when the doors opened, and forcing his way through all opposition into the street; and such was the appearance of strength and agility displayed in his frame, and of determination in his look and manner, that

I did not doubt a moment but that he might get clear through his opponents, unless they employed fatal means to stop his purpose.

It was a period of awful suspense betwixt the opening of the outward gate and that of the door of the apartment, when there appeared—no guard with bayonets fixed, or watch with clubs, bills, or partisans, but a good-looking young woman, with grogram petticoats, tucked up for trudging through the streets, and holding a lantern in her hand. This female ushered in a more important personage, in form stout, short, and somewhat corpulent; and by dignity, as it soon appeared, a magistrate, bob-wigged, bustling, and breathless with peevish impatience. My conductor, at his appearance, drew back as if to escape observation; but he could not elude the penetrating twinkle with which this dignitary reconnoitered the whole apartment.

'A bonny thing it is, and a beseeming, that I should be kept at the door half an hour, Captain Stanchells,'* said he, addressing the principal jailor, who now showed himself at the door as if in attendance on the great man, 'knocking as hard to get into the tolbooth as ony body else wad to get out of it, could that avail them, poor fallen creatures!—And how's this?—how's this?—strangers in the jail after lock-up hours, and on the Sabbath evening!—I shall look after this, Stanchells, you may depend on't—Keep the door locked, and I'll speak to these gentlemen in a gliffing—But first I maun hae a crack wi' an auld acquaintance here.—Mr Owen, Mr Owen, how's a' wi' ye, man?'

'Pretty well in body, I thank you, Mr Jarvie,' drawled out poor Owen, 'but sore afflicted in spirit.'

'Nae doubt, nae doubt—ay, ay—it's an awfu' whummle—and for ane that held his head sae high too—human nature, human nature—Ay, ay, we're a' subject to a downcome. Mr Osbaldistone is a gude honest gentleman; but I aye said he was ane o' them wad make a spune or spoil a horn,* as my father the worthy deacon* used to say. The deacon used to say to me, "Nick—young Nick," (his name was Nicol as weel as mine; sae folk ca'd us in their daffin' young Nick and auld Nick)—"Nick," said he, "never put out your arm farther than ye can draw it easily back again." I hae said sae to Mr Osbaldistone, and he didna seem to take it a'thegether sae kind as I wished—but it was weel meant—weel meant.'

This discourse, delivered with prodigious volubility, and a great appearance of self-complacency, as he recollected his own advice and

predictions, gave little promise of assistance at the hands of Mr Jarvie.
Yet it soon appeared rather to proceed from a total want of delicacy
than any deficiency of real kindness; for when Owen expressed himself
somewhat hurt that these things should be recalled to memory in his
present situation, the Glaswegian took him by the hand, and bade him
'Cheer up a gliff! D'ye think I wad hae comed out at twal o'clock at
night, and amaist broken the Lord's-day, just to tell a fa'en man o' his
backslidings? Na, na, that's no Bailie Jarvie's gate, nor was't his worthy
father's the deacon afore him. Why, man! it's my rule never to think on
warldly business on the Sabbath, and though I did a' I could to keep
your note that I gat this morning out o' my head, yet I thought mair on
it a' day, than on the preaching—And it's my rule to gang to my bed wi'
the yellow curtains preceesely at ten o'clock—unless I were eating a
haddock wi' a neighbour, or a neighbour wi' me—ask the lass-quean
there, if it isna a fundamental rule in my household; and here hae I sitten up reading gude books, and gaping as if I wad swallow St Enox
Kirk, till it chappit twal, whilk was a lawfu' hour to gie a look at my
ledger just to see how things stood between us; and then, as time and
tide wait for no man, I made the lass get the lantern, and came slipping
my ways here to see what can be dune anent your affairs. Bailie Jarvie
can command entrance into the tolbooth at ony hour, day or night;
sae could my father the deacon in his time, honest man, praise to his
memory.'

Although Owen groaned at the mention of the ledger, leading me
grievously to fear that here also the balance stood in the wrong column;
and although the worthy magistrate's speech expressed much self-
complacency, and some ominous triumph in his own superior judgment, yet it was blended with a sort of frank and blunt good-nature,
from which I could not help deriving some hopes. He requested to see
some papers he mentioned, snatched them hastily from Owen's hand,
and sitting on the bed, to 'rest his shanks,' as he was pleased to express
the accommodation which that posture afforded him, his servant girl
held up the lantern to him, while, pshawing, muttering, and sputter-
ing, now at the imperfect light, now at the contents of the packet, he
ran over the writings it contained.

Seeing him fairly engaged in this course of study, the guide who had
brought me hither seemed disposed to take an unceremonious leave.
He made a sign to me to say nothing, and intimated, by his change of
posture, an intention to glide towards the door in such a manner as to

attract the least possible observation. But the alert magistrate (very different from my old acquaintance Mr Justice Inglewood) instantly detected and interrupted his purposes. 'I say, look to the door, Stanchells—shut and lock it, and keep watch on the outside.'

The stranger's brow darkened, and he seemed for an instant again to meditate the effecting his retreat by violence; but ere he had determined, the door closed, and the ponderous bolt revolved. He muttered an exclamation in Gaelic, strode across the floor, and then, with an air of dogged resolution, as if fixed and prepared to see the scene to an end, sate himself down on the oak table and whistled a strathspey.

Mr Jarvie, who seemed very alert and expeditious in going through business, soon showed himself master of that which he had been considering, and addressed himself to Mr Owen in the following strain: 'Weel, Mr Owen, weel—your house are awin certain sums to Messrs MacVittie and MacFin (shame fa' their souple snouts! they made that and mair out o' a bargain about the aik-woods at Glen-Cailziechat, that they took out atween my teeth—wi' help o' your gude word, I maun needs say, Mr Owen—but that makes nae odds now.)—Weel, sir, your house awes them this siller; and for this, and relief of other engagements they stand in for you, they hae putten a double turn o' Stanchells' muckle key on ye.—Weel, sir, ye awe this siller—and maybe ye awe some mair to some other body too—maybe ye awe some to mysell, Bailie Nicol Jarvie.'

'I cannot deny, sir, but the balance may of this date be brought out against us, Mr Jarvie,' said Owen; 'but you'll please to consider'——

'I hae nae time to consider e'enow, Mr Owen—Sae near Sabbath at e'en, and out o' ane's warm bed at this time o' night, and a sort o' drow in the air besides—there's nae time for considering—But, sir, as I was saying, ye awe me money—it winna deny—ye awe me money, less or mair, I'll stand by it—But then, Mr Owen, I canna see how you, an active man that understands business, can redd out the business ye're come down about, and clear us a' aff—as I have gritt hope ye will—if ye're keepit lying here in the tolbooth of Glasgow.—Now, sir, if you can find caution *judicio sisti*, that is, that ye winna flee the country, but appear and relieve your caution when ca'd for in our legal courts, ye may be set at liberty this very morning.'

'Mr Jarvie,' said Owen, 'if any friend would become surety for me to that effect, my liberty might be usefully employed, doubtless, both for the house and all connected with it.'

'Aweel, sir,' continued Jarvie, 'and doubtless such a friend wad expect ye to appear when ca'd on, and relieve him o' his engagement.'

'And I should do so as certainly, bating sickness or death, as that two and two make four.'

'Aweel, Mr Owen,' resumed the citizen of Glasgow, 'I dinna misdoubt ye, and I'll prove it, sir—I'll prove it. I am a carefu' man, as is weel kend, and industrious, as the hale town can testify; and I can win my crowns, and keep my crowns, and count my crowns, wi' ony body in the Saut-Market, or it may be in the Gallowgate. And I'm a prudent man, as my father the deacon was before me; but rather than an honest civil gentleman, that understands business, and is willing to do justice to all men, should lie by the heels this gate, unable to help himsell or ony body else—why, conscience, man! I'll be your bail mysell—But ye'll mind it's a bail *judicio sisti*, as our town-clerk says, not *judicatum solvi*;* ye'll mind that, for there's muckle difference.'

Mr Owen assured him, that as matters then stood, he could not expect any one to become security for the actual payment of the debt, but that there was not the most distant cause for apprehending loss from his failing to present himself when lawfully called upon.

'I believe ye—I believe ye. Eneugh said—eneugh said. We'se hae your legs loose by breakfast-time,—And now let's hear what thir chamber chiels o' yours hae to say for themselves, or how, in the name of unrule, they got here at this time o' night.'

CHAPTER XXIII

Hame came our gudeman at e'en,
    And hame came he,
And there he saw a man
    Where a man suldna be.
'How's this now, kimmer?
How's this? quo he,—
How came this carle here
Without the leave o' me?'

*Old Song**

THE magistrate took the light out of his servant-maid's hand, and advanced to his scrutiny, like Diogenes in the street of Athens,* lantern-in-hand, and probably with as little expectation as that of the cynic, that he was likely to encounter any especial treasure in the course of his researches. The first whom he approached was my mysterious guide, who, seated on a table as I have already described him, with his eyes firmly fixed on the wall, his features arranged into the utmost inflexibility of expression, his hands folded on his breast with an air betwixt carelessness and defiance, his heel patting against the foot of the table, to keep time with the tune which he continued to whistle, submitted to Mr Jarvie's investigation with an air of absolute confidence and assurance, which, for a moment, placed at fault the memory and sagacity of the acute and anxious investigator.

'Ah!—Eh!—Oh!' exclaimed the Bailie. 'My conscience!—it's impossible—and yet—no!—Conscience, it canna be!—and yet again—Deil hae me! that I suld say sae—Ye robber—ye cateran—ye born deevil that ye are, to a' bad ends and nae gude ane—can this be you?'

'E'en as ye see, Bailie,' was the laconic answer.

'Conscience! if I am na clean bumbaized—*you*, ye cheat-the-wuddy rogue, *you* here on your venture in the tolbooth o' Glasgow?—What d'ye think's the value o' your head?'

'Umph?—why, fairly weighed, and Dutch weight,* it might weigh down one provost's, four bailies', a town-clerk's, six deacons', besides stentmasters'——

'Ah, ye reiving villain!' interrupted Mr Jarvie. 'But tell ower your sins, and prepare ye, for if I say the word'——

'True, Bailie,' said he who was thus addressed, folding his hands behind him with the utmost *nonchalance*, 'but ye will never say that word.'

'And why suld I not, sir?' exclaimed the magistrate—'Why suld I not? Answer me that—why suld I not?'

'For three sufficient reasons, Bailie Jarvie.—First, for auld langsyne;—second, for the sake of the auld wife ayont the fire at Stuckavrallachan, that made some mixture of our bluids, to my own proper shame be it spoken! that has a cousin wi' accounts, and yarn winnles, and looms, and shuttles, like a mere mechanical person;—and lastly, Bailie, because if I saw a sign o' your betraying me, I would plaster that wa' with your harns ere the hand of man could rescue you!'

'Ye're a bauld desperate villain, sir,' retorted the undaunted Bailie; 'and ye ken that I ken ye to be sae, and that I wadna stand a moment for my ain risk.'

'I ken weel,' said the other, 'ye hae gentle bluid in your veins, and I wad be laith to hurt my ain kinsman. But I'll gang out here as free as I came in, or the very wa's o' Glasgow tolbooth shall tell o't these ten years to come.'

'Weel, weel,' said Mr Jarvie, 'bluid's thicker than water; and it liesna in kith, kin, and ally, to see motes in ilk other's een if other een see them no. It wad be sair news to the auld wife below the Ben of Stuckavrallachan, that you, ye Hieland limmer, had knockit out my harns, or that I had kilted you up in a tow. But ye'll own, ye dour deevil, that were it no your very sell, I wad hae grippit the best man in the Hielands.'

'Ye wad hae tried, cousin,' answered my guide, 'that I wot weel; but I doubt ye wad hae come aff wi' the short measure; for we gang-there-out Hieland bodies are an unchancy generation when you speak to us o' bondage. We downa bide the coercion of gude braid-claith about our hinderlins; let a be breeks o' freestone, and garters o' iron.'

'Ye'll find the stane breeks and the airn garters, ay, and the hemp cravat, for a' that, neighbour,' replied the Bailie. 'Nae man in a civilized country ever played the pliskies ye hae done—but e'en pickle in your ain pock-neuk*—I hae gi'en ye warning.'

'Well, cousin,' said the other, 'ye'll wear black at my burial?'

'Deil a black cloak will be there, Robin, but the corbies and the hoodie-craws, I'se gie ye my hand on that. But whar's the gude thousand pund Scots that I lent ye, man, and when am I to see it again?'

'Where it is,' replied my guide, after the affectation of considering for a moment, 'I cannot justly tell—probably where last year's snaw is.'

'And that's on the tap of Schehallion,* ye Hieland dog,' said Mr Jarvie; 'and I look for payment frae you where ye stand.'

'Ay,' replied the Highlander, 'but I keep neither snaw nor dollars in my sporran. And as to when you'll see it—why, just when the king enjoys his ain again, as the auld sang says.'*

'Warst of a', Robin,' retorted the Glaswegian,—'I mean, ye disloyal traitor—Warst of a'!—Wad ye bring popery in on us, and arbitrary power, and a foist and a warming-pan, and the set forms, and the curates, and the auld enormities o' surplices and cearments? Ye had better stick to your auld trade o' theft-boot, black-mail, spreaghs, and gillravaging—better stealing nowte than ruining nations.'

'Hout, man, whisht wi' your whiggery,' answered the Celt, 'we hae kend ane anither mony a lang day. I'se take care your counting-room is no cleaned out when the Gillon-a-naillie[39] come to redd up the Glasgow buiths, and clear them o' their auld shop-wares. And, unless it just fa' in the preceese way o' your duty, ye maunna see me oftener, Nicol, than I am disposed to be seen.'

'Ye are a dauring villain, Rob,' answered the Bailie; 'and ye will be hanged, that will be seen and heard tell o'; but I'se ne'er be the ill bird and foul my nest, set apart strong necessity and the skreigh of duty, which no man should hear and be inobedient.—And wha the deevil's this?' he continued, turning to me—'Some gillravager that ye hae listed, I daur say. He looks as if he had a bauld heart to the high-way, and a lang craig for the gibbet.'

'This, good Mr Jarvie,' said Owen, who, like myself, had been struck dumb during this strange recognition, and no less strange dialogue, which took place betwixt these extraordinary kinsmen—'This, good Mr Jarvie, is young Mr Frank Osbaldistone, only child of the head of our house, who should have been taken into our firm at the time Mr Rashleigh Osbaldistone, his cousin, had the luck to be taken into it'—(Here Owen could not suppress a groan)—'But, howsoever'——

'O, I have heard of that smaik,' said the Scotch merchant, interrupting him; 'it is he whom your principal, like an obstinate auld fule, wad make a merchant o', wad he or wad he no, and the lad turned a strolling stage-player, in pure dislike to the labour an honest man should live by.—Weel, sir, what say you to your handiwark? Will

Hamlet the Dane, or Hamlet's ghost, be good security for Mr Owen, sir?'

'I don't deserve your taunt,' I replied, 'though I respect your motive, and am too grateful for the assistance you have afforded Mr Owen, to resent it. My only business here was to do what I could (it is perhaps very little) to aid Mr Owen in the management of my father's affairs. My dislike of the commercial profession is a feeling of which I am the best and sole judge.'

'I protest,' said the Highlander, 'I had some respect for this callant even before I kend what was in him; but now I honour him for his contempt of weavers and spinners, and sic-like mechanical persons and their pursuits.'

'Ye're mad, Rob,' said the Bailie—'mad as a March hare,—though wherefore a hare suld be mad at March mair than at Martinmas, is mair than I can weel say. Weavers! Deil shake ye out o' the web the weaver craft made. Spinners!—ye'll spin and wind yoursell a bonny pirn. And this young birkie here, that ye're hoying and hounding on the shortest road to the gallows and the deevil, will his stage-plays and his poetries help him here, dy'e think, ony mair than your deep oaths and drawn dirks, ye reprobate that ye are?—Will *Tityre tu patulæ*,* as they ca' it, tell him where Rashleigh Osbaldistone is? or Macbeth, and all his kernes and galla-glasses,* and your awn to boot, Rob, procure him five thousand pounds to answer the bills which fall due ten days hence, were they a' rouped at the Cross,* basket-hilts, Andra-Ferraras,* leather targets, brogues, brechan, and sporrans?'

'Ten days?' I answered, and instinctively drew out Diana Vernon's packet; and the time being elapsed during which I was to keep the seal sacred, I hastily broke it open. A sealed letter fell from a blank enclosure, owing to the trepidation with which I opened the parcel. A slight current of wind, which found its way through a broken pane of the window, wafted the letter to Mr Jarvie's feet, who lifted it, examined the address with unceremonious curiosity, and, to my astonishment, handed it to his Highland kinsman, saying, 'Here's a wind has blown a letter to its right owner, though there were ten thousand chances against its coming to hand.'

The Highlander, having examined the address, broke the letter open without the least ceremony. I endeavoured to interrupt his proceeding.

'You must satisfy me, sir,' said I, 'that the letter is intended for you before I can permit you to peruse it.'

'Make yourself quite easy, Mr Osbaldistone,' replied the mountaineer, with great composure;—'remember Justice Inglewood, Clerk Jobson, Mr Morris—above all, remember your vera humble servant, Robert Cawmil, and the beautiful Diana Vernon. Remember all this, and doubt no longer that the letter is for me.'

I remained astonished at my own stupidity. Through the whole night, the voice, and even the features of this man, though imperfectly seen, haunted me with recollections to which I could assign no exact local or personal associations. But now the light dawned on me at once,—this man was Campbell himself. His whole peculiarities flashed on me at once,—the deep strong voice,—the inflexible, stern, yet considerate cast of features,—the Scottish brogue, with its corresponding dialect and imagery, which, although he possessed the power at times of laying them aside, recurred at every moment of emotion, and gave pith to his sarcasm, or vehemence to his expostulation. Rather beneath the middle size than above it, his limbs were formed upon the very strongest model that is consistent with agility, while, from the remarkable ease and freedom of his movements, you could not doubt his possessing the latter quality in a high degree of perfection. Two points in his person interfered with the rules of symmetry—his shoulders were so broad in proportion to his height, as, notwithstanding the lean and lathy appearance of his frame, gave him something the air of being too square in respect to his stature; and his arms, though round, sinewy, and strong, were so very long as to be rather a deformity. I afterwards heard that this length of arm was a circumstance on which he prided himself; that when he wore his native Highland garb, he could tie the garters of his hose without stooping; and that it gave him great advantage in the use of the broadsword, at which he was very dexterous. But certainly this want of symmetry destroyed the claim he might otherwise have set up, to be accounted a very handsome man; it gave something wild, irregular, and, as it were, unearthly, to his appearance, and reminded me involuntarily, of the tales which Mabel used to tell of the old Picts* who ravaged Northumberland in ancient times, who, according to her tradition, were a sort of half-goblin half-human beings, distinguished, like this man, for courage, cunning, ferocity, the length of their arms, and the squareness of their shoulders.

When, however, I recollected the circumstances in which we formerly met, I could not doubt that the billet was most probably designed for him. He had made a marked figure among those mysterious personages over whom Diana seemed to exercise an influence, and from whom she experienced an influence in her turn. It was painful to think that the fate of a being so amiable was involved in that of desperadoes of this man's description; yet it seemed impossible to doubt it. Of what use, however, could this person be to my father's affairs?—I could think only of one. Rashleigh Osbaldistone had, at the instigation of Miss Vernon, certainly found means to produce Mr Campbell when his presence was necessary to exculpate me from Morris's accusation—Was it not possible that her influence, in like manner, might prevail on Campbell to produce Rashleigh? Speaking on this supposition, I requested to know where my dangerous kinsman was, and when Mr Campbell had seen him. The answer was indirect.

'It's a kittle cast she has gien me to play; but yet it's fair play, and I winna baulk her. Mr Osbaldistone, I dwell not very far from hence—my kinsman can show you the way—Leave Mr Owen to do the best he can in Glasgow—do you come and see me in the glens, and it's like I may pleasure you, and stead your father in his extremity. I am but a poor man; but wit's better than wealth—and, cousin,' (turning from me to address Mr Jarvie,) 'if ye daur venture sae muckle as to eat a dish of Scotch collops, and a leg o' red-deer venison wi' me, come ye wi' this Sassenach gentleman as far as Drymen or Bucklivie, or the Clachan of Aberfoil* will be better than ony o' them, and I'll hae somebody waiting to weise ye the gate to the place where I may be for the time—What say ye, man?—There's my thumb, I'll ne'er beguile thee.'

'Na, na, Robin,' said the cautious burgher, 'I seldom like to leave the Gorbals; I have nae freedom to gang amang your wild hills, Robin, and your kilted red-shanks—it disna become my place, man.'

'The devil damn your place and you baith!' reiterated Campbell. 'The only drap o' gentle bluid that's in your body was our great granduncle's that was justified at Dumbarton, and you set yourself up to say ye wad derogate frae your place to visit me!—Hark thee, man, I owe thee a day in harst*—I'll pay up your thousan pund Scots, plack and bawbee, gin ye'll be an honest fallow for anes, and just daiker up the gate wi' this Sassenach.'

'Hout awa' wi' your gentility,' replied the Bailie; 'carry your gentle bluid to the Cross, and see what ye'll buy wi't.—But, if I *were* to come, wad ye really and soothfastly pay me the siller?'

'I swear to ye,' said the Highlander, 'upon the halidome of him that sleeps beneath the grey stane at Inch-Cailleach.'[40]

'Say nae mair, Robin,—say nae mair—We'll see what may be dune.—But ye maunna expect me to gang ower the Highland line— I'll gae beyond the line at no rate. Ye maun meet me about Bucklivie or the Clachan of Aberfoil, and dinna forget the needful.'

'Nae fear—nae fear,' said Campbell, 'I'll be as true as the steel blade that never failed its master.—But I must be budging, cousin, for the air o' Glasgow tolbooth is no that ower salutary to a Highlander's constitution.'

'Troth,' replied the merchant, 'and if my duty were to be dune, ye couldna change your atmosphere, as the minister ca's it,* this ae wee while.—Ochon, that I sud ever be concerned in aiding and abetting an escape frae justice! it will be a shame and disgrace to me and mine, and my very father's memory, for ever.'

'Hout tout, man, let that flee stick in the wa',' answered his kinsman; 'when the dirt's dry it will rub out*—Your father, honest man, could look ower a friend's fault as weel as anither.'

'Ye may be right, Robin,' replied the Bailie, after a moment's reflection; 'he was a considerate man the deacon; he kend we had a' our frailties, and he lo'ed his friends—Ye'll no hae forgotten him, Robin?' This question he put in a softened tone, conveying as much at least of the ludicrous as the pathetic.

'Forgotten him!' replied his kinsman, 'what suld ail me to forget him?—a wapping weaver he was, and wrought my first pair o' hose.— But come awa', kinsman,

'Come fill up my cap, come fill up my cann,
Come saddle my horses, and call up my man;
Come open your gates, and let me gae free,
I daurna stay langer in bonny Dundee.'*

'Whisht, sir!' said the magistrate, in an authoritative tone—'lilting and singing sae near the latter end o' the Sabbath! This house may hear ye sing anither tune yet—Aweel, we hae a' back-slidings to answer for—Stanchells, open the door.'

The jailor obeyed, and we all sallied forth. Stanchells looked with some surprise at the two strangers, wondering, doubtless, how they came into these premises without his knowledge; but Mr Jarvie's 'Friends o' mine, Stanchells—friends o' mine,' silenced all disposition to enquiries. We now descended into the lower vestibule, and hollowed more than once for Dougal, to which summons no answer was returned; when Campbell observed, with a sardonic smile, 'That if Dougal was the lad he kent him, he would scarce wait to get thanks for his ain share of the night's wark, but was in all probability on the full trot to the pass of Ballamaha'*———

'And left us—and, abune a', me, mysell, locked up in the tolbooth a' night!' exclaimed the Bailie, in ire and perturbation. 'Ca' for fore-hammers, sledge-hammers, pinches, and coulters; send for Deacon Yettlin, the smith, and let him ken that Bailie Jarvie's shut up in the tolbooth by a Hieland blackguard, whom he'll hang up as high as Haman'*———

'When ye catch him,' said Campbell, gravely; 'but stay, the door is surely not locked.'

Indeed, on examination, we found that the door was not only left open, but that Dougal in his retreat had, by carrying off the keys along with him, taken care that no one should exercise his office of porter in a hurry.

'He has glimmerings o' common sense now, that creature Dougal,' said Campbell; 'he kend an open door might hae served me at a pinch.'

We were by this time in the street.

'I tell you, Robin,' said the magistrate, 'in my puir mind, if ye live the life ye do, ye shuld hae ane o' your gillies door-keeper in every jail in Scotland, in case o' the warst.'

'Ane o' my kinsmen a bailie in ilka burgh will just do as weel, cousin Nicol—so, gude-night or gude-morning to ye; and forget not the Clachan of Aberfoil.'

And without waiting for an answer, he sprung to the other side of the street, and was lost in darkness. Immediately on his disappearance, we heard him give a low whistle of peculiar modulation; which was instantly replied to.

'Hear to the Hieland deevils,' said Mr Jarvie; 'they think themselves on the skirts of Benlomond already, where they may gang whewing and whistling about without minding Sunday or Saturday.' Here he was interrupted by something which fell with a heavy clash on the street before us—'Gude guide us! what's this mair o't?—Mattie, haud up the lantern—Conscience! if it isna the keys—Weel, that's just as weel—they cost the burgh siller, and there might hae been some clavers about the loss o' them—O, an Bailie Grahame were to get word o' this night's job, it wad be a sair hair in my neck!'*

As we were still but a few steps from the tolbooth door, we carried back these implements of office, and consigned them to the head jailor, who, in lieu of the usual mode of making good his post by turning the keys, was keeping sentry in the vestibule till the arrival of some assistant, whom he had summoned in order to replace the Celtic fugitive Dougal.

Having discharged this piece of duty to the burgh, and my road lying the same way with the honest magistrate's, I profited by the light of his lantern, and he by my arm, to find our way through the streets, which, whatever they may now be, were then dark, uneven, and ill-paved. Age is easily propitiated by attentions from the young. The Bailie expressed himself interested in me, and added, 'That since I was nane o' that play-acting and play-ganging generation, whom his saul hated, he wad be glad if I wad eat a reisted haddock, or a fresh herring, at breakfast wi' him the morn, and meet my friend, Mr Owen, whom, by that time, he would place at liberty.'

'My dear sir,' said I, when I had accepted of the invitation with thanks, 'how could you possibly connect me with the stage?'

'I watna,' replied Mr Jarvie; 'it was a bletherin' phrasin' chield they ca' Fairservice, that cam at e'en to get an order to send the crier through the toun for ye at skreigh o' day the morn. He tell't me whae ye were, and how ye were sent frae your father's house, because ye wadna be a dealer, and that ye mightna disgrace your family wi' ganging on the stage. Ane Hammorgaw, our precentor, brought him here, and said he was an auld acquaintance; but I sent them baith awa' wi' a flae in their lug for bringing me sic an errand on sic a night. But I see he's a fule-creature a'thegither, and clean mista'en about ye. I like ye, man,' he continued; 'I like a lad that will stand by his friends in trouble—I aye did it mysell, and sae did the deacon my father, rest and bless him! But ye suldna keep ower muckle company wi' Hielandmen and thae wild cattle. Can a man touch pitch and no be defiled?*—aye mind that. Nae doubt, the best and wisest may err—Once, twice, and thrice have I backslidden, man, and dune three things this night—my father wadna hae believed his een if he could hae looked up and seen me do them.'

He was by this time arrived at the door of his own dwelling. He paused, however, on the threshold, and went on in a solemn tone of deep contrition,—'Firstly, I hae thought my ain thoughts on the Sabbath—Secondly, I hae gi'en security for an Englishman—and, in the third and last place, well-a-day! I hae let an ill-doer escape from the place of imprisonment—But there's balm in Gilead,* Mr Osbaldistone—Mattie, I can let mysell in—see Mr Osbaldistone to Luckie Flyter's, at the corner o' the wynd.—Mr Osbaldistone'—in a whisper—'ye'll offer nae incivility to Mattie—she's an honest man's daughter, and a near cousin o' the Laird o' Limmerfield's.'

CHAPTER XXIV

'Will it please your worship to accept of my poor service? I
beseech that I may feed upon your bread, though it be the
brownest, and drink of your drink, though it be of the smallest; for
I will do your worship as much service for forty shillings as
another man shall for three pounds.'

GREENE'S *Tu Quoque**

I REMEMBERED the honest Bailie's parting charge, but did not conceive there was any incivility in adding a kiss to the half-crown with
which I remunerated Mattie's attendance; nor did her 'Fie for shame,
sir,' express any very deadly resentment of the affront. Repeated
knocking at Mrs Flyter's gate awakened in due order, first, one or two
stray dogs, who began to bark with all their might; next two or three
night-capped heads, which were thrust out of the neighbouring windows to reprehend me for disturbing the solemnity of the Sunday
night by that untimely noise. While I trembled lest the thunders of
their wrath might dissolve in showers like that of Xantippe,* Mrs Flyter herself awoke, and began, in a tone of objurgation not unbecoming
the philosophical spouse of Socrates, to scold one or two loiterers in
her kitchen, for not hastening to the door to prevent a repetition of my
noisy summons.

These worthies were, indeed, nearly concerned in the fracas which
their laziness occasioned, being no other than the faithful Mr Fairservice, with his friend Mr Hammorgaw, and another person, whom I
afterwards found to be the town-crier, who were sitting over a cog of
ale, as they called it, (at my expense, as my bill afterwards informed
me,) in order to devise the terms and style of a proclamation to be made
through the streets the next day, in order that 'the unfortunate young
gentleman,' as they had the impudence to qualify me, might be
restored to his friends without farther delay. It may be supposed that I
did not suppress my displeasure at this impertinent interference with
my affairs; but Andrew set up such ejaculations of transport at my
arrival, as fairly drowned my expressions of resentment. His raptures,
perchance, were partly political; and the tears of joy which he shed had
certainly their source in that noble fountain of emotion, the tankard.
However, the tumultuous glee which he felt, or pretended to feel at my

return, saved Andrew the broken head which I had twice destined him; first, on account of the colloquy he had held with the precentor on my affairs; and, secondly, for the impertinent history he had thought proper to give of me to Mr Jarvie. I however contented myself with slapping the door of my bedroom in his face as he followed me, praising Heaven for my safe return, and mixing his joy with admonitions to me to take care how I walked my own ways in future. I then went to bed, resolving my first business in the morning should be to discharge this troublesome, pedantic, self-conceited coxcomb, who seemed so much disposed to constitute himself rather a preceptor than a domestic.

Accordingly in the morning I resumed my purpose, and calling Andrew into my apartment, requested to know his charge for guiding and attending me as far as Glasgow. Mr Fairservice looked very blank at this demand, justly considering it as a presage to approaching dismission.

'Your honour,' he said, after some hesitation, 'wunna think—wunna think'——

'Speak out, you rascal, or I'll break your head,' said I, as Andrew, between the double risk of losing all by asking too much, or a part, by stating his demand lower than what I might be willing to pay, stood gasping in the agony of doubt and calculation.

Out it came with a bolt, however, at my threat; as the kind violence of a blow on the back sometimes delivers the windpipe from an intrusive morsel. 'Aughteen pennies sterling per diem—that is by the day—your honour wadna think unconscionable.'

'It is double what is usual, and treble what you merit, Andrew; but there's a guinea for you, and get about your business.'

'The Lord forgi'e us! Is your honour mad?' exclaimed Andrew.

'No; but I think you mean to make me so—I give you a third above your demand, and you stand staring and expostulating there as if I were cheating you.—Take your money, and go about your business.'

'Gude safe us!' continued Andrew, 'in what can I hae offended your honour?—Certainly a' flesh is but as flowers of the field;* but if a bed of camomile hath value in medicine, of a surety the use of Andrew Fairservice to your honour is nothing less evident—it's as muckle as your life's worth to part wi' me.'

'Upon my honour,' replied I, 'it is difficult to say whether you are more knave or fool.—So you intend then to remain with me whether I like it or no?'

'Troth, I was e'en thinking sae,' replied Andrew, dogmatically; 'for if your honour disna ken when ye hae a gude servant, I ken when I hae a gude master, and the deil be in my feet gin I leave ye*—and there's the brief and the lang o't,—besides I hae received nae regular warning to quit my place.'

'Your place, sir!' said I; 'why, you are no hired servant of mine, you are merely a guide, whose knowledge of the country I availed myself of on my road.'

'I am no just a common servant, I admit, sir,' remonstrated Mr Fairservice; 'but your honour kens I quitted a gude place at an hour's notice, to comply wi' your honour's solicitations. A man might make honestly and wi' a clear conscience, twenty sterling pounds per annum, weel counted siller, o' the garden at Osbaldistone Hall, and I wasna likely to gi'e up a' that for a guinea, I trow—I reckoned on staying wi' your honour to the term's end at the least o't; and I account upon my wage, board-wage, fee, and bountith,* ay, to that length o't at the least.'

'Come, come, sir,' replied I, 'these impudent pretensions won't serve your turn; and if I hear any more of them, I shall convince you, that Squire Thorncliffe is not the only one of my name that can use his fingers.'

While I spoke thus, the whole matter struck me as so ridiculous, that, though really angry, I had some difficulty to forbear laughing at the gravity with which Andrew supported a plea so utterly extravagant. The rascal, aware of the impression he had made on my muscles, was encouraged to perseverance. He judged it safer, however, to take his pretensions a peg lower, in case of overstraining at the same time both his plea and my patience.

'Admitting that my honour could part with a faithful servant, that had served me and mine by day and night for twenty years, in a strange place, and at a moment's warning, he was weel assured,' he said, 'it wasna in my heart, nor in no true gentleman's, to pit a puir lad like himsell, that had come forty or fifty, or say a hundred miles out o' his road purely to bear my honour company, and that had nae hauding but his penny-fee, to sic a hardship as this comes to.'

I think it was you, Will, who once told me, that, to be an obstinate man, I am in certain things the most gullable and malleable of mortals. The fact is, that it is only contradiction which makes me peremptory, and when I do not feel myself called on to give battle to any proposition, I am always willing to grant it, rather than give myself much trouble. I knew this fellow to be a greedy, tiresome, meddling coxcomb; still, however, I must have some one about me in the quality of guide and domestic, and I was so much used to Andrew's humour, that on some occasions it was rather amusing. In the state of indecision to which these reflections led me, I asked Fairservice if he knew the roads, towns, &c. in the north of Scotland, to which my father's concerns with the proprietors of Highland forests were likely to lead me. I believe if I had asked him the road to the terrestrial paradise,* he would have at that moment undertaken to guide me to it; so that I had reason afterwards to think myself fortunate in finding that his actual knowledge did not fall very much short of that which he asserted himself to possess. I fixed the amount of his wages, and reserved to myself the privilege of dismissing him when I chose, on paying him a week in advance. I gave him finally a severe lecture on his conduct of the preceding day, and then dismissed him, rejoicing at heart, though somewhat crest-fallen in countenance, to rehearse to his friend, the precentor, who was taking his morning draught in the kitchen, the mode in which he had 'cuitled up the daft young English squire.'

Agreeable to appointment, I went next to Bailie Nicol Jarvie's, where a comfortable morning's repast was arranged in the parlour, which served as an apartment of all hours, and almost all work, to that honest gentleman. The bustling and benevolent magistrate had been as good as his word. I found my friend Owen at liberty, and, conscious of the refreshments and purification of brush and basin, was of course a very different person from Owen a prisoner, squalid, heart-broken, and hopeless. Yet the sense of pecuniary difficulties arising behind, before, and around him, had depressed his spirit, and the almost paternal embrace which the good man gave me, was embittered by a sigh of the deepest anxiety. And when he sate down, the heaviness in his eye and manner, so different from the quiet composed satisfaction which they usually exhibited, indicated that he was employing his arithmetic in mentally numbering up the days, the hours, the minutes, which yet remained as an interval between the dishonour of bills and the downfall of the great commercial establishment of Osbaldistone and Tresham. It was left to me, therefore, to do honour to our landlord's hospitable cheer,—to his tea, right from China, which he got in a present from some eminent ship's-husband at Wapping,—to his coffee, from a snug plantation of his own, as he informed us with a wink, called

Salt-market Grove, in the island of Jamaica,—to his English toast and ale, his Scotch dried salmon, his Lochfine herrings, and even to the double damask tablecloth, 'wrought by no hand, as you may guess,' save that of his deceased father the worthy Deacon Jarvie.

Having conciliated our good-humoured host by those little attentions which are great to most men, I endeavoured in my turn to gain from him some information which might be useful for my guidance, as well as for the satisfaction of my curiosity. We had not hitherto made the least allusion to the transactions of the preceding night, a circumstance which made my question sound somewhat abrupt, when, without any previous introduction of the subject, I took advantage of a pause when the history of the tablecloth ended, and that of the napkins was about to commence, to enquire, 'Pray, by the by, Mr Jarvie, who may this Mr Robert Campbell be whom we met with last night?'

The interrogatory seemed to strike the honest magistrate, to use the vulgar phrase, 'all of a heap,' and instead of answering, he returned the question,—'Whae's Mr Robert Campbell?—ahem—ahay!—Whae's Mr Robert Campbell, quo' he?'

'Yes,' said I, 'I mean who, and what is he?'

'Why, he's—ahay!—he's—ahem!—Where did ye meet with Mr Robert Campbell, as ye ca' him?'

'I met him by chance,' I replied, 'some months ago, in the north of England.'

'Ou then, Mr Osbaldistone,' said the Bailie doggedly, 'ye'll ken as muckle about him as I do.'

'I should suppose not, Mr Jarvie,' I replied; 'you are his relation it seems, and his friend.'

'There is some cousin-red between us, doubtless,' said the Bailie reluctantly, 'but we hae seen little o' ilk other since Rob gae up the cattle-line o' dealing, poor fallow! he was hardly guided by them might hae used him better—and they haena made their plack a bawbee o't neither. There's mony ane this day wad rather they had never chased puir Robin frae the Cross o' Glasgow—there's mony ane wad rather see him again at the tail o' three hundred kyloes, than at the head o' thirty waur cattle.'

'All this explains nothing to me, Mr Jarvie, of Mr Campbell's rank, habits of life, and means of subsistence,' I replied.

'Rank?' said Mr Jarvie; 'he's a Hieland gentleman, nae doubt—better rank need nane to be;—and for habit, I judge he wears the

Hieland habit amang the hills, though he has breeks on when he comes to Glasgow;—and as for his subsistence, what needs we care about his subsistence, sae lang as he asks naething frae us, ye ken. But I hae nae time for clavering about him e'en now, because we maun look into your father's concerns wi' a' speed.'

So saying, he put on his spectacles, and sate down to examine Mr Owen's states, which the other thought it most prudent to communicate to him without reserve. I knew enough of business to be aware that nothing could be more acute and sagacious than the views which Mr Jarvie entertained of the matters submitted to his examination; and, to do him justice, it was marked by much fairness and even liberality. He scratched his ear indeed repeatedly, on observing the balance which stood at the debit of Osbaldistone and Tresham in account with himself personally.

'It may be a dead loss,' he observed; 'and, conscience! whate'er ane o' your Lombard-street goldsmiths may say to it, it's a snell ane in the Saut-Market o' Glasgow. It will be a heavy deficit—a staff out o' my bicker,* I trow. But what then?—I trust the house wunna coup the crans for a' that's come and gane yet; and if it does, I'll never bear sae base a mind as thae corbies in the Gallowgate—an I am to lose by ye, I'se ne'er deny I hae won by ye mony a fair pund sterling—Sae, an it come to the warst, I'se e'en lay the head o' the sow to the tail o' the grice.'[41]

I did not altogether understand the proverbial arrangement with which Mr Jarvie consoled himself, but I could easily see that he took a kind and friendly interest in the arrangement of my father's affairs, suggested several expedients, approved several plans proposed by Owen, and, by his countenance and counsel, greatly abated the gloom upon the brow of that afflicted delegate of my father's establishment.

As I was an idle spectator on this occasion, and, perhaps, as I showed some inclination more than once to return to the prohibited, and, apparently, the puzzling subject of Mr Campbell, Mr Jarvie dismissed me with little formality, with an advice to 'gang up the gate to the college, where I wad find some chields could speak Greek and Latin weel,—at least they got plenty o' siller for doing deil haet else, if they didna do that; and where I might read a spell o' the worthy Mr Zachary Boyd's translation o' the Scriptures*—better poetry need nane to be, as he had been tell'd by them that kend, or suld hae kend, about sic things.' But he seasoned this dismission with a kind and hospitable invitation, 'to come back and take part o' his family-chack, at ane pre-ceesely—there wad be a leg o' mutton, and, it might be, a tup's head, for they were in season;' but, above all, I was to return at 'ane o'clock preceesely—it was the hour he and the deacon his father aye dined at—they pat it aff for naething nor for naebody.'

CHAPTER XXV

So stands the Thracian herdsman with his spear
Full in the gap, and hopes the hunted bear;
And hears him in the rustling wood, and sees
His course at distance by the bending trees,
And thinks—Here comes my mortal enemy,
And either he must fall in fight, or I.

*Palamon and Arcite**

I TOOK the route towards the college, as recommended by Mr Jarvie, less with the intention of seeking for any object of interest or amusement, than to arrange my own ideas, and meditate on my future conduct. I wandered from one quadrangle of old-fashioned buildings to another, and from thence to the College-yards, or walking ground, where, pleased with the solitude of the place, most of the students being engaged in their classes, I took several turns, pondering on the waywardness of my own destiny.

I could not doubt, from the circumstances attending my first meeting with this person Campbell, that he was engaged in some strangely desperate courses; and the reluctance with which Mr Jarvie alluded to his person or pursuits, as well as all the scene of the preceding night, tended to confirm these suspicions. Yet to this man Diana Vernon had not, it would seem, hesitated to address herself in my behalf; and the conduct of the magistrate himself towards him showed an odd mixture of kindness, and even respect, with pity and censure. Something there must be uncommon in Campbell's situation and character; and what was still more extraordinary, it seemed that his fate was doomed to have influence over, and connexion with my own. I resolved to bring Mr Jarvie to close quarters on the first proper opportunity, and learn as much as was possible on the subject of this mysterious person, in order that I might judge whether it was possible for me, without prejudice to my reputation, to hold that degree of farther correspondence with him, to which he seemed to invite.

While I was musing on these subjects, my attention was attracted by three persons who appeared at the upper end of the walk through which I was sauntering, seemingly engaged in very earnest conversation. That intuitive impression which announces to us the approach of whomsoever we love or hate with intense vehemence, long before a more indifferent eye can recognise their persons, flashed upon my mind the sure conviction that the midmost of these three men was Rashleigh Osbaldistone. To address him was my first impulse; my second was, to watch him until he was alone, or at least to reconnoitre his companions before confronting him. The party was still at such distance, and engaged in such deep discourse, that I had time to step unobserved to the other side of a small hedge, which imperfectly screened the alley in which I was walking.

It was at this period the fashion of the young and gay to wear, in their morning walks, a scarlet cloak, often laced and embroidered, above their other dress, and it was the trick of the time for gallants occasionally to dispose it so as to muffle a part of the face. The imitating this fashion, with the degree of shelter which I received from the hedge, enabled me to meet my cousin, unobserved by him or the others, except perhaps as a passing stranger. I was not a little startled at recognising in his companions that very Morris on whose account I had been summoned before Justice Inglewood, and Mr MacVittie the merchant, from whose starched and severe aspect I had recoiled on the preceding day.

A more ominous conjunction to my own affairs, and those of my father, could scarce have been formed. I remembered Morris's false accusation against me, which he might be as easily induced to renew as he had been intimidated to withdraw; I recollected the inauspicious influence of MacVittie over my father's affairs, testified by the imprisonment of Owen; and I now saw both these men combined with one, whose talents for mischief I deemed little inferior to those of the great author of all ill, and my abhorrence of whom almost amounted to dread.

When they had passed me for some paces, I turned and followed them unobserved. At the end of the walk they separated, Morris and MacVittie leaving the gardens, and Rashleigh returning alone through the walks. I was now determined to confront him, and demand reparation for the injuries he had done my father, though in what form redress was likely to be rendered remained to be known. This, however, I trusted to chance; and, flinging back the cloak in which I was muffled, I passed through a gap of the low hedge, and presented myself before Rashleigh, as, in a deep reverie, he paced down the avenue.

Rashleigh was no man to be surprised or thrown off his guard by sudden occurrences. Yet he did not find me thus close to him, wearing undoubtedly in my face the marks of that indignation which was glowing in my bosom, without visibly starting at an apparition so sudden and so menacing.

'You are well met, sir,' was my commencement; 'I was about to take a long and doubtful journey in quest of you.'

'You know little of him you sought then,' replied Rashleigh, with his usual undaunted composure. 'I am easily found by my friends—still more easily by my foes;—your manner compels me to ask in which class I must rank Mr Francis Osbaldistone?'

'In that of your foes, sir,' I answered; 'in that of your mortal foes, unless you instantly do justice to your benefactor, my father, by accounting for his property.'

'And to whom, Mr Osbaldistone,' answered Rashleigh, 'am I, a member of your father's commercial establishment, to be compelled to give any account of my proceedings in those concerns, which are in every respect identified with my own?—Surely not to a young gentleman whose exquisite taste for literature would render such discussions disgusting and unintelligible.'

'Your sneer, sir, is no answer; I will not part with you until I have full satisfaction concerning the fraud you meditate—you shall go with me before a magistrate.'

'Be it so,' said Rashleigh, and made a step or two as if to accompany me; then pausing, proceeded:—'Were I inclined to do as you would have me, you should soon feel which of us had most reason to dread the presence of a magistrate. But I have no wish to accelerate your fate. Go, young man! amuse yourself in your world of poetical imaginations, and leave the business of life to those who understand and can conduct it.'

His intention, I believe, was to provoke me, and he succeeded. 'Mr Osbaldistone,' I said, 'this tone of calm insolence shall not avail you. You ought to be aware that the name we both bear never submitted to insult, and shall not in my person be exposed to it.'

'You remind me,' said Rashleigh, with one of his blackest looks, 'that it was dishonoured in my person!—and you remind me also by whom! Do you think I have forgotten the evening at Osbaldistone Hall, when you cheaply and with impunity played the bully at my expense? For that insult—never to be washed out but by blood!—for the various times you have crossed my path, and always to my preju-dice—for the persevering folly with which you seek to traverse schemes, the importance of which you neither know nor are capable of estimating,—for all these, sir, you owe me a long account, for which there shall come an early day of reckoning.'

'Let it come when it will,' I replied, 'I shall be willing and ready to meet it. Yet you seem to have forgotten the heaviest article—that I had the pleasure to aid Miss Vernon's good sense and virtuous feeling in extricating her from your infamous toils.'

I think his dark eyes flashed actual fire at this home-taunt, and yet his voice retained the same calm expressive tone with which he had hitherto conducted the conversation.

'I had other views with respect to you, young man,' was his answer; 'less hazardous for you, and more suitable to my present character and former education. But I see you will draw on yourself the personal chastisement your boyish insolence so well merits. Follow me to a more remote spot, where we are less likely to be interrupted.'

I followed him accordingly, keeping a strict eye on his motions, for I believed him capable of the very worst actions. We reached an open spot in a sort of wilderness, laid out in the Dutch taste, with clipped hedges, and one or two statues. I was on my guard, and it was well with me that I was so; for Rashleigh's sword was out and at my breast ere I could throw down my cloak, or get my weapon unsheathed, so that I only saved my life by springing a pace or two backwards. He had some advantage in the difference of our weapons; for his sword, as I recol-lect, was longer than mine, and had one of those bayonet or three-cornered blades which are now generally worn; whereas, mine was what we then called a Saxon blade—narrow, flat, and two-edged, and scarcely so manageable as that of my enemy. In other respects we were pretty equally matched; for what advantage I might possess in super-ior address and agility, was fully counter-balanced by Rashleigh's great strength and coolness. He fought, indeed, more like a fiend than a man—with concentrated spite and desire of blood, only allayed by that cool consideration which made his worst actions appear yet worse from the air of deliberate premeditation which seemed to accompany them. His obvious malignity of purpose never for a moment threw him off his guard, and he exhausted every feint and stratagem proper to the science of defence; while, at the same time, he meditated the most desperate catastrophe to our rencounter.

On my part, the combat was at first sustained with more moderation. My passions, though hasty, were not malevolent; and the walk of two or three minutes' space gave me time to reflect that Rashleigh was my father's nephew, the son of an uncle, who after his fashion had been kind to me, and that his falling by my hand could not but occasion much family distress. My first resolution, therefore, was to attempt to disarm my antagonist; a manœuvre in which, confiding in my superiority of skill and practice, I anticipated little difficulty. I found, however, I had met my match; and one or two foils which I received, and from the consequences of which I narrowly escaped, obliged me to observe more caution in my mode of fighting. By degrees I became exasperated at the rancour with which Rashleigh sought my life, and returned his passes with an inveteracy resembling in some degree his own; so that the combat had all the appearance of being destined to have a tragic issue. That issue had nearly taken place at my expense. My foot slipped in a full lounge which I made at my adversary, and I could not so far recover myself as completely to parry the thrust with which my pass was repaid. Yet it took but partial effect, running through my waistcoat, grazing my ribs, and passing through my coat behind. The hilt of Rashleigh's sword, so great was the vigour of his thrust, struck against my breast with such force as to give me great pain, and confirm me in the momentary belief that I was mortally wounded. Eager for revenge, I grappled with my enemy, seizing with my left hand the hilt of his sword, and shortening my own with the purpose of running him through the body. Our death-grapple was interrupted by a man who forcibly threw himself between us, and pushing us separate from each other, exclaimed, in a loud and commanding voice, 'What! the sons of those fathers who sucked the same breast shedding each other's bluid as it were strangers'!—By the hand of my father, I will cleave to the brisket the first man that mints another stroke!'

I looked up in astonishment. The speaker was no other than Campbell. He had a basket-hilted broadsword drawn in his hand, which he made to whistle around his head as he spoke, as if for the purpose of enforcing his mediation. Rashleigh and I stared in silence at this unexpected intruder, who proceeded to exhort us alternately: 'Do you, Maister Francis, opine that ye will re-establish your father's credit by cutting your kinsman's thrapple, or getting your ain sneckit instead thereof in the College-yards of Glasgow?—Or do you, Mr Rashleigh, think men will trust their lives and fortunes wi' ane, that, when in point of trust and in point of confidence wi' a great political interest, gangs about brawling like a drunken gillie?—Nay, never look gash or grim at me, man—if ye're angry, ye ken how to turn the buckle o' your belt behind you.'*

'You presume on my present situation,' replied Rashleigh, 'or you would have hardly dared to interfere where my honour is concerned.'

'Hout, tout, tout!—Presume?—And what for should it be presuming?—Ye may be the richer man, Mr Osbaldistone, as is maist likely; and ye may be the mair learned man, whilk I dispute not: but I reckon ye are neither a prettier man nor a better gentleman than mysell—and it will be news to me when I hear ye are as gude. And *dare* too?— Muckle daring there's about it—I trow here I stand, that hae slashed as het a haggis* as ony o' the twa o' ye, and thought nae muckle o' my morning's wark when it was dune. If my foot were on the heather as it's on the causeway, or this pickle gravel, that's little better, I hae been waur mistrysted than if I were set to gie ye baith your ser'ing o't.'

Rashleigh had by this time recovered his temper completely. 'My kinsman,' he said, 'will acknowledge he forced this quarrel on me. It was none of my seeking. I am glad we are interrupted before I chastised his forwardness more severely.'

'Are ye hurt, lad?' enquired Campbell of me, with some appearance of interest.

'A very slight scratch,' I answered, 'which my kind cousin would not long have boasted of had not you come between us.'

'In troth, and that's true, Maister Rashleigh,' said Campbell; 'for the cauld iron and your best bluid were like to hae become acquaint when I mastered Mr Frank's right hand. But never look like a sow playing upon a trump* for the luve o' that, man—come and walk wi' me. I hae news to tell ye, and ye'll cool and come to yoursell, like MacGibbon's crowdy,* when he set it out at the window-bole.'

'Pardon me, sir,' said I. 'Your intentions have seemed friendly to me on more occasions than one; but I must not, and will not, quit sight of this person, until he yields up to me those means of doing justice to my father's engagements, of which he has treacherously possessed himself.'

'Ye're daft, man,' replied Campbell, 'it will serve ye naething to follow us e'enow; ye hae just enow o'ae man, wad ye bring twa on your head, and might bide quiet?'

'Twenty,' I replied, 'if it be necessary.'

I laid my hand on Rashleigh's collar, who made no resistance, but said, with a sort of scornful smile, 'You hear him, MacGregor! he rushes on his fate—will it be my fault if he falls into it?—The warrants are by this time ready, and all is prepared.'

The Scotchman was obviously embarrassed. He looked around, and before, and behind him, and then said: 'The ne'er a bit will I yield my consent to his being ill-guided, for standing up for the father that got him—and I gie God's malison and mine to a' sort o' magistrates, justices, bailies, sheriffs, sheriff-officers, constables, and sic-like black cattle, that hae been the plagues o' puir auld Scotland this hunder year;—it was a merry warld when every man held his ain gear wi' his ain grip, and when the country side wasna fashed wi' warrants and poindings and apprizings,* and a' that cheatry craft. And ance mair I say it, my conscience winna see this puir thoughtless lad ill-guided, and especially wi' that sort o' trade. I wad rather ye fell till't again, and fought it out like douce honest men.'

'Your conscience, MacGregor!' said Rashleigh; 'you forget how long you and I have known each other.'

'Yes, my conscience,' reiterated Campbell, or MacGregor, or whatever was his name; 'I hae such a thing about me, Maister Osbaldistone; and therein it may weel chance that I hae the better o' you. As to our knowledge of each other,—if ye ken what I am, ye ken what usage it was made me what I am; and, whatever you may think, I would not change states with the proudest of the oppressors that hae driven me to tak the heather-bush for a beild. What *you* are, Maister Rashleigh, and what excuse ye hae for being *what* you are, is between your ain heart and the lang day.—And now, Maister Francis, let go his collar; for he says truly, that ye are in mair danger from a magistrate than he is, and were your cause as straight as an arrow, he wad find a way to put you wrang—So let go his craig, as I was saying.'

He seconded his words with an effort so sudden and unexpected, that he freed Rashleigh from my hold, and securing me, notwithstanding my struggles, in his own Herculean gripe, he called out, 'Take the bent, Mr Rashleigh. Make ae pair o' legs worth twa pair o' hands; ye hae dune that before now.'

'You may thank this gentleman, kinsman,' said Rashleigh, 'if I leave any part of my debt to you unpaid; and if I quit you now, it is only in the hope we shall soon meet again without the possibility of interruption.'

He took up his sword, wiped it, sheathed it, and was lost among the bushes.

The Scotchman, partly by force, partly by remonstrance, prevented my following him; indeed, I began to be of opinion my doing so would be to little purpose.

'As I live by bread,' said Campbell, when, after one or two struggles in which he used much forbearance towards me, he perceived me inclined to stand quiet, 'I never saw sae daft a callant! I wad hae gien the best man in the country the breadth o' his back gin he had gien me sic a kemping as ye hae dune. What wad ye do?—Wad ye follow the wolf to his den?—I tell ye, man, he has the auld trap set for ye—He has got the collector-creature Morris to bring up a' the auld story again, and ye maun look for nae help frae me here, as ye got at Justice Inglewood's—It isna good for my health to come in the gate o' the whigamore bailie bodies. Now gang your ways hame, like a gude bairn—jouk and let the jaw gae by*—Keep out o' sight o' Rashleigh, and Morris, and that MacVittie animal—Mind the Clachan of Aberfoil, as I said before, and, by the word of a gentleman, I wunna see ye wranged. But keep a calm sough till we meet again—I maun gae and get Rashleigh out o' the town afore waur comes o't, for the neb o' him's never out o' mischief—Mind the Clachan of Aberfoil.'

He turned upon his heel, and left me to meditate on the singular events which had befallen me. My first care was to adjust my dress and re-assume my cloak, disposing it so as to conceal the blood which flowed down my right side. I had scarcely accomplished this, when, the classes of the College being dismissed, the gardens began to be filled with parties of the students. I therefore left them as soon as possible; and in my way towards Mr Jarvie's, whose dinner hour was now approaching, I stopped at a small unpretending shop, the sign of which intimated the indweller to be Christopher Nielson, surgeon and apothecary. I requested of a little boy who was pounding some stuff in a mortar, that he would procure me an audience of this learned pharmacopolist. He opened the door of the back-shop, where I found a lively elderly man, who shook his head incredulously at some idle account I gave him of having been wounded accidentally by the button breaking off my antagonist's foil while I was engaged in a fencing match. When he had applied some lint and somewhat else he thought proper to the trifling wound I had received, he observed, 'There never was button on the foil that made this hurt. Ah! young blood! young blood!—But we surgeons are a secret generation—If it werena for hot blood and ill blood, what would become of the twa learned faculties?'

With which moral reflection he dismissed me; and I experienced very little pain or inconvenience afterwards from the scratch I had received.

CHAPTER XXVI

An iron race the mountain-cliffs maintain,
Foes to the gentler genius of the plain.
   *   *   *   *   *   *
Who, while their rocky ramparts round they see,
The rough abode of want and liberty,
As lawless force from confidence will grow,
Insult the plenty of the vales below.

GRAY*

WHAT made ye sae late?' said Mr Jarvie, as I entered the dining-parlour of that honest gentleman; 'it is chappit ane the best feck o' five minutes by-gane. Mattie has been twice at the door wi' the dinner, and weel for you it was a tup's head, for that canna suffer by delay. A sheep's head ower muckle boiled is rank poison, as my worthy father used to say—he likit the lug o' ane weel, honest man.'

I made a suitable apology for my breach of punctuality, and was soon seated at table, where Mr Jarvie presided with great glee and hospitality, compelling, however, Owen and myself to do rather more justice to the Scottish dainties with which his board was charged, than was quite agreeable to our southern palates. I escaped pretty well, from having those habits of society which enable one to elude this species of well-meant persecution. But it was ridiculous enough to see Owen, whose ideas of politeness were more rigorous and formal, and who was willing, in all acts of lawful compliance, to evince his respect for the friend of the firm, eating, with rueful complaisance, mouthful after mouthful of singed wool, and pronouncing it excellent, in a tone in which disgust almost overpowered civility.

When the cloth was removed, Mr Jarvie compounded with his own hands a very small bowl of brandy-punch, the first which I had ever the fortune to see.

'The limes,' he assured us, 'were from his own little farm yonder-awa,' (indicating the West Indies with a knowing shrug of his shoulders,) 'and he had learned the art of composing the liquor from auld Captain Coffinkey, who acquired it,' he added in a whisper, 'as maist folk thought, amang the Buccaniers. But it's excellent liquor,' said he, helping us round; 'and good ware has aften come frae a wicked market. And as for Captain Coffinkey, he was a decent man when I kent him, only he used to swear awfully—But he's dead, and gaen to his account, and I trust he's accepted—I trust he's accepted.'

We found the liquor exceedingly palatable, and it led to a long conversation between Owen and our host on the opening which the Union had afforded to trade between Glasgow and the British colonies in America and the West Indies, and on the facilities which Glasgow possessed of making up *sortable* cargoes for that market. Mr Jarvie answered some objection which Owen made on the difficulty of sorting a cargo for America, without buying from England, with vehemence and volubility.

'Na, na, sir, we stand on our ain bottom—we pickle in our ain pockneuk—We hae our Stirling serges, Musselburgh stuffs, Aberdeen hose, Edinburgh shalloons,* and the like, for our woollen or worsted goods—and we hae linens of a' kinds better and cheaper than you hae in Lunnon itsell—and we can buy your north o' England wares, as Manchester wares, Sheffield wares, and Newcastle earthen-ware, as cheap as you can at Liverpool—And we are making a fair spell at cottons and muslins—Na, na! let every herring hing by its ain head, and every sheep by its ain shank, and ye'll find, sir, us Glasgow folk no sae far ahint but what we may follow.—This is but poor entertainment for you, Mr Osbaldistone,' (observing that I had been for some time silent,) 'but ye ken cadgers maun aye be speaking about cart-saddles.'

I apologized, alleging the painful circumstances of my own situation, and the singular adventures of the morning, as the causes of my abstraction and absence of mind. In this manner I gained what I sought—an opportunity of telling my story distinctly and without interruption. I only omitted mentioning the wound I had received, which I did not think worthy of notice. Mr Jarvie listened with great attention and apparent interest, twinkling his little grey eyes, taking snuff, and only interrupting me by brief interjections. When I came to the account of the rencounter, at which Owen folded his hands and cast up his eyes to Heaven, the very image of woful surprise, Mr Jarvie broke in upon the narration with 'Wrang now—clean wrang—to draw a sword on your kinsman is inhibited by the laws o' God and man; and to draw a sword on the streets of a royal burgh, is punishable by fine and imprisonment—and the College-yards are nae better privileged—they should be a place of peace and quietness, I trow. The College didna get gude £600 a-year out o' bishops' rents, (sorrow fa' the brood o' bishops and their rents too!) nor yet a lease o' the Archbishoprick o' Glasgow the sell o't,* that they suld let folk tuilzie in their yards, or the wild callants bicker there wi' snaw-ba's as they whiles do, that when Mattie and I gae through, we are fain to make a baik and a bow, or rin the risk o' our harns being knocked out—it suld be looked to.[42] But come awa' wi' your tale—what fell neist?'

On my mentioning the appearance of Mr Campbell, Jarvie arose in great surprise, and paced the room, exclaiming, 'Robin again!— Robert's mad—clean wud, and waur—Rob will be hanged and disgrace a' his kindred, and that will be seen and heard tell o'. My father the deacon wrought him his first hose—odd, I am thinking Deacon Threeplie, the rape-spinner,* will be twisting his last cravat. Ay, ay, puir Robin is in a fair way o' being hanged—But come awa'—come awa'—let's hear the lave o't.'

I told the whole story as pointedly as I could; but Mr Jarvie still found something lacking to make it clear, until I went back, though with considerable reluctance, on the whole story of Morris, and of my meeting with Campbell at the house of Justice Inglewood. Mr Jarvie inclined a serious ear to all this, and remained silent for some time after I had finished my narrative.

'Upon all these matters I am now to ask your advice, Mr Jarvie, which, I have no doubt, will point out the best way to act for my father's advantage and my own honour.'

'Ye're right, young man—ye're right,' said the Bailie. 'Aye take the counsel of those who are aulder and wiser than yoursell, and binna like the godless Rehoboam, who took the advice o' a wheen beardless callants, neglecting the auld counsellors who had sate at the feet o' his father Solomon,* and, as it was weel put by Mr Meiklejohn, in his lecture on the chapter, were doubtless partakers of his sapience. But I maun hear naething about honour—we ken naething here but about credit. Honour is a homicide and a bloodspiller, that gangs about making frays in the street; but Credit is a decent honest man, that sits at hame and makes the pat play.'

'Assuredly, Mr Jarvie,' said our friend Owen, 'credit is the sum total; and if we can but save that, at whatever discount'——

'Ye are right, Mr Owen—ye are right; ye speak weel and wisely; and I trust bowls will row right, though they are awee ajee e'enow. But touching Robin, I am of opinion he will befriend this young man if it is in his power. He has a gude heart, puir Robin; and though I lost a matter o' twa hunder punds wi' his former engagements, and haena muckle expectation ever to see back my thousand pund Scots that he promises me e'enow, yet I will never say but what Robin means fair by a' men.'

'I am then to consider him,' I replied, 'as an honest man?'

'Umph!' replied Jarvie, with a precautionary sort of cough,—'Ay, he has a kind o' Hieland honesty—he's honest after a sort, as they say. My father the deacon used aye to laugh when he tauld me how that by-word came up. Ane Captain Costlett was cracking crouse about his loyalty to King Charles, and Clerk Pettigrew (ye'll hae heard mony a tale about him) asked him after what manner he served the king, when he was fighting again him at Wor'ster in Cromwell's army; and Captain Costlett was a ready body, and said that he served him *after a sort*. My honest father used to laugh weel at that sport—and sae the by-word came up.'

'But do you think,' I said, 'that this man will be able to serve me after a sort, or should I trust myself to this place of rendezvous which he has given me?'

'Frankly and fairly, it's worth trying. Ye see yoursell there's some risk in your staying here. This bit body Morris has gotten a custom-house place doun at Greenock—that's a port on the Firth doun by here; and tho' a' the warld kens him to be but a twa-leggit creature, wi' a goose's head and a hen's heart, that goes about on the quay plaguing folk about permits, and cockits, and dockits, and a' that vexatious trade, yet if he lodge an information—ou, nae doubt a man in magis-terial duty maun attend to it, and ye might come to be clapped up between four wa's, whilk wad be ill-convenient to your father's affairs.'

'True,' I observed; 'yet what service am I likely to render him by leaving Glasgow, which, it is probable, will be the principal scene of Rashleigh's machinations, and committing myself to the doubtful faith of a man of whom I know little but that he fears justice, and has doubtless good reasons for doing so; and that for some secret, and probably dangerous purpose, he is in close league and alliance with the very person who is like to be the author of our ruin?'

'Ah! but ye judge Rob hardly,' said the Bailie,—'ye judge him hardly, puir chield; and the truth is, that ye ken naething about our hill coun-try, or Hielands, as we ca' them. They are clean anither set frae the like o' huz; there's nae bailie-courts amang them—nae magistrates that dinna bear the sword in vain, like the worthy deacon that's awa'—and, I may say't, like mysell and other present magistrates in this city—But it's just the laird's command, and the loon maun loup; and the never another law hae they but the length o' their dirks—the broadsword's pursuer, or plaintiff, as you Englishers ca' it, and the target is defender; the stoutest head bears langest out—and there's a Hieland plea for ye.'

Owen groaned deeply; and I allow that the description did not greatly increase my desire to trust myself in a country so lawless as he described these Scottish mountains.

'Now, sir,' said Jarvie, 'we speak little o' thae things, because they are familiar to oursells; and where's the use o' vilifying ane's country, and bringing a discredit on ane's kin, before southrons and strangers? It's an ill bird that files its ain nest.'

'Well, sir, but as it is no impertinent curiosity of mine, but real necessity, that obliges me to make these enquiries, I hope you will not be offended at my pressing for a little farther information. I have to deal, on my father's account, with several gentlemen of these wild countries, and I must trust your good sense and experience for the requisite lights upon the subject.'

This little morsel of flattery was not thrown out in vain.

'Experience!' said the Bailie, 'I hae had experience, nae doubt, and I hae made some calculations—Ay, and to speak quietly amang oursells, I hae made some perquisitions through Andrew Wylie,* my auld clerk; he's wi' MacVittie and Co. now—but he whiles drinks a gill on the Saturday afternoons wi' his auld master. And since ye say ye are willing to be guided by the Glasgow weaver-body's advice, I am no the man that will refuse it to the son of an auld correspondent, and my father the deacon was nane sic afore me. I have whiles thought o' letting my lights burn before the Duke of Argyle, or his brother Lord Ilay, (for wherefore should they be hidden under a bushel?) but the like o' thae grit men wadna mind the like o' me, a puir wabster-body—they think mair o' wha says a thing than o' what the thing is that's said. The mair's the pity—mair's the pity. Not that I wad speak ony ill of this MacCallum More—"Curse not the rich in your bedchamber," saith the son of Sirach,* for a bird of the air shall carry the clatter, and pint-stoups hae lang lugs.'

I interrupted these prolegomena, in which Mr Jarvie was apt to be somewhat diffuse, by praying him to rely upon Mr Owen and myself as perfectly secret and safe confidents.

'It's no for that,' he replied, 'for I fear nae man—what for suld I?— I speak nae treason—Only thae Hielandmen hae lang grips, and

I whiles gang a wee bit up the glens to see some auld kinsfolks, and I wadna willingly be in bad blude wi' ony o' their clans. Howsumever, to proceed—Ye maun understand I found my remarks on figures, whilk, as Mr Owen here weel kens, is the only true demonstrable root of human knowledge.'

Owen readily assented to a proposition so much in his own way, and our orator proceeded.

'These Hielands of ours, as we ca' them, gentlemen, are but a wild kind of warld by themsells, full of heights and howes, woods, caverns, lochs, rivers, and mountains, that it wad tire the very deevil's wings to flee to the tap o' them.* And in this country, and in the isles, whilk are little better, or, to speak the truth, rather waur than the mainland, there are about twa hunder and thirty parochines,* including the Orkneys, where, whether they speak Gaelic or no, I wotna, but they are an uncivilized people.—Now, sirs, I sall haud ilk parochine at the moderate estimate of eight hunder examinable persons, deducting children under nine years of age, and then adding one-fifth to stand for bairns of nine years auld, and under, the whole population will reach to the sum of—let us add one-fifth to 800 to be the multiplier, and 230 being the multiplicand'——

'The product,' said Mr Owen, who entered delightedly into these statistics of Mr Jarvie, 'will be 230,000.'

'Right, sir—perfectly right; and the military array of this Hieland country, were a' the men-folk between aughteen and fifty-six brought out that could bear arms, couldna come weel short of fifty-seven thousand five hundred men. Now, sir, it's a sad and awfu' truth, that there is neither wark, nor the very fashion nor appearance of wark, for the tae half of thae puir creatures; that is to say, that the agriculture, the pasturage, the fisheries, and every species of honest industry about the country, cannot employ the one moiety of the population, let them work as lazily as they like, and they do work as if a pleugh or a spade burnt their fingers. Aweel, sir, this moiety of unemployed bodies, amounting to'——

'To one hundred and fifteen thousand souls,' said Owen, 'being the half of the above product.'

'Ye hae't, Maister Owen—ye hae't—whereof there may be twenty-eight thousand seven hundred able-bodied gillies fit to bear arms, and that do bear arms, and will touch or look at nae honest means of livelihood even if they could get it—which, lack-a-day, they cannot.'

'But is it possible,' said I, 'Mr Jarvie, that this can be a just picture of so large a portion of the island of Britain?'

'Sir, I'll make it as plain as Peter Pasley's pikestaff—I will allow that ilk parochine, on an average, employs fifty pleughs, whilk is a great proportion in sic miserable soil as thae creatures hae to labour, and that there may be pasture eneugh for pleugh-horses, and owsen, and forty or fifty cows; now, to take care o' the pleughs and cattle, we'se allow seventy-five families of six lives in ilk family, and we'se add fifty mair to make even numbers, and ye hae five hundred souls, the tae half o' the population, employed and maintained in a sort o' fashion, wi' some chance of sour-milk and crowdie; but I wad be glad to ken what the other five hunder are to do?'

'In the name of God!' said I, 'what *do* they do, Mr Jarvie? It makes me shudder to think of their situation.'

'Sir,' replied the Bailie, 'ye wad maybe shudder mair if ye were living near-hand them. For, admitting that the tae half of them may make some little thing for themsells honestly in the Lowlands by shearing in harst, droving, hay-making, and the like; ye hae still mony hundreds and thousands o' lang-legged Hieland gillies that will neither work nor want, and maun gang thigging and sorning[43] about on their acquaintance, or live by doing the laird's bidding, be't right or be't wrang. And mair especially, mony hundreds o' them come down to the borders of the low country, where there's gear to grip, and live by stealing, reiving, lifting cows, and the like depredations! A thing deplorable in ony Christian country—the mair especially, that they take pride in it, and reckon driving a spreagh (whilk is, in plain Scotch, stealing a herd of nowte) a gallant, manly action, and mair befitting of pretty[44] men (as sic reivers will ca' themsells) than to win a day's wage by ony honest thrift. And the lairds are as bad as the loons; for if they dinna bid them gae reive and harry, the deil a bit they forbid them; and they shelter them, or let them shelter themsells, in their woods, and mountains, and strongholds, whenever the thing's dune. And every ane o' them will maintain as mony o' his ain name, or his clan, as we say, as he can rap and rend means for; or, whilk's the same thing, as mony as can in ony fashion, fair or foul, mainteen themsells—and there they are wi' gun and pistol, dirk and dourlach, ready to disturb the peace o' the country whenever the laird likes; and that's the grievance of the Hielands, whilk are, and hae been for this thousand years by-past, a bike o' the maist lawless unchristian limmers that ever disturbed a douce, quiet, Godfearing neighbourhood, like this o' ours in the west here.'

'And this kinsman of yours, and friend of mine, is he one of those great proprietors who maintain the household troops you speak of?' I enquired.

'Na, na,' said Bailie Jarvie; 'he's nane o' your great grandees o' chiefs, as they ca' them, neither. Though he is weel born, and lineally descended frae auld Glenstrae—I ken his lineage—indeed he is a near kinsman, and, as I said, of gude gentle Hieland blude, though ye may think weel that I care little about that nonsense—it's a' moonshine in water—waste threads and thrums, as we say—but I could show ye letters frae his father, that was the third aff Glenstrae, to my father Deacon Jarvie, (peace be wi' his memory!) beginning, Dear Deacon, and ending, your loving kinsman to command,—they are amaist a' about borrowed siller, sae the gude deacon, that's dead and gane, keepit them as documents and evidents—He was a carefu' man.'

'But if he is not,' I resumed, 'one of their chiefs or patriarchal leaders, whom I have heard my father talk of, this kinsman of yours has, at least, much to say in the Highlands, I presume?'

'Ye may say that—nae name better kend between the Lennox and Breadalbane. Robin was anes a weel-doing, pains-taking drover, as ye wad see amang ten thousand—It was a pleasure to see him in his belted plaid and brogues, wi' his target at his back, and claymore and dirk at his belt, following a hundred Highland stots, and a dozen o' the gillies, as rough and ragged as the beasts they drave. And he was baith civil and just in his dealings, and if he thought his chapman had made a hard bargain, he wad gie him a luck-penny* to the mends. I hae kend him gie back five shillings out o' the pund sterling.'

'Twenty-five per cent,' said Owen—'a heavy discount.'

'He wad gie it though, sir, as I tell ye; mair especially if he thought the buyer was a puir man, and couldna stand by a loss. But the times cam hard, and Rob was venturesome. It wasna my faut—it wasna my faut; he canna wyte me. I aye tauld him o't—And the creditors, mair especially some grit neighbours o' his, grippit to his living and land; and they say his wife was turned out o' the house to the hill-side, and sair misguided to the boot. Shamefu'! shamefu'!—I am a peacefu' man and a magistrate, but if ony ane had guided sae muckle as my servant quean, Mattie, as it's like they guided Rob's wife, I think it suld hae set the shabble⁴⁵ that my father the deacon had at Bothwell brig* a-walking again. Weel, Rob cam hame, and fand desolation, God pity us! where he left plenty; he looked east, west, south, north, and saw neither hauld nor hope—neither beild nor shelter; sae he e'en pu'd the bonnet ower his brow, belted the broadsword to his side, took to the brae-side, and became a broken-man.'[46]

The voice of the good citizen was broken by his contending feelings. He obviously, while he professed to contemn the pedigree of his Highland kinsman, attached a secret feeling of consequence to the connexion, and he spoke of his friend in his prosperity with an overflow of affection, which deepened his sympathy for his misfortunes, and his regret for their consequences.

'Thus tempted, and urged by despair,' said I, seeing Mr Jarvie did not proceed in his narrative, 'I suppose your kinsman became one of those depredators you have described to us?'

'No sae bad as that,' said the Glaswegian,—'no a'thegither and outright sae bad as that; but he became a levier of black-mail, wider and farther than ever it was raised in our day, a' through the Lennox and Menteith, and up to the gates o' Stirling Castle.'

'Black-mail?*—I do not understand the phrase,' I remarked.

'Ou, ye see, Rob soon gathered an unco band o' blue-bonnets at his back, for he comes o' a rough name when he's kent by his ain, and a name that's held its ain for mony a lang year, baith again king and parliament, and kirk too, for aught I ken—an auld and honourable name, for as sair as it has been worried and hadden down and oppressed. My mother was a MacGregor—I carena wha kens it—And sae Rob had soon a gallant band; and as it grieved him (he said) to see sic *hership*, and waste, and depredation to the south o' the Hieland line, why, if ony heritor or farmer wad pay him four punds Scots out of each hundred punds of valued rent, whilk was doubtless a moderate consideration, Rob engaged to keep them scaithless—let them send to him if they lost sae muckle as a single cloot by thieving, and Rob engaged to get them again, or pay the value—and he aye keepit his word—I canna deny but he keepit his word—a' men allow Rob keeps his word.'

'This is a very singular contract of assurance,' said Mr Owen.

'It's clean again our statute law, that must be owned,' said Jarvie, 'clean again law; the levying and the paying black-mail are baith punishable: but if the law canna protect my barn and byre, whatfor suld I no engage wi' a Hieland gentleman that can?—answer me that.'

'But,' said I, 'Mr Jarvie, is this contract of black-mail, as you call it, completely voluntary on the part of the landlord or farmer who pays the insurance? or what usually happens, in case any one refuses payment of this tribute?'

'Aha, lad!' said the Bailie, laughing, and putting his finger to his nose, 'ye think ye hae me there. Troth, I wad advise ony friends o' mine to gree wi' Rob; for, watch as they like, and do what they like, they are sair apt to be harried[47] when the lang nights come on. Some o' the Grahame and Cohoon* gentry stood out; but what then?—they lost their haill stock the first winter; sae maist folks now think it best to come into Rob's terms. He's easy wi' a' body that will be easy wi' him; but if ye thraw him, ye had better thraw the deevil.'

'And by his exploits in these vocations,' I continued, 'I suppose he has rendered himself amenable to the laws of the country?'

'Amenable?—ye may say that; his craig wad ken the weight o' his hurdies if they could get haud o' Rob. But he has gude friends amang the grit folks; and I could tell ye o' ae grit family that keeps him up as far as they decently can, to be a thorn in the side of another. And then he's sic an auld-farran lang-headed chield as never took up the trade o' cateran in our time; mony a daft reik he has played—mair than wad fill a book, and a queer ane it wad be—as gude as Robin Hood, or William Wallace—a' fu' o' venturesome deeds and escapes, sic as folk tell ower at a winter-ingle in the daft days.* It's a queer thing o' me, gentlemen, that am a man o' peace mysell, and a peacefu' man's son, for the deacon my father quarrelled wi' nane out o' the town-council—it's a queer thing, I say, but I think the Hieland blude o' me warms at thae daft tales, and whiles I like better to hear them than a word o' profit, gude forgie me!—But they are vanities—sinfu' vanities—and, moreover, again the statute law—again the statute and gospel law.'

I now followed up my investigation, by enquiring what means of influence this Mr Robert Campbell could possibly possess over my affairs, or those of my father.

'Why, ye are to understand,' said Mr Jarvie, in a very subdued tone—'I speak amang friends, and under the rose—Ye are to understand, that the Hielands hae been keepit quiet since the year aughty-nine—that was Killiecrankie year.* But how hae they been keepit quiet, think ye? By siller, Mr Owen—by siller, Mr Osbaldistone. King William caused Breadalbane distribute twenty thousand gude punds sterling amang them, and it's said the auld Hieland Earl keepit a lang lug o't in his ain sporran. And then Queen Anne, that's dead, gae the chiefs bits o' pensions,* sae they had wherewith to support their gillies and caterans that work nae wark, as I said afore; and they lay by quiet eneugh, saving some spreagherie on the Lowlands, whilk is their use and wont, and some cutting o' thrapples amang themsells, that nae civilized body kens or cares ony thing anent.—Weel, but there's a new warld come up wi' this King George, (I say, God bless him, for ane,)— there's neither like to be siller nor pensions gaun amang them; they haena the means o' mainteening the clans that eat them up, as ye may guess frae what I said before; their credit's gane in the Lowlands; and a man that can whistle ye up a thousand or feifteen hundred linking lads to do his will, wad hardly get fifty punds on his band at the Cross o' Glasgow—This canna stand lang—there will be an outbreak for the Stewarts—there will be an outbreak—they will come down on the Low Country like a flood, as they did in the waefu' wars o' Montrose,* and that will be seen and heard tell o' ere a twalmonth gangs round.'

'Yet still,' I said, 'I do not see how this concerns Mr Campbell, much less my father's affairs.'

'Rob can levy five hundred men, sir, and therefore war suld concern him as muckle as maist folk,' replied the Bailie; 'for it is a faculty that is far less profitable in time o' peace. Then, to tell ye the truth, I doubt he has been the prime agent between some o' our Hieland chiefs and the gentlemen in the north o' England. We a' heard o' the public money that was taen frae the chield Morris somewhere about the fit o' Cheviot by Rob and ane o' the Osbaldistone lads; and, to tell ye the truth, word gaed that it was yourself, Mr Francis, and sorry was I that your father's son suld hae taen to sic practices—Na, ye needna say a word about it— I see weel I was mistaen; but I wad believe ony thing o' a stage-player, whilk I concluded ye to be. But now, I doubtna, it has been Rashleigh himsell, or some other o' your cousins—they are a' tarr'd wi' the same stick—rank jacobites and papists, and wad think the government siller and government papers lawfu' prize. And the creature Morris is sic a cowardly caitiff, that to this hour he daurna say that it was Rob took the portmanteau aff him; and troth he's right, for your customhouse and excise cattle are ill liket on a' sides, and Rob might get a back-handed lick at him, before the Board, as they ca't, could help him.'

'I have long suspected this, Mr Jarvie,' said I, 'and perfectly agree with you; but as to my father's affairs'——

'Suspected it?—it's certain—it's certain—I ken them that saw some of the papers that were taen aff Morris—it's needless to say where. But to your father's affairs—Ye maun think that in thae twenty years be-gane, some o' the Hieland lairds and chiefs hae come to some sma' sense o' their ain interest—your father and others hae bought the woods of Glen-Disseries, Glen Kissoch, Tober-na-Kippoch, and mony mair besides, and your father's house has granted large bills in payment,—and as the credit o' Osbaldistone and Tresham was gude—for I'll say before Mr Owen's face as I wad behind his back, that, bating misfortunes o' the Lord's sending, nae men could be mair honourable in business—the Hieland gentlemen, holders o' thae bills, hae found credit in Glasgow and Edinburgh—(I might amaist say in Glasgow wholly, for it's little the pridefu' Edinburgh folk do in real business)—for all, or the greater part of the contents o' thae bills.—So that—Aha! d'ye see me now?'

I confessed I could not quite follow his drift.

'Why,' said he, 'if these bills are not paid, the Glasgow merchant comes on the Hieland lairds, whae hae deil a boddle o' siller, and will like ill to spew up what is item a' spent—They will turn desperate—five hundred will rise that might hae sitten at hame—the deil will gae ower Jock Wabster—and the stopping of your father's house will hasten the outbreak that's been sae lang biding us.'

'You think, then,' said I, surprised at this singular view of the case, 'that Rashleigh Osbaldistone has done this injury to my father, merely to accelerate a rising in the Highlands, by distressing the gentlemen to whom these bills were originally granted?'

'Doubtless—doubtless—it has been one main reason, Mr Osbaldistone. I doubtna but what the ready money he carried off wi' him might be another. But that makes comparatively but a sma' part o' your father's loss, though it might make the maist part o' Rashleigh's direct gain. The assetts he carried off are of nae mair use to him than if he were to light his pipe wi' them. He tried if MacVittie and Co. wad gie him siller on them—that I ken by Andro Wylie—but they were ower auld cats to draw that strae afore them*—they keepit aff and gae fair words. Rashleigh Osbaldistone is better kend than trusted in Glasgow, for he was here about some jacobitical papistical troking in seventeen hundred and seven,* and left debt ahint him. Na, na, he canna pit aff the paper here; folk will misdoubt him how he came by it. Na, na, he'll hae the stuff safe at some o' their haulds in the Hielands, and I daur say my cousin Rob could get at it gin he liked.'

'But would he be disposed to serve us in this pinch, Mr Jarvie?' said I. 'You have described him as an agent of the Jacobite party, and deeply connected in their intrigues; will he be disposed for my sake, or, if you please, for the sake of justice, to make an act of restitution, which, supposing it in his power, would, according to your view of the case, materially interfere with their plans?'

'I canna preceesely speak to that—the grandees among them are doubtfu' o' Rob, and he's doubtfu' o' them—and he's been weel friended wi' the Argyle family, wha stand for the present model of government.—If he was freed o' his hornings and captions, he wad rather be on Argyle's side than he wad be on Breadalbane's, for there's auld ill-will between the Breadalbane family and his kin and name. The truth is, that Rob is for his ain hand, as Henry Wynd feught[48]—he'll take the side that suits him best; if the deil was laird, Rob wad be for being tenant, and ye canna blame him, puir fallow, considering his circumstances. But there's ae thing sair again ye—Rob has a grey mear in his stable at hame.'

'A grey mare*?' said I. 'What is that to the purpose?'

'The wife, man—the wife,—an awfu' wife she is. She downa bide the sight o' a kindly Scot, if he come frae the Lowlands, far less of an Inglisher, and she'll be keen for a' that can set up King James, and ding down King George.'

'It is very singular,' I replied, 'that the mercantile transactions of London citizens should become involved with revolutions and rebellions.'

'Not at a', man—not at a',' returned Mr Jarvie, 'that's a' your silly prejudications. I read whiles in the lang dark nights, and I hae read in Baker's Chronicle* that the merchants o' London could gar the Bank of Genoa break their promise to advance a mighty sum to the King of Spain, whereby the sailing of the Grand Spanish Armada was put aff for a haill year—What think you of that, sir?'

'That the merchants did their country golden service, which ought to be honourably remembered in our histories.'

'I think sae too; and they wad do weel, and deserve weel baith o' the state and o' humanity, that wad save three or four honest Hieland gentlemen frae louping heads ower heels into destruction, wi' a' their puir sackless[49] followers, just because they canna pay back the siller they had reason to count upon as their ain—and save your father's credit—and my ain gude siller that Osbaldistone and Tresham awes me into the bargain—I say if ane could manage a' this, I think it suld be done and said unto him, even if he were a puir ca'-the-shuttle body, as unto one whom the king delighteth to honour.'*

'I cannot pretend to estimate the extent of public gratitude,' I replied; 'but our own thankfulness, Mr Jarvie, would be commensurate with the extent of the obligation.'

'Which,' added Mr Owen, 'we would endeavour to balance with a *per contra*, the instant our Mr Osbaldistone returns from Holland.'

'I doubtna—I doubtna—he is a very worthy gentleman, and a sponsible, and wi' some o' my lights might do muckle business in Scotland—Weel, sir, if these assetts could be redeemed out o' the hands o' the Philistines, they are gude paper—they are the right stuff when they are in the right hands, and that's yours, Mr Owen.—And I'se find ye three men in Glasgow, for as little as ye may think o' us, Mr Owen,—that's Sandie Steenson in the Trade's-Land, and John Pirie in Candleriggs, and another, that sall be nameless at this present, sall advance what soums are sufficient to secure the credit of your house, and seek nae better security.'

Owen's eyes sparkled at this prospect of extrication; but his countenance instantly fell on recollecting how improbable it was that the recovery of the assetts, as he technically called them, should be successfully achieved.

'Dinna despair, sir—dinna despair,' said Mr Jarvie; 'I hae taen sae muckle concern wi' your affairs already, that it maun een be ower shoon ower boots* wi' me now. I am just like my father the deacon, (praise be wi' him!) I canna meddle wi' a friend's business, but I aye end wi' making it my ain—Sae, I'll een pit on my boots the morn, and be jogging ower Drymen-Muir wi' Mr Frank here; and if I canna mak Rob hear reason, and his wife too, I dinna ken wha can—I hae been a kind freend to them afore now, to say naething o' ower-looking him last night, when naming his name wad hae cost him his life—I'll be hearing o' this in the council maybe frae Bailie Grahame, and Mac-Vittie, and some o' them. They hae coost up my kindred to Rob to me already—set up their nashgabs! I tauld them I wad vindicate nae man's faults; but set apart what he had done again the law o' the country, and the hership o' the Lennox, and the misfortune o' some folk losing life by him, he was an honester man than stude on ony o' their shanks—And whatfor suld I mind their clavers?—If Rob is an outlaw, to himsell be it said—there is nae laws now about reset of intercommuned persons,* as there was in the ill times o' the last Stewarts—I trow I hae a Scotch tongue in my head—if they speak, I'se answer.'

It was with great pleasure that I saw the Bailie gradually surmount the barriers of caution, under the united influence of public spirit and good-natured interest in our affairs, together with his natural wish to avoid loss and acquire gain, and not a little harmless vanity. Through the combined operation of these motives he at length arrived at the doughty resolution of taking the field in person, to aid in the recovery of my father's property. His whole information led me to believe, that if the papers were in possession of this Highland adventurer, it might be possible to induce him to surrender what he could not keep with any prospect of personal advantage; and I was conscious that the presence of his kinsman was likely to have considerable weight with him. I therefore cheerfully acquiesced in Mr Jarvie's proposal, that we should set out early next morning.

That honest gentleman was indeed as vivacious and alert in preparing to carry his purpose into execution, as he had been slow and cautious in forming it. He roared to Mattie to 'air his trot-cosey, to have his jack-boots greased and set before the kitchen-fire all night, and to see that his beast be corned, and a' his riding gear in order.' Having agreed to meet him at five o'clock next morning, and having settled that Owen, whose presence could be of no use to us upon this expedition, should await our return at Glasgow, we took a kind farewell of this unexpectedly zealous friend. I installed Owen in an apartment in my lodgings, contiguous to my own, and, giving orders to Andrew Fairservice to attend me next morning at the hour appointed, I retired to rest with better hopes than it had lately been my fortune to entertain.

CHAPTER XXVII

Far as the eye could reach no tree was seen,
Earth, clad in russet, scorn'd the lively green;
No birds, except as birds of passage, flew;
No bee was heard to hum, no dove to coo;
No streams, as amber smooth—as amber clear,
Were seen to glide, or heard to warble here.

*Prophecy of Famine**

IT was in the bracing atmosphere of a harvest morning, that I met by appointment Fairservice, with the horses, at the door of Mr Jarvie's house, which was but little space distant from Mrs Flyter's hotel. The first matter which caught my attention was, that whatever were the deficiencies of the pony which Mr Fairservice's legal adviser, Clerk Touthope, generously bestowed upon him in exchange for Thorncliff's mare, he had contrived to part with it, and procure in its stead an animal with so curious and complete a lameness, that it seemed only to make use of three legs for the purpose of progression, while the fourth appeared as if meant to be flourished in the air by way of accompaniment. 'What do you mean by bringing such a creature as that here, sir? and where is the pony you rode to Glasgow upon?' were my very natural and impatient enquiries.

'I sell't it, sir. It was a slink beast, and wad hae eaten its head aff, standing at Luckie Flyter's at livery. And I hae bought this on your honour's account. It's a grand bargain—cost but a pund sterling the foot—that's four a'thegither. The stringhalt will gae aff when it's gaen a mile; it's a weel-kend ganger; they ca' it Souple Tam.'

'On my soul, sir!' said I, 'you will never rest till my supple-jack and your shoulders become acquainted. If you do not go instantly and procure the other brute, you shall pay the penalty of your ingenuity.'

Andrew, notwithstanding my threats, continued to battle the point, as he said it would cost him a guinea of rue-bargain* to the man who had bought his pony before he could get it back again. Like a true Englishman, though sensible I was duped by the rascal, I was about to pay his exaction rather than lose time, when forth sallied Mr Jarvie, cloaked, mantled, hooded, and booted, as if for a Siberian winter, while two apprentices, under the immediate direction of Mattie, led forth the decent ambling steed which had the honour on such occasions to support the person of the Glasgow magistrate. Ere he 'clombe to the saddle,'* an expression more descriptive of the Bailie's mode of mounting than that of the knights-errant to whom Spenser applies it, he enquired the cause of the dispute betwixt my servant and me. Having learned the nature of honest Andrew's manœuvre, he instantly cut short all debate by pronouncing, that if Fairservice did not forthwith return the three-legged palfrey, and produce the more useful quadruped which he had discarded, he would send him to prison, and amerce him in half his wages. 'Mr Osbaldistone,' said he, 'contracted for the service of both your horse and you—twa brutes at ance—ye unconscionable rascal!—but I'se look weel after you during this journey.'

'It will be nonsense fining me,' said Andrew doughtily, 'that hasna a grey groat to pay a fine wi'—it's ill taking the breeks aff a Hielandman.'*

'If ye hae nae purse to fine, ye hae flesh to pine,' replied the Bailie, 'and I will look weel to ye getting your deserts the tae way or the tither.'

To the commands of Mr Jarvie, therefore, Andrew was compelled to submit, only muttering between his teeth, 'Ower mony maisters—ower mony maisters, as the paddock said to the harrow, when every tooth gae her a tig.'

Apparently he found no difficulty in getting rid of Supple Tam, and recovering possession of his former Bucephalus, for he accomplished the exchange without being many minutes absent; nor did I hear further of his having paid any smart-money for breach of bargain.

We now set forward, but had not reached the top of the street in which Mr Jarvie dwelt, when a loud hallooing, and breathless call of 'Stop, stop!' was heard behind us. We stopped accordingly, and were overtaken by Mr Jarvie's two lads, who bore two parting tokens of Mattie's care for her master. The first was conveyed in the form of a voluminous silk handkerchief, like the main-sail of one of his own West-Indiamen, which Mrs Mattie particularly desired he would put about his neck, and which, thus entreated, he added to his other integuments. The second youngster brought only a verbal charge (I thought I saw the rogue disposed to laugh as he delivered it) on the part of the housekeeper, that her master would take care of the waters. 'Pooh! pooh! silly hussy,' answered Mr Jarvie; but added, turning to me, 'it shows a kind heart though—it shows a kind heart in sae young a quean—Mattie's a carefu' lass.' So speaking, he pricked the sides of his palfrey, and we left the town without farther interruption.

While we paced easily forward, by a road which conducted us north-eastward from the town, I had an opportunity to estimate and admire the good qualities of my new friend. Although, like my father, he considered commercial transactions the most important objects of human life, he was not wedded to them so as to undervalue more general knowledge. On the contrary, with much oddity and vulgarity of manner,—with a vanity which he made much more ridiculous by disguising it now and then under a thin veil of humility, and devoid as he was of all the advantages of a learned education, Mr Jarvie's conversation showed tokens of a shrewd, observing, liberal, and, to the extent of its opportunities, a well-improved mind. He was a good local antiquary, and entertained me, as we passed along, with an account of remarkable events which had formerly taken place in the scenes through which we passed. And as he was well acquainted with the ancient history of his district, he saw with the prospective eye of an enlightened patriot, the buds of many of those future advantages, which have only blossomed and ripened within these few years. I remarked also, and with great pleasure, that although a keen Scotchman, and abundantly zealous for the honour of his country, he was disposed to think liberally of the sister kingdom. When Andrew Fairservice (whom, by the way, the Bailie could not abide) chose to impute the accident of one of the horses casting his shoe to the deteriorating influence of the Union, he incurred a severe rebuke from Mr Jarvie.

'Whisht, sir!—whisht! it's ill-scraped tongues like yours, that make mischief atween neighbourhoods and nations. There's naething sae gude on this side o' time but it might hae been better, and that may be said o' the Union. Nane were keener against it than the Glasgow folk, wi' their rabblings and their risings, and their mobs, as they ca' them now-a-days.* But it's an ill wind blaws naebody gude—Let ilka ane roose the ford as they find it—I say, Let Glasgow flourish! whilk is judiciously and elegantly putten round the town's arms, by way of by-word.—Now, since St Mungo catched herrings in the Clyde, what was ever like to gar us flourish like the sugar and tobacco-trade? Will ony body tell me that, and grumble at the treaty that opened us a road west-awa' yonder?'

Andrew Fairservice was far from acquiescing in these arguments of expedience, and even ventured to enter a grumbling protest, 'That it was an unco change to hae Scotland's laws made in England; and that, for his share, he wadna for a' the herring-barrels in Glasgow, and a' the tobacco-casks to boot, hae gien up the riding o' the Scots Parliament,* or sent awa' our crown, and our sword, and our sceptre, and Mons Meg,[50] to be keepit by thae English pock-puddings in the Tower o' Lunnon. What wad Sir William Wallace, or auld Davie Lindsay, hae said to the Union, or them that made it?'

The road which we travelled, while diverting the way with these discussions, had become wild and open, as soon as we had left Glasgow a mile or two behind us, and was growing more dreary as we advanced. Huge continuous heaths spread before, behind, and around us in hopeless barrenness, now level and interspersed with swamps, green with treacherous verdure, or sable with turf, or, as they call them in Scotland, peat-bogs, and now swelling into huge heavy ascents, which wanted the dignity and form of hills, while they were still more toilsome to the passenger. There were neither trees nor bushes to relieve the eye from the russet livery of absolute sterility. The very heath was of that stinted imperfect kind which has little or no flower, and affords the coarsest and meanest covering, which, as far as my experience enables me to judge, mother Earth is ever arrayed in. Living thing we saw none, except occasionally a few straggling sheep of a strange diversity of colours, as black, bluish, and orange. The sable hue predominated, however, in their faces and legs. The very birds seemed to shun these wastes, and no wonder, since they had an easy method of escaping from them; at least I only heard the monotonous and plaintive cries of the lapwing and curlew, which my companions denominated the peasweep and whaup.

At dinner, however, which we took about noon, at a most miserable alehouse, we had the good fortune to find that these tiresome screamers of the morass were not the only inhabitants of the moors. The goodwife told us, that 'the gudeman had been at the hill;' and well for us that he had been so, for we enjoyed the produce of his *chasse* in the shape of some broiled moor-game, a dish which gallantly eked out the ewe-milk cheese, dried salmon, and oaten bread, being all besides that the house afforded. Some very indifferent two-penny ale, and a glass of excellent brandy, crowned our repast; and as our horses had, in the meantime, discussed their corn, we resumed our journey with renovated vigour.

I had need of all the spirits a good dinner could give, to resist the dejection which crept insensibly on my mind, when I combined the strange uncertainty of my errand with the disconsolate aspect of the country through which it was leading me. Our road continued to be, if possible, more waste and wild than that we had travelled in the forenoon. The few miserable hovels that showed some marks of human habitation, were now of still rarer occurrence; and at length, as we began to ascend an uninterrupted swell of moorland, they totally disappeared. The only exercise which my imagination received was, when some particular turn of the road gave us a partial view, to the left, of a large assemblage of dark-blue mountains stretching to the north and north-west, which promised to include within their recesses, a country as wild perhaps, but certainly differing greatly in point of interest, from that which we now travelled. The peaks of this screen of mountains were as wildly varied and distinguished as the hills which we had seen on the right were tame and lumpish; and while I gazed on this Alpine region, I felt a longing to explore its recesses, though accompanied with toil and danger, similar to that which a sailor feels when he wishes for the risks and animation of a battle or a gale, in exchange for the insupportable monotony of a protracted calm. I made various enquiries of my friend Mr Jarvie, respecting the names and positions of these remarkable mountains; but it was a subject on which he had no information, or did not choose to be communicative. 'They're the Hieland hills—the Hieland hills—Ye'll see and hear eneugh about them before ye see Glasgow Cross again—I downa look at them—I never see them but they gar me grew.—It's no for fear—no for fear, but just for grief, for the puir blinded half-starved creatures that inhabit them—But say nae mair about it—it's ill speaking o' Hielandmen sae near the line. I hae kend mony an honest man wad na hae ventured this length without he had made his last will and testament—Mattie had ill-will to see me set awa on this ride, and grat awee, the sillie tawpie; but it's nae mair ferlie to see a woman greet than to see a goose gang barefit.'*

I next attempted to lead the discourse on the character and history of the person whom we were going to visit; but on this topic Mr Jarvie was totally inaccessible, owing perhaps in part to the attendance of Mr Andrew Fairservice, who chose to keep so close in our rear that his ears could not fail to catch every word which was spoken, while his tongue assumed the freedom of mingling in our conversation as often as he saw an opportunity. For this he occasionally incurred Mr Jarvie's reproof.

'Keep back, sir, as best sets ye,' said the Bailie, as Andrew pressed forward to catch the answer to some question I had asked about Campbell.—'Ye wad fain ride the fore-horse, an ye wist how—That chield's aye for being out o' the cheese-fat he was moulded in.—Now, as for your questions, Mr Osbaldistone, now that chield's out of ear-shot, I'll just tell ye it's free to you to speer, and it's free to me to answer, or no—Gude I canna say muckle o' Rob, puir chield; ill I winna say o' him, for, forby that he's my cousin, we're coming near his ain country, and there may be ane o' his gillies ahint every whin-bush for what I ken—And if ye'll be guided by my advice, the less ye speak about him, or where we are gaun, or what we are gaun to do, we'll be the mair likely to speed us in our errand. For it's like we may fa' in wi' some o'his unfreends—there are e'en ower mony o' them about—and his bonnet sits even on his brow yet for a' that; but I doubt they'll be upsides wi' Rob at the last—air day or late day, the fox's hide finds aye the flaying knife.'

'I will certainly,' I replied, 'be entirely guided by your experience.'

'Right, Mr Osbaldistone—right,—but I maun speak to this gabbling skyte too, for bairns and fules speak at the Cross what they hear at the ingle side.—D'ye hear, you, Andrew—What's your name—Fairservice!'

Andrew, who at the last rebuff had fallen a good way behind, did not choose to acknowledge the summons.

'Andrew, ye scoundrel!' repeated Mr Jarvie; 'here, sir! here!'

'Here is for the dog,' said Andrew, coming up sulkily.

'I'll gie you dog's wages, ye rascal, if ye dinna attend to what I say t'ye—We are gaun into the Hielands a bit'——

'I judged as muckle,' said Andrew.

'Haud your peace, ye knave, and hear what I have to say till ye—We are gaun a bit into the Hielands'——

'Ye tauld me sae already,' replied the incorrigible Andrew.

'I'll break your head,' said the Bailie, rising in wrath, 'if ye dinna haud your tongue.'

'A hadden tongue,' replied Andrew, 'makes a slabbered mouth.'

It was now necessary I should interfere, which I did by commanding Andrew, with an authoritative tone, to be silent at his peril.

'I am silent,' said Andrew. 'I'se do a' your lawfu' bidding without a nay-say.—My puir mither used aye to tell me,

> "Be it better, be it worse,
> Be ruled by him that has the purse."*

Sae ye may e'en speak as lang as ye like, baith the tane and the tither o'
you, for Andrew.'

Mr Jarvie took the advantage of his stopping after quoting the above
proverb, to give him the requisite instructions.

'Now, sir, it's as muckle as your life's worth—that wad be dear o' little siller, to be sure—but it is as muckle as a' our lives are worth, if ye
dinna mind what I say to ye. In this public whar we are gaun to, and
whar it is like we may hae to stay a' night, men o' a' clans and kindred—
Hieland and Lawland—tak up their quarters—And whiles there are
mair drawn dirks than open Bibles amang them, when the usquebaugh
gets uppermost. See ye neither meddle nor mak, nor gie nae offence
wi' that clavering tongue o' yours, but keep a calm sough, and let ilka
cock fight his ain battle.'

'Muckle needs to tell me that,' said Andrew contemptuously, 'as if
I had never seen a Hieland-man before, and kend nae how to manage
them. Nae man alive can cuitle up Donald* better than mysell—I
hae bought wi' them, sauld wi' them, eaten wi' them, drucken wi'
them'——

'Did ye ever fight wi' them?' said Mr Jarvie.

'Na, na,' answered Andrew, 'I took care o' that; it wad ill hae set me,
that am an artist and half a scholar to my trade, to be fighting amang a
wheen kilted loons that dinna ken the name o' a single herb or flower in
braid Scots, let abee in the Latin tongue.'

'Then,' said Mr Jarvie, 'as ye wad keep either your tongue in your
mouth, or your lugs in your head, (and ye might miss them, for as
saucy members as they are,) I charge ye to say nae word, gude or bad,
that ye can weel get by, to ony body that may be in the Clachan. And
ye'll specially understand that ye're no to be bleezing and blasting
about your master's name and mine, or saying that this is Mr Bailie
Nicol Jarvie o' the Saut-Market, son o' the worthy Deacon Nicol
Jarvie, that a' body has heard about; and this is Mr Frank Osbaldistone,
son of the managing partner of the great house of Osbaldistone and
Tresham, in the City.'

'Eneuch said,' answered Andrew—'eneuch said! What need ye
think I wad be speaking about your names for?—I hae mony things
o'mair importance to speak about, I trow.'

'It's thae very things of importance that I am feared for, ye blethering goose; ye maunna speak ony thing, gude or bad, that ye can by any possibility help.'

'If ye dinna think me fit,' replied Andrew, in a huff, 'to speak like ither folk, gie me my wages and my board-wages, and I'se gae back to Glasgow—There's sma' sorrow at our parting, as the auld mear said to the broken cart.'

Finding Andrew's perverseness again rising to a point which threatened to occasion me inconvenience, I was under the necessity of explaining to him, that he might return if he thought proper, but that in that case I would not pay him a single farthing for his past services. The argument *ad crumenam*,* as it has been called by jocular logicians, has weight with the greater part of mankind, and Andrew was in that particular far from affecting any trick of singularity. He 'drew in his horns,' to use the Bailie's phrase, on the instant, professed no intention whatever to disoblige, and a resolution to be guided by my commands, whatever they might be.

Concord being thus happily restored to our small party, we continued to pursue our journey. The road, which had ascended for six or seven English miles, began now to descend for about the same space, through a country which, neither in fertility or interest, could boast any advantage over that which we had passed already, and which afforded no variety, unless when some tremendous peak of a Highland mountain appeared at a distance. We continued, however, to ride on without pause; and even when night fell and overshadowed the desolate wilds which we traversed, we were, as I understood from Mr Jarvie, still three miles and a bittock distant from the place where we were to spend the night.

CHAPTER XXVIII*

Baron of Bucklivie,
May the foul fiend drive ye,
And a' to pieces rive ye,
For building sic a town,
Where there's neither horse meat, nor man's meat,
    nor a chair to sit down.

*Scottish Popular Rhymes on a bad Inn**

THE night was pleasant, and the moon afforded us good light for our journey. Under her rays, the ground over which we passed assumed a more interesting appearance than during the broad daylight, which discovered the extent of its wasteness. The mingled light and shadows gave it an interest which naturally did not belong to it; and, like the effect of a veil flung over a plain woman, irritated our curiosity on a subject which had in itself nothing gratifying.

The descent, however, still continued, turned, winded, left the more open heaths, and got into steeper ravines, which promised soon to lead us to the banks of some brook or river, and ultimately made good their presage. We found ourselves at length on the bank of a stream, which rather resembled one of my native English rivers than those I had hitherto seen in Scotland. It was narrow, deep, still, and silent; although the imperfect light, as it gleamed on its placid waters, showed also that we were now among the lofty mountains which formed its cradle. 'That's the Forth,' said the Bailie, with an air of reverence, which I have observed the Scotch usually pay to their distinguished rivers. The Clyde, the Tweed, the Forth, the Spey, are usually named by those who dwell on their banks with a sort of respect and pride, and I have known duels occasioned by any word of disparagement. I cannot say I have the least quarrel with this sort of harmless enthusiasm. I received my friend's communication with the importance which he seemed to think appertained to it. In fact, I was not a little pleased, after so long and dull a journey, to approach a region which promised to engage the imagination. My faithful squire, Andrew, did not seem to be quite of the same opinion, for he received the solemn information, 'That is the Forth,' with a 'Umph!—an he had said that's the public house, it wad hae been mair to the purpose.'

The Forth, however, as far as the imperfect light permitted me to judge, seemed to merit the admiration of those who claimed an interest in its stream. A beautiful eminence of the most regular round shape, and clothed with copsewood of hazels, mountain-ash, and dwarf-oak, intermixed with a few magnificent old trees, which, rising above the underwood, exposed their forked and bared branches to the silver moonshine, seemed to protect the sources from which the river sprung. If I could trust the tale of my companion, which, while professing to disbelieve every word of it, he told under his breath, and with an air of something like intimidation, this hill, so regularly formed, so richly verdant, and garlanded with such a beautiful variety of ancient trees and thriving copsewood, was held by the neighbourhood to contain, within its unseen caverns, the palaces of the fairies; a race of airy beings, who formed an intermediate class between men and demons, and who, if not positively malignant to humanity, were yet to be avoided and feared, on account of their capricious, vindictive, and irritable disposition.[51]

'They ca' them,' said Mr Jarvie, in a whisper, '*Daoine Schie*, whilk signifies, as I understand, men of peace; meaning thereby to make their gude-will. And we may e'en as weel ca' them that too, Mr Osbaldistone, for there's nae gude in speaking ill o' the laird within his ain bounds.' But he added presently after, on seeing one or two lights which twinkled before us, 'It's deceits o' Satan, after a', and I fearna to say it—for we are near the manse now, and yonder are the lights in the Clachan of Aberfoil.'

I own I was well pleased at the circumstance to which Mr Jarvie alluded; not so much that it set his tongue at liberty, in his opinion, with all safety to declare his real sentiments with respect to the *Daoine Schie*, or fairies, as that it promised some hours' repose to ourselves and our horses, of which, after a ride of fifty miles and upwards, both stood in some need.

We crossed the infant Forth by an old-fashioned stone bridge, very high and very narrow. My conductor, however, informed me, that to get through this deep and important stream, and to clear all its tributary dependencies, the general pass from the Highlands to the southward lay by what was called the Fords of Frew, at all times deep and difficult of passage, and often altogether unfordable. Beneath these fords there was no pass of general resort until so far east as the bridge of Stirling; so that the river of Forth forms a defensible line betwixt the Highlands and Lowlands of Scotland, from its source nearly to the Frith, or inlet of the ocean, in which it terminates. The subsequent events which we witnessed led me to recall with attention what the shrewdness of Bailie Jarvie suggested, in his proverbial expression, that 'Forth bridles the wild Highlandman.'

About half a mile's riding, after we crossed the bridge, placed us at the door of the public-house where we were to pass the evening. It was a hovel rather worse than better than that in which we had dined; but its little windows were lighted up, voices were heard from within, and all intimated a prospect of food and shelter, to which we were by no means indifferent. Andrew was the first to observe that there was a peeled willow-wand placed across the half-open door of the little inn. He hung back, and advised us not to enter. 'For,' said Andrew, 'some of their chiefs and grit men are birling at the usquebaugh in by there, and dinna want to be disturbed; and the least we'll get, if we gang ram-stam in on them, will be a broken head, to learn us better havings, if we dinna come by the length of a cauld dirk in our wame, whilk is just as likely.'

I looked at the Bailie, who acknowledged, in a whisper, 'that the gowk had some reason for singing, ance in the year.'

Meantime a staring half-clad wench or two came out of the inn and the neighbouring cottages, on hearing the sound of our horses' feet. No one bade us welcome, nor did any one offer to take our horses, from which we had alighted; and to our various enquiries, the hopeless response of 'Ha niel Sassenach,'* was the only answer we could extract. The Bailie, however, found (in his experience) a way to make them speak English. 'If I gie ye a bawbee,' said he to an urchin of about ten years old, with a fragment of a tattered plaid about him, 'will you understand Sassenach?'

'Ay, ay, that will I,' replied the brat, in very decent English.

'Then gang and tell your mammy, my man, there's twa Sassenach gentlemen come to speak wi' her.'

The landlady presently appeared, with a lighted piece of split fir blazing in her hand. The turpentine in this species of torch (which is generally dug from out the turf-bogs) makes it blaze and sparkle readily, so that it is often used in the Highlands in lieu of candles. On this occasion such a torch illuminated the wild and anxious features of a female, pale, thin, and rather above the usual size, whose soiled and ragged dress, though aided by a plaid or tartan screen, barely served the purposes of decency, and certainly not those of comfort. Her black hair, which escaped in uncombed elf-locks from under her coif, as well as the strange and embarrassed look with which she regarded us, gave me the idea of a witch disturbed in the midst of her unlawful rites. She plainly refused to admit us into the house. We remonstrated anxiously, and pleaded the length of our journey, the state of our horses, and the certainty that there was not another place where we could be received nearer than Callander, which the Bailie stated to be seven Scots miles* distant. How many these may exactly amount to in English measurement, I have never been able to ascertain, but I think the double *ratio* may be pretty safely taken as a medium computation. The obdurate hostess treated our expostulation with contempt.—'Better gang farther than fare waur,' she said, speaking the Scottish Lowland dialect, and being indeed a native of the Lennox district,—'Her house was taen up wi'them wadna like to be intruded on wi' strangers.—She didna ken wha mair might be there—redcoats, it might be, frae the garrison.' (These last words she spoke under her breath, and with very strong emphasis.) 'The night,' she said, 'was fair abune head—a night amang the heather wad caller our bloods—we might sleep in our claes as mony a gude blade does in the scabbard—there wasna muckle flowmoss in the shaw, if we took up our quarters right, and we might pit up our horses to the hill, naebody wad say naething against it.'

'But, my good woman,' said I, while the Bailie groaned and remained undecided, 'it is six hours since we dined, and we have not taken a morsel since. I am positively dying with hunger, and I have no taste for taking up my abode supperless among these mountains of yours. I positively must enter; and make the best apology you can to your guests for adding a stranger or two to their number.—Andrew, you will see the horses put up.'

The Hecate* looked at me with surprise, and then ejaculated, 'A wilfu' man will hae his way—them that will to Cupar maun to Cupar!*—To see thae English belly-gods—he has had ae fu' meal the day already, and he'll venture life and liberty rather than he'll want a het supper! Set roasted beef and pudding on the opposite side o' the pit o' Tophet,* and an Englishman will mak a spang at it—But I wash my hands o't—Follow me, sir,' (to Andrew,) 'and I'se show ye where to pit the beasts.'

I own I was somewhat dismayed at my landlady's expressions, which seemed to be ominous of some approaching danger. I did not, however, choose to shrink back after having declared my resolution, and accordingly I boldly entered the house; and after narrowly escaping breaking my shins over a turf back and a salting tub, which stood on either side of the narrow exterior passage, I opened a crazy half-decayed door, constructed not of plank, but of wicker, and, followed by the Bailie, entered into the principal apartment of this Scottish caravansary.*

The interior presented a view which seemed singular enough to southern eyes. The fire, fed with blazing turf and branches of dried wood, blazed merrily in the centre; but the smoke, having no means to escape but through a hole in the roof, eddied round the rafters of the cottage, and hung in sable folds at the height of about five feet from the floor. The space beneath was kept pretty clear, by innumerable currents of air which rushed towards the fire from the broken panel of basket-work which served as a door, from two square holes, designed as ostensible windows, through one of which was thrust a plaid, and through the other a tattered great-coat; and moreover, through various less distinguishable apertures, in the walls of the tenement, which, being built of round stones and turf, cemented by mud, let in the atmosphere at innumerable crevices.

At an old oaken table, adjoining to the fire, sat three men, guests apparently, whom it was impossible to regard with indifference. Two were in the Highland dress; the one, a little dark-complexioned man, with a lively, quick, and irritable expression of features, wore the trews, or close pantaloons, wove out of a sort of chequered stocking stuff. The Bailie whispered me, that 'he behoved to be a man of some consequence, for that naebody but their Duinhéwassels* wore the trews; they were ill to weave exactly to their Highland pleasure.'

The other mountaineer was a very tall, strong man, with a quantity of reddish hair, freckled face, high cheek-bones, and long chin—a sort of caricature of the national features of Scotland. The tartan which he wore differed from that of his companion, as it had much more scarlet in it, whereas the shades of black and dark-green predominated in the chequers of the other. The third, who sate at the same table, was in the Lowland dress,—a bold, stout-looking man, with a cast of military daring in his eye and manner, his riding-dress showily and profusely laced, and his cocked hat of formidable dimensions. His hanger and a pair of pistols lay on the table before him. Each of the Highlanders had their naked dirks stuck upright in the board beside him,—an emblem, I was afterwards informed, but surely a strange one, that their compotation was not to be interrupted by any brawl. A mighty pewter measure, containing about an English quart of usquebaugh, a liquor nearly as strong as brandy, which the Highlanders distil from malt, and drink undiluted in excessive quantities, was placed before these worthies. A broken glass, with a wooden foot, served as a drinking cup to the whole party, and circulated with a rapidity, which, considering the potency of the liquor, seemed absolutely marvellous. These men spoke loud and eagerly together, sometimes in Gaelic, at other times in English. Another Highlander, wrapt in his plaid, reclined on the floor, his head resting on a stone, from which it was only separated by a wisp of straw, and slept, or seemed to sleep, without attending to what was going on around him. He also was probably a stranger, for he lay in full dress, and accoutred with the sword and target, the usual arms of his countrymen when on a journey. Cribs there were of different dimensions beside the walls, formed, some of fractured boards, some of shattered wicker-work or plaited boughs, in which slumbered the family of the house, men, women, and children, their places of repose only concealed by the dusky wreaths of vapour which arose above, below, and around them.

Our entrance was made so quietly, and the carousers I have described were so eagerly engaged in their discussions, that we escaped their notice for a minute or two. But I observed the Highlander who lay beside the fire raise himself on his elbow as we entered, and, drawing his plaid over the lower part of his face, fix his look on us for a few seconds, after which he resumed his recumbent posture, and seemed again to betake himself to the repose which our entrance had interrupted.

We advanced to the fire, which was an agreeable spectacle after our late ride, during the chillness of an autumn evening among the mountains, and first attracted the attention of the guests who had preceded us, by calling for the landlady. She approached, looking doubtfully and timidly, now at us, now at the other party, and returned a hesitating and doubtful answer to our request to have something to eat.

'She didna ken,' she said, 'she wasna sure there was ony thing in the house,' and then modified her refusal with the qualification,—'that is, ony thing fit for the like of us.'

I assured her we were indifferent to the quality of our supper; and looking round for the means of accommodation, which were not easily to be found, I arranged an old hen-coop as a seat for Mr Jarvie, and turned down a broken tub to serve for my own. Andrew Fairservice entered presently afterwards, and took a place in silence behind our backs. The natives, as I may call them, continued staring at us with an air as if confounded by our assurance, and we, at least I myself, disguised as well as we could, under an appearance of indifference, any secret anxiety we might feel concerning the mode in which we were to be received by those whose privacy we had disturbed.

At length, the lesser Highlander, addressing himself to me, said, in very good English, and in a tone of great haughtiness, 'Ye make yourself at home, sir, I see.'

'I usually do so,' I replied, 'when I come into a house of public entertainment.'

'And did she na see,' said the taller man, 'by the white wand at the door, that gentlemans had taken up the public-house on their ain business?'

'I do not pretend to understand the customs of this country; but I am yet to learn,' I replied, 'how three persons should be entitled to exclude all other travellers from the only place of shelter and refreshment for miles round.'

'There's nae reason for't, gentlemen,' said the Bailie; 'we mean nae offence—but there's neither law nor reason for't—but as far as a stoup o' gude brandy wad make up the quarrel, we, being peaceable folk, wad be willing'——

'Damn your brandy, sir!' said the Lowlander, adjusting his cocked-hat fiercely upon his head; 'we desire neither your brandy nor your company,' and up he rose from his seat. His companions also arose, muttering to each other, drawing up their plaids, and snorting and snuffing the air after the manner of their countrymen when working themselves into a passion.

'I tauld ye what wad come, gentlemen,' said the landlady, 'an ye wad hae been tauld—get awa' wi' ye out o' my house, and make nae disturbance here—there's nae gentleman be disturbed at Jeanie MacAlpine's an she can hinder. A wheen idle English loons, gaun about the country under cloud o' night, and disturbing honest peaceable gentlemen that are drinking their drap drink at the fireside!'

At another time I should have thought of the old Latin adage,

'Dat veniam corvis, vexat censura columbas'*——

But I had not any time for classical quotation, for there was obviously a fray about to ensue, at which, feeling myself indignant at the inhospitable insolence with which I was treated, I was totally indifferent, unless on the Bailie's account, whose person and qualities were ill qualified for such an adventure. I started up, however, on seeing the others rise, and dropped my cloak from my shoulders, that I might be ready to stand on the defensive.

'We are three to three,' said the lesser Highlander, glancing his eyes at our party; 'if ye be pretty men, draw!' and, unsheathing his broadsword, he advanced on me. I put myself in a posture of defence, and, aware of the superiority of my weapon, a rapier or small-sword, was little afraid of the issue of the contest. The Bailie behaved with unexpected mettle. As he saw the gigantic Highlander confront him with his weapon drawn, he tugged for a second or two at the hilt of his *shabble*, as he called it; but finding it loth to quit the sheath, to which it had long been secured by rust and disuse, he seized, as a substitute, on the red-hot coulter of a plough which had been employed in arranging the fire by way of a poker, and brandished it with such effect, that at the first pass he set the Highlander's plaid on fire, and compelled him to keep a respectful distance till he could get it extinguished. Andrew, on the contrary, who ought to have faced the Lowland champion, had, I grieve to say it, vanished at the very commencement of the fray. But his antagonist, crying, 'Fair play! fair play!' seemed courteously disposed to take no share in the scuffle. Thus we commenced our rencontre on fair terms as to numbers. My own aim was, to possess myself, if possible, of my antagonist's weapon; but I was deterred from closing for fear of the dirk which he held in his left hand, and used in parrying the thrusts of my rapier. Meantime the Bailie, notwithstanding the success of his first onset, was sorely bested. The weight of his weapon, the corpulence of his person, the very effervescence of his own passions, were rapidly exhausting both his strength and his breath, and he was almost at the mercy of his antagonist, when up started the sleeping Highlander from the floor on which he reclined, with his naked sword and target in his hand, and threw himself between the discomfited magistrate and his assailant, exclaiming, 'Her nainsell has eaten the town pread at the Cross o' Glasgow, and py her troth she'll fight for Bailie Sharvie at the Clachan of Aberfoil—tat will she e'en!' And seconding his words with deeds, this unexpected auxiliary made his sword whistle about the ears of his tall countryman, who, nothing abashed, returned his blows with interest. But being both accoutred with round targets made of wood, studded with brass, and covered with leather, with which they readily parried each other's strokes, their combat was attended with much more noise and clatter than serious risk of damage. It appeared, indeed, that there was more of bravado than of serious attempt to do us any injury; for the Lowland gentleman, who, as I mentioned, had stood aside for want of an antagonist when the brawl commenced, was now pleased to act the part of moderator and peace-maker.

'Haud your hands—haud your hands—eneugh done—eneugh done!—the quarrel's no mortal. The strange gentlemen have shown themselves men of honour, and gien reasonable satisfaction. I'll stand on mine honour as kittle as ony man, but I hate unnecessary bloodshed.'

It was not, of course, my wish to protract the fray—my adversary seemed equally disposed to sheath his sword—the Bailie, gasping for breath, might be considered as *hors de combat*, and our two sword-and-buckler men gave up their contest with as much indifference as they had entered into it.

'And now,' said the worthy gentleman who acted as umpire, 'let us drink and gree like honest fellows—The house will haud us a'.' I propose that this good little gentleman that seems sair forfoughen, as I may say, in this tuilzie, shall send for a tass o' brandy, and I'll pay for another, by way of archilowe,[52] and then we'll birl our bawbees a' round about, like brethren.'

'And fa's to pay my new ponnie plaid,' said the larger Highlander, 'wi' a hole burnt in't ane might put a kail-pat through? Saw ever ony body a decent gentleman fight wi' a firebrand before?'

'Let that be nae hinderance,' said the Bailie, who had now recovered his breath, and was at once disposed to enjoy the triumph of having behaved with spirit, and avoid the necessity of again resorting to such hard and doubtful arbitrement;—'Gin I hae broken the head,' he said, 'I sall find the plaister. A new plaid sall ye hae, and o' the best—your ain clan-colours, man—an ye will tell me where it can be sent t'ye frae Glasco.'

'I needna name my clan—I am of a king's clan, as is weel kend,' said the Highlander; 'but ye may tak a bit o' the plaid—figh, she smells like a singit sheep's head!—and that'll learn ye the sett*—and a gentleman, that's a cousin o' my ain, that carries eggs doun frae Glencroe, will ca' for't about Martimas, an ye will tell her where ye bide. But, honest gentleman, neist time ye fight, an ye hae ony respect for your athversary, let it be wi' your sword, man, since ye wear ane, and no wi' thae het culters and fireprands, like a wild Indian.'

'Conscience!' replied the Bailie, 'every man maun do as he dow—my sword hasna seen the light since Bothwell Brigg, when my father, that's dead and gane, ware it; and I kenna weel if it was forthcoming than either, for the battle was o' the briefest—At ony rate, it's glewed to the scabbard now beyond my power to part them; and, finding that, I e'en grippit at the first thing I could make a fend wi'. I trow my fighting days is done, though I like ill to take the scorn, for a' that.—But where's the honest lad that tuik my quarrel on himsell sae frankly?—I'se bestow a gill o' aquavitæ on him, an I suld never ca' for anither.'

The champion for whom he looked around was, however, no longer to be seen. He had escaped, unobserved by the Bailie, immediately when the brawl was ended, yet not before I had recognised, in his wild features and shaggy red hair, our acquaintance Dougal, the fugitive turnkey of the Glasgow jail. I communicated this observation in a whisper to the Bailie, who answered in the same tone, 'Weel, weel, I see that him that ye ken o' said very right. There *is* some glimmering o' common sense about that creature Dougal; I maun see and think o' something will do him some gude.'

Thus saying, he sat down, and fetching one or two deep aspirations, by way of recovering his breath, called to the landlady; 'I think, Luckie, now that I find that there's nae hole in my wame, whilk I had muckle reason to doubt frae the doings o' your house, I wad be the better o' something to pit intill't.'

The dame, who was all officiousness so soon as the storm had blown over, immediately undertook to broil something comfortable for our supper. Indeed, nothing surprised me more, in the course of the whole matter, than the extreme calmness with which she and her household seemed to regard the martial tumult that had taken place. The good woman was only heard to call to some of her assistants, 'Steek the door—steek the door!—Kill or be killed, let naebody pass out till they hae paid the lawin.' And as for the slumberers in those lairs by the wall, which served the family for beds, they only raised their shirtless bodies to look at the fray, ejaculated, 'Oigh! oigh!' in the tone suitable to their respective sex and ages, and were, I believe, fast asleep again, ere our swords were well returned to their scabbards.

Our landlady, however, now made a great bustle to get some victuals ready, and, to my surprise, very soon began to prepare for us, in the frying-pan, a savoury mess of venison collops, which she dressed in a manner that might well satisfy hungry men, if not epicures. In the meantime the brandy was placed on the table, to which the Highlanders, however partial to their native strong waters, showed no objection, but much the contrary; and the Lowland gentleman, after the first cup had passed round, became desirous to know our profession, and the object of our journey.

'We are bits o' Glasgow bodies, if it please your honour,' said the Bailie, with an affectation of great humility, 'travelling to Stirling to get in some siller that is awing us.'

I was so silly as to feel a little disconcerted at the unassuming account which he chose to give of us; but I recollected my promise to be silent, and allow the Bailie to manage the matter his own way. And really, when I recollected, Will, that I had not only brought the honest man a long journey from home, which even in itself had been some inconvenience, (if I were to judge from the obvious pain and reluctance with which he took his seat or arose from it,) but had also put him within a hair's-breadth of the loss of his life, I could hardly refuse him such a compliment. The spokesman of the other party, snuffing up his breath through his nose, repeated the words with a sort of sneer;— 'You Glasgow tradesfolks hae naething to do but to gang frae the tae end o' the west o' Scotland to the ither, to plague honest folks that may chance to be awee ahint the hand, like me.'

'If our debtors were a' sic honest gentlemen as I believe you to be, Garschattachin,' replied the Bailie, 'conscience! we might save ourselves a labour, for they wad come to seek us.'

'Eh! what! how!' exclaimed the person whom he had addressed, 'as I shall live by bread, (not forgetting beef and brandy,) it's my auld friend Nicol Jarvie, the best man that ever counted doun merks on a band till a distressed gentleman. Were ye na coming up my way?— were ye na coming up the Endrick to Garschattachin?'

'Troth no, Maister Galbraith,' replied the Bailie, 'I had other eggs on the spit—and I thought ye wad be saying I cam to look about the annual rent that's due on the bit heritable band that's between us.'

'Damn the annual rent!' said the laird, with an appearance of great heartiness,—'Deil a word o' business will you or I speak, now that ye're sae near my country—To see how a trot-cosey and a joseph can disguise a man—that I suldna ken my auld feal friend the deacon!'

'The bailie, if ye please,' resumed my companion; 'but I ken what gars ye mistak—the band was granted to my father that's happy, and he was deacon; but his name was Nicol as weel as mine. I dinna mind that there's been a payment of principal sum or annual rent on it in my day, and doubtless that has made the mistake.'

'Weel, the devil take the mistake and all that occasioned it!' replied Mr Galbraith. 'But I am glad ye are a bailie. Gentlemen, fill a brimmer—this is my excellent friend, Bailie Nicol Jarvie's health—I kend him and his father these twenty years. Are ye a' cleared kelty aff?—Fill anither. Here's to his being sune provost—I say provost—Lord Provost Nicol Jarvie!—and them that affirms there's a man walks the Hie-street o' Glasgow that's fitter for the office, they will do weel not to let me, Duncan Galbraith of Garschattachin, hear them say sae—that's all.' And therewith Duncan Galbraith martially cocked his hat, and placed it on one side of his head with an air of defiance.

The brandy was probably the best recommendation of these complimentary toasts to the two Highlanders, who drank them without appearing anxious to comprehend their purport. They commenced a conversation with Mr Galbraith in Gaelic, which he talked with perfect fluency, being, as I afterwards learned, a near neighbour to the Highlands.

'I kend that Scant-o'-grace weel eneugh frae the very outset,' said the Bailie, in a whisper to me; 'but when blude was warm, and swords were out at ony rate, wha kens what way he might hae thought o' paying his debts? it will be lang or he does it in common form. But he's an honest lad, and has a warm heart too; he disna come often to the Cross o' Glasgow, but mony a buck and blackcock he sends us doun frae the hills. And I can want my siller weel eneugh. My father the deacon had a great regard for the family of Garschattachin.'

Supper being now nearly ready, I looked round for Andrew Fairservice; but that trusty follower had not been seen by any one since the beginning of the rencontre. The hostess, however, said that she believed our servant had gone into the stable, and offered to light me to the place, saying that 'no entreaties of the bairns or hers could make him give any answer; and that truly she caredna to gang into the stable hersell at this hour. She was a lone woman, and it was weel kend how the Brownie of Ben-ye-gask guided the gudewife of Ardnagowan;* and it was aye judged there was a Brownie in our stable, which was just what garr'd me gie ower keeping an hostler.'

As, however, she lighted me towards the miserable hovel into which they had crammed our unlucky steeds, to regale themselves on hay, every fibre of which was as thick as an ordinary goose quill, she plainly showed me that she had another reason for drawing me aside from the company than that which her words implied. 'Read that,' she said, slipping a piece of paper into my hand as we arrived at the door of the shed; 'I bless God I am rid o't. Between sogers and Saxons, and cat-erans and cattle-lifters, and hership and bluidshed, an honest woman wad live quieter in hell than on the Highland line.'

So saying, she put the pine-torch into my hand, and returned into the house.

CHAPTER XXIX

Bagpipes, not lyres, the Highland hills adorn,
MacLean's loud hollo, and MacGregor's horn.

*John Cooper's Reply to Allan Ramsay**

I STOPPED in the entrance of the stable, if indeed a place be entitled to that name where horses were stowed away along with goats, poultry, pigs, and cows, under the same roof with the mansion-house; although, by a degree of refinement unknown to the rest of the hamlet, and which I afterwards heard was imputed to an overpride on the part of Jeanie MacAlpine, our landlady, the apartment was accommodated with an entrance different from that used by her biped customers. By the light of my torch, I deciphered the following billet, written on a wet, crumpled, and dirty piece of paper, and addressed, 'For the honoured hands of Mr F. O. a Saxon young gentleman—These.' The contents were as follows:

'SIR,
'There are night-hawks abroad, so that I cannot give you and my respected kinsman, B. N. J., the meeting at the Clachan of Aberfoil, whilk was my purpose. I pray you to avoid unnecessary communication with those you may find there, as it may give future trouble. The person who gives you this is faithful, and may be trusted, and will guide you to a place where, God willing, I may safely give you the meeting, when I trust my kinsman and you will visit my poor house, where, in despite of my enemies, I can still promise sic cheer as ane Hielandman may gie his friends, and where we will drink a solemn health to a certain D. V. and look to certain affairs whilk I hope to be your aidance in; and I rest, as is wont among gentlemen, your servant to command,
                                                                    R. M. C.'

I was a good deal mortified at the purport of this letter, which seemed to adjourn to a more distant place and date the service which I had hoped to receive from this man Campbell. Still, however, it was some comfort to know that he continued to be in my interest, since without him I could have no hope of recovering my father's papers.

I resolved, therefore, to obey his instructions; and, observing all caution before the guests, to take the first good opportunity I could find to procure from the landlady directions how I was to obtain a meeting with this mysterious person.

My next business was to seek out Andrew Fairservice, whom I called several times by name, without receiving any answer, surveying the stable all round, at the same time, not without risk of setting the premises on fire, had not the quantity of wet litter and mud so greatly counterbalanced two or three bunches of straw and hay. At length my repeated cries of 'Andrew Fairservice—Andrew! Fool—Ass, where are you?' produced a doleful 'Here,' in a groaning tone, which might have been that of the Brownie itself. Guided by this sound, I advanced to the corner of a shed, where, ensconced in the angle of the wall, behind a barrel full of the feathers of all the fowls which had died in the cause of the public for a month past, I found the manful Andrew; and partly by force, partly by command and exhortation, compelled him forth into the open air. The first words he spoke were, 'I am an honest lad, sir.'

'Who the devil questions your honesty?' said I; 'or what have we to do with it at present? I desire you to come and attend us at supper.'

'Yes,' reiterated Andrew, without apparently understanding what I said to him, 'I am an honest lad, whatever the Bailie may say to the contrary. I grant the warld and the warld's gear sits ower near my heart whiles, as it does to mony a ane—But I am an honest lad; and, though I spak o' leaving ye in the muir, yet God knows it was far frae my purpose, but just like idle things folk says when they're driving a bargain, to get it as far to their ain side as they can—And I like your honour weel for sae young a lad, and I wadna part wi' ye lightly.'

'What the deuce are you driving at now?' I replied. 'Has not every thing been settled again and again to your satisfaction? And are you to talk of leaving me every hour, without either rhyme or reason?'

'Ay, but I was only making fashion before,' replied Andrew; 'but it's come on me in sair earnest now—Lose or win, I daur gae nae farther wi' your honour; and if ye'll tak my foolish advice, ye'll bide by a broken tryste, rather than gang forward yoursell—I hae a sincere regard for ye, and I'm sure ye'll be a credit to your friends if ye live to saw out your wild aits, and get some mair sense and steadiness—But I can follow ye nae farther, even if ye suld founder and perish from the way for lack of guidance and counsel—to gang into Rob Roy's country is a mere tempting o' Providence.'

'Rob Roy?' said I, in some surprise; 'I know no such person. What new trick is this, Andrew?'

'It's hard,' said Andrew—'very hard, that a man canna be believed when he speaks Heaven's truth, just because he's whiles owercome, and tells lees a little when there is necessary occasion. Ye needna ask whae Rob Roy is, the reiving lifter that he is—God forgie me! I hope naebody hears us—when ye hae a letter frae him in your pouch. I heard ane o'his gillies bid that auld rudas jaud of a gudewife gie ye that. They thought I didna understand their gibberish; but, though I canna speak it muckle, I can gie a gude guess at what I hear them say— I never thought to hae tauld ye that, but in a fright a' things come out that suld be keepit in. O, Maister Frank, a' your uncle's follies, and a' your cousins' pliskies, were naething to this!—Drink clean cap-out, like Sir Hildebrand; begin the blessed morning with brandy sops, like Squire Percy; swagger, like Squire Thorncliffe; rin wud amang the lasses, like Squire John; gamble, like Richard; win souls to the pope and the deevil, like Rashleigh; rive, rant, break the Sabbath, and do the pope's bidding, like them a' put thegither—But, merciful Providence! take care o' your young bluid, and gang nae near Rob Roy!'

Andrew's alarm was too sincere to permit me to suppose he counterfeited. I contented myself, however, with telling him, that I meant to remain in the alehouse that night, and desired to have the horses well looked after. As to the rest, I charged him to observe the strictest silence upon the subject of his alarm, and he might rely upon it I would not incur any serious danger without due precaution. He followed me with a dejected air into the house, observing between his teeth, 'Man suld be served afore beast—I haena had a morsel in my mouth, but the rough legs o' that auld muircock, this haill blessed day.'

The harmony of the company seemed to have suffered some interruption since my departure, for I found Mr Galbraith and my friend the Bailie high in dispute.

'I'll hear nae sic language,' said Mr Jarvie, as I entered, 'respecting the Duke o' Argyle and the name o' Campbell. He's a worthy public-spirited nobleman, and a credit to the country, and a friend and benefactor to the trade o' Glasgow.'

'I'll sae naething against MacCallum More and the Slioch-nan-Diarmid,'* said the lesser Highlander, laughing. 'I live on the wrang side of Glencroe to quarrel with Inverara.'

'Our loch ne'er saw the Cawmil lymphads,'[53] said the bigger High-lander. 'She'll speak her mind and fear naebody—She doesna value a Cawmil mair as a Cowan, and ye may tell MacCallum More that Allan Iverach said sae—It's a far cry to Lochow.'[54]

Mr Galbraith, on whom the repeated pledges which he had quaffed had produced some influence, slapped his hand on the table with great force, and said in a stern voice, 'There's a bloody debt due by that family, and they will pay it one day—The banes of a loyal and a gallant Grahame hae lang rattled in their coffin for vengeance on thae Dukes of Guile and Lords for Lorn.* There ne'er was treason in Scotland but a Cawmil was at the bottom o't; and now that the wrang side's uppermost, wha but the Cawmils for keeping down the right? But this warld winna last lang, and it will be time to sharp the maiden[55] for shearing o' craigs and thrapples. I hope to see the auld rusty lass linking at a bluidy harst again.'

'For shame, Garschattachin!' exclaimed the Bailie; 'fy for shame, sir; wad ye say sic things before a magistrate, and bring yoursell into trouble?—How d'ye think to mainteen your family and satisfy your creditors, (mysell and others,) if ye gang on in that wild way, which cannot but bring you under the law, to the prejudice of a' that's con-nected wi' ye?'

'D—n my creditors,' retorted the gallant Galbraith, 'and you, if ye be ane o' them. I say there will be a new warld sune—And we shall hae nae Cawmils cocking their bonnet sae hie, and hounding their dogs where they daurna come themsells, nor protecting thieves, nor mur-derers, and oppressors, to harry and spoil better men and mair loyal clans than themsells.'

The Bailie had a great mind to have continued the dispute, when the savoury vapour of the broiled venison, which our landlady now placed before us, proved so powerful a mediator, that he betook himself to his trencher with great eagerness, leaving the strangers to carry on the dispute among themselves.

'And tat's true,' said the taller Highlander, whose name I found was Stewart, 'for we suldna be plagued and worried here wi' meetings to pit down Rob Roy, if the Cawmils didna gie him refutch. I was ane o' thirty o' my ain name—part Glenfinlas, and part men that came down frae Appine. We shased the MacGregors as ye wad shase rae-deer, till we came into Glenfalloch's country, and the Cawmils raise and wadna let us pursue nae farder, and sae we lost our labour; but her wad gie twa and a plack to be as near Rob as she was tat day.'

It seemed to happen very unfortunately, that in every topic of discourse which these warlike gentlemen introduced, my friend the Bailie found some matter of offence. 'Ye'll forgie me speaking my mind, sir; but ye wad maybe hae gien the best bowl in your bonnet to hae been as far awa frae Rob as ye are e'en now—Odd, my het pleughculter wad hae been naething to his claymore.'

'She had better speak nae mair about her culter, or, by G—, her will gar her eat her words, and twa handfuls o' cauld steel to drive them ower wi'!' And, with a most inauspicious and menacing look, the mountaineer laid his hand on his dagger.

'We'll hae nae quarrelling, Allan,' said his shorter companion; 'and if the Glasgow gentleman has ony regard for Rob Roy, he'll maybe see him in cauld irons the night, and playing tricks on a tow the morn; for this country has been ower lang plagued wi' him, and his race is nearhand run—And it's time, Allan, we were ganging to our lads.'

'Hout awa, Inverashalloch,' said Galbraith. 'Mind the auld saw, man—It's a bauld moon, quoth Bennygask—another pint, quoth Lesley*—we'll no start for another chappin.'

'I hae had chappins eneugh,' said Inverashalloch; 'I'll drink my quart of usquebaugh or brandy wi' ony honest fellow, but the deil a drap mair, when I hae wark to do in the morning. And, in my puir thinking, Garschattachin, ye had better be thinking to bring up your horsemen to the Clachan before day, that we may a' start fair.'

'What the deevil are ye in sic a hurry for?' said Garschattachin; 'meat and mass never hindered wark. An it had been my directing, deil a bit o' me wad hae fashed ye to come down the glens to help us. The garrison and our ain horse could hae taen Rob Roy easily eneugh. There's the hand,' he said, holding up his own, 'should lay him on the green, and never ask a Hielandman o' ye a' for his help.'

'Ye might hae loot us bide still where we were, then,' said Inverashalloch. 'I didna come sixty miles without being sent for. But an ye'll hae my opinion, I redd ye keep your mouth better steekit, if ye hope to speed. Shored folk live lang, and sae may him ye ken o'. The way to catch a bird is no to fling your bannet at her. And also thae gentlemen hae heard some things they suldna hae heard, an the brandy hadna been ower bauld for your brain, Major Galbraith.—Ye needna cock your hat and bully wi' me, man, for I will not bear it.'

'I hae said it,' said Galbraith, with a solemn air of drunken gravity, 'that I will quarrel no more this night either with broadcloth or tartan.

When I am off duty, I'll quarrel with you or ony man in the Hielands or Lowlands, but not on duty—no—no.—I wish we heard o' these red-coats.—If it had been to do ony thing against King James, we wad hae seen them lang syne—but when it's to keep the peace o' the country, they can lie as lound as their neighbours.'

As he spoke, we heard the measured footsteps of a body of infantry on the march; and an officer, followed by two or three files of soldiers, entered the apartment. He spoke in an English accent, which was very pleasant to my ears, now so long accustomed to the varying brogue of the Highland and Lowland Scotch.

'You are, I suppose, Major Galbraith, of the squadron of Lennox Militia, and these are the two Highland gentlemen with whom I was appointed to meet in this place?'

They assented, and invited the officer to take some refreshments, which he declined.

'I have been too late, gentlemen, and am desirous to make up time. I have orders to search for and arrest two persons guilty of treasonable practices.'

'We'll wash our hands o' that,' said Inverashalloch. 'I came here wi' my men to fight against the red MacGregor that killed my cousin seven times removed, Duncan MacLaren in Invernenty;[56] but I will hae nothing to do touching honest gentlemen that may be gaun through the country on their ain business.'

'Nor I neither,' said Iverach.

Major Galbraith took up the matter more solemnly, and, premising his oration with a hiccup, spoke to the following purpose:

'I shall say nothing against King George, Captain, because, as it happens, my commission may rin in his name—but one commission being good, sir, does not make another bad; and some think that James may be just as good a name as George. There's the king that is—and there's the king that suld of right be—I say, an honest man may and suld be loyal to them both, Captain.—But I am of the Lord-Lieutenant's opinion for the time, as it becomes a militia officer and a depute-lieutenant,—and about treason and all that, it's lost time to speak of it—least said is sunest mended.'

'I am sorry to see how you have been employing your time, sir,' replied the English officer,—as indeed the honest gentleman's reasoning had a strong relish of the liquor he had been drinking, 'and I could wish, sir, it had been otherwise on an occasion of this consequence.

I would recommend to you to try to sleep for an hour—Do these gentlemen belong to your party?'—looking at the Bailie and me, who, engaged in eating our supper, had paid little attention to the officer on his entrance.

'Travellers, sir,' said Galbraith—'lawful travellers by sea and land, as the prayer-book hath it.'

'My instructions,' said the Captain, taking a light to survey us closer, 'are to place under arrest an elderly and a young person, and I think these gentlemen answer nearly the description.'

'Take care what you say, sir,' said Mr Jarvie; 'it shall not be your red coat nor your laced hat shall protect you, if you put any affront on me. I'se convene ye baith in an action of scandal and false imprisonment— I am a free burgess and a magistrate o' Glasgow; Nicol Jarvie is my name, sae was my father's afore me—I am a bailie, be praised for the honour, and my father was a deacon.'

'He was a prick-eared cur,'* said Major Galbraith, 'and fought agane the King at Bothwell Brigg.'

'He paid what he ought and what he bought, Mr Galbraith,' said the Bailie, 'and was an honester man than ever stude on your shanks.'

'I have no time to attend to all this,' said the officer; 'I must positively detain you, gentlemen, unless you can produce some respectable security that you are loyal subjects.'

'I desire to be carried before some civil magistrate,' said the Bailie,—'the sherra or the judge of the bounds—I am not obliged to answer every red-coat that speers questions at me.'

'Well, sir, I shall know how to manage you if you are silent—And you, sir,' (to me) 'what may your name be?'

'Francis Osbaldistone, sir.'

'What, a son of Sir Hildebrand Osbaldistone, of Northumberland?'

'No, sir,' interrupted the Bailie; 'a son of the great William Osbaldistone, of the House of Osbaldistone and Tresham, Crane-Alley, London.'

'I am afraid, sir,' said the officer, 'your name only increases the suspicions against you, and lays me under the necessity of requesting that you will give up what papers you have in charge.'

I observed the Highlanders look anxiously at each other when this proposal was made. 'I had none,' I replied, 'to surrender.'

The officer commanded me to be disarmed and searched. To have resisted would have been madness. I accordingly gave up my arms, and submitted to a search, which was conducted as civilly as an operation of the kind well could. They found nothing except the note which I had received that night through the hand of the landlady.

'This is different from what I expected,' said the officer; 'but it affords us good grounds for detaining you. Here I find you in written communication with the outlawed robber, Robert MacGregor Campbell, who has been so long the plague of this district—How do you account for that?'

'Spies of Rob!' said Inverashalloch—'we wad serve them right to strap them up till the neist tree.'

'We are gaun to see after some gear o' our ain, gentlemen,' said the Bailie, 'that's fa'en into his hands by accident—there's nae law agane a man looking after his ain, I hope?'

'How did you come by this letter?' said the officer, addressing himself to me.

I could not think of betraying the poor woman who had given it to me, and remained silent.

'Do you know any thing of it, fellow?' said the officer, looking at Andrew, whose jaws were chattering like a pair of castanets at the threats thrown out by the Highlander.

'O ay, I ken a' about it—It was a Hieland loon gied the letter to that lang-tongued jaud the gudewife there—I'll be sworn my maister kend naething about it. But he's wilfu' to gang up the hills and speak wi' Rob; and O, sir, it wad be a charity just to send a wheen o' your red-coats to see him safe back to Glasgow again whether he will or no—And ye can keep Mr Jarvie as lang as ye like—He's responsible eneugh for ony fine ye may lay on him—and so's my master for that matter—for me, I'm just a puir gardener lad, and no worth your steering.'

'I believe,' said the officer, 'the best thing I can do is to send these persons to the garrison under an escort. They seem to be in immediate correspondence with the enemy, and I shall be in no respect answerable for suffering them to be at liberty.—Gentlemen, you will consider yourselves as my prisoners. So soon as dawn approaches I will send you to a place of security. If you be the persons you describe yourselves, it will soon appear, and you will sustain no great inconvenience from being detained a day or two.—I can hear no remonstrances,' he continued, turning away from the Bailie, whose mouth was open to address him, 'the service I am on gives me no time for idle discussions.'

'Aweel—aweel, sir,' said the Bailie, 'you're welcome to a tune on your ain fiddle; but see if I dinna gar ye dance till't afore a's dune.'

An anxious consultation now took place between the officer and the Highlanders, but carried on in so low a tone, that it was impossible to catch the sense. So soon as it was concluded they all left the house. At their departure, the Bailie thus expressed himself: 'Thae Hielandmen are o' the westland clans, and just as light-handed as their neighbours, an a' tales be true, and yet ye see they hae brought them frae the head o' Argyleshire to make war wi' puir Rob for some auld ill-will that they hae at him and his sirname—And there's the Grahames, and the Buchanans, and the Lennox gentry, a' mounted and in order.—It's weel kend their quarrel—and I dinna blame them—naebody likes to lose his kye—and then there's sodgers, puir things, hoyed out frae the garrison at a'body's bidding—Puir Rob will hae his hands fu' by the time the sun comes ower the hill. Weel—it's wrang for a magistrate to be wishing ony thing agane the course o' justice, but deil o' me an I wad break my heart to hear that Rob had gien them a' their paiks!'

CHAPTER XXX

———General,
Hear me, and mark me well, and look upon me
Directly in my face—my woman's face—
See if one fear, one shadow of a terror,
One paleness dare appear, but from my anger,
To lay hold on your mercies.

*Bonduca**

WE were permitted to slumber out the remainder of the night in the best manner that the miserable accommodations of the alehouse permitted. The Bailie, fatigued with his journey and the subsequent scenes, less interested also in the event of our arrest, which to him could only be a matter of temporary inconvenience, perhaps less nice than habit had rendered me about the cleanliness or decency of his couch, tumbled himself into one of the cribs which I have already described, and soon was heard to snore soundly. A broken sleep, snatched by intervals, while I rested my head upon the table, was my only refreshment. In the course of the night I had occasion to observe, that there seemed to be some doubt and hesitation in the motions of the soldiery. Men were sent out as if to obtain intelligence, and returned apparently without bringing any satisfactory information to their commanding officer. He was obviously eager and anxious, and again dispatched small parties of two or three men, some of whom, as I could understand from what the others whispered to each other, did not return again to the Clachan.

The morning had broken, when a corporal and two men rushed into the hut, dragging after them, in a sort of triumph, a Highlander, whom I immediately recognised as my acquaintance the ex-turnkey. The Bailie, who started up at the noise with which they entered, immediately made the same discovery, and exclaimed, 'Mercy on us! they hae grippit the puir creature Dougal—Captain, I will put in bail—sufficient bail, for that Dougal creature.'

To this offer, dictated undoubtedly by a grateful recollection of the late interference of the Highlander in his behalf, the Captain only answered, by requesting Mr Jarvie to 'mind his own affairs, and remember that he was himself for the present a prisoner.'

'I take you to witness, Mr Osbaldistone,' said the Bailie, who was probably better acquainted with the process in civil than in military cases, 'that he has refused sufficient bail. It's my opinion that the creature Dougal will have a good action of wrongous imprisonment and damages agane him, under the Act seventeen hundred and one,* and I'll see the creature righted.'

The officer, whose name I understood was Thornton, paying no attention to the Bailie's threats or expostulations, instituted a very close enquiry into Dougal's life and conversation, and compelled him to admit, though with apparent reluctance, the successive facts,—that he knew Rob Roy MacGregor—that he had seen him within these twelve months—within these six months—within this month— within this week; in fine, that he had parted from him only an hour ago. All this detail came like drops of blood from the prisoner, and was, to all appearance, only extorted by the threat of an halter and the next tree, which Captain Thornton assured him should be his doom, if he did not give direct and special information.

'And now, my friend,' said the officer, 'you will please inform me how many men your master has with him at present.'

Dougal looked in every direction except at the querist, and began to answer, 'She canna just be sure about that.'

'Look at me, you Highland dog,' said the officer, 'and remember your life depends on your answer. How many rogues had that outlawed scoundrel with him when you left him?'

'Ou, no aboon sax rogues when I was gane.'

'And where are the rest of his banditti?'

'Gane wi' the Lieutenant agane ta westland carles.'

'Against the westland clans?' said the Captain. 'Umph—that is likely enough; and what rogue's errand were you dispatched upon?'

'Just to see what your honour and ta gentlemen red-coats were doing doun here at ta Clachan.'

'The creature will prove fause-hearted after a',' said the Bailie, who by this time had planted himself close behind me; 'it's lucky I didna pit mysell to expenses anent him.'

'And now, my friend,' said the Captain, 'let us understand each other. You have confessed yourself a spy, and should string up to the next tree—but come, if you will do me one good turn, I will do you another. You, Donald—you shall just in the way of kindness carry me and a small party to the place where you left your master, as I wish to speak a few words with him on serious affairs; and I'll let you go about your business, and give you five guineas to boot.'

'Oigh! oigh!' exclaimed Dougal, in the extremity of distress and perplexity, 'she canna do tat—she canna do tat—she'll rather be hanged.'

'Hanged, then, you shall be, my friend,' said the officer; 'and your blood be upon your own head.—Corporal Cramp, do you play Provost-Marshal—away with him!'

The corporal had confronted poor Dougal for some time, ostentatiously twisting a piece of cord which he had found in the house into the form of a halter. He now threw it about the culprit's neck, and, with the assistance of two soldiers, had dragged Dougal as far as the door, when overcome with the terror of immediate death, he exclaimed, 'Shentlemans, stops—stops!—She'll do his honour's bidding—stops!'

'Awa wi' the creature!' said the Bailie, 'he deserves hanging mair now than ever—awa wi' him, corporal—why dinna ye tak him awa?'

'It's my belief and opinion, honest gentleman,' said the corporal, 'that if you were going to be hanged yourself, you would be in no such d——d hurry.'

This by-dialogue prevented my hearing what passed between the prisoner and Captain Thornton, but I heard the former snivel out, in a very subdued tone, 'And ye'll ask her to gang nae farther than just to show ye where the MacGregor is?—Ohon! ohon!'

'Silence your howling, you rascal—No; I give you my word I will ask you to go no farther.—Corporal, make the men fall-in in front of the houses. Get out these gentlemen's horses; we must carry them with us. I cannot spare any men to guard them here.—Come, my lads, get under arms.'

The soldiers bustled about, and were ready to move. We were led out, along with Dougal, in the capacity of prisoners. As we left the hut, I heard our companion in captivity remind the Captain of 'ta foive kuineas.'

'Here they are for you,' said the officer, putting gold into his hand; 'but observe, that if you attempt to mislead me, I will blow your brains out with my own hand.'

'The creature,' said the Bailie, 'is waur than I judged him—it is a warldly and a perfidious creature—O the filthy lucre of gain that men gies themsells up to! My father the deacon used to say, the penny siller slew mair souls than the naked sword slew bodies.'

The landlady now approached, and demanded payment of her reckoning, including all that had been quaffed by Major Galbraith and his Highland friends. The English officer remonstrated, but Mrs MacAlpine declared, if she 'hadna trusted to his honour's name being used in their company, she wad never hae drawn them to stoup o' liquor; for Mr Galbraith, she might see him again, or she might no, but weel did she wot she had sma' chance of seeing her siller—and she was a puir widow, had naething but her custom to rely on.'

Captain Thornton put a stop to her remonstrances by paying the charge, which was only a few English shillings, though the amount sounded very formidable in Scottish denominations. The generous officer would have included Mr Jarvie and me in this general acquittance; but the Bailie, disregarding an intimation from the landlady, to 'make as muckle of the Inglishers as we could, for they were sure to gie us plague eneugh,' went into a formal accounting respecting our share of the reckoning, and paid it accordingly. The Captain took the opportunity to make us some slight apology for detaining us. 'If we were loyal and peaceable subjects,' he said, 'we would not regret being stopped for a day, when it was essential to the king's service; if otherwise, he was acting according to his duty.'

We were compelled to accept an apology which it would have served no purpose to refuse, and we sallied out to attend him on his march.

I shall never forget the delightful sensation with which I exchanged the dark, smoky, smothering atmosphere of the Highland hut, in which we had passed the night so uncomfortably, for the refreshing fragrance of the morning air, and the glorious beams of the rising sun, which, from a tabernacle of purple and golden clouds, were darted full on such a scene of natural romance and beauty as had never before greeted my eyes. To the left lay the valley, down which the Forth wandered on its easterly course, surrounding the beautiful detached hill, with all its garland of woods. On the right, amid a profusion of thickets, knolls, and crags, lay the bed of a broad mountain lake, lightly curled into tiny waves by the breath of the morning breeze, each glittering in its course under the influence of the sunbeams. High hills, rocks, and banks, waving with natural forests of birch and oak, formed the borders of this enchanting sheet of water; and, as their leaves rustled to the wind and twinkled in the sun, gave to the depth of solitude a sort of life and vivacity. Man alone seemed to be placed in a state of inferiority, in a scene where all the ordinary features of nature were raised and exalted. The miserable little *bourocks*, as the Bailie termed them, of which about a dozen formed the village called the Clachan of Aberfoil, were composed of loose stone, cemented by clay instead of mortar, and thatched by turfs, laid rudely upon rafters formed of native and unhewn birches and oaks from the woods around. The roofs approached the ground so nearly, that Andrew Fairservice observed we might have ridden over the village the night before, and never found out we were near it, unless our horses' feet had 'gane through the riggin'.'

From all we could see, Mrs MacAlpine's house, miserable as were the quarters it afforded, was still by far the best in the hamlet; and I dare say (if my description gives you any curiosity to see it) you will hardly find it much improved at the present day, for the Scotch are not a people who speedily admit innovation, even when it comes in the shape of improvement.[57]

The inhabitants of these miserable dwellings were disturbed by the noise of our departure; and as our party of about twenty soldiers drew up in rank before marching off, we were reconnoitred by many a beldam from the half-opened door of her cottage. As these sibyls thrust forth their grey heads, imperfectly covered with close caps of flannel, and showed their shrivelled brows, and long skinny arms, with various gestures, shrugs, and muttered expressions in Gaelic addressed to each other, my imagination recurred to the witches of Macbeth, and I imagined I read in the features of these crones the malevolence of the weird sisters. The little children also, who began to crawl forth, some quite naked, and others very imperfectly covered with tatters of tartan stuff, clapped their tiny hands, and grinned at the English soldiers, with an expression of national hate and malignity which seemed beyond their years. I remarked particularly that there were no men, nor so much as a boy of ten or twelve years old, to be seen among the inhabitants of a village which seemed populous in proportion to its extent; and the idea certainly occurred to me, that we were likely to receive from them, in the course of our journey, more effectual tokens of ill-will than those which lowered on the visages, and dictated the murmurs, of the women and children.

It was not until we commenced our march that the malignity of the elder persons of the community broke forth into expressions. The last file of men had left the village, to pursue a small broken track, formed by the sledges in which the natives transported their peats and turfs, and which led through the woods that fringed the lower end of the lake, when a shrilly sound of female exclamation broke forth, mixed with the screams of children, the hooping of boys, and the clapping of hands with which the Highland dames enforce their notes, whether of rage or lamentation. I asked Andrew, who looked as pale as death, what all this meant.

'I doubt we'll ken that ower sune,' said he. 'Means?—It means that the Highland wives are cursing and banning the red-coats, and wishing ill-luck to them, and ilka ane that ever spoke the Saxon tongue. I have heard wives flyte in England and Scotland—it's nae marvel to hear them flyte ony gate—but sic ill-scrapit tongues as thae Hieland carlines'—and sic grewsome wishes, that men should be slaughtered like sheep—and that they may lapper their hands to the elbows in their heart's blude—and that they suld dee the death of Walter Cuming of Guiyock,[58] wha hadna as muckle o' him left thegither as would supper a messan-dog—sic awsome language as that I ne'er heard out o' a human thrapple;—and, unless the deil wad rise amang them to gie them a lesson, I thinkna that their talent at cursing could be amended. The warst o't is, they bid us aye gang up the loch, and see what we'll land in.'

Adding Andrew's information to what I had myself observed, I could scarce doubt that some attack was meditated upon our party. The road, as we advanced, seemed to afford every facility for such an unpleasant interruption. At first it winded apart from the lake through marshy meadow ground, overgrown with copsewood, now traversing dark and close thickets which would have admitted an ambuscade to be sheltered within a few yards of our line of march, and frequently crossing rough mountain torrents, some of which took the soldiers up to the knees, and ran with such violence, that their force could only be stemmed by the strength of two or three men holding fast by each other's arms. It certainly appeared to me, though altogether unacquainted with military affairs, that a sort of half-savage warriors, as I had heard the Highlanders asserted to be, might, in such passes as these, attack a party of regular forces with great advantage. The Bailie's good sense and shrewd observation had led him to the same conclusion, as I understood from his requesting to speak with the Captain, whom he addressed nearly in the following terms:— 'Captain, it's no to fleech ony favour out o' ye, for I scorn it—and it's under protest that I reserve my action and pleas of oppression and wrongous imprisonment;—but, being a friend to King George and his army, I take the liberty to speer—Dinna ye think ye might tak a better time to gang up this glen? If ye are seeking Rob Roy, he's kend to be better than half a hunder men strong when he's at the fewest; and if he brings in the Glengyle folk, and the Glenfinlas and Balquidder lads, he may come to gie you your kail through the reek;* and it's my sincere advice, as a king's friend, ye had better tak back again to the Clachan, for thae women at Aberfoil are like the scarts and sea-maws at the Cumries,* there's aye foul weather follows their skirling.'

'Make yourself easy, sir,' replied Captain Thornton, 'I am in the execution of my orders. And as you say you are a friend to King George, you will be glad to learn, that it is impossible that this gang of ruffians, whose license has disturbed the country so long, can escape the measures now taken to suppress them. The horse squadron of militia, commanded by Major Galbraith, is already joined by two or more troops of cavalry, which will occupy all the lower passes of this wild country; three hundred Highlanders, under the two gentlemen you saw at the inn, are in possession of the upper part, and various strong parties from the garrison are securing the hills and glens in different directions. Our last accounts of Rob Roy correspond with what this fellow has confessed, that, finding himself surrounded on all sides, he had dismissed the greater part of his followers, with the purpose either of lying concealed, or of making his escape through his superior knowledge of the passes.'

'I dinna ken,' said the Bailie; 'there's mair brandy than brains in Garschattachin's head this morning—And I wadna, an I were you, Captain, rest my main dependence on the Hielandmen—hawks winna pike out hawks' een. They may quarrel amang themsells, and gie ilk ither ill names, and maybe a slash wi' a claymore; but they are sure to join in the lang run against a' civilized folk, that wear breeks on their hinder ends, and hae purses in their pouches.'

Apparently these admonitions were not altogether thrown away on Captain Thornton. He reformed his line of march, commanded his soldiers to unsling their firelocks and fix their bayonets, and formed an advanced and rear-guard, each consisting of a non-commissioned officer and two soldiers, who received strict orders to keep an alert look-out. Dougal underwent another and very close examination, in which he steadfastly asserted the truth of what he had before affirmed;

and being rebuked on account of the suspicious and dangerous appearance of the route by which he was guiding them, he answered with a sort of testiness that seemed very natural, 'Her nainsell didna mak ta road—an shentlemans likit grand roads, she suld hae pided at Glasco.'

All this passed off well enough, and we resumed our progress.

Our route, though leading towards the lake, had hitherto been so much shaded by wood, that we only from time to time obtained a glimpse of that beautiful sheet of water.* But the road now suddenly emerged from the forest ground, and, winding close by the margin of the loch, afforded us a full view of its spacious mirror, which now, the breeze having totally subsided, reflected in still magnificence the high dark heathy mountains, huge grey rocks, and shaggy banks, by which it is encircled. The hills now sunk on its margin so closely, and were so broken and precipitous, as to afford no passage except just upon the narrow line of the track which we occupied, and which was overhung with rocks, from which we might have been destroyed merely by rolling down stones, without much possibility of offering resistance. Add to this, that, as the road winded round every promontory and bay which indented the lake, there was rarely a possibility of seeing a hundred yards before us. Our commander appeared to take some alarm at the nature of the pass in which he was engaged, which displayed itself in repeated orders to his soldiers to be on the alert, and in many threats of instant death to Dougal, if he should be found to have led them into danger. Dougal received these threats with an air of stupid impenetrability, which might arise either from conscious innocence, or from dogged resolution.

'If shentlemans were seeking ta Red Gregarach,' he said, 'to be sure they couldna expect to find her without some wee danger.'

Just as the Highlander uttered these words, a halt was made by the corporal commanding the advance, who sent back one of the file who formed it, to tell the Captain that the path in front was occupied by Highlanders, stationed on a commanding point of particular difficulty. Almost at the same instant a soldier from the rear came to say, that, they heard the sound of a bagpipe in the woods through which we had just passed. Captain Thornton, a man of conduct as well as courage, instantly resolved to force the pass in front, without waiting till he was assailed from the rear; and, assuring his soldiers that the bagpipes which they heard were those of the friendly Highlanders who

Rob Roy

were advancing to their assistance, he stated to them the importance of advancing and securing Rob Roy, if possible, before these auxiliaries should come up to divide with them the honour, as well as the reward which was placed on the head of this celebrated freebooter. He therefore ordered the rear-guard to join the centre, and both to close up to the advance, doubling his files, so as to occupy with his column the whole practicable part of the road, and to present such a front as its breadth admitted. Dougal, to whom he said in a whisper, 'You dog, if you have deceived me you shall die for it!' was placed in the centre, between two grenadiers, with positive orders to shoot him if he attempted an escape. The same situation was assigned to us, as being the safest, and Captain Thornton, taking his half-pike from the soldier who carried it, placed himself at the head of his little detachment, and gave the word to march forward.

The party advanced with the firmness of English soldiers. Not so Andrew Fairservice, who was frightened out of his wits; and not so, if truth must be told, either the Bailie or I myself, who, without feeling the same degree of trepidation, could not with stoical indifference see our lives exposed to hazard in a quarrel with which we had no concern. But there was neither time for remonstrance nor remedy.

We approached within about twenty yards of the spot where the advanced-guard had seen some appearance of an enemy. It was one of those promontories which run into the lake, and round the base of which the road had hitherto winded in the manner I have described. In the present case, however, the path, instead of keeping the water's edge, scaled the promontory by one or two rapid zigzags, carried in a broken track along the precipitous face of a slaty grey rock, which would otherwise have been absolutely inaccessible. On the top of this rock, only to be approached by a road so broken, so narrow, and so precarious, the corporal declared he had seen the bonnets and long-barrelled guns of several mountaineers, apparently couched among the long heath and brushwood which crested the eminence. Captain Thornton ordered him to move forward with three files, to dislodge the supposed ambuscade, while at a more slow but steady pace, he advanced to his support with the rest of his party.

The attack which he meditated was prevented by the unexpected apparition of a female upon the summit of the rock. 'Stand!' she said, with a commanding tone, 'and tell me what ye seek in MacGregor's country?'

I have seldom seen a finer or more commanding form than this woman. She might be between the term of forty and fifty years, and had a countenance which must once have been of a masculine cast of beauty; though now, imprinted with deep lines by exposure to rough weather, and perhaps by the wasting influence of grief and passion, its features were only strong, harsh, and expressive. She wore her plaid, not drawn around her head and shoulders, as is the fashion of the women in Scotland, but disposed around her body as the Highland soldiers wear theirs. She had a man's bonnet, with a feather in it, an unsheathed sword in her hand, and a pair of pistols at her girdle.

'It's Helen Campbell, Rob's wife,' said the Bailie, in a whisper of considerable alarm; 'and there will be broken heads amang us or it's lang.'

'What seek ye here?' she asked again of Captain Thornton, who had himself advanced to reconnoitre.

'We seek the outlaw, Rob Roy MacGregor Campbell,' answered the officer, 'and make no war on women; therefore offer no vain opposition to the king's troops, and assure yourself of civil treatment.'

'Ay,' retorted the Amazon, 'I am no stranger to your tender mercies. Ye have left me neither name nor fame—my mother's bones will shrink aside in their grave when mine are laid beside them—Ye have left me and mine neither house nor hold, blanket nor bedding, cattle to feed us, or flocks to clothe us—Ye have taken from us all—all!—The very name of our ancestors have ye taken away, and now ye come for our lives.'

'I seek no man's life,' replied the Captain; 'I only execute my orders. If you are alone, good woman, you have nought to fear—if there are any with you so rash as to offer useless resistance, their own blood be on their own heads—Move forward, sergeant.'

'Forward—march,' said the non-commissioned officer. 'Huzza, my boys, for Rob Roy's head and a purse of gold!'

He quickened his pace into a run, followed by the six soldiers; but as they attained the first traverse of the ascent, the flash of a dozen of firelocks from various parts of the pass parted in quick succession and deliberate aim. The sergeant, shot through the body, still struggled to gain the ascent, raised himself by his hands to clamber up the face of the rock, but relaxed his grasp, after a desperate effort, and falling, rolled from the face of the cliff into the deep lake, where he perished. Of the soldiers three fell, slain or disabled; the others retreated on their main body, all more or less wounded.

'Grenadiers, to the front!' said Captain Thornton.—You are to re-collect, that in those days this description of soldiers actually carried that destructive species of fire-work from which they derive their name. The four grenadiers moved to the front accordingly. The officer commanded the rest of the party to be ready to support them, and only saying to us, 'Look to your safety, gentlemen,' gave, in rapid succession, the word to the grenadiers; 'Open your pouches—handle your grenades—blow your matches—fall on.'

The whole advanced with a shout, headed by Captain Thornton, the grenadiers preparing to throw their grenades among the bushes where the ambuscade lay, and the musketeers to support them by an instant and close assault. Dougal, forgotten in the scuffle, wisely crept into the thicket which overhung that part of the road where we had first halted, which he ascended with the activity of a wild cat. I followed his example, instinctively recollecting that the fire of the Highlanders would sweep the open track. I clambered until out of breath; for a continued spattering fire, in which every shot was multiplied by a thousand echoes, the hissing of the kindled fusees of the grenades, and the successive explosion of those missiles, mingled with the huzzas of the soldiers, and the yells and cries of their Highland antagonists, formed a contrast which added—I do not shame to own it—wings to my desire to reach a place of safety. The difficulties of the ascent soon increased so much that I despaired of reaching Dougal, who seemed to swing himself from rock to rock, and stump to stump, with the facility of a squirrel, and I turned down my eyes to see what had become of my other companions. Both were brought to a very awkward stand-still.

The Bailie, to whom I suppose fear had given a temporary share of agility, had ascended about twenty feet from the path, when his foot slipping, as he straddled from one huge fragment of rock to another, he would have slumbered with his father the deacon, whose acts and words he was so fond of quoting, but for a projecting branch of a ragged thorn, which, catching hold of the skirts of his riding coat, supported him in mid air, where he dangled not unlike to the sign of the Golden Fleece over the door of a mercer in the Trongate of his native city.

As for Andrew Fairservice, he had advanced with better success, until he had attained the top of a bare cliff, which, rising above the wood, exposed him, at least in his own opinion, to all the dangers of the neighbouring skirmish, while, at the same time, it was of such a precipitous and impracticable nature, that he dared neither to advance nor retreat. Footing it up and down upon the narrow space which the top of the cliff afforded, (very like a fellow at a country-fair dancing upon a trencher,) he roared for mercy in Gaelic and English alternately, according to the side on which the scale of victory seemed to predominate, while his exclamations were only answered by the groans of the Bailie, who suffered much, not only from apprehension, but from the pendulous posture in which he hung suspended by the loins.

On perceiving the Bailie's precarious situation, my first idea was to attempt to render him assistance; but this was impossible without the concurrence of Andrew, whom neither sign, nor entreaty, nor command, nor expostulation, could inspire with courage to adventure the descent from his painful elevation, where, like an unskilful and obnoxious minister of state, unable to escape from the eminence to which he had presumptuously ascended, he continued to pour forth piteous prayers for mercy, which no one heard, and to skip to and fro, writhing his body into all possible antick shapes to avoid the balls which he conceived to be whistling around him.

In a few minutes this cause of terror ceased, for the fire, at first so well sustained, now sunk at once, a sure sign that the conflict was concluded. To gain some spot from which I could see how the day had gone was now my object, in order to appeal to the mercy of the victors, who, I trusted, (whichever side might be gainers,) would not suffer the honest Bailie to remain suspended, like the coffin of Mahomet,* between heaven and earth, without lending a hand to disengage him. At length, by dint of scrambling, I found a spot which commanded a view of the field of battle. It was indeed ended; and, as my mind already augured, from the place and circumstances attending the contest, it had terminated in the defeat of Captain Thornton. I saw a party of Highlanders in the act of disarming that officer, and the scanty remainder of his party. They consisted of about twelve men, most of whom were wounded, who, surrounded by treble their number, and without the power either to advance or retreat, exposed to a murderous and well-aimed fire, which they had no means of returning with effect, had at length laid down their arms by the order of their officer, when he saw that the road in his rear was occupied, and that protracted resistance would be only wasting the lives of his brave followers. By the Highlanders, who fought under cover, the victory was cheaply bought, at the expense of one man slain and two wounded by the grenades. All this I learned afterwards. At present I only comprehended the general result of the day, from seeing the English officer, whose face was covered with blood, stripped of his hat and arms, and his men, with sullen and dejected countenances, which marked their deep regret, enduring, from the wild and martial figures who surrounded them, the severe measures to which the laws of war subject the vanquished for security of the victors.

CHAPTER XXXI

'Woe to the vanquish'd!' was stern Brenno's word,
When sunk proud Rome beneath the Gallic sword—
'Woe to the vanquish'd!' when his massive blade
Bore down the scale against her ransom weigh'd;
And on the field of foughten battle still,
Woe knows no limit save the victor's will.

*The Gaulliad**

I ANXIOUSLY endeavoured to distinguish Dougal among the victors.
I had little doubt that the part he had played was assumed, on purpose
to lead the English officer into the defile, and I could not help admir-
ing the address with which the ignorant, and apparently half-brutal
savage, had veiled his purpose, and the affected reluctance with which
he had suffered to be extracted from him the false information which
it must have been his purpose from the beginning to communicate. I
foresaw we should incur some danger on approaching the victors in
the first flush of their success, which was not unstained with cruelty,
for one or two of the soldiers, whose wounds prevented them from rising, were poniarded by the victors, or rather by some ragged Highland
boys who had mingled with them. I concluded, therefore, it would be
unsafe to present ourselves without some mediator; and as Campbell,
whom I now could not but identify with the celebrated freebooter Rob
Roy, was nowhere to be seen, I resolved to claim the protection of his
emissary, Dougal.

After gazing everywhere in vain, I at length retraced my steps to see
what assistance I could individually render to my unlucky friend,
when, to my great joy, I saw Mr Jarvie delivered from his state of suspense; and though very black in the face, and much deranged in the
garments, safely seated beneath the rock, in front of which he had
been so lately suspended. I hastened to join him and offer my con-
gratulations, which he was at first far from receiving in the spirit of
cordiality with which they were offered. A heavy fit of coughing scarce
permitted him breath enough to express the broken hints which he
threw out against my sincerity.

'Uh! uh! uh! uh!—they say a friend—uh! uh!—a friend sticketh
closer than a brither—uh! uh! uh!—When I came up here, Maister

Osbaldistone, to this country, cursed of God and man—uh! uh!—
Heaven forgie me for swearing—on nae man's errand but yours, d'ye
think it was fair—uh! uh!—to leave me, first, to be shot or drowned
atween red-wud Highlanders and red-coats; and next, to be hung up
between heaven and earth, like an auld potato-bogle, without sae
muckle as trying—uh! uh!—sae muckle as trying to relieve me?'

I made a thousand apologies, and laboured so hard to represent the
impossibility of my affording him relief by my own unassisted exertions, that at length I succeeded, and the Bailie, who was as placable as
hasty in his temper, extended his favour to me once more. I next took
the liberty of asking him how he had contrived to extricate himself.

'Me extricate! I might hae hung there till the day of judgment, or I
could hae helped mysell, wi' my head hinging down on the tae side,
and my heels on the tother, like the yarn scales in the weigh-house. It
was the creature Dougal that extricated me, as he did yestreen—he
cuttit aff the tails o' my coat wi' his durk, and another gillie and him set
me on my legs as cleverly as if I had never been aff them.—But to see
what a thing gude braid claith is—had I been in ony o' your rotten
French camlets now, or your drab-de-berries,* it would hae screeded
like an auld rag wi' sic a weight as mine.—But fair fa' the weaver that
wrought the weft o't—I swung and bobbit yonder as safe as a gabbart[59]
that's moored by a three-plie cable at the Broomie-law.'*

I now enquired what had become of his preserver.

'The creature,' so he continued to call the Highlandman, 'contrived
to let me ken there wad be danger in gaun near the leddy till he came
back, and bade me stay here—I am o' the mind,' he continued, 'that
he's seeking after you—it's a considerate creature—and troth, I wad
swear he was right about the leddy as he ca's her, too—Helen Campbell was nane o' the maist douce maidens, nor meekest wives neither,
and folk say that Rob himsell stands in awe o' her. I doubt she winna
ken me, for it's mony years since we met—I am clear for waiting for the
Dougal creature or we gang near her.'

I signified my acquiescence in this reasoning; but it was not the will
of fate that day that the Bailie's prudence should profit himself or any
one else.

Andrew Fairservice, though he had ceased to caper on the pinnacle
upon the cessation of the firing, which had given occasion for his
whimsical exercise, continued, as perched on the top of an exposed
cliff, too conspicuous an object to escape the sharp eyes of the

Highlanders, when they had time to look a little around them. We were apprized he was discovered, by a wild and loud halloo set up among the assembled victors, three or four of whom instantly plunged into the copsewood, and ascended the rocky side of the hill in different directions towards the place where they had discovered this whimsical apparition.

Those who arrived first within gunshot of poor Andrew, did not trouble themselves to offer him any assistance in the ticklish posture of his affairs, but levelling their long Spanish-barrelled guns, gave him to understand by signs, which admitted of no misconstruction, that he must contrive to come down and submit himself to their mercy, or be marked at from beneath, like a regimental target set up for ball-practice. With such a formidable hint for venturous exertion, Andrew Fairservice could no longer hesitate; the more imminent peril overcame his sense of that which seemed less inevitable, and he began to descend the cliff at all risks, clutching to the ivy and oak stumps, and projecting fragments of rock, with an almost feverish anxiety, and never failing, as circumstances left him a hand at liberty, to extend it to the plaided gentry below in an attitude of supplication, as if to deprecate the discharge of their levelled fire-arms. In a word, the fellow, under the influence of a counteracting motive for terror, achieved a safe descent from his perilous eminence, which, I verily believe, nothing but fear of instant death could have moved him to attempt. The awkward mode of Andrew's descent greatly amused the Highlanders below, who fired a shot or two while he was engaged in it, without the purpose of injuring him, as I believe, but merely to enhance the amusement they derived from his extreme terror, and the superlative exertions of agility to which it excited him.

At length he attained firm and comparatively level ground, or rather, to speak more correctly, his foot slipping at the last point of descent, he fell on the earth at his full length, and was raised by the assistance of the Highlanders, who stood to receive him, and who, ere he gained his legs, stripped him not only of the whole contents of his pockets, but of periwig, hat, coat, doublet, stockings, and shoes, performing the feat with such admirable celerity, that, although he fell on his back a well-clothed and decent burgher-seeming serving-man, he arose a forked, uncased, bald-pated, beggarly-looking scarecrow. Without respect to the pain which his undefended toes experienced from the sharp encounter of the rocks over which they hurried him, those who had detected Andrew proceeded to drag him downward towards the road through all the intervening obstacles.

In the course of their descent, Mr Jarvie and I became exposed to their lynx-eyed observation, and instantly half-a-dozen armed Highlanders thronged around us, with drawn dirks and swords pointed at our faces and throats, and cocked pistols presented against our bodies. To have offered resistance would have been madness, especially as we had no weapons capable of supporting such a demonstration. We therefore submitted to our fate; and, with great roughness on the part of those who assisted at our toilette, were in the act of being reduced to as unsophisticated a state (to use King Lear's phrase) as the plumeless biped* Andrew Fairservice, who stood shivering between fear and cold at a few yards' distance. Good chance, however, saved us from this extremity of wretchedness; for, just as I had yielded up my cravat, (a smart Steinkirk,* by the way, and richly laced,) and the Bailie had been disrobed of the fragments of his riding-coat—enter Dougal, and the scene was changed. By a high tone of expostulation, mixed with oaths and threats, as far as I could conjecture the tenor of his language from the violence of his gestures, he compelled the plunderers, however reluctant, not only to give up their further depredations on our property, but to restore the spoil they had already appropriated. He snatched my cravat from the fellow who had seized it, and twisted it (in the zeal of his restitution) around my neck with such suffocating energy, as made me think that he had not only been, during his residence at Glasgow, a substitute of the jailor, but must moreover have taken lessons as an apprentice of the hangman. He flung the tattered remnants of Mr Jarvie's coat around his shoulders, and as more Highlanders began to flock towards us from the high road, he led the way downwards, directing and commanding the others to afford us, but particularly the Bailie, the assistance necessary to our descending with comparative ease and safety. It was, however, in vain that Andrew Fairservice employed his lungs in obsecrating a share of Dougal's protection, or at least his interference, to procure restoration of his shoes.

'Na, na,' said Dougal in reply, 'she's nae gentle body, I trow; her petters hae ganged parefoot, or she's muckle mista'en.' And, leaving Andrew to follow at his leisure, or rather at such leisure as the surrounding crowd were pleased to indulge him with, he hurried us down to the pathway in which the skirmish had been fought, and hastened to present us as additional captives to the female leader of his band.

We were dragged before her accordingly, Dougal fighting, struggling, screaming, as if he were the party most apprehensive of hurt, and repulsing, by threats and efforts, all those who attempted to take a nearer interest in our capture than he seemed to do himself. At length we were placed before the heroine of the day, whose appearance, as well as those of the savage, uncouth, yet martial figures who surrounded us, struck me, to own the truth, with considerable apprehension. I do not know if Helen MacGregor had personally mingled in the fray, and indeed I was afterwards given to understand the contrary; but the specks of blood on her brow, her hands and naked arms, as well as on the blade of the sword which she continued to hold in her hand—her flushed countenance, and the disordered state of the raven locks which escaped from under the red bonnet and plume that formed her head-dress, seemed all to intimate that she had taken an immediate share in the conflict. Her keen black eyes and features expressed an imagination inflamed by the pride of gratified revenge, and the triumph of victory. Yet there was nothing positively sanguinary, or cruel, in her deportment; and she reminded me, when the immediate alarm of the interview was over, of some of the paintings I had seen of the inspired heroines in the catholic churches of France. She was not, indeed, sufficiently beautiful for a Judith, nor had she the inspired expression of features which painters have given to Deborah, or to the wife of Heber the Kenite,* at whose feet the strong oppressor of Israel, who dwelled in Harosheth of the Gentiles, bowed down, fell, and lay a dead man. Nevertheless, the enthusiasm by which she was agitated, gave her countenance and deportment, wildly dignified in themselves, an air which made her approach nearly to the ideas of those wonderful artists, who gave to the eye the heroines of Scripture history.

I was uncertain in what terms to accost a personage so uncommon, when Mr Jarvie, breaking the ice with a preparatory cough, (for the speed with which he had been brought into her presence had again impeded his respiration,) addressed her as follows:—'Uh! uh! &c. &c. I am very happy to have this joyful opportunity,' (a quaver in his voice strongly belied the emphasis which he studiously laid on the word joyful)—'this *joyful* occasion,' he resumed, trying to give the adjective a more suitable accentuation, 'to wish my kinsman Robin's wife a very good morning—Uh! uh!—How's a' wi' ye' (by this time he had talked himself into his usual jog-trot manner, which exhibited a mixture of

familiarity and self-importance)—'How's a' wi' ye this lang time?—
Ye'll hae forgotten me, Mrs MacGregor Campbell, as your cousin—
uh! uh!—but ye'll mind my father, Deacon Nicol Jarvie, in the Saut
Market o' Glasgow?—an honest man he was, and a sponsible, and
respectit you and yours—Sae, as I said before, I am right glad to see
you, Mrs MacGregor Campbell, as my kinsman's wife. I wad crave the
liberty of a kinsman to salute you, but that your gillies keep such a
dolefu' fast haud o' my arms; and, to speak Heaven's truth and a
magistrate's, ye wadna be the waur of a cogfu' o' water before ye welcomed your friends.'

There was something in the familiarity of this introduction which
ill suited the exalted state of temper of the person to whom it was
addressed, then busied with distributing dooms of death, and warm
from conquest in a perilous encounter.

'What fellow are you,' she said, 'that dare to claim kindred with the
MacGregor, and neither wear his dress nor speak his language?—
What are you, that have the tongue and the habit of the hound, and yet
seek to lie down with the deer?'

'I dinna ken,' said the undaunted Bailie, 'if the kindred has ever
been weel redd out to you yet, cousin—but it's kend and can be proved.
My mother, Elspeth MacFarlane, was the wife of my father, Deacon
Nicol Jarvie—peace be wi' them baith—and Elspeth was the daughter
of Parlane MacFarlane, at the Sheeling o' Loch Sloy. Now, this Parlane
MacFarlane, as his surviving daughter, Maggy MacFarlane, alias
MacNab, wha married Duncan MacNab o' Stuckavrallachan, can
testify, stood as near to your gudeman, Robin MacGregor, as in the
fourth degree of kindred, for'—

The virago lopped the genealogical tree, by demanding haughtily,
'If a stream of rushing water acknowledged any relation with the portion withdrawn from it for the mean domestic uses of those who dwelt
on its banks?'

'Vera true, kinswoman,' said the Bailie; 'but for a' that, the burn wad
be glad to hae the milldam back again in simmer, when the chuckie
stanes are white in the sun. I ken weel eneugh you Hieland folk haud us
Glasgow people light and cheap for our language and our claes; but
every body speaks their native tongue that they learned in infancy; and
it would be a daft-like thing to see me wi' my fat wame in a short
Hieland coat, and my puir short houghs gartered below the knee,
like ane o' your lang-legged gillies—Mair by token, kinswoman,' he

continued, in defiance of various intimations by which Dougal seemed to recommend silence, as well as of the marks of impatience which the Amazon evinced at his loquacity, 'I wad hae ye to mind that the king's errand whiles comes in the cadger's gate, and that, for as high as ye may think o' the gudeman, as it's right every wife should honour her husband—there's Scripture warrant for that—yet as high as ye haud him, as I was saying, I hae been serviceable to Rob ere now;—forbye a set o' pearlins I sent yoursell when ye was gaun to be married, and when Rob was an honest weel-doing drover, and nane o' this unlawfu' wark, wi' fighting, and flashes, and fluf-gibs, disturbing the king's peace and disarming his soldiers.'

He had apparently touched on a key which his kinswoman could not brook. She drew herself up to her full height, and betrayed the acuteness of her feelings by a laugh of mingled scorn and bitterness.

'Yes,' she said, 'you, and such as you, might claim a relation to us when we stooped to be the paltry wretches fit to exist under your dominion, as your hewers of wood and drawers of water*—to find cattle for your banquets, and subjects for your laws to oppress and trample on—But now we are free—free by the very act which left us neither house nor hearth, food nor covering—which bereaved me of all—of all—and makes me groan when I think I must still cumber the earth for other purposes than those of vengeance. And I will carry on the work this day has so well commenced, by a deed that shall break all bands between MacGregor and the Lowland churles.—Here—Allan—Dougal—bind these Sassenachs neck and heel together, and throw them into the Highland loch to seek for their Highland kinsfolk.'

The Bailie, alarmed at this mandate, was commencing an expostulation, which probably would have only inflamed the violent passions of the person whom he addressed, when Dougal threw himself between them, and in his own language, which he spoke with a fluency and rapidity strongly contrasted by the slow, imperfect, and idiot-like manner in which he expressed himself in English, poured forth what I doubt not was a very animated pleading in our behalf.

His mistress replied to him, or rather cut short his harangue, by exclaiming in English, (as if determined to make us taste in anticipation the full bitterness of death,) 'Base dog, and son of a dog, do you dispute my commands?—Should I tell ye to cut out their tongues and put them into each other's throats, to try which would there best knap

Southron, or to tear out their hearts and put them into each other's breasts, to see which would there best plot treason against the Mac-Gregor—and such things have been done of old in the day of revenge, when our fathers had wrongs to redress—Should I command you to do this, would it be your part to dispute my orders?'

'To be sure, to be sure,' Dougal replied, with accents of profound submission; 'her pleasure suld be done—tat's but reason—but an it were—tat is, an it could be thought the same to her to coup the ill-faured loon of ta red-coat Captain, and hims corporal Cramp, and twa three o' the red-coats into the loch, hersell wad do't wi' muckle mair great satisfaction than to hurt ta honest civil shentlemans as were friends to the Gregarach, and came up on the Chief's assurance, and not to do no treason, as hersell could testify.'

The lady was about to reply, when a few wild strains of a pibroch were heard advancing up the road from Aberfoil, the same probably which had reached the ears of Captain Thornton's rear-guard, and determined him to force his way onward rather than return to the village, on finding the pass occupied. The skirmish being of very short duration, the armed men who followed this martial melody, had not, although quickening their march when they heard the firing, been able to arrive in time sufficient to take any share in the rencontre. The victory, therefore, was complete without them, and they now arrived only to share in the triumph of their countrymen.

There was a marked difference betwixt the appearance of these new comers and that of the party by which our escort had been defeated, and it was greatly in favour of the former. Among the Highlanders who surrounded the Chieftainess, if I may presume to call her so without offence to grammar,* were men in the extremity of age, boys scarce able to bear a sword, and even women—all, in short, whom the last necessity urges to take up arms; and it added a shade of bitter shame to the dejection which clouded Thornton's manly countenance, when he found that the numbers and position of a foe, otherwise so despicable, had enabled them to conquer his brave veterans. But the thirty or forty Highlanders who now joined the others, were all men in the prime of youth or manhood, active clean-made fellows, whose short hose and belted plaids set out their sinewy limbs to the best advantage. Their arms were as superior to those of the first party as their dress and appearance. The followers of the female Chief had axes, scythes, and other antique weapons, in aid of their guns, and some had only clubs, daggers, and long knives. But of the second party, most had pistols at the belt, and almost all had dirks hanging at the pouches which they wore in front. Each had a good gun in his hand, and a broadsword by his side, besides a stout round target, made of light wood, covered with leather, and curiously studded with brass, and having a steel pike screwed into the centre. These hung on the left shoulder during a march, or while they were engaged in exchanging fire with the enemy, and were worn on the left arm when they charged with sword in hand.

But it was easy to see that this chosen band had not arrived from a victory such as they found their ill-appointed companions possessed of. The pibroch sent forth occasionally a few wailing notes, expressive of a very different sentiment from triumph, and when they appeared before the wife of their Chieftain, it was in silence, and with downcast and melancholy looks. They paused when they approached her, and the pipes again sent forth the same wild and melancholy strain.

Helen rushed towards them with a countenance in which anger was mingled with apprehension. 'What means this, Allaster?' she said to the minstrel. 'Why a lament in the moment of victory?—Robert—Hamish—Where's the MacGregor?—where's your father?'

Her sons, who led the band, advanced with slow and irresolute steps towards her, and murmured a few words in Gaelic, at hearing which she set up a shriek that made the rocks ring again, in which all the women and boys joined, clapping their hands and yelling, as if their lives had been expiring in the sound. The mountain echoes, silent since the military sounds of battle had ceased, had now to answer these frantic and discordant shrieks of sorrow, which drove the very night-birds from their haunts in the rocks, as if they were startled to hear orgies more hideous and ill-omened than their own, performed in the face of open day.

'Taken!' repeated Helen, when the clamour had subsided—'Taken!—captive!—and you live to say so?—Coward dogs! did I nurse you for this, that you should spare your blood on your father's enemies? or see him prisoner, and come back to tell it?'

The sons of MacGregor,* to whom this expostulation was addressed, were youths, of whom the eldest had hardly attained his twentieth year. *Hamish*, or James, the elder of these youths, was the tallest by a head, and much handsomer than his brother; his light-blue eyes, with a profusion of fair hair, which streamed from under his smart blue bonnet, made his whole appearance a most favourable specimen of the Highland youth. The younger was called Robert; but, to distinguish him from his father, the Highlanders added the epithet, *Oig*, or the young. Dark hair, and dark features, with a ruddy glow of health and animation, and a form strong and well-set beyond his years, completed the sketch of the young mountaineer.

Both now stood before their mother with countenances clouded with grief and shame, and listened, with the most respectful submission, to the reproaches with which she loaded them. At length, when her resentment appeared in some degree to subside, the eldest, speaking in English, probably that he might not be understood by their followers, endeavoured respectfully to vindicate himself and his brother from his mother's reproaches. I was so near him as to comprehend much of what he said; and, as it was of great consequence to me to be possessed of information in this strange crisis, I failed not to listen as attentively as I could.

'The MacGregor,' his son stated, 'had been called out upon a trysting with a Lowland hallion, who came with a token from'—he muttered the name very low, but I thought it sounded like my own.—'The MacGregor,' he said, 'accepted of the invitation, but commanded the Saxon who brought the message to be detained, as a hostage that good faith should be observed to him. Accordingly he went to the place of appointment,' (which had some wild Highland name that I cannot remember,) 'attended only by Angus Breck and little Rory, commanding no one to follow him. Within half an hour Angus Breck came back with the doleful tidings that the MacGregor had been surprised and made prisoner* by a party of Lennox militia, under Galbraith of Garschattachin.' He added, 'that Galbraith, on being threatened by MacGregor, who, upon his capture, menaced him with retaliation on the person of the hostage, had treated the threat with great contempt, replying, "Let each side hang his man; we'll hang the thief, and your catherans may hang the gauger, Rob, and the country will be rid of two damned things at once, a wild Highlander and a revenue officer." Angus Breck, less carefully looked to than his master, contrived to escape from the hands of the captors, after having been in their custody long enough to hear this discussion and to bring off the news.'

'And did you learn this, you false-hearted traitor,' said the wife of MacGregor, 'and not instantly rush to your father's rescue to bring him off, or leave your body on the place?'

The young MacGregor modestly replied, by representing the very superior force of the enemy, and stated, that as they made no preparation for leaving the country, he had fallen back up the glen with the purpose of collecting a band sufficient to attempt a rescue with some tolerable chance of success. At length he said, 'The militiamen would quarter, he understood, in the neighbouring house of Gartartan, or the old castle in the port of Monteith, or some other stronghold, which, although strong and defensible, was nevertheless capable of being surprised, could they but get enough of men assembled for the purpose.'

I understood afterwards that the rest of the freebooter's followers were divided into two strong bands, one destined to watch the remaining garrison of Inversnaid,* a party of which, under Captain Thornton, had been defeated; and another to show front to the Highland clans who had united with the regular troops and Lowlanders in this hostile and combined invasion of that mountainous and desolate territory, which, lying between the lakes of Loch-Lomond, Loch-Katrine, and Loch-Ard, was at this time currently called Rob Roy's, or the MacGregor, country. Messengers were dispatched in great haste, to concentrate, as I supposed, their forces, with a view to the purposed attack on the Lowlanders; and the dejection and despair, at first visible on each countenance, gave place to the hope of rescuing their leader, and to the thirst of vengeance. It was under the burning influence of the latter passion that the wife of MacGregor commanded that the hostage exchanged for his safety should be brought into her presence. I believe her sons had kept this unfortunate wretch out of her sight, for fear of the consequences; but if it was so, their humane precaution only postponed his fate. They dragged forward at her summons a wretch already half dead with terror, in whose agonized features I recognised, to my horror and astonishment, my old acquaintance Morris.

He fell prostrate before the female Chief with an effort to clasp her knees, from which she drew back, as if his touch had been pollution, so that all he could do in token of the extremity of his humiliation, was to kiss the hem of her plaid. I never heard entreaties for life poured forth with such agony of spirit. The ecstasy of fear was such, that, instead of paralyzing his tongue, as on ordinary occasions, it even rendered him eloquent; and, with cheeks pale as ashes, hands compressed in agony, eyes that seemed to be taking their last look of all mortal objects, he protested, with the deepest oaths, his total ignorance of any

design on the person of Rob Roy, whom he swore he loved and honoured as his own soul. In the inconsistency of his terror, he said, he was
but the agent of others, and he muttered the name of Rashleigh. He
prayed but for life—for life he would give all he had in the world: it was
but life he asked—life, if it were to be prolonged under tortures and
privations: he asked only breath, though it should be drawn in the
damps of the lowest caverns of their hills.

It is impossible to describe the scorn, the loathing, and contempt,
with which the wife of MacGregor regarded this wretched petitioner
for the poor boon of existence.

'I could have bid you live,' she said, 'had life been to you the same
weary and wasting burden that it is to me—that it is to every noble and
generous mind. But you—wretch! you could creep through the world
unaffected by its various disgraces, its ineffable miseries, its constantly
accumulating masses of crime and sorrow: you could live and enjoy
yourself, while the noble-minded are betrayed—while nameless
and birthless villains tread on the neck of the brave and the long-
descended: you could enjoy yourself, like a butcher's dog in the shambles, battening on garbage, while the slaughter of the oldest and best
went on around you! This enjoyment you shall not live to partake of;
you shall die, base dog, and that before yon cloud has passed over the
sun.'

She gave a brief command in Gaelic to her attendants, two of whom
seized upon the prostrate suppliant, and hurried him to the brink of a
cliff which overhung the flood. He set up the most piercing and dreadful cries that fear ever uttered—I may well term them dreadful, for
they haunted my sleep for years afterwards. As the murderers, or executioners, call them as you will, dragged him along, he recognised me
even in that moment of horror, and exclaimed, in the last articulate
words I ever heard him utter, 'O, Mr Osbaldistone, save me!—save
me!'

I was so much moved by this horrid spectacle, that, although in
momentary expectation of sharing his fate, I did attempt to speak in his
behalf, but, as might have been expected, my interference was sternly
disregarded. The victim was held fast by some, while others, binding a
large heavy stone in a plaid, tied it round his neck, and others again
eagerly stripped him of some part of his dress. Half-naked, and thus
manacled, they hurled him into the lake, there about twelve feet deep,
with a loud halloo of vindictive triumph, above which, however, his

last death-shriek, the yell of mortal agony, was distinctly heard. The heavy burden splashed in the dark-blue waters, and the Highlanders, with their pole-axes and swords, watched an instant, to guard, lest, extricating himself from the load to which he was attached, the victim might have struggled to regain the shore. But the knot had been securely bound; the wretched man sunk without effort; the waters, which his fall had disturbed, settled calmly over him, and the unit of that life for which he had pleaded so strongly, was for ever withdrawn from the sum of human existence.

CHAPTER XXXII

And be he safe restored ere evening set,
Or, if there's vengeance in an injured heart,
And power to wreak it in an armed hand,
Your land shall ache for't.

*Old Play**

I KNOW not why it is, that a single deed of violence and cruelty affects our nerves more than when these are exercised on a more extended scale. I had seen that day several of my brave countrymen fall in battle—it seemed to me that they met a lot appropriate to humanity; and my bosom, though thrilling with interest, was affected with nothing of that sickening horror with which I beheld the unfortunate Morris put to death without resistance, and in cold blood. I looked at my companion, Mr Jarvie, whose face reflected the feelings which were painted in mine. Indeed, he could not so suppress his horror, but that the words escaped him in a low and broken whisper,——

'I take up my protest against this deed, as a bloody and cruel murder—it is a cursed deed, and God will avenge it in his due way and time.'

'Then you do not fear to follow?' said the virago, bending on him a look of death, such as that with which a hawk looks at his prey ere he pounces.

'Kinswoman,' said the Bailie, 'nae man willingly wad cut short his thread of life before the end o' his pirn was fairly measured off on the yarn-winles—And I hae muckle to do, an I be spared, in this warld—public and private business, as weel that belanging to the magistracy as to my ain particular—and nae doubt I hae some to depend on me, as puir Mattie, wha is an orphan—She's a far-awa' cousin o' the Laird o' Limmerfield—Sae that, laying a' this thegither—skin for skin, yea all that a man hath will he give for his life.'

'And were I to set you at liberty,' said the imperious dame, 'what name would you give to the drowning of that Saxon dog?'

'Uh! uh!—hem! hem!' said the Bailie, clearing his throat as well as he could, 'I suld study to say as little on that score as might be—least said is sunest mended.'

'But if you were called on by the courts, as you term them, of justice,' she again demanded, 'what then would be your answer?'

The Bailie looked this way and that way, like a person who meditates an escape, and then answered in the tone of one who, seeing no means of accomplishing a retreat, determines to stand the brunt of battle,—'I see what you are driving me to the wa' about. But I'll tell you't plain, kinswoman, I behoved just to speak according to my ain conscience; and though your ain gudeman, that I wish had been here for his ain sake and mine, as weel as the puir Hieland creature Dougal, can tell ye that Nicol Jarvie can wink as hard at a friend's failings as ony body, yet I'se tell ye, kinswoman, mine's ne'er be the tongue to belie my thought; and sooner than say that yonder puir wretch was lawfully slaughtered, I wad consent to be laid beside him—though I think ye are the first Hieland woman wad mint sic a doom to her husband's kinsman but four times removed.'

It is probable that the tone of firmness assumed by the Bailie in his last speech was better suited to make an impression on the hard heart of his kinswoman than the tone of supplication he had hitherto assumed, as gems can be cut with steel, though they resist softer metals. She commanded us both to be placed before her. 'Your name,' she said to me, 'is Osbaldistone?—the dead dog, whose death you have witnessed, called you so.'

'My name *is* Osbaldistone,' was my answer.

'Rashleigh, then, I suppose, is your Christian name?' she pursued.

'No; my name is Francis.'

'But you know Rashleigh Osbaldistone?' she continued. 'He is your brother, if I mistake not, at least your kinsman and near friend.'

'He is my kinsman,' I replied, 'but not my friend. We were lately engaged together in a rencontre, when we were separated by a person whom I understand to be your husband. My blood is hardly yet dried on his sword, and the wound on my side is yet green. I have little reason to acknowledge him as a friend.'

'Then,' she replied, 'if a stranger to his intrigues, you can go in safety to Garschattachin and his party, without fear of being detained, and carry them a message from the wife of the MacGregor?'

I answered, 'That I knew no reasonable cause why the militia gentlemen should detain me; that I had no reason, on my own account, to fear being in their hands; and that if my going on her embassy would act as a protection to my friend and servant, who were her prisoners, I was ready to set out directly.' I took the opportunity to say, 'That I had come into this country on her husband's invitation, and his assurance that he would aid me in some important matters in which I was interested; that my companion, Mr Jarvie, had accompanied me on the same errand.'

'And I wish Mr Jarvie's boots had been fu' o' boiling water when he drew them on for sic a purpose,' interrupted the Bailie.

'You may read your father,' said Helen MacGregor, turning to her sons, 'in what this young Saxon tells us—Wise only when the bonnet is on his head, and the sword is in his hand, he never exchanges the tartan for the broad-cloth, but he runs himself into the miserable intrigues of the Lowlanders, and becomes again, after all he has suffered, their agent—their tool—their slave.'

'Add, madam,' said I, 'and their benefactor.'

'Be it so,' she said; 'for it is the most empty title of them all, since he has uniformly sown benefits to reap a harvest of the most foul ingratitude.—But enough of this.—I shall cause you to be guided to the enemy's outposts—ask for their commander, and deliver him this message from me, Helen MacGregor;—that if they injure a hair of MacGregor's head, and if they do not set him at liberty within the space of twelve hours, there is not a lady in the Lennox but shall before Christmas cry the coronach for them she will be loath to lose,—there is not a farmer but shall sing well-a-wa over a burnt barnyard and an empty byre,—there is not a laird nor heritor shall lay his head on the pillow at night with the assurance of being a live man in the morning,—and, to begin as we are to end, so soon as the term is expired, I will send them this Glasgow Bailie, and this Saxon Captain, and all the rest of my prisoners, each bundled in a plaid, and chopped into as many pieces as there are checks in the tartan.'

As she paused in her denunciation, Captain Thornton, who was within hearing, added with great coolness, 'Present my compliments—Captain Thornton's, of the Royals, compliments—to the commanding officer, and tell him to do his duty and secure his prisoner, and not waste a thought upon me. If I have been fool enough to have been led into an ambuscade by these artful savages, I am wise enough to know how to die for it without disgracing the service. I am only sorry for my poor fellows,' he said, 'that have fallen into such butcherly hands.'

'Whisht! whisht!' exclaimed the Bailie; 'are ye weary o' your life?—Ye'll gie *my* service to the commanding officer, Mr Osbaldistone—Bailie Nicol Jarvie's service, a magistrate o' Glasgow, as his father the deacon was before him—and tell him, here are a wheen honest men in great trouble, and like to come to mair; and the best thing he can do for the common good, will be just to let Rob come his wa's up the glen, and nae mair about it—There's been some ill dune here already, but as it has lighted chiefly on the gauger, it winna be muckle worth making a stir about.'

With these very opposite injunctions from the parties chiefly interested in the success of my embassy, and with the reiterated charge of the wife of MacGregor, to remember and detail every word of her injunctions, I was at length suffered to depart; and Andrew Fairservice, chiefly, I believe, to get rid of his clamorous supplications, was permitted to attend me. Doubtful, however, that I might use my horse as a means of escape from my guides, or desirous to retain a prize of some value, I was given to understand that I was to perform my journey on foot, escorted by Hamish MacGregor, the elder brother, who, with two followers, attended, as well to show me the way, as to reconnoitre the strength and position of the enemy. Dougal had been at first ordered on this party, but he contrived to elude the service, with the purpose, as we afterwards understood, of watching over Mr Jarvie, whom, according to his wild principles of fidelity, he considered as entitled to his good offices, from having once acted in some measure as his patron or master.

After walking with great rapidity about an hour, we arrived at an eminence covered with brushwood, which gave us a commanding prospect down the valley, and a full view of the post which the militia occupied. Being chiefly cavalry, they had judiciously avoided any attempt to penetrate the pass which had been so unsuccessfully assayed by Captain Thornton. They had taken up their situation with some military skill, on a rising ground in the centre of the little valley of Aberfoil, through which the river Forth winds its earliest course, and which is formed by two ridges of hills, faced with barricades of limestone rock, intermixed with huge masses of brescia, or pebbles imbedded in some softer substance which has hardened around them like mortar; and surrounded by the more lofty mountains in the distance. These ridges, however, left the valley of breadth enough to secure the cavalry from any sudden surprise by the mountaineers, and they had stationed sentinels and outposts at proper distances from this main body, in every direction, so that they might secure full time to mount and get under arms upon the least alarm. It was not indeed expected at that time, that Highlanders would attack cavalry in an open plain, though late events have shown that they may do so with success.[60] When I first knew the Highlanders, they had almost a superstitious dread of a mounted trooper, the horse being so much more fierce and imposing in his appearance than the little *shelties* of their own hills, and moreover being trained, as the more ignorant mountaineers believed, to fight with his feet and his teeth.

The appearance of the picqueted horses, feeding in this little vale; the forms of the soldiers, as they sate, stood, or walked, in various groups in the vicinity of the beautiful river, and of the bare yet romantic ranges of rock which hedge in the landscape on either side, formed a noble foreground, while far to the eastward the eye caught a glance of the lake of Menteith; and Stirling Castle, dimly seen along with the blue and distant line of the Ochill Mountains, closed the scene.*

After gazing on this landscape with great earnestness, young Mac-Gregor intimated to me that I was to descend to the station of the militia and execute my errand to their commander, enjoining me at the same time, with a menacing gesture, neither to inform them who had guided me to that place, nor where I had parted from my escort. Thus tutored, I descended towards the military post, followed by Andrew, who, only retaining his breeches and stockings of the English costume, without a hat, bare-legged, with brogues on his feet, which Dougal had given him out of compassion, and having a tattered plaid to supply the want of all upper garments, looked as if he had been playing the part of a Highland Tom-of-Bedlam.* We had not proceeded far before we became visible to one of the videttes, who, riding towards us, presented his carabine and commanded me to stand. I obeyed, and when the soldier came up, desired to be conducted to his commanding officer. I was immediately brought where a circle of officers, sitting upon the grass, seemed in attendance upon one of superior rank. He wore a cuirass of polished steel, over which were drawn the insignia of the ancient Order of the Thistle.* My friend Garschattachin, and many other gentlemen, some in uniform, others in their ordinary dress, but all armed and well attended, seemed to receive their orders from this person of distinction. Many servants in rich liveries, apparently a part of his household, were also in waiting.

Having paid to this nobleman the respect which his rank appeared to demand, I acquainted him that I had been an involuntary witness to the king's soldiers having suffered a defeat from the Highlanders at the pass of Loch-Ard, (such I had learned was the name of the place where Mr Thornton was made prisoner,) and that the victors threatened every species of extremity to those who had fallen into their power, as well as to the Low Country in general, unless their Chief, who had that morning been made prisoner, were returned to them uninjured. The Duke (for he whom I addressed was of no lower rank) listened to me with great composure, and then replied, that he should be extremely sorry to expose the unfortunate gentlemen who had been made prisoners to the cruelty of the barbarians into whose hands they had fallen, but that it was folly to suppose that he would deliver up the very author of all these disorders and offences, and so encourage his followers in their license. 'You may return to those who sent you,' he proceeded, 'and inform them, that I shall certainly cause Rob Roy Campbell, whom they call MacGregor, to be executed, by break of day, as an outlaw taken in arms, and deserving death by a thousand acts of violence; that I should be most justly held unworthy of my situation and commission did I act otherwise; that I shall know how to protect the country against their insolent threats of violence; and that if they injure a hair of the head of any of the unfortunate gentlemen whom an unlucky accident has thrown into their power, I will take such ample vengeance, that the very stones of their glens shall sing woe for it this hundred years to come!'

I humbly begged leave to remonstrate respecting the honourable mission imposed on me, and touched upon the obvious danger attending it, when the noble commander replied, 'that, such being the case, I might send my servant.'

'The deil be in my feet,' said Andrew, without either having respect to the presence in which he stood, or waiting till I replied—'the deil be in my feet, if I gang my tae's length. Do the folk think I hae another thrapple in my pouch after John Highlandman's sneckit this ane wi' his joctaleg? or that I can dive doun at the tae side of a Highland loch and rise at the tother, like a shell-drake? Na, na—ilk ane for himsell, and God for us a'. Folk may just mak a page o' their ain age, and serve themsells till their bairns grow up, and gang their ain errands for Andrew. Rob Roy never came near the parish of Dreepdaily, to steal either pippin or pear frae me or mine.'

Silencing my follower with some difficulty, I represented to the Duke the great danger Captain Thornton and Mr Jarvie would certainly be exposed to, and entreated he would make me the bearer of such modified terms as might be the means of saving their lives. I assured him I should decline no danger if I could be of service; but from what I had heard and seen, I had little doubt they would be instantly murdered should the chief of the outlaws suffer death.

The Duke was obviously much affected. 'It was a hard case,' he said, 'and he felt it as such; but he had a paramount duty to perform to the country—Rob Roy must die!'

I own it was not without emotion that I heard this threat of instant death to my acquaintance Campbell, who had so often testified his good-will towards me. Nor was I singular in the feeling, for many of those around the Duke ventured to express themselves in his favour. 'It would be more advisable,' they said, 'to send him to Stirling Castle, and there detain him a close prisoner, as a pledge for the submission and dispersion of his gang. It were a great pity to expose the country to be plundered, which, now that the long nights approached, it would be found very difficult to prevent, since it was impossible to guard every point, and the Highlanders were sure to select those that were left exposed.' They added, that there was great hardship in leaving the unfortunate prisoners to the almost certain doom of massacre denounced against them, which no one doubted would be executed in the first burst of revenge.

Garschattachin ventured yet farther, confiding in the honour of the nobleman whom he addressed, although he knew he had particular reasons for disliking their prisoner. 'Rob Roy,' he said, 'though a kittle neighbour to the Low Country, and particularly obnoxious to his Grace, and though he maybe carried the catheran trade farther than ony man o' his day, was an auld-farrand carle, and there might be some means found of making him hear reason; whereas his wife and sons were reckless fiends, without either fear or mercy about them, and, at the head of a' his limmer loons, would be a worse plague to the country than ever he had been.'

'Pooh! pooh!' replied his Grace, 'it is the very sense and cunning of this fellow which has so long maintained his reign—a mere Highland robber would have been put down in as many weeks as he has flourished years. His gang, without him, is no more to be dreaded as a permanent annoyance—it will no longer exist—than a wasp without its head, which may sting once perhaps, but is instantly crushed into annihilation.'

Garschattachin was not so easily silenced. 'I am sure, my Lord Duke,' he replied, 'I have no favour for Rob, and he as little for me, seeing he has twice cleaned out my ain byres, beside skaith amang my tenants; but, however'———

'But, however, Garschattachin,' said the Duke, with a smile of peculiar expression, 'I fancy you think such a freedom may be pardoned in a friend's friend, and Rob's supposed to be no enemy to Major Galbraith's friends over the water.'*

'If it be so, my lord,' said Garschattachin, in the same tone of jocularity, 'it's no the warst thing I have heard of him. But I wish we heard some news from the clans, that we have waited for sae lang. I vow to God they'll keep a Hielandman's word wi' us—I never kend them better—it's ill drawing boots upon trews.'*

'I cannot believe it,' said the Duke; 'these gentlemen are known to be men of honour, and I must necessarily suppose they are to keep their appointment. Send out two more horsemen to look for our friends. We cannot, till their arrival, pretend to attack the pass where Captain Thornton has suffered himself to be surprised, and which, to my knowledge, ten men on foot might make good against a regiment of the best horse in Europe—Meanwhile let refreshments be given to the men.'

I had the benefit of this last order, the more necessary and acceptable, as I had tasted nothing since our hasty meal at Aberfoil the evening before. The videttes who had been dispatched, returned without tidings of the expected auxiliaries, and sunset was approaching, when a Highlander belonging to the clans whose co-operation was expected, appeared as the bearer of a letter, which he delivered to the Duke with a most profound congé.

'Now will I wad a hogshead of claret,' said Garschattachin, 'that this is a message to tell us that these cursed Highlandmen, whom we have fetched here at the expense of so much plague and vexation, are going to draw off, and leave us to do our own business if we can.'

'It is even so, gentlemen,' said the Duke, reddening with indignation, after having perused the letter, which was written upon a very dirty scrap of paper, but most punctiliously addressed, 'For the much-honoured hands of Ane High and Mighty Prince, the Duke, &c. &c. &c.' 'Our allies,' continued the Duke, 'have deserted us, gentlemen, and have made a separate peace with the enemy.'

'It's just the fate of all alliances,' said Garschattachin; 'the Dutch were gaun to serve us the same gate, if we had not got the start of them at Utrecht.'*

'You are facetious, sir,' said the Duke, with a frown which showed how little he liked the pleasantry, 'but our business is rather of a grave cast just now.—I suppose no gentleman would advise our attempting to penetrate farther into the country, unsupported either by friendly Highlanders, or by infantry from Inversnaid?'

A general answer announced that the attempt would be perfect madness.

'Nor would there be great wisdom,' the Duke added, 'in remaining exposed to a night-attack in this place. I therefore propose that we should retreat to the house of Duchray and that of Gartartan,* and keep safe and sure watch and ward until morning. But before we separate, I will examine Rob Roy before you all, and make you sensible, by your own eyes and ears, of the extreme unfitness of leaving him space for farther outrage.' He gave orders accordingly, and the prisoner was brought before him, his arms belted down above the elbow, and secured to his body by a horse-girth buckled tight behind him. Two non-commissioned officers had hold of him, one on each side, and two file of men with carabines and fixed bayonets attended for additional security.

I had never seen this man in the dress of his country, which set in a striking point of view the peculiarities of his form. A shock-head of red hair, which the hat and periwig of the Lowland costume had in a great measure concealed, was seen beneath the Highland bonnet, and verified the epithet of *Roy*, or Red, by which he was much better known in the Low Country than by any other, and is still, I suppose, best remembered. The justice of the appellation was also vindicated by the appearance of that part of his limbs, from the bottom of his kilt to the top of his short hose, which the fashion of his country dress left bare, and which was covered with a fell of thick, short, red hair, especially around his knees, which resembled in this respect, as well as from their sinewy appearance of extreme strength, the limbs of a red-coloured Highland bull. Upon the whole, betwixt the effect produced by the change of dress, and by my having become acquainted with his real and formidable character, his appearance had acquired to my eyes something so much wilder and more striking than it before presented, that I could scarce recognise him to be the same person.

His manner was bold, unconstrained unless by the actual bonds, haughty, and even dignified. He bowed to the Duke, nodded to Garschattachin and others, and showed some surprise at seeing me among the party.

'It is long since we have met, Mr Campbell,' said the Duke.

'It is so, my Lord Duke; I could have wished it had been,' (looking at the fastening on his arms,) 'when I could have better paid the compliments I owe to your Grace—but there's a gude time coming.'

'No time like the time present, Mr Campbell,' answered the Duke, 'for the hours are fast flying that must settle your last account with all mortal affairs. I do not say this to insult your distress; but you must be aware yourself that you draw near the end of your career. I do not deny that you may sometimes have done less harm than others of your unhappy trade, and that you may occasionally have exhibited marks of talent, and even of a disposition which promised better things. But you are aware how long you have been the terror and the oppressor of a peaceful neighbourhood, and by what acts of violence you have maintained and extended your usurped authority. You know, in short, that you have deserved death, and that you must prepare for it.'

'My lord,' said Rob Roy, 'although I may well lay my misfortunes at your Grace's door, yet I will never say that you yourself have been the wilful and witting author of them. My lord, if I had thought sae, your Grace would not this day have been sitting in judgment on me; for you have been three times within good rifle distance of me when you were thinking but of the red deer, and few people have kend me miss my aim. But as for them that have abused your Grace's ear, and set you up against a man that was ance as peacefu' a man as ony in the land, and made your name the warrant for driving me to utter extremity,—I have had some amends of them, and, for a' that your Grace now says, I expect to live to hae mair.'

'I know,' said the Duke, in rising anger, 'that you are a determined and impudent villain, who will keep his oath if he swears to mischief; but it shall be my care to prevent you. You have no enemies but your own wicked actions.'

'Had I called myself Grahame, instead of Campbell, I might have heard less about them,' answered Rob Roy, with dogged resolution.

'You will do well, sir,' said the Duke, 'to warn your wife and family and followers, to beware how they use the gentlemen now in their hands, as I will requite tenfold on them, and their kin and allies, the slightest injury done to any of his majesty's liege subjects.'

'My lord,' said Roy in answer, 'none of my enemies will allege that I have been a bloodthirsty man, and were I now wi' my folk, I could rule four or five hundred wild Hielanders as easy as your Grace those eight or ten lackeys and foot-boys. But if your Grace is bent to take the head away from a house, ye may lay your account there will be misrule amang the members.—However, come o't what like, there's an honest man, a kinsman o' my ain, maun come by nae skaith.—Is there ony body here wad do a gude deed for MacGregor?—he may repay it, though his hands be now tied.'

The Highlander who had delivered the letter to the Duke replied, 'I'll do your will for you, MacGregor; and I'll gang back up the glen on purpose.'

He advanced, and received from the prisoner a message to his wife, which, being in Gaelic, I did not understand, but I had little doubt it related to some measures to be taken for the safety of Mr Jarvie.

'Do you hear the fellow's impudence?' said the Duke; 'he confides in his character of a messenger. His conduct is of a piece with his masters', who invited us to make common cause against these freebooters, and have deserted us so soon as the MacGregors have agreed to surrender the Balquidder lands they were squabbling about.

"No truth in plaids, no faith in tartan trews!
Cameleon-like, they change a thousand hues."'*

'Your great ancestor never said so, my lord,' answered Major Galbraith; 'and, with submission, neither would your Grace have occasion to say it, wad ye but be for beginning justice at the well-head—Gie the honest man his mear again—Let every head wear its ain bannet, and the distractions o' the Lennox wad be mended wi' them o' the land.'

'Hush! hush! Garschattachin,' said the Duke; 'this is language dangerous for you to talk to any one, and especially to me; but I presume you reckon yourself a privileged person. Please to draw off your party towards Gartartan; I shall myself see the prisoner escorted to Duchray, and send you orders to-morrow. You will please grant no leave of absence to any of your troopers.'

'Here's auld ordering and counter-ordering,' muttered Garschattachin between his teeth. 'But patience! patience!—we may ae day play at Change seats, the king's coming.'

The two troops of cavalry now formed, and prepared to march off the ground, that they might avail themselves of the remainder of daylight to get to their evening quarters. I received an intimation, rather than an invitation, to attend the party; and I perceived, that, though no longer considered as a prisoner, I was yet under some sort of suspicion. The times were indeed so dangerous,—the great party questions of Jacobite and Hanoverian divided the country so effectually,—and the constant disputes and jealousies between the Highlanders and Lowlanders, besides a number of inexplicable causes of feud which separated the great leading families in Scotland from each other, occasioned such general suspicion, that a solitary and unprotected stranger was almost sure to meet with something disagreeable in the course of his travels.

I acquiesced, however, in my destination with the best grace I could, consoling myself with the hope that I might obtain from the captive freebooter some information concerning Rashleigh and his machinations. I should do myself injustice did I not add, that my views were not merely selfish. I was too much interested in my singular acquaintance not to be desirous of rendering him such services as his unfortunate situation might demand, or admit of his receiving.

CHAPTER XXXIII

And when he came to broken brigg,
He bent his bow and swam;
And when he came to grass growing,
Set down his feet and ran.

Gil Morrice*

THE echoes of the rocks and ravines, on either side, now rang to the trumpets of the cavalry, which, forming themselves into two distinct bodies, began to move down the valley at a slow trot. That commanded by Major Galbraith soon took to the right hand, and crossed the Forth, for the purpose of taking up the quarters assigned them for the night, when they were to occupy, as I understood, an old castle in the vicinity. They formed a lively object while crossing the stream, but were soon lost in winding up the bank on the opposite side, which was clothed with wood.

We continued our march with considerable good order. To ensure the safe custody of the prisoner, the Duke had caused him to be placed on horseback behind one of his retainers, called, as I was informed, Ewan of Brigglands, one of the largest and strongest men who were present. A horse-belt, passed round the bodies of both, and buckled before the yeoman's breast, rendered it impossible for Rob Roy to free himself from his keeper. I was directed to keep close beside them, and accommodated for the purpose with a troop-horse. We were as closely surrounded by the soldiers as the width of the road would permit, and had always at least one, if not two, on each side with pistol in hand. Andrew Fairservice, furnished with a Highland pony of which they had made prey somewhere or other, was permitted to ride among the other domestics, of whom a great number attended the line of march, though without falling into the ranks of the more regularly trained troopers.

In this manner we travelled for a certain distance, until we arrived at a place where we also were to cross the river.* The Forth, as being the outlet of a lake, is of considerable depth, even where less important in point of width, and the descent to the ford was by a broken precipitous ravine, which only permitted one horseman to descend at once. The rear and centre of our small body halting on the bank while the front files passed down in succession, produced a considerable delay, as is usual on such occasions, and even some confusion; for a number of those riders, who made no proper part of the squadron, crowded to the ford without regularity, and made the militia cavalry, although tolerably well drilled, partake in some degree of their own disorder.

It was while we were thus huddled together on the bank that I heard Rob Roy whisper to the man behind whom he was placed on horse-back, 'Your father, Ewan, wadna hae carried an auld friend to the shambles, like a calf, for a' the Dukes in Christendom.'

Ewan returned no answer, but shrugged, as one who would express by that sign that what he was doing was none of his own choice.

'And when the MacGregors come down the glen, and ye see toom faulds, a bluidy hearth-stane, and the fire flashing out between the rafters o' your house, ye may be thinking then, Ewan, that were your friend Rob to the fore, you would have had that safe which it will make your heart sair to lose.'

Ewan of Brigglands again shrugged and groaned, but remained silent.

'It's a sair thing,' continued Rob, sliding his insinuations so gently into Ewan's ear that they reached no other but mine, who certainly saw myself in no shape called upon to destroy his prospects of escape—'It's a sair thing, that Ewan of Brigglands, whom Roy Mac-Gregor has helped with hand, sword, and purse, suld mind a gloom from a great man mair than a friend's life.'

Ewan seemed sorely agitated, but was silent. We heard the Duke's voice from the opposite bank call, 'Bring over the prisoner.'

Ewan put his horse in motion, and just as I heard Roy say, 'Never weigh a MacGregor's bluid against a broken whang o' leather, for there will be another accounting to gie for it baith here and hereafter,' they passed me hastily, and, dashing forward rather precipitately, entered the water.

'Not yet, sir—not yet,' said some of the troopers to me, as I was about to follow, while others pressed forward into the stream.

I saw the Duke on the other side, by the waning light, engaged in commanding his people to get into order, as they landed dispersedly, some higher, some lower. Many had crossed, some were in the water, and the rest were preparing to follow, when a sudden splash warned me that MacGregor's eloquence had prevailed on Ewan to give him freedom and a chance for life. The Duke also heard the sound, and instantly guessed its meaning. 'Dog!' he exclaimed to Ewan as he landed, 'where is your prisoner?' and, without waiting to hear the apology which the terrified vassal began to falter forth, he fired a pistol at his head, whether fatally I know not, and exclaimed, 'Gentlemen, disperse and pursue the villain—An hundred guineas for him that secures Rob Roy!'

All became an instant scene of the most lively confusion. Rob Roy, disengaged from his bonds, doubtless by Ewan's slipping the buckle of his belt, had dropped off at the horse's tail, and instantly dived, passing under the belly of the troop-horse which was on his left hand. But as he was obliged to come to the surface an instant for air, the glimpse of his tartan plaid drew the attention of the troopers, some of whom plunged into the river with a total disregard to their own safety, rushing, according to the expression of their country, through pool and stream, sometimes swimming their horses, sometimes losing them and struggling for their own lives. Others less zealous, or more prudent, broke off in different directions, and galloped up and down the banks, to watch the places at which the fugitive might possibly land. The hollowing, the whooping, the calls for aid at different points, where they saw, or conceived they saw, some vestige of him they were seeking,— the frequent report of pistols and carabines, fired at every object which excited the least suspicion,—the sight of so many horsemen riding about, in and out of the river, and striking with their long broadswords at whatever excited their attention, joined to the vain exertions used by their officers to restore order and regularity; and all this in so wild a scene, and visible only by the imperfect twilight of an autumn evening, made the most extraordinary hubbub I had hitherto witnessed. I was indeed left alone to observe it, for our whole cavalcade had dispersed in pursuit, or at least to see the event of the search. Indeed, as I partly suspected at the time, and afterwards learned with certainty, many of those who seemed most active in their attempts to waylay and recover the fugitive, were, in actual truth, least desirous that he should be taken, and only joined in the cry to increase the general confusion, and to give Rob Roy a better opportunity of escaping.

Escape, indeed, was not difficult for a swimmer so expert as the freebooter, as soon as he had eluded the first burst of pursuit. At one time he was closely pressed, and several blows were made which flashed in the water around him; the scene much resembling one of the otter-hunts which I had seen at Osbaldistone-Hall, where the animal is detected by the hounds from his being necessitated to put his nose above the stream to vent or breathe, while he is enabled to elude them by getting under water again so soon as he has refreshed himself by respiration. MacGregor, however, had a trick beyond the otter; for he contrived, when very closely pursued, to disengage himself unobserved from his plaid, and suffer it to float down the stream, where in its progress it quickly attracted general attention; many of the horsemen were thus put upon a false scent, and several shots or stabs were averted from the party for whom they were designed.

Once fairly out of view, the recovery of the prisoner became almost impossible, since, in so many places, the river was rendered inaccessible by the steepness of its banks, or the thickets of alders, poplars, and birch, which, overhanging its banks, prevented the approach of horsemen. Errors and accidents had also happened among the pursuers, whose task the approaching night rendered every moment more hopeless. Some got themselves involved in the eddies of the stream, and required the assistance of their companions to save them from drowning. Others, hurt by shots or blows in the confused melée, implored help or threatened vengeance, and in one or two instances such accidents led to actual strife. The trumpets, therefore, sounded the retreat, announcing that the commanding officer, with whatsoever unwillingness, had for the present relinquished hopes of the important prize which had thus unexpectedly escaped his grasp, and the troopers began slowly, reluctantly, and brawling with each other as they returned, again to assume their ranks. I could see them darkening, as they formed on the southern bank of the river, whose murmurs, long drowned by the louder cries of vengeful pursuit, were now heard hoarsely mingling with the deep, discontented, and reproachful voices of the disappointed horsemen.

Hitherto I had been as it were a mere spectator, though far from an uninterested one, of the singular scene which had passed. But now I heard a voice suddenly exclaim, 'Where is the English stranger?—It was he gave Rob Roy the knife to cut the belt.'

'Cleave the pock-pudding to the chafts!' cried one voice.

'Weize a brace of balls through his harn-pan!' said a second.

'Drive three inches of cauld airn into his breaskit!' shouted a third.

And I heard several horses galloping to and fro, with the kind purpose, doubtless, of executing these denunciations. I was immediately awakened to the sense of my situation, and to the certainty that armed men, having no restraint whatever on their irritated and inflamed passions, would probably begin by shooting or cutting me down, and afterwards investigate the justice of the action. Impressed by this belief, I leaped from my horse, and turning him loose, plunged into a bush of alder-trees, where, considering the advancing obscurity of the night, I thought there was little chance of my being discovered. Had I been near enough to the Duke to have invoked his personal protection, I would have done so; but he had already commenced his retreat, and I saw no officer on the left bank of the river of authority sufficient to have afforded protection, in case of my surrendering myself. I thought there was no point of honour which could require, in such circumstances, an unnecessary exposure of my life. My first idea, when the tumult began to be appeased, and the clatter of the horses' feet was heard less frequently in the immediate vicinity of my hiding-place, was to seek out the Duke's quarters, when all should be quiet, and give myself up to him, as a liege subject, who had nothing to fear from his justice, and a stranger, who had every right to expect protection and hospitality. With this purpose I crept out of my hiding-place, and looked around me.

The twilight had now melted nearly into darkness; few or none of the troopers were left on my side of the Forth, and of those who were already across it, I only heard the distant trample of the horses' feet, and the wailing and prolonged sound of their trumpets, which rung through the woods to recall stragglers. Here, therefore, I was left in a situation of considerable difficulty. I had no horse, and the deep and wheeling stream of the river, rendered turbid by the late tumult of which its channel had been the scene, and seeming yet more so under the doubtful influence of an imperfect moonlight, had no inviting influence for a pedestrian by no means accustomed to wade rivers, and who had lately seen horsemen weltering, in this dangerous passage, up to the very saddle-laps. At the same time, my prospect, if I remained on the side of the river on which I then stood, could be no other than of concluding the various fatigues of this day and the preceding night, by passing that which was now closing, in *al fresco* on the side of a Highland hill.

After a moment's reflection, I began to consider that Fairservice, who had doubtless crossed the river with the other domestics, according to his forward and impertinent custom of putting himself always among the foremost, could not fail to satisfy the Duke, or the competent authorities, respecting my rank and situation; and that, therefore, my character did not require my immediate appearance, at the risk of being drowned in the river,—of being unable to trace the march of the squadron in case of my reaching the other side in safety,—or, finally, of being cut down, right or wrong, by some straggler, who might think such a piece of good service a convenient excuse for not sooner rejoining his ranks. I therefore resolved to measure my steps back to the little inn, where I had passed the preceding night. I had nothing to apprehend from Rob Roy. He was now at liberty, and I was certain, in case of my falling in with any of his people, the news of his escape would ensure me protection. I might thus also show, that I had no intention to desert Mr Jarvie in the delicate situation in which he had engaged himself, chiefly on my account. And lastly, it was only in this quarter that I could hope to learn tidings concerning Rashleigh and my father's papers, which had been the original cause of an expedition so fraught with perilous adventure. I therefore abandoned all thoughts of crossing the Forth that evening; and, turning my back on the Fords of Frew, began to retrace my steps towards the little village of Aberfoil.

A sharp frost-wind, which made itself heard and felt from time to time, removed the clouds of mist which might otherwise have slumbered till morning on the valley; and, though it could not totally disperse the clouds of vapour, yet threw them in confused and changeful masses, now hovering round the heads of the mountains, now filling, as with a dense and voluminous stream of smoke, the various deep gullies where masses of the composite rock, or brescia, tumbling in fragments from the cliffs, have rushed to the valley, leaving each behind its course a rent and torn ravine resembling a deserted water-course. The moon, which was now high, and twinkled with all the vivacity of a frosty atmosphere, silvered the windings of the river and the peaks and precipices which the mist left visible, while her beams seemed as it were absorbed by the fleecy whiteness of the mist, where it lay thick and condensed; and gave to the more light and vapoury specks, which were elsewhere visible, a sort of filmy transparency resembling the lightest veil of silver gauze. Despite the uncertainty of my situation, a view so romantic, joined to the active and inspiring influence of the frosty atmosphere, elevated my spirits while it braced my nerves. I felt an inclination to cast care away, and bid defiance to danger, and involuntarily whistled, by way of cadence to my steps, which my feeling of the cold led me to accelerate, and I felt the pulse of existence beat prouder and higher in proportion as I felt confidence in my own strength, courage, and resources. I was so much lost in these thoughts, and in the feelings which they excited, that two horsemen came up behind me without my hearing their approach, until one was on each side of me, when the left-hand rider, pulling up his horse, addressed me in the English tongue. 'So ho, friend, whither so late?'

'To my supper and bed at Aberfoil,' I replied.

'Are the passes open?' he enquired, with the same commanding tone of voice.

'I do not know,' I replied; 'I shall learn when I get there; but,' I added, the fate of Morris recurring to my recollection, 'if you are an English stranger, I advise you to turn back till daylight; there has been some disturbance in this neighbourhood, and I should hesitate to say it is perfectly safe for strangers.'

'The soldiers had the worst?—had they not?' was the reply.

'They had indeed; and an officer's party were destroyed or made prisoners.'

'Are you sure of that?' replied the horseman.

'As sure as that I hear you speak,' I replied. 'I was an unwilling spectator of the skirmish.'

'Unwilling?' continued the interrogator. 'Were you not engaged in it then?'

'Certainly no,' I replied; 'I was detained by the king's officer.'

'On what suspicion? and who are you? or what is your name?' he continued.

'I really do not know, sir,' said I, 'why I should answer so many questions to an unknown stranger. I have told you enough to convince you that you are going into a dangerous and distracted country. If you choose to proceed, it is your own affair; but as I ask you no questions respecting your name and business, you will oblige me by making no enquiries after mine.'

'Mr Francis Osbaldistone,' said the other rider, in a voice the tones of which thrilled through every nerve of my body, 'should not whistle his favourite airs when he wishes to remain undiscovered.'

And Diana Vernon—for she, wrapped in a horseman's cloak, was the last speaker—whistled in playful mimicry the second part of the tune, which was on my lips when they came up.

'Good God!' I exclaimed, like one thunder-struck, 'can it be you, Miss Vernon, on such a spot—at such an hour—in such a lawless country—in such'——

'In such a masculine dress, you would say.—But what would you have?—The philosophy of the excellent Corporal Nym is the best after all—things must be as they may—*pauca verba*.'*

While she was thus speaking, I eagerly took advantage of an unusually bright gleam of moonshine, to study the appearance of her companion; for it may be easily supposed, that finding Miss Vernon in a place so solitary, engaged in a journey so dangerous, and under the protection of one gentleman only, were circumstances to excite every feeling of jealousy, as well as surprise. The rider did not speak with the deep melody of Rashleigh's voice; his tones were more high and commanding; he was taller, moreover, as he sate on horseback, than that first-rate object of my hate and suspicion. Neither did the stranger's address resemble that of any of my other cousins; it had that indescribable tone and manner by which we recognise a man of sense and breeding, even in the first few sentences he speaks.

The object of my anxiety seemed desirous to get rid of my investigation.

'Diana,' he said, in a tone of mingled kindness and authority, 'give your cousin his property, and let us not spend time here.'

Miss Vernon had in the meantime taken out a small case, and leaning down from her horse towards me, she said, in a tone in which an effort at her usual quaint lightness of expression contended with a deeper and more grave tone of sentiment, 'You see, my dear coz, I was born to be your better angel. Rashleigh has been compelled to yield up his spoil, and had we reached this same village of Aberfoil last night, as we purposed, I should have found some Highland sylph to have wafted to you all these representatives of commercial wealth. But there were giants and dragons in the way; and errant-knights and damsels of modern times, bold though they be, must not, as of yore, run into useless danger—Do not you do so either, my dear coz.'

'Diana,' said her companion, 'let me once more warn you that the evening waxes late, and we are still distant from our home.'

'I am coming, sir, I am coming—consider,' she added, with a sigh, 'how lately I have been subjected to control—besides, I have not yet given my cousin the packet—and bid him farewell—for ever.—Yes, Frank,' she said, '*for ever!*—there is a gulf between us—a gulf of absolute perdition—where we go, you must not follow—what we do, you must not share in—farewell—be happy!'

In the attitude in which she bent from her horse, which was a

Highland pony, her face, not perhaps altogether unwillingly, touched mine—She pressed my hand, while the tear that trembled in her eye found its way to my cheek instead of her own. It was a moment never to be forgotten—inexpressibly bitter, yet mixed with a sensation of pleasure so deeply soothing and affecting, as at once to unlock all the flood-gates of the heart. It was *but* a moment, however; for, instantly recovering from the feeling to which she had involuntarily given way, she intimated to her companion she was ready to attend him, and putting their horses to a brisk pace, they were soon far distant from the place where I stood.

Heaven knows, it was not apathy which loaded my frame and my tongue so much, that I could neither return Miss Vernon's half embrace, nor even answer her farewell. The word, though it rose to my tongue, seemed to choke in my throat like the fatal *guilty*, which the delinquent who makes it his plea knows must be followed by the doom of death. The surprise—the sorrow, almost stupified me. I remained motionless with the packet in my hand, gazing after them, as if endeavouring to count the sparkles which flew from the horses' hoofs. I continued to look after even these had ceased to be visible, and to listen for their footsteps long after the last distant trampling had died in my ears. At length, tears rushed to my eyes, glazed as they were by the exertion of straining after what was no longer to be seen. I wiped them mechanically, and almost without being aware that they were flowing, but they came thicker and thicker. I felt the tightening of the throat and breast, the *hysterica passio* of poor Lear;* and, sitting down by the wayside, I shed a flood of the first and most bitter tears which had flowed from my eyes since childhood.

CHAPTER XXXIV

Dangle. Egad, I think the interpreter is the harder to be understood of the two.

*Critic**

I HAD scarce given vent to my feelings in this paroxysm, ere I was ashamed of my weakness. I remembered that I had been for some time endeavouring to regard Diana Vernon, when her idea intruded itself on my remembrance, as a friend, for whose welfare I should indeed always be anxious, but with whom I could have little further communication. But the almost unrepressed tenderness of her manner, joined to the romance of our sudden meeting where it was so little to have been expected, were circumstances which threw me entirely off my guard. I recovered, however, sooner than might have been expected, and without giving myself time accurately to examine my motives, I resumed the path on which I had been travelling when overtaken by this strange and unexpected apparition.

I am not, was my reflection, transgressing her injunction so pathetically given, since I am but pursuing my own journey by the only open route. If I have succeeded in recovering my father's property, it still remains incumbent on me to see my Glasgow friend delivered from the situation in which he has involved himself on my account; besides, what other place of rest can I obtain for the night excepting at the little inn of Aberfoil? They also must stop there, since it is impossible for travellers on horseback to go farther—Well then we shall meet again—meet for the last time perhaps—but I shall see and hear her—I shall learn who this happy man is who exercises over her the authority of a husband—I shall learn if there remains, in the difficult course in which she seems engaged, any difficulty which my efforts may remove, or aught that I can do to express my gratitude for her generosity—for her disinterested friendship.—

As I reasoned thus with myself, colouring with every plausible pretext which occurred to my ingenuity, my passionate desire once more to see and converse with my cousin, I was suddenly hailed by a touch on the shoulder; and the deep voice of a Highlander, who, walking still faster than I, though I was proceeding at a smart pace, accosted me with, 'A braw night, Maister Osbaldistone—we have met at the mirk hour before now.'

There was no mistaking the tone of MacGregor; he had escaped the pursuit of his enemies, and was in full retreat to his own wilds and to his adherents. He had also contrived to arm himself, probably at the house of some secret adherent, for he had a musket on his shoulder, and the usual Highland weapons by his side. To have found myself alone with such a character in such a situation, and at this late hour in the evening, might not have been pleasant to me in any ordinary mood of mind; for, though habituated to think of Rob Roy in rather a friendly point of view, I will confess frankly that I never heard him speak but that it seemed to thrill my blood. The intonation of the mountaineers gives a habitual depth and hollowness to the sound of their words, owing to the guttural expression so common in their native language, and they usually speak with a good deal of emphasis. To these national peculiarities Rob Roy added a sort of hard indifference of accent and manner, expressive of a mind neither to be daunted, nor surprised, nor affected, by what passed before him, however dreadful, however sudden, however afflicting. Habitual danger, with unbounded confidence in his own strength and sagacity, had rendered him indifferent to fear; and the lawless and precarious life he led had blunted, though its dangers and errors had not destroyed, his feelings for others. And it was to be remembered, that I had very lately seen the followers of this man commit a cruel slaughter on an unarmed and suppliant individual.

Yet such was the state of my mind, that I welcomed the company of the outlaw leader as a relief to my own overstrained and painful thoughts; and was not without hopes, that through his means I might obtain some clew of guidance through the maze in which my fate had involved me. I therefore answered his greeting cordially, and congratulated him on his late escape in circumstances when escape seemed impossible.

'Ay,' he replied, 'there is as much between the craig and the woodie[61] as there is between the cup and the lip. But my peril was less than you may think, being a stranger to this country. Of those that were summoned to take me, and to keep me, and to retake me again, there was a moiety, as cousin Nicol Jarvie calls it, that had nae will that I suld be either taen, or keepit fast, or retaen; and of t'other moiety, there was ae half was feared to stir me; and so I had only like the fourth part of fifty or sixty men to deal withal.'

'And enough too, I should think,' replied I.

'I dinna ken that,' said he; 'but I ken, that turn every ill-willer that I had amang them out upon the green before the Clachan of Aberfoil, I wad find them play with broadsword and target, one down and another come on.'

He now enquired into my adventures since we entered his country, and laughed heartily at my account of the battle we had in the inn, and at the exploits of the Bailie with the red-hot poker.

'Let Glasgow Flourish!'* he exclaimed. 'The curse of Cromwell* on me, if I wad hae wished better sport than to see cousin Nicol Jarvie singe Iverach's plaid, like a sheep's head between a pair of tongs. But my cousin Jarvie,' he added more gravely, 'has some gentleman's bluid in his veins, although he has been unhappily bred up to a peaceful and mechanical craft, which could not but blunt any pretty man's spirit.— Ye may estimate the reason why I could not receive you at the Clachan of Aberfoil, as I purposed. They had made a fine hose-net for me when I was absent twa or three days at Glasgow, upon the king's business— but I think I broke up the league about their lugs—they'll no be able to hound one clan against another as they hae dune.—I hope soon to see the day when a' Hielandmen will stand shouther to shouther.—But what chanced next?'

I gave him an account of the arrival of Captain Thornton and his party, and the arrest of the Bailie and myself, under pretext of our being suspicious persons; and upon his more special enquiry, I recollected the officer had mentioned that, besides my name sounding suspicious in his ears, he had orders to secure an old and young person, resembling our description. This again moved the outlaw's risibility.

'As man lives by bread,' he said, 'the buzzards have mistaen my friend the Bailie for his Excellency, and you for Diana Vernon—O, the most egregious night-howlets!'

'Miss Vernon?' said I, with hesitation, and trembling for the answer—'Does she still bear that name?—She passed but now, along with a gentleman who seemed to use a style of authority.'

'Ay, ay!' answered Rob, 'she's under lawfu' authority now; and full time, for she was a daft hempie—But she's a mettle quean. It's a pity his Excellency is a thought eldern. The like o' yoursell, or my son Hamish, wad be mair sortable in point of years.'

Here, then, was a complete downfall of those castles of cards which my fancy had, in despite of my reason, so often amused herself with building. Although in truth I had scarcely any thing else to expect, since I could not suppose that Diana could be travelling in such a country, at such an hour, with any but one who had a legal title to protect her, I did not feel the blow less severely when it came, and Mac-Gregor's voice, urging me to pursue my story, sounded in my ears without conveying any exact import to my mind.

'You are ill,' he said, at length, after he had spoken twice without receiving an answer; 'this day's wark has been ower muckle for ane doubtless unused to sic things.'

The tone of kindness in which this was spoken recalling me to myself, and to the necessities of my situation, I continued my narrative as well as I could.—Rob Roy expressed great exultation at the successful skirmish in the pass.

'They say,' he observed, 'that king's chaff is better than other folk's corn; but I think that canna be said o' king's soldiers, if they let themselves be beaten wi' a wheen auld carles that are past fighting, and bairns that are no come till't, and wives wi' their rocks and distaffs, the very wally-draigles o' the country-side—and Dougal Gregor, too, wha wad hae thought there had been as muckle sense in his tatty pow, that ne'er had a better covering than his ain shaggy hassock of hair!—But say away—though I dread what's to come neist,—for my Helen's an incarnate devil when her bluid's up—puir thing, she has ower muckle reason.'

I observed as much delicacy as I could in communicating to him the usage we had received, but I obviously saw the detail gave him great pain.

'I wad rather than a thousand merks,' he said, 'that I had been at hame! To misguide strangers, and forbye a', my ain natural cousin, that had showed me sic kindness—I wad rather they had burned half the Lennox in their folly! But this comes o' trusting women and their bairns, that have neither measure nor reason in their dealings—however, it's a' owing to that dog of a gauger, wha betrayed me by pretending a message from your cousin Rashleigh, to meet him on the king's affairs, whilk I thought was very like to be anent Garschattachin and a party of the Lennox declaring themselves for King James. Faith, but I kend I was clean beguiled when I heard the Duke was there; and when they strapped the horse-girth ower my arms, I might hae judged what was biding me; for I kend your kinsman, being, wi' pardon, a slippery loon himsell, is prone to employ those of his ain kidney—I wish he mayna hae been at the bottom o' the ploy himsell—I thought the chield Morris looked devilish queer when I determined he should remain a wad, or hostage, for my safe back-coming. But I *am* come back, nae thanks to him, or them that employed him, and the question is, how the collector-loon is to win back himsell—I promise him it will not be without ransom.'

'Morris,' said I, 'has already paid the last ransom which mortal man can owe.'

'Eh! What?' exclaimed my companion hastily; 'What d'ye say? I trust it was in the skirmish he was killed?'

'He was slain in cold blood, after the fight was over, Mr Campbell.'

'Cold blood?—Damnation!'—he said, muttering betwixt his teeth—'How fell that, sir?—Speak out, sir, and do not Maister or Campbell me—my foot is on my native heath, and my name is Mac-Gregor!'*

His passions were obviously irritated; but, without noticing the rudeness of his tone, I gave him a short and distinct account of the death of Morris. He struck the but of his gun with great vehemence against the ground, and broke out, 'I vow to God, such a deed might make one forswear kin, clan, country, wife, and bairns!—and yet the villain wrought long for it. And what is the difference between warsling below the water wi' a stane about your neck, and wavering in the wind wi' a tether round it?—it's but choking after a', and he drees the doom he ettled for me. I could have wished, though, they had rather putten a ball through him, or a dirk; for the fashion of remov-ing him will give rise to mony idle clavers—But every wight has his weird, and we maun a' dee when our day comes—And naebody will deny that Helen MacGregor has deep wrongs to avenge.'

So saying, he seemed to dismiss the theme altogether from his mind, and proceeded to enquire how I got free from the party in whose hands he had seen me.

My story was soon told; and I added the episode of my having recovered the papers of my father, though I dared not trust my voice to name the name of Diana.

'I was sure ye wad get them,' said MacGregor; 'the letter ye brought me contained his Excellency's pleasure to that effect; and nae doubt it was my will to have aided in it. And I asked ye up into this glen on the very errand. But it's like his Excellency has forgathered wi' Rashleigh sooner than I expected.'

The first part of this answer was what most forcibly struck me.

'Was the letter I brought you, then, from this person you call his Excellency? Who is he? and what is his rank and proper name?'

'I am thinking,' said MacGregor, 'that since ye dinna ken them already, they canna be o' muckle consequence to you, and sae I shall say naething on that score. But weel I wot the letter was frae his ain hand, or, having a sort of business of my ain on my hands, being, as ye weel may see, just as much as I can fairly manage, I canna say I would hae fashed mysell sae muckle about the matter.'

I now recollected the lights seen in the library—the various circumstances which had excited my jealousy—the glove—the agitation of the tapestry which covered the secret passage from Rashleigh's apartment; and, above all, I recollected that Diana retired, in order to write, as I then thought, the billet to which I was to have recourse in case of the last necessity. Her hours, then, were not spent in solitude, but in listening to the addresses of some desperate agent of Jacobitical treason, who was a secret resident within the mansion of her uncle! Other young women have sold themselves for gold, or suffered themselves to be seduced from their first love from vanity; but Diana had sacrificed my affections and her own to partake the fortunes of some desperate adventurer—to seek the haunts of freebooters through midnight deserts, with no better hopes of rank or fortune than that mimicry of both which the mock court of the Stewarts at St Germains had in their power to bestow.

'I will see her,' I said internally, 'if it be possible, once more. I will argue with her as a friend—as a kinsman—on the risk she is incurring, and I will facilitate her retreat to France, where she may, with more comfort and propriety, as well as safety, abide the issue of the turmoils which the political trepanner, to whom she has united her fate, is doubtless busied in putting into motion.

'I conclude, then,' I said to MacGregor, after about five minutes' silence on both sides, 'that his Excellency, since you give me no other name for him, was residing in Osbaldistone Hall at the same time with myself?'

'To be sure—to be sure—and in the young lady's apartment, as best reason was.' This gratuitous information was adding gall to bitterness. 'But few,' added MacGregor, 'kend he was derned there, save Rashleigh and Sir Hildebrand; for you were out o' the question; and the young lads haena wit eneugh to ca' the cat frae the cream—But it's a bra' auld-fashioned house; and what I specially admire, is the abundance o' holes and bores and concealments—ye could put twenty or thirty men in ae corner, and a family might live a week without finding them out—whilk, nae doubt, may on occasion be a special convenience. I wish we had the like o' Osbaldistone-Hall on the braes o' Craig Royston—But we maun gar woods and caves serve the like o' us puir Hieland bodies.'

'I suppose his Excellency,' said I, 'was privy to the first accident which befell'——

I could not help hesitating a moment.

'Ye were going to say Morris,' said Rob Roy coolly, for he was too much accustomed to deeds of violence for the agitation he had at first expressed to be of long continuance. 'I used to laugh heartily at that reik, but I'll hardly hae the heart to do't again, since the ill-far'd accident at the Loch—Na, na, his Excellency kend nought o' that ploy—it was a' managed atween Rashleigh and mysell. But the sport that came after—and Rashleigh's shift o' turning the suspicion aff himsell upon you, that he had nae grit favour to frae the beginning—and then Miss Die, she maun hae us sweep up a' our spiders' webs again, and set you out o' the Justice's claws—and then the frightened craven, Morris, that was scared out o' his seven senses by seeing the real man when he was charging the innocent stranger—and the gowk of a clerk—and the drunken carle of a justice—Ohon! ohon!—mony a laugh that job's gien me—and now, a' that I can do for the puir devil is to get some messes said for his soul.'

'May I ask,' said I, 'how Miss Vernon came to have so much influence over Rashleigh and his accomplices, as to derange your projected plan?'

'Mine? it was none of mine. No man can say I ever laid my burden on other folk's shoulders—it was a' Rashleigh's doings—But, undoubtedly, she had great influence wi' us baith on account of his Excellency's affection, as weel as that she kend far ower mony secrets to be lightlied in a matter o' that kind.—Deil tak him,' he ejaculated, by way of summing up, 'that gies women either secret to keep or power to abuse—fules shouldna hae chapping sticks.'

We were now within a quarter of a mile from the village, when three Highlanders, springing upon us with presented arms, commanded us to stand and tell our business. The single word *Gregaragh*, in the deep and commanding voice of my companion, was answered by a shout, or rather yell, of joyful recognition. One, throwing down his firelock, clasped his leader so fast round the knees, that he was unable to extricate himself, muttering, at the same time, a torrent of Gaelic gratulation, which every now and then rose into a sort of scream of gladness. The two others, after the first howling was over, set off literally with the speed of deers, contending which should first carry to the village, which a strong party of the MacGregors now occupied, the joyful news of Rob Roy's escape and return. The intelligence excited such shouts of jubilation that the very hills rung again, and young and old, men, women, and children, without distinction of sex or age, came running down the vale to meet us, with all the tumultuous speed and clamour of a mountain torrent. When I heard the rushing noise and yells of this joyful multitude approach us, I thought it a fitting precaution to remind MacGregor that I was a stranger, and under his protection. He accordingly held me fast by the hand, while the assemblage crowded around him with such shouts of devoted attachment, and joy at his return, as were really affecting; nor did he extend to his followers what all eagerly sought, the grasp, namely, of his hand, until he had made them understand that I was to be kindly and carefully used.

The mandate of the Sultan of Delhi* could not have been more promptly obeyed. Indeed, I now sustained nearly as much inconvenience from their well-meant attentions as formerly from their rudeness. They would hardly allow the friend of their leader to walk upon his own legs, so earnest were they in affording me support and assistance upon the way; and at length, taking advantage of a slight stumble which I made over a stone, which the press did not permit me to avoid, they fairly seized upon me, and bore me in their arms in triumph towards Mrs MacAlpine's.

On arrival before her hospitable wigwam, I found power and popularity had its inconveniences in the Highlands, as everywhere else; for, before MacGregor could be permitted to enter the house where he was to obtain rest and refreshment, he was obliged to relate the story of his escape at least a dozen times over, as I was told by an officious old man, who chose to translate it at least as often for my edification, and to whom I was in policy obliged to seem to pay a decent degree of attention. The audience being at length satisfied, group after group departed to take their bed upon the heath, or in the neighbouring huts, some cursing the Duke and Garschattachin, some lamenting the probable danger of Ewan of Brigglands, incurred by his friendship to

MacGregor, but all agreeing that the escape of Rob Roy himself lost nothing in comparison with the exploit of any one of their chiefs since the days of Dougal-Ciar, the founder of his line.*

The friendly outlaw, now taking me by the arm, conducted me into the interior of the hut. My eyes roved round its smoky recesses in quest of Diana and her companion; but they were nowhere to be seen, and I felt as if to make enquiries might betray some secret motives, which were best concealed. The only known countenance upon which my eyes rested, was that of the Bailie, who, seated on a stool by the fire-side, received, with a sort of reserved dignity, the welcomes of Rob Roy, the apologies which he made for his indifferent accommodation, and his enquiries after his health.

'I am pretty weel, kinsman,' said the Bailie, 'indifferent weel, I thank ye; and for accommodations, ane canna expect to carry about the Saut-Market at his tail, as a snail does his caup—and I am blythe that ye hae gotten out o' the hands o' your unfreends.'

'Weel, weel, then,' answered Roy, 'what is't ails ye, man?—a's weel that ends weel!—the warld will last our day—come, take a cup o' brandy—your father the deacon could tak ane at an orra time.'

'It might be he might do sae, Robin, after fatigue—whilk has been my lot mair ways than ane this day. But,' he continued, slowly filling up a little wooden stoup which might hold about three glasses, 'he was a moderate man of his bicker, as I am mysell—Here's wussing health to ye, Robin,' (a sip,) 'and your weelfare here and hereafter,' (another taste,) 'and also to my cousin Helen—and to your twa hopefu' lads, of whom mair anon.'

So saying, he drank up the contents of the cup with great gravity and deliberation, while MacGregor winked aside to me, as if in ridicule of the air of wisdom and superior authority which the Bailie assumed towards him in their intercourse, and which he exercised when Rob was at the head of his armed clan, in full as great, or a greater degree, than when he was at the Bailie's mercy in the Tolbooth of Glasgow. It seemed to me, that MacGregor wished me, as a stranger, to understand, that if he submitted to the tone which his kinsman assumed, it was partly out of deference to the rights of hospitality, but still more for the jest's sake.

As the Bailie set down his cup he recognised me, and giving me a cordial welcome on my return, he waived farther communication with me for the present.

'I will speak to your matters anon; I maun begin, as in reason, wi' those of my kinsman.—I presume, Robin, there's naebody here will carry aught o' what I am gaun to say, to the town-council or elsewhere, to my prejudice or to yours?'

'Make yourself easy on that head, cousin Nicol,' answered Mac-Gregor; 'the tae half o' the gillies winna ken what ye say, and the tother winna care—besides, that I wad stow the tongue out o' the head o' ony o' them that suld presume to say ower again ony speech held wi' me in their presence.'

'Aweel, cousin, sic being the case, and Mr Osbaldistone here being a prudent youth, and a safe friend—I'se plainly tell ye, ye are breeding up your family to gang an ill gate.'—Then clearing his voice with a preliminary hem, he addressed his kinsman, checking, as Malvolio proposed to do when seated in his state, his familiar smile with an austere regard of control.*—'Ye ken yoursell ye haud light by the law—and for my cousin Helen, forbye that her reception o' me this blessed day, whilk I excuse on account of perturbation of mind, was muckle on the north side o' *friendly*, I say (out-putting this personal reason of complaint) I hae that to say o' your wife'——

'Say *nothing* of her, kinsman,' said Rob, in a grave and stern tone, 'but what is befitting a friend to say, and her husband to hear. Of me you are welcome to say your full pleasure.'

'Aweel, aweel,' said the Bailie, somewhat disconcerted, 'we'se let that be a pass-over—I dinna approve of making mischief in families—But here are your twa sons, Hamish and Robin, whilk signifies, as I'm gien to understand, James and Robert—I trust ye will call them sae in future—there comes nae gude o' Hamishes, and Eachines, and Angusses, except that they're the names ane aye chances to see in the indictments at the Western Circuits for cow-lifting, at the instance of his majesty's advocate for his majesty's interest—aweel, but the twa lads, as I was saying, they haena sae muckle as the ordinar grunds, man, of liberal education—they dinna ken the very multiplication-table itself, whilk is the root of a' usefu' knowledge, and they did naething but laugh and fleer at me when I tauld them my mind on their ignorance—It's my belief they can neither read, write, nor cipher, if sic a thing could be believed o' ane's ain connexions in a Christian land.'

'If they could, kinsman,' said MacGregor, with great indifference, 'their learning must have come o' free will, for whar the deil was I to get them a teacher?—wad ye hae had me put on the gate o' your Divinity-Hall at Glasgow College, "Wanted, a tutor for Rob Roy's bairns?"'

'Na, kinsman,' replied Mr Jarvie, 'but ye might hae sent the lads whar they could hae learned the fear o' God, and the usages of civilized creatures. They are as ignorant as the kyloes ye used to drive to market, or the very English churls that ye sauld them to, and can do naething whatever to purpose.'

'Umph!' answered Rob; 'Hamish can bring doun a black-cock when he's on the wing wi' a single bullet, and Rob can drive a dirk through a twa-inch board.'

'Sae muckle the waur for them, cousin! Sae muckle the waur for them baith!' answered the Glasgow merchant in a tone of great decision; 'an they ken naething better than that, they had better no ken that neither. Tell me yoursell, Rob, what has a' this cutting, and stabbing, and shooting, and driving of dirks, whether through human flesh or fir deals, dune for yoursell? and werena ye a happier man at the tail o' your nowte-bestial, when ye were in an honest calling, than ever ye hae been since, at the head o' your Hieland kernes and gally-glasses?'

I observed that MacGregor, while his well-meaning kinsman spoke to him in this manner, turned and writhed his body like a man who indeed suffers pain, but is determined no groan shall escape his lips; and I longed for an opportunity to interrupt the well-meant, but, as it was obvious to me, quite mistaken strain, in which Jarvie addressed this extraordinary person. The dialogue, however, came to an end without my interference.

'And sae,' said the Bailie, 'I hae been thinking, Rob, that as it may be ye are ower deep in the black book to win a pardon, and ower auld to mend yoursell, that it wad be a pity to bring up twa hopefu' lads to sic a godless trade as your ain, and I wad blithely tak them for prentices at the loom, as I began mysell and my father the deacon afore me, though, praise to the Giver, I only trade now as wholesale dealer—And—and'——

He saw a storm gathering on Rob's brow, which probably induced him to throw in, as a sweetener of an obnoxious proposition, what he had reserved to crown his own generosity, had it been embraced as an acceptable one;—'and Robin, lad, ye needna look sae glum, for I'll pay the prentice-fee, and never plague ye for the thousand merks neither.'

'*Ceade millia diaoul*, hundred thousand devils!' exclaimed Rob, rising and striding through the hut. 'My sons weavers!—*Millia molligheart!** but I wad see every loom in Glasgow, beam, traddles, and shuttles, burnt in hell-fire sooner!'

With some difficulty I made the Bailie, who was preparing a reply, comprehend the risk and impropriety of pressing our host on this topic, and in a minute he recovered, or reassumed, his serenity of temper.

'But ye mean weel—ye mean weel,' said he; 'so gie me your hand, Nicol, and if ever I put my sons apprentice, I will gie you the refusal o' them. And, as you say, there's the thousand merks to be settled between us.—Here, Eachin MacAnaleister, bring me my sporran.'

The person he addressed, a tall, strong mountaineer, who seemed to act as MacGregor's lieutenant, brought from some place of safety a large leathern pouch, such as Highlanders of rank wear before them when in full dress, made of the skin of the sea otter, richly garnished with silver ornaments and studs.

'I advise no man to attempt opening this sporran till he has my secret,' said Rob Roy; and then twisting one button in one direction, and another in another, pulling one stud upward, and pressing another downward, the mouth of the purse, which was bound with massive silver-plate, opened and gave admittance to his hand. He made me remark, as if to break short the subject on which Bailie Jarvie had spoken, that a small steel pistol was concealed within the purse, the trigger of which was connected with the mounting, and made part of the machinery, so that the weapon would certainly be discharged, and in all probability its contents lodged in the person of any one, who, being unacquainted with the secret, should tamper with the lock which secured his treasure. 'This,' said he, touching the pistol—'this is the keeper of my privy purse.'

The simplicity of the contrivance to secure a furred pouch, which could have been ripped open without any attempt on the spring, reminded me of the verses in the Odyssey,* where Ulysses, in a yet ruder age, is content to secure his property by casting a curious and involved complication of cordage around the sea-chest in which it was deposited.

The Bailie put on his spectacles to examine the mechanism, and when he had done, returned it with a smile, and a sigh, observing, 'Ah! Rob, had ither folk's purses been as weel guarded, I doubt if your sporran wad hae been as weel filled as it kythes to be by the weight.'

'Never mind, kinsman,' said Rob, laughing, 'it will aye open for a friend's necessity, or to pay a just due—and here,' he added, pulling out a rouleau of gold, 'here is your ten hundred merks—count them, and see that you are full and justly paid.'

Mr Jarvie took the money in silence, and weighing it in his hand for an instant, laid it on the table, and replied, 'Rob, I canna tak it—I downa intromit with it—there can nae gude come o't—I hae seen ower weel the day what sort of a gate your gowd is made in—ill-got gear ne'er prospered; and, to be plain wi' you, I winna meddle wi't—it looks as there might be bluid on't.'

'Troutsho!'* said the outlaw, affecting an indifference which, perhaps, he did not altogether feel, 'it's gude French gowd, and ne'er was in Scotchman's pouch before mine—look at them, man—they are a' louis d'ors, bright and bonnie as the day they were coined.'

'The waur, the waur—just sae muckle the waur, Robin,' replied the Bailie, averting his eyes from the money, though, like Cæsar on the Lupercal,* his fingers seemed to itch for it—'Rebellion is waur than witchcraft, or robbery either; there's gospel warrant for't.'*

'Never mind the warrant, kinsman,' said the freebooter; 'you come by the gowd honestly, and in payment of a just debt—it came from the one king, you may gie it to the other, if ye like; and it will just serve for a weakening of the enemy, and in the point where puir King James is weakest too, for, God knows, he has hands and hearts eneugh, but I doubt he wants the siller.'

'He'll no get mony Hielanders then, Robin,' said Mr Jarvie, as, again replacing his spectacles on his nose, he undid the rouleau, and began to count its contents.

'Nor Lowlanders neither,' said MacGregor, arching his eyebrow, and, as he looked at me, directing a glance towards Mr Jarvie, who, all unconscious of the ridicule, weighed each piece with habitual scrupulosity; and having told twice over the sum, which amounted to the discharge of his debt, principal and interest, he returned three pieces to buy his kinswoman a gown, as he expressed himself, and a brace more for the twa bairns, as he called them, requesting they might buy any thing they liked with them except gunpowder. The Highlander stared at his kinsman's unexpected generosity, but courteously accepted his gift, which he deposited for the time in his well-secured pouch.

The Bailie next produced the original bond for the debt, on the back of which he had written a formal discharge, which, having subscribed himself, he requested me to sign as a witness. I did so, and Bailie Jarvie was looking anxiously around for another, the Scottish law requiring the subscription of two witnesses to validate either a bond or acquittance. 'You will hardly find a man that can write save ourselves within these three miles,' said Rob, 'but I'll settle the matter as easily;' and, taking the paper from before his kinsman, he threw it in the fire. Bailie Jarvie stared in his turn, but his kinsman continued, 'That's a Hieland settlement of accounts—the time might come, cousin, were I to keep a' these charges and discharges, that friends might be brought into trouble for having dealt with me.'

The Bailie attempted no reply to this argument, and our supper now appeared in a style of abundance, and even delicacy, which, for the place, might be considered as extraordinary. The greater part of the provisions were cold, intimating they had been prepared at some distance; and there were some bottles of good French wine to relish pasties of various sorts of game, as well as other dishes. I remarked that MacGregor, while doing the honours of the table with great and anxious hospitality, prayed us to excuse the circumstance that some particular dish or pasty had been infringed on before it was presented to us. 'You must know,' said he to Mr Jarvie, but without looking towards me, 'you are not the only guests this night in the MacGregor's country, whilk, doubtless, ye will believe, since my wife and the twa lads would otherwise have been maist ready to attend you, as weel beseems them.'

Bailie Jarvie looked as if he felt glad at any circumstance which occasioned their absence; and I should have been entirely of his opinion, had it not been that the outlaw's apology seemed to imply they were in attendance on Diana and her companion, whom even in my thoughts I could not bear to designate as her husband.

While the unpleasant ideas arising from this suggestion counteracted the good effects of appetite, welcome, and good cheer, I remarked that Rob Roy's attention had extended itself to providing us better bedding than we had enjoyed the night before. Two of the least fragile of the bedsteads, which stood by the wall of the hut, had been stuffed with heath, then in full flower, so artificially arranged, that, the flowers being uppermost, afforded a mattress at once elastic and fragrant. Cloaks, and such bedding as could be collected, stretched over this vegetable couch, made it both soft and warm. The Bailie seemed exhausted by fatigue. I resolved to adjourn my communication to him until next morning; and therefore suffered him to betake himself to bed so soon as he had finished a plentiful supper. Though tired and harassed, I did not myself feel the same disposition to sleep, but rather a restless and feverish anxiety, which led to some farther discourse betwixt me and MacGregor.

CHAPTER XXXV

A hopeless darkness settles o'er my fate;
I've seen the last look of her heavenly eyes,—
I've heard the last sound of her blessed voice,—
I've seen her fair form from my sight depart:
My doom is closed.

*Count Basil**

'I KEN not what to make of you, Mr Osbaldistone,' said MacGregor, as he pushed the flask towards me. 'You eat not, you show no wish for rest; and yet you drink not, though that flask of Bourdeaux might have come out of Sir Hildebrand's ain cellar. Had you been always as abstinent, you would have escaped the deadly hatred of your cousin Rashleigh.'

'Had I been always prudent,' said I, blushing at the scene he recalled to my recollection, 'I should have escaped a worse evil—the reproach of my own conscience.'

MacGregor cast a keen and somewhat fierce glance on me, as if to read whether the reproof, which he evidently felt, had been intentionally conveyed. He saw that I was thinking of myself, not of him, and turned his face towards the fire with a deep sigh. I followed his example, and each remained for a few minutes wrapt in his own painful reverie. All in the hut were now asleep, or at least silent, excepting ourselves.

MacGregor first broke silence, in the tone of one who takes up his determination to enter on a painful subject. 'My cousin Nicol Jarvie means well,' he said, 'but he presses ower hard on the temper and situation of a man like me, considering what I have been—what I have been forced to become—and, above all, that which has forced me to become what I am.'

He paused; and, though feeling the delicate nature of the discussion in which the conversation was likely to engage me, I could not help replying, that I did not doubt his present situation had much which must be most unpleasant to his feelings. 'I should be happy to learn,' I added, 'that there is an honourable chance of your escaping from it.'

'You speak like a boy,' returned MacGregor, in a low tone that growled like distant thunder—'like a boy, who thinks the auld gnarled oak can be twisted as easily as the young sapling. Can I forget that I have been branded as an outlaw,—stigmatized as a traitor,—a price set on my head as if I had been a wolf,—my family treated as the dam and cubs of the hill-fox, whom all may torment, vilify, degrade, and insult,—the very name which came to me from a long and noble line of martial ancestors, denounced, as if it were a spell to conjure up the devil with?'

As he went on in this manner, I could plainly see, that, by the enumeration of his wrongs, he was lashing himself up into a rage, in order to justify in his own eyes the errors they had led him into. In this he perfectly succeeded; his light grey eyes contracting alternately and dilating their pupils, until they seemed actually to flash with flame, while he thrust forward and drew back his foot, grasped the hilt of his dirk, extended his arm, clenched his fist, and finally rose from his seat.

'And they *shall* find,' he said, in the same muttered, but deep tone of stifled passion, 'that the name they have dared to proscribe—that the name of MacGregor—*is* a spell to raise the wild devil withal.— *They* shall hear of my vengeance, that would scorn to listen to the story of my wrongs—The miserable Highland drover, bankrupt, barefooted,—stripped of all, dishonoured and hunted down, because the avarice of others grasped at more than that poor all could pay, shall burst on them in an awful change. They that scoffed at the grovelling worm, and trode upon him, may cry and howl when they see the stoop of the flying and fiery-mouthed dragon.—But why do I speak of all this?' he said, sitting down again, and in a calmer tone—'Only ye may opine it frets my patience, Mr Osbaldistone, to be hunted like an otter, or a sealgh, or a salmon upon the shallows, and that by my very friends and neighbours; and to have as many sword-cuts made, and pistols flashed at me, as I had this day in the ford of Avondow, would try a saint's temper, much more a Highlander's, who are not famous for that gude gift, as ye may hae heard, Mr Osbaldistone.—But ae thing bides wi' me o' what Nicol said.—I'm vexed for the bairns—I'm vexed when I think o' Hamish and Robert living their father's life.' And yielding to despondence on account of his sons, which he felt not upon his own, the father rested his head upon his hand.

I was much affected, Will. All my life long I have been more melted by the distress under which a strong, proud, and powerful mind is compelled to give way, than by the more easily excited sorrows of softer dispositions. The desire of aiding him rushed strongly on my mind, notwithstanding the apparent difficulty, and even impossibility, of the task.

'We have extensive connexions abroad,' said I; 'might not your sons, with some assistance—and they are well entitled to what my father's house can give—find an honourable resource in foreign service?'

I believe my countenance showed signs of sincere emotion; but my companion, taking me by the hand, as I was going to speak farther, said, 'I thank—I thank ye—but let us say nae mair o' this. I did not think the eye of man would again have seen a tear on MacGregor's eye-lash.' He dashed the moisture from his long grey eye-lash and shaggy red eye-brow with the back of his hand. 'Tomorrow morning,' he said, 'we'll talk of this, and we will talk, too, of your affairs—for we are early starters in the dawn, even when we have the luck to have good beds to sleep in. Will ye not pledge me in a grace cup?' I declined the invitation.

'Then, by the soul of St Maronoch!* I must pledge myself,' and he poured out and swallowed at least half a quart of wine.

I laid myself down to repose, resolving to delay my own enquiries until his mind should be in a more composed state. Indeed, so much had this singular man possessed himself of my imagination, that I felt it impossible to avoid watching him for some minutes after I had flung myself on my heath mattress to seeming rest. He walked up and down the hut, crossed himself from time to time, muttering over some Latin prayer of the Catholic church; then wrapped himself in his plaid, with his naked sword on one side, and his pistol on the other, so disposing the folds of his mantle, that he could start up at a moment's warning, with a weapon in either hand, ready for instant combat. In a few minutes his heavy breathing announced that he was fast asleep. Overpowered by fatigue, and stunned by the various unexpected and extraordinary scenes of the day, I, in my turn, was soon overpowered by a slumber deep and overwhelming, from which, notwithstanding every cause for watchfulness, I did not awake until the next morning.

When I opened my eyes, and recollected my situation, I found that MacGregor had already left the hut. I awakened the Bailie, who, after many a snort and groan, and some heavy complaints of the soreness of his bones, in consequence of the unwonted exertions of the preceding day, was at length able to comprehend the joyful intelligence, that the assets carried off by Rashleigh Osbaldistone had been safely recovered. The instant he understood my meaning he forgot all his grievances, and, bustling up in a great hurry, proceeded to compare the contents of the packet, which I put into his hands, with Mr Owen's memorandums, muttering as he went on, 'Right, right—the real thing—Baillie and Whittington—where's Baillie and Whittington?—seven hundred, six, and eight—exact to a fraction—Pollock and Peelman—twenty-eight, seven—exact—Praise be blest!—Grub and Grinder—better men cannot be—three hundred and seventy—Gliblad—twenty, I doubt Gliblad's ganging—Slipprytongue—Slipprytongue's gaen—but they are sma' sums—sma' sums—the rest's a' right—Praise be blest! we have got the stuff, and may leave this doleful country. I shall never think on Loch-Ard but the thought will gar me grew again.'

'I am sorry, cousin,' said MacGregor, who entered the hut during the last observation, 'I have not been altogether in the circumstances to make your reception sic as I could have desired—natheless, if you would condescend to visit my puir dwelling'——

'Muckle obliged, muckle obliged,' answered Mr Jarvie, very hastily. 'But we maun be ganging—we maun be jogging, Mr Osbaldistone and me—business canna wait.'

'Aweel, kinsman,' replied the Highlander, 'ye ken our fashion—foster the guest that comes—further him that maun gang.—But ye cannot return by Drymen—I must set ye on Loch Lomond, and boat ye down to the Ferry o' Balloch,* and send your nags round to meet ye there—It's a maxim of a wise man never to return by the same road he came, providing another's free to him.'

'Ay, ay, Rob,' said the Bailie, 'that's ane o' the maxims ye learned when ye were a drover—ye caredna to face the tenants where your beasts had been taking a rug of their moorland grass in the by-ganging—and I doubt your road's waur marked now than it was then.'

'The mair need not to travel it ower often, kinsman,' replied Rob; 'but I'se send round your nags to the ferry wi' Dougal Gregor, wha is converted for that purpose into the Bailie's man, coming—not, as ye may believe, from Aberfoil or Rob Roy's country, but on a quiet jaunt from Stirling.—See, here he is.'

'I wadna hae kend the creature,' said Mr Jarvie; nor indeed was it easy to recognise the wild Highlander, when he appeared before the door of the cottage, attired in a hat, periwig, and riding coat, which had once called Andrew Fairservice master, and mounted on the Bailie's horse, and leading mine. He received his last orders from his master to avoid certain places where he might be exposed to suspicion—to collect what intelligence he could in the course of his journey, and to await our coming at an appointed place, near the Ferry of Balloch.

At the same time, MacGregor invited us to accompany him upon our own road, assuring us that we must necessarily march a few miles before breakfast, and recommending a dram of brandy as a proper introduction to the journey, in which he was pledged by the Bailie, who pronounced it 'an unlawful and perilous habit to begin the day wi' spirituous liquors, except to defend the stomach (whilk was a tender part) against the morning mist; in whilk case his father the deacon had recommended a dram, by precept and example.'

'Very true, kinsman,' replied Rob, 'for which reason we, who are Children of the Mist,* have a right to drink brandy from morning till night.'

The Bailie, thus refreshed, was mounted on a small Highland pony; another was offered for my use, which, however, I declined, and we resumed, under very different guidance and auspices, our journey of the preceding day.

Our escort consisted of MacGregor, and five or six of the handsomest, best armed, and most athletic mountaineers of his band, and whom he had generally in immediate attendance upon his own person.

When we approached the pass, the scene of the skirmish of the preceding day, and of the still more direful deed which followed it, MacGregor hastened to speak, as if it were rather to what he knew must be necessarily passing in my mind, than to any thing I had said—he spoke, in short, to my thoughts, and not to my words.

'You must think hardly of us, Mr Osbaldistone, and it is not natural that it should be otherwise. But remember, at least, we have not been unprovoked—we are a rude and an ignorant, and it may be a violent and passionate, but we are not a cruel people—the land might be at peace and in law for us, did they allow us to enjoy the blessings of peaceful law. But we have been a persecuted generation.'

'And persecution,' said the Bailie, 'maketh wise men mad.'*

'What must it do then to men like us, living as our fathers did a thousand years since, and possessing scarce more lights than they did?— Can we view their bluidy edicts against us—their hanging, heading, hounding, and hunting down an ancient and honourable name, as deserving better treatment than that which enemies give to enemies?—

Here I stand, have been in twenty frays, and never hurt man but when I was in het bluid; and yet they wad betray me and hang me like a masterless dog, at the gate of ony great man that has an ill will at me.'

I replied, 'that the proscription of his name and family sounded in English ears as a very cruel and arbitrary law;' and having thus far soothed him, I resumed my propositions of obtaining military employment for himself, if he chose it, and his sons in foreign parts. MacGregor shook me very cordially by the hand, and detaining me, so as to permit Mr Jarvie to precede us, a manœuvre for which the narrowness of the road served as an excuse, he said to me, 'You are a kind-hearted and an honourable youth, and understand, doubtless, that which is due to the feelings of a man of honour.—But the heather that I have trod upon when living, must bloom ower me when I am dead—my heart would sink, and my arm would shrink and wither like fern in the frost, were I to lose sight of my native hills; nor has the world a scene that would console me for the loss of the rocks and cairns, wild as they are, that you see around us.—And Helen—what could become of her, were I to leave her the subject of new insult and atrocity?—or how could she bear to be removed from these scenes, where the remembrance of her wrongs is aye sweetened by the recollection of her revenge?—I was once so hard put at by my Great enemy, as I may well ca' him, that I was forced e'en to gie way to the tide, and removed myself and my people and family from our dwellings in our native land, and to withdraw for a time into MacCallum More's country—and Helen made a Lament on our departure, as weel as MacRimmon[62] himsell could hae framed it—and so piteously sad and waesome, that our hearts amaist broke as we sate and listened to her—it was like the wailing of one that mourns for the mother that bore him—the tears came down the rough faces of our gillies as they hearkened—and I wad not have the same touch of heartbreak again, no, not to have all the lands that ever were owned by MacGregor.'

'But your sons,' I said, 'they are at the age when your countrymen have usually no objection to see the world?'

'And I should be content,' he replied, 'that they pushed their fortune in the French or Spanish service, as is the wont of Scottish cavaliers of honour, and last night your plan seemed feasible enough—But I hae seen his Excellency this morning before ye were up.'

'Did he then quarter so near us?' said I, my bosom throbbing with anxiety.

'Nearer than ye thought,' was MacGregor's reply; 'but he seemed rather in some shape to jalouse your speaking to the young leddy; and so you see'——

'There was no occasion for jealousy,' I answered, with some haughtiness; 'I should not have intruded on his privacy.'

'But ye must not be offended, or look out from amang your curls then, like a wild-cat out of an ivy-tod, for ye are to understand that he wishes most sincere weel to you, and has proved it. And it's partly that whilk has set the heather on fire e'en now.'

'Heather on fire?' said I. 'I do not understand you.'

'Why,' resumed MacGregor, 'ye ken weel eneuch that women and gear are at the bottom of a' the mischief in this warld—I hae been misdoubting your cousin Rashleigh since ever he saw that he wasna to get Die Vernon for his marrow, and I think he took grudge at his Excellency mainly on that account. But then came the splore about the surrendering your papers—and we hae now gude evidence, that, sae soon as he was compelled to yield them up, he rade post to Stirling, and tauld the government all, and mair than all, that was gaun doucely on amang us hill-folk; and, doubtless, that was the way that the country was laid to take his Excellency and the leddy, and to make sic an unexpected raid on me. And I hae as little doubt that the poor deevil Morris, whom he could gar believe ony thing, was egged on by him, and some of the Lowland gentry, to trepan me in the gate he tried to do. But if Rashleigh Osbaldistone were baith the last and best of his name; and granting that he and I ever forgather again, the fiend go down my weasand with a bare blade at his belt, if we part before my dirk and his best bluid are weel acquainted thegither!'

He pronounced the last threat with an ominous frown, and the appropriate gesture of his hand upon his dagger.

'I should almost rejoice at what has happened,' said I, 'could I hope that Rashleigh's treachery might prove the means of preventing the explosion of the rash and desperate intrigues, in which I have long suspected him to be a prime agent.'

'Trow ye na that,' said Rob Roy; 'traitor's word never yet hurt honest cause. He was ower deep in our secrets, that's true; and had it not been so, Stirling and Edinburgh Castles would have been baith in our hands by this time, or briefly hereafter, whilk is now scarce to be hoped for. But there are ower many engaged, and far ower gude a cause to be gien up for the breath of a traitor's tale, and that will be seen and heard of ere it be lang. And so, as I was about to say, the best of my thanks to you for your offer anent my sons, whilk last night I had some thoughts to have embraced in their behalf. But I see that this villain's treason will convince our great folks that they must instantly draw to a head, and make a blow for it, or be taen in their houses, coupled up like hounds, and driven up to London like the honest noblemen and gentlemen in the year seventeen hundred and seven.* Civil war is like a cockatrice; we have sitten hatching the egg that held it for ten years, and might hae sitten on for ten years mair, when in comes Rashleigh, and chips the shell, and out bangs the wonder amang us, and cries to fire and sword. Now in sic a matter I'll hae need o' a' the hands I can mak; and, nae disparagement to the Kings of France and Spain, whom I wish very weel to, King James is as gude a man as ony o' them, and has the best right to Hamish and Rob, being his natural-born subjects.'

I easily comprehended that these words boded a general national convulsion; and, as it would have been alike useless and dangerous to have combatted the political opinions of my guide, at such a place and moment, I contented myself with regretting the promiscuous scene of confusion and distress likely to arise from any general exertion in favour of the exiled royal family.

'Let it come, man—let it come,' answered MacGregor; 'ye never saw dull weather clear without a shower; and if the world is turned upside down, why, honest men have the better chance to cut bread out of it.'

I again attempted to bring him back to the subject of Diana; but although on most occasions and subjects he used a freedom of speech which I had no great delight in listening to, yet upon that alone, which was most interesting to me, he kept a degree of scrupulous reserve, and contented himself with intimating, 'that he hoped the leddy would be soon in a quieter country than this was like to be for one while.' I was obliged to be content with this answer, and to proceed in the hope that accident might, as on a former occasion, stand my friend, and allow me at least the sad gratification of bidding farewell to the object who had occupied such a share of my affections, so much beyond even what I had supposed, till I was about to be separated from her for ever.

We pursued the margin of the lake for about six English miles, through a devious and beautifully variegated path, until we attained a sort of Highland farm, or assembly of hamlets, near the head of that fine sheet of water, called, if I mistake not, Lediart, or some such name. Here a numerous party of MacGregor's men were stationed in order, to receive us. The taste, as well as the eloquence of tribes, in a savage, or, to speak more properly, in a rude state, is usually just, because it is unfettered by system and affectation;* and of this I had an example in the choice these mountaineers had made of a place to receive their guests. It has been said that a British monarch would judge well to receive the embassy of a rival power in the cabin of a man-of-war; and a Highland leader acted with some propriety in choosing a situation, where the natural objects of grandeur proper to his country might have the full effect on the mind of his guests.

We ascended about two hundred yards from the shores of the lake, guided by a brawling brook, and left on the right hand four or five Highland huts, with patches of arable land around them, so small as to show that they must have been worked with the spade rather than the plough, cut as it were out of the surrounding copsewood, and waving with crops of barley and oats. Above this limited space the hill became more steep; and on its edge we descried the glittering arms and waving drapery of about fifty of MacGregor's followers. They were stationed on a spot, the recollection of which yet strikes me with admiration.* The brook, hurling its waters downwards from the mountain, had in this spot encountered a barrier rock, over which it had made its way by two distinct leaps. The first fall, across which a magnificent old oak, slanting out from the farther bank, partly extended itself as if to shroud the dusky stream of the cascade, might be about twelve feet high; the broken waters were received in a beautiful stone basin, almost as regular as if hewn by a sculptor; and after wheeling around its flinty margin, they made a second precipitous dash, through a dark and narrow chasm, at least fifty feet in depth, and from thence, in a hurried, but comparatively a more gentle course, escaped to join the lake.

With the natural taste which belongs to mountaineers, and especially to the Scottish Highlanders, whose feelings I have observed are often allied with the romantic and poetical, Rob Roy's wife and followers had prepared our morning repast, in a scene well calculated to impress strangers with some feelings of awe. They are also naturally a grave and proud people, and, however rude in our estimation, carry their ideas of form and politeness to an excess that would appear overstrained, except from the demonstration of superior force which accompanies the display of it; for it must be granted that the air of punctilious deference and rigid etiquette which would seem ridiculous in an ordinary peasant, has, like the salute of a *corps-de-garde*, a propriety when tendered by a Highlander completely armed. There was, accordingly, a good deal of formality in our approach and reception.

The Highlanders, who had been dispersed on the side of the hill, drew themselves together when we came in view, and, standing firm and motionless, appeared in close column behind three figures, whom I soon recognised to be Helen MacGregor and her two sons. MacGregor himself arranged his attendants in the rear, and, requesting Mr Jarvie to dismount where the ascent became steep, advanced slowly, marshalling us forward at the head of the troop. As we advanced, we heard the wild notes of the bagpipes, which lost their natural discord from being mingled with the dashing sound of the cascade. When we came close, the wife of MacGregor came forward to meet us: Her dress was studiously arranged in a more feminine taste than it had been on the preceding day, but her features wore the same lofty, unbending, and resolute character; and as she folded my friend the Bailie in an unexpected and apparently unwelcome embrace, I could perceive, by the agitation of his wig, his back, and the calves of his legs, that he felt much like to one who feels himself suddenly in the gripe of a she-bear, without being able to distinguish whether the animal is in kindness or in wrath.

'Kinsman,' she said, 'you are welcome—and you too, stranger,' she added, releasing my alarmed companion, who instinctively drew back and settled his wig, and addressing herself to me,—'You also are welcome. You came,' she added, 'to our unhappy country, when our bloods were chafed, and our hands were red. Excuse the rudeness that gave you a rough welcome, and lay it upon the evil times, and not upon us.' All this was said with the manners of a princess, and in the tone and style of a court. Nor was there the least tincture of that vulgarity, which we naturally attach to the Lowland Scottish. There was a strong provincial accentuation, but, otherwise, the language rendered by Helen MacGregor, out of the native and poetical Gaelic, into English, which she had acquired as we do learned tongues, but had probably never heard applied to the mean purposes of ordinary life, was graceful, flowing, and declamatory. Her husband, who had in his time played many parts, used a much less elevated and emphatic dialect,—but even *his* language rose in purity of expression, as you may have remarked, if I have been accurate in recording it, when the affairs which he discussed were of an agitating and important nature; and it appears to me in his case, and in that of some other Highlanders whom I have known, that, when familiar and facetious, they used the Lowland Scottish dialect,—when serious and impassioned, their thoughts arranged themselves in the idiom of their native language; and in the latter case, as they uttered the corresponding ideas in English, the expressions sounded wild, elevated, and poetical. In fact, the language of passion is almost always pure as well as vehement, and it is no uncommon thing to hear a Scotchman, when overwhelmed by a countryman with a tone of bitter and fluent upbraiding, reply by way of taunt to his adversary, 'You have gotten to your English.'

Be this as it may, the wife of MacGregor invited us to a refreshment spread out on the grass, which abounded with all the good things their mountains could offer, but was clouded by the dark and undisturbed gravity which sat on the brow of our hostess, as well as by our deep and anxious recollection of what had taken place on the preceding day. It was in vain that the leader exerted himself to excite mirth: A chill hung over our minds as if the feast had been funereal; and every bosom felt light when it was ended.

'Adieu, cousin,' she said to Mr Jarvie, as we rose from the entertainment; 'the best wish Helen MacGregor can give to a friend is, that he may see her no more.'

The Bailie struggled to answer, probably with some common-place maxim of morality; but the calm and melancholy sternness of her countenance bore down and disconcerted the mechanical and formal importance of the magistrate. He coughed,—hemmed,—bowed,— and was silent. 'For you, stranger,' she said, 'I have a token, from one whom you can never'——

'Helen,' interrupted MacGregor, in a loud and stern voice, 'what means this?—have you forgotten the charge?'

'MacGregor,' she replied, 'I have forgotten nought that is fitting for me to remember. It is not such hands as these,' and she stretched forth her long, sinewy, and bare arm, 'that are fitting to convey love-tokens, were the gift connected with aught but misery.—Young man,' she said, presenting me with a ring, which I well remembered as one of the few ornaments that Miss Vernon sometimes wore, 'this comes from one whom you will never see more. If it is a joyless token, it is well fitted to pass through the hands of one to whom joy can never be known. Her last words were—'Let him forget me for ever.'

'And can she,' I said, almost without being conscious that I spoke, 'suppose that is possible?'

'All may be forgotten,' said the extraordinary female who addressed me,—'all—but the sense of dishonour, and the desire of vengeance.'

'*Seid suas!*'[63] cried the MacGregor, stamping with impatience. The bagpipes sounded, and, with their thrilling and jarring tones, cut short our conference. Our leave of our hostess was taken by silent gestures; and we resumed our journey, with an additional proof on my part, that I was beloved by Diana, and was separated from her for ever.

CHAPTER XXXVI

Farewell to the land where the clouds love to rest,
Like the shroud of the dead, on the mountain's cold breast;
To the cataract's roar where the eagles reply,
And the lake her lone bosom expands to the sky.*

OUR route lay through a dreary, yet romantic country, which the distress of my own mind prevented me from remarking particularly, and which, therefore, I will not attempt to describe. The lofty peak of Ben Lomond, here the predominant monarch of the mountains, lay on our right hand, and served as a striking land-mark. I was not awakened from my apathy, until, after a long and toilsome walk, we emerged through a pass in the hills, and Loch Lomond opened before us. I will spare you the attempt to describe what you would hardly comprehend without going to see it. But certainly this noble lake, boasting innumerable beautiful islands, of every varying form and outline which fancy can frame,—its northern extremity narrowing until it is lost among dusky and retreating mountains,—while, gradually widening as it extends to the southward, it spreads its base around the indentures and promontories of a fair and fertile land, affords one of the most surprising, beautiful, and sublime spectacles in nature. The eastern side, peculiarly rough and rugged, was at this time the chief seat of Mac-Gregor and his clan, to curb whom a small garrison had been stationed in a central position betwixt Loch Lomond and another lake. The extreme strength of the country, however, with the numerous passes, marshes, caverns, and other places of concealment or defence, made the establishment of this little fort seem rather an acknowledgment of the danger, than an effectual means of securing against it.

On more than one occasion, as well as on that which I witnessed, the garrison suffered from the adventurous spirit of the outlaw and his followers. These advantages were never sullied by ferocity when he himself was in command; for, equally good-tempered and sagacious, he understood well the danger of incurring unnecessary odium. I learnt with pleasure that he had caused the captives of the preceding day to be liberated in safety; and many traits of mercy, and even generosity, are recorded of this remarkable man on similar occasions.

A boat waited for us in a creek beneath a huge rock, manned by four lusty Highland rowers; and our host took leave of us with great cordiality, and even affection. Betwixt him and Mr Jarvie, indeed, there seemed to exist a degree of mutual regard, which formed a strong contrast to their different occupations and habits. After kissing each other very lovingly, and when they were just in the act of parting, the Bailie, in the fulness of his heart, and with a faltering voice, assured his kinsman, 'that if ever an hundred pund, or even twa hundred, would put him or his family in a settled way, he need but just send a line to the Saut-Market;' and Rob, grasping his basket-hilt with one hand, and shaking Mr Jarvie's heartily with the other, protested, 'that if ever any body should affront his kinsman, an he would but let him ken, he would stow his lugs out of his head, were he the best man in Glasgow.'

With these assurances of mutual aid and continued good-will, we bore away from the shore, and took our course for the south-western angle of the lake, where it gives birth to the river Leven. Rob Roy remained for some time standing on the rock from beneath which we had departed, conspicuous by his long gun, waving tartans, and the single plume in his cap, which in those days denoted the Highland gentleman and soldier; although I observe the present military taste has decorated the Highland bonnet with a quantity of black plumage,* resembling that which is borne before funerals. At length, as the distance increased between us, we saw him turn and go slowly up the side of the hill, followed by his immediate attendants or body guard.

We performed our voyage for a long time in silence, interrupted only by the Gaelic chant which one of the rowers sung in low irregular measure, rising occasionally into a wild chorus, in which the others joined.

My own thoughts were sad enough; yet I felt something soothing in the magnificent scenery with which I was surrounded; and thought, in the enthusiasm of the moment, that had my faith been that of Rome, I could have consented to live and die a lonely hermit in one of the romantic and beautiful islands amongst which our boat glided.

The Bailie had also his speculations, but they were of somewhat a different complexion; as I found when, after about an hour's silence, during which he had been mentally engaged in the calculations necessary, he undertook to prove the possibility of draining the lake, and 'giving to plough and harrow many hundred, ay, many a thousand acres, from whilk no man could get earthly gude e'enow, unless it were a gedd,[64] or a dish of perch now and then.'

Amidst a long discussion, which he 'crammed into mine ear against the stomach of my sense,'* I only remember, that it was part of his project to preserve a portion of the lake just deep enough and broad enough for the purposes of water-carriage, so that coal-barges and gabbards should pass as easily between Dunbarton and Glenfalloch as between Glasgow and Greenock.*

At length we neared our distant place of landing, adjoining to the ruins of an ancient castle, and just where the lake discharges its superfluous waters into the Leven. There we found Dougal with the horses. The Bailie had formed a plan with respect to 'the creature,' as well as upon the draining of the lake; and, perhaps, in both cases, with more regard to the utility than to the practical possibility of his scheme. 'Dougal,' he said, 'ye are a kindly creature, and hae the sense and feeling o' what is due to your betters—and I'm e'en wae for you, Dougal, for it canna be but that in the life ye lead you suld get a Jeddart cast* ae day, suner or later. I trust, considering my services as a magistrate, and my father the deacon's afore me, I hae interest eneugh in the council to gar them wink a wee at a waur faut than yours. Sae I hae been thinking that if ye will gang back to Glasgow wi' us, being a strong-backit creature, ye might be employed in the warehouse till something better suld cast up.'

'Her nainsell muckle obliged till the Bailie's honour,' replied Dougal; 'but teil be in her shanks fan she gangs on a causeway'd street, unless she be drawn up the Gallowgate wi' tows, as she was before.'

In fact, I afterwards learned that Dougal had originally come to Glasgow as a prisoner, from being concerned in some depredation, but had somehow found such favour in the eyes of the jailor, that, with rather overweening confidence, he had retained him in his service as one of the turnkeys; a task which Dougal had discharged with sufficient fidelity, so far as was known, until overcome by his clannish prejudices on the unexpected appearance of his old leader.

Astonished at receiving so round a refusal to so favourable an offer, the Bailie, turning to me, observed, that the 'creature was a natural-born idiot.' I testified my own gratitude in a way which Dougal much better relished, by slipping a couple of guineas into his hand. He no sooner felt the touch of the gold, than he sprung twice or thrice from the earth with the agility of a wild buck, flinging out first one heel and then another, in a manner which would have astonished a French dancing-master. He ran to the boatmen to show them the prize, and a small gratuity made them take part in his raptures. He then, to use a favourite expression of the dramatic John Bunyan, 'went on his way, and I saw him no more.'*

The Bailie and I mounted our horses, and proceeded on the road to Glasgow. When we had lost the view of the lake, and its superb amphitheatre of mountains, I could not help expressing, with enthusiasm, my sense of its natural beauties, although I was conscious that Mr Jarvie was a very uncongenial spirit to communicate with on such a subject.

'Ye are a young gentleman,' he replied, 'and an Englishman, and a' this may be very fine to you; but for me, wha am a plain man, and ken something o' the different values of land, I wadna gie the finest sight we hae seen in the Hielands, for the first keek o' the Gorbals o' Glasgow; and if I were ance there, it suldna be every fule's errand, begging your pardon, Mr Francis, that suld take me out o' sight o' Saint Mungo's steeple again!'

The honest man had his wish; for, by dint of travelling very late, we arrived at his own house that night, or rather on the succeeding morning. Having seen my worthy fellow-traveller safely consigned to the charge of the considerate and officious Mattie, I proceeded to Mrs Flyter's, in whose house, even at this unwonted hour, light was still burning. The door was opened by no less a person than Andrew Fairservice himself, who, upon the first sound of my voice, set up a loud shout of joyful recognition, and without uttering a syllable, ran up stairs towards a parlour on the second floor, from the windows of which the light proceeded. Justly conceiving that he went to announce my return to the anxious Owen, I followed him upon the foot. Owen was not alone,—there was another in the apartment,—it was my father.

The first impulse was to preserve the dignity of his usual equanimity,—'Francis, I am glad to see you.'—The next was to embrace me tenderly,—'My dear—dear son!'—Owen secured one of my hands, and wetted it with his tears, while he joined in gratulating my return. These are scenes which address themselves to the eye and to the heart, rather than to the ear.—My old eye-lids still moisten at the recollection of our meeting; but your kind and affectionate feelings can well imagine what I should find it impossible to describe.

When the tumult of our joy was over, I learnt that my father had arrived from Holland shortly after Owen had set off for Scotland.

Determined and rapid in all his movements, he only stopped to provide the means of discharging the obligations incumbent on his house.
By his extensive resources, with funds enlarged, and credit fortified,
by eminent success in his continental speculation, he easily accomplished what perhaps his absence alone rendered difficult, and set out
for Scotland to exact justice from Rashleigh Osbaldistone, as well as to
put order to his affairs in that country. My father's arrival in full credit,
and with the ample means of supporting his engagements honourably,
as well as benefiting his correspondents in future, was a stunning blow
to MacVittie and Company, who had conceived his star set for ever.
Highly incensed at the usage his confidential clerk and agent had
received at their hands, Mr Osbaldistone refused every tender of apology and accommodation; and, having settled the balance of their
account, announced to them, that, with all its numerous contingent
advantages, that leaf of their ledger was closed for ever.

While he enjoyed this triumph over false friends, he was not a little
alarmed on my account. Owen, good man, had not supposed it possible that a journey of fifty or sixty miles, which may be made with so
much ease and safety in any direction from London, could be attended
with any particular danger. But he caught alarm, by sympathy, from
my father, to whom the country, and the lawless character of its inhabitants, were better known.

These apprehensions were raised to agony, when, a few hours
before I arrived, Andrew Fairservice made his appearance, with a dismal and exaggerated account of the uncertain state in which he had left
me. The nobleman with whose troops he had been a sort of prisoner,
had, after examination, not only dismissed him, but furnished him
with the means of returning rapidly to Glasgow, in order to announce
to my friends my precarious and unpleasant situation.

Andrew was one of those persons who have no objection to the sort
of temporary attention and woful importance which attaches itself to
the bearer of bad tidings, and had therefore by no means smoothed
down his tale in the telling, especially as the rich London merchant
himself proved unexpectedly one of the auditors. He went at great
length into an account of the dangers I had escaped, chiefly, as he insinuated, by means of his own experience, exertion, and sagacity.

'What was to come of me now, when my better angel, in his
(Andrew's) person, was removed from my side, it was,' he said, 'sad
and sair to conjecture; that the Bailie was nae better than just naebody

at a pinch, or something waur, for he was a conceited body—and Andrew hated conceit—but certainly atween the pistols and the cara- bines of the troopers, that rappit aff the tane after the tother as fast as hail, and the dirks and claymores o' the Hielanders, and the deep waters and weils o' the Avondow, it was to be thought there wad be a puir account of the young gentleman.'

This statement would have driven Owen to despair, had he been alone and unsupported; but my father's perfect knowledge of mankind enabled him easily to appreciate the character of Andrew, and the real amount of his intelligence. Stripped of all exaggeration, however, it was alarming enough to a parent. He determined to set out in person to obtain my liberty, by ransom or negotiation, and was bus- ied with Owen till a late hour, in order to get through some necessary correspondence, and devolve on the latter some business which should be transacted during his absence; and thus it chanced that I found them watchers.

It was late ere we separated to rest, and, too impatient long to endure repose, I was stirring early the next morning. Andrew gave his attendance at my levee, as in duty bound, and, instead of the scarecrow figure to which he had been reduced at Aberfoil, now appeared in the attire of an undertaker, a goodly suit, namely, of the deepest mourn- ing. It was not till after one or two queries, which the rascal affected as long as he could to misunderstand, that I found out he 'had thought it but decent to put on mourning, on account of my inexpressible loss; and as the broker at whose shop he had equipped himself, declined to receive the goods again, and as his own garments had been destroyed or carried off in my honour's service, doubtless I and my honourable father, whom Providence had blessed wi' the means, wadna suffer a puir lad to sit down wi' the loss; a stand o' claes was nae great matter to an Osbaldistone, (be praised for't!) especially to an auld and attached servant o' the house.'

As there was something of justice in Andrew's plea of loss in my ser- vice, his finesse succeeded; and he came by a good suit of mourning, with a beaver and all things conforming, as the exterior signs of woe for a master who was alive and merry.

My father's first care, when he arose, was to visit Mr Jarvie, for whose kindness he entertained the most grateful sentiments, which he expressed in very few but manly and nervous terms. He explained the altered state of his affairs, and offered the Bailie, on such terms as could not but be both advantageous and acceptable, that part in his concerns which had been hitherto managed by MacVittie and Company. The Bailie heartily congratulated my father and Owen on the changed posture of their affairs, and, without affecting to disclaim that he had done his best to serve them, when matters looked otherwise, he said, 'He had only just acted as he wad be done by—that, as to the extension of their correspondence, he frankly accepted it with thanks. Had MacVittie's folk behaved like honest men,' he said, 'he wad hae liked ill to hae come in ahint them, and out afore them, this gate. But it's otherwise, and they maun e'en stand the loss.'

The Bailie then pulled me by the sleeve into a corner, and, after again cordially wishing me joy, proceeded in rather an embarrassed tone.

'I wad heartily wish, Maister Francis, there suld be as little said as possible about the queer things we saw up yonder awa—There's nae gude, unless ane were judicially examinate, to say ony thing about that awfu' job o' Morris—and the members o' the council wadna think it creditable in ane of their body to be fighting wi' a wheen Hielandmen, and singeing their plaidens—And abune a', though I am a decent sponsible man, when I am on my right end, I canna but think I maun hae made a queer figure without my hat and my periwig, hinging by the middle like bawdrons, or a cloak flung ower a cloak-pin. Bailie Grahame wad hae an unco hair in my neck an he got that tale by the end.'

I could not suppress a smile when I recollected the Bailie's situation, although I certainly thought it no laughing matter at the time. The good-natured merchant was a little confused, but smiled also when he shook his head. 'I see how it is—I see how it is. But say naething about it—there's a gude callant; and charge that lang-tongued, conceited, upsetting serving-man o' yours, to say naething neither. I wadna for ever sae muckle that even the lassock Mattie kend ony thing about it. I wad never hear an end o't.'

He was obviously relieved from his impending fears of ridicule, when I told him it was my father's intention to leave Glasgow almost immediately. Indeed he had now no motive for remaining, since the most valuable part of the papers carried off by Rashleigh had been recovered. For that portion which he had converted into cash and expended in his own or on political intrigues, there was no mode of recovering it but by a suit at law, which was forthwith commenced, and proceeded, as our law-agents assured us, with all deliberate speed.

We spent, accordingly, one hospitable day with the Bailie, and took leave of him, as this narrative now does. He continued to grow in wealth, honour, and credit, and actually rose to the highest civic honours in his native city. About two years after the period I have mentioned, he tired of his bachelor life, and promoted Mattie from her wheel by the kitchen fire, to the upper end of his table, in the character of Mrs Jarvie. Bailie Grahame, the MacVitties, and others, (for all men have their enemies, especially in the council of a royal burgh,) ridiculed this transformation. 'But,' said Mr Jarvie, 'let them say their say. I'll ne'er fash mysell, nor lose my liking for sae feckless a matter as a nine days' clash. My honest father the deacon had a byword,

> "Brent brow and lily skin,
> A loving heart, and a leal within,
> Is better than gowd or gentle kin."*

Besides,' as he always concluded, 'Mattie was nae ordinary lassock-quean; she was akin to the Laird o' Limmerfield.'

Whether it was owing to her descent or her good gifts, I do not presume to decide; but Mattie behaved excellently in her exaltation, and relieved the apprehensions of some of the Bailie's friends, who had deemed his experiment somewhat hazardous. I do not know that there was any other incident of his quiet and useful life worthy of being particularly recorded.

CHAPTER XXXVII

'Come ye hither, my "six" good sons,
    Gallant men I trow ye be,
How many of you, my children dear,
    Will stand by that good Earl and me?'

' "Five" of them did answer make—
"Five" of them spoke hastily,
O father, till the day we die,
    We'll stand by that good Earl and thee.'
                        *The Rising in the North**

On the morning when we were to depart from Glasgow, Andrew Fairservice bounced into my apartment like a madman, jumping up and down, and singing, with more vehemence than tune,

> 'The kiln's on fire*—the kiln's on fire—
> The kiln's on fire—she's a' in a lowe.'

With some difficulty I prevailed on him to cease his confounded clamour, and explain to me what the matter was. He was pleased to inform me, as if he had been bringing the finest news imaginable, 'that the Hielands were clean broken out every man o' them, and that Rob Roy, and a' his breekless bands, wad be down upon Glasgow, or twenty-four hours o' the clock gaed round.'

'Hold your tongue,' said I, 'you rascal! You must be drunk or mad; and if there is any truth in your news, is it a singing matter, you scoundrel?'

'Drunk or mad? nae doubt,' replied Andrew, dauntlessly; 'ane's aye drunk or mad if he tells what grit folks dinna like to hear—Sing? odd, the clans will make us sing on the wrang side o' our mouth, if we are sae drunk or mad as to bide their coming.'

I rose in great haste, and found my father and Owen also on foot, and in considerable alarm.

Andrew's news proved but too true in the main. The great rebellion which agitated Britain in the year 1715 had already broken out, by the unfortunate Earl of Mar's setting up the standard of the Stewart family in an ill-omened hour, to the ruin of many honourable families, both in England and Scotland. The treachery of some of the Jacobite agents,

(Rashleigh among the rest,) and the arrest of others, had made George the First's government acquainted with the extensive ramifications of a conspiracy long prepared, and which at last exploded prematurely, and in a part of the kingdom too distant to have any vital effect upon the country, which, however, was plunged into much confusion.*

This great public event served to confirm and elucidate the obscure explanations I had received from MacGregor; and I could easily see why the westland clans, who were brought against him, should have waived their private quarrel, in consideration that they were all shortly to be engaged in the same public cause. It was a more melancholy reflection to my mind, that Diana Vernon was the wife of one of those who were most active in turning the world upside down, and that she was herself exposed to all the privations and perils of her husband's hazardous trade.

We held an immediate consultation on the measures we were to adopt in this crisis, and acquiesced in my father's plan, that we should instantly get the necessary passports, and make the best of our way to London. I acquainted my father with my wish to offer my personal service to the government in any volunteer corps, several being already spoken of. He readily acquiesced in my proposal; for, though he disliked war as a profession, yet upon principle, no man would have exposed his life more willingly in defence of civil and religious liberty.

We travelled in haste and in peril through Dumfries-shire and the neighbouring counties of England. In this quarter, gentlemen of the Tory interest were already in motion mustering men and horses, while the Whigs assembled themselves in the principal towns, armed the inhabitants, and prepared for civil war. We narrowly escaped being stopped on more occasions than one, and were often compelled to take circuitous routes to avoid the points where forces were assembling.

When we reached London, we immediately associated with those bankers and eminent merchants who agreed to support the credit of government, and to meet that run upon the funds, on which the conspirators had greatly founded their hopes of furthering their undertaking, by rendering the government, as it were, bankrupt. My father was chosen one of the members of this formidable body of the monied interest, as all had the greatest confidence in his zeal, skill, and activity. He was also the organ by which they communicated with government, and contrived, from funds belonging to his own house, or over which he had command, to find purchasers for a quantity of the

national stock, which was suddenly flung into the market at a depreciated price when the rebellion broke out. I was not idle myself, but
obtained a commission, and levied, at my father's expense, about two
hundred men, with whom I joined General Carpenter's army.*

The rebellion, in the meantime, had extended itself to England.
The unfortunate Earl of Derwentwater had taken arms in the cause,
along with General Foster. My poor uncle, Sir Hildebrand, whose
estate was reduced to almost nothing by his own carelessness and the
expense and debauchery of his sons and household, was easily persuaded to join that unfortunate standard. Before doing so, however, he
exhibited a degree of precaution of which no one could have suspected
him—he made his will!

By this document he devised his estates at Osbaldistone-Hall, and
so forth, to his sons successively, and their male heirs, until he came to
Rashleigh, whom, on account of the turn he had lately taken in politics,
he detested with all his might,—he cut him off with a shilling, and settled the estate on me, as his next heir. I had always been rather a
favourite of the old gentleman; but it is probable that, confident in the
number of gigantic youths who now armed around him, he considered
the destination as likely to remain a dead letter, which he inserted
chiefly to show his displeasure at Rashleigh's treachery, both public
and domestic. There was an article, by which he bequeathed to the
niece of his late wife, Diana Vernon, now Lady Diana Vernon
Beauchamp, some diamonds belonging to her late aunt, and a great silver ewer, having the arms of Vernon and Osbaldistone quarterly
engraven upon it.

But Heaven had decreed a more speedy extinction of his numerous
and healthy lineage than, most probably, he himself had reckoned on.
In the very first muster of the conspirators at a place called Green-
Rigg,* Thorncliffe Osbaldistone quarrelled about precedence with a
gentleman of the Northumbrian border, to the full as fierce and
intractable as himself. In spite of all remonstrances, they gave their
commander a specimen of how far their discipline might be relied
upon, by fighting it out with their rapiers, and my kinsman was killed
on the spot. His death was a great loss to Sir Hildebrand, for, notwithstanding his infernal temper, he had a grain or two of more sense than
belonged to the rest of the brotherhood, Rashleigh always excepted.

Perceval, the sot, died also in his calling. He had a wager with
another gentleman, who, from his exploits in that line, had acquired

the formidable epithet of Brandy Swalewell, which should drink the largest cup of strong liquor when King James was proclaimed by the insurgents at Morpeth. The exploit was something enormous. I forget the exact quantity of brandy which Percie swallowed, but it occasioned a fever, of which he expired at the end of three days, with the word, *water*, *water*, perpetually on his tongue.

Dickon broke his neck near Warrington Bridge,* in an attempt to show off a foundered blood-mare, which he wished to palm upon a Manchester merchant who had joined the insurgents. He pushed the animal at a five-barred gate; she fell in the leap, and the unfortunate jockey lost his life.

Wilfred the fool, as sometimes befalls, had the best fortune of the family. He was slain at Proud Preston,* in Lancashire, on the day that General Carpenter attacked the barricades, fighting with great bravery, though I have heard he was never able exactly to comprehend the cause of quarrel, and did not uniformly remember, on which king's side he was engaged. John also behaved very boldly in the same engagement, and received several wounds, of which he was not happy enough to die on the spot.

Old Sir Hildebrand, entirely broken-hearted by these successive losses, became, by the next day's surrender, one of the unhappy prisoners, and was lodged in Newgate with his wounded son John.

I was now released from my military duty, and lost no time, therefore, in endeavouring to relieve the distresses of these near relations. My father's interest with government, and the general compassion excited by a parent who had sustained the successive loss of so many sons within so short a time, would have prevented my uncle and cousin from being brought to trial for high treason; but their doom was given forth from a greater tribunal. John died of his wounds in Newgate, recommending to me, with his last breath, a cast of hawks which he had at the Hall, and a black spaniel bitch, called Lucy.

My poor uncle seemed beaten down to the very earth by his family calamities, and the circumstances in which he unexpectedly found himself. He said little, but seemed grateful for such attentions as circumstances permitted me to show him. I did not witness his meeting with my father for the first time for so many years, and under circumstances so melancholy; but judging from my father's extreme depression of spirits, it must have been melancholy in the last degree. Sir Hildebrand spoke with great bitterness against Rashleigh, now his only surviving child; laid upon him the ruin of his house, and the deaths of all his brethren, and declared, that neither he nor they would have plunged into political intrigue, but for that very member of his family who had been the first to desert them. He once or twice mentioned Diana, always with great affection; and once he said, while I sate by his bedside—'Nevoy, since Thorncliffe and all of them are dead, I am sorry you cannot have her.'

The expression affected me much at the time; for it was a usual custom of the poor old Baronet's,* when joyously setting forth upon the morning's chase, to distinguish Thorncliffe, who was a favourite, while he summoned the rest more generally; and the loud jolly tone in which he used to hollo, 'Call Thornie—call all of them,' contrasted sadly with the wobegone and self-abandoning note in which he uttered the disconsolate words which I have above quoted. He mentioned the contents of his will, and supplied me with an authenticated copy—the original he had deposited with my old acquaintance Mr Justice Inglewood, who, dreaded by no one, and confided in by all as a kind of neutral person, had become, for aught I know, the depositary of half the wills of the fighting men of both factions in the county of Northumberland.

The greater part of my uncle's last hours were spent in the discharge of the religious duties of his church, in which he was directed by the chaplain of the Sardinian ambassador,* for whom, with some difficulty, we obtained permission to visit him. I could not ascertain by my own observation, or through the medical attendants, that Sir Hildebrand Osbaldistone died of any formed complaint, bearing a name in the science of medicine. He seemed to me completely worn out and broken down by fatigue of body and distress of mind, and rather ceased to exist than died of any positive struggle; just as a vessel, buffeted and tossed by a succession of tempestuous gales, her timbers overstrained, and her joints loosened, will sometimes spring a leak and founder, when there are no apparent causes for her destruction.

It was a remarkable circumstance that my father, after the last duties were performed to his brother, appeared suddenly to imbibe a strong anxiety that I should act upon the will, and represent his father's house, which had hitherto seemed to be the thing in the world which had least charms for him. But formerly, he had been only like the fox in the fable,* contemning what was beyond his reach; and, moreover, I doubt not that the excessive dislike which he entertained against Rashleigh (now Sir Rashleigh) Osbaldistone, who loudly threatened to attack his father Sir Hildebrand's will and settlement, corroborated my father's desire to maintain it.

'He had been most unjustly disinherited,' he said, 'by his own father—his brother's will had repaired the disgrace, if not the injury, by leaving the wreck of the property to Frank, the natural heir, and he was determined the bequest should take effect.'

In the meantime, Rashleigh was not altogether a contemptible personage as an opponent. The information he had given to government was critically well-timed, and his extreme plausibility, with the extent of his intelligence, and the artful manner in which he contrived to assume both merit and influence, had, to a certain extent, procured him patrons among ministers. We were already in the full tide of litigation with him on the subject of his pillaging the firm of Osbaldistone and Tresham; and, judging from the progress we made in that comparatively simple lawsuit, there was a chance that this second course of litigation might be drawn out beyond the period of all our natural lives.

To avert these delays as much as possible, my father, by the advice of his counsel learned in the law, paid off and vested in my person the rights to certain large mortgages, affecting Osbaldistone-Hall. Perhaps, however, the opportunity to convert a great share of the large profits which accrued from the rapid rise of the funds upon the suppression of the rebellion, and the experience he had so lately had of the perils of commerce, encouraged him to realize, in this manner, a considerable part of his property. At any rate, it so chanced, that, instead of commanding me to the desk, as I fully expected, having intimated my willingness to comply with his wishes, however they might destine me, I received his directions to go down to Osbaldistone-Hall, and take possession of it as the heir and representative of the family. I was directed to apply to Squire Inglewood for the copy of my uncle's will deposited with him, and take all necessary measures to secure that possession, which sages say makes nine points of the law.

At another time I should have been delighted with this change of destination. But now Osbaldistone-Hall was accompanied with many painful recollections. Still, however, I thought, that in that neighbourhood only I was likely to acquire some information respecting the fate of Diana Vernon. I had every reason to fear it must be far different from what I could have wished it. But I could obtain no precise information on the subject.

It was in vain that I endeavoured, by such acts of kindness as their situation admitted, to conciliate the confidence of some distant relations who were among the prisoners in Newgate. A pride which I could not condemn, and a natural suspicion of the Whig, Frank Osbaldistone, cousin to the double-distilled traitor Rashleigh, closed every heart and tongue, and I only received thanks, cold and extorted, in exchange for such benefits as I had power to offer. The arm of the law was also gradually abridging the numbers of those whom I endeavoured to serve, and the hearts of the survivors became gradually more contracted towards all whom they conceived to be concerned with the existing government. As they were led gradually, and by detachments, to execution, those who survived lost interest in mankind, and the desire of communicating with them. I shall long remember what one of them, Ned Shafton by name, replied to my anxious enquiry, whether there was any indulgence I could procure him? 'Mr Frank Osbaldistone, I must suppose you mean me kindly, and therefore I thank you. But, by G——, men cannot be fattened like poultry, when they see their neighbours carried off day by day to the place of execution, and know that their own necks are to be twisted round in their turn.'

Upon the whole, therefore, I was glad to escape from London, from Newgate, and from the scenes which both exhibited, to breathe the free air of Northumberland. Andrew Fairservice had continued in my service more from my father's pleasure than my own. At present there seemed a prospect that his local acquaintance with Osbaldistone-Hall and its vicinity might be useful; and, of course, he accompanied me on my journey, and I enjoyed the prospect of getting rid of him, by establishing him in his old quarters. I cannot conceive how he could prevail upon my father to interest himself in him, unless it were by the art, which he possessed in no inconsiderable degree, of affecting an extreme attachment to his master, which theoretical attachment he made compatible in practice with playing all manner of tricks without scruple, providing only against his master being cheated by any one but himself.

We performed our journey to the North without any remarkable adventure, and we found the country, so lately agitated by rebellion, now peaceful and in good order. The nearer we approached to Osbaldistone-Hall, the more did my heart sink at the thought of entering that deserted mansion; so that, in order to postpone the evil day, I resolved first to make my visit at Mr Justice Inglewood's.

That venerable person had been much disturbed with thoughts of what he had been, and what he now was; and natural recollections of the past had interfered considerably with the active duty, which, in his present situation, might have been expected from him. He was fortunate, however, in one respect: he had got rid of his clerk, Jobson, who had finally left him in dudgeon at his inactivity, and become legal assistant to a certain Squire Standish, who had lately commenced operations in those parts as a justice, with a zeal for King George and the Protestant succession, which, very different from the feelings of his old patron, Mr Jobson had more occasion to restrain within the bounds of the law, than to stimulate to exertion.

Old Justice Inglewood received me with great courtesy, and readily exhibited my uncle's will, which seemed to be without a flaw. He was for some time in obvious distress, how he should speak and act in my presence; but when he found, that though a supporter of the present government upon principle, I was disposed to think with pity on those who had opposed it on a mistaken feeling of loyalty and duty, his discourse became a very diverting medley of what he had done, and what he had left undone,—the pains he had taken to prevent some squires from joining, and to wink at the escape of others, who had been so unlucky as to engage in the affair.

We were *tête-à-tête*, and several bumpers had been quaffed by the Justice's special desire, when, on a sudden, he requested me to fill a *bona fide* brimmer to the health of poor dear Die Vernon, the rose of the wilderness, the heath-bell of Cheviot, and the blossom that's transplanted to an infernal convent.

'Is not Miss Vernon married then?' I exclaimed, in great astonishment. 'I thought his Excellency'——

'Pooh! pooh! his Excellency and his Lordship's all a humbug now, you know—mere St Germains titles—Earl of Beauchamp, and ambassador plenipotentiary from France, when the Duke Regent of Orleans scarce knew that he lived, I daresay. But you must have seen old Sir Frederick Vernon at the hall, when he played the part of Father Vaughan?'

'Good Heavens! then Vaughan was Miss Vernon's father!'

'To be sure he was,' said the Justice, coolly; 'There's no use in keeping the secret now, for he must be out of the country by this time—otherwise, no doubt, it would be my duty to apprehend him.—Come, off with your bumper to my dear lost Die!

> And let her health go round, around, around,
> And let her health go round;
> For though your stocking be of silk,
> Your knees near kiss the ground, aground, aground.'[65]

I was unable, as the reader may easily conceive, to join in the Justice's jollity. My head swam with the shock I had received. 'I never heard,' I said, 'that Miss Vernon's father was living.'

'It was not our government's fault that he is,' replied Inglewood, 'for the devil a man there is whose head would have brought more money. He was condemned to death for Fenwick's plot, and was thought to have had some hand in the Knightsbridge affair,* in King William's time; and as he had married in Scotland a relation of the house of Breadalbane, he possessed great influence with all their chiefs. There was a talk of his being demanded to be given up at the Peace of Ryswick,* but he shammed ill, and his death was given publicly out in the French papers. But when he came back here on the old score, we old cavaliers knew him well,—that is to say, I knew him, not as being a cavalier myself, but no information being lodged against the poor gentleman, and my memory being shortened by frequent attacks of the gout, I could not have sworn to him, you know.'

'Was he, then, not known at Osbaldistone-Hall?' I enquired.

'To none but to his daughter, the old knight, and Rashleigh, who had got at that secret as he did at every one else, and held it like a twisted cord about poor Die's neck. I have seen her one hundred times she would have spit at him, if it had not been fear for her father, whose life would not have been worth five minutes' purchase if he had been discovered to the government—But don't mistake me, Mr Osbaldistone; I say the government is a good, a gracious, and a just government; and if it has hanged one-half of the rebels, poor things, all will acknowledge they would not have been touched had they staid peaceably at home.'

Waiving the discussion of these political questions, I brought back Mr Inglewood to his subject, and I found that Diana, having positively refused to marry any of the Osbaldistone family, and expressed her particular detestation of Rashleigh, he had from that time begun to cool in zeal for the cause of the Pretender; to which, as the youngest of six brethren, and bold, artful, and able, he had hitherto looked forward as the means of making his fortune. Probably the compulsion with which he had been forced to render up the spoils which he had abstracted from my father's counting-house by the united authority of Sir Frederick Vernon and the Scottish Chiefs, had determined his resolution to advance his progress by changing his opinions, and betraying his trust. Perhaps also, for few men were better judges where his interest was concerned, he considered their means and talents to be, as they afterwards proved, greatly inadequate to the important task of overthrowing an established government. Sir Frederick Vernon, or, as he was called among the Jacobites, his Excellency Viscount Beauchamp, had, with his daughter, some difficulty in escaping the consequences of Rashleigh's information. Here Mr Inglewood's information was at fault; but he did not doubt, since we had not heard of Sir Frederick being in the hands of the government, he must be by this time abroad, where, agreeable to the cruel bond he had entered into with his brother-in-law, Diana, since she had declined to select a husband out of the Osbaldistone family, must be confined to a convent. The original cause of this singular agreement Mr Inglewood could not perfectly explain; but he understood it was a family compact, entered into for the purpose of securing to Sir Frederick the rents of the remnant of his large estates, which had been vested in the Osbaldistone family by some legal manœuvre; in short, a family compact, in which, like many of those undertaken at that time of day, the feelings of the principal parties interested were no more regarded than if they had been a part of the live-stock upon the lands.

I cannot tell, such is the waywardness of the human heart, whether this intelligence gave me joy or sorrow. It seemed to me, that, in the knowledge that Miss Vernon was eternally divided from me, not by marriage with another, but by seclusion in a convent, in order to fulfil an absurd bargain of this kind, my regret for her loss was aggravated rather than diminished. I became dull, low-spirited, absent, and unable to support the task of conversing with Justice Inglewood, who in his turn yawned, and proposed to retire early. I took leave of him over night, determining the next day, before breakfast, to ride over to Osbaldistone-Hall.

Mr Inglewood acquiesced in my proposal. 'It would be well,' he said, 'that I made my appearance there before I was known to be in the country, the more especially as Sir Rashleigh Osbaldistone was now, he understood, at Mr Jobson's house, hatching some mischief doubtless.—They were fit company,' he added, 'for each other, Sir Rashleigh having lost all right to mingle in the society of men of honour;

but it was hardly possible two such d——d rascals should collogue
together without mischief to honest people.'

He concluded, by earnestly recommending a toast and tankard, and
an attack upon his venison pasty, before I set out in the morning, just
to break the cold air on the wolds.

CHAPTER XXXVIII

His master's gone, and no one now
Dwells in the halls of Ivor;
Men, dogs, and horses, all are dead,
He is the sole survivor.

WORDSWORTH*

THERE are few more melancholy sensations than those with which we regard scenes of past pleasure, when altered and deserted. In my ride to Osbaldistone-Hall, I passed the same objects which I had seen in company with Miss Vernon on the day of our memorable ride from Inglewood Place. Her spirit seemed to keep me company on the way; and, when I approached the spot where I had first seen her, I almost listened for the cry of the hounds and the notes of the horn, and strained my eye on vacant space, as if to descry the fair huntress again descend like an apparition from the hill. But all was silent, and all was solitary. When I reached the Hall, the closed doors and windows, the grass-grown pavement, the courts, which were now so silent, presented a strong contrast to the gay and bustling scene I had so often seen them exhibit, when the merry hunters were going forth to their morning sport, or returning to the daily festival. The joyous bark of the fox-hounds as they were uncoupled, the cries of the huntsman, the clang of the horses' hoofs, the loud laugh of the old knight at the head of his strong and numerous descendants, were all silenced now and for ever.

While I gazed round the scene of solitude and emptiness, I was inexpressibly affected, even by recollecting those whom, when alive, I had no reason to regard with affection. But the thought that so many youths of goodly presence, warm with life, health, and confidence, were within so short a time cold in the grave, by various yet all violent and unexpected modes of death, afforded a picture of mortality at which the mind trembled. It was little consolation to me that I returned a proprietor to the halls, which I had left almost like a fugitive. My mind was not habituated to regard the scenes around as my property, and I felt myself an usurper, at least an intruding stranger, and could hardly divest myself of the idea, that some of the bulky forms of my deceased kinsmen were, like the gigantic spectres of a romance, to appear in the gateway, and dispute my entrance.

While I was engaged in these sad thoughts, my follower, Andrew, whose feelings were of a very different nature, exerted himself in thundering alternately on every door in the building, calling, at the same time, for admittance, in a tone so loud as to intimate, that *he*, at least, was fully sensible of his newly acquired importance, as squire of the body to the new lord of the manor. At length, timidly and reluctantly, Anthony Syddall, my uncle's aged butler and major-domo, presented himself at a lower window, well fenced with iron bars, and enquired our business.

'We are come to tak your charge aff your hand, my auld friend,' said Andrew Fairservice; 'ye may gie up your keys as sune as ye like—ilka dog has his day. I'll tak the plate and napery aff your hand. Ye hae had your ain time o't, Mr Syddall; but ilka bean has its black,* and ilka path has its puddle; and it will just set you henceforth to sit at the board-end, as weel as it did Andrew lang syne.'

Checking with some difficulty the forwardness of my follower, I explained to Syddall the nature of my right, and the title I had to demand admittance into the Hall, as into my own property. The old man seemed much agitated and distressed, and testified manifest reluctance to give me entrance, although it was couched in a humble and submissive tone. I allowed for the agitation of natural feelings, which really did the old man honour; but continued peremptory in my demand of admittance, explaining to him that his refusal would oblige me to apply for Mr Inglewood's warrant, and a constable.

'We are come from Mr Justice Inglewood's this morning,' said Andrew, to enforce the menace, 'and I saw Archie Rutledge, the constable, as I came up by—the country's no to be lawless as it has been, Mr Syddall, letting rebels and papists gang on as they best listed.'

The threat of the law sounded dreadful in the old man's ears, conscious as he was of the suspicion under which he himself lay, from his religion and his devotion to Sir Hildebrand and his sons. He undid, with fear and trembling, one of the postern entrances, which was secured with many a bolt and bar, and humbly hoped that I would excuse him for fidelity in the discharge of his duty.—I reassured him, and told him I had the better opinion of him for his caution.

'Sae have not I,' said Andrew; 'Syddall is an auld sneck-drawer; he wadna be looking as white as a sheet, and his knees knocking together, unless it were for something mair than he's like to tell us.'

'Lord forgive you, Mr Fairservice,' replied the butler, 'to say such things of an old friend and fellow-servant!—Where,'—following me humbly along the passage, 'where would it be your honour's pleasure to have a fire lighted? I fear me you will find the house very dull and dreary—But perhaps you mean to ride back to Inglewood Place to dinner?'

'Light a fire in the library,' I replied.

'In the library!'—answered the old man; 'nobody has sat there this many a day, and the room smokes, for the daws have built in the chimney this spring, and there were no young men about the Hall to pull them down.'

'Our ain reek's better than other folk's fire,'* said Andrew; 'his honour likes the library. He's nane o' your Papishers, that delight in blinded ignorance, Mr Syddall.'

Very reluctantly, as it appeared to me, the butler led the way to the library, and, contrary to what he had given me to expect, the interior of the apartment looked as if it had been lately arranged, and made more comfortable than usual. There was a fire in the grate, which burned clearly, notwithstanding what Syddall had reported of the vent. Taking up the tongs, as if to arrange the wood, but rather perhaps to conceal his own confusion, the butler observed, 'it was burning clear now, but had smoked woundily in the morning.'

Wishing to be alone, till I recovered myself from the first painful sensations which every thing around me recalled, I desired old Syddall to call the land-steward, who lived at about a quarter of a mile from the Hall. He departed with obvious reluctance. I next ordered Andrew to procure the attendance of a couple of stout fellows upon whom he could rely, the population around being Papists, and Sir Rashleigh, who was capable of any desperate enterprise, being in the neighbourhood. Andrew Fairservice undertook this task with great cheerfulness, and promised to bring me up from Trinlay-Knowe, 'twa true-blue Presbyterians* like himsell, that would face and out-face baith the Pope, the devil, and the Pretender—and blythe will I be o' their company mysell, for the very last night that I was at Osbaldistone-Hall, the blight be on ilka blossom in my bit yard, if I didna see that very picture' (pointing to the full-length portrait of Miss Vernon's grandfather) 'walking by moonlight in the garden! I tauld your honour I was fleyed wi' a bogle that night, but ye wadna listen to me—I aye thought there was witchcraft and deevilry amang the Papishers, but I ne'er saw't wi' bodily een till that awfu' night.'

'Get along, sir,' said I, 'and bring the fellows you talk of; and see they have more sense than yourself, and are not frightened at their own shadow.'

'I hae been counted as gude a man as my neighbours ere now,' said Andrew, petulantly; 'but I dinna pretend to deal wi' evil spirits.' And so he made his exit, as Wardlaw the land-steward made his appearance.

He was a man of sense and honesty, without whose careful management my uncle would have found it difficult to have maintained himself a housekeeper so long as he did. He examined the nature of my right of possession carefully, and admitted it candidly. To any one else the succession would have been a poor one, so much was the land encumbered with debt and mortgage. Most of these, however, were already vested in my father's person, and he was in a train of acquiring the rest; his large gains, by the recent rise of the funds, having made it a matter of ease and convenience for him to pay off the debt which affected his patrimony.

I transacted much necessary business with Mr Wardlaw, and detained him to dine with me. We preferred taking our repast in the library, although Syddall strongly recommended our removing to the Stone-Hall, which he had put in order for the occasion. Meantime Andrew made his appearance with his true-blue recruits, whom he recommended in the highest terms, as 'sober decent men, weel founded in doctrinal points, and, above all, as bold as lions.' I ordered them something to drink, and they left the room. I observed old Syddall shake his head as they went out, and insisted upon knowing the reason.

'I maybe cannot expect,' he said, 'that your honour should put confidence in what I say, but it is Heaven's truth for all that—Ambrose Wingfield is as honest a man as lives, but if there is a false knave in the country, it is his brother Lancie—the whole country knows him to be a spy for Clerk Jobson on the poor gentlemen that have been in trouble—But he's a dissenter, and I suppose that's enough now-a-days.'

Having thus far given vent to his feelings, to which, however, I was little disposed to pay attention, and having placed the wine on the table, the old butler left the apartment.

Mr Wardlaw having remained with me until the evening was somewhat advanced, at length bundled up his papers, and removed himself to his own habitation, leaving me in that confused state of mind in which we can hardly say whether we desire company or solitude. I had not, however, the choice betwixt them; for I was left alone in the room, of all others most calculated to inspire me with melancholy reflections.

As twilight was darkening the apartment, Andrew had the sagacity to advance his head at the door, not to ask if I wished for lights, but to recommend them as a measure of precaution against the bogles which still haunted his imagination. I rejected his proffer somewhat peevishly, trimmed the wood-fire, and placing myself in one of the large leathern chairs which flanked the old Gothic chimney, I watched unconsciously the bickering of the blaze which I had fostered. 'And this,' said I alone, 'is the progress and the issue of human wishes! Nursed by the merest trifles, they are first kindled by fancy, nay, are fed upon the vapour of hope till they consume the substance which they inflame; and man, and his hopes, passions, and desires, sink into a worthless heap of embers and ashes!'

There was a deep sigh from the opposite side of the room, which seemed to reply to my reflections. I started up in amazement—Diana Vernon stood before me, resting on the arm of a figure so strongly resembling that of the portrait so often mentioned, that I looked hastily at the frame, expecting to see it empty.* My first idea was, either that I had gone suddenly distracted, or that the spirits of the dead had arisen and been placed before me. A second glance convinced me of my being in my senses, and that the forms which stood before me were real and substantial. It was Diana herself, though paler and thinner than her former self; and it was no tenant of the grave who stood beside her, but Vaughan, or rather Sir Frederick Vernon, in a dress made to imitate that of his ancestor, to whose picture his countenance possessed a family resemblance. He was the first that spoke, for Diana kept her eyes fast fixed on the ground, and astonishment actually riveted my tongue to the roof of my mouth.

'We are your suppliants, Mr Osbaldistone,' he said, 'and we claim the refuge and protection of your roof till we can pursue a journey, where dungeons and death gape for me at every step.'

'Surely,' I articulated with great difficulty—'Miss Vernon cannot suppose—you, sir, cannot believe, that I have forgot your interference in my difficulties, or that I am capable of betraying any one, much less you?'

'I know it,' said Sir Frederick; 'yet it is with the most inexpressible reluctance that I impose on you a confidence, disagreeable perhaps—certainly dangerous—and which I would have specially wished to have conferred on some one else. But my fate, which has chased me through a life of perils and escapes, is now pressing me hard, and I have no alternative.'

At this moment the door opened, and the voice of the officious Andrew was heard. 'A'm bringin' in the caunles—Ye can light them gin ye like—Can do is easy carried about wi' ane.'*

I ran to the door, which, as I hoped, I reached in time to prevent his observing who were in the apartment. I turned him out with hasty violence, shut the door after him, and locked it—then instantly remembering his two companions below, knowing his talkative humour, and recollecting Syddall's remark, that one of them was supposed to be a spy, I followed him as fast as I could to the servants' hall, in which they were assembled. Andrew's tongue was loud as I opened the door, but my unexpected appearance silenced him.

'What is the matter with you, you fool?' said I; 'you stare and look wild, as if you had seen a ghost.'

'N—n—no—nothing,' said Andrew; 'but your worship was pleased to be hasty.'

'Because you disturbed me out of a sound sleep, you fool. Syddall tells me he cannot find beds for these good fellows to-night, and Mr Wardlaw thinks there will be no occasion to detain them. Here is a crown-piece for them to drink my health, and thanks for their goodwill.—You will leave the Hall immediately, my good lads.'

The men thanked me for my bounty, took the silver, and withdrew, apparently unsuspicious and contented. I watched their departure until I was sure they could have no further intercourse that night with honest Andrew. And so instantly had I followed on his heels, that I thought he could not have time to speak two words with them before I interrupted him. But it is wonderful what mischief may be done by only two words. On this occasion they cost two lives.

Having made these arrangements, the best which occurred to me upon the pressure of the moment, to secure privacy for my guests, I returned to report my proceedings, and added, that I had desired Syddall to answer every summons, concluding that it was by his connivance they had been secreted in the Hall. Diana raised her eyes to thank me for the caution.

'You now understand my mystery,' she said; 'you know, doubtless, how near and dear that relative is who has so often found shelter here; and will be no longer surprised, that Rashleigh, having such a secret at his command, should rule me with a rod of iron.'

Her father added, 'that it was their intention to trouble me with their presence as short a time as was possible.'

I entreated the fugitives to waive every consideration but what affected their safety, and to rely on my utmost exertions to promote it. This led to an explanation of the circumstances under which they stood.

'I always suspected Rashleigh Osbaldistone,' said Sir Frederick; 'but his conduct towards my unprotected child, which with difficulty I wrung from her, and his treachery in your father's affairs, made me hate and despise him. In our last interview I concealed not my sentiments, as I should in prudence have attempted to do; and in resentment of the scorn with which I treated him, he added treachery and apostasy to his catalogue of crimes. I at that time fondly hoped that his defection would be of little consequence. The Earl of Mar had a gallant army in Scotland, and Lord Derwentwater, with Forster, Kenmure, Winterton, and others, were assembling forces on the Border. As my connexions with these English nobility and gentry were extensive, it was judged proper that I should accompany a detachment of Highlanders, who, under Brigadier MacIntosh of Borlum, crossed the Frith of Forth, traversed the low country of Scotland, and united themselves on the Borders with the English insurgents. My daughter accompanied me through the perils and fatigues of a march so long and difficult.'

'And she will never leave her dear father!' exclaimed Miss Vernon, clinging fondly to his arm.

'I had hardly joined our English friends when I became sensible that our cause was lost. Our numbers diminished instead of increasing, nor were we joined by any except of our own persuasion. The Tories of the High Church remained in general undecided, and at length we were cooped up by a superior force in the little town of Preston. We defended ourselves resolutely one day. On the next, the hearts of our leaders failed, and they resolved to surrender at discretion. To yield myself up on such terms, were to have laid my head on the block. About twenty or thirty gentlemen were of my mind: We mounted our horses, and placed my daughter, who insisted on sharing my fate, in the centre of our little party. My companions, struck with her courage and filial piety, declared that they would die rather than leave her behind. We rode in a body down a street called Fishergate, which leads to a marshy ground or meadow, extending to the river Ribble, through which one of our party promised to show us a good ford. This marsh had not been strongly invested by the enemy, so that we had only an affair with a patrol of Honeywood's dragoons, whom we dispersed and cut to pieces. We crossed the river, gained the high road to Liverpool, and then dispersed to seek several places of concealment and safety. My fortune led me to Wales, where there are many gentlemen of my religious and political opinions. I could not, however, find a safe opportunity of escaping by sea, and found myself obliged again to draw towards the North. A well-tried friend has appointed to meet me in this neighbourhood, and guide me to a seaport on the Solway, where a sloop is prepared to carry me from my native country for ever. As Osbaldistone-Hall was for the present uninhabited, and under the charge of old Syddall, who had been our confident on former occasions, we drew to it as to a place of known and secure refuge. I resumed a dress which had been used with good effect to scare the superstitious rustics, or domestics, who chanced at any time to see me; and we expected from time to time to hear by Syddall of the arrival of our friendly guide, when your sudden coming hither, and occupying this apartment, laid us under the necessity of submitting to your mercy.'

Thus ended Sir Frederick's story, whose tale sounded to me like one told in a vision; and I could hardly bring myself to believe, that I saw his daughter's form once more before me in flesh and blood, though with diminished beauty and sunk spirits. The buoyant vivacity with which she had resisted every touch of adversity, had now assumed the air of composed and submissive, but dauntless resolution and constancy. Her father, though aware and jealous of the effect of her praises on my mind, could not forbear expatiating upon them.

'She has endured trials,' he said, 'which might have dignified the history of a martyr;—she has faced danger and death in various shapes;—she has undergone toil and privation, from which men of the strongest frame would have shrunk;—she has spent the day in darkness, and the night in vigil, and has never breathed a murmur of weakness or complaint. In a word, Mr Osbaldistone,' he concluded, 'she is a worthy offering to that God, to whom,' crossing himself, 'I shall dedicate her, as all that is left dear or precious to Frederick Vernon.'

There was a silence after these words, of which I well understood the mournful import. The father of Diana was still as anxious to destroy my hopes of being united to her now, as he had shown himself during our brief meeting in Scotland.

'We will now,' said he to his daughter, 'intrude no farther on Mr Osbaldistone's time, since we have acquainted him with the circumstances of the miserable guests who claim his protection.'

I requested them to stay, and offered myself to leave the apartment. Sir Frederick observed, that my doing so could not but excite my attendant's suspicion; and that the place of their retreat was in every respect commodious, and furnished by Syddall with all they could possibly want. 'We might perhaps have even contrived to remain there, concealed from your observation; but it would have been unjust to decline the most absolute reliance on your honour.'

'You have done me but justice,' I replied. 'To you, Sir Frederick, I am but little known; but Miss Vernon, I am sure, will bear me witness that'——

'I do not want my daughter's evidence,' he said politely, but yet with an air calculated to prevent my addressing myself to Diana, 'since I am prepared to believe all that is worthy of Mr Francis Osbaldistone. Permit us now to retire; we must take repose when we can, since we are absolutely uncertain when we may be called upon to renew our perilous journey.'

He drew his daughter's arm within his, and, with a profound reverence, disappeared with her behind the tapestry.

CHAPTER XXXIX

But now the hand of fate is on the curtain,
And gives the scene to light.

DON SEBASTIAN*

I FELT stunned and chilled as they retired. Imagination, dwelling on an absent object of affection, paints her not only in the fairest light, but in that in which we most desire to behold her. I had thought of Diana as she was, when her parting tear dropped on my cheek; when her parting token, received from the wife of MacGregor, augured her wish to convey into exile and conventual seclusion the remembrance of my affection. I saw her; and her cold passive manner, expressive of little except composed melancholy, disappointed, and, in some degree, almost offended me. In the egotism of my feelings, I accused her of indifference—of insensibility. I upbraided her father with pride, with cruelty, with fanaticism; forgetting that both were sacrificing their interest, and Diana her inclination, to the discharge of what they regarded as their duty.

Sir Frederick Vernon was a rigid Catholic, who thought the path of salvation too narrow to be trodden by an heretic; and Diana, to whom her father's safety had been for many years the principal and moving spring of thoughts, hopes, and actions, felt that she had discharged her duty in resigning to his will, not alone her property in the world, but the dearest affections of her heart. But it was not surprising that I could not, at such a moment, fully appreciate these honourable motives; yet my spleen sought no ignoble means of discharging itself.

'I am contemned, then,' I said, when left to run over the tenor of Sir Frederick's communications, 'I am contemned, and thought unworthy even to exchange words with her. Be it so; they shall not at least prevent me from watching over her safety. Here will I remain as an outpost, and, while under my roof at least, no danger shall threaten her, if it be such as the arm of one determined man can avert.'

I summoned Syddall to the library. He came, but came attended by the eternal Andrew, who, dreaming of great things in consequence of my taking possession of the Hall and the annexed estates, was resolved to lose nothing for want of keeping himself in view; and, as often happens to men who entertain selfish objects, overshot his mark, and rendered his attentions tedious and inconvenient.

His unrequired presence prevented me from speaking freely to Syddall, and I dared not send him away for fear of increasing such suspicions as he might entertain from his former abrupt dismissal from the library. 'I shall sleep here, sir,' I said, giving them directions to wheel nearer to the fire an old-fashioned day-bed, or settee. 'I have much to do, and shall go late to bed.'

Syddall, who seemed to understand my look, offered to procure me the accommodation of a mattress and some bedding. I accepted his offer, dismissed my attendant, lighted a pair of candles, and desired that I might not be disturbed till seven in the ensuing morning.

The domestics retired, leaving me to my painful and ill-arranged reflections, until nature, worn out, should require some repose.

I endeavoured forcibly to abstract my mind from the singular circumstances in which I found myself placed. Feelings which I had gallantly combated while the exciting object was remote, were now exasperated by my immediate neighbourhood to her whom I was so soon to part with for ever. Her name was written in every book which I attempted to peruse; and her image forced itself on me in whatever train of thought I strove to engage myself. It was like the officious slave of Prior's Solomon,*—

> Abra was ready ere I named her name,
> And when I call'd another, Abra came.

I alternately gave way to these thoughts, and struggled against them, sometimes yielding to a mood of melting tenderness of sorrow which was scarce natural to me, sometimes arming myself with the hurt pride of one who had experienced what he esteemed unmerited rejection. I paced the library until I had chafed myself into a temporary fever. I then threw myself on the couch, and endeavoured to dispose myself to sleep; but it was in vain that I used every effort to compose myself—that I lay without movement of finger or of muscle, as still as if I had been already a corpse—that I endeavoured to divert or banish disquieting thoughts, by fixing my mind on some act of repetition or arithmetical process. My blood throbbed, to my feverish apprehension, in pulsations which resembled the deep and regular strokes of a distant fulling-mill, and tingled in my veins like streams of liquid fire.

At length I arose, opened the window, and stood by it for some time in the clear moonlight, receiving, in part at least, that refreshment and dissipation of ideas from the clear and calm scene, without which they had become beyond the command of my own volition. I resumed my place on the couch with a heart, Heaven knows, not lighter, but firmer, and more resolved for endurance. In a short time a slumber crept over my senses; still, however, though my senses slumbered, my soul was awake to the painful feelings of my situation, and my dreams were of mental anguish and external objects of terror.

I remember a strange agony, under which I conceived myself and Diana in the power of MacGregor's wife, and about to be precipitated from a rock into the lake; the signal was to be the discharge of a cannon, fired by Sir Frederick Vernon, who, in the dress of a cardinal, officiated at the ceremony. Nothing could be more lively than the impression which I received of this imaginary scene. I could paint, even at this moment, the mute and courageous submission expressed in Diana's features—the wild and distorted faces of the executioners, who crowded around us with 'mopping and mowing;'* grimaces ever changing, and each more hideous than that which preceded. I saw the rigid and inflexible fanaticism painted in the face of the father—I saw him lift the fatal match—the deadly signal exploded—It was repeated again and again and again, in rival thunders, by the echoes of the surrounding cliffs, and I awoke from fancied horror to real apprehension.

The sounds in my dream were not ideal. They reverberated on my waking ears, but it was two or three minutes ere I could collect myself so as distinctly to understand that they proceeded from a violent knocking at the gate. I leaped from my couch in great apprehension, took my sword under my arm, and hastened to forbid the admission of any one. But my route was necessarily circuitous, because the library looked not upon the quadrangle, but into the gardens. When I had reached a staircase, the windows of which opened upon the entrance court, I heard the feeble and intimidated tones of Syddall expostulating with rough voices, which demanded admittance, by the warrant of Justice Standish, and in the King's name, and threatened the old domestic with the heaviest penal consequences, if he refused instant obedience. Ere they had ceased, I heard, to my unspeakable provocation, the voice of Andrew bidding Syddall stand aside, and let him open the door.

'If they come in King George's name, we have naething to fear—we

hae spent baith bluid and gowd for him—We dinna need to darn ourselves like some folks, Mr Syddall—We are neither Papists nor Jacobites, I trow.'

It was in vain I accelerated my pace down stairs; I heard bolt after
bolt withdrawn by the officious scoundrel, while all the time he was
boasting his own and his master's loyalty to King George; and I could
easily calculate that the party must enter before I could arrive at the
door to replace the bars. Devoting the back of Andrew Fairservice to
the cudgel so soon as I should have time to pay him his deserts, I ran
back to the library, barricaded the door as I best could, and hastened to
that by which Diana and her father entered, and begged for instant
admittance. Diana herself undid the door. She was ready dressed, and
betrayed neither perturbation nor fear.

'Danger is so familiar to us,' she said, 'that we are always prepared
to meet it—My father is already up—he is in Rashleigh's apartment—We will escape into the garden, and thence by the postern-
gate (I have the key from Syddall in case of need) into the wood—I
know its dingles better than any one now alive—Keep them a few
minutes in play.—And, dear, dear Frank, once more, fare thee well!'

She vanished like a meteor to join her father, and the intruders were
rapping violently, and attempting to force the library door by the time
I had returned into it.

'You robber dogs!' I exclaimed, wilfully mistaking the purpose of
their disturbance, 'if you do not instantly quit the house I will fire my
blunderbuss through the door.'

'Fire a fule's bauble!' said Andrew Fairservice; 'it's Mr Clerk Jobson, with a legal warrant'—

'To search for, take, and apprehend,' said the voice of that execrable
pettifogger, 'the bodies of certain persons in my warrant named,
charged of high treason under the 13th of King William, chapter
third.'*

And the violence on the door was renewed. 'I am rising, gentlemen,' said I, desirous to gain as much time as possible—'commit no
violence—give me leave to look at your warrant; and, if it is formal and
legal, I shall not oppose it.'

'God save great George our King!'* ejaculated Andrew. 'I tauld ye
that ye would find nae Jacobites here.'

Spinning out the time as much as possible, I was at length compelled to open the door, which they would otherwise have forced.

Mr Jobson entered, with several assistants, among whom I discovered the younger Wingfield, to whom, doubtless, he was obliged for his information, and exhibited his warrant, directed not only against Frederick Vernon, an attainted traitor, but also against Diana Vernon, spinster, and Francis Osbaldistone, gentleman, accused of misprision of treason. It was a case in which resistance would have been madness; I therefore, after capitulating for a few minutes' delay, surrendered myself a prisoner.

I had next the mortification to see Jobson go straight to the chamber of Miss Vernon, and I learned that from thence, without hesitation or difficulty, he went to the room where Sir Frederick had slept. 'The hare has stolen away,' said the brute, 'but her form is warm—the greyhounds will have her by the haunches yet.'

A scream from the garden announced that he prophesied too truly. In the course of five minutes, Rashleigh entered the library with Sir Frederick Vernon and his daughter as prisoners. 'The fox,' he said, 'knew his old earth, but he forgot it could be stopped by a careful huntsman—I had not forgot the garden gate, Sir Frederick—or, if that title suits you better, most noble Lord Beauchamp.'

'Rashleigh,' said Sir Frederick, 'thou art a detestable villain!'

'I better deserved the name, Sir Knight, or my Lord, when, under the direction of an able tutor, I sought to introduce civil war into the bosom of a peaceful country. But I have done my best,' said he, looking upwards, 'to atone for my errors.'

I could hold no longer. I had designed to watch their proceedings in silence, but I felt that I must speak or die. 'If hell,' I said, 'has one complexion more hideous than another, it is where villainy is masked by hypocrisy.'

'Ha! my gentle cousin,' said Rashleigh, holding a candle towards me, and surveying me from head to foot; 'right welcome to Osbaldistone-Hall!—I can forgive your spleen—It is hard to lose an estate and a mistress in one night; for we shall take possession of this poor manor-house in the name of the lawful heir, Sir Rashleigh Osbaldistone.'

While Rashleigh braved it out in this manner, I could see that he put a strong force upon his feelings, both of anger and shame. But his state of mind was more obvious when Diana Vernon addressed him. 'Rashleigh,' she said, 'I pity you—for, deep as the evil is which you have laboured to do me, and the evil you have actually done, I cannot hate you so much as I scorn and pity you. What you have now done may be the work of an hour, but will furnish you with reflection for your life—of what nature I leave to your own conscience, which will not slumber for ever.'

Rashleigh strode once or twice through the room, came up to the side-table, on which wine was still standing, and poured out a large glass with a trembling hand; but when he saw that we observed his tremor, he suppressed it by a strong effort, and, looking at us with fixed and daring composure, carried the bumper to his head without spilling a drop.

'It is my father's old burgundy,' he said, looking to Jobson; 'I am glad there is some of it left—You will get proper persons to take care of the house and property in my name, and turn out the doating old butler, and that foolish Scotch rascal. Meanwhile, we will convey these persons to a more proper place of custody.—I have provided the old family coach for your convenience,' he said, 'though I am not ignorant that even the lady could brave the night air on foot or on horseback, were the errand more to her mind.'

Andrew wrung his hands.—'I only said that my master was surely speaking to a ghaist in the library—and the villain Lancie to betray an auld friend, that sang aff the same Psalm-book wi' him every Sabbath for twenty years!'

He was turned out of the house, together with Syddall, without being allowed to conclude his lamentation. His expulsion, however, led to some singular consequences. Resolving, according to his own story, to go down for the night where Mother Simpson would give him a lodging for old acquaintance' sake, he had just got clear of the avenue, and into the old wood as it was called, though it was now used as pasture-ground rather than woodland, when he suddenly lighted on a drove of Scotch cattle, which were lying there to repose themselves after the day's journey. At this, Andrew was in no way surprised, it being the well-known custom of his countrymen, who take care of those droves, to quarter themselves after night upon the best unenclosed grass-ground they can find, and depart before daybreak to escape paying for their night's lodgings. But he was both surprised and startled, when a Highlander, springing up, accused him of disturbing the cattle, and refused him to pass forward till he had spoken to his master. The mountaineer conducted Andrew into a thicket, where he found three or four more of his countrymen. 'And,' said Andrew, 'I saw sune they were ower mony men for the drove; and from the questions they put to me, I judged they had other tow on their rock.'*

They questioned him closely about all that had passed at Osbaldistone-Hall, and seemed surprised and concerned at the report he made to them.

'And troth,' said Andrew, 'I tauld them a' I kend; for dirks and pistols were what I could never refuse information to in a' my life.'

They talked in whispers among themselves, and at length collected their cattle together, and drove them close up to the entrance of the avenue, which might be half a mile distant from the house. They proceeded to drag together some felled trees which lay in the vicinity, so as to make a temporary barricade across the road, about fifteen yards beyond the avenue. It was now near daybreak, and there was a pale eastern gleam mingled with the fading moonlight, so that objects could be discovered with some distinctness. The lumbering sound of a coach, drawn by four horses, and escorted by six men on horseback, was heard coming up the avenue. The Highlanders listened attentively. The carriage contained Mr Jobson and his unfortunate prisoners. The escort consisted of Rashleigh, and several horsemen, peace-officers and their assistants. So soon as we had passed the gate at the head of the avenue, it was shut behind the cavalcade by a Highlandman, stationed there for that purpose. At the same time the carriage was impeded in its farther progress by the cattle, amongst which we were involved, and by the barricade in front. Two of the escort dismounted to remove the felled trees, which they might think were left there by accident or carelessness. The others began with their whips to drive the cattle from the road.

'Who dare abuse our cattle?' said a rough voice.—'Shoot him, Angus.'

Rashleigh instantly called out, 'A rescue—a rescue!' and, firing a pistol, wounded the man who spoke.

'*Claymore!*' cried the leader of the Highlanders, and a scuffle instantly commenced. The officers of the law, surprised at so sudden an attack, and not usually possessing the most desperate bravery, made but an imperfect defence, considering the superiority of their numbers. Some attempted to ride back to the Hall, but on a pistol being fired from behind the gate, they conceived themselves surrounded, and at length galloped off in different directions. Rashleigh, meanwhile, had dismounted, and on foot had maintained a desperate and single-handed conflict with the leader of the band. The window of the carriage, on my side, permitted me to witness it. At length Rashleigh dropped.

'Will you ask forgiveness for the sake of God, King James, and auld friendship?' said a voice which I knew right well.

'No, never,' said Rashleigh, firmly.

'Then, traitor, die in your treason!' retorted MacGregor, and plunged his sword in his prostrate antagonist.

In the next moment he was at the carriage door—handed out Miss Vernon, assisted her father and me to alight, and dragging out the attorney, head foremost, threw him under the wheel.

'Mr Osbaldistone,' he said, in a whisper, 'you have nothing to fear—I must look after those who have—Your friends will soon be in safety—Farewell, and forget not the MacGregor.'

He whistled—his band gathered round him, and, hurrying Diana and her father along with him, they were almost instantly lost in the glades of the forest. The coachman and postilion had abandoned their horses, and fled at the first discharge of firearms; but the animals, stopped by the barricade, remained perfectly still; and well for Jobson that they did so, for the slightest motion would have dragged the wheel over his body. My first object was to relieve him, for such was the rascal's terror that he never could have risen by his own exertions. I next commanded him to observe, that I had neither taken part in the rescue, nor availed myself of it to make my escape, and enjoined him to go down to the Hall, and call some of his party, who had been left there, to assist the wounded. But Jobson's fears had so mastered and controlled every faculty of his mind, that he was totally incapable of moving. I now resolved to go myself, but in my way I stumbled over the body of a man, as I thought, dead or dying. It was, however, Andrew Fairservice, as well and whole as ever he was in his life, who had only taken this recumbent posture to avoid the slashes, stabs, and pistol-balls, which, for a moment or two, were flying in various directions. I was so glad to find him that I did not enquire how he came thither, but instantly commanded his assistance.

Rashleigh was our first object. He groaned when I approached him, as much through spite as through pain, and shut his eyes, as if determined, like Iago, to speak no word more.* We lifted him into the carriage, and performed the same good office to another wounded man of his party, who had been left on the field. I then with difficulty made

Jobson understand that he must enter the coach also, and support Sir Rashleigh upon the seat. He obeyed, but with an air as if he but half comprehended my meaning. Andrew and I turned the horses' heads round, and, opening the gate of the avenue, led them slowly back to Osbaldistone-Hall.

Some fugitives had already reached the Hall by circuitous routes, and alarmed its garrison by the news that Sir Rashleigh, Clerk Jobson, and all their escort, save they who escaped to tell the tale, had been cut to pieces at the head of the avenue, by a whole regiment of wild Highlanders. When we reached the mansion, therefore, we heard such a buzz as arises when bees are alarmed, and mustering in their hives. Mr Jobson, however, who had now in some measure come to his senses, found voice enough to make himself known. He was the more anxious to be released from the carriage, as one of his companions (the peace-officer) had, to his inexpressible terror, expired by his side with a hideous groan.

Sir Rashleigh Osbaldistone was still alive, but so dreadfully wounded that the bottom of the coach was filled with his blood, and long traces of it left from the entrance-door into the Stone-Hall, where he was placed in a chair, some attempting to stop the bleeding with cloths, while others called for a surgeon, and no one seemed willing to go to fetch one.

'Torment me not,' said the wounded man. 'I know no assistance can avail me. I am a dying man.' He raised himself in his chair, though the damps and chill of death were already on his brow, and spoke with a firmness which seemed beyond his strength. 'Cousin Francis,' he said, 'draw near to me.' I approached him as he requested.—'I wish you only to know that the pangs of death do not alter one iota of my feelings towards you. I hate you!' he said, the expression of rage throwing a hideous glare into the eyes which were soon to be closed for ever—'I hate you with a hatred as intense, now while I lie bleeding and dying before you, as if my foot trode on your neck.'

'I have given you no cause, sir,' I replied, 'and for your own sake I could wish your mind in a better temper.'

'You *have* given me cause,' he rejoined—'in love, in ambition, in the paths of interest, you have crossed and blighted me at every turn. I was born to be the honour of my father's house—I have been its disgrace—and all owing to you.—My very patrimony has become yours—Take it,' he said, 'and may the curse of a dying man cleave to it!'

In a moment after he had uttered this frightful wish, he fell back in the chair; his eyes became glazed, his limbs stiffened, but the grin and glare of mortal hatred survived even the last gasp of life. I will dwell no longer on so painful a picture, nor say any more of the death of Rashleigh, than that it gave me access to my rights of inheritance without farther challenge, and that Jobson found himself compelled to allow, that the ridiculous charge of misprision of high-treason was got up on an affidavit which he made with the sole purpose of favouring Rashleigh's views, and removing me from Osbaldistone-Hall. The rascal's name was struck off the list of attorneys, and he was reduced to poverty and contempt.

I returned to London when I had put my affairs in order at Osbaldistone-Hall, and felt happy to escape from a place which suggested so many painful recollections. My anxiety was now acute to learn the fate of Diana and her father. A French gentleman who came to London on commercial business, was intrusted with a letter to me from Miss Vernon, which put my mind at rest respecting their safety.

It gave me to understand, that the opportune appearance of MacGregor and his party was not fortuitous. The Scottish nobles and gentry, engaged in the insurrection, as well as those of England, were particularly anxious to further the escape of Sir Frederick Vernon, who, as an old and trusted agent of the house of Stewart, was possessed of matter enough to have ruined half Scotland. Rob Roy, of whose sagacity and courage they had known so many proofs, was the person whom they pitched upon to assist his escape, and the place of meeting was fixed at Osbaldistone-Hall. You have already heard how nearly the plan had been disconcerted by the unhappy Rashleigh. It succeeded, however, perfectly; for when once Sir Frederick and his daughter were again at large, they found horses prepared for them, and, by MacGregor's knowledge of the country,—for every part of Scotland, and of the north of England, was familiar to him,—were conducted to the western sea-coast, and safely embarked for France. The same gentleman told me, that Sir Frederick was not expected to survive for many months a lingering disease, the consequence of late hardships and privations. His daughter was placed in a convent, and although it was her father's wish she should take the veil, he was understood to refer the matter entirely to her own inclinations.

When these news reached me, I frankly told the state of my affections to my father, who was not a little startled at the idea of my marrying a Roman Catholic. But he was very desirous to see me 'settled in life,' as he called it; and he was sensible that, in joining him with heart and hand in his commercial labours, I had sacrificed my own inclinations. After a brief hesitation, and several questions asked and answered to his satisfaction, he broke out with—'I little thought a son of mine should have been Lord of Osbaldistone Manor, and far less that he should go to a French convent for a spouse. But so dutiful a daughter cannot but prove a good wife. You have worked at the desk to please me, Frank; it is but fair you should wive to please yourself.'

How I sped in my wooing, Will Tresham, I need not tell you. You know, too, how long and happily I lived with Diana. You know how I lamented her. But you do not—cannot know, how much she deserved her husband's sorrow.

I have no more of romantic adventure to tell, nor, indeed, any thing to communicate farther, since the latter incidents of my life are so well known to one who has shared, with the most friendly sympathy, the joys, as well as the sorrows, by which its scenes have been chequered. I often visited Scotland, but never again saw the bold Highlander who had such an influence on the early events of my life. I learned, however, from time to time, that he continued to maintain his ground among the mountains of Loch Lomond, in despite of his powerful enemies, and that he even obtained, to a certain degree, the connivance of government to his self-elected office of Protector of the Lennox, in virtue of which he levied black-mail with as much regularity as the proprietors did their ordinary rents. It seemed impossible that his life should have concluded without a violent end. Nevertheless, he died in old age and by a peaceful death, some time about the year 1733,* and is still remembered in his country as the Robin Hood of Scotland, the dread of the wealthy, but the friend of the poor, and possessed of many qualities, both of head and heart, which would have graced a less equivocal profession than that to which his fate condemned him.

Old Andrew Fairservice used to say, that 'There were many things ower bad for blessing, and ower gude for banning, like ROB ROY.'

[Here the original manuscript ends somewhat abruptly. I have reason to think that what followed related to private affairs.]

POSTSCRIPT

THE second article of the Appendix to the Introduction to Rob Roy, p. 55, contains two curious letters respecting the arrest of Mr Grahame of Killearn by that daring freebooter, while levying the Duke of Montrose's rents. These were taken from scroll copies in the possession of his Grace the present Duke, who kindly permitted the use of them in the present publication. Both volumes of the Novel had but just passed through the press, when the Right Honourable Mr Peel—whose important state avocations do not avert his attention from the interests of literature—transmitted to the author copies of the original letters and enclosure, of which he possessed only the rough draught. The originals were discovered in the State Paper Office, by the indefatigable researches of Mr Lemon, who is daily throwing more light on that valuable collection of records. From the documents with which the author has been thus kindly favoured, he is enabled to fill up the addresses which were wanting in the scrolls. That of the 21st Nov. 1716, is addressed to Lord Viscount Townshend, and is accompanied by one of the same date to Robert Pringle, Esquire, Under-Secretary of State, which is here inserted as relative to so curious an incident.

Letter from the DUKE OF MONTROSE to ROBERT PRINGLE, Esq., Under-Secretary to Lord Viscount Townshend.

'*Glasgow,* 21 *Nov.* 1716.

'Sᴿ,

'HAVEING had so many dispatches to make this night, I hope ye'l excuse me that I make use of another hand to give yow a short account of the occasion of this express, by which I have written to my Ld. Duke of Roxburgh, and my Lord Townshend, which I hope ye'l gett carefully deleivered.

'Mr Graham, younger of Killearn, being on Munday last in Monteith att a country house, collecting my rents, was about nine o'clock that same night surprised by Rob Roy with a party of his men in arms, who, haveing surrounded the house and secured the avenues, presented their guns in at the windows, while he himself entered the room with some others with cokt pistolls, and seased Killearn with all his money, books, papers, and bonds, and carryed all away with him to the hills, at the same time ordering Killearn to write a letter to me, (of which ye have the copy inclosed,) proposeing a very honourable treaty to me. I must say this story was as surprising to me as it was insolent; and it must bring a very great concern upon me, that this gentleman, my near relation, should be brought to suffer all the barbaritys and crueltys, which revenge and mallice may suggest to these miscreants, for his haveing acted a faithfull part in the service of the government, and his affection to me in my concerns.

'I need not be more particular to you, since I know that my Letter to my Lord Townshend will come into your hands, so shall only now give you the assurances of my being, with great sincerity,

'S^r, y^r most humble servant,

(Signed)　　　　　　　　　　　　　　　　'MONTROSE.

'I long exceedingly for a return of my former dispatches to the Secretary's about Methven and Col^{ll} Urquhart, and my wife's cousins, Balnamoon and Phinaven.

'I must beg yow'll give my humble service to Mr Secretary Methven, and tell him that I must referr him to what I have written to My Lord Townshend in this affair of Rob Roy, believing it was needless to trouble both with letters.'

Examined,　　　　　　　　　　　　　　　ROBT. LEMON,
　　　　　　　　　　　　　　　　Deputy Keeper of State Papers.

STATE PAPER OFFICE,
Nov. 4, 1829.

NOTE.—The enclosure referred to in the preceding letter, is another copy of the letter which Mr Grahame of Killearn was compelled by Rob Roy to write to the Duke of Montrose, and is exactly the same as the one enclosed in his Grace's letter to Lord Townshend, dated November 21st, 1716.

R. L.

The last letter in the Appendix, p. 58, (28th November,) acquainting the Government with Killearn's being set at liberty, is also addressed to the Under-Secretary of State, Mr Pringle.

The author may also here remark, that immediately previous to the insurrection of 1715, he perceives, from some notes of information given to Government, that Rob Roy appears to have been much employed and trusted by the Jacobite party, even in the very delicate task of transporting *specie* to the Earl of Breadalbane, though it might have somewhat resembled trusting Don Raphael and Ambrose de Lamela with the church-treasure.*

SCOTT'S NOTES

Notes present in the early editions are marked (1822); all other notes were added in 1829.

1. As it may be necessary, in the present Edition, to speak upon the square, the Author thinks it proper to own, that the communication alluded to is entirely imaginary.

2. I have been informed, that, at no very remote period, it was proposed to take this large stone, which marks the grave of Dugald Ciar Mohr, and convert it to the purpose of the lintel of a window, the threshold of a door, or some such mean use. A man of the clan MacGregor, who was somewhat deranged, took fire at this insult; and when the workmen came to remove the stone, planted himself upon it, with a broad axe in his hand, swearing he would dash out the brains of any one who should disturb the monument. Athletic in person, and insane enough to be totally regardless of consequences, it was thought best to give way to his humour; and the poor madman kept sentinel on the stone day and night, till the proposal of removing it was entirely dropped.

3. The above is the account which I find in a manuscript history of the clan Mac-Gregor, of which I was indulged with a perusal by Donald MacGregor, Esq. late Major of the 33d regiment, where great pains have been taken to collect traditions and written documents concerning the family. But an ancient and constant tradition, preserved among the inhabitants of the country, and particularly those of the clan, MacFarlane, relieves Dugald Ciar Mohr of the guilt of murdering the youths, and lays the blame on a certain Donald or Duncan Lean, who performed the act of cruelty, with the assistance of a gillie who attended him, named Charlioch, or Charlie. They say that the homicides dared not again join their clan, but that they resided in a wild and solitary state as outlaws, in an unfrequented part of the MacFarlanes' territory. Here they lived for some time undisturbed, till they committed an act of brutal violence on two defenceless women, a mother and daughter of the MacFarlane clan. In revenge of this atrocity, the MacFarlanes hunted them down and shot them. It is said the younger ruffian, Charlioch, might have escaped, being remarkably swift of foot. But his crime became his punishment, for the female whom he had outraged had defended herself desperately, and had stabbed him with his own dirk on the thigh. He was lame from the wound, and was the more easily overtaken and killed. I incline to think that this last is the true edition of the story, and that the guilt was transferred to Dugald Ciar Mohr, as a man of higher name. Or it is possible these subordinate persons had only executed his orders.

   [The MS referred to in this note was by John Gregorson of Ardtornish; see Scott's *Letters* xi. 288–9, 301–2; xii. 6. Scott says he heard the tradition 40 years earlier 'in the vicinity of Glenfruin'.]

4. See Statistical Account of Scotland, vol. xviii. page 332. Parish of Kippen.

5. See Appendix, No. I.

6. His courage and affectation of foppery were united, which is less frequently the case, with a spirit of innate modesty. He is thus described in Lord Binning's satirical verses, entitled 'Argyle's Levee.'

> 'Six times had Harry bow'd unseen
>   Before he dared advance;
> The Duke then, turning round well pleased,
>   Said, 'Sene you've been in France,
> A more polite and jaunty man
>   I never saw before;'
> Then Harry bow'd, and blush'd, and bow'd,
>   And strutted to the door.'

See a Collection of Original Poems, by Scotch Gentlemen, vol. ii. page 125. [Despite the attribution of Scott's source, *A Collection of Original Poems by the Rev. Mr Blacklock and other Scotch Gentlemen*, vol. 2 (1762), 'The Duke of Argyll's Levee' is in fact by Joseph Mitchell (1684–1738) and was published in *The Gentleman's Magazine* in 1740 (*DNB*). Original reads 'durst' for 'dared', 'Sure' for 'Sene', 'mien' for 'man'.]

7. Mr Grahame of Gartmore's Causes of the Disturbances in the Highlands. See Jamieson's edition of Burt's Letters from the North of Scotland, Appendix, vol. ii. p. 348.
[Scott drew the attention of the Gartmore MS, 'An Inquiry into the Causes which facilitate the Rise and Progress of Rebellions and Insurrections in the Highlands of Scotland' (1747), to Robert Jamieson, who printed extracts in the 5th edn. (1818) of Burt's *Letters*.]

8. 'At night they arrived at Luss, where they were joined by Sir Humphry Colquhoun of Luss, and James Grant of Plascander, his son-in-law, followed by forty or fifty stately fellows in their short hose and belted plaids, armed each of them with a well-fixed gun on his shoulder, a strong handsome target, with a sharp-pointed steel of above half an ell in length screwed into the navel of it, on his left arm, a sturdy claymore by his side, and a pistol or two, with a dirk and knife, in his belt.'—*Rae's History of the Rebellion*, 4to, p. 287.
[Scott had the 2nd edn. (1746) of the Revd Peter Rae's *A History of the Rebellion raised against his Majesty by the friends of the Popish Pretender.*]

9. The Loch Lomond expedition was judged worthy to form a separate pamphlet, which I have not seen, but, as quoted by the historian Rae, it must be delectable.
   'On the morrow, being Thursday the 13th, they went on their expedition, and about noon came to Inversnaid, the place of danger, where the Paisley men and those of Dumbarton, and several of the other companies, to the number of an hundred men, with the greatest intrepidity leapt on shore, got up to the top of the mountains, and stood a considerable time, beating their drums all the while; but no enemy appearing, they went in quest of their boats, which the rebels had seized, and having casually lighted on some ropes and oars hid among the shrubs, at length they found the boats drawn up a good way on the land, which they

hurled down to the loch. Such of them as were not damaged they carried off with them, and such as were, they sank and hewed to pieces. That same night they returned to Luss, and thence next day to Dumbarton, from whence they had first set out, bringing along with them the whole boats they found in their way on either side of the loch, and in the creeks of the isles, and mooring them under the cannon of the castle. During this expedition the pinnaces discharging their patararoes, and the men their small-arms, made such a thundering noise, through the multiplied rebounding echoes of the vast mountains on both sides of the loch, that the MacGregors were cowed and frighted away to the rest of the rebels who were encamped at Strath Fillan.'—*Rae's History of the Rebellion*, 4to, p. 287.

10. The first of these anecdotes, which brings the highest pitch of civilisation so closely in contact with the half-savage state of society, I have heard told by the late distinguished Dr Gregory; and the members of his family have had the kindness to collate the story with their recollections and family documents, and furnish the authentic particulars. The second rests on the recollection of an old man, who was present when Rob took French leave of his literary cousin on hearing the drums beat, and communicated the circumstance to Mr Alexander Forbes, a connexion of Dr Gregory by marriage, who is still alive.

11. The reader will find two original letters of the Duke of Montrose, with that which Mr Graham of Killearn dispatched from his prison-house by the Outlaw's command, in the Appendix, No. II.

12. About 1792, when the author chanced to pass that way while on a tour through the Highlands, a garrison, consisting of a single veteran, was still maintained at Inversnaid. The venerable warder was reaping his barley croft in all peace and tranquillity; and when we asked admittance to repose ourselves, he told us we would find the key of *The Fort* under the door.

13. Letters from the North of Scotland, vol. ii. pp. 344–5.

14. Mad herdsmen, a name given to cattle stealers.

15. The winds which sweep a wild glen in Badenoch are so called.

16. Appendix, No. III.

17. Such an admission is ascribed to the robber, Donald Bean Lean, in Waverley, vol. ii. p. 309.
[See Chapter XLII (World's Classics edn., p. 289).]

18. Some accounts state, that Appin himself was Rob Roy's antagonist on this occasion. My recollection, from the account of Invernahyle himself, was as stated in the text. But the period when I received the information is now so distant, that it is possible I may be mistaken. Invernahyle was rather of low stature, but very well made, athletic, and an excellent swordsman.

19. This fatal piece was taken from Robin Oig, when he was seized many years afterwards. It remained in possession of the magistrates, before whom he was brought for examination, and now makes part of a small collection of arms belonging to the author. It is a Spanish-barrelled gun, marked with the letters R.M.C. for Robert MacGregor Campbell.
[Scott acquired Rob Roy's gun in 1811; see *Letters* iii. 99.]

20. The author is uncertain whether it is worth while to mention, that he had a personal opportunity of observing even in his own time, that the king's writ did not pass quite current in the Braes of Balquhidder. There were very considerable debts due by Stewart of Appin (chiefly to the author's family,) which were likely to be lost to the creditors, if they could not be made available out of this same farm of Invernenty, the scene of the murder done upon MacLaren.

His family, consisting of several strapping deer-stalkers, still possessed the farm, by virtue of a long lease, for a trifling rent. There was no chance of any one buying it with such an encumbrance, and a transaction was entered into by the MacLarens, who, being desirous to emigrate to America, agreed to sell their lease to the creditors for L.500, and to remove at the next term of Whitsunday. But whether they repented their bargain, or desired to make a better, or whether from a mere point of honour, the MacLarens declared they would not permit a summons of removal to be executed against them, which was necessary for the legal completion of the bargain. And such was the general impression that they were men capable of resisting the legal execution of warning by very effectual means, no king's messenger would execute the summons without the support of a military force. An escort of a sergeant and six men was obtained from a Highland regiment lying in Stirling; and the author, then a writer's apprentice, equivalent to the honourable situation of an attorney's clerk, was invested with the superintendance of the expedition, with directions to see that the messenger discharged his duty fully, and that the gallant sergeant did not exceed his part by committing violence or plunder. And thus it happened, oddly enough, that the author first entered the romantic scenery of Loch Katrine, of which he may perhaps say he has somewhat extended the reputation, riding in all the dignity of danger, with a front and rear guard, and loaded arms. The sergeant was absolutely a Highland Sergeant Kite, full of stories of Rob Roy and of himself, and a very good companion. We experienced no interruption whatever, and when we came to Invernenty, found the house deserted. We took up our quarters for the night, and used some of the victuals which we found there. On the morning we returned as unmolested as we came.

The MacLarens, who probably never thought of any serious opposition, received their money and went to America, where, having had some slight share in removing them from their *paupera regna*, I sincerely hope they prospered.

The rent of Invernenty instantly rose from L.10 to L.70 or L.80; and when sold, the farm was purchased (I think by the late Laird of MacNab) at a price higher in proportion than what even the modern rent authorised the parties interested to hope for.

[This adventure took place during Scott's apprenticeship to his father, *c.*1788. He 'extended the reputation' of Loch Katrine in *The Lady of the Lake* (1810). For *Sergeant Kite*, see Farquhar, *The Recruiting Officer* (1705), III. i.]

21. Published in Blackwood's Magazine, vol. ii. page 228.
[The letters are printed in the last instalment of 'Memoir of Rob Roy MacGregor, and some branches of his family', in *Blackwood's Edinburgh Magazine*, 2 (1817), 288–93. The letter Scott quotes from below (pp. 51–2) is on p. 293.]

22. Childe Harold's Pilgrimage, Canto II.

23. See Appendix, No. V.

24. Such, at least, was his general character; for when James Mohr, while perpetrating the violence at Edinbilly, called out, in order to overawe opposition, that Glengyle was lying in the moor with a hundred men to patronise his enterprise, Jean Key told him he lied, since she was confident Glengyle would never countenance so scoundrelly a business.

25. Allan Breck Stewart was a man likely in such a matter to keep his word. James Drummond MacGregor and he, like Katherine and Petruchio, were well matched 'for a couple of quiet ones.' Allan Breck lived till the beginning of the French Revolution. About 1789, a friend of mine, then residing at Paris, was invited to see some procession which was supposed likely to interest him, from the windows of an apartment occupied by a Scottish Benedictine priest. He found, sitting by the fire, a tall, thin, raw-boned, grim-looking old man, with the petit croix of St Louis. His visage was strongly marked by the irregular projections of the cheek-bones and chin. His eyes were grey. His grizzled hair exhibited marks of having been red, and his complexion was weather-beaten, and remarkably freckled. Some civilities in French passed between the old man and my friend, in the course of which they talked of the streets and squares of Paris, till at length the old soldier, for such he seemed, and such he was, said with a sigh, in a sharp Highland accent, 'Deil ane o' them a' is worth the Hie street of Edinburgh!' On enquiry, this admirer of Auld Reekie, which he was never to see again, proved to be Allan Breck Stewart. He lived decently on his little pension, and had, in no subsequent period of his life, shown anything of the savage mood, in which he is generally believed to have assassinated the enemy and oppressor, as he supposed him, of his family and clan.

26. The Trials of the Sons of Rob Roy, with Anecdotes of Himself and his Family, were published at Edinburgh, 1818, in 12mo.

27. James died near three months before, but his family might easily remain a long time without the news of that event.

28. It does not appear to whom this letter was addressed. Certainly, from its style and tenor, it was designed for some person high in rank and office—perhaps the King's Advocate for the time.
[The letter was addressed to Viscount Charles Townshend, Secretary of State for the Northern Departments; see Scott's 'Postscript', below. Montrose was so perturbed he wrote three drafts; Scott prints the version which was sent (Murray, 211–14).]

29. This curious epistle is copied from an authentic narrative of Marshal Wade's proceedings in the Highlands, communicated by the late eminent antiquary, George Chalmers, Esq. to Mr Robert Jamieson of the Register House, Edinburgh, and published in the Appendix to an Edition of Burt's Letters from the North of Scotland. 2 vols. 8vo. Edinburgh, 1818.

30. A pass on the eastern margin of Loch Lomond, and an entrance to the Highlands.

31. The introduction of gaugers, supervisors, and examiners, was one of the great complaints of the Scottish nation, though a natural consequence of the Union.

32. This seems to have been written about the time of Wilkes and Liberty.

    [(1822) The radical John Wilkes, subsequently Mayor of London, stirred up English xenophobia against the Scots in his journal *The North Briton* (1763) as part of a campaign against the ministry of Lord Bute.]

33. Now called Don Juan.

    [(1822) 'The Stone Guest', title of a play by Molière (1655), is a source for the famous opera by Da Ponte and Mozart. Don Juan invites the statue of the Commandant, whom he has killed in a duel, to supper; the statue shows up and carries him to hell.]

34. Perhaps from the French *Justaucorps*.

    [(1822) A close-fitting, knee-length coat.]

35. On occasions of public alarm, in the beginning of the eighteenth century, the horses of the Catholics were often seized upon, as they were always supposed to be on the eve of rising in rebellion.

36. The nunnery of Wilton was granted to the Earl of Pembroke upon its dissolution, by the magisterial authority of Henry VIII., or his son Edward VI. On the accession of Queen Mary, of Catholic memory, the Earl found it necessary to re-instal the Abbess and her fair recluses, which he did with many expressions of his remorse, kneeling humbly to the vestals, and inducting them into the convent and possessions from which he had expelled them. With the accession of Elizabeth, the accommodating Earl again resumed his Protestant faith, and a second time drove the nuns from their sanctuary. The remonstrances of the Abbess, who reminded him of his penitent expressions on the former occasion, could wring from him no other answer than that in the text—'Go spin, you jade—Go spin.'

37. I have in vain laboured to discover this gentleman's name, and the period of his incumbency. I do not, however, despair to see these points, with some others which may elude my sagacity, satisfactorily elucidated by one or other of the periodical publications which have devoted their pages to explanatory commentaries on my former volumes; and whose research and ingenuity claim my peculiar gratitude, for having discovered many persons and circumstances connected with my narratives, of which I myself never so much as dreamed.

    [(1822) In his edition of *Rob Roy* John Sutherland notes that W. Forbes Gray, undeterred by Scott's irony, identified the preacher as the Revd James Stirling (*A Guide to Edinburgh, Abbotsford, and the 'Rob Roy' Country* (1932)).]

38. This I believe to be an anachronism, as Saint Enoch's Church was not built at the date of the story.

39. The lads with the kilts or petticoats.

40. Inch Cailleach is an island in Lochlomond, where the clan of MacGregor were wont to be interred, and where their sepulchres may still be seen. It formerly contained a nunnery; hence the name Inch-Cailleach, or the Island of Old Women. [See also Scott's n. 35 to *The Lady of the Lake*.]

41. Anglicé, the head of the sow to the tail of the pig.

    [Proverbial, meaning 'balance your Loss with your Gain' (James Kelly, *A Complete Collection of Scotish Proverbs* (1721)).]

42. The boys in Scotland used formerly to make a sort of Saturnalia in a snow-storm, by pelting passengers with snowballs. But those exposed to that annoyance were excused from it on the easy penalty of a baik (curtsey) from a female, or a bow from a man. It was only the refractory who underwent the storm.

43. *Thigging* and *sorning* was a kind of genteel begging, or rather something between begging and robbing, by which the needy in Scotland used to extort cattle, or the means of subsistence, from those who had any to give.

44. The word *pretty* is, or was, used in Scotch, in the sense of the German *prachtig*, and meant a gallant, alert fellow, prompt and ready at his weapons.

45. Cutlass.

46. An outlaw.

47. Plundered.

48. Two great clans fought out a quarrel with thirty men of a side, in presence of the king, on the North Inch of Perth, on or about the year 1392; a man was amissing on one side, whose room was filled by a little bandy-legged citizen of Perth. This substitute, Henry Wynd—or, as the Highlanders called him, *Gow Chrom*, that is, the bandy-legged smith—fought well, and contributed greatly to the fate of the battle, without knowing which side he fought on—so, to fight for your own hand, like Henry Wynd, passed into a proverb.
[Scott would make this the climactic episode of *The Fair Maid of Perth* (1827). The proverb was a favourite of Scott's, especially in the period following his ruin.]

49. Sackless, that is, innocent.

50. Mons Meg was a large old-fashioned piece of ordnance, a great favourite with the Scottish common people; she was fabricated at Mons, in Flanders, in the reign of James IV. or V. of Scotland. This gun figures frequently in the public accounts of the time, where we find charges for grease to grease Meg's mouth withal, (to increase, as every schoolboy knows, the loudness of the report,) ribands to deck her carriage, and pipes to play before her when she was brought from the Castle to accompany the Scottish army on any distant expedition. After the Union, there was much popular apprehension that the Regalia of Scotland, and the sub-ordinate Palladium, Mons Meg, would be carried to England to complete the odious surrender of national independence. The Regalia, sequestered from the sight of the public, were generally supposed to have been abstracted in this man-ner. As for Mons Meg, she remained in the Castle of Edinburgh, till, by order of the Board of Ordnance, she was actually removed to Woolwich about 1757. The Regalia, by his Majesty's special command, have been brought forth from their place of concealment in 1818, and exposed to the view of the people, by whom they must be looked upon with deep associations; and, in this very winter of 1828-9, Mons Meg has been restored to the country, where that, which in every other place or situation was a mere mass of rusty iron, becomes once more a curi-ous monument of antiquity.
[Scott himself directed the rediscovery of the Scottish Regalia in 1818, and inter-ceded with George IV for the return of Mons Meg on the royal visit to Edin-burgh in 1822.]

51. THE lakes and precipices amidst which the Avon-Dhu, or river Forth, has its birth, are still, according to popular tradition, haunted by the Elfin people, the most peculiar, but most pleasing, of the creations of Celtic superstitions. The opinions entertained about these beings, are much the same with those of the Irish, so exquisitely well narrated by Mr Crofton Croker. An eminently beautiful little conical hill, near the eastern extremity of the valley of Aberfoil, is supposed to be one of their peculiar haunts, and is the scene which awakens, in Andrew Fairservice, the terror of their power. It is remarkable, that two successive clergymen of the parish of Aberfoil have employed themselves in writing about this fairy superstition. The eldest of these was Robert Kirke, a man of some talents, who translated the Psalms into Gaelic verse. He had formerly been minister at the neighbouring parish of Balquidder, and died at Aberfoil in 1688, at the early age of forty-two.

He was author of the Secret Commonwealth, which was printed after his death, in 1691, an edition which I have never seen, and was reprinted in Edinburgh, 1815. This is a work concerning the fairy people, in whose existence Mr Kirke appears to have been a devout believer. He describes them with the usual powers and qualities ascribed to such beings in Highland tradition.

But what is sufficiently singular, the Rev. Robert Kirke, author of the said treatise, is believed himself to have been taken away by the fairies, in revenge, perhaps, for having let in too much light upon the secrets of their commonwealth. We learn this catastrophe from the information of his successor, the late amiable and learned Dr Patrick Grahame, also minister at Aberfoil, who, in his Sketches of Perthshire, has not forgotten to touch upon the *Daoine Shie*, or men of peace.

The Rev. Robert Kirke was, it seems, walking upon a little eminence to the west of the present manse, which is still held a *Dun Shie*, or fairy mound, when he sunk down, in what seemed to mortals a fit, and was supposed to be dead. This, however, was not his real fate.

'Mr Kirke was the near relation of Graham of Duchray, the ancestor of the present General Graham Stirling. Shortly after his funeral, he appeared in the dress in which he had sunk down, to a mutual relation of his own, and of Duchray. 'Go,' said he to him, 'to my cousin Duchray, and tell him that I am not dead. I fell down in a swoon, and was carried into Fairyland, where I now am. Tell him, that when he and my friends are assembled at the baptism of my child, (for he had left his wife pregnant,) I will appear in the room, and that if he throws the knife which he holds in his hand over my head, I will be released, and restored to human society.' The man, it seems, neglected, for some time, to deliver the message. Mr Kirke appeared to him a second time, threatening to haunt him night and day till he executed his commission, which at length he did. The time of the baptism arrived. They were seated at table; the figure of Mr Kirke entered, but the Laird of Duchray, by some unaccountable fatality, neglected to perform the prescribed ceremony. Mr Kirke retired by another door, and was seen no more. It is firmly believed that he is, at this day, in Fairyland.'—(*Sketches of Perthshire*, p. 254.)

[In this note Scott refers to T. Crofton Croker, *Researches in the South of Ireland*

(1814), 79–82, and Patrick Grahame, *Sketches of Perthshire* (2nd edn., 1812), 243–55.]

52. Archilowe, of unknown derivation, signifies a peace-offering.

53. *Lymphads*. The galley which the family of Argyle and others of the Clan-Campbell carry in their arms.
[(1822) The galley signifies the Campbell ('Cawmil') dominion over Lorne.]

54. Lochow and the adjacent districts formed the original seat of the Campbells. The expression of a 'far cry to Lochow' was proverbial.
[(1822) See *A Legend of the Wars of Montrose*, Chapter 12: 'meaning that their ancient hereditary domains lay beyond the reach of an invading enemy.' Here it has the reverse sense, that a Campbell need not be feared outside his domains.]

55. A rude kind of guillotine formerly used in Scotland.

56. This, as appears from the introductory matter to this Tale, is an anachronism. The slaughter of MacLaren, a retainer of the chief of Appine, by the Mac-Gregors, did not take place till after Rob Roy's death, since it happened in 1736.

57. I do not know how this might stand in Mr Osbaldistone's day, but I can assure the reader, whose curiosity may lead him to visit the scenes of these romantic adventures, that the Clachan of Aberfoil now affords a very comfortable little inn. If he chances to be a Scottish antiquary, it will be an additional recommendation to him, that he will find himself in the vicinity of the Rev. Dr Patrick Grahame, minister of the gospel at Aberfoil, whose urbanity in communicating information on the subject of national antiquities, is scarce exceeded even by the stores of legendary lore which he has accumulated.—*Orig. Note.* The respectable clergyman alluded to has been dead for some years.
[After the 1829 edition went to press Scott discovered that the Revd Grahame was still alive, and wrote him a letter of apology; Grahame replied graciously (*Letters* xi. 288 n. 1). In his 1830 introduction to *A Legend of Montrose* Scott took the opportunity to correct the error. Scott's descriptions of 'Rob Roy country' (including the detail about the 'comfortable inn . . . lately built by his Grace the Duke of Montrose') rely heavily on Grahame's *Sketches of Perthshire* (2nd edn., 1812).]

58. A great feudal oppressor, who, riding on some cruel purpose through the forest of Guiyock, was thrown from his horse, and, his foot being caught in the stirrup, was dragged along by the frightened animal till he was torn to pieces. The expression, Walter of Guiyock's curse, is proverbial.

59. A kind of lighter used in the river Clyde, probably from the French *gabare*.

60. The affairs of Prestonpans and Falkirk are probably alluded to, which marks the time of writing the Memoirs as subsequent to 1745.
[Prestonpans and Falkirk were battles (Sept. 1745 and Jan. 1746) in which the Jacobite army defeated government forces. In this note, added in 1829, Scott seems to have forgotten his 1818 note to Chapter IV ('Wilkes and Liberty'), which dated Frank's narrative shortly after 1762–3.]

61. *i. e.* The throat and the withy. Twigs of willow, such as bind fagots, were often used for halters in Scotland and Ireland, being a sage economy of hemp.

62. The MacRimmons or MacCrimonds were hereditary pipers to the chiefs of MacLeod, and celebrated for their talents. The pibroch said to have been composed by Helen MacGregor is still in existence. See the Introduction to this Novel.

[This replaces a note in earlier editions (1818–22) which read: 'This Lament is said still to be preserved, a circumstance which cannot fail to give authenticity to these Memoirs.—EDITOR.']

63. 'Strike up.'

64. A pike.

65. This pithy verse occurs, it is believed, in Shadwell's play of Bury Fair.

[The verse is not printed in Shadwell's *Bury Fair*. Nina Prytula suggests that the song, or one like it, may have been inserted in I. i, or that Scott may have misremembered the passage, as follows: '*Wild*: A fellow that has one leg shorter than another, will never stand still; but Hop, hop, hop, round, round, round. *Bell*: Observe any fellow that has a stinking breath . . . will speak in your very nose: and turn round as often as you will, he turns with you, and your Nostrils must have it. Come, begin.—*Song*.—*Wild*: 'Tis very pretty, and delicately sung.']

EDITOR'S NOTES

'If Shakespeare is worth reading, he is worth explaining' (Thomas Warton, *Observations on the Faerie Queene of Spenser*, 1754). The annotator of Scott could go on forever, and I have tried to be concise. I have not been able to identify all the citations and allusions in the text; some of the epigraphs and quoted verses are likely to be by Scott himself, who not only quoted freely from memory (drawing on oral as well as written sources) but would often supply his own improvisations. *Rob Roy* is unusually rich in Scots proverbs, only some of which I have remarked here. In compiling these notes I have been much assisted by the ongoing Edinburgh Edition of the Waverley novels, and by four previous editions of *Rob Roy*: John Sutherland's Everyman edition (1995), Andrew Lang's Border edition (1892), the Dryburgh edition (1893), and, especially, an earlier Oxford University Press edition copiously annotated by C. B. Wheeler (1914). The first and last of these are cited here as 'Sutherland' and 'Wheeler'. Among other sources frequently cited, 'Chambers' refers to Robert Chambers, *Popular Rhymes of Scotland* (1870), 'Burt' to Robert Jamieson's edition of Edward Burt, *Letters from a Gentleman in the North of Scotland to his Friend in London* (1818), 'Kelly' to James Kelly, *A Complete Collection of Scotish Proverbs* (1721), 'Letters' to H. J. C. Grierson, ed., *Letters of Sir Walter Scott* (1932), and 'Murray' to W. H. Murray, *Rob Roy MacGregor: His Life and Times* (1982). Scots words and phrases, and some foreign and technical terms, are explained in a separate glossary.

1 *epigraph*: William Wordsworth, 'Rob Roy's Grave' (1807), lines 37–40.

3 *in his present capacity*: in his prefatory 'Advertisement' to *The Antiquary* (1816) 'the Author of "Waverley" ' had taken a 'respectful leave' of his public, 'as one who is not likely again to solicit their favour'. Under a different, more complicated system of aliases, and with a new publisher, William Blackwood, Scott went on to publish *Tales of My Landlord, First Series*, at the end of that year. Dissatisfied with Blackwood, Scott struck a new deal with Constable (see below) for his return as 'the Author of Waverley' in *Rob Roy*.

Junius: author of a series of political satires, *Letters of Junius*, that appeared in the *Public Advertiser* between 1769 and 1772. His (or her) identity has never been satisfactorily established.

3 *honest Benedict . . . live to be married*: Shakespeare, *Much Ado About Nothing*, II. iii. 220–1: 'When I said I would die a bachelor, I did not think I should live till I were married.'

some distinguished contemporaries: such as Byron, who had resumed *Childe Harold's Pilgrimage* in 1816 (Canto 3); or, Fiona Robertson has suggested to me, Scott himself, who had made several comebacks under his own name as poet (most recently in *Harold the Dauntless*, 1817) after bidding farewell to the 'Harp of the North' at the end of *The Lady of the Lake* (1810).

5 *late Mr Constable*: Archibald Constable (1774–1827), Scott's principal publisher. 'Constable said the name of the real hero would be the best possible name for the book. "Nay," answered Scott, "never let me have to write up to a name. You well know I have generally adopted a title that told nothing."—The bookseller, however, persevered; and after the trio had dined, these scruples gave way' (J. G. Lockhart, *Life of Sir Walter Scott, Bart.*; 1896 edn., ch. 38).

an American Indian: the comparison was a commonplace of Scottish Enlightenment anthropology. See Roger Emerson, 'American Indians, Frenchmen, and Scots Philosophers', *Studies in Eighteenth-Century Culture* (1979), vol. 9, 211–36, and Peter Womack, *Improvement and Romance* (1989), 20–4. More topically, Scott had likened the Highland clans to 'Afghaun tribes': 'Culloden Papers', *Quarterly Review*, 28 (1816), 288–9.

the Highland line: the border between Lowlands and Highlands, extending from the Moray firth southwest along the Grampians to the mouth of the Clyde.

Rob Roy's name: Wordsworth, 'Rob Roy's Grave', final stanza (lines 117–20). The third line reads: 'The proud heart flashing through the eyes.'

6 *cor a glaive*: *coir a' cleadhmaimh*: Scott's Gaelic tends to be phonetic and approximate and I shall not correct future examples.

7 *horrid circumstances*: the MacGregors hacked off Drummond's head, wrapped it in a plaid and carried it into the house of the dead man's sister, where they presented it to her at table, cramming bread and cheese into the mouth; maddened with horror, the lady fled into the woods. Scott adapted the incident in his *A Legend of the Wars of Montrose* (1819). The *present edition of these Novels* (below) refers to the 'Magnum Opus' edition, 1830.

an expressive Scottish phrase: Scott recalls one of his main sources, Burt's *Letters*: 'they are hounded (as they phrase it) into the Bounds of an other chief' (*OED*). The phrase is 'expressive' because literal: MacGregors were often pursued by bloodhounds, used in Scotland for tracking fugitives.

8 *Sir Humphrey Colquhoun*: according to Murray this should be Sir Alexander Colquhoun. Scott conflates the MacGregors' raid on Luss, 7 December 1602, with the battle of Glen Fruin, 7 February 1603.

9 '*babe unborn*': perhaps a reminiscence of *Henry V*, I. ii: 'some are yet ungotten and unborn | that shall have cause to curse . . .'.

the historian Johnston, and a Professor Ross: Scott owned Robert Johnston's *Historia Rerum Britannicarum* (1655), but according to Wheeler this does not mention the battle of Glenfruin. Alexander Ross's *History of the Family of*

Sutherland (1631) does contain an account of the battle, which Scott quotes in his n. 23 to *The Lady of the Lake*.

10 *made desolate*: Scott's source is Sir Robert Gordon, *A Genealogical History of the Earldom of Sutherland* (1813), 393.

11 *a Highlandman's promise with them*: 'Sua he keipit ane Hielandman's promis': entry for 2 October 1603, *The Diary of Robert Birrel . . . from 1532 until 1605*, in Sir John Graham Dalyell, *Fragments of Scottish History* (1798), 60–1.

12 *crossed saltire wise*: i.e. diagonally, as in the cross of St Andrew, patron of Scotland.

14 *an influence . . . the massacre of Glencoe*: Sir John Dalrymple, Master of Stair and Secretary of State for Scotland, who instigated the infamous massacre of the clan MacDonald, 13 February 1692. Wheeler suggests that 'upon the Restoration' must be a slip for 'upon the Revolution' (of 1688).

Commissioners of supply: assessors of land tax.

This statute . . . was passed: on 29 November 1774.

15 *Glenfalloch*: i.e. Margaret Campbell MacGregor (d. 1691), daughter of Archibald Campbell. Rob Roy's father Donald Glas (d. 1702) was titled lieutenant-colonel 'from his command of a regiment of foot in the army of Charles II following the Restoration of 1660' (Murray, 2). They were married in 1656.

16 *the middle of the 17th century*: Rob Roy was born in late February 1671 and died in the last days of December 1734 (Murray).

Red Robert: i.e. *Rab ruadh* (Gaelic).

cold iron rang: Samuel Butler, *Hudibras*, I. ii. 832–3 (slightly misquoted). But see Scott's tragic treatment of one of these quarrels in his tale 'The Two Drovers' (1827).

17 *already mentioned*: Archibald of Kilmanan, 10th MacGregor of Glenstrae and clan chief, deeded the property to Rob Roy in December 1701. A *wadset* is a kind of mortgage in Scots law.

James first Duke of Montrose: James Graham, 1st Duke and 4th Marquis of Montrose (d. 1742).

totally insolvent: on Rob Roy's ruin see Murray, 144–53, who assigns blame to the shadowy MacDonald. Rob Roy had secured the £1,000 advance from Montrose with a wadset on Craig Royston. When MacDonald disappeared Rob began efforts to pay Montrose back, but Montrose, regardless, started proceedings against him. At the end of Feb. 1713 Montrose was able to assert his legal claim on Rob Roy's property and have him outlawed as an absconding debtor.

18 *a popular exaggeration*: according to the account transmitted in the Revd William Nimmo's *History of Stirlingshire* (2nd edn. by William MacGregor Stirling, 1817), Helen Mary MacGregor (m. 1693) was beaten, raped, and branded with a hot iron by Montrose's goons ('Lictoribus verenda detexit; ferro dein candente pubem ambussit', 713). But Murray thinks this extremity of abuse unlikely: when Rob Roy later kidnapped Montrose's factor, John Graham of Killearn, who had directed the eviction, he released him unharmed without

exacting any vengeance. Nevertheless, wife and children were turned out on to the hillside in March, the bleakest month of the Highland winter.

18 *The Duke of Argyle*: John Campbell, 2nd Duke of Argyll and Duke of Greenwich (1678–1743). Rob sought his protection and adopted his name because his mother was a Campbell, as well as to exploit the traditional rivalry between Argyll and Montrose.

not likely to be forgotten: James Graham (1612–50), 5th Earl and 1st Marquis of Montrose, was the most formidable of the Royalist generals in Scotland during the civil war; Archibald Campbell (1598–1661), 8th Earl and 1st Duke of Argyll, supported the Covenanters. The harrying of Argyll's domains in Lorn in 1644 preceded the defeat of his forces by Montrose at Inverlochy the following year. Argyll lived to savour Montrose's execution by the victorious Covenanting party in 1650, but was in his turn beheaded at the Restoration.

19 *letters of horning and caption*: legal writs proclaiming a debtor's outlaw status if he failed to pay his debts, and warranting the seizure of his person and property.

professed himself a Jacobite: as Scott acknowledges in the 'Postscript' (here printed following the text of the novel, pp. 453–5), Rob Roy had been a Jacobite agent for some time—his droving expeditions made him useful as an emissary and intelligence-gatherer.

Dr Johnson . . . nearest to the Lowland line: 'These prejudices are wearing fast away; but so much of them still remains, that when I asked a very learned minister in the islands, which they considered as their most savage clans: "Those", said he, "that live next the Lowlands."' *A Journey to the Western Islands of Scotland* (1774), 'Anoch'.

21 *my gifted friend Wordsworth*: Scott quotes lines 17–60 of 'Rob Roy's Grave'; line 29 should read 'thus' for 'then', line 42 'A signal this which all can see', and line 68 'summer heat and winter snow'.

23 *John Ramsay of Ochtertyre*: (1736–1814). Scott heard this story on a visit to Ochtertyre in 1793.

Nimmo's Stirlingshire: on p. 717.

Little John: the famous henchman of Robin Hood.

25 '*drowning his sounding steps amid the din of general war*': source not traced.

26 *little risk of danger*: these actions took place between 29 September and 13 October 1715.

the inventor of the reflecting telescope: the members of the scientific dynasty mentioned here, all named James Gregory, are Dr James Gregory (1638–1675), who projected the new telescope in his *Optica Promota* (1663); he was the father of Dr James Gregory (d. 1731), the Aberdeen Professor of Medicine, companion of Rob Roy, and father of James (d. 1755), Rob Roy's near-recruit and also Professor of Medicine at Aberdeen; this was the uncle of 'the late distinguished' Dr James Gregory, Professor at Edinburgh (1753–1821).

27 *educated by Rob Roy*: Scott's MS has an additional sentence: 'If we can suppose that the youth who escaped this mountain promotion was the author of the

celebrated legacy from a father to his daughters it may be curious to reflect how the morality of the work might have been improved by a trip to the Lennox on Rob Roy's [illegible word].' Scott had thought that the youth might be James's brother John Gregory, author of *A Father's Legacy to his Daughters* (1774).

28 *was seen no more*: compare the departure of Pliable, early in *The Pilgrim's Progress*: 'So away he went, and Christian saw him no more.'

battle of Sherriff-muir: 13 November 1715.

29 *on both sides*: Murray (who accuses Scott of 'defamation') gives a detailed defence of Rob Roy's conduct at Sherriffmuir (189–90).

ballad on the battle of Sherriff-muir: printed in David Herd, *Ancient and Modern Scottish Songs* (1776), i. 104, which gives the quoted stanza as follows:

> Rob Roy stood watch
> On a hill for to catch
> The booty for ought that I fa', man,
> For he ne'er advanced,
> From the place he was stanc'd,
> 'Till no more to do there at a', man.

offending clans: Rob's house was burnt on 5 April 1716, and again at the end of September.

Col. Patrick Campbell of Finnah: this should be Alexander Campbell of Fonab.

31 *destroy the fortification*: this took place on 8 August 1718.

32 *General Wolfe*: (1727–59) commander of the army that took Quebec from the French; he was killed in the action.

notes on that work: see *Waverley*, ch. 15, and 'Notes to the edition of 1829', nos. 26 and 29 (World Classics edn., pp. 67–73, 394–5).

36 *a singular composition*: the letter is reprinted in Appendix No. IV. It was Wade's policy to accept letters of submission from the Highland chiefs and forward them to the king for the grant of clemency. Murray (who gives the date as 15 September 1725) conjectures that Argyll had his lawyers draft the letter and that Rob signed it as a formality, with scant regard for the contents.

37 *as black as rebellion could make it*: compare *2 Henry IV*, I. ii. 68–73: 'Doth not the king lack subjects? Do not the rebels need soldiers? Though it be a shame to be on any side but one, it is worse shame to beg than to be on the worst side, were it worse than the name of rebellion can tell how to make it.'

the Highland Rogue: the Abbotsford library catalogue lists a copy of *The Highland Rogue; or, the Memorable Actions of the celebrated Rob Roy Macgregor, commonly called Rob Roy* (London, 1723). Although modern scholars did for a while attribute this publication to Defoe, it is now thought not to be his.

38 *Mrs Cole's principle*: see Samuel Foote, *The Minor* (1760), I: 'One time, I thought of dying a Roman, which is truly a comfortable communion enough for one of us.' Mrs Cole is a bawd.

his mode of religion: Murray gives 1730 as the date of Rob's 'conversion'; he made confession at Drummond Castle, seat of James Drummond, 4th Duke of Perth.

38 *quit-rent*: 'rent of small amount paid by a freeholder or copyholder in place of services which might be demanded of him' (Wheeler).

Invernahyle: Scott stayed with Alexander (Alastair) Stewart of Invernahyle (1707–95), a legal client of his father's, on his first excursion to the Highlands in 1787; he was an invaluable source of anecdotes about Highland Jacobites and the '45 rebellion.

39 *before the dirge was finished*: the *Caledonian Mercury* of 9 January 1735 reported Rob Roy's death as having occurred one week earlier, i.e. 28 December 1734. The Gaelic 'Cha till mi tuilleadh' means 'I shall return no more'; see the last sentence of Scott's 'Culloden Papers' article (1816) and his coronach imitation, 'Mackrimmon's Lament' (1818).

40 *an Até 'stirring up to blood and strife'*: compare *King John*, II. i. 63 (reading 'stirring him'). Até was a Homeric personification of impulsive mischief and wanton destruction.

41 *Not Proven*: verdict allowed by Scots law as an alternative to 'not guilty'.

42 *Chevalier Johnstone*: aide-de-camp to Charles Edward Stuart at Culloden; Scott refers to the English edition of his *Memoirs of the Rebellion in 1745 and 1746* (1820). Prestonpans and Culloden were battles in the '45 rising; in the first the Jacobite army won a surprise victory over Hanoverian forces, in the second it suffered a crushing defeat.

43 *when Previsa fell*: from the Albanian war-song in Byron, *Childe Harold's Pilgrimage*, II. lxxii. 8: 'Remember the moment when Previsa fell . . . The wealthy we slaughter'd, the lovely we spared.'

rape of the Sabines . . . Book of Judges: according to Livy's *History*, the early Roman settlers supplied themselves with wives by inviting their Sabine neighbours to their games and carrying off their women; for the kidnapping of the daughters of Shiloh by the sons of Benjamin, see Judges 21: 19–23.

'pretty Fanny's way': Thomas Parnell, 'An Elegy. To an Old Beauty', lines 33–4: 'And all that's madly wild or oddly gay, | We call it only pretty Fanny's way'.

a respectable woman: in his 'Culloden Papers' article Scott refers to this informant as 'a woman on the banks of Loch Lomond, herself the daughter of such a marriage': *Quarterly Review*, 26 (1816), 318.

44 *Professor William Richardson of Glasgow*: (1743–1814). His 'Ode on the Prospect of Leaving Britain' celebrates the beauties of 'Rob Roy country'—in particular, the scenery around his birthplace, Aberfoyle.

47 *those who had so deeply injured her*: Scott's humane emphasis on the sufferings of Jean Key, based on a careful review of the evidence, should be read in the context of other contemporaneous accounts of the affair, which suggest her complicity in the rape (e.g. K. MacLeay, *Historical Memoirs of Rob Roy and the Clan MacGregor*, 1818).

48 *a special verdict*: 'one which declares as to the fact, but leaves the determining of the law to the judge' (Wheeler). The *panel* is the accused.

49 *a remarkable Highland story . . . alluded to*: these events are the basis for Robert Louis Stevenson's romances *Kidnapped* (1886) and *Catriona* (1893).

50 *Ancient Pistol standing upon his reputation*: the cowardly braggart of Shakespeare's *Henry V*: 'Old do I wax; and from my weary limbs | Honour is cudgell'd . . .', v. i. 78–9.

 Don Bernard de Castel Blazo . . . Alguazils: in Le Sage's *Gil Blas*, III. iii, Don Bernard dismisses Gil Blas from his service because he objects to his consorting with an alguazil (police constable): 'I cannot put up with a servant who has such honourable acquaintances' (trans. Smollett, i. 232).

53 *ITE. CONCLAMATUM EST*: 'go, it is proclaimed'; formula used to dismiss mourners at the Roman Catholic funeral service.

59 *invasion from Spain*: in fact Rob Roy took part in the abortive Jacobite rising of 1719, in which Spanish troops actually landed in the north of Scotland and were defeated by a government force at Glen Shiel. Thanks to Argyll's protection no reprisals were taken against him.

61 *Songs*: Robert Jamieson, *Popular Ballads and Songs* (1800), ii. 135.

63 *note on Waverley*: n. 60, 1829 edn. (World's Classics edn., 399).

65 *epigraph*: Beaumont and Fletcher, *Monsieur Thomas* (printed 1639), I. ii. Scott omits a line between 'mine own' and 'My grand curse'.

66 *bestow all my tediousness upon you*: compare *Much Ado About Nothing*, III. v. 20, 'If I were as tedious as a king, I could find it in my heart to bestow it all of your worship'.

 Sully's Memoirs: Scott owned the first two volumes of the Duc de Sully's *Mémoires des Sages et Royales Œconomies d'Estat Domestiques de Henry le Grand* (1634).

67 *P. P., Clerk of our Parish*: Alexander Pope's *Memoirs of P. P. Clerk of this Parish* (1727), a burlesque on Bishop Burnet's *History of His Own Time* (1724), was advertised as an illustration of 'The Importance of a Man to Himself'.

68 *in my mind's eye*: *Hamlet*, I. ii. 185: referring to the hero's dead father.

70 *he should engross*: Pope, 'An Epistle to Dr Arbuthnot', lines 17–18 (reading 'foredoom'd' for 'condemn'd', 'pens' for 'penned'). To 'engross' means to write out in legal form.

71 *the falling Atlas*: Atlas was a Titan condemned to hold up the heavens; Hercules took his place so that Atlas could go and fetch him the golden apples of the Hesperides.

72 *Corneille and Boileau*: the foremost tragic dramatist (1606–84) and poet-critic (1636–1711) of the seventeenth-century French Classical revival.

 Postlethwayte . . . Savary: Malachy Postlethwayte (1707–67), author of *The Universal Dictionary of Trade and Commerce* (1751; Scott had the 3rd edn. of 1766). This was based on *Le Parfait Négociant* (1675) by Jacques Savary des Brulons.

72 *Addison himself*: Joseph Addison's journal *The Spectator* (1711–20) was devoted to the formation of a polite style for the middle classes.

73 *epigraph*: Ben Jonson, *Bartholomew Fair*, III. v (slightly adapted).

agio, tariffs, tare and tret: percentage charged for exchanging currencies, or changing paper money into cash; excise duties; rule for computing weight of packaging and waste in the transportation of goods.

depreciation of the louis d'or: notoriously unstable, the French currency was depreciated several times during the reign of Louis XIV. The revolution referred to is the so-called 'Glorious Revolution' of 1688–9. But the phrase (and the novel's general preoccupation with matters of credit and circulation) would have had a topical resonance for Scott's readers, in the heated post-war debate about returning British currency to the gold standard; many feared that the measure (passed in 1819) would bring about a depreciation.

arret . . . parteur: decree . . . bearer of a bill.

74 *Grand Monarque*: Louis XIV.

the golden rule: Matthew 7: 12: 'Therefore all things whatsoever ye would that men should do to you, do ye even so to them.'

76 *Barils and barricants, also tonneaux*: different measures of cask for wine or brandy. Of the terms that follow (taken from Postlethwayte), *velle* and *barique* are also liquid measures; *cockets* are warrants certifying that customs duties have been paid; *Isingham* and *Gentish* are kinds of Flemish linen; *titling, cropling* and *lub-fish* are different sizes of *stock-fish*, fish dried in the air without salt.

Saxby's Tables: Henry Saxby's *The British Customs* was not published until 1757.

Castle of the Trompette—Palace of Gallienus: monuments in Bordeaux; the Palais Gallien was supposed to have been erected by the third-century Roman Emperor Gallienus.

77 *led their lives and employed their talents*: Frank refers to the licentious verse and lifestyle of Restoration poets such as John Wilmot, Earl of Rochester (1648–80).

Fontarabian echoes borne: Scott travesties his own *Marmion* (1808), VI. xxxiii:

> O, for a blast of that dread horn,
> On Fontarabian echoes borne,
> That to King Charles did come,
> When Rowland brave, and Olivier,
> And every paladin and peer,
> On Roncesvalles died!

'Fontarabian echoes' refers to the euphonious liberty Milton took with the story of the fall of Roland at Roncesvalles, in *Paradise Lost*, I. 586–7: 'When Charlemain with all his peerage fell | By Fontarabbia.'

78 *the bellman writes better lines*: perhaps an (anachronistic) allusion to Dougal Graham (1724–79), 'the Glasgow Bellman', author of a verse 'History of the Rise, Progress and Extinction of the Late Rebellion in Britain, in the years 1745 and 1746'.

the Gazette: an official newspaper which published a list of bankruptcies.

79 *Jacobites*: from the Latin, *Jacobus*: supporters of the exiled James VII and II (1633–1701) and the claim of his Stuart descendants to the British crown. Following the death without issue of Queen Anne in 1714, George, Elector of Hanover, became king of Britain; James's son, James Francis Stuart (1688–1766), maintained a rival court (as the Chevalier de St George) at St-Germains in France. With varying degrees of *éclat* and French aid the Jacobites would attempt to rise in 1708, 1715, 1719, and 1745. Throughout the eighteenth century Oxford was notorious for its Jacobite and High-Church leanings.

Lilly's Grammar and Accidence: William Lily's Latin *Rudiments of Grammar* (with John Colet, 1534) and John Stanbridge's *Accidence* (1505) were the basis of school texts for the following two centuries.

82 *Orlando Furioso*: verse romance by Lodovico Ariosto (1515), one of the favourite works of Scott's youth; he outraged one of his professors by declaring Ariosto superior to Homer.

83 *stuck in my throat*: compare *Macbeth*, II. ii. 32: ' "Amen" stuck in my throat.'

85 *epigraph*: John Gay, *Fables*, Second Part, Fable V, 'The Bear in a Boat'; last line reading 'his oar' for 'the oar'.

Prince Prettyman: see Buckingham's *The Rehearsal* (1671), III. iv: 'But, Mr Bayes, is not this some disparagement to a prince to pass for a fisherman's son?'

future Lord Mayor: Richard Whittington (d. 1423), historical Mayor of London who attained legendary status as a rags-to-riches hero; plays and ballads about him are recorded from 1605. According to the traditional rhyme, he was quitting London in disappointment when the bells of Bow church recalled him to his destiny: 'Turn again, Whittington, | Thrice Mayor of London.'

86 *foris-familiation*: legal term for a father's final settlement of property on his son, excluding him from further claims.

the north road: now the A1, the principal road from London to York and Edinburgh.

87 *a siege, or battle, in Flanders*: in the lately concluded War of the Spanish Succession, 1702–13.

Beggar's Opera heroes: the robber-captain Macheath is the hero of John Gay's 'Newgate pastoral', *The Beggar's Opera* (1728). *The Golden Farmer*, alias William Davis, was a farmer who practised highway robbery for forty years until he was detected and hanged in 1690; the *Flying Highwayman* was William Harrow, hanged for housebreaking in 1763.

household words: see *Henry V*, IV. iii. 52.

89 *division of labour*: term made famous by Adam Smith in *The Wealth of Nations* (1776).

White's ... Marybone: White's was a fashionable chocolate-house in St James's Street, founded in 1693; Marylebone Gardens was a pleasure-garden, opened in 1650. Both establishments were notorious gambling dens; Hogarth featured White's in *The Rake's Progress* (1735), while Gay made Marylebone Gardens a resort of Macheath in *The Beggar's Opera*.

Anthony-a-Wood: Frank refers to Wood's diary entry for 25 July 1654. See

The Life and Times of Anthony Wood, antiquary, of Oxford, 1632–1695, described by Himself (Oxford, 1891), i. 186.

89 '*the mad Prince and Poins*': Prince Hal and Poins join in Falstaff's highway robbery for a prank, which they enhance by robbing the other robbers, in *1 Henry IV*, II. ii.

Gibbet in the Beaux Stratagem: by Thomas Farquhar (1707): 'There's a great deal of Address and good Manners in robbing a Lady, I am the most a Gentleman that way that ever travell'd the Road' (IV. ii).

90 *Bucephalus*: the wonderful steed of Alexander the Great.

92 *epigraph*: Charles Churchill's obnoxious anti-Scots satire *The Prophecy of Famine: A Scots Pastoral* (1763), 190–3.

93 *North Briton*: the expression (for 'Scotsman') became current right after the Union—*OED* records usages from 1707 and 1717.

though clad in rags, as the poet saith: see John Dryden, 'Absalom and Achitophel', line 87: 'And virtue, though clad in rags, will keep me warm.'

94 *Change*: the Royal Exchange in the City of London, where stocks were traded.

I inclined my ear much more seriously: compare *Othello*, I. iii. 145–6: 'This to hear | Would Desdemona seriously incline.'

95 *Oh, the oak, the ash, and the bonny ivy tree*: traditional song; see Chambers, *Popular Rhymes of Scotland*, 204.

the Black Douglas: traditional name for the great Border clan (distinguishing them from 'the red Douglas' of Angus), but usually referring to 'Good Sir James' Douglas (1286?–1330), the follower of Robert Bruce; he is featured in Scott's late novel *Castle Dangerous* (1832), as well as James Hogg's *The Three Perils of Man* (1821).

Wat the Devil: perhaps fictitious, but reminiscent of many Border reivers, such as Scott's own ancestor Wat of Harden. 'Hogs' are not pigs but yearling sheep.

Chryseis and Briseis of old: maidens taken captive in the Trojan war, objects of the quarrel between Achilles and Agamemnon (Homer, *Iliad*, i).

Sinons: Sinon the Greek, pretending to be a renegade, tricked the Trojans into admitting the fatal wooden horse into their city (Virgil, *Aeneid*, ii); ever since, his name has been a byword for deceit.

97 *the regency of that kingdom*: Philippe d'Orleans did not assume the regency until 1 September 1715, following the death of his uncle Louis XIV.

The divisions of Whig and Tory . . . just established on the throne: George I, Elector of Hanover, assumed the throne in 1714 following the death of Queen Anne. The decisive support of the Whigs ensured their return to power after four years of Tory ascendancy (1710–14). The reluctance of many of the Tory ministers to pledge allegiance to the new king, followed by the complicity of party grandees in the 1715 Jacobite rising, effectively destroyed the chances of a Tory ministry for the next half century.

Common Council: of the City of London.

97 *the barber*: Wheeler cites a characterization in P. Stubbes, *The Anatomy of Abuses* (1583): 'snap go the fingers, god wot' (Part II, p. 50 in 1882 reprint).

98 *King and Prince of Skinkers*: i.e. of those who pour out liquor.

Whitson-Tryste: fair held at Whitsuntide, around the first Sunday after Easter, at Wooler, near Berwick.

99 *my uncle's seat*: sometimes identified with Chillingham Castle (Charles S. Olcott, *The Country of Sir Walter Scott*, 1913); Wheeler raises objections and proposes Biddlestone Hall, near Harbottle.

100 *epigraph*: William Somerville, *The Chace*, iii. 43–7, reading 'strokes' for 'sweeps'.

102 *The mode . . . new to me*: *The Spectator*, No. 104 (1711), comments: 'The Model of this Amazonian Hunting-Habit for Ladies, was, as I take it, first imported from France.' But it appears that ladies began to wear the masculine *justaucorps*, or close-fitting jacket, with vest and hat, and a long skirt below, from the mid-1660s (*OED*).

Phœbe: one of the names of Diana, goddess of hunting and chastity in the Graeco-Roman pantheon.

103 *Markham*: Gervase Markham (1568?–1637), author of several treatises on husbandry, farriery, and equitation.

Alcoran: the Qur'ān or Koran, the holy book of Islam.

Gibson and Bartlett: anachronisms. William Gibson's *The Farrier's New Guide* was first published in 1720, while J. Bartlett's *The Gentleman's Farriery; or, a practical treatise on the diseases of horses* did not appear until 1754.

give a ball . . . mash . . . horn: administer a pill to a horse, or mix him a warm preparation of boiled grain, or play on a hunting horn.

worm . . . dew-claws: cut the ligament under a dog's tongue (a prophylactic against madness), remove the rudimentary inner toe.

reclaim . . . casting-stones . . . sealed: to reclaim a hawk is to tame it; casting-stones are pellets administered to help the bird disgorge waste matter; to seal a hawk is to sow its eyelids shut.

106 *Orsons*: 'bear's sons', from the popular old romance of *Valentine and Orson* (Scott owned a 1632 chapbook version). They were royal twins, born in the woods; Valentine was reclaimed by his uncle and raised at court, but Orson was raised by bears.

King Willie: William of Orange, whose accession in 1688 effectively marked the end of the Stuart dynasty in Britain.

an unusual severity of decorum: in *The Age of Louis XIV* Voltaire ascribes the French court's 'refinement of manners' to the influence of Anne of Austria and the ladies of the court, and mentions the substitution of matrons of the palace for maids of honour out of a concern for propriety.

107 *the hunting of Chevy Chace*: the occasion of the most famous of the English ballads (it is the first selection printed in Thomas Percy's *Reliques of Ancient English Poetry*, 1765). Chevy Chase (the deer forest of Cheviot) was a hunting ground near the Scottish border, the site of a great battle between the Northumbrian Percy and the Scot Douglas.

108 *'the clamour much of men and dogs'*: James Thomson, 'Summer', line 377: 'The clamour much, of men, and boys, and dogs.'

109 *epigraph*: an approximate quotation (doubtless from memory) of Thomas Penrose's 'The Carousal of Odin', from *Flights of Fancy* (1775). Original reads:

> The portal hinges grate,—they come—
> The din of voices rocks the dome.
> In stalk the various forms, and drest
> In various armour, various vest,
> With helm and morion, targe and shield,
> Some quivering lances couch, some biting maces wield:
> All march with haughty step, all proudly shake the crest.

previous to the Revolution: in 1686 James II drew up an army on Hounslow Heath, outside London, with the object of intimidating the refractory city and parliament. He disbanded it two years later when it became clear that he could not rely on the loyalty of his troops. In the ensuing crisis William of Orange was invited in to protect the Protestant religion, and James fled the country without a fight.

110 *Gyas . . . Cloanthus*: 'fortemque Gyan, fortemque Cloanthum' (*Aeneid* i. 222), followers of Aeneas who vie with one another in the boat race in Book V.

Anak: 'a people great and tall', Deut. 9: 2.

111 *cannon ball*: Butler, *Hudibras*, II. i. 872–3, reading 'Like Feather-bed betwixt a wall'.

112 *a fool positive*: 'this Patroclus is a fool positive', *Troilus and Cressida*, II. iii. 61.

changed into pieces of slate: I have not found a source for this.

113 *Spectator*: the daily paper edited by Addison and Steele paid particular attention to the regulation of female manners, as part of its programme for the formation of middle-class politeness.

Sancho in the Sierra Morena: in *Don Quixote*, I. 25.

114 *the bird of the air will not carry the matter*: Eccles. 10: 20: 'Curse not the king . . . for a bird of the air shall carry the voice, and that which hath wings shall tell the matter.'

cour plénière: full court or assembly.

117 *wild beasts at Ephesus*: 1 Cor. 15: 32.

118 *the first gardener's quarrel to them*: i.e. Adam's; a 'quarrel' because he was led into temptation by Eve (the 'slice o' the spare rib': see Gen. 2: 21–2).

119 *Marmontel's late novel*: *Bélisaire* (1767), ch. 2. Gerimer, king of the Vandals, is overthrown by the Byzantine general Belisarius, and becomes a humble farmer. Many years later he meets Belisarius, whom imperial disfavour has reduced to blindness and beggary. After they part he resumes his spade, musing on the consolations of his lot.

120 *epigraph*: 1 *Henry IV*, II. iv. 465, reading 'most monstrous'.

fed at his cost: see *Henry V*, IV. iii. 25: 'Nor care I who doth feed upon my cost'.

120 *rowelling horses*: inserting a leather disc (the rowel) under the skin so as to discharge fluid from swellings.

121 *May chance to catch a fall*: source not traced.

122 *after the fashion of Nimrod*: the 'mighty hunter before the Lord', Gen. 10: 9.

123 *a miller's word*: millers were proverbially deceitful: 'an honest miller has a golden
thumb', 'many a miller, many a thief.'

   via: 'Off with you' (Italian).

   scout-master: chief of spies.

124 *the licentiate Pedro Garcias*: see the 'Address to the Reader' prefacing Le Sage's
Gil Blas (1715). A leather purse containing 100 ducats was buried under a head-
stone inscribed 'Here is interred the soul of the Licentiate Pedro Garcias'.

125 *leap a five-barred gate*: Sutherland points out Diana's descent from Farquhar's
Silvia, in *The Recruiting Officer*, I. ii: 'I can gallop all the morning after the Hunting Horn ... In short, I can do every thing with my Father but drink and shoot
flying.'

126 *playing booty*: playing falsely; according to *OED*, playing badly on purpose so as
to lose the game, but Scott appears to use it here and in his introduction to mean
playing on the wrong side or playing a double part.

127 *non-juror*: one who refused to take the oaths of Allegiance (to William III or the
Hanoverians) and Abjuration (of the Stuarts), required of office-holders.

   palladium: shrine of Pallas Athena, supposed to protect the city of Troy.

129 *epigraph*: Butler, *Hudibras*, III. iii. 675–8, reading 'can wish' for 'could wish'.

131 *O, in Skipton-in-Craven*: source not traced.

132 *canet*: 'let him sing' (Latin).

   Good people all, I pray give ear: source not traced.

133 *Gorgon's head*: the head of the Gorgon Medusa petrified all who looked upon it.

   contra pacem domini regis: 'against the peace of our lord the king' (Latin).

134 *quorum and custos rotulorum*: respectively, justices of the peace, whose presence
was necessary for certain business transactions, and the chief justice of the
county, 'keeper of the rolls' or session records.

   so it be duly executed: Jobson cites Part IV, ch. 31 of Coke's *Institutes of the Laws
of England* (1628–44): 'no part of the Christian world hath the like, if the same
be duly executed'.

   knight of the sorrowful countenance: epithet for Don Quixote.

   art and part of: planner and participator in (Scots law term).

   Johnson's Lives of the Highwaymen: Capt. Charles Johnson, *The History of the
Lives and Actions of the Most Famous Highwaymen, Street-Robbers, &c.*, not
recorded before 1724.

   Themis, or Comus: Classical deities of, respectively, law and revelry.

135 *sits the wind in that quarter?*: compare *Much Ado About Nothing*, II. iii. 90, 'Sits the
wind in that corner?'

135 *She show'd him the way to woo*: exact source not traced, although the lines are reminiscent of many lyrics, e.g. Burns, 'O John, Come Kiss Me Now': 'For well ye ken the way to woo.' See also 'O Tell Me How to Woo Thee' in Scott's *Minstrelsy of the Scottish Border*, Part II.

Dalton: Michael Dalton's *The Countrey Justice* (1618) was reprinted until 1746. Jobson gives the gist of the argument in Chapter XII, 'Bailment', interpolating, however, the detail about paying the clerk.

136 *34 Edward III*: statute (1360) establishing justices of the peace.

137 *3d of King Edward*: defining which offences are bailable. 'Commandment' means inciting another person to break the law.

main pernor, or bailsman: one who gives surety for the prisoner's appearance in court (*replevisable* = subject to bail).

138 *take up this matter*: come to a settlement.

140 *epigraph*: Jonson, Fletcher, and Middleton, *The Widow* (1652), III. i.

142 *the Duke of Argyle*: John Campbell, 2nd Duke of Argyll, the most powerful supporter of the Hanoverian government in the Highlands, and Rob Roy's protector (see Scott's introduction). *MacCallum More*, or *MacCailein Mor*, 'Son of Colin the Great', was the traditional Gaelic name of the descendants of the thirteenth-century magnate Colin Campbell of Lochawe. Argyll 'unhorsed' Marlborough, whom he detested, by blocking a parliamentary vote of thanks to him for his conduct of the war in 1710. This eased the ascendancy of the new Tory ministry, which expressed its gratification by making Argyll a Knight of the Garter. Far from being one of their party, Argyll was largely responsible for outmanœuvering the Jacobite interest at the death of Queen Anne and securing the Hanover succession. James, 2nd Duke of *Ormond* (1665–1745), was one of the Tory grandees impeached for treason on George's accession; he fled to France and helped instigate the 1715 rising. Justice Inglewood must mean 1710, not 1714, as the epoch of Argyll's 'Toryism'; even so his rustication grants the Justice a curiously long retrospective on events of only five years ago ('those days').

144 *unlucky affair of Sir John Fenwick's*: a thwarted conspiracy to assassinate William III in 1696, which cost Fenwick his head.

145 *Think of this as you take tobacco*: a version of this popular song, recorded from the early seventeenth century, is printed in Thomas D'Urfey's *Wit and Mirth, or Pills to Purge Melancholy*, 1719, which Scott owned. It varies quite a bit from the verse printed here, which Scott may have got from an alternative source in printed broadsides or chap-books, or else improvised from memory. See Robert Bell (ed.), *Ancient Poems and Songs of the Peasantry of England* (London, 1862), 39–41, 232–33.

146 *trusses a partridge*: seizes it in flight with its talons.

'bloody with spurring, fiery-red with haste': *Richard II*, II. iii. 58.

bam . . . bite: compare Scott's *Guy Mannering*, ch. 3: 'what were then called bites and bams, since denominated hoaxes and quizzes.'

147 *Trigesimo Septimo . . . Primo Gulielmi*: statutes (37 Henry VIII and 1 William &
    Mary, c. 21) providing for the appointment and dismissal of the Clerk of the
    Peace by the Custos Rotulorum (Wheeler).

   wooden shoes and warming pans: a taunt against Papists and Jacobites, alluding to
   the clogs worn by peasants in Catholic Europe, and to the malicious rumour that
   James III was not the legitimate child of his parents but a changeling smuggled
   into the royal bedchamber in a warming pan.

148 *the taking away of your good name . . . with all my heart*: perhaps a distant remin-
    iscence of *Othello*, III. iii. 162–5: 'he that filches from me my good name | Robs
    me of that which not enriches him | And makes me poor indeed.'

   third and fourth Edward VI . . . portuasses: an early Protestant statute 'for the abolishing and putting away of divers books and images'. The list that follows identifies various Roman Catholic liturgical and devotional books. Of the other
   statutes Jobson mentions, 'the first of his present Majesty' (George I) orders all
   remaining papists to take the oath of allegiance, while the statutes of Elizabeth
   and James I specify measures to penalize the observance of Mass.

   femme couverte: legal term for a married ('covered' or protected) woman. The
   following threat refers to 35 Elizabeth, c. 2, a statute for confining Catholics to
   their places of abode. The details about waiting for ferries and wading up to the
   knees are sadistic embellishments, however; Jobson gets them from the oath of
   abjuration of the realm which felons were required to swear after taking sanctuary (Wheeler).

149 *Helots*: vassals, after the caste of serfs in ancient Sparta.

150 *beating hemp, or drawing out flax*: kinds of labour assigned to women in prisons or
    bridewells.

   a frank and unreserved disposition: another echo of Farquhar's *The Recruiting
   Officer*: 'I love Silvia, I admire her frank, generous Disposition', II. i.

152 *Ourang-Outangs*: late eighteenth-century natural philosophers speculated about
    the possible kinship between mankind and the anthropoid apes; the Scottish
    judge James Burnet, Lord Monboddo achieved notoriety by arguing that orang-
    utans lacked only speech, which they could be taught, to make them fully human
    (*Of the Origin and Progress of Language*, 1773).

153 *epigraph*: source not identified; probably by Scott himself. According to J. G.
    Lockhart, Scott began the practice of making up his own mottoes while working
    on *The Antiquary*: 'from that hour, whenever memory failed to suggest an
    appropriate epigraph, he had recourse to the inexhaustible mines of "old play"
    or "old ballad", to which we owe some of the most exquisite verses that ever
    flowed from his pen' (*Life of Scott*, ch. 37).

   folios . . . quartos and octavos . . . duodecimos and pamphlets: sizes of book, defined
   by how many times the printed sheet would be folded before binding; folios
   were folded in two, quartos in four, etc.

154 *in the varsal world*: period catchphrase; *OED* cites usages from Vanbrugh and
    Swift. Scott's use of 'varsal' to mean 'every single' at the end of Chapter XIV is
    anomalous, however.

155 *Will Shakspeare*: see *1 Henry IV*, v. v. One of Hotspur's allies in the northern rising against Henry IV, Sir Richard Vernon was executed after the battle of Shrewsbury (1403).

while others plundered: this appears to be a Spenserian pastiche of Scott's own.

new martingale ... Duke of Newcastle's: William Cavendish (1592–1676), Duke of Newcastle, occupied his retirement with the revision of his *A New Method and Extraordinary Invention ... to Dress Horses* (1667).

156 *Vernon semper viret*: 'Vernon always flourishes', ominously punning on the Latin proverb, 'Ver non semper viret', 'Spring does not flourish forever'.

two meanings in one word: compare *Richard III*, III. i. 82–3: 'like the formal vice, Iniquity, | I moralize two meanings in one word.'

hieroglyphics ... pyramids of Egypt: highly topical at the time of writing (following the Napoleonic occupation of Egypt, 1798–1801). In 1821 Champollion began deciphering the Rosetta stone, acquired by the British in 1801.

Gwillym: John Guillim, Pursuivant at Arms, pen-name of John Barkham (1572?–1642), author of *A Display of Heraldry* (1610); Scott had the 6th edn. (1724).

157 *the misfortunes of Charles I*: imprisonment and execution.

College of St Omers: Jesuit school for Irish and English students at the Pas-de-Calais, France.

161 *wrathful dove, or most magnanimous mouse*: *2 Henry IV*, III. ii. 157.

162 *piqueing, repiqueing, or capotting his adversary*: scores in the card game picquet. To pique is to score 30 points against one's opponent before he scores, to repique is to score 30 points from one's own hand, and to capot is to win all 12 tricks and score 40.

164 *epigraph*: source not traced; perhaps this is by Scott.

165 *the Goddess in the Dunciad*: 'More she had spoke, but yawn'd—All Nature nods: | What mortal can resist the yawn of Gods?' Alexander Pope, *The Dunciad* (1743), iv. 605–6.

166 *a spoiling of the Amalekites*: the Amalekites were a rival tribe exterminated, with divine sanction, by the Israelites; as Wheeler suggests, Rashleigh confounds them with the 'spoiling of the Egyptians' in Exod. 12: 36.

the wind bloweth where it listeth: John 3: 8.

Ovid in Thrace ... Tristia: the *Tristia*, 'Sorrows', was a collection of poems written by Ovid after his banishment from Rome to the shores of the Black Sea, one of the northernmost reaches of the empire.

to build the lofty rhyme: Milton, 'Lycidas', line 11—in which the poet examines his vocation.

him who decorated the shades of Twickenham: Alexander Pope, who built a famous grotto at his villa there.

167 *Button's coffee-house*: in Russell Street, Covent Garden; one of the most famous of the literary coffee-houses of the Augustan era, patronized by Addison and Steele from 1712.

167 *'set their sandall'd feet on princes'*: source not traced.

168 *Mazarin, or Alberoni*: both men rose from humble origins to become Cardinals and Prime Ministers, Jules Mazarin to Louis XIII of France, Alberoni to Philip V of Spain. Jason Hartford has pointed out to me that Rashleigh's name is reminiscent of the still more famous and powerful (but well-born) Cardinal Armand Jean du Plessis, duc de Richelieu (1585–1642), Prime Minister to Louis XIII before Mazarin.

highflying or Tory principles: High-Church, supporting the authority of the Church of England and its bishops; not to be confused with the opposite sense of 'highflying', meaning attached to the Evangelical wing of the Church of Scotland, after the mid-eighteenth century.

169 *Isle of Calypso*: Ogygia, where the nymph Calypso detained Odysseus for seven years.

170 *Plutus*: the deity of wealth in the Classical pantheon.

172 *epigraph*: *Othello*, II. iii. 270.

173 *points at thee for his!*: parody of *Macbeth* IV. i. 121–4: 'Horrible sight! Now I see 'tis true; | For the blood-bolter'd Banquo smiles upon me, | And points at them for his.'

174 *But with the morning cool repentance came*: compare Nicholas Rowe, *The Fair Penitent* (1703), I. i. 162: 'At length the morn and cold indifference came.' Scott was fond of the tag—see also *The Antiquary*, ch. 5.

175 *full divan*: full council (Turkish, from the Ottoman imperial court).

toast and tankard: the practice of dunking a piece of toast in one's ale gave rise to the modern usage, 'the name of a lady being supposed to flavour a bumper like a spiced toast in the drink' (*OED*).

177 *'black he stood as night!'*: compare Milton's description of Death in *Paradise Lost*, ii. 670 (reading 'it' for 'he').

nothing wherefore: see *Othello*, II. iii. 277–9.

Lombard Street: the principal banking thoroughfare in the City of London.

178 *Divina Commédia of Dante*: this expresses a recondite taste for the period. Dante would not become fashionable until the end of the century, with the first English translation of the *Commedia* appearing in 1782, and Henry Cary producing the definitive version for Scott's generation in 1805–14.

the new turnips, and the rats, and the Hanoverians: the turnip and the brown or Norway rat, both recently introduced to Britain, were popularly associated with the new dynasty. Compare the exchange between Squire Western and his sister in Fielding's *Tom Jones* (VI. xiv): 'I hope to zee it . . . before the *Hannover* Rats have eat up all our Corn, and left us nothing but Turneps to feed upon. . . . Your jargon of Turneps and *Hannover* Rats, is to me perfectly unintelligible.'

179 *false archimage*: the evil shape-shifting warlock in Spenser's *Faerie Queene*, Book I.

180 *epigraph*: source not traced; perhaps by Scott.

Shakspeare's authority: see *Othello*, II. iii. Iago's apology is at line 298; Cassio's denunciation of alcohol precedes it (rather than follows it) at 267–83; 'O thou

invisible spirit of wine, if thou hast no name to be known by, let us call thee
devil! . . . O God, that men should put an enemy into their mouths to steal away
their brains! That we should with joy, pleasance, revel and applause, transform
ourselves into beasts!'

182 *Camilla*: Volscian warrior-princess, remarkable for her valour and fleetness of
foot, in Virgil's *Aeneid*, Book VII.

183 *Black Bear of Norway*: Scottish folktale of the 'Beauty and the Beast' type.
Scott's protégé John Leyden refers to 'The Black Bull of Norroway' in his edition (1801) of *The Compleynt of Scotland* (1548); see Chambers, *Popular Rhymes
of Scotland*, 95. In *The Lilac Fairy Book* Andrew Lang relates a West Highland
variant, 'The Brown Bear of Norway'. The detail about the princess being
teased appears to be Scott's own fancy.

185 *as the poet says*: Ovid, *Ars Amatoria*, i. 720: 'intret amicitiae nomine tectus
amore', 'Let Love make his entrance concealed beneath the name of friendship'
(trans. H. T. Riley, 1896). An example of the unsuitable literature with which
Rashleigh has been plying Diana.

191 *Chapter XIV*: vol. 2 of the first edition (1818) began here.

epigraph: source not traced. Perhaps by Scott.

193 *the deil's over Jock Wabster*: all Hell has broken loose. One of the many proverbial expressions with which this servant, like Sancho Panza, colours his speech.

Misegun beans: a variety of broad bean, after Mazagan, a port in Morocco.

194 *Culross to the East Nuik*: respectively, a royal burgh near the western border of
Fife, and the county's easternmost extension into the North Sea.

195 *the English measure*: the Scots ell measured 37.2 inches.

196 *Sir John the Græme*: compare 'On the Death of Sir John the Grame', Watson's
Choice Collection of Comic and Serious Scots Poems, Part III (1711): 'Here lies Sir
John the *Grame*, baith wight and wise'. Sir John Graham, the companion of
Wallace, was killed at the battle of Falkirk in 1298; the phrase 'Wight, wise,
worthy trust' was engraved on his sword.

198 *'sport toward'*: compare *A Midsummer Night's Dream*, III. i. 70: 'What, a play
toward!'

199 *barghaist . . . dobbie*: in his *Letters on Witchcraft and Demonology* Scott describes
both as northern regional names for 'a local spectre which haunts a particular
spot under various forms' (Letter 3).

200 *whisk and swabbers*: an old form of whist, in which certain cards (the swabbers)
entitled the holder to part of the stakes.

201 *News-Letter*: twice-weekly record of parliamentary and court news, precursor
of the newspapers.

202 *epigraph*: Satan's challenge to Death, *Paradise Lost*, ii. 681.

205 *the learned names o' the plants*: according to the pre-Linnaean taxonomy of John
Ray (1627–1705), presumably.

207 *the sweet youth was in love*: *Much Ado About Nothing*, III. ii. 37, 47.

208 *epigraph*: the most famous moment in Defoe's novel (1719), slightly misquoted.

209 *I sing*: Scott's own translation, no doubt, of the opening of Ariosto's *Orlando Furioso*.

211 *urge doubts to those that fear*: *Richard II*, II. i. 299, reading 'them that fear'.

212 *'Dead for a ducat'*: see *Hamlet*, III. iv. 23–4: 'How now! a rat? | Dead, for a ducat, dead!' Hamlet runs his sword through the arras and kills the eavesdropping Polonius.

215 *epigraph*: Thomas Tickell, 'Colin and Lucy, A Ballad', ii. 25–8.

217 *Mess John Quackleben's*: this seems to be an invention of Scott's. He used the facetious name again (for a doctor) in *St Ronan's Well* (1824).

221 *overcrowed, as Spenser would have termed it*: see *Faerie Queene*, I. ix. 50; *Shepheardes Calender*, 'Februarie', line 43.

Pacolet: dwarf in the romance of *Valentine and Orson*, who assists the brothers with a magical wooden horse.

224 *epigraph*: conflation of stanza 37, lines 1–2, and stanza 49, lines 4 and 3, of *William and Helen*, Scott's translation of Gottfried Bürger's 'Lenore' and his first published book (1796).

226 *Doctor Lightfoot*: perhaps John Lightfoot (1602–75), author of *Harmony of the Four Evangelists* (1647).

227 *better a finger aff as aye wagging*: literally, better to take a severed finger completely off than leave it dangling. Proverbial: 'Better put an end to a troublesome business, than to be always vex'd with it' (Kelly).

229 *drowsy ear of night*: conflation of *A Midsummer Night's Dream*, v. i, 'The iron tongue of midnight hath told twelve', and *Henry V*, IV, Prol. 16, 'the third hour of drowsy morning.'

the Middle Marches: the wildest part of the English–Scottish Border, comprising the Cheviot Hills and the headwaters of the Tyne.

230 *Hotspur*: nickname of Harry Percy, the warlike son of the Earl of Northumberland in Shakespeare's *1 Henry IV*, renowned for his bold horsemanship.

231 *taen the bent . . . taen my morning*: gone to the open country . . . taken my morning dram.

232 *All their clan shall never get her*: source not traced.

jurisdictiones fandandy causey: 'iurisdictionis fundandae causa', in order to establish a right of action. Here *writer* refers to the Scottish title for a solicitor, not to an author.

233 *club-law*: law according to physical force, law of the strongest.

234 *hure o' Babylon*: 'whore of Babylon' (Rev. 17: 1, 5)—a favourite Presbyterian epithet for the Church of Rome.

235 *epigraph*: John Langhorne, *Fables of Flora* (1771), No. VII, 'The Wall-Flower', opening lines; reading 'that' for 'yon' and 'thought' for 'thoughts'.

twelve shillings (Scotch): the Scots pound was worth only one-twelfth of the English pound, making this equivalent to just one English shilling.

237 *a place of considerable rank and importance*: Glasgow had doubled in size between the Union of Crowns in 1603 and the Union of Parliaments in 1707, when its population reached 13,000, making it the second city in Scotland and the tenth in Great Britain. Glasgow merchants were prompt to exploit the opening to the transatlantic colonies created by the Union, and the city's economic boom, fuelled by the Virginia tobacco and West India sugar trades, took off in the mid-1740s. By the mid-1760s, when Frank is narrating, the population of Glasgow had grown to 28,300. It would triple by the end of the century, when the development of the Lanarkshire iron and coal foundries and steam-powered cotton-spinning marked the advent of the industrial era.

St Mungo's favourite city: Kentigern, popularly known as St Mungo, is supposed to have been the first bishop of Glasgow at the end of the sixth century.

promising circumstances: for the description that follows, compare Daniel Defoe, *A Tour Through the Whole Island of Great Britain* (1726, Letter 12): 'the four principal streets are the fairest for breadth, and the finest built that I have ever seen in one city together. The houses are all of stone, and generally equal and uniform in height, as well as in front . . . in a word, 'tis the cleanest and beautifullest, and best built city in Britain, London excepted.' Glasgow's four principal streets, Trongate, High, Gallowgate, and Saltmarket Streets, formed a cross on the north bank of the Clyde; the Cathedral marked the city's northern limit.

238 *a Saturday evening*: in early editions Scott had Frank and Andrew arrive in Glasgow on a Thursday morning, 'alluding to the Presbyterian custom of the fast-Thursday which preceded a communion Sunday'. Rather than explain all this to his English readers in 1829 he changed it to the more immediately comprehensible eve of the Sabbath (see Iain Gordon Brown (ed.), *Scott's Interleaved Waverley Novels*, p. 72).

Ostelere of old father Chaucer: the Chaucerian spelling (referring to a male figure) is 'hostiler'.

Barony Laigh Kirk: a correspondent in *Blackwood's Magazine* (2 (1818)) complained 'that though we have both a Barony Kirk and a Laigh Kirk, Glasgow never possessed any place of worship which could lay claim to the compound designation in your text' (163). The Laigh (Low) or Tron Church stood downhill from the Cathedral in the Trongate. Wheeler explains Scott's usage: 'It was burnt down in 1793, and while it was being rebuilt its congregation met in the crypt of the Cathedral, to which for the time they applied the name of their church. Scott has transferred this temporary occupation to the early part of the century.'

239 *mourning and woe*: Ezek. 2: 10.

240 *as others had done elsewhere*: the story of the rallying of the Glasgow guilds in 1578 to defend the cathedral against a sentence of demolition drawn up by the Presbyterian authorities is apparently apocryphal.

241 *epigraph*: William Congreve, *The Mourning Bride* (1697), II. i, reading 'my trembling heart'.

searchers . . . idlers in kirk-time: 3 James I, c. 4, made all who failed to attend

Sunday service liable to a fine. Officers or 'compurgators' patrolled Glasgow on the sabbath until the mid-eighteenth century.

242 *'princes in Israel'*: Wheeler suggests an allusion to 2 Sam. 3: 38, 'Know ye not there is a prince fallen in Israel?'

243 *Paul preaching at Athens*: Raphael's cartoons, made for the tapestries of the Sistine Chapel in the Vatican, 1515–16; acquired by Charles I, they are now in the Victoria and Albert Museum, London.

248 *a kirk wi' a chimley in't*: a tavern.

249 *epigraph*: Otway, *Venice Preserv'd* (1682), Act I.

the valley of the shadow of death: Ps. 23: 4.

250 *on the northern bank of the Clyde*: the Low Green, east of the old bridge.

252 *Diana of the Ephesians*: Ephesus was a major centre of the cult of Diana or Artemis, denounced by the apostle Paul; see Acts 19: 27–8.

the Psalms of David were excellent poetry: Frank subscribes to the fashionable aesthetic of the sublime, which found its highest instances in the parts of scripture composed by Moses and David. Rather avant-garde at the beginning of the century, this view had become conventional by the time Frank is supposed to be telling the story. See John Dennis, *The Advancement and Reformation of Modern Poetry* (1701), chs. 2 and 5.

Davie Lindsay: Sir David Lindsay (*c.*1490–1555), poet and statesman; no doubt Fairservice reveres him as the author of *Ane Pleasant Satire of the Thrie Estates* (1540), which excoriates the corruption of the pre-Reformation church.

253 *Mirza . . . Bagdad*: Addison published the first (and only) of 'The Visions of Mirzah' in *The Spectator*, No. 159, 1 Sept. 1711; the bridge, with its threescore and ten arches, is an allegorical representation of human life.

257 *Ha nun Gregarach*: 'It is the MacGregor.'

258 *epigraph*: source not traced; probably by Scott.

259 *Irish, Earse, or Gaelic*: terms then used interchangeably to denote the language of the Highlanders.

She's sleeping: Scott's characterization of Highland speech, including the general-purpose pronoun 'she' (and the cognate 'her nainsell') and the representation of unvoiced consonants ('f' for 'w', 't' for 'd', etc.), draws on 'a highly developed literary convention [which] can often be remote from reality', dating back to the seventeenth century (Graham Tulloch, *The Language of Walter Scott*, 254–5).

260 *omnium*: Stock Exchange expression for all the articles included in a contract between government and the subscribers to a loan.

battle of Almanza: 25 April 1707; the British and their allies were defeated by a Franco-Spanish force under the Duke of Berwick, an illegitimate son of James II.

263 *departing from the realm*: a warrant *in meditatione fugae* (or 'fugie warrant'), issued for the arrest of a debtor whom the creditor suspects of intent to flee the country.

264 *O hon-a-ri!... Ahellanay!*: supposedly Gaelic expressions of lamentation.

265 *make a spune or spoil a horn*: proverbial: succeed utterly in an enterprise or botch it.

deacon: in Scotland, the president of an incorporated craft or trade.

Stanchells: i.e. 'stanchions', window-bars.

268 *judicio sisti... judicatum solvi*: Jarvie will go bail for Owen's appearance in court, but he will not assume liability for any debts or costs he might have incurred.

269 *epigraph*: variant lines from 'Our goodman came hame at e'en', in David Herd, *Ancient and Modern Scottish Songs* (1776), ii. 172–5.

Diogenes in the streets of Athens: in response to popular adulation of the Athenian demagogues, the Cynic philosopher Diogenes 'lit a lamp in broad daylight and said, as he went about, "I am looking for a man." ' Diogenes Laertius, *Lives of the Philosophers* (trans. R. D. Hicks, London, 1925), vi. 41.

Dutch weight: or Scotch Troy weight, in which the pound was slightly lighter than the English (Wheeler).

270 *pickle in your ain pock-neuk*: literally, 'peck in the bottom of your own bag'— depend upon your own resources. This is the first recorded usage of this proverbial-seeming expression.

271 *Schehallion*: distinctive peak, 3547 ft., between Lochs Tay and Rannoch in Perthshire.

as the auld sang says: 'The king shall enjoy his own again', Song No. 1 in James Hogg, *The Jacobite Relics of Scotland* (1819), vol. 1.

272 *Tityre tu patulæ*: opening words of Virgil's first *Eclogue*, representing poetic ease: 'Thou, Tityrus, reclining under the shade of the wide-spreading beech...'

kernes and galla-glasses: a Gaelic chieftain's footsoldiers; in the passage referred to (*Macbeth*, I. ii) they actually belong to Macbeth's antagonist, 'the merciless Macdonwald.'

the Cross: the Market Cross in Glasgow, where the city's main streets meet.

Andra-Ferraras: generic name for high-quality broadswords in Scotland throughout the seventeenth and eighteenth centuries, after the sixteenth-century Venetian swordsmith Andrea Ferrara.

273 *the old Picts*: there was some confusion in the period about the identity of the Picts. Scott believed that the Scots and Picts were the original inhabitants of the country, and that the Scots exterminated the Picts or drove them underground after the Anglo–Saxon conquest (*Tales of a Grandfather*, ch. i). In any case Scott alludes here to the reputation of the proscribed MacGregors for being the last pure-blooded specimens of 'the ancient Celtic race' (see Burt, I. xxii–xxiii).

274 *Drymen or Bucklivie, or the Clachan of Aberfoil*: the first two are villages on the Highland line and the southern border of 'Rob Roy's country'—north of Glasgow, between the eastern banks of Loch Lomond and Stirling. Aberfoyle is several miles to the north of them, on the edge of the Trossachs; 'clachan' is Gaelic for a small village or hamlet.

274 *I owe thee a day in harst*: i.e. a day's work at harvest. Proverbial: 'spoken of one to
     whom I owe a good turn' (Kelly).

275 *atmosphere, as the minister ca's it*: the *OED*'s first citation of this usage, meaning
     the air in a particular room, is from *Sermons to Young Women* (1767) by James
     Fordyce, a Scots minister.

     let that flee stick in the wa' ... *when the dirt's dry it will rub out*: proverbial: 'it's not
     worth bothering about; there's no harm done in the end.'

     bonny Dundee: the version of the popular song quoted here is 'Bonny *Dundee*: Or,
     Jockey's Deliverance', in *A Collection of Old Ballads* (London, 1723–5), i. 275–7;
     with the last line of the chorus reading 'For Ise gang no more to bonny *Dundee*'.
     Scott later wrote his own text to the song for his drama *The Doom of Devorgoil*
     (1830).

276 *pass of Ballamaha*: Balmaha, on the shore of Loch Lomond above Drymen.

     high as Haman: on a gallows 50 cubits high; Esther 7: 9–10.

     a sair hair in my neck: proverbial for a severe irritant.

277 *touch pitch and no be defiled*: Ecclcus. 13: 1.

278 *balm in Gilead*: Jer. 8: 22.

279 *epigraph*: from John Cooke, Greene's *Tu Quoque, or, The City Gallant* (publ.
     posth. 1614), p. 3. Scott's quotation omits several words and phrases.

     Xantippe: shrewish wife of the philosopher Socrates: 'When Xanthippe first
     scolded him and then drenched him with water, his rejoinder was, "Did I not say
     that Xanthippe's thunder would end in rain?" ' Diogenes Laertius, *Lives of the
     Philosophers*, ii. 36.

280 *flowers of the field*: Isa. 40: 6.

281 *if your honour disna ken* ... *gin I leave ye*: Wheeler notes that Scott is adapting
     Antonio's speech in Beaumarchais, *The Marriage of Figaro*, II. xxi: 'If you
     haven't enough [sense] to keep a good servant, I'm not so stupid as to dismiss
     such a good master.'

     fee, and bountith: wages due to a servant, and a supplementary gratuity.

282 *terrestrial paradise*: the legendary site of the Garden of Eden.

284 *a staff out o' my bicker*: a bicker was a bowl made of wooden staves bound
     together.

     Mr Zachary Boyd's translation o' the Scriptures: Boyd (1585?–1653) made verse
     translations of the scriptures, some of them unintentionally ludicrous, in *Zion's
     Flowers* (1644) and *The Psalmes of David in Meeter* (1646). Trevor Royle, *The
     Macmillan Companion to Scottish Literature* (1983), quotes a few lines:

                          There was a man called Job,
                          Dwelt in the land of Uz;
                          He had the gift of the gob;
                          The same case happen us!

286 *epigraph*: from *Palamon and Arcite*, Dryden's modernization of Chaucer's *The Knight's Tale*, ii. 181–6, reading 'rustling in the wood' for 'in the rustling wood'.

291 *ye ken how to turn the buckle o' your belt behind you*: Wheeler cites Oliver Cromwell's speech of 17 September 1656, 'if any man be angry at it—I am plain and shall use an homely expression: Let him turn the buckle of his girdle behind him.' There is some ambiguity as to whether the phrase means 'prepare for' or 'refrain from' fighting.

slashed as het a haggis: been embroiled in as desperate a business, with (here) a connotation of bloody swordplay; a haggis is a pudding made of a sheep's stomach stuffed with oatmeal and minced organ meat. Kelly cites a proverbial expression, 'A Hardy man to draw a sword to a haggish', which he glosses as 'An ironical ridicule upon a braggadochio'.

sow playing upon a trump: proverbial (Kelly) for wearing an astounded or offended expression.

come to yoursell, like MacGibbon's crowdy: proverbial: 'Spoken when people are angry without a Cause; as if you would say, let him settle himself, for I value not his anger' (Kelly). Crowdie is an oatmeal porridge.

292 *poindings and apprizings*: proceedings for the seizure and sale of a debtor's property.

293 *jouk and let the jaw gae by*: proverbial: 'Duck and let the wave pass over you.'

295 *epigraph*: Thomas Gray, 'The Alliance of Education and Government: A Fragment' (1748), 88–9, 96–9, reading 'And while' for 'Who, while' in the third line.

296 *shalloons*: closely-woven woollen material, used for linings. Jarvie's speech closely follows a passage in Defoe's *Tour* (Letter 12), defending Glasgow's ability to supply 'a sortable cargo without buying [goods] from England': 'They have several woollen manufactures . . . such as the Sterling serges, Musclebrow stuffs, Aberdeen stockings, Edinburgh shalloons, blankets, &c. . . . The trade with England being open, they have now, all the Manchester wares, Sheffield wares, and Newcastle hard wares . . . as cheap brought to them by horse-packs as they can be carried to London . . . They have linens of most kinds . . . not known in England, cheaper than England . . . and for muslins, their own are very acceptable, and cheaper than in England' (Penguin edn. (1971), 608–9).

297 *the sell o't*: after the Reformation Glasgow College was endowed with a share of the Cathedral estates, as well as the kirk livings which had been granted to the city by Queen Mary.

the rape-spinner: master of the guild of rope-makers, which would supply the city hangman.

Rehoboam . . . Solomon: see 1 Kings 12: 6–14.

299 *Andrew Wylie*: John Galt would use the name for the hero of his comic novel, *Sir Andrew Wylie of that Ilk* (1822).

the son of Sirach: Jesus Ben Sirach, author of the apocryphal Ecclesiasticus or Book of Wisdom. But Jarvie's phrase comes from Eccles. 10: 20 (see above, p. 114).

300 *heights and howes . . . it wad tire the very deevil's wings to flee to the tap o' them*: perhaps a reminiscence of Milton, *Paradise Lost*, ii. 618–21.

300 *twa hunder and thirty parochines*: for the statistical account of the Highlands that follows, Scott draws on the Gartmore MS, 'Causes of the present disorderly State of the Highlands of Scotland', printed in Burt, ii. 355–8.

302 *luck-penny*: a small sum returned from the seller to the buyer.

 Bothwell brig: decisive battle (1676) in which the Covenanters were defeated by a Royalist army under the Duke of Monmouth. See Scott's *Old Mortality*, chs. 30–2.

303 *Black-mail*: see Author's Introduction for a full account. This is the origin of the term.

304 *Cohoon*: phonetic variant of Colquhoun.

 daft days: the holiday period around Christmas and the New Year.

 Killiecrankie year: in 1689 a Jacobite Highland army defeated a much larger government force at the pass of Killiecrankie, near Blair Athol in Perthshire; but their commander, Viscount Dundee (Graham of Claverhouse), was killed in the action, which turned out to be the last armed resistance to the new order on British soil until the 1715 rising.

305 *pensions*: Breadalbane was allotted between £12,000 and £20,000 to distribute among the chieftains; during Anne's reign about £4,000, or £360 per chief, was disbursed annually (Scott, *Tales of a Grandfather*, chs. 57, 65).

 waefu' wars o' Montrose: during his campaign, 1644–5, Montrose led a Highland army into the Lowlands, sacking Aberdeen, Dundee, and much of Perthshire and Fife along the way, until his defeat at Philiphaugh in the Borders.

306 *ower auld cats to draw that strae afore them*: proverbial: 'too old to be imposed upon. A young cat will jump at a straw drawn before her, but not an old one; nothing being more playful than a young cat, and nothing more dull than an old one' (Kelly).

 seventeen hundred and seven: Jarvie refers to the intrigues surrounding the abortive Jacobite rising that followed the Act of Union, in 1708. *Troking* means fraud, deceit.

307 *A grey mare*: proverbial: 'The gray Mare is the better Horse', meaning, 'the good Wife is Master' (Kelly).

 Baker's Chronicle: Sir Richard Baker, *A Chronicle of the Kings of England from the Time of the Romans Government to the Raigne of King Charles* (1643). Scott had a later continuation (1730).

308 *whom the king delighteth to honour*: Esther 6: 6.

 ower shoon ower boots: proverbial: in for a penny, in for a pound.

309 *reset of intercommuned persons*: dealings with outlaws.

310 *epigraph*: Churchill, *The Prophecy of Famine*, ii. 295–6, 301–4, reading 'heard' for 'known' in the fourth line.

 rue-bargain: forfeit paid for cancelling a deal; also 'smart-money', below.

311 *'clombe to the saddle'*: see Spenser, *Faerie Queene*, IV. v. 46: 'Unto his lofty steede he clombe anone'.

311 *it's ill taking the breeks aff a Hielandman*: Scott bowdlerizes the proverb, 'It is ill to take Breeks off a bare Arse' (Kelly).

312 *mobs, as they ca' them now-a-days*: *OED* records the vernacular abbreviation of '*mobile vulgus*', 'mutable crowd', from 1688, with complaints against this immediately fashionable usage from Addison (1711) and Swift (1738).

313 *riding o' the Scots parliament*: ceremonial cavalcade to mark the opening of parliament. Andrew's complaints against the Union are in the tradition of Smollett's Lieut. Lismahago in *Humphry Clinker* (1771).

314 *nae mair ferlie to see a woman greet than to see a goose gang barefit*: proverbial: no more wonderful to see a woman weep than to see a goose walk barefoot (Kelly).

316 *Be ruled by him that has the purse*: proverbial rhyme, cited by Kelly and by Allan Ramsay, *A Collection of Scots Proverbs* (1737).

Donald: generic name for a Highlandman.

317 *ad crumenam*: referring to the purse.

318 *Chapter XXVIII*: vol. 3 of the first edition (1818) began here.

epigraph: 'Scott had heard it several years before from the Revd Mr Macfarlane, minister of Drymen (afterwards Principal of Glasgow University), in the course of a forenoon ride through that part of Stirlingshire in which Bucklyvie is situated' (Chambers, *Popular Rhymes of Scotland*, 292–3). Chambers identifies the 'Baron of Bucklivie' as one Buchanan, 'a cadet of the family of Kippen'.

320 *Ha niel Sassenach*: roughly, 'I can't speak English'.

321 *Scots miles*: about 220 yards longer than the English—but notoriously variable in the Highlands.

Hecate: here, after *Macbeth*, the deity of the witches; originally, Diana in her dark, nocturnal aspect.

them that will to Cupar maun to Cupar!: the speaker herself glosses the proverb. Cupar is a royal burgh in Fife; Wheeler suggests an allusion to going to law, since it was the seat of the County Court.

pit o' Tophet: abyss of Hell, after the valley near Jerusalem where human sacrifices were offered to the pagan deity Moloch.

322 *caravansary*: inn for the accommodation of travellers, from the Persian, 'hotel for caravans'. Another of the allusions to barbaric, savage, or pagan cultures clustered in this part of the novel.

Duinhéwassels: 'gentlemen' (Gaelic), usually denoting secondary rank to the Chief.

324 *Dat veniam corvis, vexat censura columbas*: Juvenal, *Satires*, II. 63: 'The judgment pardons the crows and condemns the doves.'

326 *king's clan . . . sett*: the scarlet, noted earlier, marks the Stewart tartan. But the custom of wearing a design peculiar to a family or district seems to be quite recent, following the use of regimental tartans in the later eighteenth century.

329 *how the Brownie of Ben-ye-gask guided the gudewife of Ardnagowan*: I have not

been able to identify a source for this. The Brownie was a household demon that performed domestic and agricultural tasks by night.

331 *epigraph*: John Couper, 'Bag-pipes no Musick: A Satyre on Scots Poetry' (1720), reading: 'Low Bells, not Lyres, the Highland Cliffs adorn, | *Macklean*'s loud halloo, or *Mackgregor*'s Horn.' In fact it was Ramsay who wrote a reply to Couper, 'In Answer to Bagpipes no Musick' (1720).

333 *Slioch-nan-Diarmid*: 'children of Diarmid', a reference to the Campbell clan's supposed descent from the Ossianic hero Diarmaid Ua Duibhne.

334 *Dukes of Guile and Lords for Lorn*: Scott gets this pun (on 'Dukes of Argyll and Lords of Lorn') from a poem by Alexander Craig of Rose-Craig, 'On the Earl of Argyll', printed in *The Staggering State of Scots Statesmen*, by Sir John Scot of Scotstarvet (1754): 'Now Earl of Guile, and Lord ForLorn thou goes, | Quitting thy Prince, to serve his Spanish foes.' For the continuation see below, p. 376.

335 *it's a bauld moon, quoth Bennygask—another pint, quoth Lesley*: proverbial. 'Spoken when people encourage themselves to stay a little longer in the Alehouse, because they have Moonlight' (Kelly).

337 *prick-eared cur*: Royalist epithet for Puritans and Presbyterians, referring to their close-cropped hair and (hence) conspicuous ears.

340 *epigraph*: Beaumont and Fletcher, *Bonduca* (publ. 1719), v. i. Scott elides three lines between 'woman's face' and 'See if one fear'.

341 *the Act seventeen hundred and one*: statute of the Scottish parliament 'for preventing wrongous imprisonment' (Wheeler).

346 *gie you your kail through the reek*: proverbial: give you a hiding.

    the Cumries: islets, Great and Little Cumbrae, in the Firth of Clyde.

347 *that beautiful sheet of water*: Loch Ard, west of Aberfoyle.

351 *coffin of Mahomet*: according to legend the prophet's coffin hovered above the floor in his tomb at Medina.

353 *epigraph*: unidentified; probably by Scott. 'Woe to the vanquish'd' is a translation of the famous *vae victis* of Livy, *History*, v. xlviii. 9.

354 *camlets . . . drab-de-berries*: a light wool spun from the angora goat, and a thick woollen cloth from Berry, near Orleans. Jarvie's eulogy anticipates Robert Fergusson's poem, 'Braid Claith' (1772).

    the Broomie-law: the quay of Glasgow, at that period west of the city.

356 *unsophisticated a state (to use King Lear's phrase) as the plumeless biped*: see *King Lear*, III. iv. 105–7: 'here's three on's are sophisticated! . . . unaccommodated man is no more but such a poor, bare, forked animal as thou art.' Meanwhile, 'Plato had defined Man as an animal, biped and featherless': Diogenes Laertius, *Lives of the Philosophers*, VI. 40.

    Steinkirk: loosely knotted, fancy cravat, imitating the mode of French officers at the Battle of Steinkirk (1692).

357 *Judith . . . Deborah . . . the wife of Heber the Kenite*: sanguinary heroines of the Old Testament. Judith decapitated Holofernes, the Assyrian general (the Book of

Judith in the Apocrypha); the prophetess Deborah directed the overthrow of the Canaanite captain, Sisera (Judg.: 4); Jael, the wife of Heber, butchered the fugitive Sisera as he rested: 'At her feet he bowed, he fell, he lay down; at her feet he bowed, he fell; where he bowed, there he fell down dead' (Judg. 5: 27).

359 *hewers of wood and drawers of water*: Josh. 9: 21.

360 *Chieftainess . . . offence to grammar*: 'apparently the word after being long obsolete was formed anew by Scott' (*OED*).

361 *sons of MacGregor*: for their subsequent fates see 'Author's Introduction'. In 1829 Scott corrected their birth order, which he had reversed in earlier editions.

362 *surprised and made prisoner*: loosely based on a historical incident, except that the troops caught Rob Roy in bed.

363 *Inversnaid*: Rob Roy's former home, on the northern tip of Loch Lomond, east bank; for the garrison see 'Author's Introduction.'

366 *epigraph*: unidentified; probably by Scott.

370 *closed the scene*: compare Patrick Grahame, *Sketches of Perthshire* (2nd edn., 1812): 'Looking eastward, you have the windings of the Forth, deep skirted with woods, in birds'-eye prospect; the lake of Menteith . . . the great mass, with Stirling castle and the Ochills, in the back-ground' (180–1).

Tom-of-Bedlam: name for a ragged crazy beggar, assumed by the fugitive Edgar in *King Lear*.

Order of the Thistle: this is James Grahame, 1st Duke of Montrose, Rob Roy's inveterate enemy; see Author's Introduction. In the novel Scott plays down their personal feud.

373 *friends over the water*: Jacobites, in exile in France.

it's ill drawing boots upon trews: it's no good trying to civilize a Highlander. For 'a Hielandman's word' see note to p. 11, above.

374 *Utrecht*: the Treaty of Utrecht, which ended the War of the Spanish Succession in 1713, was actually a series of separate agreements; the alliance had been weakened in 1712 when the British, impatient with the reluctant Dutch, began negotiating on their own.

Duchray . . . Gartartan: castles, situated (respectively) a mile south-east of Loch Ard and about three miles south of Aberfoyle, towards Drymen.

376 *they change a thousand hues*: Montrose quotes the third and fourth lines of the poem by Alexander Craig cited in Chapter XXXII, 'On the Earl of Argyll': 'No faith in plaids, no trust in Highland trews, | Camelion-like, they change to many hues.' Montrose's 'great ancestor' is his great-grandfather, the 1st Marquis.

378 *epigraph*: 'Gil Morrice: A Scottish Ballad', in Thomas Percy, *Reliques of Ancient English Poetry* (1765),lines 51–4. Scott has modernized the spelling.

cross the river: the Fords of Frew, east of Loch Ard. For the historical basis of the episode that follows, see Author's Introduction.

385 *things must be as they may—pauca verba*: see *Henry V*, II. i. 20, 'things must be as they may'. One of Scott's favourite tags (see *Journal*, ed. W. E. K. Anderson

(1972), 175, 596). For 'pauca verba', Latin for 'few words', see *Merry Wives of Windsor*, I. i, where Sir Hugh Evans says, 'Pauca verba, Sir John' (l. 109), and Corporal Nym echoes him: 'pauca, pauca' (l. 119).

386 *the hysterica passio of poor Lear*: see *King Lear*, II. iv. 55–7.

> O, how this mother swells up toward my heart!
> Hysterica passio—down, thou climbing sorrow,
> Thy element's below.

The medical account of hysteria was in a confused, transitional state in Scott's day; in the 1780s the influential Scots physician William Cullen had revived the ancient uterine theory of hysteria as a primarily female-sexual disturbance, not entirely displacing, however, earlier modern accounts of a nervous imbalance that could also afflict men (hypochondriasis). Frank seems to experience the upsurge of an archaic, feminine organism—the wandering womb of a pre-modern physiology. See Ilza Veith, *Hysteria: The History of a Disease* (Chicago, 1965).

387 *epigraph*: Sheridan, *The Critic*, I. ii, reading 'hardest' for 'harder'.

389 *Let Glasgow Flourish!*: as Jarvie reminded Fairservice in Chapter XXVII, this is the motto on the city's coat of arms.

The curse of Cromwell: the Scots, like the Irish, had bitter memories of the atrocities perpetrated by Cromwell's troops in their country, e.g. the sack of Dundee, 1651.

391 *my foot is on my native heath, and my name is MacGregor!*: this became a catchphrase, partly thanks to Pocock's dramatization (where the line is spoken by Helen MacGregor). It was echoed and parodied for the next hundred years or so, as in Dickens's *David Copperfield* (1851): 'On Monday next, on the arrival of the four o'clock afternoon coach at Canterbury, my foot will be on my native heath—my name, Micawber!' (ch. 36).

394 *Sultan of Delhi*: proverbial Asiatic despot.

395 *the founder of his line*: see Author's Introduction.

396 *Malvolio . . . control*: see *Twelfth Night*, II. v. 62: 'quenching my familiar smile with an austere regard of control.'

398 *Millia molligheart!*: a thousand curses!

Odyssey: see *Odyssey*, viii. 463–5: 'Noble Odysseus . . . battened the lid down with a lightning knot | learned, once, long ago, from the Lady Kirke' (trans. Robert Fitzgerald, 1961). In 1817 Scott acquired Rob Roy's sporran ('which no one can find the means of opening') for his cabinet of relics at Abbotsford (*Letters* iv. 540–1).

399 *Troutsho!*: an exclamation apparently coined by Scott.

Cæsar on the Lupercal: in *Julius Caesar*, I. ii, Casca tells how Caesar's supporters three times offered him a crown, and how he refused it with increasing reluctance: 'to my thinking, he was very loath to lay his fingers off it'.

gospel warrant for't: see 1 Sam. 15: 23, 'rebellion is as the sin of witchcraft.'

402 *epigraph*: Joanna Baillie, *Count Basil* (1798), reading 'sounds' (for 'sound') in the third line.

404 *St Maronoch*: 'The parish of Kilmaronock, at the eastern extremity of Loch Lomond, derives its name from a cell or chapel, dedicated to Saint Maronock, or Marnock, or Maronnan, about whose sanctity very little is now remembered' (Scott, *The Lady of the Lake*, n. 17).

405 *Balloch*: at the southern tip of Loch Lomond.

406 *Children of the Mist*: 'MacEagh', name for the line of Clan MacGregor excluded from the chieftainship by the Campbells in 1519, and subsequently proscribed; see Author's Introduction. According to the Edinburgh editor of *A Tale of the Wars of Montrose*, J. H. Alexander, MacEagh more likely derives from 'son of the wolf' than 'son of the mist'.

persecution . . . maketh wise men mad: compare Eccles. 7: 7, 'oppression maketh a wise man mad.'

409 *seventeen hundred and seven*: after an abortive French invasion, meant to exploit opposition to the Act of Union, prominent Scottish Jacobites were arrested and taken down to London for trial. In a conciliatory spirit the government refrained from bringing evidence against them and they were acquitted. Rashleigh's involvement in the affair has been hinted at earlier.

410 *The taste, as well as the eloquence of tribes . . . unfettered by system and affectation*: a view coming into fashion at the time Frank is writing: see Hugh Blair, 'A Critical Dissertation on the Poems of Ossian' (1765); Adam Ferguson, *An Essay on the Progress of Civil Society*, III. viii (1767).

the recollection of which yet strikes me with admiration: Scott had already used the Falls of Lediart, near the north side of Loch Ard, as a setting for the famous scene in *Waverley*, ch. 22, in which Flora MacIvor plays and sings to the hero. See the World's Classics edn., pp. 105–6 and 397 (n. 25 to the 1829 edition).

414 *epigraph*: unidentified; probably by Scott.

415 *present military taste . . . black plumage*: banned after 1746, the Highland dress was sanctioned for military apparel when Pitt raised nine Highland regiments to fight in the Seven Years War, 1756–63.

416 *'crammed into mine ear against the stomach of my sense'*: from *The Tempest*, II. i. 100–1: 'You cram these words into mine ears against | the stomach of my sense'.

Dunbarton and Glenfalloch . . . Glasgow and Greenock: from the Clyde to the head of Loch Lomond; Greenock is on the Firth of Clyde.

a Jeddart cast: a Jedburgh fate. In *Tales of a Grandfather*, ch. 37, Scott describes the pacification of the Borders under James VI: 'these judicial measures were conducted so severely as to give rise to the proverb of Jeddart (or Jedburgh) justice, by which it is said a criminal was hanged first and tried afterwards.'

417 *'went on his way, and I saw him no more'*: compare the departure of Pliable, early in *The Pilgrim's Progress*: 'So away he went, and Christian saw him no more.'

421 *better than gowd or gentle kin*: source not identified.

422 *epigraph*: 'The Rising in the North', from Percy's *Reliques*, lines 65–72; Scott modernizes the spelling and changes the numbers, originally nine and eight.

The kiln's on fire: proverbial, according to Wheeler.

423 *much confusion*: Mar raised the standard on 6 September 1715, and three weeks later occupied Perth. But Argyll held Edinburgh, and Mar's following disintegrated after the inconclusive battle of Sherriffmuir, 13 November.

424 *General Carpenter's army*: Carpenter's regiments marched against a Jacobite army in the north of England led by the Earl of Derwentwater and Thomas Forster. Blockaded at Preston, the Jacobites surrendered on 13 November, the same day as Sherriffmuir.

Green-Rigg: this took place on 6 October 1715.

425 *Warrington Bridge*: the English Jacobites intended to take Warrington Bridge, with a view to occupying Liverpool, before they were stopped at Preston.

Proud Preston: ballad epithet, as in 'On the First Rebellion—1715': 'The earl of Mar did vow and swear, | That if e'er proud Preston he did come near', John Bell (ed.), *Rhymes of Northern Bards* (1812), 223. Carpenter attacked on 12 November.

426 *Baronet's*: as Wheeler points out, Sir Hildebrand is here referred to as a baronet, and Rashleigh inherits his title, yet elsewhere he has been described as a mere knight.

the chaplain of the Sardinian ambassador: foreign embassies were exempted from the penal laws against Roman Catholics.

the fox in the fable: who disdained the grapes as sour because they were out of his reach, in Aesop's 'The Fox and the Grapes'.

430 *Knightsbridge affair*: Jacobite plot to assassinate William III at Knightsbridge, when he returned from hunting, in 1694. The chief conspirators were Sir William Barclay and Sir William Perkins. For *Fenwick's plot* see note to p. 144, above.

Peace of Ryswick: between France and England, 1697; Louis XIV agreed to renounce his support of the Stuarts and recognize William III.

433 *epigraph*: Wordsworth, 'Simon Lee, the Old Huntsman', lines 29–32, reading 'dead' for 'gone' in the first line and 'Hall' for 'halls' in the following.

434 *ilka bean has its black*: proverbial: every bean has its speck, i.e. there is some misfortune in every lot.

435 *Our ain reek's better than other folk's fire*: proverbial: better discomfort at home than comfort in someone else's house.

true-blue Presbyterians: compare Butler's *Hudibras*, I. i. 189–96: 'For his Religion . . . | 'Twas Presbyterian true Blue'.

437 *I looked hastily at the frame, expecting to see it empty*: a Gothic trope from Horace Walpole, *The Castle of Otranto* (1765). As Manfred makes his illicit advances to Isabella he is startled to see the portrait of his grandfather 'quit its pannel, and descend on the floor with a grave and melancholy air.'

438 *Can do is easy carried about wi'ane*: proverbial. Ramsay glosses, 'Cunning is no burthen' (*A Collection of Scottish Proverbs*, 23).

442 *epigraph*: Dryden, *Don Sebastian* (1691), Act IV, second line reading, 'And draws the scene to sight'.

443 *Prior's Solomon*: II. ii. 362–3, reading 'call'd her name' and 'tho' I call'd another'.

444 *'mopping and mowing'*: grimacing: see *King Lear*, IV. i. 62.

445 *the 13th of King William, chapter third*: the Act attainting the Old Pretender and declaring all who intercommuned with him guilty of high treason.

   God save great George our King!: the second line of 'God Save the King' as it was first sung in London theatres during the 1745 Jacobite rising—marking the loyalist appropriation of what had formerly been a Jacobite song. (Percy A. Scholes, *God Save the Queen! The History and Romance of the World's First National Anthem*, 1954).

448 *other tow on their rock*: proverbial: 'other flax on their distaff', other fish to fry.

449 *speak no word more*: see *Othello*, V. ii. 307: 'From this time forth I never will speak word.'

452 *some time about the year 1733*: Scott's 1829 emendation, from '1736' in earlier editions. In fact Rob Roy died at the end of 1734; see note to p. 39, above.

455 *Don Raphael and Ambrose de Lamela*: thieves and tricksters in *Gil Blas*, I. xv–xvi, and v. i–ii.

GLOSSARY

a': all
abee: alone
a'body: everybody
abune: above, over
ahint: behind
aiblins: perhaps
aik: oak; *aik-snag*: knotty stick or stump of oak
ain: own
air: early
airn: iron
aits: oats; *ait, aiten*: oaten
ajee: awry, off-balance, disordered
amaist: almost
ance, anes: once; *ance and awa*: now and then
anent: about, concerning
aneuch: enough
anker: cask of wine or spirits, containing about 8 gallons
auld-farran, auld-farrand: shrewd, wise.
auld-warld: old-fashioned, ancient
awe: owe
ayont: beside, beyond

baik: curtsey
bailie: alderman or magistrate
bairn: child
baith: both
ban: curse
band: bond, covenant
bang: spring, bound
barefit: barefoot
barkit: stripped of bark
barm: yeast
bauld: bold, full
bawbee: sixpence Scots or a halfpenny sterling; *plack and bawbee*: to the last penny
bawdrons: familiar name for a cat
beild: shelter

bent: moorland, open country
bicker: wooden bowl or vessel
bicker: throw stones, quarrel; (of a flame) flicker or quiver
bide: wait, stay
bide tryst: keep an appointment
Bienséance: decorum, propriety
bigging: building
bike: nest, swarm
binna: do not be
birkie: lively lad, 'spark'
birl: toss, carouse, booze
bit: adjective indicating smallness, familiarity, or contempt
bittock: a short distance
black-game: black grouse
bleeze, bleize: blaze
bleezing and blasting: talking loudly, showing off
blether, blethers: idle talk, nonsense
blood-tit: small thoroughbred horse
blude, bluid: blood
bobbit: bobbed up and down
boddle, bodle: copper coin of small value (two Scots pence)
bogle: goblin, scarecrow
bole: recess or aperture in a wall
bourock: heap of stones, small hut
bowl: ball, button
bra', braw: fine, brave
braid-claith: broadcloth, a fine black woollen cloth
brechan: tartan plaid
breeks: breeches
brent: smooth
brig: bridge
brisket: breast
brochan: gruel
brogue: deerskin moccasin worn by Highlanders
brose: porridge made by pouring boiling water over oatmeal

brownie: household goblin or sprite
buith: booth, shop
bumbaized: astounded
burn: stream
by: besides
by-gane: ago
byre: cowshed

ca': call, drive, work
ca'-the-shuttle: weaver
cadger: carrier, itinerant dealer
callant: lad
caller: cool, fresh, or freshen
canny: prudent, sensible, skilful, shrewd
cap-out; to drink clean cap-out: to drain to the last drop
carle: fellow
carline: old woman, hag
carte du pays: map of the country
castor: fine fur hat
cateran: Highland bandit
cauldrife: cold
caunle: candle
caup: shell
chack: snack
chafts: jaws
chamber chiels: fellow lodgers
chap: strike (of a clock)
chapman: pedlar
chappin: quart measure
chapping-sticks: cudgels
chappit: struck
cheatry: deceitful
cheat-the-wuddy rogue: gallows-bird (lit. 'cheat-the-gallows')
chiel, chield: fellow
chimley: chimney
choul: jowl
chuckie-stanes: pebbles
clachan: hamlet
claes: clothes
clash: gossip, scandal
clauts: clots, scrapings
clavers: gossip, idle talk; *took out our clavers*: finished off our gossip
clean cap out: empty the cup

clerkit: wrote
clinkum-clankum: jingling
cloot: hoof
clout: piece of cloth
clow: clove
cocket: customs seal or warrant
cockle-headed: whimsical, eccentric
codlings: baking apples
cog: wooden cup or bowl; *cogfu'*: bowl-ful
coif: close-fitting cap
collogue: speak privately together, intrigue
compearance: making a formal appearance in court
coost: cast
corbie: crow or raven
coronach: Highland lament for the dead
costard: head (facetious)
coulter: cutting blade on a plough
coup: upset, spill
coup the crans: be overturned
coup the creels: tumble head over heels
coupit ower craig: spilt down a throat
cousin-red: kinship
cowe: stalk, twig
crack: chat, gossip
cracking crouse: boasting
craig: neck, throat; crag, precipice
creagh: Highland raid
creel: basket carried on the back
crouse: smart, complacent
crowdy: thick oatmeal porridge
cuitle up: wheedle, coax, tickle
curliewurlies: elaborate ornamental carving

daffin': chaffing, teasing
daft: crazy
daiker: saunter, loiter
darn, dern: conceal
demit: resign an office
ding: beat, knock down
dirdum: fuss
divot: lump of turf or peat
dooms: very
douce: gentle, sedate, sober

douncome: downfall

dour: stubborn, reluctant, sullen

dourlach: knapsack

dousely: soberly, quietly

dow: be able; *downa*: cannot

dow'd: withered

dree: suffer, endure

drow: cold mist, drizzle

eclaircissement: clarification, explanation

een: eyes

e'en: even

e'enow: just now

eneuch, eneugh, enow: enough

ettled: intended

even: compare, match

evidents: proofs

fa': befall; also who

fa'ard: favoured; *ill-fa'ared*: ugly

fadeurs: insipidities

fash: trouble, bother; *fasheous*: annoying

Fasterns's-e'en: Shrove Tuesday

fat: vat

fauld: fold

fause-face: mask, vizor

feal: loyal

feck: part

feckless: trifling, useless, weak

fend: defend, shift

ferlie: wonder, wonderful

feught: fought

file: defile

fizzenless: sapless, spiritless

flae: flea

fleech: coax

fleer: jeer

fleg: fright

fley: frighten

flit: move house

flow-moss: quagmire, marsh

fluf-gib: explosion of gunpowder

flyte: scold, abuse

forbye: besides

forfoughen: out of breath, winded

forgather: encounter

forpit: fourth of a peck

foundered: lame

fozy: soft, spongy

fu': full

fule: fool

fusionless: withered, sapless, useless

gabble: jabber, nonsensical talk

gae: gave

gaed: went; *gaen*: gone

gang: go

gang-there-out: wandering, vagrant

gar: make

gash: shrewd, acute; sour-looking

gate: way, manner

gauger: excise-man, customs officer

gaun: going

gaunt: yawn

gear: affair, business; moveable prop-
    erty, livestock

gedd: pike

Geneva cloak: black clerical-style cloak

gien: given

gillies: Highland retainers

gillravaging: raiding, plundering

gin: if, suppose

girdle-cakes: thin oatcakes cooked on a
    griddle or iron plate

glee'd: crooked, astray

gleg: smooth, quick, active, bright

gliff, gliffing: moment, short while

glisk: glimpse

gloaming: fitful, faint

gloom: frown

glowr: stare

gomeril: blockhead

gowd: gold

gowk: cuckoo, fool

gowling and routing: scolding, yelling at

grat: wept; *greet*: weep, cry

gree: agree

grew: shiver, shudder

grice: sucking pig

grilse: young salmon

grit: great

gude: God

gudeman: husband, head of household

guide: deal with, use, employ

gutty: paunchy

ha': hall
hadden: held
hae: have
haet: trifle, bit
halidome: sanctity
haill, hale: whole
hallion: fellow, rogue
ha'narra: have never a
hantle: a lot, many, much
harn-pan: brain-pan, skull
harns: brains
harried: raided
harst: harvest
haud: hold; *neither to haud nor to bind*: fit to be tied
hauding: means
hauld: habitation
havings: behaviour, manners
heather-cowe: sprig of heather
heckle: comb used for cleaning flax
hempie: wild, mischievous, unruly
herd: cowherd
herd-widdiefows: cattle-rustlers; *widdiefou* = one who deserves the gallows
heritor: landholder
hership: raid, pillage
het: hot
hie: high
hinderlins: backside
hirdy-girdy: upset
hog: unshorn yearling sheep
hoodie-craw: hooded crow
hose-net: small net used for fishing in streams; entanglement, confusion
hough: thigh, hamstring
howe: hollow
howlet: owl
hoy: urge on, call
hurdies: haunches, buttocks
hure: whore
huz: us

ilk, ilka: each, every
impetrate: obtain by petition
ingan: onion

ingle: fireplace
intromit: meddle with another's business or property (Scots law term)
I'se: I'll
ivy-tod: ivy-bush

jalouse: be suspicious of
jannock: bannock, oatcake
jaud: jade
jaw: dash; wave
joctaleg: large clasp-knife
joseph: riding-cloak
jouk: duck, dodge
jowing: tolling a large bell by moving the tongue
justified: executed

kail: cabbage; *kail-pat*: pot for boiling vegetables
kailyard: cabbage-patch
kaim: comb
kale: greens, broth
keek: peep, glimpse
kelty aff: glass quite empty
kemping: struggle
ken: know
kend: knew, known
kenna: don't know
kilted: tucked up, lifted
kimmer: gossip
kinrick: kingdom
kirk: church
kittle: sensitive, difficult, troublesome; *kittle cast*: tricky part
knap Southron: speak English
kraemes: warehouses; row of booths or stalls
kye: cows
kyloes: Highland cattle
kynrik: kingdom
kythe: seem

laigh: low
laird: squire, lord of the manor
laith: loath
lang-kale: colewort
lang lug: a great deal

lang-nebbit: long-nosed
lapper: smear
lassie, lassock: little girl
lave: rest
lawin, lawing: bill, reckoning
leasing-making: slander, treason
leddy: lady
lee: lie
leg-bail: leave to run away
let a be: let alone
liesna: lies not, is not
lightlied: slighted
limmer: jade, rogue
linking: stirring briskly
loon: fellow, rogue
loot: let
lound: quiet
loup: leap
lowe: blaze
luckie: widow; term of address to landlady or housewife in general
lug: ear

main: cast of dice
mainprize: bail
mair: more; *mair by token*: all the more,
 moreover
malison: curse
manse: parsonage
marrow: marriage partner
Martimas: Feast of St Martin, 11
 November
maun: must; *maunna*: mustn't
maw: mow
mear: mare
mense: good manners, tact
messan: cur, little dog
mickle: much, large
midden: dunghill; *middenstead*: site of
 dunghill
mint: make, attempt
mirk: dark
misguide: maltreat
mistryst: alarm
mouls: mould, earth
muckle: much
mull: snuff-box

mutch: woman's linen or muslin cap

nae: no
naig: nag
napery: table linen
nash-gab: impertinent chatter
natheless: nevertheless
neb: nose
neist: next
neuk: nook, corner
nevoy: nephew
nipperty-tipperty: fussy, fancy
nowte, nolt: black cattle, oxen

open-steek: ornamental stitch
opine: suppose, presume
orra: occasional, odd
owsen: oxen

paddock: toad
paiks: beating, punishment
parochine: parish
parritch: porridge
pat: pot; *pat play*: pot boil
pearlins: lace made from thread or silk
peers: pears
penny-fee: wages
penny-wedding: wedding at which the
 guests help pay the expenses
pickle: little bit of; peck, rummage
pickthank: toady
pide: stay
pike: peck
pinch: iron crowbar or lever
pirn: reel, bobbin
pis aller: last resort
plack: fourpence Scots or one-third of
 an English penny; *plack and bawbee*:
 the full sum
pleugh: plough
pliskie: trick, prank
ploy: prank, frolic
pockmanty: portmanteau, travelling-
 bag
pock-pudding: steamed pudding; abu-
 sive term for the English, referring to
 their supposed gluttony

poind: distrain

pootry: poultry

potato-bogle: scarecrow

pou'd, pu'd: pulled

pow: head

pretty: brave, gallant, alert

professors: those who profess a trade or vocation

puir: poor

quean: wench

queez-maddam: French pear, jargonelle

raddle: beat, riddle

ram-stam: headlong

rant: romp, frolic

rap aff: rush off noisily

rap and rend: rob with violence

rathe: early, ready

rax: stretch

redd: clear up, advise

red-wud: stark raving mad

reek: smoke

reft: seized, robbed

refutch: refuge

reik: prank, adventure

reisted: roasted, smoked

reive: pillage, break

remeed: remedy

replevisable: subject to bail

rigg: ridge

rigging: top of house

rived and ruggit: torn and tugged about

rock: distaff, spindle

roose: praise

roosted: rusted

roup: sell by auction

row: roll

rubbit: robbed

rudas: coarse, stern; haggard or masculine-looking woman

sackless: innocent, simple, feeble, silly

sain: bless

sair: sore

sap: blockhead

sark: shirt

saut: salt

saw: sow

scart: cormorant

scaur: frighten

screed: tear

sea-coal: mineral coal (as distinct from charcoal)

seamaws: seagulls

sell o't: itself

ser'ing: serving

set: become, be suitable

sett: pattern

shaw: wood, flat ground at base of hill

shelty: pony, especially the Shetland breed

sherra: sheriff

ship's husband: official in charge of provisioning, repairing, and clearing vessels

shoon: shoes

shore: threaten

shoutha: shoulder

sic, siccan: such

siller: money

singit: singed

skaith: harm, damage

skart: scratch

skeps: beehives

skirl: scream

skreigh: call; *skreigh-o'-day*: crack of dawn

skyte: wretch

slabber: slobber

slink: worthless creature

smaik: fool

sneck: notch, slash

sneck-drawer: sly fellow

snell: sharp, drastic, severe

sodgers: soldiers

soothfast: honest

sorn: beg in a bullying manner

sort: accommodate, manage

sortable: (of a cargo) properly assorted, composed of suitable sorts

sough; keep a calm sough: keep quiet about it

soum: sum

souple: active, supple; cunning, subtle

spang: leap, spring

sparry-grass: asparagus

speer: inquire

speerings: tidings

splore: uproar

sporran: purse

spreagh: cattle-rustling

states: statements

stead: be of use

steek: shut

steer: stir, meddle, interfere with, pester

stent-masters: officials appointed to assess taxes in a town or parish

stibbler: clergyman on probation

stickit: botched

stint: stop, hang back

stock: neck-cloth

stot: bullock

stoup: liquid measure

stow: cut off

strae: straw

stricken: fought

suld: should

supple-jack: strong pliant cane

sybo: spring onion

syne: since, ago

tae: toe

tae, tane: the one

taen: taken

tass: glass, cup

tatty-pow: potato-head

tawpie: silly girl

thae: these, those

thegither: together

thigging: begging

theft-boot: hush-money, bribe for receiving stolen goods

thrang: busy, pressed with work

thrapple: throat, windpipe

thraw: thwart, oppose, cross

throughgaun: cross-examination

throughstane: flat gravestone

thrum: story

thrums: loose ends of woven fabric

tig: touch, tap

till: to; *till't*: to it

tither: the other

tod: fox; bush

tolbooth: gaol

took: tuck, drumbeat

toom: empty

toupet: wig or hairpiece

tow: rope, hemp

town: house and outbuildings

troking: deceit, fraud

trot-cosey: riding-hood

trow: trust

tryste: appointment

tuik: took

tuilzie: tussle, scuffle

tup: ram

turf back: tub containing peat for fuel

twa and a plack: a bit of money

twal: twelve

twasome: pair, couple

tyke: dog

uncased: undressed

unchancy: unlucky, dangerous

unco: uncommon, considerable; *unco thing*: sad thing

unfreend: enemy

usquebaugh: whisky

vivers: victuals

wa': wall, way

wabster: weaver

wad: would; bet; hostage

wae: sorry; *waesome*: sorrowful

wally-draigle: weakling, unfit specimen

wame: belly; hollow

wapping: stout, resourceful

warsle: wrestle, struggle

wat: wet

watna: don't know

waur: worse

wean: child

weasand: windpipe

wedder: wether, male sheep

weil: eddy

weird: destiny

weise, weize: guide, direct

we'se: we'll

whang: thong

wheen: a few, some

whigmaleerie: fanciful ornamentation

while syne: some time ago

whiles: sometimes

whilk: which

whin: gorse

whisht: hush, be quiet

whummle: overturn, upset

whuppit awa': whipped away, carried off

wight: valiant, brave

winna: will not

winle: frame for winding yarn

wist: knew

witting: knowledge

won: get, reach

woodie, wuddie: withy, halter made of willow twigs

woundly: very much, dreadfully

wud: mad

wush: recommend

wuss: wish

wyte: blame

yestreen: last night

yett: gate, door

yill: ale

Zookers: 'Gadzooks', God's hooks (= nails)

Zounds: God's wounds

American Literature

British and Irish Literature

Children's Literature

Classics and Ancient Literature

Colonial Literature

Eastern Literature

European Literature

Gothic Literature

History

Medieval Literature

Oxford English Drama

Poetry

Philosophy

Politics

Religion

The Oxford Shakespeare

A complete list of Oxford World's Classics, including Authors in Context, Oxford English Drama, and the Oxford Shakespeare, is available in the UK from the Marketing Services Department, Oxford University Press, Great Clarendon Street, Oxford OX2 6DP, or visit the website at www.oup.com/uk/worldsclassics.

In the USA, visit www.oup.com/us/owc for a complete title list.

Oxford World's Classics are available from all good bookshops. In case of difficulty, customers in the UK should contact Oxford University Press Bookshop, 116 High Street, Oxford OX1 4BR.

JANE AUSTEN	Emma
	Mansfield Park
	Persuasion
	Pride and Prejudice
	Sense and Sensibility
MRS BEETON	Book of Household Management
LADY ELIZABETH BRADDON	Lady Audley's Secret
ANNE BRONTË	The Tenant of Wildfell Hall
CHARLOTTE BRONTË	Jane Eyre
	Shirley
	Villette
EMILY BRONTË	Wuthering Heights
SAMUEL TAYLOR COLERIDGE	The Major Works
WILKIE COLLINS	The Moonstone
	No Name
	The Woman in White
CHARLES DARWIN	The Origin of Species
CHARLES DICKENS	The Adventures of Oliver Twist
	Bleak House
	David Copperfield
	Great Expectations
	Nicholas Nickleby
	The Old Curiosity Shop
	Our Mutual Friend
	The Pickwick Papers
	A Tale of Two Cities
GEORGE DU MAURIER	Trilby
MARIA EDGEWORTH	Castle Rackrent

A SELECTION OF **OXFORD WORLD'S CLASSICS**

GEORGE ELIOT	Daniel Deronda
	The Lifted Veil and Brother Jacob
	Middlemarch
	The Mill on the Floss
	Silas Marner
SUSAN FERRIER	Marriage
ELIZABETH GASKELL	Cranford
	The Life of Charlotte Brontë
	Mary Barton
	North and South
	Wives and Daughters
GEORGE GISSING	New Grub Street
	The Odd Woman
THOMAS HARDY	Far from the Madding Crowd
	Jude the Obscure
	The Mayor of Casterbridge
	The Return of the Native
	Tess of the d'Urbervilles
	The Woodlanders
WILLIAM HAZLITT	Selected Writings
JAMES HOGG	The Private Memoirs and Confessions of a Justified Sinner
JOHN KEATS	The Major Works
	Selected Letters
CHARLES MATURIN	Melmoth the Wanderer
WALTER SCOTT	The Antiquary
	Ivanhoe
	Rob Roy
MARY SHELLEY	Frankenstein
	The Last Man

ROBERT LOUIS STEVENSON	**Kidnapped and Catriona** **The Strange Case of Dr Jekyll and Mr Hyde and Weir of Hermiston** **Treasure Island**
BRAM STOKER	**Dracula**
WILLIAM MAKEPEACE THACKERAY	**Vanity Fair**
OSCAR WILDE	**Complete Shorter Fiction** **The Major Works** **The Picture of Dorian Gray**
DOROTHY WORDSWORTH	**The Grasmere and Alfoxden Journals**
WILLIAM WORDSWORTH	**The Major Works**

TROLLOPE IN OXFORD WORLD'S CLASSICS

ANTHONY TROLLOPE

An Autobiography
The American Senator
Barchester Towers
Can You Forgive Her?
The Claverings
Cousin Henry
Doctor Thorne
The Duke's Children
The Eustace Diamonds
Framley Parsonage
He Knew He Was Right
Lady Anna
The Last Chronicle of Barset
Orley Farm
Phineas Finn
Phineas Redux
The Prime Minister
Rachel Ray
The Small House at Allington
The Warden
The Way We Live Now

A SELECTION OF   OXFORD WORLD'S CLASSICS

HANS CHRISTIAN ANDERSEN	Fairy Tales
J. M. BARRIE	Peter Pan in Kensington Gardens and Peter and Wendy
L. FRANK BAUM	The Wonderful Wizard of Oz
FRANCES HODGSON BURNETT	The Secret Garden
LEWIS CARROLL	Alice's Adventures in Wonderland and Through the Looking-Glass
CARLO COLLODI	The Adventures of Pinocchio
KENNETH GRAHAME	The Wind in the Willows
ANTHONY HOPE	The Prisoner of Zenda
THOMAS HUGHES	Tom Brown's Schooldays

A SELECTION OF   OXFORD WORLD'S CLASSICS

ANTON CHEKHOV
Early Stories
Five Plays
The Princess and Other Stories
The Russian Master and Other Stories
The Steppe and Other Stories
Twelve Plays
Ward Number Six and Other Stories

FYODOR DOSTOEVSKY
Crime and Punishment
Devils
A Gentle Creature and Other Stories
The Idiot
The Karamazov Brothers
Memoirs from the House of the Dead
Notes from the Underground and
The Gambler

NIKOLAI GOGOL
Dead Souls
Plays and Petersburg Tales

ALEXANDER PUSHKIN
Eugene Onegin
The Queen of Spades and Other Stories

LEO TOLSTOY
Anna Karenina
The Kreutzer Sonata and Other Stories
The Raid and Other Stories
Resurrection
War and Peace

IVAN TURGENEV
Fathers and Sons
First Love and Other Stories
A Month in the Country

Six French Poets of the Nineteenth Century

HONORÉ DE BALZAC   Cousin Bette
Eugénie Grandet
Père Goriot

CHARLES BAUDELAIRE   The Flowers of Evil
The Prose Poems and Fanfarlo

BENJAMIN CONSTANT   Adolphe

DENIS DIDEROT   Jacques the Fatalist
The Nun

ALEXANDRE DUMAS (PÈRE)   The Black Tulip
The Count of Monte Cristo
Louise de la Vallière
The Man in the Iron Mask
La Reine Margot
The Three Musketeers
Twenty Years After
The Vicomte de Bragelonne

ALEXANDRE DUMAS (FILS)   La Dame aux Camélias

GUSTAVE FLAUBERT   Madame Bovary
A Sentimental Education
Three Tales

VICTOR HUGO   The Essential Victor Hugo
Notre-Dame de Paris

J.-K. HUYSMANS   Against Nature

PIERRE CHODERLOS   Les Liaisons dangereuses
DE LACLOS

MME DE LAFAYETTE   The Princesse de Clèves

GUILLAUME DU LORRIS   The Romance of the Rose
and JEAN DE MEUN

A SELECTION OF   **OXFORD WORLD'S CLASSICS**

GUY DE MAUPASSANT   **A Day in the Country and Other Stories**
A Life
Bel-Ami
Mademoiselle Fifi and Other Stories
Pierre et Jean

PROSPER MÉRIMÉE   **Carmen and Other Stories**

MOLIÈRE   **Don Juan and Other Plays**
**The Misanthrope, Tartuffe, and Other
Plays**

BLAISE PASCAL   **Pensées and Other Writings**

ABBÉ PRÉVOST   **Manon Lescaut**

JEAN RACINE   **Britannicus, Phaedra, and Athaliah**

ARTHUR RIMBAUD   **Collected Poems**

EDMOND ROSTAND   **Cyrano de Bergerac**

MARQUIS DE SADE   **The Crimes of Love**
**The Misfortunes of Virtue and Other Early
Tales**

GEORGE SAND   **Indiana**

MME DE STAËL   **Corinne**

STENDHAL   **The Red and the Black**
The Charterhouse of Parma

PAUL VERLAINE   **Selected Poems**

JULES VERNE   **Around the World in Eighty Days**
Captain Hatteras
Journey to the Centre of the Earth
Twenty Thousand Leagues under the Seas

VOLTAIRE   **Candide and Other Stories**
Letters concerning the English Nation

A SELECTION OF OXFORD WORLD'S CLASSICS

ÉMILE ZOLA
L'Assommoir
The Attack on the Mill
La Bête humaine
La Débâcle
Germinal
The Kill
The Ladies' Paradise
The Masterpiece
Nana
Pot Luck
Thérèse Raquin

A SELECTION OF   **OXFORD WORLD'S CLASSICS**

THOMAS AQUINAS   Selected Philosophical Writings

FRANCIS BACON   The Essays

WALTER BAGEHOT   The English Constitution

GEORGE BERKELEY   Principles of Human Knowledge and
                            Three Dialogues

EDMUND BURKE   A Philosophical Enquiry into the Origin of
                            Our Ideas of the Sublime and Beautiful
                          Reflections on the Revolution in France

CONFUCIUS   The Analects

ÉMILE DURKHEIM   The Elementary Forms of Religious Life

FRIEDRICH ENGELS   The Condition of the Working Class in
                            England

JAMES GEORGE FRAZER   The Golden Bough

SIGMUND FREUD   The Interpretation of Dreams

THOMAS HOBBES   Human Nature and De Corpore Politico
                          Leviathan

JOHN HUME   Selected Essays

NICCOLO MACHIAVELLI   The Prince

THOMAS MALTHUS   An Essay on the Principle of Population

KARL MARX   Capital
                          The Communist Manifesto

J. S. MILL   On Liberty and Other Essays
                          Principles of Political Economy and
                            Chapters on Socialism

FRIEDRICH NIETZSCHE   Beyond Good and Evil
                          The Birth of Tragedy
                          On the Genealogy of Morals
                          Twilight of the Idols

A SELECTION OF   OXFORD WORLD'S CLASSICS

THOMAS PAINE — **Rights of Man, Common Sense, and Other Political Writings**

JEAN-JACQUES ROUSSEAU — **The Social Contract**
Discourse on the Origin of Inequality

ADAM SMITH — **An Inquiry into the Nature and Causes of the Wealth of Nations**

MARY WOLLSTONECRAFT — **A Vindication of the Rights of Woman**